Between
Summer's Longing
and Winter's End

Between Summer's Longing and Winter's End

THE STORY OF A CRIME

Leif GW Persson

Translated from the Swedish by Paul Norlen

Pantheon Books

NEW YORK

Translation copyright © 2010 by Pantheon Books, a division of Random House, Inc.

All rights reserved. Published in the United States by Pantheon Books, a division of Random House, Inc., New York, and in Canada by Random House of Canada Limited, Toronto. Originally published in Sweden as *Mellan sommarens längtan och vinterns köld: en roman om ett brott* by Piratförlaget, Stockholm, in 2002. Copyright © 2002 by Leif GW Persson.

Pantheon Books and colophon are registered trademarks of Random House, Inc.

Library of Congress Cataloging-in-Publication Data

Persson, Leif GW
[Mellan sommarens längtan och vinterns köld. English]
Between summer's longing and winter's end : the story of a crime / Leif GW Persson ;
translated from the Swedish by Paul Norlen.
p. cm.
"Originally published in Sweden by Piratförlaget in 2002."
ISBN 978-0-307-37745-6
I. Norlen, Paul R.   II. Title.
PT9876.26.E7225M45 2010
833'.914—dc22   2010004678

www.pantheonbooks.com

Book design by Virginia Tan

Printed in the United States of America

First American Edition

9 8 7 6 5 4 3 2 1

To the Bear and Mikael

The best informant is the one who hasn't understood
the significance of what he has told.

The Professor

Between Summer's Longing and Winter's End

CHAPTER I

Free falling, as in a dream

Stockholm in November

It was Charlie, age thirteen, who saved the life of Vindel, age fifty-five. At least that's how Vindel described it at the preliminary police hearing.

"If Charlie hadn't looked up and pulled me to the side, that damn thing would've hit me right in the skull and I wouldn't be sitting here now."

It was a peculiar story right from the start, for three main reasons.

First, Charlie was thought to be deaf in both ears. Not least by Vindel himself, who was convinced that the only things Charlie understood nowadays were eye contact, sign language, and physical touch. It's true that Vindel talked with him more than ever, but that's only to be expected when someone you liked grew old and slowed down, and Vindel had always been kind to Charlie. Just what you would expect.

Second, it is a long-established axiom in Western physics that a free-falling body precedes the sound that said body produces by friction against the surrounding atmosphere. Thus, according to said physics, there would have been no noticeable sound whatsoever.

Third, and this was the most remarkable. If Charlie had heard something, noticed the danger, pulled Vindel aside, and thereby saved his life . . . why didn't he hear the sound of the victim's left shoe, which, only a few seconds later, struck him right in the neck and killed him on the spot?

[FRIDAY, NOVEMBER 22]

Between 19:56 and 20:01 hours on Friday the twenty-second of November, three calls were routed via emergency number 90 000 to the command center of the Stockholm Police.

The first came from a retired lawyer who had seen the entire incident in detail from his balcony at Valhallavägen 38. The lawyer introduced himself by name and title and appeared not the least bit upset. His story was wordy and systematically outlined. Factually, it was completely off the wall.

In summary, the premise was that a lunatic dressed in a long black coat and a ski cap with earflaps had just shot down a poor dog owner and his dog. Now the lunatic was running around in circles, shouting incoherently; the reason that the lawyer found himself out on his balcony with the temperature below freezing was that his wife suffered from asthma and cigarette smoke had an unpleasant tendency to cling to the curtains: "If you are wondering about that, sergeant?"

The second call came from the taxi switchboard. One of their drivers had picked up an older woman at Valhallavägen 46, and as he held open the door to help his passenger into the backseat, he noticed from the corner of his eye "a poor fellow who fell down from the roof of that tall building where all the students live." The driver was forty-five years old and had come to Sweden from Turkey twenty years earlier. He had seen worse things as a child and had learned early on that there is a time and a place for everything; that is why he called the switchboard on the radio, told what he had seen, and asked them to call the police, while he drove the old woman to her daughter, who lived on a farm outside of Märsta. It was a good fare and life went on.

Phone call number three came from a man who, judging by his voice, seemed to be middle-aged. He refused to say what his name was and where he was calling from, but he sounded exhilarated in a way that indicated that he had ingested some stimulating substance. In addition he had some good advice. "Now one of those crazy students has jumped off the roof again. Don't forget to bring a few buckets along when you come to pick him up."

At the command center everything was running along tracks laid down long ago. When the on-duty operator sent out an area alert on the radio, she had already lowered the priority of the verbose lawyer and raised that of the taxi driver and the exhilarated man with the good advice about buckets; she omitted the shooting, the dog, and the buckets.

Her message was that a person had fallen or jumped from the student dormitory called Rosehip on Körsbärsvägen and landed on the walkway above the parking lot across the street from the intersection of Valhallavägen and Frejgatan. A lifeless body would be found at the scene and a distraught male, dressed in a black coat and a peaked cap, wandering around in the vicinity. Was there a patrol car in the area that could take care of the whole thing?

There was one, only a hundred yards farther down Valhallavägen. It belonged to the Östermalm precinct—VD 2—and at the moment the alarm went out over the radio, the car was stopping in front of the hot-dog stand at the driveway to the Roslagstull hospital. In the car were two of the Stockholm Police Department's finest. In the driver's seat sat police officer in training Oredsson, age twenty-four. He was blond, blue-eyed, and broad-shouldered. He was doing his last round as a trainee and in a month he would become a police officer. A conviction also burned in Oredsson's soul that, once he joined the police force, the struggle against the steadily increasing crime rate would enter a decisive phase in which good would come out the victor.

In the passenger seat beside him sat his immediate superior, police assistant Stridh, who was almost twice Oredsson's age and went by the name Peace at Any Price among his older colleagues. Ever since they started their beat two hours ago his thoughts had focused exclusively on the plump sausage with mashed potatoes, cucumber-and-shrimp salad, mustard, and ketchup that would provide at least temporary relief from his miserable existence. Now he could smell it, but in the struggle over the microphone that was placed between him and Oredsson he had, of course, lost.

"Two thirty-five here. We're listening," answered Oredsson. Energetic and alert as always.

.   .   .

Approximately at the same time as the retired lawyer contacted the female radio operator at the police department's command center, police superintendent Lars M. Johansson ("M" for Martin), head of the National Bureau of Criminal Investigation, stepped out through the entryway of his residence on Wollmar Yxkullsgatan in Södermalm. Johansson disappeared down the street with brisk steps and in an excellent mood, en route to his first date with a woman who he knew was lovely to look at and in all likelihood nice to talk with as well. This would take place in a neighborhood restaurant nearby with food both excellent and reasonably priced. Outside it was a cold and starry evening without the least fleck of snow on the streets and sidewalks; all in all an almost ideal combination for a person who wanted to keep his head clear, his spirits high, and his feet dry.

Lars Martin Johansson was a solitary man. In the legal sense he had been so since the day almost ten years ago when his first, and so far only, wife left him, took their two children with her, and moved in with a new man, to a new life in a new house. In a spiritual sense he had been solitary his entire life, in spite of the fact that he'd grown up with six siblings and two parents who had met more than fifty years ago, were still married to each other, and would remain so until death did them part. In Johansson's case, loneliness was not something inherited. It wasn't security, intimacy, and companionship that he lacked when he was growing up. Those had been there to excess and were still to be had, if that was what he wanted, but when as an adult he started to ransack his consciousness for happy memories from his childhood, the only ones he found were times when he'd been left entirely in peace. When he stood alone on the stage, the only actor in the piece, by himself.

It would be quite an understatement to maintain that Johansson felt at home in his solitude. According to conventional models of human coexistence, it was considerably worse than that. Solitude was the necessary prerequisite for Johansson to function, in the ordinary human sense of shaping the days into a respectable life or in the purely professional sense of acquitting oneself well before other people without consideration for family and friends and feelings in the most general sense. In that respect, his wife's having left him and taken the children with her made existence almost ideal.

Two years after the divorce his then seven-year-old daughter had given him an LP record, *A Single Man* by Elton John, for Christmas. Apart from feeling his heart wrench as he read the words on the cover, he saw evidence of unusual human insight for someone her age. As an adult she would either become very strong and independent or else run the risk of being crushed under her own insight.

What disturbed the whole equation—this secure, controlled, pre-dictable life—was his interest in women: their scent, their soft skin, the hollow in the neck between the hairline and the slender throat. It sought him out in dreams at night when he couldn't defend himself other than by rolling the sheets into a sweaty cord in the middle of the bed; it sought him out in broad daylight; awake, sober, and clearheaded, he would twist his neck out of its socket for a regal posture and a pair of tanned legs he would never see again.

Now a specific example of this interest of his was sitting half an arm's length away at the same table in a neighborhood restaurant where excellent food was served at a very reasonable price. He had met her two days earlier when he gave a lecture to a group of police chiefs with a legal education on the operation of the National Bureau of Criminal Investigation. Now she was eating her pasta with shellfish and mush-rooms with evident enjoyment, which made him happy. It was a good sign. If a woman poked at her food, it was a bad indication of something other than food.

The first time they talked to each other was at the break between the two hours of his lecture. About the obvious tedium of staying at a hotel in Stockholm when your life, home, and friends were in Sundsvall. Then to the point.

"If you don't have anything better to do on Friday evening, there's a very good restaurant in my neighborhood." Johansson nodded, looking down into his white plastic coffee cup. His Norrland dialect was some-what more marked than usual.

"I thought you'd never dare ask. Where, when, and how?"

Now she was sitting there, half an arm's length away.

I really ought to say something about my solitude, thought Johans-son. Warn her, in case I become really fond of her and she of me.

"Pasta, olive oil, basil, tomato, shellfish, and a little mushroom.

What's wrong with potato pancakes and fried bacon? I was brought up on that kind of thing."

Johansson nodded and laid down his fork. "I think you know. Otherwise I wouldn't be sitting here."

She had set aside her fork and looked rather charmed.

Okay, thought Johansson. Shook his head and tilted his wineglass.

"I don't have the faintest idea. I'm a simple country boy. Tell me about it."

Seven minutes past eight, only two minutes after they'd responded to the alarm, Stridh and Oredsson arrived at the scene. Oredsson had driven in on the walkway that ran above the parking lot parallel to Valhallavägen, and before he stopped the car he turned on the searchlights. A few yards in front of the car sat an older man in a peaked cap and dark coat. He was rocking his upper body; in his arms he was hugging a dog that looked like a small German shepherd. He didn't seem to have even noticed their arrival. Some ten yards farther away, exactly at the border between the walkway and the grassy area leading to the nearby wall of the building, lay a lifeless body. Around the head a pool of blood with a radius of close to half a yard shone like melted pewter in the beam of the headlights.

"I can check if he's alive." Oredsson looked inquiringly at Stridh while he was undoing his seat belt.

"If you think it's unpleasant I can do it." Stridh nodded with a certain emphasis. He was still the boss.

Oredsson shook his head and opened the car door.

"It's okay. I've seen much worse, actually."

Stridh contented himself with nodding. Didn't ask where a twenty-four-year-old police trainee might have picked up such experience.

It must have been somewhere. When he reported to the command center a few minutes later he was concise and clear and his voice didn't sound the least bit shaken. At the scene was a dead male, therefore an ambulance was not needed. Judging by the extensive injuries and the position of the body it appeared most probable that the male in question had fallen or jumped from one of the upper floors in the adjacent apartment building, a high-rise of at least twenty stories that contained student apartments and for unclear reasons was named the Rosehip. There was a witness at the scene, an older man who had been out walking his dog. His colleague Stridh had just spoken with him. It would be great if they could send someone from the after-hours unit plus a technician. Meanwhile, Oredsson would set up the cordon around the dead body, but no other reinforcements were required, in any event not at the present time.

"Yes. That's the situation," concluded Oredsson. I'm not going to bother saying anything about the mutt being dead too, he thought.

Police Inspector Bäckström was sitting in the break room at the after-hours unit, staring at the TV; up until now everything had gone well. For a Friday evening it had been unusually calm, and when the riot squad had carried in a street brawler half an hour earlier, Bäckström had seen what was coming and managed to sneak into the restroom. One of his colleagues would have to take care of that piece of crap. A gook, of course, and just as messy as those types always were.

Normally Bäckström worked with the homicide squad, but because he was always in financial straits, he was forced to work a great deal of overtime. True, only fools slaved at the after-hours unit on a Friday evening, but three days before payday he had no choice. Everything had gone fine—up until now, that is, when the chief inspector on duty stood in the door looking just as surly as usual while staring urgently at Bäckström.

"I've got a corpse for you, Bäckström. Seems to be lying on the walkway below that student skyscraper above the parking lot at Valhallavägen and Frejgatan. I've talked with Wiijnbladh at tech. You can ride with him."

Bäckström lightened up a little and nodded. A do-it-yourselfer, he thought. One of those student reds who jumped because he didn't get his welfare on time. I've still got a good chance to finish my shift before the bars close.

· · ·

It took a good long while before Bäckström and Wiijnbladh showed up—a do-it-yourselfer wasn't going to run away from you, and an extra cup of coffee was never a bad thing—but neither Stridh nor Oredsson had been idle. Oredsson had cordoned off the area around the place where the body was lying. At the criminal technology course at school he'd learned that police officers almost always cordoned off too small an area, so he'd used a little extra and the blue-and-white-striped barricade tape was neatly stretched between suitable light posts and trees. A few curiosity seekers had arrived while he was doing that, but after a quick look at the dead body all of them had turned and gone away. He had of course not touched the body. He'd learned that in the same course.

In the meantime Stridh consoled Vindel. After some coaxing he had persuaded him to sit in the backseat of the car, allowing him to bring the dog with him. They had also helped wrap the mutt in Stridh's own blanket, which he always brought with him on long nighttime work shifts, for reasons that he shared with no one. There was a plastic sheet in the car that was usually spread out in the backseat when they transported drunks, but that was nothing you would wrap a dead body in, especially not in sight of a near relation.

"His name is Charlie," Vindel explained with tears in his eyes. "He's a Pomeranian, although I think there's a little foxhound in him too. He turned thirteen last summer but he's a frisky rascal."

Vindel snuffled and fell silent while Stridh squeezed his shoulder. After that he began his initial questioning.

"Vindel" was not his real name. He was just called that. His name was Gustav Adolf Nilsson; he was born in 1930 and had come to Stockholm in 1973 to go to a retraining course at AMS—an unemployed construction worker from Norrland and that's the way it remained, for he never got a new job.

"It was my buddies at the course," Vindel explained. "You see, I was born and raised in those parts and we talked quite a lot about how it was at home. So then it became Vindel. As in the Vindel River, you know?"

Stridh nodded. He knew.

Vindel explained that he and Charlie lived nearby, two floors above the courtyard at Surbrunnsgatan 4. After they'd eaten their dinner and before it was time to watch the evening news on TV, they would take their usual evening walk. They always took the same route. First across

Valhallavägen at the intersection with Surbrunnsgatan, then the walkway parallel to Valhallavägen down to Roslagstull, where they would turn and walk home again. If it was nice weather, however, they might walk farther.

On the slope below the Rosehip dormitory Charlie had one of his favorite trees, so that's where they would take their first lengthy stop.

"It's important that they have time to nose around properly," Vindel explained. "For a dog that's like reading the newspaper."

Just as they were standing there and Charlie was reading his newspaper, Charlie had suddenly raised his head and looked straight up along the façade of the building. Suddenly Vindel was thrown backward with a powerful jerk of the leash.

"I was just about knocked to the ground. If Charlie hadn't looked up and pulled me to the side, that damn thing would've hit me right in the skull and I wouldn't be sitting here now." Vindel nodded emphatically.

"Do you believe that he heard some sound that he reacted to?" Stridh made a mark in his notebook.

"Naw." Vindel shook his head with even greater emphasis. "He's completely deaf in both ears. It must have been that sixth sense they have. Certain Pomeranians have it. A sixth sense."

Stridh nodded but said nothing.

If Charlie had had a sixth sense, it had in any case failed immediately afterward, when the victim's downward-falling left shoe struck him in the neck and killed him on the spot.

"This is too terrible," Vindel said, and he started snuffling again. "We're standing there, Charlie and I, looking at the damn thing, and suddenly his shoe comes falling."

"It came right after the body?" Stridh asked.

"Naw, not really. We stood there and watched. It took a good while."

"A minute, two minutes?"

"Naw. Not a minute, it didn't take that long, but it probably took ten, twenty seconds in all. It took that long."

"Ten to twenty seconds, you say. You don't think it could have been even shorter?"

"Well. I'm sure maybe it feels longer when you're standing like that, but probably it took quite a few seconds."

Vindel snuffled audibly and blew his nose in his hand.

While Stridh was talking with Vindel, Oredsson took the opportunity to use his blue eyes. He discovered the shoe immediately; it was lying only a few yards from the body and probably belonged to the victim, as he was missing a left shoe and the right shoe, which was still on his foot, was suspiciously like the one lying on the incline. For a moment he considered fetching a plastic bag from the car and placing the shoe in it, of course at the same spot and in the same position where it was now lying, but he abandoned that thought. In the course on criminal technology, nothing in particular had been said about the handling of shoes, but because he assumed that it should be handled like a clue in general, he let it lie where it was. There was nothing in either the weather conditions or the surrounding environment to justify a departure from the golden rule in the form of so-called special clue-securing measures.

So be it, thought Oredsson, and felt quite pleased with his decision. He would go with the golden rule about touching as few things as possible and leaving the search to the technicians.

Instead he proceeded to inspect the façade along an imagined vertical line from the place where the body had landed straight up the building. Somewhere on the fifteenth or sixteenth floor—the building foundation was on a slope, which made him uncertain how best to calculate—a window appeared to be standing open despite the cold. Approximately fifty yards' vertical drop, thought Oredsson—who was the best shot in his class and a crackerjack at judging distance—which agreed rather well with the deplorable condition of the corpse. Oredsson looked at his watch. A good half hour had elapsed since the command center promised to send the after-hours unit and technician. What are they up to? thought Oredsson with irritation.

Bäckström was small, fat, and crude, while Wiijnbladh was small, slender, and dapper, and together they complemented each other splendidly. They were also happy working together. Bäckström thought that Wiijnbladh was a cowardly half fairy—you didn't even need to raise your voice, he still did what he was told. Wiijnbladh, in turn, viewed Bäckström as mentally challenged and bad-tempered—a pure dream to work with for anyone who preferred having complete control of the situation. Because they were both solidly incompetent, no disagreements arose either on factual or other professional grounds, and to sum up, they made a real radar unit.

Exactly one hour after they received the assignment, they were on the walkway below the Rosehip, although in all fairness it should be noted that at this time of day it takes almost ten minutes to drive from the police station on Kungsholmen to the parking lot right in front of the intersection of Valhallavägen and Frejgatan, where they had chosen to position their car.

"What the hell is this?" said Bäckström, tugging crossly at the barricade tape in front of the corpse. "Have we landed in some damn war or what?" He fixed his eyes on both his uniformed colleagues.

"It's a barricade tape," Oredsson answered calmly. His blue and strangely pale eyes scrutinized Bäckström. He stood motionless with legs wide apart and with his burly arms hanging by his sides. "There's a whole roll in the car if you need more."

My God, what a sick bastard, thought Bäckström. That's not a policeman; he looks like he's acting in some old Nazi movie. What gives? Are they letting them into the corps nowadays? He decided to quickly change the subject.

"There was supposed to be a witness here. Where the hell has he taken off to?" He glared crossly at the two in uniform.

"I drove him home half an hour ago," answered the older, considerably fatter clod, who was standing next to the younger Nazi type. "He was in a bit of shock and wanted to go home; I've already talked with him. I have the name and address if you want to question him again."

"It'll work out; it'll work out," said Wiijnbladh diplomatically. "Without getting ahead of ourselves, I think this looks suspiciously like a suicide. Did you gentlemen know, by the way, that there are twenty suicides for every murder in this city?"

Judging by the shaking of their heads, they didn't seem to be aware of that fact, nor particularly interested in pursuing the matter further.

"There's a window standing wide open on the fifteenth or possibly the sixteenth floor, depending on how you calculate." Oredsson pointed up toward the façade of the building. "It's been standing open since we got here. Despite the cold."

"But that sounds just great," answered Wiijnbladh with genuine warmth in his voice. "My good men, let's take a look at the corpse. Maybe if we're lucky he has something in his pockets. Hurry down and get my camera." Wiijnbladh nodded encouragingly toward Oredsson. "It's in the backseat. Bring the bag from the trunk too."

Oredsson nodded without answering. In due course we'll take care of your type, he thought, but for the time being I'm only a simple soldier and it's a matter of placing yourself in the ranks without being noticed. But in due course. . . .

Something doesn't add up, thought Johansson. He had talked about Italian food, about a recent long trip to Southeast Asia, and in answer to a direct question, he had told her about his growing up in Norrland. He had done so in a quiet and humorous way, and for anyone who could read between the lines it was obvious that Lars Martin Johansson was educated, talented, and pleasant, successful, with money in the bank, and—most important of all—unmarried and unattached as well as highly capable in the purely physical relations between man and woman.

His dinner guest seemed both pleased and interested, the signals she gave were clear enough, but still something didn't add up. She had responded by sharing her own background: daughter of an attorney in Östersund, mother a housewife, one older and one younger sister, studied law in Uppsala, practiced for a time with the prosecutor's office, became interested in police work and applied to police chief training. For anyone with eyes to see and ears to hear with it was quite obvious that she was beautiful and educated, talented and pleasant, and certainly a very agreeable partner in the purely physical relations between woman and man.

You've got a guy, thought Johansson, and the reason you don't want to talk about it is that you're a bit too well-brought-up, a bit too conventional, and a bit too inclined to bet on the sure thing. You could imagine a discreet affair, but if you should venture beyond that, you'd first want to be sure you were going to get more out of it in the end than you already have.

Johansson could certainly imagine a discreet affair—he had even

carried out one or two—but when it concerned female police officers there were obvious complications. Almost all female police officers
went out with male police officers, and because there were ten men to
every woman within the corps, the pressure from the demand side was
both huge and insatiable. Johansson's oldest brother was a property
owner and car dealer. He was rich, shrewd, uneducated, and crude and
could see right through both friends and foes. Once Johansson had
teased him about his beautiful blonde secretary. Well? What was the real
story?

"Let me give you some good advice." His older brother looked at
him seriously. "You should never shit where you eat."

High time for a so-called table-turning, thought Johansson. Such a tactic
might work even on hardened criminals, so there was really no reason
why it shouldn't work on a female interim police superintendent from
Sundsvall as well.

"A completely different matter," said Johansson with a relaxed smile.
"How's it going with your guy nowadays? I haven't seen him for a long
time."

She took it well. Concealed her surprise nicely, with the help of the
wineglass. Looked at him and smiled with a little worried wrinkle on
her forehead.

"I'm sure things are going well with him. I didn't know that you
knew each other."

"Did he get that job he applied for?" countered Johansson, who
wanted to quickly feel solid ground under his feet.

"Do you mean as assistant county police chief?" No more wrinkle.
Johansson nodded.

"He started last summer. He's as happy as a fish in water. I don't
know if that's due to the distance between Växjö and Sundsvall. . . . I
can't really say that it has exactly contributed to developing our relationship, but perhaps that was the idea." Now she smiled again.

"We don't know each other that well." Johansson raised his glass.
How can you stay with that idiot? he thought.

. . .

On the walkway below the dormitory Bäckström and Wiijnbladh speedily and vigorously began their investigation of the cause of death. First Wiijnbladh flashed off a few photos toward the dead body and as soon as he lowered the camera and started mumbling something inaudibly into a little pocket tape recorder, Bäckström started rooting through the corpse's clothing. This was quickly done. The body was dressed in a pair of blue jeans, a white T-shirt, and over that a dark-gray V-neck pullover, on the right foot a sock and a powerful bootlike shoe, on the left foot only a sock. In the right side pocket of the jeans Bäckström found a wallet. He looked through the contents while he smacked his lips with delight.

"Come here, boys, and see." Bäckström waved toward Stridh and Oredsson. "I believe we have an investigative breakthrough in the making."

Bäckström held up a plastic ID card with photo.

"John P. Krassner . . . b period . . . that probably means 'borned' . . . July fifteen one thousand nine hundred fifty-three," Bäckström read in bad English. John P. Krassner, born July 15, 1953, he translated with satisfaction. "Obviously some damn American who decided to close up shop. Some damn professional student who lost his way in all those books."

Stridh and Oredsson contented themselves with nodding neutrally, but Bäckström didn't give up. He leaned forward and held up the ID card against the head of the body. Clearly it was the head that had taken the first impact against the ground. It appeared to have been crushed diagonally from above, from the crown toward the chin; face and hair were covered with dried blood, the face pressed together and the facial features impossible to make out. Bäckström grinned delightedly.

"What do you say, boys? I'd say they're as alike as two peas."

Stridh made a grimace of displeasure but said nothing. Oredsson stared at Bäckström without changing expression. Swine, he thought.

"Okay." Bäckström straightened up and looked at his watch. Already 9:30, he thought. Now it was crucial to put the machinery in motion. "If you boys see to it that we get the corpse on its way to the coroner's office, then Wiijnbladh and I will take a look at that apartment."

"What do we do with the shoe?" wondered Oredsson.

"Put it in a bag and send it with the body," Wiijnbladh said before Bäckström had time to say anything and create unnecessary problems. "And since you'll be talking with the dispatcher anyway . . . see to it that they send someone here from the street department who'll clean up."

"Exactly," Bäckström agreed. "It looks like hell. And you"—he looked at Oredsson—"don't forget to take that fucking barricade with you."

"Sure," Oredsson said, and nodded. One day I'm going to get you in town for drunkenness, he thought. And when you start messing around and whining that you're a policeman I'll stuff a whole roll of tape up your rear end. "Goes without saying." Oredsson smiled, and nodded at Bäckström, "Remove the barricade. I got it, sir."

That guy is not all there, thought Bäckström. God help you if you were an average citizen and met up with that idiot.

According to the bulletin board in the lobby, the room behind the open window was on the sixteenth floor: one of eight student rooms along the same corridor and with a common kitchen. In spite of the fact that it was Friday evening, the command center managed to get hold of the building superintendent, who was sitting in his little office in an adjacent building only a hundred yards from there. He sighed—it wasn't the first time something like this had happened—and promised to show up in a jiffy. Five minutes later he was opening the corridor door to the area where the room was. He pointed at the door in question and gave the key to Wiijnbladh.

"You'll get along fine without me, won't you?" he asked rhetorically. "I want the key back when you're through."

It was Wiijnbladh who opened. Inside the door was a coat closet and to the right a bathroom with a shower. Straight ahead a smaller room where the only window was wide open. Altogether it might amount to at the most sixty square feet.

"You may as well talk to his neighbors while I take a few pictures." Wiijnbladh looked inquiringly at Bäckström.

Bäckström nodded in agreement. This suited him fine. It was cold as an Eskimo's asshole in there and damned if he was going to get pneumonia on account of a crazy window jumper.

While Wiijnbladh took his pictures Bäckström's luck continued to hold. He looked in the kitchen—empty—and, to be on the safe side, in the refrigerator. Nothing appeared especially tempting, however, and the milk cartons, plastic-wrapped cucumbers, and various cans with contents unknown were all labeled with the names of students. My God, what pigs, thought Bäckström. Not even a beer or a soda for a thirsty policeman. He knocked and tried all the doors. They were locked, and if there was anyone home, he or she clearly didn't intend to open the door in any event. Luck was still on his side.

The room was small, untidy, and sparsely furnished, with the standard assortment of worn-out furniture: a bed, a nightstand, a wall-mounted bed lamp, in the opposite corner a simple reading chair with a floor lamp, toward the window wall a bookshelf, and on the other side of the window a desk and a chair.

"Damn, what a cozy place he has," said Bäckström.

People who didn't work, students for example, shouldn't have food or a roof over their head, but if necessary he could tolerate this. The present occupant didn't seem to have settled in for a long stay, and he didn't seem to be especially orderly. The personal effects were few: a suitcase, a few clothes, some books with titles in English. On the unmade bed was a short quilted jacket, under the bed a pair of well-worn shoes. It was no opium den, but if the person who was living here didn't pull himself together it would soon be a lot like one.

The desk was the most organized. There were papers and envelopes, pens, paper clips, an eraser, and a few cassettes with colored ribbon for the handy little portable electric typewriter that was placed in the middle of the desk. In addition a paper with a text in English was sitting in the typewriter cylinder, only a half dozen lines but revealing enough for a pro like Wiijnbladh.

"If I were to summarize," Wiijnbladh began with a contented expression, "I think probably all we have seen speaks for a suicide. If you see the window there," Wiijnbladh pointed toward the now-closed window, where the broken window catch lay on the floor below, "you see that he has broken the catch loose. Otherwise it can only be opened a few inches. If you want to air out or something."

Bäckström nodded contentedly. Wiijnbladh was certainly a long-winded bastard, but this sounded like music to his ears.

"Yes, and then you have the message he left in the typewriter. It's in English and I would definitely say that it exudes a great weariness with life, a sort of . . ."

Wiijnbladh looked for words, but since his knowledge of English was limited, to put it mildly, it wasn't all that easy.

"Yes, a typical suicide note, quite simply." Wiijnbladh nodded with extra emphasis.

Bäckström nodded too. They were in the same boat, after all, so he could grant him that. "Yes, then we mustn't forget the front door. It was locked from inside," he said.

"Certainly." Wiijnbladh nodded. With a common, patented catch, he thought. How stupid can you really be?

"Okay then. I think we're about done here." Bäckström looked at his watch. It was only a quarter past ten, and if he hurried back to the after-hours unit he should even have time to call the old man with the dog who'd seen him jump—that little extra concluding detail that was the mark of a completely unobjectionable investigation—and soon he'd be sitting in the bar, enjoying a well-earned beer.

Johansson and his companion had left the restaurant in the good spirits that naturally arise when certain not entirely simple decisions have been postponed while at the same time possibilities for choice still remain. They walked together to her hotel down by Slussen, and Johansson wasn't hard to convince when she suggested a last beer in the hotel bar.

"The course ends in a week. Any chance you'll show up then?" The tensions had relaxed. She sat leaning forward. She smiled and lightly drew her nails over the back of Johansson's right hand. She herself had narrow, strong hands.

Johansson shook his head regretfully.

"In a week I'll be sitting on a plane to the U.S. I'm going to meet a lot of people from Interpol and the FBI." Johansson gave a faint sigh. Sometimes I wonder if there's someone up there who's actively out to get me, or if I'm just bad at planning.

She sighed too. "You certainly are leading a boring life. I'm going to a course in Härnösand with our civilian employees. It's going to be really exciting." Now she smiled again.

Johansson saw the opportunity and laced his hand into hers. Just lightly, though, very lightly. Skin touching skin. No pressure.

"I'm going to buy something nice for you as a Christmas present. Something we don't have here."

"A solid gold sheriff's badge?" She giggled and squeezed his hand harder.

"Yes," said Johansson. "Or perhaps one of those blue baseball caps that say FBI."

Bäckström was still at the after-hours unit despite the fact that it was half an hour past midnight, and he was sour as vinegar. Wijnbladh and he had sealed the door to the do-it-yourselfer's room before ten-thirty, and by dawn next day the whole sorry story would be lying on the desk of the officer in charge at Östermalm. Real policemen like him and Wijnbladh shouldn't be involved with this kind of shit. The peasant police in the local precincts could deal with it.

Everything had gone like a charm, and they were just about to close the door to the corridor when that damn black guy had shown up together with some Swedish student whore with purple lipstick, and you didn't have to be a policeman to figure out what the two of them had in mind. He'd also been obstinate in some incoherent African English. He refused to move and wanted to know what the hell they were doing in his corridor. Bäckström's only thought was to bypass the piece of shit and take the elevator down, although he really ought to have called for a patrol car with two types like Oredsson in it, but naturally the coward Wijnbladh got involved. He had shown his ID and started negotiating with the gook in his own lousy English. Then the whore had interfered too, partly in Swedish and partly in English, and the misery had broken loose in earnest. He couldn't have taken his own life, he was a really fine guy, not the least bit depressed, blah blah blah.

Finally Bäckström had been forced to crack down. He'd told them to call on Monday, and to be on the safe side he'd given them the name and extension of a colleague in the bureau who was almost always on sick leave this time of year because of his severe alcohol problem. They were finally able to drive away after a quarter hour of his life had gone down the toilet.

When at last he sat down behind his desk to tie up all the loose threads in this sorry story, it was time for the next lunatic. That fat clod Stridh clearly had his work orders turned upside down and had submitted an interrogation with the witness. Two closely spaced typewritten pages, for something you could be done with in ten lines, and completely incomprehensible throughout. According to the witness, the early retired Gustav Adolf Nilsson, it was clearly not he but his mutt who had heard that lunatic Krassner jump out the window. The same mutt who, despite his good hearing, had been killed by a mysteriously falling shoe.

What do you mean, early-retired? thought Bäckström. Social Swedish for a drunk who didn't want to pay his way, but was still able to cheat the pants off some naïve socialist bastard at the unemployment office. Up yours, thought Bäckström as he dialed Vindel's home number.

A quarter of an hour later the whole thing was signed, sealed, and delivered, as always when a real pro was at work. Bäckström pulled the report from the cylinder of the typewriter and made corrections with his ballpoint pen while he read the brief, clarifying text, in which, by the way, there was not the least trace of an as yet unburied dog.

"Upon questioning by telephone the witness Nilsson states the following in summary. Circa 19:50 the witness found himself below the student dormitory the Rosehip on Körsbärsvägen. The witness states that at that point he became aware of a sound from one of the upper stories of the building. When he looked up he observed the body of a male person who had jumped out of a window, fallen straight down along the façade of the building, and struck the ground only a few yards from the place where the witness was standing. The witness has had this questioning read to him by telephone and has approved it."

The last was a complete lie, but because Nilsson was hardly the type who recorded his telephone conversations with the police, no damage was done. In addition, the old fart had sounded completely confused when Bäckström was talking with him. He ought to be grateful that someone helped him put the pieces in place, thought Bäckström, while he put the papers into a plastic sleeve and applied a handwritten slip of paper for the officer in charge at Östermalm.

Bäckström looked at the clock. Five past one but still there was no great hurry. There was even time to carry out a little idea he'd had while he wrote out the interview with Nilsson. A stitch in time, thought Bäckström, as he folded up his overcoat and hid it in an empty binder that he'd found on the bookshelf. Bäckström took the binder under his arm and the plastic sleeve in his other hand, sneaked out to reception, and placed the plastic sleeve farthest down in the pile in the Östermalm police in-box. After that he stuck his head in through the door to the on-duty chief inspector's office.

"It's about that suicide you sent me out on." Bäckström nodded toward the binder, which he was carrying under his arm.

"Are there any problems?" The on-duty chief inspector wrinkled his brow.

"No. It's completely clear that it's a suicide, but it concerns an American citizen and that can be sensitive, you know. There are a few things I was thinking about checking in the register."

"What's the problem?" The on-duty chief inspector looked inquiringly at him, but the wrinkle in his brow was gone.

"I was thinking about overtime. I should have gone off duty more than an hour ago."

"It's okay. Put down whatever time it takes."

I'll be damned, thought the on-duty chief inspector, looking after Bäckström's quickly vanishing backside. Of all the chiselers. Maybe he's gotten religion, he thought, but at the same moment the phone rang and he had other things to think about.

Finally free, thought Bäckström as he slipped out through the gate to Kungsholmsgatan and set out toward the bar. He tossed the empty binder into the nearest garbage can.

.   .   .

At midnight Lars Martin Johansson was already in his bed on Wollmar Yxkullsgatan, listening to the bells ring in Maria Church. A nice-looking woman, he thought. She was nice to talk with too, although a police officer, of course. Wonder if she's married to that idiot in Växjö or if they only live together? You can't have it all, thought Johansson and sighed. Or can you? Perhaps you can have it all? This new thought cheered him up markedly. Tomorrow was a new day, he thought, and then perhaps he would have it all? Johansson stretched out his arm and turned out the bed lamp, lay on his right side with his arm under the pillow, and within a few minutes he was sleeping as soundly as he always did.

Vindel was standing in the parlor. He'd lifted Charlie's basket up onto the oak table by the window. He stroked the soft fur and Charlie lay as quietly as if he were sleeping. Tomorrow he would arrange the funeral. Time will tell, thought Vindel, although just now it didn't feel so merry. He wiped away a tear with the back of his hand. Best to open the window a little, he thought. Pomeranians don't like it when it gets too warm.

Police Assistant Stridh had gone home directly after his shift. Made himself a substantial and nutritious sandwich, topped with a well-considered mixture of the goodies to be found in his generously supplied refrigerator. Plus a cold beer. Now he was lying on the sofa in his living room, reading Winston Churchill's biography of his ancestor the Duke of Marlborough. It was in four volumes and almost three thousand pages long, but because he didn't need to be at work before Monday afternoon he had all the time in the world. A great man, thought Stridh, in contrast to that mustache-wearing lunatic who tried to set the whole world on fire and would just about have succeeded if it hadn't been for old Winston. Strange that he wasn't a bachelor, thought Stridh, while he made himself comfortable on the couch and looked up the place in the second volume where he'd stopped reading the last time he'd gone off duty.

. . .

His young colleague Oredsson had changed into workout clothes after his shift and gone straight down to the gym in the cellar. There the lights were always off this time of day; lifting weights after completed service had become like a purifying bath for him. It helped him to arrange all the new impressions and experiences into a larger context. He'd understood from the first day that it was foreigners who were responsible for almost all crimes being committed in today's Sweden, but how could the problem itself be solved? Just sending them home, which would have been the simplest, was unthinkable in the current political climate. But what should be done instead, and how could they achieve a political climate in which necessary changes would even become possible? That was worth thinking about, thought Oredsson, and discussing with trusted colleagues. Because he had also understood on that first day that he was not alone.

At home in his bedroom Wiijnbladh lay and masturbated while he thought about what his wife had been doing that night. He'd figured out several years ago that she wasn't out with her girlfriends. Then he'd borrowed a service car and followed her. She had gone straight home to a recently divorced colleague out in Älvsjö, and because the lights in his apartment were turned out almost immediately you didn't need to be a policeman to understand that this wasn't a first visit. He had remained sitting there half the night in the cold car while he stared at the black windows and thoughts were coursing like tracers in his head. Then he'd driven home, never said a word on the subject, and never showed by his expression what he knew and thought.

He didn't know where and with whom she was tonight. She wasn't with his colleague in Älvsjö in any event, for he'd hanged himself half a year ago, and it was Wiijnbladh who'd had the exquisite pleasure of cutting him down from the pipe in the ceiling of the laundry room where he'd secured the rope. A heavy duty, even for the hardened investigators on the tech squad. But necessary, and Wiijnbladh had volunteered.

How could something that started so well end so damn badly? thought Bäckström, staring drunkenly down into the beer glass that he'd succeeded in grabbing hold of at the bar while the rightful owner was out on the dance floor. He'd gone to a place with good prospects down on Kungsgatan that was mostly frequented by police and an assortment of firemen, security guards, and ambulance drivers. Plus a hellish lot of hospital orderlies, and for a scarred champion like himself the competition hardly seemed overwhelming.

Everything had started perfectly too. He had run into a younger officer from the bureau in Farsta who wanted to get onto the homicide squad at any price and had also gotten the idea that Bäckström was the right man to arrange the matter. Two paltry beers he'd paid for, that stingy bastard, so he could forget that business with homicide. Then he'd encountered a fat Finnish woman he'd screwed last summer. She was working as a bedpan changer at Sabbatsberg hospital and lived in a filthy three-room apartment far out in hell somewhere in the southern suburbs. Single mother of course; he could still feel the LEGO pieces crunching under the soles of his feet when he slipped out the following morning. She clearly also had a faulty memory, for despite the previous visit, he had succeeded in borrowing a twenty from her. He also got a wet kiss on the cheek, but now even she had taken off. The only people remaining in the almost empty place were a bunch of drunks plus a worn-down hag who'd fallen asleep on a couch.

What a fucking society, what fucking people, and what a fucking life they're living, thought Bäckström. The only thing you could hope for was a really juicy murder so you got something substantial to bite into.

[SATURDAY, NOVEMBER 23]

Police Inspector Bo Jarnebring of the Stockholm Police Department's central surveillance squad was not one to work on a Saturday if he had the choice, but for the past fourteen days such an option had been considerably reduced: He'd started a new job as chief inspector and head of the local detective unit with the Östermalm police. It was a temporary appointment, to be sure, and, he hoped, only for a short time, but everyone around him had nonetheless been greatly surprised. Jarnebring was generally known as the direct opposite of a careerist; he always spit upward and seldom missed an opportunity to chew out both bosses and semi-bosses. In addition, his work as a detective was perhaps the most important part of his identity. He had worked with the central surveillance squad for more than fifteen years, and he held an unquestioned conviction that, as far as his life as a policeman was concerned, he couldn't imagine anything better than to live and die that way.

A month ago he and a number of colleagues within the surveillance operation had taken the Finland ferry to Helsinki for a work conference. These meetings had long been a tradition and a necessary, recurring element of the planning that must take place, even within so-called surveillance, all the bohemian and impressionistic aspects of the occupation aside.

As always, it had been pleasant. Nothing but known quantities and guys you could trust. In the morning criminals old and new had been discussed, the usual heroic stories had been told, after which the proceedings were interrupted for a generously ample lunch, something which of course had been taken into account when the afternoon program had been determined. Among the invitees was the head of the detective unit of the Östermalm police, who would recount a few varied experiences from the local surveillance operation. He was a white man, a funny S.O.B., and despite the fact that he had departed from the true doctrine he was still an old detective in heart and soul. As the first item on the program after lunch he was absolutely perfect. He was a very entertaining lecturer, and afterward you could never remember a word he'd said. What the whole thing was about was actually something else: getting to meet friends and colleagues under somewhat more easygoing conditions, and perhaps having the opportunity during the evening to discuss something other than old crooks.

This time, unfortunately, things had really gone south. In the wee hours the elite few who were still standing on two feet had gathered in the conference leaders' cabin for a last round, and to make a long and nowadays thoroughly hushed-up story short, Jarnebring had torn the Achilles tendon of the chief of the Östermalm police detective unit. For the latter was not only an entertaining lecturer; he was also known as a strongman and past master at both arm-wrestling and Indian wrestling. Jarnebring was the last one standing, the same Jarnebring who twenty-five years earlier used to run the second leg of the short relay in the Finnish Games and had made it a habit never to give up.

The official version was somewhat different: *During the day's concluding remarks, one of the lecturers unfortunately happened to twist his ankle
when he stood to summarize the discussion up at the blackboard. Everyone had
of course been completely sober, but because the rough sea had been annoying at
times, misfortune nonetheless managed to rear its ugly head. A typical injury in
the line of duty, therefore, which was some consolation at least if you were
forced to go around in a cast for a few months.*

Jarnebring was a man who lived by simple and obvious rules. Discretion was a matter of honor. If you got involved in something, you made
a point of cleaning up after yourself, and when it really counted was
when your buddies were involved. Therefore, for the past fourteen days,
he had been filling in as head of the local detective unit with the Östermalm police and that was that.

Unfortunately, however, this had affected his life. His most recent
girlfriend, who worked as a uniformed police officer at Norrmalm, had
left early in the morning on a sudden call to duty, so he could forget that
type of activity. Exercising was not an option either, for you did that sort
of thing while on duty, and as an old elite athlete he knew the value of
holding yourself to a carefully determined exercise schedule. Paying a
call on his plaster-casted colleague in misfortune was also out of the
question. He had taken his wife along and gone to a health resort in
Värmland in order to rehabilitate himself in earnest, at the department's
expense.

After he showered, had breakfast, and leafed through the morning
paper, it was still only nine o'clock, and ahead of him stretched an
entirely free day, long as a marathon and hardly enticing for an old
sprinter like Jarnebring. At that point he decided to call his best friend
and former colleague, Police Superintendent Lars Martin Johansson, at
the National Bureau of Criminal Investigation. This decision had
demanded a good deal of inner persuasion, for the last time they had
met there had been a serious falling-out. Over a trifle, at that, a Yugoslav
thug whom Jarnebring and his colleagues, with considerable effort and
slightly unconventional methods, had finally succeeded in placing in the
criminal detention center where he ought to have been from the very
beginning. No big deal in itself, but Johansson, who had shown disturb-

ing signs of wavering conviction since he'd left the field campaign against criminality to take it easy behind a series of ever-larger desks, had gone completely crazy, bawled him out, and marched off in the middle of a nice dinner.

One time doesn't count, and I'm not one to dwell on the past, thought Jarnebring generously while he dialed his old friend and colleague's home number. But no one answered, and before Jarnebring realized it, he was suddenly striding through the doors to the reception area at the Östermalm police station on Tulegatan. He nodded toward the officer in uniform who was sitting behind the counter and in turn nodded back.

"How's it going?" asked Jarnebring. "Anything happened?"

The officer shook his head while he checked off his list. "A few car prowls, fistfights, and property damage at some bar over on Birger Jarlsgatan, an executive on Karlavägen who beat up his wife, although homicide should have taken care of that of course, yes." He leafed through his papers. "Then we have a suicide too. Some crazy American who jumped from that student dormitory up on Valhallavägen."

"American, from the U.S.?"

The officer in uniform nodded in confirmation.

"American citizen. Born in '53, I believe. The papers are in your box. I got them from the after-hours unit this morning."

Olle Hultman, thought Jarnebring and brightened up. It'll soon be Christmas, after all.

Johansson had already been at work for more than an hour when Jarnebring phoned him at home. Christmas was drawing near, soon he would be changing jobs, and both old and new needed to be in order before then. I'm living in a time of change, he thought while he leafed through the pile of papers on his desk. First he had cleared up the final planning of his trip. This was something he was looking forward to. Flight from Stockholm to New York, direct connection to Washington, D.C., and after that pickup by car for transport to the FBI Academy in Quantico, Virginia. Five-day-long conference on the most up-to-date methods in the struggle against the steadily increasing crime rate—that's what it said in the program, anyway—and then back to New York, where he had the weekend free. Johansson was already rubbing his hands with delight. He liked New York. He'd been there once before. Undeniably certain differences compared to both Näsåker and Stockholm, but just right for a person who was trying to expand his awareness.

After that he started writing a statement in connection with the investigation of a triple murder in Stockholm's southern suburbs just over a year before. The investigators and technicians of the Stockholm police had unfortunately missed two of the corpses. The third was lying in the building elevator, so they had found that one, but because the elevator was rather small the perpetrator had dumped the other two in the elevator shaft, and unfortunately it was the building superintendent who had found them a few days later. To make matters worse, the police department ombudsman got wind of the matter and for once he was so well informed that there was reason to suspect that a fifth columnist was running loose like a mad dog, striking wildly around himself in his own flock. He hadn't been found either.

"It's probably someone who feels he's been passed over," Wiijnbladh had suggested as they were having coffee at the technical squad, and all the officers had nodded in agreement. Even that idiot Olsson, who got the position as assistant head of the squad that Wiijnbladh should have had. If there had been any justice in this world.

The ombudsman had in turn requested a statement from the National Police Board: Could this be considered consistent with professional police work?

The chief of national police was a highly placed attorney with a background in government, and he didn't know a thing about police work; nor did anyone around him, for that matter.

"Perhaps we should ask Johansson," suggested the chief of national police. "They say he was something of a legend during his time at the bureau." No one in the group had raised any objections whatsoever.

The chief of national police was delighted with Johansson. Not only was he a "real policeman," he looked like a real policeman, and even spoke with a Norrland accent. In addition he was completely understandable both when he spoke and when he wrote. A remarkable man, the chief of national police had thought on more than one occasion. He even seemed . . . well . . . educated.

Johansson was completely unaware of these bureaucratic considerations as he plowed his way with a groan through the files that the Stockholm Police Department had handed over: a balancing act between the frying pan of collegiality and the fire of professionalism. Maybe I could make a joke of it, thought Johansson. The three victims were Turks, as was the perpetrator; what it concerned was what was summarized in police-speak as a showdown in narcotics circles. Turks, as was well known, tended to be small, dark, and hard to discover, especially in an elevator shaft. Here was an excellent occasion, after ten years' absence, once again to share a front seat with Jarnebring and meet his other old comrades from surveillance. Johansson sighed, clasped his hands behind his head, and tipped his chair back. I have to weigh every word with the utmost care here, he thought.

Olle Hultman was an old detective, of course. What else would you expect? A detective of the really old school who not only knew every crook by name and number but also every tattoo on their needle-marked arms. When Jarnebring was new to surveillance, Olle Hultman had become his mentor, and the generally accepted opinion was that Hultman would live and die with his squad.

"When he's been kicked out after retirement he'll sit in the park outside the police station and feed the pigeons, and within half a year he'll be dead," his boss declared in confidence to Jarnebring. "So take the opportunity and learn. People like Olle don't grow on trees."

But his boss had been wrong. Completely wrong. Olle Hultman had taken the first opportunity for retirement at fifty-nine and immediately started working in the porter's office at the American embassy. There he had soon made himself indispensable in matters both large and small; for several years now he had been the informal head of the embassy's so-

called cigar-and-delicatessen department. Regardless of what annoyances might afflict embassy personnel and American citizens on
Swedish soil, Olle Hultman was the Right Man to deal with them. Olle
knew absolutely everyone and everyone liked him. All police officers did
of course, but in addition he had strategic contacts all the way from the
coast guard and customs through the tax and enforcement authorities
and down to the street department's meter maids.

This time she'd come home at three-thirty in the morning and it took a
good while before she came into the bedroom and crept into bed. Wijnbladh pretended to sleep; by and by he must have done so for real. He
woke up by eight o'clock and despite the lack of sleep he felt completely
clear in the head. His wife slept deeply. She snored a little and had
drooled on the pillow. I ought to kill her, thought Wijnbladh, silently
collecting his clothes. He slipped out into the living room and got
dressed. He decided to go to work, despite the fact that it was still many
hours before he needed to head for his after-hours shift.

At approximately the time that Wijnbladh woke up, Stridh set aside his
book, adjusted himself on the couch, and fell asleep. In spite of the fact
that he looked like King Oscar II he felt like a prince. In his dreams he
intended to visit Blenheim Palace, wander through the high, light halls,
stop for a while in the room where Winston had been born, and then
have a nourishing lunch at a nearby pub.

Jarnebring had called Hultman's pager and within a minute Hultman
had phoned back. After another minute Jarnebring had told him what it
was about: dead American citizen, white, born in '53, and according to as
of yet unconfirmed reports, possibly active as a journalist; a press pass
had been found among his belongings. According to the after-hours unit
it was a suicide, but he had nevertheless decided to take a look at the
matter himself, and if Hultman wanted to come along that would be
just fine. Services and counter-services, thought Jarnebring.

"You suspect something fishy?" asked Hultman.

"No," answered Jarnebring, "but I have nothing better to do."

"I'll gladly tag along," Hultman said warmly. "You should know that sometimes I wish I were back. I suggest we take my car, in case he has things that I can drive to the embassy. I can be there in ten minutes."

"See you outside," said Jarnebring and hung up. He got up, flexed his broad shoulders, took the holster with his service weapon, and snapped it securely to his left thigh. There now, he thought, grinning contentedly.

Bäckström woke up at roughly the time when he should have been at work. He had felt better. The bedroom reeked of sweat and old binges, and when he tested his breath against the palm of his hand he realized that the situation was critical. I've got to shower, thought Bäckström, in spite of the fact that only homos showered more than once a week: tooth-brushing, gargling, throat lozenges, at least one pack in his pocket. At work the same nondenominational preacher/chief inspector that he'd been forced to schmooze with the night before was waiting, and Bäckström was not one to take unnecessary risks. What the hell do they want? he thought while the water sprinkled over his white body. Here you work the whole night and what do you get for that? At the same moment the phone rang. It was the preacher calling. His voice sounded acid and he wondered if something had happened.

"Nothing other than that I worked until five in the morning and happened to oversleep," an offended Bäckström replied. "But now I'm on my way."

How stupid can you get? he thought smugly. The dolt had even begged pardon.

Now it was just a matter of finding a pair of clean underwear. The ones he'd had on yesterday didn't smell too confidence-inspiring. Bäckström poked around in the pile of dirty laundry and finally found a pair that didn't seem to be coming direct from the cheese shop. This is going to work out, he thought. As always when a real pro is at work.

It was true that Jarnebring looked like a badass, talked like a badass, and all too often behaved like a badass, but as a policeman he didn't leave much to be desired. He was quick, shrewd, efficient, and had the preda-tor's nose for human weakness. Together with Hultman he made one half of an odd couple. Jarnebring was large and burly, dressed in a winter coat that extended below the waist in order to conceal his service weapon, blue jeans, and shoes with rubber soles that gave a sure footing if he needed to run after someone. Hultman was small and slim, looked younger than his sixty-four years, wore a single-breasted gray suit with a vest and a blue topcoat against the November wind.

While they stood observing the place where Krassner had hit the ground, an older woman stopped on the gravel walk below.

"Are you from the police?" she asked. Jarnebring noticed with a cer-tain enjoyment that it was Hultman who'd received the question.

"Yes," said Hultman with a competent funeral director's ingratiating smile. "We're in the process of investigating a death. But it's nothing you need to worry yourself about."

The old lady shook her head mournfully.

"I heard from a neighbor that it was one of those poor students who jumped out the window. It's just all so sad, isn't it? Young people."

Now Jarnebring nodded in the same way as his old mentor. The lady shook her head, smiled weakly, and went on.

In total it had taken them four hours, from the time Hultman picked Jarnebring up outside the Östermalm police station until he dropped him off at the same place; during that time they had accomplished a great deal. First they had visited the place where Krassner had died. After that they had looked in his apartment and spoken with a couple of the students who were living on the same corridor. No one they spoke with had known him especially well. He had only lived there, on a sub-lease, for a little more than a month and hadn't appeared to be particu-larly interested in associating with anyone. In addition he had been considerably older than the others on the corridor. The one they had talked with the most was a South African student who had expressed strong doubt that Krassner had taken his own life, but when Jarnebring pressed him he hadn't been able to explain why. It was more a feeling that he had.

They had devoted most of their time to searching through Krassner's apartment. Between the bathroom cabinet and the wall Jarnebring found a plastic bag with five marijuana cigarettes—not the first time in that particular spot—which Bäckström and Wiijnbladh had obviously missed, but otherwise there was nothing sensational to report. Most of the time had been spent gathering together Krassner's personal belongings and dividing them into two piles. One pile Hultman could take with him to the embassy to send home to Krassner's relatives in the United States and a significantly smaller pile that Jarnebring needed to retain until the investigation was complete. In the first and larger pile were mostly clothes and in the second, smaller pile mostly personal papers. Hultman had done this before. Jarnebring wrote the confiscation report while Hultman divided the respective piles and dictated what went where. Jarnebring had not had any objections.

After the visit to the apartment they had gone to the home of the witness, Gustav Adolf Nilsson, who lived on Surbrunnsgatan right in the vicinity. Both Jarnebring and Hultman had met Nilsson previously while on duty, but because Nilsson didn't appear to remember them, they didn't mention it. Nilsson, or Vindel, as he preferred to be called, had been depressed but at the same time relieved. He had succeeded in arranging a place for his dog at the animal cemetery, and a few of the neighbors would be present at the burial.

"I've set him on the balcony for the time being," said Vindel, nodding toward the balcony door. "Pomeranians don't like it if it gets too hot," he added in explanation.

The rest had been purely routine. First they had driven out to the embassy and dropped off those of Krassner's effects that were not needed for the investigation. True, the police station was closer, but because Jarnebring had accepted with pleasure a guided tour of the embassy, he would have to be dropped off afterward in reverse order. Thus, almost exactly four hours after Hultman had picked him up outside the Östermalm police station, they were back at the same spot.

Hultman stopped. Turned off the motor and smiled amiably toward Jarnebring.

"Scotch or bourbon?" he asked.

"Can't you get a mixed case?" Jarnebring asked in return. "My lady isn't too thrilled about whiskey and it's almost Christmas."

"No problem. A mixed case. A completely different matter," Hultman looked at Jarnebring and smiled paternally. "Are you doing anything in particular this evening?"

Jarnebring shook his head.

"You don't happen to have a suit with a white shirt and a tie?"

Jarnebring nodded. He knew what was coming.

"Then I thought to ask if I might have the pleasure of treating you to a nice dinner."

"Certainly." Jarnebring smiled. "Should I bring along a couple of young ladies? Mine is on assignment, of course, but she has a couple of colleagues who are really something."

"Old memories." Hultman nodded, mostly to himself, it seemed. "First we talk about old memories, and then you tell me what has happened since I quit while we have a really good dinner. What you do after that doesn't concern me, as long as you take care of yourself."

Johansson sat the whole day and worked on his statement about the two missed murder victims. He wasn't done until about seven—thinking, that is; the actual writing of his viewpoints would have to wait until tomorrow. After that he took a taxi home, prepared a simple meal, and spent the rest of the evening watching TV. At midnight he was sleeping deeply, on his right side with his right arm tucked under the pillow.

Hultman had kept his promise. They started eating at seven-thirty and it was not until just before midnight that Hultman looked at his watch and took out his gold card. They said goodbye on the street outside the restaurant with mutual marks of respect and promises to see each other again soon. After that Hultman went home while Jarnebring wandered further out into the Stockholm night.

· · ·

Stridh woke up just in time for the morning news on the radio. After that he had hash with eggs and red beets and two beers. Now he was lying on the couch again and it was time to start on volume three. Finally, he thought, making himself comfortable, finally time to study the political intrigues in early-eighteenth-century Holland that preceded the battle of Blenheim.

Wiijnbladh's day had been a day of personal suffering, as was often the case. First he had pondered various ways to put his wife to death, but because none of them was painful enough and certain enough—after all, he couldn't assume that Bäckström and his colleagues would be in charge of the investigation—it had only granted him minor relief. When he'd finally pulled himself together and driven home, a note from his wife stuck to the mirror in the hall reported that she'd gone to visit her sister in Sollentuna. Wonder what they talk about? thought Wiijnbladh with a shiver.

Bäckström had had a good day, even if it had appeared threatening at the start when his boss foisted a wife-abuse case off on him. What do you mean, wife abuse? thought Bäckström. Every policeman worth his badge knew that these were only drunken hags who wanted nothing better than to have their drunken husbands beat them up. All women liked a little whipping (Bäckström knew that from personal experience), but certain specimens persisted in spicing up marital coexistence by running off now and then to Mister Policeman to complain. They should have a damn good beating instead, thought Bäckström while he steered his service car to the victim's residence. Strangely enough she lived on fashionable Karlavägen, which had made him sufficiently curious to show up for questioning at the residence.

What a hell of an apartment, thought Bäckström when he had finally sunk down into the victim's sofa. There was no shortage of dough here, and most likely she was trying to squeeze her man for even more and he'd quite simply taken a swing at her, but without a doubt the case offered certain openings. She didn't look too bad either, thought Bäckström. Certainly over forty, but she had big knockers and could surely get good speed going on her little mouse if a real pro like Bäckström was at the stick.

"Yes, Mrs. Östergren," said Bäckström gently. "If you would be so kind as to tell me what happened. You can take your time and try to take it from the beginning, even if it feels terribly difficult just now."

Mrs. Östergren nodded and snuffled. I do believe, God help me, that I'm sitting here making myself horny, thought Bäckström contentedly with his head slightly to one side.

"There there, Mrs. Östergren," he said consolingly. "This is going to work out. I'll see to it personally. Soon we're going to see the light at the end of the tunnel," he added. When I'm looking into your pussy, you fucking sow, he thought.

Three hours later Bäckström was sitting at the after-hours unit, writing out his report. If our friend the executive doesn't get locked up for this then he never will be, thought Bäckström. His dear old lady had gotten both Bäckström's work and home numbers, so that part the dear spouse didn't need to think about. If she just rises to the bait I'll be greasing up her snout, thought Bäckström, and he pulled the last piece of paper from the typewriter. High time for a beer or two, he added to himself, looking at the clock while making the most necessary corrections with his ballpoint pen.

Oredsson had spent the day with ten or so of his closest cohorts, all of them officers with the uniformed police, of course. Three were actually women but completely okay despite that fact. One of his friends had gotten the use of an abandoned hut from an older relative, and there they had practiced breaking in and freeing hostages (blank ammunition, of course) and then they'd barbecued and finished a couple cases of beer while they chatted about this and that.

"This sort of thing should be cleared up before it happens," explained Mikkelson, who worked with the riot squad and knew what he was talking about. "It's nothing that needs to be fussed about when it's already happened."

A white man, thought Oredsson, and in the evening they would be meeting again, go out on the town, and show the colors.

A spot with better prospects than this probably doesn't exist, thought Jarnebring contentedly, looking around the large bar. He had found a dive on Kungsgatan where mostly police and a few firemen, security guards, and other assorted folks went, plus at least a few battalions of female nursing personnel. He'd gotten results right away. Two female officers from the police cavalry, at least one of whom seemed firmly determined to ride down his on-duty girlfriend.

"You're looking nice," she said approvingly. "I've never seen you in a suit before, but it looks good on you."

"Business," said Jarnebring and shrugged his broad shoulders apologetically. "I'm at Östermalm now, so the American embassy invited me to dinner. Think about that, ladies, when you're galloping around out on Djurgården. See to it that you behave yourselves." Jarnebring gave them a quarter of a wolfish grin.

"And if we don't do that?"

Damn she's good-looking, thought Jarnebring. The night has hardly begun and I'm already home.

Jarnebring increased the power to half a wolfish grin. Leaned over and whispered in her ear. She giggled but her friend suddenly looked wary. A possible leak there, thought Jarnebring, and how do I seal it?

When Bäckström came in he was in an excellent mood. En route to the bar he had already planned the first gentlemen's dinner for his colleagues in homicide in his new apartment on Karlavägen. They're going to shit their pants, those fucking paupers, thought Bäckström delightedly while he slipped past the coat check. He had left his coat at work on Kungsholmsgatan. Who the hell wants to pay for something like that? thought Bäckström, staring at the coat checker. Fucking loan shark.

Because he was completely broke, not a fucking kopeck in his pockets, he had immediately started scouting around for a suitable victim that he could borrow a little from, but the pickings looked thin. On the other hand it was booming like hell out on the dance floor and there was a good pull from the bar; plenty of abandoned bottles and glasses. Bäckström made an evasive maneuver behind a burly type in a suit who was standing with his back to him chatting with a couple of blondes that he had a vague memory he'd seen somewhere. Some damn security guard who's been at daddy's funeral and wants to show off that he has a suit, thought Bäckström as his fat fingers wrapped themselves around an almost full half liter of strong beer. There it is, thought Bäckström. Carefully pulled the beer toward him and turned around, back against back. A sure trick that always worked. He sighed silently with pleasure and raised his well-earned malt.

Suddenly the suit reached out a hand, big as a hairy Christmas ham with fingers on top of it, and grabbed hold of his beer.

"Watch out, you bastard, I'm a cop," Bäckström threatened, and at the same moment he saw that it was Jarnebring. Has that bastard started sneaking around in disguise? thought Bäckström. He knew perfectly well who Jarnebring was. All policemen knew that. Only a month ago the fucking psychopath had torn the leg of an older colleague from Östermalm in order to get at his job. Wonder how many people he's beaten to death? thought Bäckström, and suddenly it felt as if he had a large black hole in his chest approximately where his heart used to be.

Jarnebring sipped his regained beer, smiled his wolfish grin, and nodded toward the mirror wall behind the rows of bottles standing on the bar.

"Do you see that mirror? I've been watching you since you came in."

Bäckström had a good reply on the tip of his tongue but for some reason that was never really clear to him he refrained from it and contented himself with nodding.

"I think you should go home," Jarnebring continued. "You seem a bit overworked." Jarnebring exchanged a glance with the bartender, who nodded, eyeing Bäckström.

"Go home and sleep," said the bartender. "And listen, I believe this place will get along fine without you. Just so you know."

Bäckström shrugged his shoulders, turned on his heels, and left. Actually he had only intended to make an evasive maneuver, but that damn gorilla standing in the doorway clearly had an eye on him. He smiled broadly toward Bäckström, held the front door with an exaggerated bow, and showed the way out with a sweeping right arm.

"Thank you for joining us, police inspector."

I'm going to kill you bastards, thought Bäckström.

Oredsson and his comrades had been sitting at a table only a few yards from the bar and they had seen the whole thing. Wonder if he thinks like we do? thought Oredsson. Everything I've heard about him seems to add up, and we work at the same place. He felt the excitement growing in his chest.

When Bäckström came out on Kungsgatan it was snowing. Large white flakes floating like moist reminders, unclear of what, from the great infinity up there. Suddenly he started weeping. Hell. He was weeping like a little bastard, like a fucking hag. Bastards, he thought. I'm going to kill those bastards.

"I'm going to kill you bastards," Bäckström roared straight out toward the empty street and a passing taxi. What fucking people, what a fucking society, and what a fucking life they're living, he thought.

[SUNDAY, NOVEMBER 24]

Johansson devoted Sunday to writing out his statement on the two missed murder victims. He weighed every word with utmost care, and as such things took their sweet time, it was already seven o'clock in the evening when he returned to his apartment. After that he prepared a simple meal, read a book in English about the international narcotics trade, and at midnight he was sleeping deeply, according to already long-established routine.

You're starting to get old, thought Jarnebring gloomily as he leafed through the papers on John P. Krassner's death. The night before, everything had gone without a hitch. They hadn't even had to dance with each other, but instead had sat at a table in the quietest corner available, while her friend excused herself and slipped away with a well-known local stud from the Södermalm riot squad. Then he had gone home with her. They had walked the whole way in spite of the fact that she lived way up at Gärdet, and when they were finally standing in her doorway there was only one decision he needed to make.

She smiled at him but in her eyes there was another, more evaluating expression.

"Well," she said, giggling. "What do we do? Will you come up and have a cup of tea? Are you going home? Or do you want more time to think it over?"

First he had considered using having to work the next day as an excuse. Instead he shook his head.

"I'm going home," answered Jarnebring. "It may be that I've got a big hole in my head, but considering . . . well, I'm sure you know . . . so I guess I'll go home."

She had had difficulty concealing her surprise. Then she had shrugged her shoulders, smiled at him, leaned over, and given him a kiss right on the mouth.

"Suit yourself," she said and disappeared through the doorway.

You're a coward, thought Jarnebring as he was walking down the street. Or else you're starting to get old. That thought, however, was so unpleasant that he immediately dismissed it.

Now he was sitting here, behind a desk where he didn't need to be. Like a male counterpart to Busy Lizzie—and as a chief inspector and boss he didn't even get overtime. I'm starting to get like Johansson, thought Jarnebring, leafing further in his papers. There are three possibilities, he thought: murder, suicide, or accident.

It seemed extremely unlikely that this was an accident. Krassner was five feet eight inches tall; the window was relatively high up on the wall and well above Krassner's waist. Besides, it was equipped with a catch, which meant that it could only be opened a few inches. The same window catch that someone had broken loose with force, and the break marks in the wood seemed brand new. It even smelled of wood in the holes from the pulled-out screws. Assume that he'd had a sudden, compulsive need for a breath of fresh air, broken the catch, and leaned out. Even then he shouldn't have tipped over and fallen out. Forget that, thought Jarnebring, crossing out the third alternative.

Murder or suicide remained. What argued for murder? Nothing, thought Jarnebring. No signs of trespass, no signs of struggle, no known, visible, or even plausible motive, no murder weapon, hardly even any opportunity. What kind of murderer went into a student room and, without a sound or a trace, murdered the person who was living there? Eight small rooms with thin walls crowded along a common corridor, and a potential murderer could scarcely control the fact that Krassner was the only one there when the whole thing happened. You can just forget murder, thought Jarnebring with a slight feeling of regret that he couldn't help, occupationally injured as he was.

That left suicide, thought Jarnebring, and what argued for that? Everything we're aware of, he thought, and it's not our fault that we don't know too much about Krassner himself. A vacuum that, by the way, Hultman would be filling for him rather soon. He harbored no doubts on that point. Alone in the room, depressed or on a sudden gloomy impulse, he writes a suicide note—that was still the way it had to be interpreted—breaks the window catch, takes a deep breath, and jumps. There were certainly better ways, not least considering those who would have to clean up afterward, but not for Krassner, not this time. No pills had been found that he might have ingested, no knife or other sharp object that would have worked against wrists or neck, no rope to hang himself with, not even a place where he could have fastened the noose. Definitely no firearm.

Suicide, thought Jarnebring and nodded, and now it was only a matter of straightening out three remaining question marks. The first regarded Krassner as an individual. Who was he and what was he actually doing here? Hultman and the embassy will take care of that, and I'll chew my service revolver if they come up with anything that makes a mess of things for me, thought Jarnebring.

The second concerned Vindel's testimony about the victim's mysterious left shoe, which had come tumbling down a good while after

Krassner himself and unfortunately killed Vindel's best friend. An admittedly old Pomeranian, thought Jarnebring, and even if this was punishable, there was no suspect that could be held responsible.

The distance in time from the moment the victim hit the ground to the time his left shoe did was the question they had talked about most when they questioned Vindel. It was a matter of less than a minute, less than half a minute, but it wasn't a matter of a mere few seconds and Vindel was quite certain on that point.

"Yes, first I just stood there staring. I was in shock, of course, and it took a few seconds for sure, and it's not really so strange if it seemed longer to me." Vindel cleared his throat, sighed, and tried again. "Yes. Then I stood there looking at the guy who fell, and it was not a pretty sight, I can assure you, officers. I've only seen something like that once before and it was a good many years ago. A buddy of mine at work who fell down from a bridge span and landed in the cargo hold of a working tug anchored in the river under us. It was up at Älvkarleby. We were doing some maintenance work."

Vindel sighed again and nodded.

"Ten seconds. Say it took ten seconds before Charlie got the shoe on his head." Vindel snuffled and his eyes became moist.

When they'd left Vindel and were en route to the embassy they'd discussed the mysterious shoe. Hultman had also come up with an explanation that wasn't too bad.

"Do you recall that crazy who jumped from his private plane and landed in a flower bed out in Hässelby?" asked Hultman.

Jarnebring remembered him, with a wry smile besides, occupationally injured as he was.

"The guy who was buck naked when he landed," Jarnebring said, nodding.

"I seem to recall that he had one sock on," said Hultman. "He had those knee-length ones with garters. I seem to recall that he was some kind of executive."

Jarnebring nodded again. That was right. He too had made note of the garter.

"All of his clothes peeled off on the way down from the draft."

"On that occasion it was a fall of six hundred yards," said Hultman, "before all his clothes were pulled off. This time we're talking about fifty yards. Fifty yards ought to be enough to pull off a shoe, shouldn't it?"

"I think so too," said Jarnebring, nodding in agreement. "But how do we explain the difference in time? I've only seen the shoes in pictures, but they seem to be sturdy things, boots almost. Ought to fall just as fast as a body. If they hadn't hit . . ." Jarnebring was thinking out loud but Hultman was there first.

"For example, a window ledge or something else on the way down," Hultman concluded.

"Not at all unlikely," said Jarnebring.

"Highly probable, if you ask me," said Hultman.

The third question mark remained. There were four witnesses to the occurrence itself; four known witnesses. First Vindel, then the three who had contacted the command center, and as far as the time was concerned they were of one voice and were quite certainly correct. About four minutes before eight in the evening Krassner had begun his fall, and scarcely four seconds later he hit the ground. Think if you were able to fall free for the time it took to run a hundred yards, thought Jarnebring. That would give the others something to chew on.

In addition there was a fifth witness. A student from South Africa who was living on the same corridor as Krassner. Some time about six-thirty in the evening he had greeted Krassner as the latter was on his way out. They hadn't spoken with each other, only said hello. Dressed in out-door clothes, Krassner had then disappeared through the door to the elevators, while the student himself had gone into his room. Half an hour later—approximately—the witness had left the corridor. He was going to meet a girl at seven o'clock at a student restaurant that was in an adjacent building and he was leaving at the last moment.

"Unfortunately I often arrive late, even if it's someone I like," he had added with an apologetic smile.

Once out on the street he had almost run into Krassner, who was on his way into the building again. Dressed in the same outdoor clothes, according to the witness's recollection. Krassner had said hello, shaken his head, and said something in English about a bad memory being good if you wanted to keep your legs in good shape. "A bad memory keeps your legs in good shape."

"He smiled at me and didn't appear at all like he was going to rush up and take his own life," the witness had concluded, and that observation was also his point.

Jarnebring sighed. He goes out at six-thirty. Comes rushing back a half hour later, and less than an hour after that he decides to jump out the window. What is going on? thought Jarnebring, looking out his own window. At least it had stopped snowing, temperature several degrees above freezing, slushy and slippery. An impulse? "No, to hell with this. No more beers at the bar for me. High time I scurry home and jump out the window." And he'd been happy too, if that black guy was to be believed, thought Jarnebring gloomily. What if I were to phone Lidman? He was a professor, after all, and had written some sort of dissertation about what went on in the heads of all do-it-yourselfers. Jarnebring had heard him give a lecture about his findings, and regardless of the subject he had never listened to such an elated lecturer. Lidman had bubbled with enthusiasm, and the pictures he had shown had been a bit much even for the hardened policemen who made up his audience.

Jarnebring looked up Lidman's number, phoned him, talked with him for close to half an hour, of which the last five minutes were spent getting him to stop, but when he was finally able to put down the receiver he was in almost as high spirits as Lidman himself. So it wasn't any more difficult than that, thought Jarnebring contentedly. A rather classic behavior in someone who is just about to take his own life; the only thing that bothered him now was that that wretched Bäckström had come to the same conclusion as himself. Albeit in his own case it had been preceded by thorough and competent police work. How the hell can someone like that become a police officer? thought Jarnebring. Whatever, he thought. Now it was high time to drive home and meet the little lady and perhaps he ought to go by way of Åhléns department store and buy a pound of shrimp and some other foreplay goodies.

.   .   .

Jarnebring looked like a badass, talked like a badass, and all too often behaved like a badass, but as a policeman he didn't leave much to be desired. He was quick, shrewd, efficient, and had the predator's nose for human weakness. When he left the Östermalm police quarters on Tulegatan, on the afternoon of Sunday, November 24, he was in a really good mood. Suicide, he thought, and just in time for Christmas he would cash out a well-earned mixed case from his old buddy Hultman.

[MONDAY, NOVEMBER 25]

When Lars Martin Johansson's secretary arrived at work at the National Police Board at eight o'clock on Monday morning her boss had already been sitting behind his desk for more than an hour, and he was in an excellent mood.

"I have a statement here," Johansson said, handing over a plastic folder with papers. "Three things: I want you to read it, see to it that it's comprehensible, and print it out. Any questions?"

His secretary took the papers, smiled coolly, and shook her head.

"Personally I'm going to go swimming," said Johansson cheerfully.

He must have met someone new, thought his secretary.

Johansson found running for exercise difficult. What bothered him was not the physical activity itself but simply the fact that he couldn't think while he ran: a pure waste of time, in other words. On the other hand, he thought very well while walking—this applied to brisk walks as well—and he did his very best thinking while swimming. Besides, things were so practically arranged in the large police station on Kungsholmen that they had their own pool.

Johansson was an excellent swimmer. He had learned it early in a simple and unsentimental way. The summer when he was five years old his oldest brother, who was fifteen, had taken little Lars Martin with him to the laundry pier down at the river, thrown him into the water, and from the pier given him the necessary instructions.

"You shouldn't flounder so damn much, try and swim like Tarzan."

Tarzan was the family's elkhound and a past master of dog-paddling,

46

clearly better than Johnny Weissmuller, and before the week was over, Lars Martin was swimming almost as well as the mutt.

"I'll be damned, you're a real man of talent," his big brother concluded proudly. "Now you'll learn how to swim like people."

After an hour in the pool, plus five minutes in the shower and twenty in the sauna, an alert and rosy Lars Martin Johansson returned to his office. His good mood didn't get any worse from the fact that his secretary had done exactly what he'd asked her to do.

"I've said it before and I'll say it again," said Johansson, "and you know what I mean. May I treat you to lunch as a thank-you?"

He's met someone new, thought his secretary, smiling and nodding.

The lunch had been excellent; what else was to be expected on a day like this? Johansson had fried bacon with potato pancakes and uncooked lingonberries, and when he ordered a large glass of cold milk with his meal, his secretary looked at him almost lovingly. Discreetly, of course, but still; as usual, she pecked at her vegetables and boiled fish.

"There has to be milk," explained Johansson. "Although it's important that it's cold. I saw some lunatic on TV who maintained that it took away the vitamins in the lingonberries, but he's got that turned around."

"I've decided," she said. "I'm going with you to the personnel bureau."

"Good," said Johansson and raised his milk glass in a toast. "It's a kick upward for me and I'll see to it that there'll be something for you too."

And a kick away from the police job, he thought. But he didn't say that. Instead they toasted with milk and mineral water.

"Now we'll have coffee," said Johansson with a Norrland accent. He leaned forward and looked at her with fake seriousness. "Boiled coffee."

In the afternoon Johansson was visited by the head of the personnel bureau whom he would succeed in a little more than a month. It was an informal visit; the head of the personnel bureau didn't really want anything in particular, just to complain in general terms and perhaps get a cup of coffee while he did so.

"Would you like a cookie with your coffee?" asked Johansson amiably, but he only shook his head. Tired, worn out, and kind, thought Johansson, and now they're going to get rid of you.

"I need some advice," the head of the personnel bureau said. "You've worked in Stockholm for many years. Do you know an officer named Koskinen?"

The one called Koskenkorva, thought Johansson, and nodded. "He's drunk himself to death?" Johansson suggested sensitively.

"If only it were that good," the head of the personnel bureau said with a loud moan. "No, he's been appointed head of the command center, and now we've received six complaints of which one is anonymous, signed by a group of some type that calls itself the Still Functioning Uniformed Police in Stockholm. It's twenty-two pages long and contains a detailed account of Chief Inspector Koskinen's performance as on-duty commander at Norrmalm. If what's there is true, it's horrifying."

"I'm sure it's true," said Johansson.

"At the same time the union at Norrmalm supports him wholeheartedly and his bosses have given him among the best evaluations I've ever seen during my years in this office."

"Obviously," said Johansson. "How else would they get rid of him?" That's why they're called traveling testimonials, he thought, but he didn't say that.

"What advice do you have?" The head of the personnel office looked at him almost imploringly.

"None," said Johansson cheerfully. "There is none. There isn't meant to be."

How naïve can you be? thought Johansson while he picked out shirts at the men's department at NK. His impending trip demanded certain additions to his wardrobe, and besides, an old acquaintance who was head of security for the largest of the city's three commercial banks had invited him to dinner that evening. But it wasn't this business that occupied his thoughts. The Koskinen problem will solve itself according to classic Darwinist police principles, he thought. Either he drinks himself to death, puts a bullet in his head, or gets so bad that he quite simply can't go on working. On the other hand, that he would flat out be fired was less likely. As a rule there was always some colleague in the vicinity who could pull the ass of someone like that out of the fire in a pinch, and if not, then it usually wasn't very important. What might that be? What might happen here? thought Johansson while he hesitated between a dark blue shirt and one that was a somewhat lighter blue.

"I'll take both," said Johansson, and the sales clerk nodded officiously.

In the evening he had dinner with his acquaintance, an ex–police officer but nowadays head of security at the large bank. Now he was moving up, chief of staff and member of the company board, and needed a successor.

"I have an offer, Lars," he said amiably while he twirled his wineglass between his fingers. "One of those that you can't say no to."

Johansson could.

"I'm a policeman," said Johansson. "The reason that I became a policeman was that I dreamed of putting crooks in the can. What I'm doing now is something different, to be sure, but I know it's only temporary."

His acquaintance had looked surprised.

"Think it over," he said.

Jarnebring had been up to his ears in work all morning—that was how he himself summarized the whole thing. First the customary morning prayers with his coworkers in the local detective unit where they had gone over the current cases in the precinct. After that he'd planned a special effort against car break-ins, which had recently increased substantially. He had arranged a lookout where his detectives could sit to avoid freezing, which was never good for the actual surveillance, and he had borrowed equipment from the narcotics squad: cameras, extra-powerful telescopes, and better communications equipment. Now the crooks would get it in the neck.

After a quick lunch in the building he turned off his phone and turned on the red "busy" lamp on the door. Now he was going to finish up the investigation of the cause of Krassner's death. Suicide, thought

Jarnebring emphatically, and called the forensic medicine office in Solna to hear how it had gone. It had gone very well, answered the responsible forensic doctor, who had already finished the autopsy early that morning.

There were no injuries to the body that appeared to have occurred in anything other than a natural manner.

"Natural manner?" said Jarnebring inquiringly.

"As in when you dive fifty yards straight down to the street," answered the doctor and giggled.

He was from Yugoslavia; he had the nickname Esprit de Corpse and was known as something of a joker, as long as the joke wasn't on him.

"The head crushed, thirty other fractures. We human beings cannot fly."

How true, how true, thought Jarnebring and sighed silently.

"What do we do with the clothes?" asked Esprit. "I still have his shoes and clothes here."

Lazy asses, thought Jarnebring; he was thinking of his colleagues on the technical squad.

"Didn't the techs take them with them, when they took the prints?" he asked.

"They forgot the clothes," said Esprit. "They got a call."

"I'll send a car," said Jarnebring, and he started to put down the receiver.

"Excellent. You'll get a preliminary statement. Suicide. We human beings cannot fly."

"Thanks," said Jarnebring, and hung up.

It was Oredsson and Stridh who got the task of fetching Krassner's clothes and shoes at the forensic medicine office in Solna for removal to the head of the bureau at their own precinct. Stridh remained sitting in the car while Oredsson took care of the practical details. Actually he did offer, thought Stridh while observing the entrance to the forensic medicine office. Such is the way of all flesh, he thought gloomily. It was also Oredsson who took the elevator up to turn over the two bags to Jarnebring when they'd returned to the station. He offered, thought

Stridh gloomily while he remained sitting in the car down in the garage, brooding.

Where have I seen him before? thought Jarnebring, looking at the husky young police officer standing in the door to his room. He was on the phone and waved him in with his free left hand.

"Can I call you back?" said Jarnebring and hung up.

"Yes?" he said and looked inquiringly at his visitor.

"It's these clothes that you asked us to pick up at the forensic medicine office, chief. The guy who jumped from the student dormitory last Friday."

"Put them on the chair there," said Jarnebring and started dialing the number of the person he'd just been talking with.

"I was thinking about those shoes." Oredsson held out the smaller bag.

"Yes?" said Jarnebring. A pair of strong, bootlike shoes in a transparent, sealed plastic bag.

"I don't know," his visitor said hesitantly, "but these aren't normal shoes."

"Not normal shoes?" Jarnebring put the receiver down on its cradle and leaned back in his chair while he inspected young Oredsson. "You mean that this is a pair of unusual shoes?"

"Yes. If you look at this magazine, chief." His visitor held out a thick magazine with a colorful cover toward Jarnebring at the same moment as the phone rang again.

"Put it on the chair," said Jarnebring and took the receiver. "Jarnebring," he answered curtly and waved out Oredsson with a left hand that brooked no contradictions. The people they let in these days, he thought, irritated.

"The police superintendent is out and about," answered Johansson's secretary with her usual cool voice. "He had some urgent business he had to take care of. No, he's not coming back today. He can be reached tomorrow morning at eight o'clock. Yes, I promise to tell him that you called." She put back the receiver and made a note on a message pad. "Detective Chief Inspector Bo Jarnebring phoned. He wants you to call him back as soon as possible. Important, and you have the number." She looked at the clock, 3:33, and wrote the time and date on the slip of paper. Jarnebring, she thought. How could he have become a chief inspector?

Jarnebring's face was slightly red around the cheeks and earlobes. This was due to the fact that he was very surprised, and he was almost never surprised. He was often furious, but he regarded surprise as a form of enjoyment for children and intellectuals. On the table before him sat a transparent plastic bag with the seal torn open; in it was a strong, boot-like right shoe. To the side of the bag was a left shoe and closest to him on top of the desk was an open illustrated magazine which actually ought not to be found in a police station. In addition, a key that looked as though it went to a safe-deposit box or a safe, along with a small slip of paper containing two lines of handwritten text. Jarnebring stared at the slip of paper. What the hell is this? he thought. It must be some bastard who's fooling with me. With us, he corrected himself.

[TUESDAY, NOVEMBER 26]

Johansson woke up late. At the time he was rolling up the window shade in his bedroom he would usually already be on his way to work. Outside a pale morning sun was shining against a blue sky and the thermometer on the windowsill showed a few degrees above freezing. Excellent, thought Johansson, and high time to start living like a human being. First shower, then breakfast and morning paper, and after that an invigorating walk to the office. The same office that allowed you to succeed even if you did a good job, like himself, for example. Bureau head, he thought contentedly. If I start acting willful, I'll get traveling testimonials and become chief of the national police by summer.

. . .

Johansson had set a new record on the route from his residence on Woll-mar Yxkullsgatan when he entered the National Police Board on Pol-hemsgatan. Must be the swimming, thought Johansson with surprise and checked his watch one more time as he came into his secretary's office. Same cool smile, he thought as she handed over the day's mail and various other things. Nothing that seemed threatening, however.

"The chief of the national police has let it be known that he is very satisfied with your statement," she said.

Obviously, thought Johansson.

"There's an Inspector Bo Jarnebring who has called several times," she continued. "He phoned yesterday afternoon and he's called twice already this morning. It sounded very urgent."

Jarnebring, thought Johansson with mixed feelings. Still his best friend, although things hadn't gone too well last time.

"Phone him, and I'll take the call," said Johansson. Boss's privilege, he thought as he sat down behind his desk.

"Long time no see," said Jarnebring. He sounded unexpectedly cheerful. His voice is almost exhilarated, thought Johansson with surprise.

"Yes, perhaps we should meet," said Johansson.

"Exactly," said Jarnebring.

"When did you have in mind?" Johansson asked, taking a quick glance at the calendar on his desk. Just as well to clear the air, he thought.

"In fifteen minutes in my office," said Jarnebring. "I can ask one of the boys to drive you if you want a change of pace and a ride in a police car instead of a taxi."

"Has something happened?" asked Johansson with surprise.

"Frankly speaking I don't really know," answered Jarnebring. "I hope you can help me on that. So if the police superintendent will be so kind as to convey himself here I'll put the coffee on in the meantime."

Someone or something must have touched his heart when he saw his best friend coming toward him in the corridor, and the bear hug he got instead of a handshake didn't make things better.

"We'll go into my office," said Jarnebring with a wolfish grin. "I don't want the personnel to see me if I start blubbering."

"You've grown, Lars," said Jarnebring, looking at his visitor. "You're starting to get real superintendent muscles. If that button on your suit coat should pop loose and hit me in the skull, Bäckström and those other geniuses in homicide will suspect you of murder."

Johansson set his coffee cup aside and smiled more neutrally than he'd actually intended.

"Okay, Bo," he said. "Let's skip the bull, as the Americans say. Tell me now. Before you burst."

Jarnebring nodded and took a thin case folder from the pile on his desk.

"John P. Krassner. Jonathan Paul Krassner, born in fifty-three, American citizen, according to as yet unconfirmed sources some sort of freelance journalist from Albany in the state of New York, said to be a few hours north of the city with the same name." Jarnebring took a fresh look at his papers. "Came to Sweden six weeks ago."

"I see," said Johansson with surprise. And what does this have to do with me? he thought.

Jarnebring leaned forward over the desk, supported on his burly arms, while he looked at Johansson.

"How do you know him?" he asked.

What's the point? thought Johansson.

"Not the faintest idea," said Johansson. "No one that I know, as far as I know no one I've met, and I don't even recall having heard the name. How would it be if you—"

"Easy, Lars." Jarnebring smiled and raised his hand with a defensive gesture. "Forget it, and before you get as mad as last time I suggest you lean back, listen to me, and we'll help each other out."

"Why is that?" said Johansson as he made himself comfortable in the chair.

"This is going to take all of five minutes," said Jarnebring, "but I actually need your help."

"Okay," said Johansson. "Tell me."

"Approximately five minutes before eight last Friday evening the afore-mentioned Krassner fell from his room on the sixteenth floor in that student skyscraper up on Valhallavägen. He was subleasing it—it seems some international housing agency for students arranged it. Got the name of it in my papers. Anyway," said Jarnebring and looked at the ceiling while trying to collect his thoughts.

"Murder, suicide, accident," said Johansson. "What's the problem?"

"Most likely suicide," said Jarnebring. "Among other things he left behind a letter. Tech called this morning and let it be known that his prints are on the letter. Right where they should be if he'd written it himself."

"You mean the corpse's fingerprints," said Johansson. "You mean that the corpse's prints are where they ought to be, but how do you know that the corpse's prints are his?"

"They're his prints," said Jarnebring. "I already got that on the fax from the embassy yesterday."

"They had Krassner's fingerprints? Does he have a record?"

Jarnebring shook his head.

"No, but they seem to have taken prints on almost everyone over in the States. They'd taken his when he was working extra at check-in at some airport. They haven't said a peep about whether or not he might have some criminal past. Seems to have been a completely ordinary gloomy bastard."

"Suicide," repeated Johansson. "What's the problem?"

Jarnebring shrugged his shoulders.

"If there is one," he said. "For one thing I don't know who he is, although I've asked the embassy to help me with that. They promised to talk with the police where he was living and find out if they knew him."

"Okay," said Johansson.

"Then he seems to have been running in and out where he was living."

Jarnebring quickly recounted Krassner's movements and his own conversation with Professor Lidman.

"Lidman says that this isn't at all uncommon. Goes around happy

55

and energetic and smiles at everyone he meets—smiling depression I guess it's called. And then just bang, no, that's enough now, now I'm going to take my life. Can be quite irrational at the same time as they seem completely normal."

"I'll buy that," said Johansson, who'd had a cousin who had left his youngest daughter's birthday party in the best spirits to go out to the garage and hang himself.

"And then there's a shoe," said Jarnebring and recounted his and Hultman's theories without mentioning the latter by name.

"Seems highly plausible," said Johansson. "I'm in agreement with you, suicide."

He glanced furtively at his watch. The shoe bumped against a window ledge or a balcony railing or perhaps even a birdhouse that some biology student has nailed up outside his little window, thought Johansson and smiled.

"Sure," said Jarnebring. "Up until yesterday afternoon when that damn shoe started haunting me again." He nodded at Johansson and seemed both serious and sincerely concerned.

"How so?" said Johansson.

"Have you ever seen this rag here?" replied Jarnebring, handing over the August issue of the American monthly magazine *Soldier of Fortune.*

"*Soldier of Fortune,*" said Johansson, making a grimace at the camouflage-wearing characters rushing across the cover against heavy gunfire. "Isn't that one of those American neo-Nazi rags?"

"Yes," said Jarnebring. "It was one of the younger officers in the department here who tipped me off. There was a whole pile in their break room. *Soldier of Fortune, The Minuteman, Guns & Ammo, The Survivalist,*" he explained. "That kind of American extreme right-wing rag aimed at gun nuts and old Klan members and the type who just want to go out and make war in general, not exactly socialist rags, if you know what I mean."

No, thought Johansson, for how would that sort of thing wind up in a break room in a Swedish police station?

"Contains a ton of advertisements for weapons and survival gear and what you should know if the Russkies come, on how you become a mercenary and how you can fuck with the police and how you evade taxes. Yes, every kind of shit imaginable," concluded Jarnebring.

"Where does the shoe come in?" asked Johansson judiciously.

"If you look in the ad section, page eighty-nine. There's an ad for a company which is called StreetSmart, shortened SS."

Johansson had already found the ad in question; it offered all the necessities for the person who wanted to survive in the "jungle where we humans are forced to live." For reasons that, considering the context, didn't appear particularly murky, the ad had the same typeface as the two "S"s that the German Nazi Schutzstaffel had worn on their uniform lapels.

"I still don't understand," Johansson persisted.

"The damn shoe," said Jarnebring, holding out a strong left boot of brown leather with a high upper. He looked almost cheerful. "The same damn shoe that the mutt took on the head, although surely that must have been a coincidence," he thought out loud.

Jarnebring pressed his thumb against the sole, and at the same time he tugged hard with his right hand against the sturdy heel. Out fell a metal-colored key, and after that floated a small scrap of paper the size of a business card.

"Open sesame," said Jarnebring with a satisfied smile. "Shoe of the well-known brand StreetSmart with a hollow heel."

"The key appears to be for a safe-deposit box or some type of safe, most likely back in the States," Jarnebring continued, holding it up. "The embassy is working on that too, so I'm taking it easy."

"I see," said Johansson. What should he say? He'd heard and seen worse. "What was in the other shoe?"

Jarnebring shook his head.

"That one was empty," he said. "I'm guessing that he was right-handed."

Johansson nodded. That seems plausible, he thought.

"Don't you want to know what was on the paper?" Jarnebring looked at him expectantly.

Johansson showed a poker face and shrugged his shoulders. Jarnebring pushed the paper over and Johansson read the two lines of handwritten text.

An honest Swedish Cop. Police Superintendent Lars M. Johansson Wolmar Yxkulls Gata 7 A, 116 50 Stockholm.

Johansson looked at the paper again. He was holding it carefully by the edges between the nails of his thumb and index finger, from old habit. Although this time it appeared to be unnecessary. Judging by the gray-black specks, someone had already dusted it for fingerprints.

Like a calling card, thought Johansson, about five by eight centimeters. Folded in the middle.

He looked at Jarnebring, who wore the same expression that his children used to have when they were little and it was Christmas Eve.

"It's someone trying to pull our legs," said Johansson. "My leg," he corrected.

"I thought so too. At first I thought so. Now I'm pretty sure it's Krassner who wrote what's there."

"Tell me," said Johansson, leaning back in his chair. At the same time he couldn't help sneaking a glance at the little scrap of paper.

At first, Jarnebring had thought along the same lines as Johansson. When, after duly efficient investigations, he found out that the same police trainee, Oredsson, who had fetched Krassner's shoes and clothes and left them in his office had also been one half of the "first patrol car on the scene," as well as the half that had placed the aforementioned shoe in its plastic bag, sealed the bag, and sent it with the hearse to the forensic-medicine office, the matter was signed, sealed, and delivered. I'll boil that bastard for glue, thought Jarnebring, and ten minutes later Oredsson and Stridh were each sitting on a chair in the corridor outside Jarnebring's office, and it was Oredsson who got to come in first.

Calamity, thought Stridh gloomily, glancing at the closed door. Wonder if he intends to kill him, he thought. He'd heard a great deal about Jarnebring over the years, so that seemed highly likely, although no particular sounds had been heard from the other side of the door. Karate expert, thought Stridh, becoming even gloomier. One of those silent executioners.

. . .

Jarnebring had grilled Oredsson for a quarter of an hour, without mentioning the contents of the heel. Oredsson was red, sweaty, and before long, truly frightened. One thing was certain. He didn't have a clue what Jarnebring was talking about. I have listened to the voice of innocence, thought Jarnebring with surprise, sent Oredsson out, and asked him to take Stridh with him, obviously without either explanations or apologies.

"Then I called Rosengren," said Jarnebring.

"Rosengren," said Johansson. "Isn't he retired? He must be almost a hundred."

"Discretion a point of honor," said Jarnebring briefly. "I don't trust those bastards who work in tech," he explained. "Babble and gossip and leak like sieves. Besides, Rosengren is the best I've met. And he's not a hundred, he's seventy-five. And he can keep his mouth shut."

"But how did you get into the tech squad?" asked Johansson with surprise. "The paper's been dusted. For prints."

"I can tell you've never been home with Rosengren. He doesn't live in an apartment, he lives in a crime tech laboratory. The old guy makes a mint doing investigations for private clients. The whole range from employees who've left fingerprints on the company jam jar to letters from husbands who've found themselves a little beaver on the side."

"I thought he was a handwriting expert," said Johansson.

"He's that too, the best," said Jarnebring with a nod that brooked no contradictions, "and he can dust off a normal fingerprint in his sleep. I took Krassner's fingerprints along and various handwritten notes that I found among his papers."

"And?" said Johansson.

"Those are Krassner's prints, only his, and they're sitting in the right place, where they should be."

"Handwriting?" wondered Johansson.

"Also Krassner's, typically American."

Johansson looked at the paper one more time and nodded. He understood what Jarnebring meant; the way his title, the numbers, the address were written.

"Krassner seems to have liked you," said Jarnebring, grinning. "You have no idea why he did?"

"Not the foggiest." Johansson shook his head. "Might one be allowed to read that letter he wrote?"

"Obviously," said Jarnebring generously and handed over a white A4 paper in a plastic sleeve. "I thought you'd never ask."

"Did Krassner know Swedish?" asked Johansson with surprise when he saw the typewritten text.

"Nada," said Jarnebring, shaking his head. "That's a translation. I haven't gotten the original back from the tech yet. I got the information on the prints by phone. Fucking lazy asses," snorted Jarnebring. "Why didn't they take his clothes along when they were there already checking out the prints?"

"Who did the translation?" asked Johansson.

"Hultman," said Jarnebring.

"Hultman? Our Hultman?" asked Johansson.

"Yes," said Jarnebring, "and he's even more fiendish in English than you are, so you can be completely at ease."

I am, thought Johansson, and read the short text.

I have lived my life caught between the longing of summer and the cold of winter. As a young man I used to think that when summer comes I would fall in love with someone, someone I would love a lot, and then, that's when I would start living my life for real. But by the time I had accomplished all those things I had to do before, summer was already gone and all that remained was the winter cold. And that, that was not the life that I had hoped for.

Strange, thought Johansson. Exactly like those poems I used to write when I was young and I burned when I got older.

"Seems to have been the sensitive type," said Jarnebring.

"He seems to have had good judgment, though, when it comes to Swedish policemen," said Johansson and got up from his chair with a jerk. "How about having dinner tonight?"

"Gladly," said Jarnebring. "If you promise not to start throwing the china."

"Seven-thirty at my neighborhood restaurant," said Johansson. "I'll pick up the check so you can relax."

"So this is where you drag all your women," said Jarnebring, when at the appointed time they were seated at Johansson's usual table in his favorite restaurant.

"Actually there aren't that many," said Johansson.

"So they have Italian chow here," said Jarnebring, glancing furtively at the menu on the large slate board. He didn't seem entirely enthusiastic.

"Yeah," said Johansson, "and you actually ought to try it sometime, but since you're the one eating with me, I've made some special arrangements. You're going to get barbecued entrecôte with au gratin potatoes and a dessert that I know you'll appreciate. On the other hand, you don't get any herring as a starter, that went beyond the restaurant owner's threshold of pain, but instead a very fine marinated lox. Perfect with aquavit, by the way."

"I thought they'd never heard of aquavit at a dive like this," said Jarnebring.

"I come here," said Johansson, "and I've done so since they opened, so they've heard of aquavit. I brought a couple of my own aquavit glasses here too, those crystal ones with a tall base that you've drunk out of at my place. I inherited a couple dozen from my great-aunt, have I told you about her?" he asked.

In spite of the fact that he'd surely done so more than once, Jarnebring nodded at him to continue.

"She's one person you should've met, Bo," continued Johansson, "for she was in a class of her own. She ran the hotel in Kramfors back in the ration-book days, so those hold seven and a half centiliters, half a ration in the good old days." First-rate stuff in that old lady, thought Johansson.

Jarnebring shook his head. He seemed almost a bit taken.

"Lars, my friend, do you know what you are? In heart and soul?"

Johansson shook his head.

"You aren't some damn bureaucrat at the National Police Board, are you, police superintendent? In heart and soul you're a Norrland landowning farmer, one of those shrewd bastards with mile-wide forests and a sawmill down by the river. If you'd just been born a hundred years earlier you'd have been drinking with Zorn and the lads down at the Opera Bar, not with a simple constable."

Make it the Golden Peace, Rydbergs, or Berns, and you're not talking about me but rather about my grandfather, or my big brother if you disregard the time period, thought Johansson. Besides, you're wrong about me, but he didn't say any of that.

"Gentlemen," interrupted the restaurant owner with a slight throat-clearing and a deep bow. "Marinated lox according to the house recipe."

He placed the plates before them; large slices of salmon cut on the diagonal, pink with streaks of white, lemon on the side, a splash of olive oil, and a few sprigs of fresh herbs.

"Drinks, gentlemen." One of his assistants held out a tray with two large beers and two brimming-full shot glasses, which he placed with an expert hand before their place settings, first Jarnebring, then Johansson. Then he took a step back and bowed slightly.

"I wish you gentlemen *bon appétit.*"

Jarnebring nodded at Johansson and grasped the glass in his right hand.

"Skoal, chief!"

"Completely okay," said Jarnebring after finishing the appetizer and two large shots from Aunt Jenny's glass. He had, however, put the vegetables and lemon wedge into the ashtray before he tackled the lox. After that they talked about the old days. Since they were best friends it was both natural and necessary to start before their careers had separated them. While Johansson had climbed higher, Jarnebring had stayed put. It had been years since they shared the same worn-out front seat in a police car and drank the same bitter coffee in the break room at surveillance, and because they could only meet in their free time nowadays, they talked mostly about the time that they had worked together.

The theme was always the same: Things were much better before, at surveillance, at homicide, much better within the police department, to put it simply; even the crooks were understandable in the good old days.

"Do you remember Murder-Otto?" asked Jarnebring. "And the Sheriff?"

"And Dahlgren and Mattson," continued Johansson nostalgically. "And Little Gösta and Splinter and the Gook and the Knife. Bongos, do you remember Bongos, and Åström and Sally? Do you remember Sally, the one that the uniformed police always arrested first when we'd done a raid? The one we called Chief Inspector Toivonen and looked like an ordinary drunk from Karelia who'd missed the boat back."

These were all police legends and old bosses who had either closed up shop or disappeared from the story with the help of the general retirement system, but none of their younger colleagues had ever seen them sitting in the park behind the police station feeding pigeons.

"Sour old bastards," said Jarnebring, "but damn capable police officers."

"They knew what was good and bad and what was right and wrong, and then they could sort out what was important from pure nonsense," said Johansson, who was feeling more than slightly affected by Aunt Jenny's measures and tried to keep the conversation on a respectable level. On a Tuesday, thought Johansson. I can't get plastered in the middle of the week even if he's my best friend and things went south last time we met and. . . .

"Eva-Lena," interrupted Jarnebring. "Do you remember Eva-Lena?"

"Eva-Lena?" Johansson, who was of the opinion that the police profession should be practiced by men, because ninety-nine percent of the time it concerned other men, but of course he would not dream of uttering a word of that, rooted feverishly among his old police memories.

"Eva-Lena, that broad who became head of the narc squad, the first female detective chief inspector in Stockholm. In the whole country, I believe. A light-haired, thin gal, a bit too thin, perhaps, but still rather tasty, swore like a tugboat captain. You remember her, don't you?"

Johansson suddenly remembered. He had been loaned out to narcotics from surveillance in an emergency and the first night he had missed a routine tailing. Muffed it, to put it simply, because the thief was cleverer than him, because his wife had just left him, because he hadn't slept since it happened, and because his children used to phone every time he tried to sleep, and because they immediately started bawling before he had time to say anything, and because their mother managed to hang up before . . . All the same, he'd muffed it and the following morning he got his new boss's view on the matter.

"How the hell do you explain this?" she began.

Personal problems, thought Johansson. He had learned at school that that's what you should say, but as soon as he started working he realized that that was pure nonsense, so he didn't say it.

"He was better than me," said Johansson. One to nothing for me, he thought, for he had seen how surprised she was.

"He was better than you? But isn't just about everyone? Isn't that so? I've heard that you're a fucking piece of trash. That's what my boys say. Surveillance sent us a fucking piece of trash to yank our chains."

And someone ought to wash your mouth out with soap, thought Johansson, but he didn't say that either.

"Almost no one is better than me," said Johansson with an obvious Norrland accent while at the same time looking her straight in the eyes. To her credit it should be said that she hadn't backed down, just stared back, but she had still lost because she was the one who had said something first.

"Okay," she said. "You'll get another chance. See to it that you're here at seven o'clock."

Instead he'd gone to his chief, one of those old legends. Johansson had chosen the easy way out.

"She's badmouthing us here at surveillance," said Johansson. "She's badmouthing us and you too, and I won't put up with that." He added a little extra Norrland drawl at the end.

"Damn sow," said the chief, who was already red under the eyes. "Damn pushy dyke." He started to dial the number of his best friend, who was an old wrestler just like him and the head of the entire detective department, "and you," he nodded at Johansson, "stay with me, lad. It's those damn socialist bastards," he explained. "You've got to be a socialist bastard in order to arrive at something so stupid as recruiting old ladies to the police." He chuckled, leaned back in his chair, and nodded at Johansson that he could leave. Lapp bastard, he thought affectionately as Johansson left.

. . .

"Her I do remember," said Johansson. "She was good," he continued, "really good, almost as good as you and me."

So she tried to sound like you and me, and behave like you and me and all the other boys, and one day she was simply gone, he thought.

"What happened to her?" asked Johansson, despite the fact that he knew the answer.

Jarnebring shrugged his broad shoulders.

"She disappeared, she quit, nobody knows," said Jarnebring.

How the hell can you recruit women to the police? he thought, but because Johansson was after all a superintendent and as such more than halfway into politics he didn't say that.

"Skoal," said Jarnebring, raising his glass. "Skoal to all the boys in surveillance and skoal to the good old days."

Who poured more aquavit? thought Johansson, a little confused. Someone must have, for Aunt Jenny's glasses were full to the brim.

"Gustav Adolf Nilsson," said Jarnebring, smiling. They had taken a break in the middle of the entrée, Johansson was drinking wine while Jarnebring abstained to continue instead with beer, and a little extra on the side in Aunt Jenny's glass, and the whole thing was just great. "Gustav Adolf Nilsson, born in thirty," repeated Jarnebring.

"Your witness," said Johansson. "The one with the mutt who got the shoe in the head," he continued. Strange story, thought Johansson. Pure detective mystery.

"Vindel," continued Jarnebring. "Do you remember him, almost ten years ago? When we were working on that robbery over at Odenplan and the double murder where I'll be damned if it wasn't our colleague at the secret police who was the perp. Do you remember?"

"Yes," said Johansson. "I remember Vindel." That other thing he'd tried to forget. "Was he the drunk who knew the victim?"

"Not today," said Jarnebring. "The same Gustav Adolf Nilsson," continued Jarnebring delightedly. "Alias Vindel. And both you and I are bigger drunks than he is today."

"I would have thought he'd drunk himself to death a good while ago," said Johansson with surprise. "The way he looked back then."

"No way, José," said Jarnebring, shaking his head delightedly. "Six months later he got an inheritance from his oldest sister, the only remaining relative. She had married a Pentecostalist who was a hardware wholesaler and twice her age. Vindel's brother-in-law," Jarnebring clarified, "but because he'd tricked Vindel out of half his parental home as soon as he'd sunk his claws into his sister, they didn't exactly get together every day. Then the old bastard kicked the bucket, the Pentecostalist that is, and ten years later when it was time for the widow to go, she left the entire inheritance to Vindel. In spite of the fact that he hadn't heard from her in twenty years. A case of bad conscience, I suppose, the old hag."

"I'll be damned," said Johansson with genuine feeling behind his words.

"Sure," said Jarnebring. "I thought I recognized him when we were over at his place, talking about his dead dog, but it was Hultman who connected the dots when we drove away from there."

So Hultman was along, thought Johansson, but he didn't say that.

"Not so strange," continued Jarnebring, "for he looked like a damn athlete compared with when you and I saw him, and that must be almost ten years ago. Skinny, sinewy, Norrland athletic type, a real gray panther. Piles of dough from his sister and not a drop after the inheritance. He's supposed to have said something to the effect that if you had as much money as he did you were simply obligated to quit drinking. He just went on the wagon and said farewell to all of his drinking buddies, from that day on. He's still living in his old pad on Surbrunnsgatan, although now the building has been turned into condominiums, and then Vindel acquired the neighboring pad as well. Knocked out the wall and added on, treasurer of the association and loaded as a bank vault."

"I'll be damned," said Johansson. "Vindel, that old lush."

"Sure," said Jarnebring. "I forgot to tell you that when you came up, 'cause all I was thinking about was that damn shoe. What a fucking story, pure detective mystery." Jarnebring's entire upper body was shaking with delight and because he was leaning forward over the table it could be felt in the whole place.

"Yes, I still don't have the foggiest," said Johansson. "As far as I know I've never met that Krassner."

A shoe with a hollow heel, in the hollow heel a key to a safe-deposit box in the United States, and so far so good. If it hadn't been for that slip of paper, thought Johansson. The paper with his name and address, despite the fact that he wasn't in the phone book, despite the fact that extremely few people outside of his family and his closest circle of friends knew where he lived. Despite the fact that his secretary, and anyone else at his office, for that matter, would never dream of giving out his home address.

"A mystery, quite simply," said Johansson gloomily, and that was exactly what he thought. A damn mystery.

"At first I thought it was the guys in the uniformed police who wanted to mess with you," said Jarnebring.

I thought so too, thought Johansson, and nodded while he poured the last drops from the wine bottle. I should have stuck to beer like Jarnie, he thought. The same Jarnie who furthermore had replenished Aunt Jenny's glass twice but still appeared capable of an arrest or two, which of course was more than one might expect of him. They might as well write a traveling testimonial for me, he thought and immediately felt cheered at the thought.

"Where was I?" said Jarnebring, taking a large gulp from his beer glass. "Yes, the guys at the uniformed police, the ones you were giving such a hard time a few months ago."

In his capacity as head of the National Bureau of Criminal Investigation, Johansson had led an internal investigation of a unit of the Stockholm riot squad. He had proceeded harshly and they had even had to sit in the pokey a while, but now it appeared that everything was returning to normal. Released from jail, back on the job although without a police van (at least for the time being), and with an indictment in Stockholm district court that would certainly run out in the sand.

"Damn crooks," said Johansson from the depths of his heart. "How the hell can they let people like that into the corps?"

"Sure," said Jarnebring, "I'm with you, and just say the word if you want to go outside and have it out with those fucking bastards, but as far as the shoe is concerned they're innocent. They don't know a thing about it."

"I agree with you," said Johansson, nodding down into his wineglass.

"It's Krassner's shoe. And for reasons unknown, he's written down your address and put it into the heel of the shoe. Where the hell did my dessert go, by the way?"

Pure detective mystery, thought Johansson, trying to make eye contact with his friend the restaurant owner. An honest cop, he thought.

"I was thinking about that letter," said Johansson.

Jarnebring nodded. They had finished off the dessert and were working on coffee and cognac. Johansson was having it mostly for show, but after half a bottle of Ramlösa mineral water he felt significantly more alert.

"Yes," said Jarnebring, who didn't appear to notice how much he drank.

"It was an electric typewriter, you said. Did you check the ink cartridge—one of those color-ribbon cassettes, if I understood you correctly?"

"What the hell, Lars," said Jarnebring. "I *am* actually a policeman. Yes, I've checked the cartridge, and the only thing on the ribbon is just what's written in the letter. Who the hell do you think I am?" said Jarnebring, taking a large gulp from his brandy snifter at the same time that he gave his friend the familiar wolfish grin.

"The wastebasket . . ." said Johansson.

"And the wastebasket," interrupted Jarnebring. "The only thing in the wastebasket was the package the cartridge came in. As I said."

"But you said that the piece of shit has been here for a month and a half," persisted Johansson. "What's he been doing that whole time? He must have been doing something?"

"I guess he's been brooding about life and the future," said Jarnebring, shrugging his shoulders. "Apart from that, he doesn't seem to have covered much ground. I guess he had other things on his mind."

"For more than a month," said Johansson with obvious doubt in his voice.

"Just over six and a half weeks," said Jarnebring. "I've checked the date. He arrived from New York at Arlanda on Sunday, the sixth of October. Jumped on Friday, the twenty-second of November."

"Those books in his room," said Johansson. "What were they about?"

"Various things," said Jarnebring, grinning for reasons that Johansson could not readily understand. "There were some paperback mysteries in English; he seems to have read those at least, for they were fairly dog-eared. Yes," Jarnebring searched his memory, "then there were quite a few books about Sweden and Swedish history and politics, all of them in English. *Sweden the Middle Way, The Paradise of Social Democracy.* I've got a list in my report if you're interested."

Not particularly, thought Johansson.

"Damn it, Lars." Jarnebring leaned forward across the table and put his right hand on Johansson's arm. "Relax. There's bound to be some simple and obvious explanation."

"I'm listening," said Johansson; at the same time he couldn't help smiling.

"Let's suppose this," said his best friend. "Some semi-radical nitwit from the States comes here for various unclear reasons and has the exact same opinions that everyone else of his ilk has. One evening he's at the bar and meets our own talents who think like he does and they stand there shooting the breeze and feeling at home and talking about the sort of thing that unites all those types, regardless of where they come from."

"And what would that be?" asked Johansson.

"That people like you and me are real shitheads. Policemen. The biggest shitheads around."

"I know what you mean," said Johansson. He had heard it from one of his own children.

"Excellent," said Jarnebring, "and at that point it's one of our own leftist loonies who remembers that he or she—most likely it's a broad, come to think of it—has read in the paper that there are actually exceptions even among the worst of the worst."

"I see," said Johansson.

"And so she starts to tell about what she's read in the paper about you and your crusade against our colleagues at the Stockholm riot squad on account of that old drunk that they possibly beat to death, and Krassner gets completely hot in his trousers and decides that, by God, I'll make sure to take that boy with me into eternity. And he proceeds to write down your name and puts it in his secret little shoe. Damn romantic," snorted Jarnebring, "and if you don't intend to foot the bill for drinks, I'll get two with my own money. What would you like?"

"Let me think," said Johansson, whose thoughts were going in a different direction than gin and tonic.

"Okay," said Jarnebring. "Do you remember that editorial in Mini-Pravda, our beloved evening paper, the day after you put those guys in the can? Half a page. Do you remember that?"

"I have a vague memory now that you mention it," Johansson lied; he could recall the editorial in detail.

"I seem to remember that the headline was 'An Honorable Cop,' " said Jarnebring.

"Now that you mention it," said Johansson evasively.

"Exactly," said Jarnebring. "Me and the other guys almost laughed ourselves silly. Lars Martin Johansson, a completely ordinary constable, one of us, allowing for the fact that a lot of water has run under the bridge since we shared the front seat and the same lookouts, you could swear he's well on his way to becoming a government minister. The only one in Swedish police history to get a positive mention in that rag. And a real policeman besides, not one of the kind you run into nowadays."

"Was it that bad?" said Johansson, and the discomfort he felt was genuine.

"Cut it out," said Jarnebring. "It's cool. I guess we know you. What about that drink, by the way?"

"I'll take care of that in a moment," said Johansson, signaling to his friend the restaurant owner.

But how did she or he know my home address? he thought.

[WEDNESDAY, NOVEMBER 27]

The night before had been a late one. Jarnebring had gone home with him and they had stayed up drinking and talking until one o'clock. Then Johansson looked at the clock and declared that he for one had had enough and that if Jarnebring was considering staying he could choose between the couch in the living room and the one in the study. Jarnebring thanked him for the invitation, called a taxi, and went home. He was rather in the mood and she had been unusually affectionate lately. I guess she's heard all that talk about my good morals, thought Jarnebring contentedly as he journeyed through the night.

Johansson woke at six as usual, got up, took two aspirin and a large glass of water before he set the clock for eight and went back to sleep again. He had to be at a conference out on Lidingö at ten o'clock, and because he wasn't a speaker but a member of the audience, he didn't have anything in particular to be concerned about. Except for that annoying little slip of paper.

Now he was sitting where he should be according to the calendar on his desk, but as one speaker followed another at the podium, his thoughts were going their own way, and every time they came back to that slip of paper.

My address, thought Johansson, for he could not let go of that thought. How did he get hold of my address? I'm not in the phone book. I don't give it out at work, and no one in my family or among my friends would do so either. On the other hand, it would be no big deal to get hold of it for someone who really wanted to. But why would Krassner have his name and address? Johansson had a good memory for both names and people and their appearances and various dealings, as you should have if you're an old detective; he had truly ransacked his memory these past twenty-four hours. No Krassner, thought Johansson.

Assume that Jarnebring was on the right track. That Krassner was an ordinary scatterbrain, the type who liked to be a little important and secretive and could even imagine gadding about in shoes with hollow heels. Hollow heels. Johansson shook his head. Of all the thousands of crooks he'd run into during his years as a policeman, he couldn't recall any who'd had shoes with hollow heels. On the other hand there were several who hadn't had any shoes at all. Dope, thought Johansson. There were sure to be one or two who had chosen to store the goods that way. A tall tale was even circulating in the building about a black guy who was extremely tall to start with, who had tried to bring in a pound of heroin through customs at Arlanda in a pair of knee-high, crocodile-leather platform boots. He didn't know if it was true, and that wasn't the point anyway, but maybe it wouldn't hurt to talk with one of the boys in narcotics? How can I do that? thought Johansson gloomily, and if he knew Jarnebring it had already been done. Wonder what we'll get for lunch, he thought, looking at his watch.

Jarnebring was not the type to surrender unnecessarily to brooding. Krassner was a closed chapter. It only remained for him to write up the case and put it in the files. He would do that as soon as Hultman called to report on what the American police had come up with regarding Krassner, and he was already convinced that this would not essentially change anything. Suicide, concluded Jarnebring, and after that he'd devoted the morning to practical matters and the afternoon to physical training. What he was going to do after work was his own business.

Good news, thought Wiijnbladh. If police-station gossip was true, it was evidently the acting head of the National Bureau of Criminal Investigation, Lars Martin Johansson, who had written the statement about the officers who had missed the two corpses in the elevator shaft. The type who gladly steps over the bodies of his colleagues, thought Wiijnbladh, and he would scarcely miss that dilettante Olsson when he let the ax fall. True, Olsson had not been at the scene of the crime, he'd been somewhere else, which only further underscored his negligence and general incompetence, but he was still the chief of the group at the tech squad where the officers were working. The job that rightly should have been mine, thought Wiijnbladh, and yet it was clearly not too late. Now it was a matter of making an extra effort before the celebration of the chief's sixtieth birthday. I'm of course in charge of both the collection and the party, thought Wiijnbladh contentedly.

. . .

On Monday morning Bäckström had returned to his usual job as murder investigator on the homicide squad, and with him he had an as good as completely investigated case of wife abuse. Normally he wouldn't have touched shit like that with a pair of tongs. The homicide squad had yielded to political pressure from a lot of red-stockings and leftist pansies and established a special investigative group for violence against women, to which the closet fags and dykes in the corps had of course applied. Violence against women? thought Bäckström. A bunch of drunken hags who both needed and wanted a little regular ass-whipping. The problem was just this case: a pile of dough and boobs like melons and the drunk she was married to was still sitting in stir. Bäckström himself had seen to that.

First he had thought about playing the good cop and simply asking his immediate superior to let him finish up the case himself. For one thing, the investigation was as good as done, and for another, there were no fresh murders that required his efforts. Just piles of old, unsolved shit that no normal person could bear to poke into, but the problem was more complicated than that. Bäckström's boss was an old idiot, six foot six and 280 pounds who completely lacked a fuse. When Bäckström saw him on Monday he had been monumentally hungover, and only a suicidal person with impaired vision would have asked the question, so Bäckström decided to lie low and not say a peep about the matter. All he needed was a couple of extra follow-up sessions with the poor victim. He was already halfway there, he'd heard it in her voice when he was talking with her on the phone. In the worst case he could always change the date on the interviews.

Jarnebring wasn't what he seemed to be, thought Oredsson, and when he talked with his older comrades he also understood why. Jarnebring was clearly an old colleague and best friend of that fifth columnist Johansson, who was head of the National Bureau of Criminal Investigation. Too bad, thought Oredsson. If you're going to tackle crime in earnest it's important to have people like Jarnebring on the right side.

· · ·

When Stridh came home he turned on the TV to watch the evening news, but it was the same old pile of misery so he turned it off again. It never ends, thought Stridh; the only bright spot was that he would soon be off again.

[THURSDAY, NOVEMBER 28]

Hultman was not one to hesitate to pull the trigger, thought Jarnebring with delight, and the Americans weren't either. When he checked his mailbox after morning prayers he found a fax from the American embassy. A record of an interrogation carried out by the police in Albany, New York, a few short official lines from the legal attaché at the embassy, as well as a handwritten letter from Hultman that summarized the essentials: Ten years ago Krassner had tried to take his own life by jumping from the balcony of the house where he was living. The local police had pulled out an old investigation of the incident. His girlfriend at that time had also been questioned, and to make a long story short, she could confirm everything that Jarnebring had suspected right from the start. Krassner was, to say the least, a complicated person. Krassner had tried to take his life before, and in the same way as now.

As a suicide attempt it was not much to write home about. Krassner had suffered a concussion and a broken leg. This time you were more successful, thought Jarnebring; he decided to finish up the investigation of the cause of death as soon as he received the final statement from the forensic doctor. Suicide, thought Jarnebring once again, and the simplest thing would be to just forget that annoying little slip of paper with his best friend's name on it. Perhaps that ridiculous shoe with the hollow heel too, thought Jarnebring. He could, of course, have found the safe-deposit box key somewhere else, and the very simplest thing was just to include it along with everything else in the confiscation report. I'm not going to write a spy novel, thought Jarnebring, so that might as well stay between Lars Martin and me.

Johansson was bewildered and felt a growing irritation. First he'd tried to create some order in his head by seeing to it that he was fully occupied. Until lunch he had quickly and efficiently cleared away all old annoyances and the usual trifles, which could just as well have remained dormant for good, and after lunch he had started to inspect an old proposal for reorganization of the operation at the National Bureau of Criminal Investigation, which even the person who had proposed it didn't have the energy to care about anymore. . . . and then he called Jarnebring.

"Okay," said Jarnebring. "Come over and we'll talk."

Jarnebring had told him about the message from the embassy, but that didn't seem to make an impression on his best friend. Nor did the fact that in his investigation he had decided not to mention the obnoxious little scrap of paper and the shoe with the hollow heel. Johansson hadn't even heard that, it seemed.

"Okay," said Jarnebring, with a slight resignation in his voice. "How can I help you?"

"You had a photo of Krassner," said Johansson. "Could I borrow it?"

Jarnebring grinned and shrugged his shoulders.

"Who were you thinking of questioning?"

Johansson also shrugged his shoulders.

"I've been going over this in my head until I'm about to go crazy. I wasn't thinking of questioning anyone."

"Just snooping around a little?"

Johansson smiled reluctantly and Jarnebring chuckled.

"Put your ear to the rails?"

"More or less," said Johansson.

"I think you're barking up the wrong tree," said Jarnebring. "You're that type, but okay. Anything else I can help you with?"

"The letter," said Johansson. "Think I could borrow that letter he wrote?"

"I meant to put the original in his file, of course, but if you can get by with a copy? Sure," said Jarnebring.

"A copy would work fine," said Johansson.

Jarnebring grinned and nodded; apparently he was psychic, for both Krassner's photo and a photocopy of his letter were already in the plastic folder that he took out and handed over to Johansson.

"Anything else you need?" asked Jarnebring, leaning back in his desk chair with his fingers clasped behind his head.

"No, such as?"

Jarnebring shook his head, acting concerned.

"I'm worried about you, Lars," he said. "Not because you're getting unnecessarily worked up over this lunatic—you've always been the type, so that doesn't worry me—but you do seem a bit rusty. What do you think about these?"

Jarnebring took a different plastic folder out of his desk drawer and handed it to Johansson. In it were ten or so photos of men approximately Krassner's age and appearance.

Johansson smiled unwillingly.

"I wasn't thinking about questioning anyone," he said. "That's your job."

"No, certainly," said Jarnebring, "but suppose you change your mind and get it into your head to do it anyway. Would be sad if the person you're talking with didn't have any pictures to choose from." He sighed. "You're worrying yourself unnecessarily," he continued. "I want the photo array back, by the way."

"Of course," said Johansson. "There was one more thing." A thought had just occurred to him. "That ink cartridge for the typewriter, do you still have it?"

"It's one of those plastic cartridges," said Jarnebring, "for a Panasonic brand electric typewriter. The only thing it was used for was to write out that letter you got a copy of. I've checked the cartridge against the letter myself. I can assure you, Lars, that every single damn stroke on the ink cartridge, every single correction which has been made on the correction tape, I've checked off on the letter."

Jarnebring looked expectantly at Johansson, who made a deprecating gesture with his hands.

"I'll pull back," said Johansson. "Sweet Jesus," he said and smiled wryly. "I'm crawling in the dust."

Jarnebring appeared not to have heard the last. "True, I'm only a simple police inspector," he said, "and if it hadn't been for one colleague who insisted that we Indian-wrestle, there wouldn't have been any need for me even to warm this chair."

Johansson smiled and nodded. The reason for Jarnebring's sudden promotion was already part of police history as recounted among those who could trust each other.

"One thing I learned early on," continued Jarnebring, and it sounded as if he was thinking out loud. "This was even before you and I ran into each other."

Johansson nodded. "Go on."

"Well," said Jarnebring. "If you must do something that takes a little time, then see to it for Christ's sake that you do it properly, otherwise you might as well not bother at all. It took me a good hour to check off the letter against the ink cartridge and correction tape."

"Quickly done at that," said Johansson approvingly.

"Sure," said Jarnebring, grinning broadly. "Which actually might have been due to the fact that old man Rosengren helped me."

Seated in his car down in the parking garage, Johansson took the plastic folder with the letter and the photo of Krassner out of his briefcase. On the back of the photo Jarnebring had attached the irritating little scrap of paper with a paper clip. It was wrapped in plastic but Johansson could still see that it was the original.

Bo, he thought.

[FRIDAY, NOVEMBER 29]

Now the shit has hit the fan in earnest, thought Bäckström, when the chief of homicide's secretary buzzed him on his intercom and said that the chief wanted to see him immediately. That damn sow, thought Bäckström. She's knifed me in the back and what the hell am I going to come up with now?

The day before he'd set up a meeting with the crime victim on Karlavägen. They were to meet at her home and Bäckström had set the time at six o'clock in the evening. A quick questioning, a little heartwarming idle chatter, and then straight to the little red beet. So I can treat you to a trip you've never made before, thought Bäckström contentedly.

When he actually got there and rang her doorbell, no one opened.

Bäckström rang and rang and finally he peeked through the mail slot to see if anything had happened. The only thing that happened was that her neighbor stuck his ugly snout out of the door and asked if there was anything he could help him with. Sour, skinny, bald old bastard, Bäckström diagnosed, while he considered whether he should stick his badge right in his kisser or simply request that he go to hell. But before he managed to do either, the old bastard had shrieked at him to get away from there or else he would call the police.

Because he didn't have any desire to stand in the stairwell negotiating with one of those Nazis from the uniformed police—for some reason he'd started thinking about that idiot Oredsson—he had carried out an orderly retreat and trotted down to a nearby Chinese restaurant, where he placed himself in the bar to be able to think better. In the ball, thought Bäckström, grinning.

"Rarge beer, rarge stlong beer," he said to the saffron monkey in the bar, but the humorless bastard didn't even crack a smile.

After a few more beers he trotted out and scouted around her building a little. The lights were off in all the windows.

Bäckström found a new bar, downed a few more beers, and finally called her from a pay phone. No answer, and after a number of rings the answering machine came on and he hung up.

Then things had just rolled on by themselves, or so it seemed. Next bar, two more beers, another attempt at the pay phone, and suddenly he'd been standing outside the usual old dive on Kungsgatan. First he'd taken a cautious peek through the window. That fucking whore who worked at Saab—the one he'd screwed last summer—was sitting in the half-empty bar, lacing her fingers together with some fucking homo watchman. Bäckström decided to go in.

"It's full," said the half-ape who stood in the doorway, grinning.

"What do you mean, full?" said Bäckström.

"It's always full here," said the half-ape and grinned even wider. "Besides, you seem to have had a few too many already."

A few too many, thought Bäckström. Don't try and get familiar with me or I'll kill you. But he didn't say that. He just left. Finally he made it home, squeezed the last drops out of one of the bottles he had bought on payday, then called her again. No answer, so he left a message on her answering machine. And what the hell was it I said then? he thought as he walked into the chief's office.

The head of the homicide squad was named Lindberg. A few years earlier he had succeeded one of the legends of the Stockholm police, and because everyone on the squad was sick and tired of legends, a few of the old hands had a chat with the union, and that's how Lindberg had become the boss, and the good thing about him was that he had no clue at all about anything whatsoever. A little fat, incompetent old bastard, thought Bäckström, and if you fixed it that you were the last one to speak with him, then you were living in the best of all worlds.

The problem was Lindberg's own chief. He had succeeded in pressing himself down into Lindberg's visitor's armchair and already looked as if he were going to have a stroke. His name was Danielsson, Chief Inspector Danielsson according to the service register, but in the building he was generally known as Jack Daniels, which was easier to remember. Jack Daniels, thought Bäckström, nodding heartily while he sat down on an empty chair nearest the door to have his escape route secured should things get hot. Strange that you haven't drunk yourself to death.

"You wanted to speak with me, chief," said Bäckström.

"Yes, yes," said Lindberg defensively. "It's about that woman on Karlavägen, that Mrs. Östergren who was abused by her husband. Her attorney has contacted us and—"

"Have you quit homicide?" interrupted his chief.

"What do you mean?" said Bäckström.

"Now tell it like it is," said Jack Daniels. "You'd planned to talk your way into a little fling with that upper-class whore on Karlavägen. The one who tried to get her man put away."

"Oh well, oh well," said Lindberg conciliatorily. "Now let's not quarrel just because . . . because of this plaintiff. We all know how difficult they can be in these kinds of cases. Yes, Danielsson, you of all people ought to know that," he added, glancing nervously at his guest in the armchair.

How the hell could you know anything about that, Danielsson

thought morosely, for you've never investigated a crime, have you? But he didn't say that.

"You horny bastard," he said instead, giving Bäckström the evil eye.

Lucky not to have been born yesterday, thought Bäckström half an hour later when he had returned to his office. It was just as he had thought. That fucking whore had used him and tried to knife him in the back, but that was her mistake, thought Bäckström. That sort of thing didn't work with an old pro, however hard she tried. Clearly she had turned over the tape from her answering machine to her lawyer, who in turn had given it to Lindberg, whereupon his boozer of a boss had insisted that they listen to it, in spite of the fact that he and Lindberg were already in agreement that the homos in the violence-against-women group should take over the case.

But that was where you shit all over yourself, thought Bäckström, for it was at that point that he'd come up with his stroke of genius.

First they had played the tape from the answering machine, and maybe it sounded a little weird, as it well might when you're worried and call someone late at night. But Bäckström had kept his cool.

"What's the problem?" said Bäckström. "She's the one who insisted on being questioned in her own home, because she couldn't bear to go to the police station. And it's clear that I got worried when she didn't open the door."

"So you called her," said Jack Daniels softly.

"Yes," said Bäckström. "I obviously didn't have reasonable grounds for anything else, even if for a while I did fear the worst."

"At one-thirty in the morning?" said Jack Daniels.

"That must be wrong," said Bäckström. "It was much earlier than that." I'm guessing there isn't any clock on those things, he thought.

"You were so fucking loaded you can hardly hear what you're saying," interrupted Jack Daniels.

"Drunk," Bäckström burst out indignantly. "I was cold sober and standing there, brushing my teeth. I was about to go to bed. It was just past ten, I guess. I was standing there brushing my teeth, and that's no doubt why it sounds a little unclear." Ingenious, thought Bäckström.

"Yes, yes," said Lindberg, raising his hands like some fucking Pentecostal preacher. "Then I believe we're clear on this matter."

Say what you will about Bäckström, thought Lindberg's immediate supervisor, Chief Inspector Danielsson, but he's a shrewd bastard. Lazy and incompetent, but shrewd! He was horny too, the fat little devil— quite a mystery how he managed it, lush that he was. I must have a little nip myself, he thought, glancing at the binder on his bookshelf where he had hidden the office bottle. He looked at the clock. Not before twelve, he thought gloomily, and besides, he'd forgotten to buy throat lozenges. Wonder where he came up with that bit about brushing his teeth, he thought.

How come Danielsson is called Jack Daniels? Bäckström pondered. Simple. Easy to remember. How do you kill a Jack Daniels? Assume that I invite him home for dinner, buy a little herring and meatballs for the sake of appearances and a shitload of aquavit. A whole fucking case and three or four cases of strong beer. Which he gets to pour into himself until he chokes and then I help him with the last gulps. Too uncertain, decided Bäckström, and it sounds fucking expensive. Besides, it was Friday and high time to slip away for the usual business errands outside the building.

Vindel is from Norrland, thought Johansson, old dog owner and teetotaler. So he gets up early. Johansson looked at the clock and decided to talk with Vindel before he went to the office. Why should I do that? he thought, suddenly despondent as he stood on the street, waiting for his taxi.

His analysis had been correct anyway, thought Johansson as he sat in Vindel's parlor with a cup of coffee before him. Dark, old-fashioned furniture, large Oriental carpet on the floor, wall clock above the sofa, and so clean it sparkled. Johansson had already made note of the large framed portrait on the sideboard over by the window. Silver frame with ornaments.

"That's Charlie," said Vindel and sighed. "He reached thirteen before he died."

"I like Pomeranians too," said Johansson, which was perhaps not completely true, as both his father and his brothers had always kept Norwegian elkhounds and he had never objected to their choice.

"You hunt, of course," Vindel declared.

"Yeah," said Johansson, and his Norrland dialect was apparent.

"Home on the farm," said Vindel, and this was more a statement than a question.

"Yeah," said Johansson. "Both of my parents are still alive, although my dad is starting to get a little frail."

"You've done well," said Vindel, glancing at Johansson's business card, which he had placed before him on the table. "Police superintendent, that's not cat shit."

"Yeah," said Johansson. "I've done well."

"For me things almost went to hell for awhile," said Vindel.

"Your health failed you?" asked Johansson, despite the fact that he knew. Vindel shook his head.

"Booze," he said. "The greatest depravity that he-down-there ever sent us poor wretches up here. But I broke out of those chains of his and there are others besides me who can testify to the fact that it was at the last minute."

Me among them, thought Johansson and nodded, but he didn't say anything. Vindel took a cookie from the plate and suddenly smiled at Johansson.

"It's nice when things go well for us Norrlanders," he said. "We've always pulled our weight, I can tell you, but how many Norrlanders are there in the government? Stockholmers and Scanians, they're a dime a dozen, but Norrlanders?" Vindel sighed and shook his head. "Although when the wind starts to blow, then we come in handy."

So true, so true, thought Johansson, and what am I doing here, really?

. . .

Johansson had shown him the pictures anyway. The picture of Krassner and nine of the others that he had gotten from Jarnebring. Vindel only shook his head.

"He wasn't in any condition for me to recognize him," said Vindel, "and it's true I've lived here since I came to Stockholm, but I don't recall any of them." He nodded toward Johansson's photographs and shook his head.

"Which of them is it?" asked Vindel.

"That one," said Johansson, pointing to the photo of Krassner.

"I've never seen him," said Vindel. "Has he done something, or . . . ?" he asked. "More than been the death of Charlie, I mean."

"Not as far as we know," said Johansson.

"I heard he was American," said Vindel. "Your colleagues who were here over the weekend said so. There was a big husky one, a real mountain of a guy, and then he had a little dapper one with him who looked like an executive. In all fairness, though, they were both nice, I have no complaints about either of them."

I should hope not, thought Johansson.

"There's one thing I was thinking about," said Vindel as they stood in the entryway saying goodbye.

"Yes," said Johansson.

"I told my neighbor, Mrs. Carlander, fine lady, widow, although she'll soon be eighty of course . . ."

"Yes," said Johansson.

"Yes, I told her that he was an American."

"Yes," said Johansson.

"Yes, she must have seen them when they stood there talking at the place where he was killed. Your colleagues, that is."

"Yes," said Johansson as he stepped out through the door. High time to get back to work, he thought.

"She'd heard about Charlie; that's why we came to talk about it and when I told her that they'd said that he was an American."

You haven't started tippling again, have you? thought Johansson, feeling ashamed at the thought. "Absolutely no problem," he said. "It's no secret, and I'd like to say thank you for the treat."

"You're welcome," said Vindel and nodded after Johansson, who was disappearing down the stairwell.

"I think she'd spoken with some American when she was at the post office," explained Vindel to Johansson's back.

"Excuse me?" said Johansson, turning around.

"It was him," said Mrs. Carlander, pointing at the photo of Krassner. "I heard right away that he was an American but also that he spoke with a distinct upstate New York accent. My husband was head of sales for SKF in the U.S. and we lived there for quite a few years," Mrs. Carlander explained.

This can't be true, thought Lars Martin Johansson.

"Tell me," he said.

"It must have been a little over a month ago," said Mrs. Carlander. She wasn't sure of the day, but toward the end of every month she would always gather together all the bills that needed to be paid and go to the post office with them, so it must have been just around then. Besides, it was then that her husband's pension check was deposited in her account, so she didn't need to worry about making overdrafts from the bank and annoyances like that.

No doubt, thought Johansson, looking around at the tastefully decorated apartment. Mrs. Carlander has the means to get by.

"I could just write it out on my postal account and put it in the mail," she continued, "but I think there are so many newfangled things and I feel more secure going to the post office where there's always someone to ask if need be. And besides, they're so nice, the people who work there, especially the manager. She's charming."

Johansson nodded.

"Where is the post office?"

"Oh," said Mrs. Carlander. "It's our own post office, as we usually say, we older folks who live here in the neighborhood. It's that little post office on Körsbärsvägen. Right on the corner before the student dormitory, but on the other side of the street of course," she explained. "Besides, the walk there is just about right."

Johansson nodded. He had a vague recollection of having walked or driven past it at some point.

"And naturally they're going to close it," said Mrs. Carlander, with a noticeable irritation at the ravages of time.

"I see," said Johansson.

"Well," said Mrs. Carlander. "So we've started to organize a protest among us older people in the neighborhood. The politicians can't just take all local service away from us."

They certainly can, thought Johansson, but he didn't say that.

"It must have been in the morning," continued Mrs. Carlander. "That I was there, that is. There are very few people there in the morning, and of course you want to stand in line as little as possible."

"That's for sure," said Johansson. "Who wants to stand in line?"

"That's why I recall it so well," said Mrs. Carlander. "I became extremely irritated at him."

On the morning about a month earlier when Mrs. Carlander visited the post office on Körsbärsvägen, the premises had been mostly empty when she entered. There was only one man, speaking English with the cashier at the only window that was open.

"I heard right away that he was an American," said Mrs. Carlander. "My husband and I lived there for almost ten years. SKF had an office in Manhattan at that time and we lived less than an hour north, on the Hudson River outside a charming little town called Montrose. Gerhard commuted on weekdays, morning and evening, and I took care of our children. Now they're grown up and have children of their own."

Johansson nodded. He had gathered as much from the framed family pictures on her little desk.

"Where was I?" Mrs. Carlander smiled absently but then she picked up the thread again and there was a twinkle in her gray eyes. "That's what was amusing, suddenly I recognized his, well, accent. New England, although to be exact it's not really New England."

"So you, Mrs. Carlander, became irritated at him," Johansson reminded her.

"He was going to send some letter and the cashier's English no doubt could have been better—I actually became a little irritated at her too, and for a moment I thought about butting in and offering to help out by translating, but you don't want to meddle either."

No, thought Johansson. You're not the type. He nodded encouragingly.

"But finally I became thoroughly irritated in any event, for he didn't give up and it's a little hard for me to stand for longer periods, but just as I was about to say something the manager came and took over. Charming young woman, you should meet her, although that is a strange title they've given her. Postmaster. What's wrong with postmistress? After all, you say equestrienne, for example. It's not logical."

If she's married to one then it's completely okay, thought Johansson, and I'll reserve judgment on that thing about horses, but he didn't say that.

"Do you recall what kind of problem there was with that letter?" asked Johansson.

Mrs. Carlander shook her head slowly.

"No," she said hesitantly. "But if there were any I'm convinced the manager would have solved them for him."

"You don't recall her name?" asked Johansson.

"Name, name," said Mrs. Carlander vaguely. "Her first name is Pia, that much I know. But what her last name is, I know that I know but sometimes I get those, well, it's as if things just fall out of my memory. The other day I forgot the word for 'navel.' I was talking with one of my grandchildren on the phone and it was completely gone. She must have thought Grandma had gone crazy, poor thing."

"It'll be okay," said Johansson confidently. "We police find out things like that." Peppy Pia, he thought.

"I think so too," said Mrs. Carlander with conviction. "I'm quite certain you are going to take notice of her, superintendent. She has that kind of appearance that you fellows take notice of, if I may say so."

Time to say goodbye, thought Johansson and smiled in her direction.

"Yes, Mrs. Carlander, I must say thank you . . ."

"You won't say what he's done? Is it narcotics and those kinds of horrors?"

Johansson shook his head and smiled soothingly.

"No, not as far as we know," he said. "He isn't suspected of any crime."

"No," said Mrs. Carlander, and she didn't sound entirely convinced.

"No," repeated Johansson. "We're just trying to find out who he was."

Mrs. Carlander nodded again but she still didn't seem entirely convinced.

Mrs. Carlander was completely correct. Pia had the kind of appearance that fellows take notice of: dark hair cut short, blue eyes, large breasts, and a narrow waist. Her last name was Hedin. There's nothing wrong with her legs either, thought Johansson, but because they were standing on either side of the counter it wasn't particularly easy to make sure of that.

Johansson had stated his name and given her his business card. He had also noted that she became more surprised when she looked at it than was warranted by his name and title alone. Then she smiled amiably at him and nodded inquiringly.

"What can I help you with?"

Johansson handed over the photo of Krassner.

"I understand you were speaking with this person about a month ago. He wanted help sending a letter."

She took the photo in her hand and Johansson saw that she recognized the face in the picture. Then she smiled amiably again and nodded toward his business card, which she had placed on the counter.

"You don't have an ID or anything," she asked. "I don't want to seem awkward, but we do have our rules as well."

Careless of me, thought Johansson, and wondered how many courses in corporate security she'd gone to. He smiled apologetically and held out his police ID. In contrast to almost everyone else, she looked at it carefully. Then she smiled again and Johansson understood that Mrs. Carlander was a woman who knew men better than most women half her age.

"That's right," she said. "I recognize him and I was the one who helped him send the letter to you."

What the hell is she saying? thought Johansson, and apparently Pia Hedin was just as observant as he was, for she just smiled and nodded toward the back of the post office.

"Perhaps we should sit down in my office," she suggested. "So we can talk without being disturbed."

Nice legs, thought Johansson as he followed her into her office, at least one consolation in this mess.

More than a month ago, Krassner had come into the post office on Körsbärsvägen and sent a letter to the Stockholm 4 post office on Folkungagatan on the south end, poste restante, for Police Superintendent Lars Martin Johansson. She had helped him herself but she didn't go into the reasons why she'd done so.

"It was a rather strange request. We almost never get any poste restante here, and the ones we do get come as a rule from abroad. As you no doubt know, police superintendent . . ."

"Call me Lars," said Johansson, and received a smile and a nod as a reward.

"When a poste restante is sent to one of our offices, it remains there for a month—thirty days, to be exact—and then it goes back to the sender. Provided that the addressee hasn't picked it up, of course."

If he had my address, thought Johansson, why in the name of heaven didn't he send it directly home to me instead of to the post office—although he did send it to the post office I usually go to.

"I'm thinking," said Johansson, smiling his most charming smile. "I had no idea that I'd received a letter poste restante."

"I figured that out a little more than a week ago," said Pia Hedin. "When we got it back here."

Finally, thought Johansson. Soon the truth will emerge, but before that we'll take everything in the right order. Calmly and methodically.

"There are naturally no obstacles to sending local mailings poste restante, but it's not common. That I can guarantee. I recall that I offered to try to find out your address so that it would be sure to get through."

"What did he say to that?" asked Johansson.

"He explained that you'd agreed to do it this way."

I see, thought Johansson. He said that.

"Yes." She nodded and smiled again. "It's clear that I started a little at the addressee's title, your title—it was actually a little bit exciting."

"What did you think?" said Johansson. What a smile she has, he thought.

"That it was some kind of secret tip. I mean, he didn't seem like he was on drugs or strange in any way. He even wanted to show his ID to me, but I said that wasn't necessary. I understood of course that there was no dope in the letter. It was an ordinary letter. Not even especially thick, and of course I could feel that there was only paper in it. Yes. What did I think? I probably thought it was exciting. A little secret agent movie like that."

She seems rather charmed, thought Johansson.

"Okay," he said. "You wouldn't be able to fetch it so I can look at it?"

"Won't work." She smiled and shook her head. "Unfortunately."

What do you mean won't work? thought Johansson.

"He had requested particular forwarding from here, so I've already sent it to that address. It actually left here yesterday."

This is, so help me God, not true, thought Johansson, and he groaned internally.

"Why did he do that?" asked Johansson.

"I explained how it worked with poste restante and that the letter would come back here in about a month, and then he said that if he hadn't picked it up within a week he wanted me to forward it to an address in the U.S. He explained that he was living at the student dormitory right across the street but that he was planning to go home in a month, approximately. He didn't know exactly which day he would leave, and he didn't want it to remain sitting here with us and he didn't want it sent to the student dormitory because he was just living there temporarily. And because we don't want a lot of letters sitting around here either, making a mess, I did as he requested, a little special service like that." She smiled and nodded.

"Where have you sent it?" said Johansson.

"To the address in the U.S. that he gave me, and actually I thought that was a little strange too."

"How so?"

"Well, as I said, he explained that he was only here temporarily and that he was living at the dormitory right across the street and that he would probably be going home in a month. So if we were to get the letter sent back, we could hold it here for a week and then forward it to him if he hadn't picked it up by then."

"Yes," said Johansson inquiringly. "What's strange about that?"

"He wanted it forwarded to a different person," she explained. "A woman, so I thought that was probably more of that secret stuff that I shouldn't butt into, but I have both her name and address. I have a copy of the forwarding information that you can look at if it's of any help."

"Yes," said Johansson. "Gladly."

Sarah J. Weissman, read Johansson, 222 Aiken Avenue, Rensselaer, NY 12144 U.S.A. Yes, yes, yes, thought Johansson. And so who is she?

"I actually checked the address," she said. "I mean, you do get a bit curious."

It shows in your eyes. You think this is a lot more fun than I do, Johansson thought gloomily.

"And?" he asked.

"Yes, the zip code fits the address. I haven't checked if the addressee is there. I don't really know if we can do that, but the rest checks out. Rensselaer is north of New York."

Upstate New York, thought Johansson, and that much adds up.

"You seem worried, superintendent," she said. "Is there anything I can help you with?"

If the eyes are indeed the mirror of the soul, thought Johansson, you seem sufficiently talented in any case. The question is whether you are sufficiently tight-lipped.

"Perhaps," said Johansson.

"Try," she said. "Sometimes you actually have to try trusting your fellow humans."

"Are you the type of person who can . . . keep her mouth shut?" asked Johansson, and he immediately thought that perhaps he ought to have put that differently.

"Yes," she said and nodded emphatically. "I am."

"Good," said Johansson. "The problem is in brief the following. I've never met this Krassner. I didn't even know that he existed. True, I'm head of the National Bureau of Criminal Investigation"—a brief period of happiness, thought Johansson—"but," he continued, "Krassner isn't one of our informants, and if he were, it wouldn't be handled in this way.

"Explain to me," Johansson went on, "why someone sends something poste restante to a police officer they've never met without saying that they've done so. The chance that he will get what's been sent ought to be about nil."

"Certainly," she said. "But there's another thing that I don't understand."

Johansson nodded to her to continue.

"How you found out about it anyway. I mean, you show up here with me. How did you find out about it?"

You're not stupid, thought Johansson, and what do I say now without saying too much?

"By pure coincidence," he said. "Why does he send something to me in such a way that he must be almost certain that I will never receive it or even find out about it?" he continued by way of diversion.

"Wouldn't the simplest way be for you to ask him? And if he's already gone home and it's terribly important I suppose you could ask the American police for help. I mean, the police have some kind of international cooperation, don't they? Even we have within the postal service, and sometimes it actually works really well."

Now she smiled again and seemed visibly charmed.

Groan, thought Johansson. Just so she doesn't think I'm a complete idiot.

"The problem is that I can't do that," he said. And don't start harping about why, he thought.

"Are you that policeman that there was so much about in the papers a few months ago?" she asked.

Johansson nodded.

"Perhaps he's heard people talking about you in particular," she said. "There was pure adulation in several newspapers, and that isn't so common when it comes to policemen, is it? Does he understand Swedish?"

"I don't believe he does," said Johansson. "Although I'm not completely sure. It's possible of course he might have spoken with someone. Who spoke Swedish, I mean." She's thinking the same way as Jarnebring, he thought. No resemblance in other respects.

"Think if it's like this," she said, suddenly sounding eager. "Suppose he's up to something secret or something dangerous, and so he wants to get himself a kind of insurance, as it were. I've read that in mysteries many times. People who leave all their secret papers with people they can trust, lawyers and journalists and in secret safe-deposit boxes. Like a type of insurance if something should happen to them." Johansson had been struck by the same thought five minutes earlier. There was just one hitch.

"There's just one hitch," he said. "How would I have found out about it?"

"You're sitting here," she said, "so you've clearly found out about it."

"True," said Johansson, "but I still have no idea what it's about."

"Exactly," she said and sounded even more eager. "And you shouldn't, either. As long as nothing has happened, you shouldn't know a thing. He never needed his insurance. You wouldn't even be sitting here if it weren't for a pure coincidence. You've said that yourself."

Johansson nodded and tried to look as if he was doing so because of what she had said. Then he smiled.

"You've never thought about becoming a police officer?" he asked.

"No, never," she said, smiling back.

"I'd like to thank you very much for your help," said Johansson.

"It was nothing," she said, and there was no mistaking that she was charmed. "Get in touch if you happen to get stuck again."

Don't tempt me, he thought, and suddenly he felt rather miserable.

What a mess, thought Johansson. What is this really all about? First he stopped at the Östermalm police station and gave back Jarnebring's identification photos. Jarnebring wasn't in, which saved both time and explanations. After that he went to the office and now he was sitting behind his desk submerged in thought. What is it that connects me with the now deceased John Krassner and the hopefully still existing Sarah Weissman? Krassner and Weissman, Americans of whom generally speaking he knew no more than that the first was dead and that he'd probably taken his own life by jumping out the window of his student apartment. And what do you really know about yourself? thought Johansson gloomily. If you really stop to think about it? Wiklander, thought Johansson.

"Can you get hold of Wiklander," said Johansson to his secretary on the intercom, despite the fact that she was only sitting on the other side of the wall five yards away from him. Don't feel like running around today, he thought.

Wiklander was thin and dark, tall and trim and ten years younger than Johansson. He worked on the National Bureau of Criminal Investigation's own surveillance squad and was an extraordinarily competent policeman. If it would ever be necessary to put a face on discretion—which was highly unlikely, as that would be contrary to the very idea—then Wiklander was a likely candidate. Now he was standing in Johansson's office, sniffing the air like a foxhound moments before you pull off the leash.

"What can I do for you, chief?" asked Wiklander.

"Find out a telephone number and check if the address matches up," said Johansson and handed over a handwritten slip of paper.

"Sarah Weissman," said Wiklander. "Check the address and find out her telephone number. Of course," he said and almost sounded a little offended. "Nothing else?"

"Well, yes," said Johansson, "so you don't need to have that sour look. I want you to do it without a soul finding out about it."

"You mean our dear colleagues," said Wiklander, who was of course no numbskull.

"Exactly," said Johansson. "In a global sense, even. And preferably no one else either."

"Sure," said Wiklander. "If she has a telephone number, you'll get it."

"Excellent," said Johansson.

Fifteen minutes later Wiklander was back with the requested telephone number. It was written on the same piece of paper he had received from

Johansson, and if he knew Wiklander it was also the only relevant thing in writing.

"That was quick," said Johansson.

"So-so," said Wiklander modestly. "It's her number and it goes with the address."

"Tell me," said Johansson with curiosity. "How'd you go about it?" He held up his watch with an inquiring smile.

"I forget," said Wiklander. "Don't really know what you're talking about."

It would be simplest to call her. Johansson was staring gloomily at his slip of paper. What time is it there now? he thought. He checked his watch. Almost twelve here makes almost six there. That wouldn't come off too well, maybe, he thought. And tomorrow he was going to the United States.

The world is really full of strange coincidences, thought Johansson, with a heavy sigh.

Johansson hadn't called her. On the other hand, Jarnebring had called him at home that evening.

He sounded in high spirits and wondered how the investigations had gone.

"How many do you want us to arrest and do we need to request assistance from the riot squad?" he asked, chuckling into the receiver.

"No need," said Johansson. "I went by and talked with Vindel but that led nowhere."

"What do you know," said Jarnebring, faking astonishment. "That led nowhere?"

"It occurred to me that perhaps he'd run into him. That Vindel had seen Krassner before because they both moved around in the same area. Just a wild chance," said Johansson, sighing.

"You didn't find out a thing, in other words."

"Not a thing," lied Johansson.

"No need to be so hangdog," said Jarnebring. "There don't seem to be very many people who knew our man Krassner."

"No?" said Johansson. "What do you mean?"

"I spoke with the embassy this afternoon, well, with Hultman, that is, and Krassner doesn't seem to have any relatives."

"Aha," said Johansson. What do you mean? he thought.

"Yes, Hultman was a little worried because they must have someone to send his things to."

Not my problem, thought Johansson.

"And the only person the folks there could get hold of was evidently some old girlfriend. But according to her it had been ten years since the breakup between her and Krassner. According to Hultman."

Old girlfriend, thought Johansson; at the same time the well-known alarm bells started to sound inside him.

"I don't understand," said Johansson. "Has Hultman talked with Krassner's old girlfriend?"

"Are you drunk, Johansson?" asked Jarnebring politely.

"Stone sober," said Johansson. "A little tired, perhaps."

"I understand," said Jarnebring pedagogically. "Our American colleagues who tried to find out who Krassner was have spoken with an old girlfriend of his. By the way, I've received a copy of their interview with her. First she says that it was about ten years ago or so that she broke up with him—"

"Yes," said Johansson. "I'm listening."

"Stop interrupting, then," said Jarnebring. "Where was I?"

"Old girlfriend who broke up ten years ago."

"Exactly," said Jarnebring with the emphasis of someone who has just found a lost thread. "And second, she doesn't appear to have been one of his most ardent admirers."

"Maybe that's why she broke up with him," said Johansson.

"For sure," said Jarnebring, "but Krassner seems to have missed that, for he's listed her as his nearest relation, and in addition a will has been found where he leaves everything to her. I reserve judgment on what that may be, but I bet my old police helmet that we're hardly talking in the billions."

"Does she have a name?" asked Johansson innocently.

"Sarah something. I have it at work."

Sarah J. Weissman, thought Johansson but kept his mouth shut.

"I see," said Johansson. "Yes, frankly speaking I'm damn tired of this story."

"Nice to hear," said Jarnebring. "And you . . ."

"Yes," said Johansson.

"Have a nice trip and take care of yourself over there. That's why I called, actually."

"Thanks," said Johansson. "Take care of yourself too."

This gets stranger and stranger, he thought as he put down the receiver.

[SATURDAY, NOVEMBER 30]

On Saturday the thirtieth of November Lars Martin Johansson took an early morning plane to New York. As travel companions he had two chief inspectors from the National Bureau of Criminal Investigation. Exceptional police officers and nice fellows.

Fuck you, Krassner, and fuck you, Weissman, thought Johansson. Because now I'm going to have a good time and maybe even learn something new that might prove useful.

"I'm thinking of having a shot with lunch," said Johansson, smiling wryly.

His colleague from the bureau's narcotics squad nodded thoughtfully.

"The same thought actually occurred to me too."

Their colleague from the Interpol section nodded as well.

"Remarkable," he said. "I was just thinking the exact same thing. Life can be really strange sometimes."

CHAPTER II

Free falling, as in a dream

Stockholm in the 1970s and 1980s

In the fall of 1976 the secret police set up an external group to increase its organizational security. Given the working name Group for Internal Security and Protection Against Leakage, it constituted the most secret part of covert police operations. As protection against discovery, a number of measures had been taken. A private-sector management consulting firm was created as a front for its operation; its office was in the city, and no one who worked there could be traced back to the secret police's already secret lists and payrolls.

Contacts with the parent organization that the group was created to watch over and defend were, naturally, surrounded with every conceivable secrecy. To start with, the group was run solely by the head of the operations bureau, who in reality was head of the entire secret police. Because of the character of the group's mission this solution had proven to be far from ideal, primarily because it limited the opportunities for systematic insight into the various branches of the operation.

For that reason, changes were made the following year. Another special group was created within the larger organization—the Group for Organizational Protection—and on the basis of that, a network of informants had been built up in all branches of the operation. At the same time, the majority of them were—hopefully—unaware of the fact that they now had a dual function in which they not only did their work but also reported what they and their colleagues were doing via daily hour-by-hour reports and continuously updated logs of data access as well as internal and external contacts. The union had objections, of course, but because SePo's union was only a pale shadow of the uniformed police officers' professional organization—and as usual had no idea what the whole thing was really about—the new system still turned out as planned.

The external group had been retained, of course, and essentially in the same form as before. The influx of information had also increased markedly, but the price to be paid was that more people within the parent organization were now aware of the external group's existence. The entire process was a good illustration of the classic dilemma of all secret police work. Ultimately it was about putting together a puzzle, and it went without saying that the task was considerably easier if the ones doing the solving had access to all the pieces. As a method the process was a complete disaster, of course, if the intention was to simultaneously keep both the puzzle-solving and the finished puzzle secret from as many people as possible, regardless of which side they belonged to.

Among the initiated few who were aware of the external operation, it was also known that the entire construction was the idea of the bureau director, Berg. Berg was the head of the operations bureau but had never breathed a word of his role as its originator, which among his superiors was interpreted as a good sign of both discretion and personal modesty. Berg himself knew better, for he had gotten the whole concept from the German security service, from its major and minor aspects all the way down to pure details; they had a long tradition of just this aspect of secret police work.

Based on his historical knowledge and everything he knew about the work of foreign security agencies, he also had a strategy for how he might get his new operation to grow and develop. The ultimate goal he envisioned was a secret bureau, or perhaps even a separate secret organization for constitutional protection, where not only the secret police were under surveillance, but also the so-called open operation within the police, and the military, of course, as well as every other governmental authority, private organization, or sector whose activity might conceivably threaten or damage the highest political authority. This mission was the historical basis of all governmental security services, the primary task overshadowing everything else. Constitutional protection, thought Berg. An excellent phrase in a context where he had to be utterly discreet when describing his assignment to an outside world often both ignorant and hostile, and which gladly took any opportunity to portray the guardians of democracy as its enemies.

The Swedish secret police, in contrast to its counterparts in both the West and the East, was an organization made up almost exclusively of police officers. The Swedish secret police had no intellectual or academic tradition whatsoever, and it was Berg's firm conviction that this was also its main strength. No upper-class pansies from Oxford or Cambridge who might sell out the whole country to the enemy for a piece of ass at some shabby hotel in a third-world country; no overexcited theoreticians who couldn't think a single original thought without immediately broadcasting it in a seminar with a crowd of their ilk; no philosophical scatterbrains or political brooders. A completely pure organization made up solely of police officers, thought Berg.

During the following years they indeed had great and well-deserved successes, both within the organization as a whole and perhaps above all else within that part of the operation that was Berg's darling; day by day it was becoming more and more like the secret bureau for constitutional protection that he had imagined. They had good luck and they had bad luck, made use of the good and turned the bad to their advantage; in brief, they successfully managed the whole situation.

At first they had good luck, exposing a spy within their own organization. An alcoholic police officer who had sold secret information to the enemy with all the finesse of a common street peddler and whose prices weren't much higher. Life imprisonment, good press, and encouraging pats on the back from the average man on the street as well as from the political bosses.

Then they had bad luck. Hostile-minded elements on the outermost fringes of the left had spread a story that it was in reality the Israeli security service that had captured the Swedish spy. In their usual unsentimental way, their agents were said to have spirited him away at the Beirut airport and conveyed him to a suitably situated prison hole where they put the muzzle of a gun to his temple and invited him to unburden his conscience. When he was through with that, which should only have taken a few days, they had driven him back to the airport and put him on the airplane to Copenhagen, at which time they called their Swedish colleagues and informed them that they had just sent them a present.

True or not, this had caused problems. Berg was not one to debate his operation in the media, however much the media nagged, but the minister of justice, who was politically responsible, had taken up the matter at their weekly meeting, and for reasons of which only he and Berg were aware he had chosen to sound more worried than irritated. Was there any truth in these, to say the least, astounding assertions?

Berg shook his head emphatically. Not in the least, but as so often before in a situation like this the truth was such that it couldn't be told or discussed even in the most exclusive company. It was actually his internal security group that had been on the trail of the spy and the external part of that group that had carried out the practical aspects. Because the operation was so sensitive, and must be concealed at all costs, it was Berg who had made contact with the Israelis and in consultation with them worked out the actual arrest. Afterward they had collectively cooked up a kidnapping story on how it had been done and through their usual channels seen to it that the "news" spread to their opponents.

"They swallowed it all, hook, line, and sinker, so we killed two birds with one stone," Berg summarized, with a friendly nod toward the speechless minister. Just like you, but the other way around, he thought.

"You may rest assured that this will stay in this room," the minister of justice replied warmly.

Unmasking a spy in your own organization was good, but nothing you could live on until the end of time, and if there was more than one it could quickly get really bad. Besides, it was unnecessary. What security work was primarily about was refining information that was being gathered anyway, taking care to manage every conceivable risk, and exploiting this to the organization's advantage. In that way conditions for expansion could be created without a need to point out a lot of annoyances that had already occurred.

Threats and menaces, dangers and future scenarios, prognoses and preventive measures were what it was really about, and you would have to be a complete fool not to understand that a well-written, well-supported, and selectively distributed security analysis, all else aside, was far superior to any number of airplane hijackings, bombing attacks, or assassinated politicians when it was a matter of securing economic resources. We have a lot to learn from the Germans, thought Berg, who had studied in detail how they dealt with the legacy from their domestic terrorists. But we haven't been as good on that point, he thought. At the beginning of the eighties it was time for the next change of organization.

First the in-house part of the operation was renamed the Group for Departmental Protection. For one thing this sounded better, a little more diffuse, a little broader, a little more Swedish, to put it simply. Also, the workload had increased markedly and among other things a special unit had been formed to inspect and refine all the information compiled within the framework of the overarching operation. No possibilities could be left untried in the hunt for new resources. Berg had been careful to underscore this when they had an introductory kickoff. Even if he hadn't put it that way.

The external operation had been retained. True, it had grown so markedly that it became necessary to create yet another front organization, which in turn gave rise to a set of leadership and coordination problems, the solution to which was found within the framework of a foundation, but the fundamental strategy, as well as the direction of the work, remained the same as before.

The special "threat group" that he had set up—Berg often, and with pride, used to think of it as his own marketing department—also had a very successful start in its operation. First, the situation in the Balkans had been taken up. Since the early 1970s, the Yugoslavs had been a source of happiness for the Swedish secret police. Croatian extremists had shot the republic's Serbian ambassador, after which their comrades freed them from a Swedish prison by hijacking an airplane, and in the end the Swedish secret police received major appropriations to battle the new terrorism.

But the Yugoslavs had been good in more ways than that. The stream of political refugees had increased steadily, and among those who came here there were strong political divisions and a reasonable element of common career criminals who gladly sat up nights, conspiring in their smoky club quarters. Appropriations for reconnaissance and external surveillance, wiretapping, and interpreters had multiplied. Appropriations for interpreters alone had increased by more than two thousand percent in less than five years.

But then it was as though the air had been let out of them, and in melancholy moments Berg used to think that the Yugoslavs clearly couldn't handle the comfortable coziness of Sweden. The terrorist acts flagged in their forecasts had simply not happened, and while year followed year and appropriations continued to climb, the opposite side quite simply refused to deliver all the atrocities that SePo had promised its political superiors. Illegal clubs, aggravated robbery, and the occasional bloody reckoning among Yugoslavian criminals were all well and good, but in the context within which Berg was operating this was clearly insufficient. The politicians had started grumbling, and among operatives within the open operation there was a growing and increasingly vocal opinion maintaining, in complete seriousness, that they now had the Yugoslavs under control and that the secret police ought to occupy itself with other things.

The situation was not good, the trend even worse, and it was at exactly that point that his newly formed threat group, the Group for Analysis and Processing of Information, as it was called in more solemn contexts, had gone in and taken a concerted hold on the entire Balkan problem. Suitable sections of a large number of old strategic analyses acquired from the Swedish military intelligence service and their foreign colleagues had been compiled—the sections that for several years had been promising the imminent collapse of the Yugoslav republic and subsequent total chaos in the Balkans and elsewhere in Europe. With these simple means a report was produced with alarming content for the nation's guardians: highest level of secrecy, highest priority, and the most restricted distribution to political superiors. Additional appropriations had arrived like a check in the mail.

After that they quickly moved ahead and went to work on the Kurdish problem. It wasn't all peace and harmony among the Kurdish refugees elsewhere in Europe, and when conflicts flared up they did sometimes shoot each other. The problem was that they stubbornly persisted in only shooting other Kurds, which from a secret police point of view was economic madness. Berg's German colleague at Constitutional Protection had the same problem as he did, and due to the fact that the Kurds themselves clearly lacked political ambitions they decided they had to do something about this.

First, they increased the pressure on their informants among the Kurdish refugees. They were warned in no uncertain terms that if they couldn't deliver anything more than the usual nonsense on yet another impending murder of some talkative guy with a fruit stand, they might just as well pack their bags and go back to Turkey. The argument clearly hit home, for within just a few months much disturbing information had come in from several different infiltrators in both Sweden and Germany. It was obvious that extremist political groups among the Kurds were planning assassination attempts on several centrally placed domestic politicians in those countries where they had the privilege of residence as refugees. And yes, new appropriations also arrived like a check in the mail. Finally, thought Berg, who had at last succeeded in showing that there was even a way to squeeze money out of a former shepherd from the mountainous regions around Diyarbakir.

When Berg, much later, looked back at the early eighties, he would think of that period as the happy years in his life. There had been a lot to do, but it had been fun doing it and the successes had been great. Then worries started to pile up. First he was saddled with a regime change. He had calculated at an early stage that the conservatives wouldn't last forever, and he had no political opinions whatsoever, if someone were to come up with the preposterous idea of asking him, but if he were able to choose . . . of course.

The conservatives had been easy to deal with, unaccustomed as they were to people like him, but the social democrats represented a different species. That he knew from early experience. Berg had been around a good while, and six years in line for the public troughs had given them sufficient appetite when it was finally time. As soon as the election results were clear, Berg had cleaned out his calendar, taken his closest associates with him to a secure location, and devoted three whole days to analyzing the new situation. Analyze? They had gone over it down to the minutest detail. They were forewarned, and thereby forearmed.

The new government had hardly had time to take its place before the military intelligence service performed the anticipated assault, with the help of its well-trained contacts within the social democratic leadership. It was the usual old turf war, but this time Berg had been better prepared than anyone before him. The day before the meeting in the government office building he had sent over the latest analysis of the situation on the terror front and seen to it that it was well spiced with an optimal selection of the military intelligence authority's own judgments. Where was the antagonism? Berg wondered innocently. As far as he could understand, both he and his coworkers were in complete agreement with their military colleagues in their view of the matter.

Berg had chosen to head back after the meeting on foot, and as he was walking in the autumn sun between Rosenbad and his own building on Kungsholmen, he became aware that he was humming the finale from Beethoven's choral symphony. *Alle Menschen werden Brüder,* Berg hummed contentedly, and when he sat down behind his desk the papers he had requested the weekend before were already topmost on the pile.

First he went to work on the requested compilation of the new government ministers, government secretaries, and the remaining politically appointed officials and advisers who had now taken over the government office building. Up until a day ago, a good many of the latter had been found in the secret police register. For good reasons and with well-deserved thick files, thought Berg with a wry smile, but after the just-completed autumn housecleaning the archives were neat and tidy and all necessary papers that might cause unnecessary annoyance were now in secure storage outside the building. In a week he would meet with the politically appointed board for the secret police, and bets were already being made among his coworkers on which of the new board members would suggest a visit to SePo's personal archive this time. There were three to choose from, and none of them was a sure thing.

Within the external operation an analysis had been made of the key political figures with whom the parent organization would now be working. All in all it consisted of a dozen people, of which a two-thirds majority sat in Rosenbad and was divided approximately equally among the preliminary Cabinet and the justice and defense departments. All of them had been made a gift of a secret police profile, the main point of which gave a summary of their special interests and inclinations in matters of national security.

With that as a foundation, a client-oriented list of priorities had then been made of those areas and issues that might conceivably appeal to the tastes of the new consumers, and for the time being his entire analysis group was busy picking out the information that must be available when, in approximately two weeks—and here too the wagering was well under way—it would be necessary to demonstrate that these were the very problems which had been viewed for a long time with the utmost seriousness.

The list of priorities was hardly exciting for an old fox like Berg. There were all the usual old articles from the standard assortment, such as the supervision of persons with sensitive positions and the surveillance of various extreme political parties, which solely concerned their own ends regardless of political orientation. Ultimately it was only a matter of weeding a little in the flower beds and shifting perspective a few degrees; after that for the most part things could proceed as before. Obviously it was necessary to raise the priority of neo-Nazis and right-wing extremists, as much as this irked him. His resources were not inexhaustible, and it was Berg's firm conviction that there were better ways to use money than keeping an eye on a few hundred semi-retarded, misguided, snot-nosed kids who marched out of step even when they didn't have a case of strong beer under their belts. Which they no doubt usually did, Berg thought acidly. But that is how things were now and that's the way it would have to be.

His own contribution to the list of priorities was a source of satisfaction to him. It dealt with something completely new in the history of the secret police, which in the long run could prove very fortunate; the fact that it was his loser of a nephew who had given him the idea didn't make matters worse. Berg's father had been a policeman out in the country, within the old organization, long before it had been nationalized. He had had two sons who had both become policemen. Things had gone well for Berg, far beyond expectations; for his older brother things had gone badly.

When Berg left the police academy, he started out as a patrolman with the uniformed police department in Stockholm. In his free time he studied for a high school diploma by correspondence. After that he took a leave of absence from the police department and studied law full-time with money he had saved up as a constable. This degree had taken him three years as opposed to the usual five, and when he applied to the prosecutor's office they had taken him in with open arms. Several of his new colleagues had made the same class journey as he had. After ten years as a prosecutor, he had been approached by the secret police. The police force had been nationalized, and the secret police had been reorganized as a special division of the National Police Board. The old operation needed to be aired out, worn-out brooms exchanged for new ones, and Berg was one of the first to be asked. Ten years later he was in effect head of the whole thing.

His older brother got married at the same time as he finished school and started as a patrolman with the uniformed police department in Stockholm. In rapid succession he had acquired three children and problems with finances, alcohol, and his marriage. Then his wife left him and took the children with her. He had driven a patrol car under the influence, crashed into a newsstand, been fined and given a suspended sentence, disciplined in the form of suspension and payroll deductions, and finally been offered a new career as watchman at the police department's lost-and-found office. There he had remained for five years, and the summer when his own son started as a patrolman in Stockholm City he had borrowed a service vehicle, driven out to Vaxholm, and plunged straight into the water from the steamboat pier.

Berg was firmly convinced that blood was thicker than water, but when it came to his own nephew his conviction had wavered on more than one occasion. When his brother had been killed in the accident— that's of course how it was described—he had exerted himself vigorously to put some order into the life of his younger relative. Because the difference in age between them was only twelve years—in solitary moments he used to thank his creator that it wasn't greater than that— he had tried to be like an older brother to him, but with hindsight that had been wasted effort.

His nephew had had miserable grades during all of his years in school. He had already acquired a well-established reputation as a bully by the end of his first year in elementary school, and the political opinions that he often, and gladly, expressed had never fit on the map provided by the Swedish parliament.

But he was big and burly, he had a grandfather, a father, and an uncle who were policemen, and he had been welcomed into the fold when he applied to the police academy.

His career had proceeded without a hitch and after a few years he was working as commander of the garrison with by far the most complaints in the Stockholm Police Department's riot squad. Without realizing it, he had a quality that made him both useful and usable to the organization he served. Police officers like him create sufficient scope for action for all the normal, functional officers, thought Berg. In addition, he was an untapped resource for the operation that Berg represented.

An absolute majority of all police officers voted for the conservatives. Berg knew that. He also knew that a sufficient number of them did so for lack of a more extreme alternative, and with that knowledge his mission was established. So: start out by mapping antigovernment elements within the police department and gradually expand the mission to include their counterparts in the military. Several of them already associated privately across operational boundaries, so there were natural inroads and it shouldn't be too difficult.

Berg himself had written the long background section to the report on undemocratic movements and elements within the institutions whose mission it was to protect the security of the realm against external and internal attacks, and he had been careful to underscore that there were two organizations that had historically shown themselves to be extraordinarily dangerous for the politically appointed powers that be, namely the military and their own secret police. He had concluded by stating that this was an important but unfortunately overlooked issue, to which, however, significantly greater attention had been devoted for some time. He also had an explanation for why it had turned out this way. "The fact that our Swedish political democracy has been one of the most stable democracies known to twentieth-century European history is in all likelihood essentially the reason that secret police interest in this issue has previously been so low."

Twelve days, not fourteen, had passed before Berg and his coworkers had been called up to the government office building in order to give an account of the prioritized activity. Normally there would be three regular participants at these meetings—the minister of justice, the chief legal officer, and Berg himself—but this time there was an additional person in the room. A week earlier the prime minister had let Berg be informed that he had decided to elevate certain security issues to his own chancellery in the Cabinet, and that he had therefore decided that from now on his special adviser would take part in these meetings on behalf of the prime minister, and that he assumed that he would hear from Berg immediately if he had any objections to his choice of person.

It had been almost seven years since Berg had been forced to listen to the language of power from his superior, and this time, unlike before, he had also been slightly shaken and a little more worried than was pleasant. Actually he had expected something like this—he had not even ruled out the possibility that he would be called up to Rosenbad only to find out that he was being replaced—but this he hadn't foreseen, especially not the concluding portion of the prime minister's directive: "objections to my choice." To Berg's ears this sounded suspiciously like a hidden message, even a warning.

Berg, like the prime minister and his adviser, obviously knew that the latter had been classified in the highest protection category for the past several years. The question was whether the prime minister and the person this ultimately concerned also knew anything more, thought Berg. For example, that Berg had certain pieces of information removed from the adviser's personal file, which he didn't want the person the information concerned to find out that Berg knew. He had brooded half the night until he saw himself as if in a mirror that mirrored another mirror diagonally behind his back, multiplying him into infinity; the next day he had been both tired and disheartened. For a brief moment he had in complete seriousness considered summoning his most intimate coworker, Police Superintendent Waltin, the head of the external operation, to seek his advice, but this was not a time for weakness, so he had dismissed that thought. Never show what you're thinking, wait and see, thought Berg. Besides, he didn't really know if he could completely trust Waltin.

. . .

Perhaps I've been worrying unnecessarily, thought Berg; looking solely at what had actually been said, their meeting had gone smoothly and with only marginal, factual objections from his superiors. The new minister of justice had first expressed a certain surprise that the Kurds had such far-reaching plans for subversive activity, to judge by the survey of which Berg "so meritoriously" had given an account, but actually he was not so surprised after all if he could "be a little personal," for he had suspected for quite some time that "there was something fishy.

"With the Kurds, that is," he explained.

There's one I don't have to worry about, thought Berg.

The new participant at the meeting did not say much. For a while it actually appeared as if he had fallen asleep in his seat, leaning back in his chair with eyes closed, but when Berg got to his ongoing investigation of personnel hostile to democracy within the police department and the military, he suddenly revived and raised his heavy eyelids at least slightly.

Berg didn't like his look, nor his expression, for that matter. He seemed almost amused, and Berg got an unpleasant feeling that the adviser was not seeing him but rather was observing him as though he were an object and not a person. The adviser suddenly started laughing so that his fat stomach bounced; then he nodded and smiled broadly toward Berg but without moving his eyelids a millimeter.

"Hear the roar from the crater of justice," he chuckled and his fat stomach bounced again. "When will we have occasion to enjoy this good cigar? I can hardly contain myself."

"According to my colleagues, we will be able to present an initial survey at the beginning of next year," Berg answered, his expression a model of correctness.

"The age of miracles is clearly not past," said the prime minister's special adviser. He sank back in the chair again with eyelids lowered and an amused smile on his lips.

That man is not in his right mind, thought Berg. But he didn't say that.

.   .   .

The following day he met Waltin at the secure location. Waltin had brought with him the papers that had been cleaned out of the special adviser's file and were now being stored outside the building, while Berg brought what was left with him. Then he visited his workroom on the top floor and read the file while Waltin was pulling on a one-armed bandit that for some unknown reason was installed in the conference room directly below. At regular intervals a faint clanking sound forced its way through the double flooring, and on at least one occasion Waltin shouted with enthusiasm. Why did he do that? thought Berg, who knew that Waltin had his own key to the machine's coin box.

There were three documents in the file that troubled Berg and that he blamed himself for not having read before yesterday's meeting. They were all almost twenty years old and dealt with the special adviser's time as a draftee in the army. According to the first document he had been placed with a regular infantry regiment in upper Norrland. One month later he had been reassigned to general headquarters in Stockholm after a request from headquarters made directly to the regimental head. There he did service for a little more than a year with a department under the command of general headquarters that produced "non-security-classified instructional materials" for draftees and noncommissioned officers in the army. And when he was discharged, after fifteen months of service, he was still an ordinary draftee.

The second document contained two different intelligence tests that he had undergone in connection with enlistment. The first was the usual test, which everyone who enlisted had to fill out, and his results had placed him in the highest category, where roughly two percent of every batch tended to land. There was in itself nothing exceptional about that; Berg himself had been in the category just below, but considering the special adviser's placement as a regular draftee in a regular infantry regiment, there was something that didn't add up. It would have been reasonable to have at least suggested alternative placement for him, but there was not the least indication of that.

Instead he came back a week later and underwent yet another test. Berg was no expert on psychological testing, but he could read. On the last page the psychologist who had conducted the test had added a handwritten note: "The respondent has attained the maximum result on

Stanford Binet in the expanded variant. According to the distribution for the test in question, this means that he belongs to that portion of the total population which makes up circa .01% of the referenced population." One in a hundred thousand, thought Berg. One of less than a hundred Swedes, who a few months later joins up as an ordinary drafted soldier in the infantry?

The third document contained only a typewritten piece of paper and its envelope: The address was handwritten with printed letters and the letter was addressed to "Stockholm Police Department, Investigation Unit, Police Station, Kungsholmen." From there it had clearly wandered on unknown paths to the archives of the secret police. The sender was anonymous, but from the contents and between the lines it was evident that he worked as a staff officer at the training department, G.H.Q. Stockholm, where, among other things, he took care of draftees' passes.

The anonymous informant was writing to point out an obvious anomaly. On the first day at his new service location, one of the draftees had already submitted a pass which granted him leave for the following two weeks. After that he had shown up and submitted another new pass with the same wording. The staff officer interpreted this as so remarkable that he asked him to wait while he checked the pass with the officer who had signed it. He had been "particularly brusquely treated by the aforementioned officer, who in an impudent tone said to me that I should not be meddling in things that were none of my business." When he returned to his office "the draftee had already departed from quarters and as this obvious anomaly has gone on for almost a year I now turn to you, sir, to comment on the matter. The situation in my workplace is unfortunately not such that I could take up the problem with my superior."

"What do you think about this?" asked Berg.

He and Waltin were sitting on the couch in the conference room and he had time to drink half a pot of coffee while Waltin read and pondered.

"Looks as though we've got another spy on our hands," Waltin said with a wry smile.

Two or three, thought Berg, moaning to himself. The second was the minister of justice's chief legal officer, who usually attended the weekly meetings. He had done so for many years, regardless of which party the minister belonged to. In addition he had a side assignment as legal adviser for the supreme commander, with the rank of lieutenant general and placement with general headquarters.

The chief legal officer tended to be a very taciturn man. On those rare occasions when he spoke, it was usually to answer a question, and what he said always concerned formalities and judicial questions. He presented an image both agreeable and taciturn. An old-fashioned educated scribe, Berg thought, but because he was not one to fall for a pretty face, and because the chief legal officer took the minutes at their meetings—granted, these were extremely concise—Berg nonetheless had a routine check carried out. His detective had spent an entire week in a cold delivery truck in the midst of a bitterly cold winter outside the chief legal officer's magnificent villa on Lidingö without having the slightest thing to report. On the eighth night, however, things started happening with a vengeance, and according to the surveillance memorandum on Berg's desk the next morning, the following had occurred.

"At two-eighteen hours the surveillance object came out onto the balcony of his bedroom on the upper floor of the villa. Thereafter with a certain difficulty he came to so-called attention and raised a glass of champagne with his right hand, after which he proposed four cheers to His Majesty the King. He was at the time in question dressed in blue briefs with yellow stripes, an army uniform jacket with lieutenant general's rank markings, ditto cap with peak. The object had thereafter begun singing the first lines of the King's song, whereupon the door to the balcony was opened from inside the villa and a naked female person came out onto the balcony and led the object through the balcony door into the villa. The female in question is according to our evaluation identical with the object's wife, who at the moment described made an extremely exhilarated impression. Certain activity appears thereafter to have occurred in the bedroom. Because the curtains had been drawn and the door to the balcony closed, however, the more precise nature of this activity could not be ascertained. At five-thirty hours the light in the bedroom was turned off."

How could they know that it was champagne? thought Berg as he fed the surveillance memorandum into his paper shredder.

Before he and Waltin parted company they agreed to tone down the military aspect of their survey of antidemocratic elements. The minister could hardly be counted on, and two against one was one too many.

"I think it's best that we lie low until we see how this develops," said Berg.

"Yes, that's probably the safest until we know if he's fish or fowl," agreed Waltin. How can a person who is so talented be a social democrat? he thought.

Things had gone well and things had gone badly, but Berg had stayed in his position. Things had gone well and things had gone badly, but regardless of which, day had followed day and turned into months and by and by into years, and Berg was still sitting where he was. At the same time it was in some way as though his surroundings—his mission and the people who made that same mission tangible and concrete—were in the process of closing around him. But not to take him in their embrace, which would have been difficult enough, as he preferred a firm handshake at a respectful distance, but rather as preparation for something quite different. Berg had spent a day at the secure location to analyze his situation seriously and in depth, with himself as his only interlocutor.

Police Superintendent Waltin was Berg's closest man. He was ten years younger than Berg, and when Berg thought about who would become his successor, thoughts that he didn't relish, it was Waltin he envisioned. They had a history in common, they had secrets in common, on a few occasions they had even exchanged personal confidences, and in addition he was Waltin's mentor. Considering their common mission it was also Waltin to whom he had given the task of holding his protective hand around its innermost core, the most sensitive, the most secret of all things secret, that which could not be jeopardized at any price and which must never be revealed: the external operation.

Nor was there anything that indicated he couldn't trust Waltin. All the checks he had carried out on him had been completely without result, not the least hint of anything that didn't add up, if you disregarded that silly story about his secret key to the one-armed bandit and other such childishness. Still, something was wrong. He sensed that it was there and he couldn't even put his finger on it.

Berg's officers were all ambitious, meticulous, and hardworking. Those who weren't he got rid of or placed in positions in his organization where their deficiencies could be of use for his overarching purposes, but still, sometimes it went wrong.

At his last meeting with his superiors, most of the time had been devoted to discussing the disturbing reports collected by his group for the surveillance of the Kurds. This minister of justice was the latest in a line of ministers of justice, and was like his predecessors to the point of interchangeability in muddling their considerations.

"This Kudo," asked the minister of justice. "What kind of fellow is he? Kudo? It sounds foreign, almost African. Is the fellow African?"

Then he would hardly have a first name like Werner, thought Berg, but he didn't say so. Instead he shook his head politely.

"Inspector Kudo is the head of the Kurdish group's surveillance unit," said Berg. "He's the one who has compiled and written the report in question," he explained.

"Oh, I understand," said the special adviser, raising his eyelids a millimeter. "That's why he signed his name to it."

"I mean the name," said the minister of justice, who didn't give up so easily. "Kudo? Isn't that African?"

"I seem to recall that his father came here as a refugee from Estonia after the war," said Berg. "Kudo. I think the name is actually Estonian."

"Personally I would say it's an assumed name," said the special adviser, his eyelids lowered and wearing his usual irritating smile. "Let us assume, purely hypothetically, that is," he said and for some reason nodded at Berg, "that his father's name was Kurt and his mother's was Doris. So it became KuDo instead of Andersson. One ought to be grateful that he doesn't spell it with a capital 'D.' Ku-Do," said the special adviser with emphasis on both syllables, while for some reason he looked at the minister.

"Exactly," said the minister of justice and giggled. "For then I might well have thought he was Japanese. As in 'judo,' I mean," he clarified, nudging the chief legal officer, who smiled politely without saying anything.

"If this is important to you gentlemen I can of course check this out," said Berg politely. One complete fool, one who never says anything, and one who isn't in his right mind, thought Berg.

"It would be just splendid if you could do that," said the special adviser with exaggerated warmth in his voice. "I guess if necessary I can put up with the fact that the fellow can neither think nor write—what do we really have to choose from?—but I'm suspicious of types who change their names."

What is it you really want to say? thought Berg.

A hidden message, thought Berg a few hours later. He was sitting behind his desk and had just finished reading Werner Kudo's personal file. Born Werner Andersson, son of Kurt Andersson and his wife, Doris, née Svensson.

Careless of me, thought Berg.

It had been a very delicate task to recruit people to the Kurdish group. Finding people who were ambitious, meticulous, and hardworking and who at the same time could accept the ever more fantastic stories that their hard-pressed informants were delivering. Werner Kudo had fit like a hand in a glove since the day in the break room when, in utmost confidence, he had revealed to one of Berg's secret informants within the operation that there were gnomes on the farm in Småland where he had grown up. Little homespun-clad fellows who kept a watchful eye on people, livestock, and buildings at his parental home, he explained while his colleague in the break room nodded encouragingly, listened eagerly, and made a mental note of every word.

Also, it was Berg who had found the perfect partner for Kudo. His name was Christer Bülling—that name was also assumed, but because his birth name was Sprain the reason was self-explanatory. He had worked at the Solna police department's planning group before Berg sank his claws into him. It was the Stockholm chief constable who had tipped him off. During a dinner he had talked about a younger colleague from Solna whom he had met during a meeting and who had made an indelible impression on him.

"The most intelligent young man I've ever met; the others call him the Professor," the chief constable had said by way of summary. This had immediately aroused Berg's curiosity.

Berg was a man possessing great knowledge. Among other things he knew that beauty tends to dwell in the eye of the beholder, and because he was also firmly convinced that the Stockholm chief constable was the most moronic police officer he had ever met, he had contacted Waltin the very next day and asked him to make a careful survey of Christer Bülling, alias the Professor.

"Why is he called the Professor?" Berg had asked when he met Waltin a week later to go over the survey.

"According to one of his first-grade classmates, it's because he was the only one wearing glasses. He was also supposed to have horribly protruding ears and generally appeared a bit dopey," Waltin had explained. "Personally I thought it was due to his grades," he had continued, "but according to one of the psychologists we have here at the firm, children are just not capable of irony in the same way as adults."

"So he's not exactly a genius," Berg concluded.

"Not exactly," Waltin had said, and sighed. "If you want I can pull his test results when he enlisted. According to the psychologist—"

"Forget about that," Berg interrupted. "Do you have anything else?"

"Bülling was exempt from fieldwork rather early. It was the company's in-house physician who recommended it. He's said to suffer from agoraphobia and has difficulty meeting people in general. Extremely taciturn, almost autistic."

"Not one to run around and talk a lot?" Berg asked.

"No," Waltin said with conviction. "On the other hand he's almost obsessed with reading a lot of papers. That certainly fits in with his diagnosis, according to the doctor. It's supposed to relieve anxiety for people like him. At the planning group they are very satisfied with him. He gets extraordinary ratings."

I can believe that, Berg thought, but he didn't say that.

"Is this someone you're thinking of recruiting?" Waltin asked.

"To the Kurd group, as head of investigation and analysis. What do you think of that?"

Waltin nodded approvingly.

"Kudo and Bülling." Waltin savored the names. "They're going to be a real radar unit. And besides, it's a kind of radar we ordinary mortals lack."

Kudo and Bülling were turning into a problem. The whole Kurdish effort, in fact, was undoubtedly getting out of control, thought Berg, because the two of them took themselves and their assignment so damn seriously. They knew nothing about the real reason the group where they were now working had been set up, and they lacked any qualification for figuring out, on their own, how matters really stood. The most recent meeting with the minister of justice might have gone badly. Also, it was, remarkably enough, the minister of justice who had made the unpleasant discovery in the papers that Berg should have read more carefully.

"I wonder about this secret monitoring," said the minister.

"Yes," said Berg, looking at him with a neutral expression.

"How is this really?" continued the minister. "I don't find it in the legal text. Is it regulated in any of those secret statutes?"

"If it's telephone wiretapping you mean," said Berg, "then it's regulated by a special—"

"No," interrupted the minister and for once he sounded a bit irritated. "I don't mean telephones. You don't suppose they're sitting in the same room talking to each other on the phone, do you? This must be some kind of concealed monitoring device. Right, like hiding a lot of microphones in the walls and ceiling and in furniture and God knows what."

"I see," said Berg vaguely. "The legal situation is a little unclear, if I may say so. What do you say, Gustav?"

Berg looked at the chief legal officer, who was looking down at his papers and didn't seem particularly interested in delineating this particular legal situation.

"I think Gustav is the right man," urged Berg. "How many of us are there who have had the privilege of holding both the scales of justice and the sword of power in our hands?" he continued ingratiatingly, with a friendly look at his interlocutor.

What the hell does that dreadful man mean? thought the chief legal officer, feeling a shudder pass through him. Is he trying to say something or what?

He really looks strange, thought Berg. He's seemed odd for quite some time now. It may be high time for a new little check.

"Yes." The chief legal office cleared his throat. "This is, as stated, an especially intricate question that the chief has brought up here, and in order to save time, I'd like to propose that we take this up after the meeting. I'm at your disposal as soon as the chief has time and so desires. But if I may say something very briefly"—he cleared his throat again before continuing—"then I'm without a doubt in total agreement with the chief that we're faced with an especially complicated judicial matter."

The minister of justice looked as happy as when his first-grade teacher had pasted a gold star in his arithmetic book.

"Yes, I suspected as much," he said contentedly. "Now, where were we before I interrupted?"

He had been lucky, at any rate, thought Berg when he was sitting in relative security behind his desk. The prime minister's special adviser had not been present. He had reported a scheduling conflict one hour before the meeting. This, by the way, had been happening more and more often during the past year. Not that I mind, thought Berg.

The day after the chief legal officer had been appointed, the supreme commander's secretary had called and asked when he would have time to visit the tailor.

"Tailor?" asked the chief legal officer.

"To be measured for the chief legal officer's uniform," explained the secretary.

I don't want a uniform, thought the chief legal officer with distaste, but before he managed to say so, the thought occurred to him that if the nation were to end up in a war, naval or otherwise, he would quite simply be compelled to wear a uniform. There were laws about that.

He had not dared say anything to his wife. They had met at an organization for liberal attorneys a few years earlier and married the following year; to have a general in the house was in all likelihood not at the top of her marital wish list. However, one evening after a nice dinner as they were sitting in the music room enjoying an excellent recording of Mahler's second symphony, he had screwed up his courage and told her the whole dreadful story.

"Now, now, honey," she said consolingly and patted him on the arm. "It's not the end of the world, is it? Go upstairs and put it on, so I can see how you look. I promise not to start laughing."

She hadn't laughed. Instead there was a strange gleam in her eyes and she looked at him in a way she had never done before. That was how it had started.

The first time they played war. Because his mother-in-law was Norwegian and his wife spoke the language fluently, Sweden got to occupy Norway. It couldn't be helped. At first he had the whole uniform on— well, not the shoes, of course, for he had kicked them off and that damn cap had tumbled off several times, but for the most part the whole uniform. It had been an exceptional experience. Then he had gone out on the balcony to collect himself and since he was there anyway, he had taken the opportunity to propose a toast to His Majesty the King, but then his wife came out and led him in again to continue negotiations for the occupation and to establish the final terms of peace, and then it had just gone on and on. Like in a dream, thought the chief legal officer. Up until now, thought the chief legal officer in distress. For now that horrid spy character Berg had evidently got on the trail of him and his wife.

"What do we do now?" said the chief legal officer, looking mournfully at his wife. How beautiful she is, he thought. But everything that has a beginning must also have an end, he thought.

"Never mind," said his wife. "It's not the end of the world, is it? There must be lots of uniforms that you can rent."

Didn't think about that, thought the chief legal officer.

"Is there anything in particular you're thinking of," he asked cautiously.

"I'm considering becoming a nurse," his wife said with an efficient and energetic gleam in her beautiful brown eyes. "How's that, honey? Haven't you been feeling a little poorly lately?"

At the meeting the following week, the chief legal officer had introduced an item of his own for the "remaining business" part of the agenda; because this was the first time during Berg's tenure, the matter had not contributed to his peace of mind. This agenda item, cryptic to say the least, provided little indication of where it was headed, either. Berg had been on pins and needles until it was time and the only consolation in this misery was that the prime minister's special adviser had once again reported that he was prevented from attending.

"Yes," the chief legal officer said, and cleared his throat. "As I've already said to my esteemed boss"—the chief legal officer nodded to the minister of justice, who nodded back, while Berg just felt left out— "I have today resigned from my position as attorney to the supreme commander. Effective immediately, by the way; my successor will be selected by the end of the week."

"That's too bad," said Berg. What's going on? he thought.

"Oh," said the chief legal officer with an unexpected chill in his voice.

"I have made the evaluation that in light of your ongoing survey of anti-democratic elements within the police and the military, there is a risk that I might find myself in a conflict of interest and I have therefore decided to resolve it in this way."

"Perhaps that's a wise decision," Berg said in a neutral tone.

"Certainly," said the chief legal officer, looking at him. "Even if we still have nothing specific to consider, I prefer to forestall rather than be forestalled."

"Exactly what I was going to say," said the minister with false joviality in his voice. "I'm sure all of us in this building have wondered the same thing. By the way, the prime minister came to see me the other day after the governmental meeting. How is your survey coming along, Berg? It's been going on for a good while now."

What's going on? thought Berg.

"How's it going with that doggone survey of our colleagues?" said Berg when he was with Waltin a few hours later.

"Pretty well," said Waltin, shrugging his shoulders in a gesture of indifference. "Or pretty badly, if you want. It depends on how you look at it."

"Do we have anything on hand?" asked Berg. "The wolf pack down in Rosenbad has started howling."

"Plenty," said Waltin.

"Good," said Berg.

CHAPTER III

Between Summer's Longing and Winter's End

Quantico, Virginia, in December

[SUNDAY, DECEMBER 1]

Johansson had fallen asleep at ten o'clock on Saturday evening but in his head the time was four in the morning on Sunday. When he woke up the time was still four o'clock on Sunday morning, because Johansson was at the FBI Academy in Quantico, Virginia, while his head was evidently still back on Wollmar Yxkullsgatan in Stockholm, where it was almost noon; Johansson himself was bright-eyed and bushy-tailed.

Outside the window it was as black as the inside of a sack, although it would clearly be a fine day, thought Johansson. The local weather report posted on the bulletin board in the lobby promised fair weather, temperature in the lower 40s and sunshine; obviously, nothing foreseeable was left to chance in this place. Should I follow my big brother's advice? thought Johansson. Or should I take a brisk walk instead? The only problem was that there were still three hours left before dawn, and security in the area was rigorous. "High-Ranking Swedish Police Officer Shot by FBI During Morning Constitutional," thought Johansson, smiling wryly as he visualized the headline. Breakfast, too, was out of the question, as the dining room didn't open until seven, and would any reasonable person want to have breakfast at one o'clock in the afternoon? Besides, he had a room with its own shower, in contrast to his coworkers, who were not as special as him and had to share a shower with the others staying on the same corridor.

Johansson went into the shower and followed his big brother's advice while he thought about a woman with whom he had spoken only once before in his life and who was approximately five thousand miles away in a northeast direction. Wonder what she's doing now, thought Johansson. I don't expect she's sitting in the post office on a Sunday. Then he returned to his bed and finished a novel in English that he'd bought to read during the trip, and when the dining room was finally open he was one of the first in line. Big brother was right, he thought while he had scrambled eggs and fried ham with rye bread. It's even good for your appetite.

When Johansson was a child, his ten-years-older brother had been responsible for the essential aspects of his upbringing. As there were seven children—Johansson was number six—and his parents also had a large farm to run, they mostly had other things on their hands than little Lars Martin. It was not a conventional upbringing, of course, and it surely would have scared the wits out of a child psychologist, but Johansson never had any reason to complain. His oldest brother had always been kind to him. He was the first one to stop calling him Little Brother; he taught him to swim when he was five, took him hunting when he wasn't much older, and beat up his middle brothers in well-measured doses when they were mean to him. He was also the first one to initiate him into the mysteries of adult life.

When Lars Martin was seven his brother had shown him his porno magazines in an intimate moment. Fat white ladies with giant breasts and no more hair between their legs than Lars Martin himself. There was definitely some kind of cheating going on, he had thought, experienced sauna-goer that he was.

"Though you can wait to read these till you get hair on your prick," big brother explained. "Besides, you'll notice it yourself. Yeah, when your love for reading starts to flow, I mean," he added vaguely.

Lars Martin was content to nod. What could he say?

"Oh, hell," said big brother, inserting a substantial wad of snuff. "I usually look at them when I beat off. It makes it easier," he said, nodding. Mostly to himself, it seemed.

Beat off, thought Lars Martin, but he didn't ask about that.

"Oh, hell," big brother continued. "There aren't any women here. Not like in Kramfors, anyway."

For the past three months big brother had worked as a forestry apprentice at SCA paper down in Kramfors, so he was not only ten years older but well traveled too.

What's this he's saying, thought Lars Martin confusedly, no women? It's swimming with women here, Mama Elna and our sisters and Grandma and all our aunts. And the old neighbor lady Mrs. Nordlund, and say what you will about old lady Nordlund, she was even fatter than the ladies in those magazines he had just been looking at.

And it kept getting stranger and stranger.

His big brother nodded seriously at him and tousled his hair.

"You'll think about this when it's time," he said. "Forget about beating off if there are ladies around, but otherwise see to it that you jerk him off, say, two, three times a day."

Kramfors, ladies, beat off, jerk him off, thought little Lars. What's he talking about?

"For otherwise it can go straight to hell." His brother nodded in great seriousness.

"To hell?" said Lars Martin inquiringly, for he knew what that was, anyway. "How so?"

"Yeah, hell," said big brother and shrugged his broad shoulders in an eloquent gesture. "You can have pure hell with your prostrate."

"Prostrate," repeated Lars Martin vaguely.

"Yeah, you know Great-Uncle Einar. They had to take him to the hospital in the middle of the night and drive a whole canister up his prick so he could finally take a piss."

A whole canister, thought Lars Martin, and our great-uncle was certainly a full-grown man, but still, wasn't that impossible?

"A canister?"

"One of those hospital canisters," his brother clarified with a fateful voice. "It was Bergqvist who told me when I was hunting with him right afterward. Think about it. A canister, I mean, hell . . ." His brother shook his head exhaustedly.

Bergqvist was the town alcoholic but a very highly regarded district physician, and big brother used to act as a hunting helper for him, so there was nothing wrong with the informant, thought Lars Martin. But a canister? Certainly only a hospital canister, but how much smaller could it be? Doctor Bergqvist was twice as big as the teacher at school.

"So let me give you a good piece of advice, if you don't have ladies around then it's a matter of beating off. And at least two or three times a day, otherwise it can go straight to hell," big brother summarized.

So this was the mecca of the Western police world to which I've made a pilgrimage, like a pilgrim from the snow-covered North, thought Johansson, in an excellent mood as he began his brisk morning walk after finishing breakfast. But no minarets and no prayer callers, for this mecca was a little less than forty miles south of Washington, D.C., on the Potomac River, unobtrusively bedded down among Virginia's gentle, forest-covered hills.

At the heart of the premises were twenty-some buildings of brick and whitewashed stone—built in some sort of postwar functional vernacular, which at ground level were joined by a network of glassed-in corridors. There were offices, laboratory facilities, workout rooms, a swimming pool and a library, classrooms, lecture halls, and a movie theater. There was a restaurant, a cafeteria, and three large buildings for accommodations with a few hundred individual rooms of between sixty and a hundred square feet for the lecturers, students, and other guests staying at or visiting the academy.

What this looks most like is a smaller American university, thought Johansson, who had never visited such a place but still had a definite and in fact quite correct idea of how things looked at a small, modern American university. Typical campus, Johansson decided knowledgeably. Although then it no longer added up: not with a small, modern American university, in any case.

Not far from the central facilities was a small American city, Hogan's Alley, with a courthouse building, church, school, post office, bank, shops, theater, and casino, and what all those things had in common was that they weren't real. It was here that police-related arts were practiced and perfected against hired actors playing murderers, robbers, bootleggers, thieves, swindlers, and con men. A Disneyland for people who want to play cops and robbers, thought Johansson, setting a course for the surrounding terrain with its gentle, tree-covered hills.

But there were only obstacle courses, jogging paths, and shooting ranges. In any case, none of it had been intended for brisk walks under a cloudless sky. This he gathered from the muddy, run-down surface and from the glassy stares he got from the totally exhausted runners racing along across the terrain. Damn, thought Johansson. They're not even running, they're trying to do themselves in. This is no university with teachers and students. This is an army encampment for an order of knights with castles and fortifications and a jousting field and fencing halls where preparations are being made for a holy war.

When he returned from his morning walk, his good mood was gone, his feet were muddy, and he went back to his room and lay down on his bed to read. Then he must have fallen asleep, for when he opened his eyes it was getting dark outside the window and he had missed lunch. Dinner in an hour, thought Johansson, feeling a bit more alert. After dinner he and his two travel companions from the National Bureau of Criminal Investigation seated themselves at the bar, each ordering a beer, and chatted a little about things past and future. On one point they were touchingly in agreement. There was a bit too much boot camp about the place. The food was good, though, and it was clean and tidy too, and their hosts were cordial with a vengeance. Exactly as it should be in a secret order, thought Johansson.

"I took a turn on the cross-country track," said the chief inspector from the narcotics squad, who was both a brother of the order and an exercise addict. "They were running like someone was chasing them with a blow torch. I was forced to put it in overdrive to get a little peace and quiet."

"I took a brisk walk myself," said Johansson. "The main street down and back." He intended to keep his experiences of the surrounding terrain to himself.

"Hoover Road, after J. Edgar Hoover, head of the FBI for almost fifty years and the person who founded the place where we're sitting right now with our beers before going to bed." The chief inspector from the Interpol group smiled and raised his beer glass.

"I thought he founded the whole FBI," said Johansson.

"There you're mistaken, chief," said the Interpol chief inspector, wiping a little foam from his upper lip. "The FBI was founded in 1908 as a special division of their department of justice. Hoover became its sixth director in 1924. On the other hand, he did found the academy we're now visiting."

"Not a day that you don't learn something new," said Johansson, smiling a little while his colleague from narcotics leaned forward and cleared his throat conspiratorially, at the same time wiggling his right hand a little.

"I've heard he wasn't sure which locker room to use," the narcotics chief inspector said, smiling wryly.

"Yes, interesting, isn't it?" The one from the Interpol group nodded. "In the middle of everything, head of the FBI, macho man to the nth degree, deeply conservative, a believer, Christian American right wing, merciless persecutor of the least liberal peccadillo, not to mention anything to the left of that, and there he was, living in a lifelong relationship with another FBI agent. They lived in the same house, and officially he was Hoover's chauffeur, servant, and bodyguard, but anyone who knew anything knew that they were a couple. And that his boss used to change into a dress on major occasions."

"Yeah, what the hell," said the narcotics chief inspector, shaking his head. "What a life."

"Let's hope they loved each other," said Johansson in a neutral tone and raised his glass.

[MONDAY, DECEMBER 2, TO FRIDAY, DECEMBER 6]

The days had gone by quickly. Planned way in advance, scheduled down to the minute, filled with the content given in the program but only that and nothing else. Three meals a day, half an hour for breakfast in the morning, an hour for lunch, and an hour and a half to have dinner. After that the evening beer at the bar, included as a free social activity, which of course ended at ten o'clock at the latest, in spite of the fact that it didn't say in the program that it should. Conference sessions, meetings in groups, lectures, seminars, and a scheduled hour per day for physical training.

Those who were naturally a part of the place—recruits, special agents, instructors, and higher officials—all looked as if they were cloned from some type of archived agent probably stored in utmost secrecy at headquarters in Washington. Medium height, hair cut short, straight-backed, head lifted, and eyes directed toward the person with whom they were speaking, broad shoulders, narrow waists, thick thighs and calves. And almost always small feet and small, chubby hands.

The sounds, the voices, the uniforms. The irregular popping from the pistol shooting range, the crackling bursts from the sharpshooter's rifles, the coughing attacks of the automatic weapons. Wild shrieks from down at Hogan's Alley, testifying that there was a breakthrough in an ongoing hostage situation. Recruits in columns, rhythmically tread-ing marching boots, voices in chorus, the words impossible to make out, en route from one exercise to another, blue baseball caps, blue fatigues, loosely hanging trousers stuffed into the high shafts of boots. Yes, sir. Good morning, sir. No, sir. Good evening, sir.

Wednesday had been the best day. During the morning there had been two hours scheduled for physical training, and Johansson had exchanged his daily brisk walks, now always up and down the main street, for a visit to the swimming pool. The day before he had, among other things, bought a pair of swimming trunks in the academy's gift shop, which like everything else were imprinted with the FBI emblem. In addition he had hesitated before a blue baseball cap with the same emblem, and finally he bought that too. Just in case, thought Johansson.

At the swimming pool was Special Agent Backstroem, who was the assigned host for the Scandinavian delegates on the strength of his eth-nic heritage, but who in all other respects appeared to have been manu-factured at headquarters in Washington.

"Sir," said Backstroem, pulling in his stomach, sticking out his chest, and looking him right in the eyes. "You're thinking about swim-ming, sir."

No, thought Johansson, who despite the fact that it was only three full days since he had become aware of Agent Backstroem's existence already hated him with a quiet Norrland fervor. I was thinking about listening to a Vikings concert and that's why I'm at the FBI Academy's swimming pool forty miles south of Washington dressed only in bathing trunks. But he didn't say that. Instead he nodded like the country boy that he was.

"Yes," said Johansson. "I thought I'd take the opportunity to swim since I'm here anyway."

"Very good, sir," said Backstroem, at the same time glancing at the lifesaving paraphernalia hanging on a hook on the wall.

"I would be very grateful if you could time me," said Johansson.

"Yes, sir," said Backstroem. "Very good sir. How many laps, sir?"

"Fifty," said Johansson, nodding and gliding down into the water with the same controlled movements as a gray seal leaving its rock in the sea.

After forty laps Backstroem started acting crazy. He ran beside him along the edge of the pool, waving his arms. Held up the watch and displayed a varying number of fingers. When Johansson heaved himself up out of the pool and wiped the water from his hair, Backstroem was on the verge of collapse.

"Sir," panted Backstroem. "You are an exceptional swimmer, sir." He tapped the watch face with his index finger.

Johansson smiled amiably. Nodded.

"So-so," he said. "It's been a while since I was at it. Where's the shower?"

Backstroem showed him the way with a forward-leaning upper body and inviting hand movements. Just so he doesn't fall in love with me, thought Johansson.

The lecture after lunch had not been too bad either. Johansson was part of an exclusive group of invitees who were to be informed of the most recent findings of the most intellectual aspect of the ongoing fight against crime. They were to learn how to produce psychological profiles of unknown perpetrators of aggravated crimes of violence. The lecturer was an instructor at the FBI's newly established unit for behavioral science, and aside from the fact that he was twenty years older than Special Agent Backstroem, it was quite obvious that he had been manufactured at the same place. Afterward an entire half hour had been set aside for a final discussion.

I see, thought Johansson. It wasn't any more difficult than that, and as far as he could understand from the lecture, all serial murderers could be divided into six categories. Either they were asocial and didn't give a tinker's damn about what anyone around them thought or did, or they were antisocial and hated those around them, regardless of what they thought or did. And, within both categories, they could be disorganized or organized or both when push came to shove. Two times three equals six, thought Johansson, something he had already learned to do in first grade.

And what have we here? thought Johansson, observing the horrid images that the lecturer was clicking out from his slide projector with the tranquil, pathological delight that was clearly the profiling expert's badge of honor.

I see, thought Johansson. Here we have a loony who knocked on his neighbor's door because he'd just purchased a yellow canary. Hates anyone who has yellow canaries. Hates everyone. When the neighbor opened, he walloped him on the head with a pipe wrench. Dragged him into the hallway and thumped him a few more times for good measure. He got so excited by all this that he pooped on the neighbor's hallway rug and when he finally pulled up his pants he had already forgotten what it was he really wanted to say. He had even forgotten to let the little bird out of its cage. After that he had clumped right through the pools of blood, out into the stairwell and into his own place. There he sat in front of the TV stuffing himself with a bag of glazed doughnuts.

"Now then," said the lecturer in that stuck-up way characteristic of all ignoramuses who have been granted the good fortune to hold the answer sheet. "Gentlemen. What do you think about this? Any suggestions?"

Suspiciously like an antisocial, disorganized perpetrator, thought Johansson, but before he had time to raise his hand, his counterpart with the Danish Board of Police's homicide commission had already answered. He was an exceptionally surly old geezer who, despite thirty years in the profession, still persisted in chasing his targets. He also spoke surprisingly good English.

"It was the neighbor who did it."

The lecturer appeared shaken and, despite his frantic shadowboxing with single mothers, absent fathers, early attempts at treatment, bed-wetting, truancy, and repeated incidents of cruelty to animals starting in childhood, it all still only amounted to a few individual points for style.

"You had him there," said Johansson when he and his Danish counter-part, after the end of the lecture and an unusually lively discussion, were walking away to the scheduled coffee break.

"Yeah," the Dane said and grinned. "These damned academics. I hate them."

"There are only three rules," said Johansson and smiled.

"Yeah, what are they?"

"You should like the situation, don't make things unnecessarily com-plicated, and finally, you should hate chance," said Johansson.

"You're a good fellow, Johansson," said the old geezer with unex-pected warmth in his voice, putting his arm around Johansson's shoul-ders. "Now let's have a beer."

On Thursday he had called Jarnebring in Stockholm. For one thing, he wanted to hear if anything had happened. For another, he wanted Krass-ner's address. Why he didn't really know himself, but since he was here anyway he might as well take the opportunity to see how he lived. Maybe talk to a neighbor, thought Johansson vaguely. Snoop around a little. Set his ear to the rail. He already had the address of Krassner's old flame. Not clear why he had written it in his notebook before he left.

"Brother," said Jarnebring warmly. "How's it going? Is it just beer and broads or is it back to school too?"

After the usual introductory remarks Johansson got to the point.

"How's it going with that Krassner?" Johansson asked. Innocently and as though in passing.

"You never give up, Lars," said Jarnebring. "I wrote that bastard off the day before yesterday. Suicide."

"You don't have his address," said Johansson. "I mean here in the States."

"And what would you do with that?" asked Jarnebring. "Thinking about delivering a wreath, or what?"

"Nah," said Johansson. "I thought that since I was here anyway . . ."

"So you thought you'd take the opportunity to see how he lived, perhaps have a chat with a neighbor, snoop around a little . . ."

"More or less," said Johansson.

"Sure," said Jarnebring. "Just don't come up with anything stupid. I have it here. Have you got pen and paper?"

"Fire away," said Johansson.

On Friday afternoon, when Johansson and his two travel companions were sitting on the plane to New York, each with a small whiskey as a counterbalance to all the watery American beer they had been drinking that week, his colleague from narcotics suddenly started to laugh.

"Yes?" said Johansson. "Out with it, now."

The colleague from narcotics nodded.

"Yes," he said. "I was thinking about the last conference I went to. It was with the narcotics unit, on the boat to Finland."

"Yes?" said Johansson.

His colleague started laughing again.

"Yes, hell," he said. "It wasn't exactly like this one, if I may say so."

Johansson smiled and nodded.

"I know what you mean," he said.

CHAPTER IV

Free falling, as in a dream

Stockholm in autumn

There hadn't been much mushroom picking, Berg would always think when he looked back at that autumn before everything happened. He and his wife had a little cottage up in Roslagen and usually they picked quite a few mushrooms during the fall. Mushrooms are good, thought Berg, it was nice to walk around in the woods thinking while his wife darted aimlessly among the bushes. It was a small contribution to their finances as well. True, he was a department head and earned more than almost all his colleagues within the corps, but every little bit helps, he would think.

But not that autumn, for the demands of his political superiors had become more and more exacting, and the prime minister's adviser started showing up at meetings again; if he really was as intelligent as they said, Berg for one could think of better ways to make use of the gifts the good Lord had clearly bestowed on him. He wasn't even ironic anymore, just treacherous, and everything he said required Berg's entire analytical capacity simply to interpret. But after many trials and tribulations it was finally ready, the first report on "Anticonstitutional Movements and Elements Within the Open Police Operations in the Stockholm Police Department."

Toward the end of this work, he had been forced to personally intervene to organize the content and form, despite the fact that his coworkers were doing all they could and despite the fact that he assigned several of his best forces to the task. People who obviously, and preferably, should have been used on more pressing assignments. Unfortunately he was the one who had established the boundaries of the task and decided on the title of the report, something he would have to eat at numerous meetings during the fall; for a while, in fact, it threatened to paint him into a corner where he easily could have lost control of the entire ongoing process.

His wretched excuse for a nephew was of course part of the material, which he had counted on in general, but when the whole thing was done he could say that, unfortunately, this simple fact demanded as much psychic energy as the work itself. Should he set out the names of colleagues included in the material when he gave a summary of it to his superiors? Obviously not; it went against established routine, and created considerable, quite unnecessary risks. Would there be gossip and talk? Probably. Would he get any questions about this? Probably not. Would it be used against him regardless of what he did or didn't do? Certainly.

It was not a long report. Including appendices, it was just over a hundred pages, and enumerated a corresponding number of policemen, almost all of whom had in common that they worked in the uniformed police in central Stockholm and that they, individually and collectively, in various ways and with varying frequency, had expressed extreme right-wing or flat-out neo-Nazi opinions. The way in which they'd done so varied essentially. There were individual policemen who openly took the first opportunity to express themselves disparagingly or even hatefully about female colleagues, about immigrants, about the so-called clientele with whom they worked, about people in general, about social democrats, about the left in general. In short, about everyone except themselves. There were others who behaved inappropriately as soon as they were around more than two pairs of eyes in the heads of anyone other than their fellow police officers; who would wear a swastika on the inside of their coat lapel; who gave the Hitler salute at the bar, who made toasts to Adolf Hitler, or said that the prime minister ought to be shot, or that you ought to make glue out of all immigrants.

There was also a hard core, organized in various ways, that had regular gatherings and maintained high security and discretion in the presence of the world around them. Of course it was within this core that Berg found his own nephew; as a foreground figure, moreover, both a formal and an informal leader. "Policeman B appears to play a leading role in this connection. It should be pointed out, however, that his superior gives him extraordinary evaluations and among other things describes him as one of the best policemen in the district, with good judgment and good conduct."

They held meetings in rented halls as well as at the police station, had joint exercises and other open-air leisure activities, had dinner together at a so-called men's club with special invitees, listened to lectures on the good life in South Africa, on Hitler as a political thinker, on why no Nobel Prize winners were black, and on the left-wing slant in the press. German marching music was played and a joint Hitler greeting was made before, during, and after the meal. "It should, however, be noted that consumption of alcohol at these social gatherings was always moderate," Berg's infiltrator noted in one of the surveillance memoranda he submitted.

Reporting to his superiors in the blue room on the seventh floor at Rosenbad. Outside the windows a pale September sun was shining. And now the misery can begin, thought Berg.

"If I've counted right in your document," said the special adviser, observing Berg with his constant, irritating half-sneer, "which isn't always easy for the mathematically inclined," he added with a faint chuckle.

Berg was content to nod.

"So, your material includes between a hundred and five and a hundred fifteen so-called members of the Stockholm Police Department's various uniformed divisions, all of whom have in common that they seem to harbor a certain *faiblesse* for"—he savored the words almost sensuously—"for the brown and black colors on the political palette."

Berg was content to nod. Where is he going? he thought.

"How many policemen are there in the divisions included in your survey?" the special adviser asked.

"Somewhere between twelve hundred and fifteen hundred," answered Berg quickly. "I apologize that I can't give you a more exact number than that." So now he'll convert that to a percentage, he thought.

"Nine hundred seventy, according to the information which I've received from the highest leadership in the Stockholm Police Department. Which should give us a percentage of between eleven and twelve percent. If this impromptu calculation is correct."

Don't put on airs, thought Berg, but he didn't say that.

"That sounds about right," said Berg, "but I think your base sounds a little small. Just under a thousand policemen, I'm almost certain that there are considerably more."

"Which should give us a percentage of between seven and eight if there are fifteen hundred as you say. That sounds almost comforting."

Now he chuckled again.

"Seven percent is bad enough," said Berg.

"That the number should be nine hundred seventy was, by the way, a piece of information I got from the chief constable. Do you mean that he could have underestimated his own personnel by more than fifty percent?"

Sweden's most moronic police officer and the only one who votes for the social democrats, if you believe what he says himself, so he might very well have, thought Berg.

"I am the one, no doubt, who is misinformed," said Berg. "However that may be, it's bad enough."

"These hundred or so you've picked out for us"—the special adviser mostly seemed to be thinking out loud—"do they form just the tip of an iceberg or are things on the contrary so fortunate that you've managed to include pretty much all of them?"

"Unfortunately one has to account for a certain number of omissions," said Berg defensively.

"Now, if one were to harbor such opinions while observing so-called normal human behavior, that's to say without running around shouting 'Heil Hitler' and singing 'Die Fahne Hoch' while dressed in a peaked cap with a skull on it . . ."

"There is probably a risk of that, yes. Unfortunately," said Berg. Where are you going now? he thought.

"But rather, one settles for silent complicity and writes one's recommendations in one way and not another and uses simple scheduling and planning, for example, to ensure that no female officers are allowed to set foot in the field or that no immigrants are admitted to the police academy. As long as one is content with that, one doesn't end up in your survey, in any case?"

No, thought Berg. How would you be able to do that? But he didn't say that, of course.

"Answer is yes," said Berg and just as he said that he wished he had bitten off his tongue instead.

"Answer is yes," repeated the special adviser, looking as though he had just tasted something extra delicious. "It sounds like a serious deficiency in the method of investigation itself."

Get out of this, thought Berg. Turn it around.

"I interpret your comments to mean that perhaps you have been thinking about the matter, that you have some concrete suggestions?"

"I don't know about suggestions. Regardless of whether there are five or fifty percent we have to find a way to get rid of them. Preferably immediately, and in the worst case as soon as possible. We are talking about the Swedish police, not about the SS or the SA or the Gestapo. Not even about the Secret Swedish State Police, or Sestapo, which for some reason they preferred to call themselves in the good old days."

How naïve can you be? thought Berg. The union would never go along, and someone like you surely ought to have learned that, at least.

"Unfortunately I see certain problems with legislation and employment-security regulations and union interests. To only mention a few of the factors in this connection." Berg shrugged his shoulders eloquently.

It hadn't gotten better. They'd gone over time by almost two hours. And he couldn't excuse himself and leave, either. Especially not when perhaps that was precisely what they hoped he would do.

"I was thinking about your excellent memorandum, the one about the secret police and the military as the great threats against democracy," said the special adviser. "Not the ones who go around in uniforms that your survey deals with. It's not the traffic cops who keep me awake at night." Now he seemed to be thinking out loud again.

"Not me either anymore," the minister interjected happily, speaking for the first time in half an hour. "Not since I stopped driving," he said and tittered.

"No," said Berg politely. "Yes," he added inquiringly, looking at his tormentor. What are you driving at? he thought.

"Would you describe your own coworkers as more or less reliable than those characters you've just described for us?"

"That is clearly a completely different category of officer," said Berg emphatically. "Behavior, opinions, or thoughts of the type described would never be tolerated by us." Finally, solid ground under his feet, he thought.

"Secret police officers are more intelligent than regular police," the special adviser clarified. "More controlled, more reticent, completely normal in their outer, observable behavior, in short. Above all, *are* they more reticent?"

"Certainly," said Berg, in spite of the fact that he now saw the direction in which they were heading. Fortunately they're significantly more reticent than most, he thought.

"If you make the Hitler salute before a job interview you won't be working for the secret police, period," said the special adviser. "Sounds like a tricky group to investigate."

"What do you mean?" asked Berg, even though he already knew.

"More talented, reticent, discreet, quite normal in their behavior. But how do they think, in reality? They're all police officers, of course, same background, same education, same experiences. Many of them are even born and bred."

"I have complete confidence in all those who are working for us," said Berg with even more emphasis.

"It's no doubt there that we differ," said the special adviser. "Misunderstand me correctly," he added quickly. "What I mean is only that self-evident lunatics, the kind that clearly show what they think and feel and intend, have an almost calming effect on me. It's the others that disturb me."

Me too, thought Berg, but it was the last thing he would think of saying to someone like that.

Now it has to be over soon anyway, thought Berg, stealing a glance at his watch. Otherwise I'll simply have to think of something regardless of the consequences.

"A completely different matter," said the adviser, observing Berg behind half-closed eyelids.

Be content to nod, thought Berg, nodding.

"Purely concretely, and if we try to enter these people's mind-set, though apart of course from the material content and the qualitative substance. I am speaking of those so-called colleagues who are included in your investigation."

"Yes?" said Berg questioningly. You never learn, he thought with irritation.

"What do they dislike the most," he said. "Person, fact, social phenomenon, thing? What's their lowest common denominator?"

So this was where we were going, thought Berg.

"The prime minister," said Berg. "If there is a particular person that you have in mind, then unfortunately it is the case that the prime minister seems to form a recurring object of hatred."

"So that's why they use his portrait for target practice during their open-air activities," said the special adviser, and for some reason he was smiling broadly as he said it.

"I am not aware of that as a fact," answered Berg, but it didn't seem as though the other was listening: he was reclining comfortably in his chair, eyelids half-lowered, hands clasped over his fat stomach, although no longer smiling.

That man is definitely not in his right mind, thought Berg.

Before they left they agreed that this was a question to be viewed with the utmost seriousness and assigned the highest priority. In addition the survey must be broadened. How did it look in the rest of the country? How did it look within the secret police and the military? And what of that business of the threat against the prime minister and the country's highest political leadership?

They wanted a comprehensive compilation of data as soon as possible. Broadly and in depth and without wavering or shying away from any facts, however unpleasant they might be. The purely practical aspects were turned over to Berg and his coworkers with confidence. What is going on? thought Berg as he sat in the backseat of his service car en route to his office on Kungsholmen. It's already dark out; soon it will be winter, and what happened to summer, actually? Where did it go?

When he got back to work he hoped that Waltin would be there so they could discuss the new turn of events, but all there was of him was a message from Berg's secretary that Waltin had waited for the longest time but had finally been compelled to take care of an urgent errand. Unfortunately he couldn't be reached on his pager either, but he intended to be in touch early the next morning.

"If you don't have any objections I was thinking about taking off too," said his secretary with an amiable smile.

They met the following morning and Waltin was just as energetic, well-tailored, and smelling of aftershave as always. Berg himself had felt better. He had twisted and turned in bed until midnight, when he finally gave up, went into his study, and put his thoughts on paper. Then he made a fresh attempt at sleeping, with only moderate success. Not until four in the morning had he disappeared into some sort of dream-filled daze, and when he and his wife were eating breakfast she suggested that he should call in sick and stay home.

"I don't suppose there's anything I can help you with?" she asked. Berg had only shaken his head and an hour later he was sitting at his desk. As a final measure before leaving home he had fed his nighttime notes into the document shredder in his study. Waltin had to be content with a piece of paper that addressed only three points, which Berg expanded on with a brief oral account of what had occurred at yesterday's meeting.

"I see," said Waltin, handing back the paper he had just read. "Sounds as if we'd need a healthy increase in appropriations. In addition, I believe we're in dangerous territory."

Berg nodded to him to continue.

"If we take the first point—expanding, deepening, and completing our survey of certain officers, we're going to have a lot of problems, to put it mildly."

"What kind of problems?" asked Berg.

"First off, purely practical problems with our collection of data. I'll give you an example. One of my recruiters became interested in a possible informant a while ago. He'll finish police academy in a few months and is interning with a uniformed division in Östermalm and seemed tailor-made to infiltrate those circles we're investigating."

"But?"

"The problem was that he was already inside. It was by pure chance that we found out about him in time."

And how many of them are there that we've missed? thought Berg, groaning internally.

"Suppose we succeed in solving this," continued Waltin. "Really penetrate, really reel in these . . . forces . . . within the corps." Waltin smiled.

"Yes?" Berg nodded to him to continue.

"Then we need only concern ourselves with the content, and if we try to do something about it we might just as well . . ." Waltin shrugged his shoulders. "You know what I mean. Both you and I have been around awhile. And what would happen to us? Are any of us that suicidal?" And you have to know what I mean, since you've got one in your own family, he thought, but he didn't say that.

"Suggestion," said Berg.

"First of all, time," said Waltin. "We have to prolong the process. Use our difficulties to explain to them why it takes such a long time, but take enormous care to avoid doing anything about the matter itself."

"And second," asked Berg.

"See to it that we tone down what we've already given them. They've already got too much. We made a mistake there."

Berg nodded. What choice did I have? he thought. To be replaced by someone like the Stockholm chief constable?

"We'll do that," said Berg. "Can you think about the arrangements and give me a concrete proposal?"

Waltin nodded and smiled in his engaging way.

"And when did you want to have it?" he asked.

"Well, preferably right now," answered Berg, "but because it's you, you can have a breather till first thing tomorrow." Waltin is sharp, he thought. He thinks like I do. The question is whether I can rely on him the same way I rely on myself.

"It can wait," decided Berg. Good Lord, he thought. I've got ten years left, after all.

"Threats and menaces against key political persons," he continued.

"I could drown them in that," answered Waltin and for some reason he seemed almost pleased. "Letters, telephone conversations, tips, complaints, surveillance material, our eavesdropping. You name it. There's as much as you'd like."

"What do we do? Shall we frighten them or keep them calm?"

"I think we should give them a suitable selection," said Waltin. "Frighten them just enough while we explain to them that the advantage with these types is that they're all talk and they never deliver."

Berg nodded. We'll do that, he thought.

"That miserable special adviser they've foisted on us. Do we have any threats against him?"

Waltin shook his head.

"Not a peep."

"This is a generally well-regarded person? Popular in broad circles?"

"Can't imagine that," said Waltin. "The simple reason no doubt is that hardly anyone knows of his existence, and those who know about him are maybe not so well informed about his actual job description. With a few isolated highly placed exceptions. If you want I can snoop around. Hear if there's something in spite of it all." Waltin smiled a meaningful smile.

"Forget about that," said Berg, shaking his head. "I don't intend to lie awake nights for his sake."

Perhaps a bit too casual, thought Berg. That last bit, anyway, was probably unnecessary.

After lunch Berg had a last-minute meeting with Kudo and Bülling at their urgent request. What they had to report was so important that they could only do so directly to him. They were clearly punctual as well, for when Berg arrived one minute late they were already sitting at their places in his own conference room.

An odd couple, thought Berg as he greeted them. Kudo was small, dark, thin, well-trained, well-dressed, and obviously careful to make a keen impression. His entire being exuded high alert, and just like all the others in the corps who were the same way and that Berg had encountered during his more than thirty years, he tried to crush the metacarpals of the person with whom he was shaking hands. Bülling was tall, fair, and lanky, his head drooping as he peeked out obliquely when he shook hands. His thin hand was dripping with sweat, and as soon as Berg released it he quickly put it back into the pocket of his baggy Manchester corduroy jacket.

Hand sweat, thought Berg at the same time as an alarm bell started to ring inside him. "Abundant or profuse hand sweat can indicate large consumption of psychopharmaceuticals," thought Berg, who had learned that by heart at internal education in personnel defense: The course where you learned everything about how to defend yourself in good time against your own personnel. Best to make discreet contact with the bureau's psychiatrist, Berg decided, smiling extra amiably at both of his visitors. The last thing he wanted was for one of his coworkers to flip out in his office.

"Please," said Berg, indicating with his right hand. What a strange couple, he thought.

"This is about the PKK," said Kudo with fateful seriousness in his voice.

"Partiya Karkeren Kurdistan," muttered Bülling with his eyes toward the tabletop.

Damn initials, thought Berg.

"I know," he said. "The Kurdistan workers' party, previously known as Kurdistan's revolutionaries. Continue." He nodded at them.

What this was about, purely concretely, was a wiretapped telephone conversation that had been snapped up a little less than a week before, after which it had taken up the entire analysis group's combined capacity. At 22:37 hours Semir G., "known Kurdish activist," had phoned his neighbor Abdullah A., also a "known Kurdish activist," both living in the same apartment block on Terapivägen in Flemingsberg. After blathering about this and that in Kurdish for almost half an hour they suddenly got to the point.

Kudo looked at Berg with the same serious gaze as though he'd been a little homespun-clad gnome on the farm where Kudo had grown up.

"It's a wedding conversation," he said heavily.

"As you surely know, chief, 'wedding' is their code word for assassination," muttered Bülling with his gaze directed firmly at the tabletop. "It's a code word they use when they're going to shoot someone."

Berg was content to nod. He himself knew that this could also mean other things, such as a wedding, for example, or a demonstration or some other collective activity of a not more closely specified type.

"So they're planning to shoot someone," intoned Kudo with eyes black as pistol barrels.

Yes, or it's also just that someone's going to get married, and don't we all know what such things can lead to down the line, thought Berg.

"Why are they phoning each other?" asked Berg. "They live in the same building."

"We're not clear about that bit yet," said Kudo, nodding energetically.

"We're working on it," mumbled Bülling.

"Do we know who it is?" asked Berg.

"Who," mumbled Bülling, peeking nervously at the door.

"That they're planning to shoot," said Kudo, in spite of the fact that he wasn't the one who was called the Professor.

"Which of their defectors or political opponents is it that they're planning to shoot this time?" clarified Berg. "Do we know what his name is?" he added, to be on the safe side.

"This time unfortunately it doesn't concern a normal wedding," said Kudo, as he leaned forward, lowered his voice, and, in order to further underscore the seriousness of the matter, also shook his head. "They're talking about lamb," he said.

"Lamb?" Berg looked at him questioningly. "As in lamb chops?"

"Lamb," mumbled Bülling. "So we're convinced that this time they intend to shoot someone completely different, probably some highly placed person of some type. Presumably one of our own top politicians."

"Why do you think that?" asked Berg.

"They're going to bring home a lamb," mumbled Bülling. "And then they're going to buy wine and then they're going to have two poets."

It had taken Berg more than a quarter of an hour to unravel the factual basis for the conclusion that the Kurdish section's analysis group had come to, of an impending attack against a highly placed Swedish politician.

"I'll read direct from the transcript of the tape," said Kudo. "Then you can form your own impression, chief."

Do that, thought Berg, nodding wearily.

"It's Semir G. who has taken up the matter. The same Semir who is phoning," added Kudo slyly. "Word for word he says this. I'm quoting from the tape."

Just get on with it, man, thought Berg, nodding.

"Quote. We must arrange for wedding soon. We must buy cakes, pastries, and rolls, but this time we must buy a lamb too. And wine and then we must have two poets. End quote."

Kudo nodded before he continued.

"Quote. We should have two poets? End quote, Abdullah A. then asks. Quote. This time we shall buy lamb and wine and have two poets. End quote, answers Semir G. That's the whole thing," said Kudo. "Right after that the conversation ends with the usual farewell phrases."

Sigh, thought Berg.

"They've never offered lamb before," explained Kudo. "When they're going to murder their own people, they only talk about pastries and rolls and cakes. Sometimes it's just rolls."

"And how do you interpret this?" asked Berg, at the same time seeing himself in a mirror.

"That this is certainly about a highly placed person outside their own circles," said Kudo, nodding triumphantly.

"Then they'll have two poets too; they usually get by with one poet," mumbled Bülling.

"Assassins, that is," said Kudo. " 'Poet' is their code for assassin, and this business of two poets can only mean that there are bigger matters in the offing."

"The wine," mumbled Bülling with a sidelong glance at his partner.

"Exactly," said Kudo energetically, "yes, the wine. It usually isn't mentioned either, and our interpretation is this, that partly it should underscore the lamb, so to speak, partly it speaks for the fact that this isn't about a politician within their own cultural sphere."

"Mohammedans don't drink wine," mumbled Bülling, at the same time making a mysterious winding movement with his long neck.

"Yes," said Berg. He leaned back in his chair and clasped his hands over his belly. "This bears thinking about. I want you to write a memorandum and append all the supporting materials you have. As well as any material we've received through our German colleagues."

Aren't most Kurds Christians? he thought.

"Take all the time you need," he said, and looked at them seriously. "It's fine if I get it in a week."

Waltin detailed three detectives with the operational bureau's section for internal surveillance to compile the material that Berg wanted. In addition he installed one of his own analysts to lead and divide up the work. He himself had more important matters to attend to.

"The prime minister, the Cabinet, the government, senior officials in government administration, highly placed politicians regardless of party allegiance. I want the threats divided into categories, I want to know how they've come in, I want to have a picture of whoever's behind them. Hamilton, here"—he nodded toward his own coworkers—"will help you with the details. Questions?"

"How far back should we go?" The one who asked was a young female detective who looked as though she was twenty at most and barely passed for a police officer.

Pretty little piece, thought Waltin, jutting out his manly chin in order to show potency and energy.

"Go back to the last election," said Waltin.

"But there must be tons," she said with surprise.

"Exactly," said Waltin energetically. "That's just the idea." And I don't intend to go into that here, he thought.

"Are we searching for something in particular, some particular person or group or organization?" asked one of the other detectives, a young man who appeared to be twenty-five at most and wore a blue college sweatshirt that said Stanford University on it.

"No," said Waltin. "This is pure compilation. A sociological investigation, if you will."

Wonder if that sweatshirt is genuine? he thought.

"Any more questions?" Waltin looked at the third member of the group. He was a young man who looked like he played in a pop band.

"No." The one being questioned shook his head. "I never have any questions."

Good types, thought Waltin as he took the elevator down to the garage. I might recruit that dark one to my own little enterprise, he thought.

Berg had spent the weekend out at his cottage. The thought was that he and his wife should spend time together, pick a few mushrooms, have a good dinner, and perhaps stop by to see his aged parents, who lived in the vicinity. But there hadn't been any visit to his parental home or any mushroom picking. Mother and Father had gone to Åland, it turned out, and on Saturday morning when they woke up it had been pouring down rain, which had kept up the entire day. They made a fire in the fireplace; his wife had read a thick novel and scarcely answered when spoken to. And he himself had mostly sat with his own thoughts. Why didn't we ever have any children? he thought. We couldn't have our own, but why didn't we adopt while there was time? The thought of this made him so dejected that he thought about his job instead. As a rule that usually calmed him, and it did so this time as well.

For lunch his wife had made a mushroom omelet. Mushrooms that they had picked before. Butter, bread, and cheese on the side.

"Beer or water?" asked his wife.

"Do we have any red wine?" asked Berg.

His wife looked at him with surprise.

"Has something happened?"

"No," said Berg. "Why do you think that?"

"You usually don't ever drink wine with lunch," she said.

Berg shrugged his shoulders and smiled wanly.

"No," he said. "But just now I suddenly felt like it. Won't you have a glass then?" he asked.

"Gladly," she said. "If you're going to anyway, I'll gladly have a glass. There's lots left over from Midsummer, as you know."

"We can have that Spanish wine," said Berg. "The case that I got from their embassy."

It had been an excellent lunch, he thought. Afterward they had had coffee, his wife had returned to her novel, he himself had a third glass of red wine and lay down on the sofa.

What do I do with Kudo and Bülling? thought Berg. He couldn't get rid of them. The operation had already been allowed to go too far, and it would likely outlast him as well. However insignificant it might be, there was also a risk that at some point the Kurds would arrange for a wedding outside their circle, and Berg wasn't the type who planned to preside over his own funeral. A probability so small as to almost defy calculation, but which I can't disregard, he thought. And whether it was the red wine or something else, suddenly he knew exactly what to do with Kudo and Bülling.

On Monday morning he summoned them, and five minutes after his secretary had hung up the phone they were sitting in front of his desk, Kudo leaning forward ready to leap, Bülling with his gaze directed at the fringe of the carpet.

"Yes," said Berg. "I've been thinking about you gentlemen since we met last week."

"What can we do for you, chief?" said Kudo.

"I believe we'll have to inform the leadership in Stockholm," said Berg. "And with a thought for the degree of secrecy, I believe we must limit the information to the chief constable alone."

"Any further limitations?" said Kudo.

"Yes," said Berg. "The information you turned in to me last week stays here with us. On the other hand, you are free to give a general report on the activities and the persons involved."

"What do we do with Semir G. and Abdullah A.?" mumbled Bülling.

"Obviously we'll report on them too," said Berg, "on their persons and general activities. With the exception of the conversation that was discussed last time we met." And hopefully this time will be the last we see each other in this way, he thought.

Of course it was actually that fool who foisted Bülling on me, thought Berg when they had left. So it's only right that he gets him back in return, and besides, perhaps he could have some small practical use for them for once. We'll just have to see if he rises to the bait, thought Berg.

The bait had been swallowed by the next weekly meeting with the political superiors. For starters it had also gone quite well in spite of the fact that the prime minister's adviser was present. First, Berg reported on the continued survey of anticonstitutional elements within the police and the military. They were working with high urgency but because the assignment was so extraordinarily sensitive they had to proceed with extreme care. This is going to take time, Berg emphasized, and he had not acknowledged the quiet chuckle from a certain person at the table.

After that he gave a lightly retouched version of Waltin's unsuccessful attempt at recruiting. Politicians loved those kinds of stories. Berg knew that from experience, and it worked this time as well.

"That was nice to hear," sighed a relieved minister. "That you were unsuccessful this time, I mean. Yes, that you were successful in the larger context because you were unsuccessful in the smaller, if one may say so, if you understand what I mean," he clarified, looking at Berg.

Finally he had touched on the ongoing compilation of threats and menaces against the sitting government and those closest to them. And here as well they were working with high urgency.

"They're working at high urgency, and I'm actually counting on the fact that as early as our next meeting I should be able to give a summary of what we have."

"There's quite a bit, of course," said the minister.

"Unfortunately that's the way it is." Berg nodded heavily in confirmation.

"These Kurds," said the minister, who seemed unusually frisky. "Are they keeping calm or . . . ? I saw an article in *Svenskan* the other day that wasn't exactly amusing."

"Wonder how it ended up just there?" said the special adviser, with an irritating grin.

"There I would like to maintain," said Berg, "that we have good control of the situation." He nodded toward the minister; he pretended not to notice the other person.

The minister nodded gratefully while the special adviser appeared even more delighted.

"I was actually at a Kurdish wedding one time," he said while he observed Berg behind half-closed eyelids and with the same amused smile. "Nice people. They served very good food too. I recall that we had roasted lamb and some kind of wine from their home region."

Okay, thought Berg as he sat in the backseat of his car returning to Kungsholmen, now what do I know? That Kudo and Bülling, mostly Kudo—for say what you will about Bülling, he wasn't directly communicative—let their mouths run before their brains, despite instructions to the contrary. And that the moronic Stockholm chief constable evidently had a direct channel to the prime minister's special adviser. So far everything's fine and dandy, thought Berg. Such knowledge is simply power.

What is it he wants to say to me? thought Berg. It's completely clear that there's a message. Who would invite someone like that to their wedding? Not even a Kurd. What type of message is it he wants to give me? That he knows what I'm doing and that he's keeping an eye on me? Quite certainly, thought Berg. That I should watch out? Quite certainly that too. But why does he talk about it to me? Because he wants to draw attention to himself? Possibly, but scarcely probable. To get me off balance, even if that means he has to show his cards to me? Or is it so bad . . . Berg's thoughts were interrupted by a quiet throat-clearing from the driver's seat.

"Boss, excuse me for interrupting, but we're here now." The car had stopped down in the garage and his chauffeur was looking at him uneasily in the rearview mirror.

"Please excuse me," said Berg. "I'm sitting here with my own thoughts."

Is it that bad, thought Berg in the elevator on the way up to his office on the top floor, that the card he's shown me means nothing to him? That he can lay it out just to shake me up, because he's holding much better cards than that? Who? thought Berg. Who in that case is the traitor in my immediate circle? Most likely Waltin, he thought, and the sorrow he suddenly felt in passing had the same cold intensity he felt whenever he thought about the children he and his wife had never had.

At the meeting the following week he reported on Waltin's compilation of those threats and menaces directed at, or intended for, politicians and senior officials in the Cabinet, the parliament, and the authorities that were of decisive significance for the security of the realm. Waltin had done an excellent job: He had done it regardless of how things stood with his own reliability, and Berg himself was very satisfied with the way in which he had set up his report. First he had quickly peeled away the remaining authorities and the parliament in order to concentrate on the menace that concerned the Cabinet and those who worked there.

As an introduction he had sketched out the various forms this took: threats from foreign powers, political conspiracies at various levels within the realm, terrorist actions with an origin in another country, domestic terrorism, political extremist groups, and actions carried out by so-called individual lunatics, and he was very satisfied with that presentation as well. An assessment that, by the way, was quite clearly shared by the minister, who larded his summary with verbal agreement and nods. And by the legal officer as well, for this could be seen in his eyes despite his usual silence. The special adviser sat with his eyes closed and he had neither grinned, chuckled, nor had any opinions, which was probably the highest praise Berg could count on from that quarter.

"Yes," said Berg, clicking a new picture from the slide projector he had brought in. "We're starting to approach the heart of the matter, as the saying goes. As you see from the charts, the volume of threats directed at the government and persons in its vicinity has increased violently since the change of administration at the last election."

At this point the special adviser had chuckled, not said anything, but chuckled in that very unnerving way. Should I wait him out? thought Berg.

"The number of threats we've captured against the government and its affiliates has increased by more than one thousand percent since the change of government. Under the previous lot, we used to get a few hundred per year, but now it's a few thousand."

"That's just terrible," said the minister of justice. "I received a letter bomb myself about a year ago."

"That case is included here, as you no doubt know," said Berg confidently, "and we have good hope of finding the perpetrators. We know they belong to a neo-Nazi group on the extreme right-wing fringe."

"It's really nice that they're still on that fringe," said the special adviser. "You say 'bomb,' " he continued, looking at Berg. "Are we talking about that package with three fireworks in it, where some mentally challenged young man with pyrotechnic inclinations pasted match-striking surfaces on the fuse?"

"Our technicians were not that shaken up," Berg agreed. "And that's the good side of things. The volume has increased dramatically, as you see, but when we observe the various individual cases the picture begins to change. It's almost exclusively a matter of communications by telephone or various types of mailings, mostly letters; in a purely judicial sense it's most often a question of insults and slander than pure threats. The most common individual communication that we receive, for example, claims that our prime minister is a Russian spy."

"But that's shocking," said the minister.

"Stay calm," said the special adviser, leaning forward and patting the minister on the arm. "I've got my eyes on that little scoundrel."

"But, but," persisted the minister, pulling his arm away. "I'm not so amused by all these threats and my wi— yes, my partner . . . actually became quite upset when she heard about my letter bomb."

"Obviously," said the special adviser jovially. "But wasn't that a different partner? Than the one you have now, I mean." Now he was laughing so that his fat belly bounced.

"Yes, you can joke," said the minister. "Tell me, Berg," he continued, nodding amiably. "What kind of people are these, who get mixed up in such things?"

"All possible types if we're talking occupations and social groups," said Berg. "And obviously there is a significant overrepresentation of persons with psychiatric problems, but we have everything from counts and barons and doctors and executives to common laborers, students, the unemployed, people on disability, and mental patients. Many are immigrants too, it should be pointed out, but almost all in that subcategory seem to have acted more out of personal dissatisfaction than any extreme political ideology."

"Police officers," said the special adviser. "Police officers and military personnel, the ones you described to us a few weeks ago. How is it with them?"

"What I am accounting for today are almost exclusively reported cases. With or without a known perpetrator. So the persons included in my earlier account, where we ourselves sniffed out the information, are not part of these statistics." Berg nodded thoughtfully before he continued. "But certainly there are also police officers and military personnel in our material on reported cases. Here, for example, there is a detective chief inspector with the Stockholm police who called the prime minister's chancellery on his service phone and conveyed threats against the prime minister to his secretary. Still in service, by the way, case closed when the crime couldn't be confirmed against his denials."

Berg cleared his throat and continued.

"We have a half dozen officers—the highest ranking is a lieutenant colonel with a ranger unit—who have uttered, to say the least, inappropriate viewpoints about the government and its work as well as individual members of the government in the presence of draftees and subordinate personnel. In brief, quite a few," concluded Berg.

"Am I unjust if I say that the material about reported cases consists mainly of rubbish, but that at the same time you are sitting on other data that perhaps indicates a more qualified menace and with presumptive perpetrators of a quite different, and higher, quality?" The special adviser looked expectantly at Berg.

"No," said Berg. "I guess I concur unreservedly with your description. That is how I myself and my coworkers view the situation."

What is going on? thought Berg. I don't even need to say it myself. He's the one who is saying it for me.

After the meeting he met Waltin. First he complimented him for his excellent support and then briefly gave his view on how the whole thing had turned out.

"It was a good meeting," said Berg. "I got a definite sense that we're finally starting to transmit on the same wavelength."

Waltin nodded. He looked satisfied, but not in any way that appeared exaggerated or suspicious, just satisfied. I've probably been mistaken, thought Berg. What I need is a week's vacation.

Waltin of course had no idea of the suspicions that had been moving around in Berg's head lately, and even if he had he wouldn't have been overly concerned. There were other things stirring in Waltin's head. One that was stirring more and more often was that dark little thing with the boyish body and that small, small, firm rear, which just now was sitting in a small, small chair in the section for internal surveillance. Before her big, big computer. At first he had thought about finding out how old she was, but on further reflection he had decided not to. That would ruin the enjoyment, thought Waltin. She looked as though she were in high school, despite the fact that she must have turned twenty-five, and that was good enough.

Lately he had looked in on her and her coworkers more and more often, and that puritanical upper-class fairy Hamilton, who was still working directly under him, had only gotten surlier and surlier. I guess I'll have to live with that, thought Waltin, and he grinned exactly like a wolf whose fantasies were only getting better and better. This time she had been sitting alone too, so he had avoided wasting a lot of unnecessary time setting up smokescreens and conversing with her male coworkers.

"How nice that you came," she said. "I need help. There's something I have to ask you."

"I'm listening," said Waltin. He assumed a semi-profile and a manly yet easy smile as he unobtrusively moved his chair closer to hers. Little Jeanette, age seventeen, thought Waltin while his well-tailored crotch tightened a little.

"We've received a few tips that I'm not really sure about," she said, wrinkling her brow.

Delightful, thought Waltin, that little wrinkle in her forehead as she bit on the pen she was holding in her little hand. Imagine if she had a lisp too, he thought. Then he might even have considered taking responsibility for his actions.

"Tell me," said Waltin, crossing his right leg over his left while loosening the knot of his tie.

"It's about an American journalist," she said. "He arrived at Arlanda from New York last Sunday and I've already received two tips about him."

"What's his name?" asked Waltin and leaned forward to get a better look at the text on her computer screen. What a delightful scent, he thought. Like rosy, freshly bathed skin.

"Jonathan Paul Krassner, goes by John," she said. "Born in 1953."

CHAPTER V

Between Summer's Longing and Winter's End

New York, New York, in December

[FRIDAY, DECEMBER 6]

When Johansson and his companions arrived in New York they were met by a biting wind, and his first move was to buy a heavy jacket and a sturdy pair of shoes. Wonder if they have them with a hollow heel? thought Johansson, smiling to himself as he stood in the store with the robust winter shoe in his hand. Heel?

"What do you call this?" asked Johansson, indicating the heel with his thumb.

" 'Heel,' sir," the clerk said politely. "You want them with a different heel?" he asked.

Johansson shook his head and smiled.

"No," he said. "These are fine the way they are. I think I'll wear them, so you can just put the old ones in a bag."

That evening he and his two traveling companions went to a restaurant for dinner. At first they considered going to a Swedish restaurant with a good reputation located close to their hotel, but after further discussion they settled on an Italian one that the officer from the Interpol section had visited the last time he was in New York.

"It's excellent, if you like Italian food." The officer from Interpol nodded to underscore what he was saying. "A few officers here in town tipped me off about it last time I was here. It's supposed to be a frequent haunt of the local Mafia bosses, and that's a good sign, of course."

"So herring and a shot is out of the question," objected the officer from narcotics. "Instead you'll be shot from behind with your head landing in a bowl of spaghetti with meat sauce."

"You've missed the point," said Johansson jovially. "You can eat herring when you get home, can't you? You have the whole Christmas holiday ahead of you."

And because he was the boss, Italian food is what they had.

"There's a very good Italian restaurant a few blocks from where I live, but I must confess this risotto is hard to beat," said Johansson a few hours later.

"It's the truffles that do the trick," said the Interpol chief inspector, who had eaten a meal or two while in service.

"Is that those little black bits of sawdust?" asked the narcotics chief inspector suspiciously. "I was just wondering."

"It's a remarkable mushroom," said the one from Interpol. "It's said to grow best if fertilized with human blood, at least if you believe that tale, and they grow best of all, it's said, if the blood is from someone who's been murdered."

"Why don't you take it, then? If they'd been a little bigger I could have pushed them to the side, but these are way too small. Especially now when you have a little red wine under your belt." The head of the National Bureau of Criminal Investigation's narcotics squad smiled wryly and raised his glass.

"Maybe you should try grating a few truffles over the herring," said Johansson, smiling. "Combine the Swedish and Italian food cultures, if I may say so."

"The Swedish is good enough for me, herring and a shot and new potatoes with dill." The narcotics chief inspector sighed nostalgically.

"What plans do you gentlemen have for tomorrow?" asked the Interpol chief inspector, changing the subject. "If there's any interest, I can arrange a little educational field trip. I spoke with my friends this afternoon."

Sounds interesting, thought Johansson. I can phone that woman who knew Krassner in the morning. If I end up calling her at all.

"Sounds interesting," he said. "I have a few things to do in the morning, thought I'd shop for a few Christmas presents, but in the afternoon and evening I've got nothing better to do. Sure, I'll gladly put the squeeze on the local bad guys."

"Me too." The chief inspector from narcotics nodded and there was a gleam in his eyes. "It's going to look brilliant in the travel report the boss, here, is going to turn in. No rest for the wicked regardless of whether it's a Sunday or a workday or wherever on earth you are. Such is a simple constable's lot." He grinned at Johansson.

"Then it's a deal." The officer from Interpol nodded.

[SATURDAY, DECEMBER 7]

Johansson waited until ten a.m. before he phoned Krassner's ex-girlfriend. In the back of his mind he had the idea that she was probably the type who preferred to get up late if given the choice, which she no doubt could on a Saturday morning. He had brooded a good deal besides, before it even occurred to him to pick up the phone. It would be simplest, of course, to forget about the whole thing, he thought. Agree with Jarnebring's theory of a little half-crazy suicide who for unknown but probably uninteresting reasons had chosen to store a slip of paper with Johansson's complete name, title, and home address in a shoe with a hollow heel. A shoe with a heel with a hole in it, thought Johansson, and sighed.

He let go of that thought, however. Johansson had been curious even as a child, and that thing about the hollow heel was simply too much. Which was not to say that it was wise to phone her if it was his own curiosity that he wanted to appease. If he looked at the matter purely professionally it was almost always better to show up unannounced and simply knock on the door of the person in question. Or forget about knocking if that was the way it was. But this isn't the right time for that, thought Johansson, so what do I do now?

With the help of a friendly receptionist at the hotel, he had carried out certain preparatory measures the day before. First he double-checked the telephone number he got from Wiklander. Not because he didn't trust him. Wiklander was almost as capable a police officer as he himself had been at the same age, but better a check too many than one too few, thought Johansson. Weissman's telephone number was in the phone book, so that had been simple enough, and because the address was the same as in his notebook it was quite certainly correct: Sarah J. Weissman, 222 Aiken Avenue, Rensselaer, New York. In addition he realized that Rensselaer was right across the river from Albany, which clearly was the capital of the state of New York. Like Solna and Sundbyberg in relation to Stockholm, thought Johansson.

"What's the easiest way to get there?" asked Johansson.

"By train from Grand Central Station," the receptionist explained. "Takes a little less than three hours if you go on the express. I can get you a timetable. They're quite frequent even on weekends. Besides, it's a really beautiful trip along the Hudson River," she added. "Not like this," she said, nodding toward the street outside the swinging lobby doors.

Wonder if it's as beautiful as driving along the Ångerman River, thought Johansson.

I can take the train on Sunday morning, Johansson decided. Look around a little, see how he lived, perhaps exchange a few words with his ex-girlfriend since he had to be there anyway. The most practical, of course, would be to phone her ahead of time. There was nothing that suggested she was a common criminal who would cut and run if a Swedish policeman phoned to talk about an old boyfriend. Or was there? Johansson thought and sighed. Six of one, he thought, and dialed her number.

After a half dozen rings he got her answering machine. She sounded chipper and happy, so possibly he had been mistaken about her morning habits.

"Hi," she said happily. "This is Sarah and I'm not home. Leave a message."

I see, thought Johansson, crestfallen, and hung up.

During the afternoon Johansson and his two traveling companions first visited a police station in lower Manhattan. It looked like most of the other police stations Johansson had visited if you disregarded the size. This was bigger. Then the local officers took them along to a nearby restaurant where you could get a good, nutritious meal at a discount price. If you were a police officer, that is.

"Never kick ass on an empty stomach," said their host, smiling broadly at them.

Detective Lieutenant Martin Flannigan, thought Johansson while something touched his heart. You could just as well be named Bo Jarnebring and be acting head of the local detective department in Östermalm. And you have the right first name.

Lieutenant Flannigan and his colleagues had arranged for them to go along on a special exercise against street robberies in Manhattan. Street robbery was something that was viewed seriously, especially at Christmastime and at least in certain parts of Manhattan.

"It's a decoy operation," Flannigan explained. "Works very well on the dumbest crooks."

Decoy, thought Johansson. *Lockfågel.* Like when he used to shoot ducks down by the river in his youth. First he set out the decoys he had inherited from his grandfather and then he paddled the kayak and settled in among the reeds by the shore and waited for twilight and for the ducks to start flying in formation. One evening he had shot more than he was able to carry at one time. How old could I have been? thought Johansson.

As soon as darkness had set in and the crooks started to look out of their holes, they'd sought out a suitably situated back street. One of Flannigan's boys had dressed up like a bum. After that he sat down in a doorway and pretended to be unconscious and alongside him he had a paper bag with several green cigarette cartons sticking up.

"Menthol cigarettes," explained Flannigan. "Don't ask me why, but blacks are crazy about menthol cigarettes."

Johansson and Flannigan were standing by the window in a little bar diagonally across the street. Flannigan's first move had been to order each of them a beer. I've gotten the best beat, thought Johansson, for his two travel companions were huddled together with their local hosts in various vehicles arranged along the street.

"Now we'll see if they rise to the bait," said Flannigan, grinning. "Cheers," he said, raising his glass.

It had only taken a quarter of an hour, but the first fish who swallowed the bait was the wrong color: a white female addict in her thirties. First she had walked past the sleeping bum, stopped at the street corner, and looked around. Then she went back again, slowed down by the bum, checked one more time, and took the paper bag with the cigarette cartons.

"Watchful as an eagle," said Flannigan, grinning.

"Police, freeze," and one minute later she was sitting in the backseat of a dark-blue van with her hands shackled behind her back.

It kept on that way until the van was full. A female drug addict, two who really were bums, plus a few ordinary snot-nosed youths, and with one exception they'd all been the right color. They turned in the catch at the police station and then Flannigan had taken his colleagues to his regular place, where they had a large number of beers, related the usual heroic stories for each other, and generally preserved the common Western police culture.

Nice guys, Johansson thought before he fell asleep in his bed at the hotel. But a hell of a place to work.

[SUNDAY, DECEMBER 8]

On Sunday Johansson's travel companions took the early morning plane home to Stockholm. He himself walked to Grand Central Station and put himself on the train to Albany. Wonder what she's like?

he thought. Judging by her voice on the answering machine she sounds both happy and nice and completely normal. Not at all like his image of an ex-girlfriend of John P. Krassner, who had had the bad taste to go around with people's home addresses in the hollow heel of his shoe.

CHAPTER VI

Free falling, as in a dream

Stockholm in October

"It's about an American journalist," said Assistant Detective Jeanette Eriksson. "He arrived at Arlanda from New York last Sunday and I've already collected two tips about him." She indicated her computer screen while Waltin leaned forward in order to see better. Why don't I just sit on Daddy's lap? she thought.

"What's his name?" said Waltin, casually placing his right hand next to her left.

"Jonathan Paul Krassner, goes by John," said Eriksson, "born in 1953. Resident of Albany in upstate New York." Although he's actually rather a dish, she thought. If you happen to like older guys.

"Do we have anything on him?" asked Waltin while he lightly drummed his fingertips on the tabletop.

"We don't have anything in-house." Assistant Detective Eriksson shook her head. "If you want me to go outside the building, then I have to go through my chief." Wonder if that's a genuine Rolex, she thought. In which case it must have cost an arm and a leg. It looks genuine, anyway.

"Let's not be in a rush," said Waltin, smiling a white-toothed smile. "What's the problem?"

"Depends on what you mean by problem," said Eriksson, shrugging her slender shoulders. "The first tip came in the day before yesterday, and I've been content to simply make a note of it. The informant is one of our journalists at state television. This particular person I happen to know about. He seems to have problems both with alcohol and his own imagination." Wonder if he thinks I'll move my foot, she thought.

"So, what did he have to tell us?" said Waltin, smiling confidently.

"He had run into Krassner at the press club down on Vasagatan Tuesday evening. I'm guessing it was in the bar, although he doesn't say so. He wanted to get hold of his contact here but our man is out on a job and I saw no reason to bother him. In any case, our informant maintains that Krassner appears suspiciously interested—those are his own words—in our cooperation with other security services in the West. Among other things he's supposed to have talked about the Germans and how we use them as our channel to the Americans."

"What could he have meant by that?" said Waltin, shrugging his well-tailored shoulders. "What Germans?" He gave her a manly smile.

"Exactly," said Eriksson and she smiled as well.

He really is a dish, she thought.

"Then there's that other tip," she continued. "It came in a few hours ago. It's another informant, and he says we should contact him at once regarding an American journalist by the name John P. Krassner."

"Whoops," said Waltin. "And so who is he?"

"That's why I need your help," she said. "This informant has a secure identity which is beyond my authority. Highest priority both with us and with military intelligence, so I'm not finding him. But according to my instructions I should see to it that the bureau chief or you get this immediately."

Assistant Detective Eriksson nodded energetically. And it doesn't appear that you have any objections, she thought.

"And because my boss is taking a long lunch in town and then you happened to come by . . ." She smiled, with a little gleam in her eyes. You are a little interested after all, she thought.

"You can make a note that I'm informed," said Waltin efficiently and looked at the clock. "Print out a copy too, so I can take it with me, and I'll be in touch during the day. Then you can set up a surveillance file on this Krassner. And classify it up a notch until we know what this is all about."

. . .

This is going like clockwork, thought Waltin a while later. Berg hadn't had any objections; he had seemed as though he was thinking about something else, and after having found out who the informant was Waltin had become truly curious. He had met him twice before, both times at the secure location, and he had not been able to avoid noticing with what respect Berg had treated him. Of the little that Berg had told him when their guest had gone home, he had also understood that this was not any ordinary retired professor of mathematics from the technical college in Stockholm. In addition it actually appeared as if the more intricate and private question of the future handling of little Miss Jeanette Eriksson was in the process of solving itself quite naturally. Say what you will about Berg, thought Waltin, he seems to be totally uninterested in women, and of course that's good for someone like me.

When Waltin phoned the retired mathematics professor he encountered unexpected problems.

"Yes, I hear what you're saying, police superintendent," said the professor in a grumpy old man's voice, "but at the risk of appearing obstinate I would still prefer to speak directly with the bureau chief."

"The problem is that the bureau chief is out of town," Waltin lied routinely. "I have spoken with him on the phone and because you contacted us, professor, the bureau chief wanted me to make contact with you at once." And besides, I am a police superintendent, you old fart, thought Waltin, but he didn't say that.

"I hear what you're saying, superintendent," mumbled the professor.

"Yes, Bureau Chief Berg was of the firm opinion that this matter was clearly important, given that you contacted us," said Waltin in a mild voice.

"If he is of that opinion then I really don't understand why he can't drag himself over here."

"As I said before, he is unfortunately out of town." Surly old fogey who for unclear historical reasons has a completely crazy estimation of his own significance, thought Waltin. But I'm sure that can be changed.

"Where is he?" asked the professor.

"Excuse me?" said Waltin. What's he saying? he thought.

"I asked where he was, Bureau Chief Berg, that is. Is that so hard to understand? Where is Bureau Chief Berg?"

Obviously senile too, thought Waltin.

"Yes," said Waltin with feigned heartiness. "A man with your background surely understands why I can't go into that. Especially not on the phone. My suggestion is that I come to your residence so we can discuss the matter in peace and quiet. Hello?"

The old fart hung up, thought Waltin, astonished. He hung up right in my ear.

When he finally got hold of Berg in his office half the afternoon had gone to waste. In addition Berg had been amused in a manner that Waltin didn't appreciate.

"Yes, yes," said Berg, smiling. "Johan can have his ways. When he was working at the defense department's intelligence division during the war he is said to have taken a swing at a staff major who had hidden his whiskey. He was, of course, a drafted corporal, and in civilian life he was professor of mathematics at Uppsala University. Then he moved to the technical college to be closer to his beloved computers."

"If we're talking about the Second World War," said Waltin, "that might possibly explain it. After all, some water has run under the bridge since then. The years pass, if I may say so."

Berg shook his head thoughtfully.

"I doubt that he's senile. He's actually the one who set up our system of codes and encryption here at the bureau. He has saved millions for us in computer costs. We had official contact just six months ago and he was just as sharp as he's always been. Here's what we'll do," continued Berg, nodding toward Waltin. "I'll phone and talk to him, then you come along so that I see to it that you are properly introduced."

"Fine with me," said Waltin and shrugged his shoulders. What could he say?

Because I have decided to trust you, thought Berg.

Professor Emeritus Johan Forselius lived in an enormous, old-fashioned apartment on Sturegatan. It took a good while before they were let in, and then they'd had to grope their way along a darkened hallway toward a distant and well-smoked study.

"It's that damn girl from the home-care services," muttered the professor. "I've told her all fall that she should put new lightbulbs in the hall, but the woman seems to be completely stupid. Speaks some incomprehensible Polish gibberish."

Forselius blew his nose vigorously into his hand and wiped it off on his pants.

"If you gentlemen want coffee you'll have to help yourselves," he said, staring crossly at Waltin. "Personally I could fancy a small cognac."

The professor sank down into a well-broken-in leather easy chair and nodded toward Berg that he could sit down as well. After that he looked again at Waltin. More challengingly this time.

"Yes, what do you say, Claes," Berg said obligingly and nodded toward Waltin. "Wouldn't a cup of coffee taste good?"

"Yes, truly," said Waltin with warmth in his voice. "Is the kitchen in that direction?" Waltin made a head movement toward the apartment's darkened interior.

"If you find a stove, superintendent, you've come to the right place," said the professor, grinning contentedly. "The cognac is in the serving area. On second thought, bring the bottle if Erik here would like some, for it must be the superintendent who'll be driving the car afterward?"

Waltin had been content to smile amiably.

Two months earlier Professor Forselius had received a letter from the United States. The sender was a John P. Krassner, who wrote that he was a researcher and author in the process of writing a book about the politics of security in Europe after the Second World War. Now he was intending to come to Sweden and requested an interview. This was not an unusual request for a man like Forselius: rumor-shrouded codebreaker from the days of the great war, well-known speaker among military personnel and secret police officers across the Western world. Forselius received similar proposals every month, despite the fact that his war posting had ended more than forty years ago, and he had done what he always did. He tossed it into the wastebasket.

"Who the hell wants to talk to people like that?" said Forselius, taking a hefty gulp from his brandy snifter. "But then, the day before yesterday, the doorbell rang, and at first I thought the damn home-care services had sent me some new damn foreigner, and then it turns out it's that damn Krassner who'd written to me to get an interview and now he's turned up on my own doorstep."

Berg nodded understandingly. Those home-care folks, those home-care folks. "So you let him in?"

"Hmm," said Forselius from the depths of his snifter. "At first I thought about just tossing the bastard out; he's a little S.O.B. and even if I'm not as strong as I once was, it wouldn't have been any big deal." Forselius grunted contentedly and gave Waltin an almost greedy glance. "But then he said something that made me curious."

"Do tell," said Berg.

"He had greetings from an old acquaintance," said Forselius.

The professor took a fresh sip from his large snifter while giving Waltin a suspicious look over the edge of his glass.

"An old acquaintance from the war and the years after." Forselius nodded and appeared most interested in the contents of his glass.

"You really don't need to be worried about Claes here," said Berg with conviction in his voice. "Completely disregarding the fact that he is my closest man, I trust him unreservedly." Did that sound a little strange? he thought.

Forselius nodded, mostly to himself, it appeared. Then he straightened in his chair, smiled, and shook his head.

"I hear what you're saying, Erik," he said. "I hear what you're saying."

"Well," said Berg, smiling.

Forselius shook his head again and set the glass down on the table next to the easy chair.

"I'm afraid that this still must stay between the two of us," he said. "But how you deal with it later is none of my concern."

A senile old man who's trying to make himself interesting, thought Waltin with irritation as he sat in the car, trying to read the evening paper he had bought in a tobacco shop directly across the street.

It took over half an hour before Berg came out. Without asking, Waltin started the car and set a course back toward Kungsholmen, but when they got stuck in the thickening traffic over by Odenplan he couldn't contain himself any longer.

"Okay, chief," said Waltin. "Tell a simple fellow laborer in the vineyard."

Berg shook his head thoughtfully.

"I hope this doesn't upset you," said Berg, "but I have to think this through myself first. What I can give you for now is a general orientation."

Waltin nodded with his eyes fixed on the traffic lights.

"The person from whom Krassner had greetings is an old acquaintance of Forselius from the time after the Second World War. Same generation as our esteemed professor, by the way, and when he and Forselius knew one another the acquaintance was working at the American embassy here in Stockholm. If you understand what I mean."

CIA, thought Waltin nodding.

"According to Krassner this was his mother's older brother, now deceased. Supposed to have died last spring."

"Although clearly chipper enough to convey a greeting," said Waltin, smiling wryly.

"Clearly," said Berg. "It's also possibly so bad that he let the cat out of the bag."

Whoops, thought Waltin. This must be the first time in world history that that's happened.

"What do you want me to do?" asked Waltin.

"Find out what Krassner is up to here at home in our dear fatherland," said Berg, smiling faintly. "Plus the usual background, of course."

"Without contacting the Germans," said Waltin rhetorically. Who could ask the guys over there directly, which would have saved me a heckuva lot of time, he thought.

"Until we know where this is heading, it stays in-house," said Berg, nodding with a certain emphasis. "We're making no contacts whatsoever outside the building." The part about the Americans especially was sensitive as hell; the Russians were like a hungover bear about that sort of thing, thought Berg.

"Can I borrow some people from your surveillance group?" asked Waltin.

"Sure," said Berg. "Take what you need."

Jeanette, age seventeen, thought Waltin, and smiled just like a wolf whose fantasies are only getting better and better.

"Umm, there was another matter," said Berg when they had parked the car in the garage under the police building.

"I'm listening," said Waltin. Why is he smiling like that? he thought.

"Forselius noticed your watch." Berg nodded toward Waltin's gold Rolex.

"I see," said Waltin and sighed. "I suppose he assumed that I got it from the Russians?"

"More or less," said Berg and smiled. "I explained to him that you were already wearing it the first time I met you, long before you started at the bureau."

"Was he impressed?" asked Waltin.

"I don't believe he's become senile," answered Berg. "There I believe you're wrong, but his eccentricity has not exactly declined with the years."

So that's what he is, thought Waltin, eccentric, like all elitist bastards.

"I told him that the watch was a present from your old mother."

Was that what I said? thought Waltin. He was content to nod.

What do I do now? thought Berg a while later when he was sitting safely behind his large desk.

If Forselius is correct in his assumptions, there must be tremendous openings, he thought. Among other things a proper chance to put a hammerlock on that younger Forselius copy down in Rosenbad. He had already forgotten Waltin and his fancy watch. It was many years since he had stopped being irritated by it, and nowadays, since Waltin had taken over the external operation, it was to be viewed as more of an advantage.

. . .

Waltin had immediately sought out Assistant Detective Jeanette Eriksson and informed her of three things. First, that she was now working for him and only for him. Second, that it was only Krassner this concerned, and third—a not unessential practical question—that the surveillance file on Krassner should be upgraded so that only he and she had access to what was in it. A good basis for continued fellowship of a more boundary-crossing nature, thought Waltin, smiling at her.

"Would you be able to do a few rounds out in the field?" asked Waltin.

"Yes," she said, nodding. "That's no problem. I've never met a guy in my whole life who thought that I was a police officer."

Well now, well now, thought Waltin, for his fantasies were fragile things.

"Find out as much as possible, then we'll talk after the weekend." He smiled again and nodded. A little paternally, as one should smile at young girls like her. Build up trust before proceeding on to the essentials.

Assistant Detective Jeanette Eriksson was not seventeen but rather twenty-seven. When she was younger her appearance had been her main problem. Nowadays it was both an advantage and a disadvantage, and as for Waltin she was completely clear about how he saw the matter. It wasn't the first time she had encountered this reaction from men like Waltin. More important still in the context within which she operated was that she was also a very capable police officer and certainly worthy of a better fate than the one Waltin was preparing for her. After their meeting she had gone directly into her new office; now assigned to a so-called special project, she had her own so-called project room with a key of her own and her own access codes and all the formal trappings. Once there she made a list of the various things she wanted to know about Jonathan Paul Krassner, who went by John, born in 1953 in Albany, New York, USA.

First she had called a colleague with the police out at Arlanda to see if any particular notes had been made when Krassner had entered the country a little less than a week earlier. None had been made. Because he was from the United States, not even the reply to the obligatory question of whether he was here as a tourist or for work or for some other reason had been noted. Pity you're not an ordinary gook, thought Eriksson reflexively.

After that, she had spoken with a colleague who was in charge of their informant at Swedish Television and asked him, on behalf of the boss and for reasons that she didn't need to go into, to get hold of all the observations the informant had made when he met Krassner, as quickly as possible and in detail. It hadn't even crossed her mind that she could do that herself. If she needed to get physically closer to Krassner she didn't want to risk any reactions from his new acquaintances over whom she couldn't have any control, and showing her identity and her face for such a notoriously unreliable informant as was the case here was obviously unthinkable.

Already on Sunday evening, after having worked diligently the whole weekend, she knew a great deal about the person who was currently a project with a secret budget. For that reason she had also phoned Waltin to report. Waltin sounded satisfied. He wanted to meet with her the next morning already and for reasons he couldn't go into, this must take place outside the building. A company with an address on Norr Mälarstrand only five minutes' walk from the building; it was a little exciting considering what she had heard whispered in the corridors about the so-called external operation.

Daddy's clever girl, thought Assistant Detective Eriksson when she put down the phone, but at the same time the thought was not completely disagreeable. A little tingling.

Uncle Claes's clever girl, thought Waltin, and it was a very appealing thought.

Berg had spent the weekend pondering what Forselius had related to him. As always when he dealt with complicated security questions, he had closed himself up in his study at home in the villa in Bromma and made use of pen and paper. Paper that he was always careful to destroy when he was through thinking. Secret police history is very instructive in that regard, about people who were careless with their papers and other possessions and left unnecessary tracks that an opponent could make use of.

When they moved out to Bromma from the apartment in the city, his wife had sometimes teased him. "God, how nice," she used to say, "that we finally have a fireplace so I don't have to watch you starting fires in the kitchen sink." Berg had taken it with a sense of humor, for he knew better, but, with all respect to modern paper shredders—he of course had one of the latest and best models at home—when it came to destroying papers, fire was superior to anything else. First you started the fire and then you were careful to crush and powder the ashes.

There were three levels to what Forselius had said. On the first level was the basic question of whether there was any truth in his musings or whether he was just imagining things. Berg had discussed just that aspect with him extensively. Forselius was widely known for his capacity for critical thinking and not least when it came to questioning himself, his own ideas, his own intellectual capacity, his own motives. "In the world in which I live there is no room for either lies or wishful thinking," he had said to Berg the first time they met.

Of course Berg had also tried to press him on this point. How did he himself view the suspicions that Krassner had sown in his mind?

"If it was a question of placing bets I'd put my money on the fact that he knows something and he knows it's true and it's even so bad he can prove it's true."

Here Forselius had started to laugh a little while he supplied himself with a fresh cognac.

"What he knows and how much he knows?" Forselius shrugged his shoulders in an eloquent gesture.

"You have no ideas on that point?" asked Berg.

"Well," said Forselius. "If it hadn't been the case that he's related to my old acquaintance, then I probably would have decided that he was only trying to get attention. Or that he was out snooping around in the most general way, as is the custom with that kind of humanist hack."

Forselius took a hefty gulp from his large snifter.

"As I'm sure you see this hangs together," Forselius continued. "True or false? If it's false, stop and do something else instead. If it's true, completely or only partly, we go ahead. What is true and what is false? When we find that out we can swing ourselves up to the highest level. Is that which is true actually interesting and in that case to whom? Whatever the case, these are empirical questions and you of course can resort to that sly type with the watch and those fancy clothes for the real heavy work."

Here the chuckling had turned into a minor coughing attack.

"Exactly like when you break a code," said Berg.

"Well," said Forselius. "As a general description perhaps, but completely uninteresting when you're going to do it. You're a good man, Berg, and you are of course no numbskull, but in my world . . ."

Forselius made a gesture with his hands.

"I know, I know," said Berg. "Math was never my strong suit when I was in school."

That's how it'll be, thought Berg, and how do I get Waltin to do his utmost without giving him all the pieces? As far as he was concerned he knew exactly what he should do. He didn't intend to utter a syllable to anyone about Forselius's suspicions. First he would see about getting onto more solid ground, and once he had done so he could take a position on how he should act regarding the top level in his world. Whom he should inform about what.

In the elevated and beautiful world where Forselius and his ilk were, where everything, even chaos, could be ordered and described and explained with the help of symbols and functions, there was naturally no place for disturbing human factors of the type that afflicted Berg in particular when he came to his workplace on Monday morning.

"Welcome," said his secretary, smiling. "You've received an invitation to a very fine lunch."

"When?" asked Berg.

"Today," said his secretary. "The prime minister's special adviser called awhile ago and wondered if you had time to have lunch with him today. He wants you to call him."

"How did he sound?" said Berg, and even as he said it he regretted it.

"He sounded very nice," said the secretary, surprised. "Why? Has something happened?"

Berg shook his head. If I have time? What choice do I have? None, he thought.

On the surface he had been his usual self, the same half-closed eyelids, the same sarcastic curl of the lips, and the same reclining position, in spite of the fact that he was actually eating. It was his manner that bothered Berg deeply. For in a purely objective sense, if you looked at what he really said and how he said it, he had been nice to Berg. An obliging and entertaining host at a lunch, quite simply. Furthermore, in a place to which few had access. One of the government's most exclusive guest dining rooms at Rosenbad.

Both his behavior and his choice of milieu disturbed Berg more than if he had tried to grab hold of Berg and butt heads with him. That's no doubt the point of this playacting, he thought. Calm, he thought. Just calm, calm, calm.

"It was nice to get to see you for lunch, Berg," said the special adviser, raising his glass of mineral water.

"Nice to be here," said Berg neutrally, and replied by raising his near beer.

"I thought that our most recent meeting was enormously positive. I got a definite feeling that we actually started to approach those matters that both you and I are assigned to manage."

Are you being ironic, you bastard? thought Berg and contented himself with nodding.

"I'm not being ironic so don't misunderstand me," said the prime minister's special adviser, making a slightly dismissive motion with his left hand. "What I mean is that both you and I, each in his own place, are prisoners of our various contexts."

Now where are you going with this? thought Berg and was content to nod again.

"Quite a few years ago, when I was doing my military service, at the kind of place that one can't talk about—but you already know that, of course—I wrote an essay about mirror war."

"That sounds interesting. I'm listening," said Berg.

"Of course my thesis was based on the special operation in which I was serving at the time. I had a superior, if you please, and mine in particular was in a league of his own. He was a very talented and exceptionally cussed old son of a bitch, and I myself was only eighteen years old."

Forselius, thought Berg, so now I know and he knows that I know, and why does he want me to know that he knows too?

"Basically it dealt with what we say to one another, in speech, in writing, with gestures and glances and in all other manners and means. For example, by not saying or doing anything whatsoever. Or just by avoiding the reaction that our opponent is expecting." Berg contented himself with nodding; he had set his fork and knife aside.

"The ideal communication in the best of all possible worlds, populated only by good people. . . . How does that look? To begin with, it is true. The sender is not mistaken on that point. What he or she is saying is actually true. In addition it is important to both the sender and the recipient, and in the best of worlds all communications are of course good. They are of use both to the sender and to the recipient and for the world around them."

"The best of worlds," said Berg, as he experienced a remarkable sense of peace, which he hadn't felt for a long time.

"Compare that with the world in which you and I live. I couldn't help seeing what you were thinking when I mentioned that I knew Forselius, in spite of the fact that you have a face that a poker shark would give his dealing hand for."

The prime minister's special adviser smiled at Berg and nodded, and suddenly he seemed not in the least ironic.

"I thank you for the compliment," said Berg. "Would you have seen it if you hadn't talked with Forselius?"

"Probably not." The special adviser shrugged his shoulders. "I have a simple question. Is there anything to Forselius's suspicions, and by that I don't mean those kind of idiotic obviosities such as that our social-democratic government and our neutral and noble fatherland were bedfellows with the U.S. and the Western powers on security matters ever since we knew how the war would end."

"I can see that we're saving time here," said Berg, smiling faintly.

"Exactly, and I'm the one who's saying it so you can just relax and enjoy. You know, I know, all the others like you and me know. There are even editors-in-chief and professors of political science and modern history who know that their military service and placements have never been by chance, nor the psychological operations either. Even that scandal reporter Guillou knows, so it's all the same that the media hasn't informed everyone else. High time they did, by the way, so we could at least deprive that bastard of one of his conceivable arguments."

"The snag is no doubt our policy of neutrality," said Berg, feeling sharper and more secure than he had for a long time.

"Obviously. There is nothing in our world that is simply good or bad. We are also the prisoner of our compromises, and as long as we here at home are not completely sure of how it's going to go out there, we are the world leaders at compromise."

"That, I believe, is a pretty good summary of Swedish postwar politics," agreed Berg.

"And neither you nor I are the first to arrive at that."

"Certainly not," said Berg.

"But it's you and I who can end up in a jam, and it's you and I who are expected to wriggle ourselves and all the others who've given us our jobs out of the jam, and if we don't manage that then we, people like you and me, get squeezed a little more."

"Speak up if you're thinking about looking for a new job," said Berg.

"And how is it this time?" The prime minister's special adviser looked seriously at his lunch guest. "Is there any sort of confounded—sorry—personal, historically determined, private obviosity which is of sufficient interest to the mass media that we could end up in a jam?"

"That's exactly what I'm trying to find out," said Berg.

"But that's just great," his host said with emphasis. "That's what we'll do then, help each other out. Completely without the aid of mirrors."

On Monday morning right before eight o'clock Assistant Detective Jeanette Eriksson entered the building on Norr Mälarstrand where she was to meet Waltin: an Art Deco building with large balconies and the best view of the water and the rises of south Stockholm on the other side. The company to which she was going was on the third floor, but from the name placard in the lobby it appeared that there was a Waltin on the top floor of the building. And if that's where he lives he must have an amazing view, thought Assistant Detective Eriksson. The office was not bad either; small, to be sure, but light, modern, functional, and tastefully furnished. Quite certainly much more expensive than it appeared. Waltin was well dressed, newly shaved, efficient, and served freshly brewed coffee. Exciting guy, she thought. Wonder what he's really like?

"Okay, Jeanette," he said, smiling. "Tell me."

As concerned Krassner the individual there was not much to relate. Not yet, for it had been a weekend, even off in the United States, and because she couldn't take the normal shortcut, that aspect would no doubt take time. On the other hand she had found him.

"He's living in the student dormitory called the Rosehip on Körsbärsvägen, on the sixteenth floor in one of those student corridors with eight rooms and a common kitchen. He sublet the room through an international student organization."

"Who are the others living in the same corridor?" asked Waltin.

"One room is standing empty, because the person who lives there has gone home to his parents. He's studying law and is from the province of Östergötland. His mother suffered a serious traffic accident a month ago. As far as the other six go, besides Krassner, they're normal students in their twenties. All of them men, actually, although I don't believe they have gender-segregated residences. I can check that out if you want."

Waltin shook his head and smiled weakly.

"Okay," Eriksson continued. "One of the guys is at the tech college, one's in business school, one's studying at GIH, one's studying political science, one sociology, and one works with information management. All of them are Swedes except for the last, who's some type of student from South Africa. He's here on a scholarship this semester, black guy. He's older than the others, twenty-eight, born in Pretoria. He got his scholarship from the Swedish trade union federation."

Typical, thought Waltin. The social democrats and their blacks and Arabs and all those other gooks that they drag here.

"Do we have anything on any of them?" he asked.

"Not with us or within the open operation. Yes, if we include the kinds of things that all boys get involved with in their teens. The one at GIH was a little wild when he was in high school, but otherwise, no, just normal Swedish students. None of them are from Stockholm. Country boys."

Waltin nodded. A purely idiotic project that an old bastard had palmed off on Berg, he thought. The only question was how to get himself where he wanted to go without wasting time on unnecessary work.

"Do you have any ideas about how we proceed from here?" he asked.

"I thought about trying to find out who he is," said Eriksson. "As I said, that's going to take time, but I have some possibilities I thought I'd try out."

"I have an idea too." Waltin smiled and nodded.

"Tell me," said Eriksson, looking at him with curiosity.

Waltin smiled secretively and shook his head.

"Leave his biography to me, then I promise you'll get a complete description of him at the end of the week. Without cheating."

"Without cheating?" She smiled inquisitively and nodded. He actually seems super smart, thought Eriksson.

"Without cheating," said Waltin emphatically and held up his right thumb.

Half as big as mine, he thought when she held out her small thumb, and he felt the well-known arousal when he saw her before him, curled up in the corner of his big sofa with her little thumb in her little mouth while the tears ran down her small, round cheeks.

As soon as she had gone Waltin went into the office restroom for relief. He leaned her over the washbasin with a firm grip around her thin neck while he took her from behind, hard and determined so that she would be quite clear about that right from the beginning. Then he washed his hands carefully and phoned one of his many business acquaintances who had a company subsidiary in the United States.

. . .

Assistant Detective Eriksson drove straight home to her studio apartment out in Solna and changed into university student clothing. Because she had studied criminology part-time for over a year this was easy. After that she took the subway into the city; a short walk brought her to the lobby of the Roseship student dormitory on Körsbärsvägen. She knew precisely what she would do and how she would do it. The camera and the rest she had stuffed under the books in her shoulder bag.

Waltin also knew what he would do. He had asked his business acquaintance with the American subsidiary to look a little closer at a young American who was trying to sell him on a business idea. Before Waltin went any further he of course wanted to know if the young American could be trusted: "Good ideas, but of course you'd really like to know if he's fish or fowl." It was also a bit sensitive, obviously, and as always it was urgent. On the other hand, what it cost was less important as long as it was done thoroughly.

"You've turned to the right man, Claes," said his acquaintance warmly. "We have contact with a completely phenomenal private detective bureau in New York. I can get them going at once."

Wonder how much he's thinking about charging me this time, thought Waltin. Thanked him cordially for the assistance and ended the conversation.

Criminology student Jeanette Eriksson rang numerous times at the door to the corridor where Krassner was living before one of the doors was opened from inside. Out came a man in his thirties dressed in jeans, T-shirt, and in stocking feet. He was uncombed and appeared clearly irritated.

It's him, she thought, and smiled her little girl smile at him.

"Excuse me," she said, "but I'm looking for a friend who lives here. Medium height, slender build, dark hair, blue eyes, thin face with a defined jawline and a dimple on his chin." Really good-looking, she thought routinely.

Krassner—for it must be he—sighed and appeared tangibly surly.

"Sorry, I don't speak Swedish," he said, and made no sign of letting her in.

And it was at that moment that Daniel showed up.

"Maybe I can help you," he said, smiling broadly with white teeth.

All guys are the same, thought Jeanette Eriksson half an hour later when she and her new acquaintance, Daniel M'Boye, were sitting across from each other, each with a cup of bad coffee from the dormitory cafeteria. Daniel had been very helpful; the friend she had been looking for had unfortunately been forced to break off his studies when his mother met with a traffic accident.

"Is he a close friend of yours?" he asked, and the compassion in his eyes seemed completely genuine.

She had managed her retreat with flying colors: old friend from high school. Didn't know each other especially well, actually. She had heard that he was studying law and had thought about asking if she could borrow some books from him. But that was no problem at all, she assured him. She had other friends she could ask.

"Do you want a cup of coffee?" He looked at her, courteous and well-mannered.

She appeared just hesitant enough.

"I'd been thinking about going down myself and having a cup in the cafeteria." The smile was broader now and almost a little imploring.

"Okay," said Jeanette, nodding and smiling. This kind of thing is actually just too easy, she thought.

First, Daniel told about himself and then asked what she did, and she answered completely correctly. Studied criminology, it was going so-so, second year at the university, didn't really know what she wanted to be, lived in a studio in Solna, also so-so, mostly study and sleep, not so much fun but life would no doubt go on.

"Although your friend who didn't want to let me in didn't exactly seem happy either," said Jeanette and giggled. "Surly type."

"I hardly know him," said Daniel and smiled. "He's only been living there a week. He's an American. Rather mysterious."

"I thought he seemed old too," said Jeanette with the correct smile. "What's he studying?"

"He said he's writing a book. Something political, political science, about Sweden and Swedish politics. It's not exactly my thing," M'Boye said, and smiled broadly as he leaned closer to her.

Time to move, thought Jeanette, and she smiled shyly back. Of course he got her home phone number after the equally obvious evasions. The new secret number that she had already arranged on Friday afternoon and that she hoped she could soon be rid of.

The weekly meeting with his superiors had gone completely without friction for once. Berg had reported on a few mixed problems: the Yugoslavs, the Kurds, how it was going with the intensified survey of antidemocratic elements within the police and the military.

"It's going slowly," said Berg, "but it's moving forward."

The special adviser had nodded, a very slight but concurring nod.

After the meeting he had taken Berg aside.

"How's it going?" he asked.

"I hope I'll have something for you on Friday," said Berg. "We don't dare go outside the building, so it's taking time to find out who he is."

"Wise," said the special adviser, and to Berg's astonishment he had patted him on the arm.

He seems worried, thought Berg. Why? he thought. What is it he knows that I don't know?

"How's it going?" Berg asked Waltin, who was sitting on the other side of his desk, lightly pinching the already perfect creases of his trousers.

"It's going slowly, but forward," said Waltin. "Do you want to see what he looks like?"

Waltin handed over a plastic folder with photographs.

The photos of Krassner were taken with a telephoto as he went in and out of the dormitory where he was living: heavy boots, jeans, thick padded jacket, bareheaded on one occasion and with a stocking cap on another, close-ups of his face, thin, dogged. A person with an idea, thought Berg, who didn't like what he saw.

"Do you know anything about his routines?"

"Seems to mostly sit closed up in his room and type," said Waltin. "He's visited the public library, the university library, and the Royal Library. Yesterday evening he went down to the press club and had a few beers. Walked the entire way home afterward. The light wasn't turned off until around two o'clock." So little Jeanette will really have to earn her keep, he thought contentedly.

"Do you have enough people?"

"Yes," said Waltin. What is this really about? he thought.

"Do we have anyone in his vicinity?"

"Yes," said Waltin.

"One of ours?"

"Yes," said Waltin.

"What's he like then?"

"Solitary, a little mysterious, seems almost a little worked up. Says hello to his corridor neighbors but doesn't associate with anyone. Tapes hairs on his door when he goes out. You know, that type."

Berg knew exactly.

"And mostly he sits locked up in his room and writes?"

"Yes," said Waltin. "He seems to mostly sit there and peck like a sparrow on his little typewriter."

"What does he live on then?" said Berg, who didn't like what he was hearing. "Birdseed?"

"McDonald's hamburgers and the occasional pizza."

This doesn't sound good, thought Berg. This doesn't sound good at all.

On Thursday evening Waltin's contact phoned. He had a little material on Krassner, which he wondered if he should fax over. There was more on the way, but he wouldn't get that until next week.

"He seems to be a strange bird," said Waltin's contact. "May I be so bold as to ask what kind of business idea he wants to sell you on?"

"Yes, of course," said Waltin. "It's not a big secret. It deals with the media. He had some interesting ideas about how certain media products could be developed."

"Oh, I see," said the contact. "Then I would be damn careful if I were in your shoes."

Jonathan Paul Krassner, known as John, was born on July 15, 1953, in Albany, New York, the only child of a marriage between Paul Jürgen Krassner, born in 1910, and Mary Melanie Buchanan, born in 1920. His parents had married the year before he was born, and divorced the year after.

The father was said to have been a salesman. After the divorce he had moved to Fresno, California. His further fate was unknown and any contacts with his son could in any event not be established. John had grown up with his mother, who worked as a nurse at a Catholic hospital outside Albany. The mother had died of cancer in 1975.

After American elementary and secondary school, with grades that were well above average, Krassner started at the state university in Albany, where he studied political science, sociology, and journalism, and finished his degree. After that he had worked as an intern at a local newspaper, moved on to a local TV station for just over a year, then returned to the newspaper where he had started his career, but now as an investigative reporter with his own byline. And after a few years he himself had wound up in the newspaper on the basis of a grandly planned series of articles, "From Refugee to Racketeer." The English has a better bite to it than the Swedish translation, thought Waltin.

According to the newspaper's investigative reporter John P. Krassner, an economically successful and socially respected Vietnamese family had built up a local crime syndicate in Albany and its environs behind a façade of restaurants, convenience stores, and coin laundries. The local uproar had been widespread for a time. Police and prosecutors had been interested, but rather quickly shook their heads and suspended their investigations. The Vietnamese family, on the other hand, had not taken the matter so lightly. They had sued the newspaper and its owners for several million dollars for libel, reported all those involved for illegal discrimination, and started to agitate in the state legislature through their local politicians and a national organization for Vietnamese boat people. The newspaper had crept to the cross, made a public apology, and paid significant damages after a settlement. Krassner had been thrown out on his ear.

What he had done after that was less clear. First he sold the house that he had inherited from his mother and where he lived after her death, to move in with his uncle, his only remaining relative. He enrolled in the university's evening courses and gradually completed a master's degree in "investigative journalism." In addition he supported himself as some type of intellectual jack-of-all-trades with freelance assignments for various media, as a lecturer in courses on journalism, and for a short time as a copywriter at an advertising agency in Poughkeepsie, about sixty miles north of New York and roughly just as far south of Albany.

Waltin leafed among the faxed papers: the hired detective bureau's exemplary systematic summary; appended copies of the parents' wedding certificate and divorce decree; Krassner's birth certificate; his school grades and class photos from high school; a copy of his driver's license and his university degree; his mother's death certificate; and a considerable packet of copies of the offending newspaper articles. At the bottom of the pile Waltin also found an obituary of his uncle and a copy of the uncle's will, and it was now that this started to be seriously interesting.

The uncle, John Christopher Buchanan, known as John, was born in 1908 in Newark, New Jersey, and had "peacefully passed away in his home in Albany on Tuesday afternoon, April 16, 1985," almost exactly six months before Waltin had occasion to be informed of his life and work. After completing secondary school he matriculated at Columbia University and by and by earned a doctorate in political science in 1938. At the time of Pearl Harbor he was working as an instructor in the same subject at Northwestern University, outside of Chicago, but like "the true patriot that he was" he had immediately left the academic world and trained to be a reserve officer.

After staff service of an unspecified nature in Washington, D.C., he had in the final stages of the Second World War been transferred to Europe with the rank of captain. In the spring of 1947, Lieutenant Colonel Buchanan had been appointed assistant military attaché at the American embassy in Stockholm, where he stayed for more than four years. Then his history got less clear, but in any case in 1958 he left the military as a full colonel and returned to academic life in the form of a professorship in contemporary European history at the State University of New York in Albany. The same year as his twelve-years-younger sister died of cancer, 1975—probably no connection—he had retired "in order to enjoy, by virtue of his age and after an honorable life in the service of his country, his well-earned leisure."

Wonder if he drank, thought Waltin. Otherwise he ought to have done something more.

The most interesting thing was his will. After the introductory and obligatory enumeration of the possessions he had left behind—the house where he lived, various liquid assets in bank accounts and pension funds, his library, a collection of "European military collectibles from the Second World War," furniture, art, and other personal property— John C. Buchanan had willed "all of the collected property left by me, the material as well as the intellectual, to my nearest relation, dear friend, and faithful squire, John P. Krassner."

The material assets had been easy to account for. According to the court proceedings, these amounted to $129,850.50, after deductions for funeral expenses. Not one word about what the intellectual property left behind consisted of.

"But this is just fantastic," said Assistant Detective Eriksson, and she smiled with both her mouth and her eyes at her well-dressed boss. "How did you do it?" He must be supersmart, she thought.

Waltin smiled modestly and made a slight, dismissive shrug.

"We can take that up on a later occasion," he said. "I thought that you could turn in copies of everything plus your own information to Berg."

Cool, thought Eriksson. That really can't hurt in this place.

Berg didn't seem equally enthused.

" 'All of the collected property left by me, the material as well as the intellectual . . .' The intellectual? What does he mean by that?"

"The papers he left behind, his notes, his diaries, old photo albums from his active period. What do I know?" Waltin turned up his hands. Not everyone's like you, Erik, he thought.

Berg shook his head and dragged his hand along his chin.

"This doesn't sound very plausible. It's standard procedure for the responsible authority to see to such things when someone leaves. That would be violating the whole basic principle for this operation."

Sure, and the stork is the father of all children, thought Waltin.

"Okay," said Berg. "We have to find out what this character is actually up to."

"Intellectual inheritance," said the special adviser, looking at Berg with his customary wry smile. "What does he mean by that?"

"That's what we're going to find out," said Berg. "I really don't believe he's shown up here to gather material on his uncle's time with the embassy in Stockholm."

"I've read Krassner's so-called investigative reporting," said the special adviser. "The content and intellectual substance, not to mention the language, instill me with a more than slight sense of unease. Not least considering the fact that Buchanan was his uncle."

"We're going to find out what he's up to," said Berg with emphasis.

"And I should be much obliged to you if you could do that," said the special adviser and nodded without the slightest hint of a smile.

Waltin disbelieved Forselius. A senile old man who surely took every opportunity to get himself a little socializing on his own terms and at a low price in an otherwise meaningless existence. In addition he could not for his life understand what it was that could be so important. With all due respect to Sweden's political history—for Berg had hinted at that every time he asked—even the media usually let go of such things after the customary run of a few weeks, and as far as he was concerned the whole subject left him cold. Waltin preferred living in the present, but his boss hadn't given him any choice.

Despite his doubts, Waltin had been compelled to engage more people. He had viewed this as a simple and practical way to get closer to little Jeanette, who was actually only seventeen years old. What all of this was really about was just him and her, and in the scenario he had planned there was definitely no place for a lot of younger, testosterone-laden colleagues. It was bad enough that she had chosen to approach that black guy who was living in the same corridor as Krassner. Black men had gigantic cocks; Waltin knew that for he had read it in a dissertation that dealt with the length and thickness of the penises of entire groups of inducted draftees from various countries. It was an international study carried out by the U.N., and the statistics that the African member countries reported were, to put it bluntly, frightening. In addition he had seen this with his own eyes when his German colleagues at Constitutional Protection had dragged him along to a private sex club outside of Wiesbaden after a security conference a few years earlier.

It hadn't been altogether simple to scrape together a functioning and fully manned surveillance group, and before he got the whole thing in place he had been compelled to dispatch a few from his own operation. He tried to make the best of the matter and carefully informed little Jeanette that the only person she was to have personal contact with, in her new role as liaison and coordinator, was himself, but the very fact that there were others around her, young, well-trained male police officers who, when it came right down to it, had only one thought in their crew-cut heads, was enough to bother him. One of them was named Martinsson but was generally known as Strummer—an extraordinarily remarkable nickname for a policeman. He had just turned thirty, played guitar and wrote his own songs, and wore his long hair hanging loose. He had already acquired his nickname when he was in the academy and surely after having lubricated a good many female police officers. Waltin himself had picked him from the narcotics unit with the Solna police a little more than a year earlier, but this was hardly a person that he wanted to get close to a young, innocent girl like Jeanette, who was only seventeen years old.

Whatever. Early on Thursday morning, the thirty-first of October, Martinsson's immediate chief made a phone call to Waltin. Might the police superintendent have a chance to meet with him and young Martinsson? They had possibly found an in to Krassner.

"Tell me," said Waltin and nodded toward Martinsson, who was on the other side of the gigantic desk, admiring himself in the mirror on the wall behind Waltin's back. "Göransson, here," Waltin, with a turn of his head indicated Martinsson's twenty-years-older and somewhat balding boss, "is saying you've found an opening for us."

Martinsson nodded. Leafed through his black notebook with his sleeves rolled up so that the surrounding world would be able to enjoy the play of muscles on his forearms.

"I believe so, chief," said Martinsson. "It was me and the guy who took over his case yesterday evening."

"I see," said Waltin, pinching his well-pressed trousers.

"It was the press club as usual. I went along inside. He was talking with a few of our own assets and among others with that Wendell from *Expressen,* and he had some younger female hacks with him, one of them had fucking decent tits. Lots of ladies around that man—Wendell, that is."

"Yes," said Waltin and sighed quietly. Get to the point if you don't want to go back to the patrol cars, he thought.

"He left right before one, and for once he was a little drunk—he had five beers instead of the normal two. He's a little guy," Martinsson said in a tone of voice that naturally followed from the fact that he was twice as big and four times as strong.

Whatever that has to do with things, thought Waltin, who himself was just slightly above average height.

"So I followed him on foot," said Martinsson.

And here I thought you were watching him from the air, thought Waltin wearily. "Yes," he said.

"He took the direct route down to doper square and the first person he runs into is Svulle Svelander."

"Svulle?" said Waltin.

"Jan Svulle Svelander, well-known pusher, well-known junkie, he's been at it since Noah's ark. Tattooed over his whole body so he looks like a Brussels carpet. Has a rap sheet long enough to wind it twice around a hot-dog stand."

"And what did they do then?" asked Waltin, even though he already knew the answer.

"He bought grass," said Martinsson. "Krassner bought grass from Svulle. A fucking lot of grass, in fact."

CHAPTER VII

Between Summer's Longing and Winter's End

Albany, New York, in December

[SUNDAY, DECEMBER 8]

It wasn't like along the Ångerman River; there it was flatter and broader, and the water usually flowed gray and turgid between the green, forest-clad hills, which faded into blue and disappeared along with the sky far away. The sky was always blue when it was summer, and Lars Martin and Mama and Papa and all his siblings used to take the car and trailer down to Kramfors to do shopping and see Aunt Jenny and live it up in town and eat herring and meatballs and watch Papa swallow his shots from Aunt Jenny's cut-crystal glass.

"How you doing, kids?" Papa used to say and wink at them just before he drank his shot, and then he used to tousle Lars Martin's hair because he was the littlest of the ones whose hair he could still tousle. Lars Martin's little sister was of course even smaller, but she was so little that she mostly lay in her basket and peeped when she didn't get the breast from Mama, and Papa never used to tousle her hair.

One time when Lars Martin came out onto the farmyard he had seen his father lift up the whole basket and the baby carriage in which it sat, and then his father had walked around with his little sister and the basket and the baby carriage and said something that Lars Martin didn't hear. He

191

had just hugged it all and put his head down into the basket and mumbled something. Then Lars Martin got sad and decided to leave it all behind, and he walked on the old road south toward Näsåker, and when he had been walking for several hours, and there really wasn't any way back, his big brother had suddenly shown up and taken him by the arm and asked him what in the name of all the devils of hell he was up to. Then he got to sit on his big brother's shoulders the whole way home and it wasn't at all as far as he had thought. And pretty soon he stopped crying too.

But this was something else, thought Lars Martin Johansson from his comfortable window seat. For this was no river in Ångermanland but rather an American river, and sometimes it was deep and sometimes it was shallow and sometimes it was narrow and sometimes it was broad and all together it was exactly like the rivers in the matinee films that he used to see at the cinema at Folkets Hus back home in Näsåker when he was only a child. Drums were heard in the background, and Indians built fires and sent smoke signals to each other and the cavalry came galloping with only minutes to spare while the trumpets blared and he and all the other kids in Näsåker cheered.

He hadn't discovered any Indians, but after a little less than an hour's journey he had seen the star-spangled banner fluttering on a high promontory on the opposite side of the river. West Point, thought Johansson, feeling the draft from the right wing of the eagle of history sweep past him at rather close range, and less than two hours later he was there. There was whirling snow in the air and the temperature was in the midteens, and there was only one taxi in the parking lot outside the station.

"Two-hundred-and-twenty-two Aiken Avenue," said Johansson and leaned back in the seat while he pondered what he would say. If she's even home, he thought gloomily, for suddenly he regretted the entire trip and even that he had gone to the United States at all, which had actually been decided long before and didn't have a thing to do with his private expedition.

. . .

Best to let the taxi wait until I see that she's home, thought Johansson when they had stopped outside a large white house with a porch, mansard roof, at least two bay windows, and a tree decorated with lights on the drive.

"Can you wait?" Johansson asked the taxi driver, who nodded, shrugged his shoulders, and mumbled something he didn't hear.

Big house, thought Johansson. It stands to reason that she would have a family, although she was listed alone in the phone book; if there was a man in the house, snow-shoveling was clearly not his great passion. Johansson congratulated himself yet again on the purchase of his new American shoes, and now he was standing on her porch and lights were on inside and he even heard music, and there really was no going back. Johansson sighed, took a deep breath, and rang the doorbell.

She was small, with a mop of frizzy red hair. Rather pretty, thought Johansson when she nodded at him with polite expectation, making note of his taxi down on the driveway from the corner of her eyes.

"I am looking for Sarah Weissman," said Johansson politely.

"Yes," she said. "That's me."

"My name is Lars M. Johansson," said Johansson.

"Finally," she said and smiled broadly with white teeth. "An honorable Swedish cop. Guess if I've been waiting."

CHAPTER VIII

Free falling, as in a dream

Stockholm in November

Waltin's entire childhood had revolved around illness, suffering, and death; it was his mother who led him onto that path at an early stage. As long as he could recall—his first memories went back to the age of three—she had been steadily dying of everything that could possibly be looked up from A to Z in *The Home Medical Book,* and treatment or relief were all too seldom to be found in her own dog-eared copy of *The Complete Drug Reference.* There was a daily drama in their existence together as they were tossed between her acute gallstone inflammations, colic, migraines, and asthma attacks. There was also a more drawn-out suffering in the form of a cancer that was eating her up from the inside while psoriasis, all kinds of allergies, and common eczema nibbled away at her exterior. There was also a mother's heart, which like a flickering flame pressed her thin blood cells through hopelessly atrophied and calcified blood vessels while her lungs, liver, and kidneys continuously failed. She spent most of her time at various hospitals, rest homes, and doctor's offices while little Claes and his upbringing were left to a slightly retarded housekeeper his mother had inherited from her father, who, practically enough, had been a wealthy man who had had the good taste to die early.

Waltin had few memories of his own father, because for the most part he had been absent until he disappeared for good when little Claes was about five and his father moved to Skåne to marry his mistress. It was then that his mother had finally been offered the opportunity to add a more psychiatrically oriented aspect to her disease profile.

Waltin promised his mother at an early age that he would become a doctor when he grew up. When he and his playmates captured bumble-bees and grasshoppers in matchboxes, his friends used to play radio, but he chalked a red cross on the matchbox and used it as an ambulance. The patients were often in bad shape and they were immediately transported to the Claes Waltin Clinic, where the professor and head of the clinic himself operated on them with a surgical kit he had borrowed from his mother's sewing box, but despite all the resources that he brought to bear, as a rule all was in vain and mortality was total. It was only dear mother who survived, year after year after year, completely against the astronomical odds of her continual and immediate demise.

When at last his mother departed earthly life, it was in the most unexpected and banal manner. Bloated on port wine and high on pills, she had fallen off the platform at the Östermalm subway station en route to her daily visit to the doctor; it had taken a whole train to put an end to her lifelong suffering. Claes was at the university, studying law. He had given up his plans to become a doctor long before, which was practical considering his wretched grades. As a human being he was fully formed; lies were the breath of life for him; he was a warm and very charming psychopath with a strong interest in women, whom he hated deeply and heartily, without realizing it. When his dear mother finally died it had been the first real step forward in his life.

He had also found her will in the nick of time, which undoubtedly spared him a great deal of hardship. It was twenty pages long and began with a long list of donations to various organizations for the most frequently occurring causes of death, with the exception of tropical diseases. The funeral was not to be shabby either, and the list of specially invited mourners included fifty-some members of the capital's medical profession in private practice. He himself chose a more practical solution: a coffin of pressed cardboard with a funeral pall that the parish loaned out for free, no flowers, and no one invited and how sweet the sound, and as soon as the touching ceremony was over and done with—he had wept for joy the whole time—he had seen to it that they cremated the old lady and tossed out the ashes in a wooded area of the northern cemetery where there was no risk that he would end up even by chance.

· · ·

His good luck had also held up during the following years. He had completed a degree in law so mediocre that he would scarcely have been able to serve in court in Haparanda. He couldn't even intern in a prosecutor's office, so the only thing that remained was to apply to police-chief training. This he had managed brilliantly, and he had celebrated his degree by sticking a chair leg up the vagina of a simple woman of the people, just a little too far. But fortunately she had the good judgment not to file a complaint, contenting herself with financial compensation that he could easily afford. He decided to truly exert himself in the future to improve his precision in the sexual arena. His fantasies were fragile things, his sexual instincts a constant balancing act, difficult enough without an unsympathetic environment becoming informed of his somewhat special preferences.

Then he met Berg, who wasn't even half as shrewd as everyone believed, and Berg had picked him for the secret police. Then when the time was ripe and the external operation started to be built up he had become its first head, and as such he was successful, well liked, and in all essentials invulnerable. Certainly there were problems, but problems existed to be solved and he had seldom lost the game. He wasn't planning to do so now either, when it was a matter of finding out what this mysterious character John P. Krassner was actually up to with his wanderings from the student dormitory where he was living to various libraries and archives, and regular evening visits to the press club's bar on Vasagatan.

That fool Martinsson had given him a possible way in, and because this was Berg's project he had discussed it with him thoroughly. What did Berg think about turning the matter into a normal narcotics case? A simple house search where first you put Krassner in the pokey and scared the shit out of him, then went through his earthly and intellectual possessions in peace and quiet. Berg had been unencouraging to say the least, and in a way that signaled that he had carefully prepared his counterarguments.

Krassner was a very sly type, Berg maintained, however it was he knew that—for according to Waltin's own little female informant he seemed mostly nervous, high-strung, and increasingly paranoid—and under no circumstances was he to be alerted before they had found out what little secrets he was sitting on. Should it prove that these were

pure products of imagination, Berg obviously had no objections to concluding the whole thing with an indictment for narcotics-related crimes
for which Krassner would get a month or two at a Swedish correctional
facility before being deported. But that was out of the question before
they were completely sure of the matter. If Krassner was dealing in hard
goods, a narcotics intervention could even backfire and be seen as an
unadulterated provocation on the part of the secret police, a planting of
evidence with the simple intention of concealing shocking things of a
completely different magnitude.

"We both well know how such things are," Berg asserted. "Just think
about those so-called Information Bureau whistle-blowers. They were
out and running around again before the ink had time to dry on their
convictions. One year for spying, that's not even a bad joke."

Waltin contented himself with nodding, for he already saw the practical consequences, and, as he was the one who would be handling
them, there was no reason at all to discuss them with anyone, least of all
with the person who was his boss.

"I'm counting on you, Claes, and I also believe we're starting to be
short on time." Berg nodded seriously, and with that, everything that
needed to be said was said.

What remained was quite simply an ordinary break-in, thought
Waltin. Or more correctly stated, an uncommon break-in, as the victim
of the crime wouldn't even be allowed to suspect that he had had a visitor in that home, which, however temporary, was nonetheless his castle.
This wasn't the first time Waltin had planned such an effort. On the contrary, he had done it so often that nowadays he only had an approximate
sense of the number of "concealed house searches" in his top-secret personal record. No big deal about that, besides, for the classified special
legislation that the government had put in the hands of the organization
he served gave him and his cohorts all the room for action they needed.

It wasn't the legal problems that worried him. It was the purely practical execution of the effort that seriously disturbed him. To enter
through a window bolted from the inside situated on the sixteenth story
was completely out of the question, even if he had the option of lowering someone from the room above. But because it was rented out to a
known left-wing activist who used his free time to sell *The Proletarian*

outside the city's state liquor stores and was otherwise always sitting home thinking up various activities to bring down society, he didn't even need to consider that alternative. Besides, hundreds of people lived on the other side of the street; based on experience, at least a few of them would discover what was going on and immediately contact the police department's central switchboard. And as there was a good chance that the person concerned might fall and be killed, there would certainly be no lack of available patrol cars that would pounce on such a call.

What remained was to go in the normal way. Through the door to the corridor where eight rooms and seven different renters were squeezed together into just over a thousand square feet. Krassner's room was at the far end. These were not ordinary renters, either. Two of them were in SePo's register of various leftist movements. The third was that South African the socialist union had dragged here, and you hardly needed to work for the secret police to calculate where he stood politically. The fourth was Krassner himself, almost paranoid according to the operative on the scene. Remaining were an apparently well-trained student at GIH who had head-butted a security guard when he was in high school, along with a technologist and a student at the business school about whom he didn't know anything negative that was documented. A real dream audience for a break-in, Waltin thought.

The lock itself wasn't a complicated one, and copies of the keys to the corridor door and to Krassner's room had been acquired with the help of an upright coworker at the property-management company that took care of the building. Of course he had done his part for the police detectives in their fight against drugs. He had kids himself and knew what it was about. "Just squeeze those damn pushers." At the same time keys were the least problem when you were working at Waltin's level; there were other things that troubled him more. How could he see to it that one of his most reliable officers could, undisturbed, make his way into Krassner's room to go through his papers and other belongings in peace and quiet? He would need at least an hour. Little Jeanette Eriksson had offered to do it herself, but that was completely out of the question for reasons that didn't have anything to do with risks. In Waltin's world this was not something that young women should be involved in. It was bad enough that she had made use of that black guy in order to get in the vicinity of Krassner. Now it was a matter of bringing her back home to headquarters as quickly as possible.

Krassner appeared extremely suspicious, hardly surprising considering whose "faithful squire" he had been, and one of the first days when Jeanette had visited the South African and contrived an errand to the kitchen, she had observed how he "taped a strand of hair" on the door when he went out.

In this case it was a little paper flag he had placed on the door's overhang, which of course would not still be there if anyone opened the door while he was away. A simple, standard measure among policemen, criminals, and those who were simply generally suspicious.

That suspiciousness also argued against emptying the corridor where Krassner and the others were living by creating some emergency situation, for example a false fire alarm. Such a solution also went against the principle of discretion, which Waltin placed uppermost in his professional practice. Involve as few as possible, do as little as possible, and be seen as little as possible. Microsurgery, quite simply, he thought.

Friday evening was the right time for a home visit to Krassner. The students would as a rule be out partying if they didn't have an exam or had decided to have a party in their own corridor. Friday evening, the twenty-second of November, thought Waltin after having looked at his calendar and consulted with little Jeanette. Then at least two of them would be going home to their parents, one would be at a party outside the building, and another two would receive free tickets to a pop concert that they themselves hadn't been able to acquire. Jeanette would take care of the South African. Krassner himself was his problem. Forselius, thought Waltin. It really was high time for the surly old bastard to pull his weight. One thing remained—finding a sufficiently capable operative to carry out such an operation. It was then that he happened to think of Hedberg. Quite naturally, because Hedberg was the only person he really trusted.

CHAPTER IX

Between Summer's Longing and Winter's End

Albany, New York, in December

[SUNDAY, DECEMBER 8]

The room they were sitting in was large and light, with a fireplace and generously proportioned bay window, walls covered with books, a giant-sized sofa in front of the fireplace, large easy chairs with footrests. Quite obvious that it had been furnished by someone considerably older than Johansson's hostess, and judging by her clothes by someone with considerably more conventional taste. Her parental home, thought Johansson. Educated, intellectual people with good finances.

She had offered him a cup of tea, and because Johansson didn't want to unnecessarily complicate things that were inherently simple he had accepted, despite the fact that he would have preferred coffee.

"Although perhaps you'd rather have coffee," she suggested as she served his tea in a large ceramic cup.

"Tea is just fine," said Johansson politely.

The cups were hers, in any case, he thought. Although otherwise there wasn't much that added up. If Krassner really was the scatterbrain that he had imagined, it agreed very poorly with the woman sitting in front of him: smiling, leaning slightly forward, palpably present and with curiosity shining from her big brown eyes. Hardly a deeply mourning ex-girlfriend for example, thought Johansson.

"Tell me," she said. "Before I die of curiosity."

Wonder if I can trust her? thought Johansson.

"Well," he said hesitantly. "I don't really know where I should begin."

"Begin at the beginning," she said, smiling even more broadly. "That's always the easiest."

Okay, thought Johansson and nodded. What do I really have to lose?

"It all begins with a shoe with a heel with a hole in it."

"A shoe with a heel with a hole in it? You mean a shoe with a hollow heel?"

So that's what it's called, of course, thought Johansson.

"Hollow heel, yes," said Johansson.

"Oh, Jesus," she said with delight. "And I'll bet it was on John's foot."

"Yes," said Johansson and nodded. "It was, but that's not the reason I'm here."

Naturally that's the pattern, thought Johansson a half hour later. You should always start at the beginning. He had told about the annoying little scrap of paper with his name, title, and home address that they had found in the hollow heel, about Krassner's suicide, about Krassner's letter that had gone astray and that he hadn't yet been able to read, about the actual reason for his visit to the United States, about his own private reasons for now sitting on her couch. On the other hand, he hadn't said a word about the worry that he had also felt.

She hadn't said anything. Just listened and nodded while she let her tea stand, untouched. When he told about Krassner's suicide she stopped smiling and contented herself with nodding now and then. Serious, attentive eyes.

"Well, I guess that's all," said Johansson, making an explanatory gesture with his hands.

"Good that you came here," she said. "I've actually been trying to get hold of you."

Heavens, things are moving fast here.

"You'll be able to read his letter soon," she said. "I'm afraid that it's not especially enlightening, even if it does say quite a lot about John," she added, smiling again.

"But first you were thinking of saying a little about yourself," said Johansson.

"Exactly," she said. "And all policemen aren't stupid, are they?"

"Not all," said Johansson, shaking his head.

Then she told about herself and about her ex-boyfriend John P. Krassner, and if she had done so in the same way during an ordinary police interrogation, she would have bestowed eternal and everlasting credit on her interrogator.

Sarah J. Weissman, J. for Judith, was born in 1955. She was an only child; her parents had been divorced for the past ten years. Her mother had remarried and lived in New York, where she was working as an editor. Her father was a professor of economics, and the house they were sitting in was his. Five years earlier he was granted a professorship at Princeton and his daughter had moved in temporarily until he decided whether to sell his house. And because he was still thinking, she had stayed.

"A typical Jewish family," Sarah summarized, smiling broadly. "Not in that correct, tiresome way but rather more practically Jewish. You noticed the Christmas tree," she said, and giggled. "Here it's important to have a Christmas tree."

"Yes," said Johansson.

"And snow-shoveling," she said. "My neighbor usually shovels for me, despite the fact that his wife yells at him, but now they've gone to Florida."

"I can take care of that if you'd like," said Johansson, for he had learned to do that even as a little boy. Both what he should say and how he should do it.

"I can certainly believe that," she said, nodding, "but it will get warmer after the weekend so I think I'll take a chance and wait."

"What kind of work do you do yourself?" asked Johansson.

A little bit of everything, it appeared. Since she completed her degree in English and history at the university she had started working freelance for several book publishers in New York; it was her mother who had opened the door to that line of business, and her main activity the last few years had been collecting information and fact-checking.

"Both nonfiction and novels. Just now I'm working on a novel about the Civil War, by one of the publisher's best-selling authors. The author is quite pleased with me. Refuses to work with anyone else."

I can imagine that, thought Johansson.

"She's even proposed," said Sarah, giggling with delight. "So just now we're having a little crisis."

Then she suddenly became serious again.

"John," she continued. "I'm going to tell about John, I promise to pull myself together."

Then she told about John. It took only a quarter of an hour and when she was through, Johansson had put all the pieces in place. I wasn't far off, he thought.

"Now you've pieced it together, right?" she asked, looking at him contentedly.

"Yes," said Johansson and smiled reluctantly. "Now it makes more sense."

"I saw that on your face at the start," she said. "That you hadn't really pieced it together."

Sarah and John had met at the university. She was eighteen, young and inexperienced. He was two years older and, if one were to believe everything he said, which she did at that time, he was a very experienced and exciting young man besides. In addition he looked good, so when her parents separated, she responded by moving into a student apartment at the university with John.

"Dad really hated John," she said delightedly, "and because I always loved my dad more than anyone else it was actually rather logical. That John and I moved in together, I mean. My dad is a very wise man," she added, serious again. "He's so wise that he's actually never accomplished anything practical, and where John was concerned he was completely right."

She sat silent a moment before she continued.

"John's dad disappeared with another woman when John was very small, so he grew up with his mom and her brother. Uncle John. John was christened after his uncle; he was the one who became his father figure when he was growing up."

"Yes," said Johansson. What should I say? he thought.

"Two of those kind of shrewd, dishonest, really thirsty, and naturally prejudiced Irishmen. You can become a Jew for less," summarized Sarah without the least hint of a smile. "His mom died from cirrhosis of the liver a few years after we'd met and her brother no doubt simply drank himself to death, if I may say so. He died last spring. He was a really horrid sort. He was a professor here at our own university, SUNY Albany, but they were forced to fire him in spite of the fact that he had a really special background and in spite of the fact that it was no doubt our own government that paid his salary."

"Why is that?" said Johansson. What does she mean? he thought.

"I'm getting to that," said Sarah calmly.

The apple hadn't fallen far from the tree, and if that was due to inheritance or environment or a little of each was actually uninteresting because either way she was the one who had to suffer. Young John had a great amount of knowledge, to a small degree factual but in everything essential fictional. He'd been involved in one thing after another and borrowed almost everything from other people, and mostly from his uncle.

She figured that out quite soon after they moved in together, and then it had only gotten worse. Already that first year, although he was still so young, he had started drinking heavily like the Irishman he was and smoking even more, and finally he hit her, for that's what a real man did when she talked back.

"That was why I broke up with him," she said, looking seriously at Johansson. "He hit me good and hard and afterward I thanked God for every punch. Then I broke up with him. Although it took more than two years."

"I see," said Johansson.

"So then he tried to take his own life," said Sarah. "It wasn't a bad performance, I can assure you. We were living on the third floor. It was, maximum, fifteen feet from the balcony to the lawn below, so it was completely impossible to kill yourself and it was certainly my fault, that too. As a suicide attempt it was exactly like everything else he dreamed up."

"And yet you became his heir," said Johansson. When he did it for real, he thought.

"Yes, he was like that. If there was something that didn't fit, he just thought it away. He never got over my breaking up with him. He's kept in contact the whole time, even though it's been ten years. He'd call me in the middle of the night, often just to tell me that he had met a new girlfriend." Sarah sighed, with a certain feeling, as it appeared. "And to anyone who could bear to listen, he always said that we were still together."

"I see," said Johansson.

What do you say about such things? he thought.

"He seems to have been a little strange," said Johansson, smiling tentatively.

"He was completely nuts," said Sarah. "But that wasn't the biggest problem."

"So what was it?" asked Johansson.

"In four words," she said, "he was no good." She put emphasis on each syllable.

"That letter he wrote," said Johansson divertingly. "Might one be able to take a look at that?"

"Certainly," said Sarah. "I'll get it right away, but there's one thing I don't really understand."

"Shoot," said Johansson, smiling.

"You say that he took his own life. How sure are you of that?"

Murder, suicide, accident, thought Johansson. Then he recounted Jarnebring's and his own conclusions, with special emphasis on the note that Krassner had left behind.

"The paper was sitting in his own typewriter, it's typed on the same machine, we've compared the text with the impressions on the color ribbon that was in the typewriter. In addition, his own fingerprints are on the letter. In just those places where they should be."

"A suicide note," said Sarah. "So John is supposed to have left a letter where he said he was going to take his own life?"

"Yes," said Johansson. "A suicide note, that's how we interpret it."

"May I take a look at that letter?" said Sarah.

"Of course," said Johansson. "I brought a copy with me—a photocopy of the original," he clarified. "The original is still in Stockholm. It's in the investigation file."

Johansson took out the copy from the inner pocket of his sport coat and handed it over to Sarah.

"Here it is," he said.

"I have lived my life caught between the longing of summer and the cold of winter. As a young man I used to think that when summer comes I would fall in love with someone, someone I would love a lot, and then, that's when I would start living my life for real. But by the time I had accomplished all those things I had to do before, summer was already gone and all that remained was the winter cold. And that, that was not the life that I had hoped for."

Sarah set aside the letter and looked seriously at Johansson.

"And this is the letter that you believe John would have written?"

"Yes," said Johansson.

"He didn't," said Sarah, shaking her head decisively.

"Why do you think that?"

"I don't think," said Sarah. "I know, and I can give you a million reasons."

"I'm listening," said Johansson.

"It isn't that I'm jealous," she said and smiled wryly. "It isn't that he harped on for ten years that I was the only woman in his life, for he did that even when he'd hit me. It's not that."

What is it then? thought Johansson and contented himself with nodding. I'm not the one who was together with that bastard, he thought, suddenly feeling a slight irritation.

"I'm not a police officer but I'm good at English," said Sarah. "American English, British English, pidgin English, slang English, go-fuck-yourself English, you-name-it English. I'm even good at Her Majesty the Queen's English."

She smiled as she looked at Johansson with her large brown eyes.

"How shall I put it?" she said. "John was no better at English than most Americans, and he definitely didn't write this."

"He didn't?"

"No way," said Sarah, "and because you're still wondering if you can ask, I'm telling you that the person who wrote this is neither an American nor an Englishman. If I were to guess, I'd say someone who does not speak English as their native language, but who still writes and speaks it more or less fluently. A man, definitely a man, who in addition seems to have a poetic disposition or, more correctly, a poetic ambition."

Like those poems I wrote when I was a boy, thought Johansson, nodding as he tried hard to appear sharp. She's a little too clever, he thought. It's crucial to be on your guard here.

"It's nothing you recognize," said Johansson. "A quotation, I mean."

"No," said Sarah, shaking her head. "It's not that good."

"Hm," said Johansson, looking as though he were thinking deeply. "I still think it was your old boyfriend who wrote it. Purely technically, I mean," he added quickly when he saw that she was preparing to object.

"What I mean is the following," Johansson clarified. "I believe that he's the one who sat and wrote this on his own typewriter. He's the one who put the paper in the typewriter and wrote out the text. He even made a few corrections that you do when you're copying off of something and discover that you've made a typo. And I don't believe that anyone forced him to do it."

Sarah nodded. Didn't appear completely dismissive of the idea.

"Could it be that he copied something written by someone else?"

Sarah suddenly looked rather pleased.

"I could certainly imagine that. That sounds just like John."

"So why did he do it?" asked Johansson.

"Don't know," said Sarah, shrugging her shoulders. "But that's not the big problem."

"What is it then? The big problem?"

"John would never take his own life," said Sarah and nodded with emphasis.

"How do you know that?"

"He was far too pleased with himself," said Sarah. "He would rather die than take his own life," she said, smiling.

So he would, thought Johansson, but he didn't say that. He contented himself with nodding.

"That letter he sent me," he reminded her.

"I'll get it," she said. "I have it in my office."

Perhaps a bit too round, thought Johansson, looking after her back as she disappeared out into the hall. Although she moves easily. Whatever that has to do with anything, he thought.

Finally, thought Johansson when just over three minutes later he was sitting with Krassner's letter in his hands.

A common white envelope covered with postmarks, stamps, various internal postal notations, and three handwritten addresses. In addition it was opened, neatly opened with the aid of a letter opener.

"I'm the one who opened it. We'll discuss that later. Read."

Judging by the first postmark it had been sent from the post office on Körsbärsvägen to Johansson's own post office on Folkungagatan on Södermalm in Stockholm, Friday, the eighteenth of October. Poste restante Police Superintendent Lars M. Johansson. The recipient's title and name were written in a neat female hand.

Pia Hedin, thought Johansson as his heart, for reasons which weren't really clear to him, beat a little faster.

Monday, the eighteenth of November, it had been returned, judging by the postmark, to the post office on Körsbärsvägen. There it had remained until Thursday, the twenty-eighth of November, when the same neat female hand had taken care of forwarding it to John P. Krassner, care of Sarah J. Weissman, 222 Aiken Avenue, Rensselaer, NY 12144 USA.

You can forget about fingerprints on the envelope, thought Johansson, but nevertheless as a matter of routine he held it by its farthest left corner between the nails of his left thumb and index finger while he carefully slid out the typewritten paper that lay inside, folded in the middle.

"You're doing it cop style," asserted an apparently charmed Sarah.

"Yes," said Johansson, unfolding his letter. "It's an old occupational injury that I have."

"I love the way you're doing that," said Sarah, giggling. "Are Swedish detectives always that gentle with their hands?"

"Not all," said Johansson, smiling wanly.

The short text seemed to have been written on Krassner's typewriter. The letter was dated Thursday, October 17, addressed to Police Superintendent Lars M. Johansson; Johansson translated as he read:

Dear Police Superintendent Lars M. Johansson,

My name is John P. Krassner. I am a researcher and journalist from the U.S. We don't know one another, but I got your name from one of my Swedish contacts, a very well-known Swedish journalist who mentioned that he knew you well and that you were an honorable, uncorrupted, and very capable Swedish police officer who doesn't shy away from the truth no matter how frightening it might be.

I've written this letter as a kind of security measure, and if you have the occasion to read it, unfortunately it means that I have most probably been killed by persons within the Swedish military intelligence service or the Swedish secret police or the Soviet military intelligence service GRU.

The reason for my being in your country is that I am in the process of finishing a large-scale investigative report that I have worked on for several years. I am going to publish my investigation in the form of a book early next year. It is going to be published by a large American publisher but at the present time I am prevented from saying which publisher this concerns. The facts that I recount are however such that they are going to alter the entire security and political situation in northern Europe and not least in your own country.

I have comprehensive documentation to support what you'll be able to read in my book. These are in secure storage along with the manuscript of the book, in a secret safe-deposit box which I have the use of. I have instructed my old girlfriend Sarah

Weissman to turn these papers over to you, so that you can see to it that justice is done in your own country.

Sincerely,

John P. Krassner

What the hell is this? thought Johansson and looked inquiringly at his hostess.

"It's a typical John P. Krassner letter," said Sarah Weissman and smiled faintly, as if she were a mind reader. "I know, because I've received a few hundred in the past ten years."

So that's how it is, thought Johansson.

"I don't understand what he means," said Johansson. "It's true that Sweden has both a military-intelligence service and a secret police, but I can assure you that they really don't run around murdering people. Least of all American journalists."

"Ah! You think the Russkies did it," said Sarah and winked.

"That I find extremely hard to believe," said Johansson. "Considering how he died, I mean."

"Me too," said Sarah. "And if I hadn't found out that he actually had died, I would have thrown it away, just as I've done with all his other letters. It was in my mailbox when I came home from New York last Friday. I was there working for a few days. I don't usually read other people's letters, actually, but considering what's happened . . . well, you understand."

"I understand," said Johansson, nodding.

"He sent a similar letter to me about a month ago," said Sarah. "In that one he reported that he was in Sweden on a secret assignment. He was like that. John's entire life was a Top Secret Mission. He could be completely out of it. When we moved in together he used to tape strands of hair on the door if we went out, to check if anyone had sneaked in while we were gone. I hardly dared sleep at night."

"Did it say anything else?" said Johansson.

"It said something about you," said Sarah, smiling. "It said that one of his, quote, secret Swedish informants, end quote, had given him the name of a, quote, honorable Swedish cop, end quote. And if something happened to him I was to see to it that you got the letter that he sent to you poste restante, which was I suppose almost a guarantee that you never would have received it, but because John was the way he was . . ." Sarah shrugged her shoulders in a meaningful way.

"Tough shit," said Johansson, smiling.

"To say the least," said Sarah. "In addition I was to make copies of all of his secret documents for you," she continued. "So that my mom and I could arrange a publisher for him and his so-called book."

"I understand," said Johansson. The fellow doesn't seem to have been quite right in the head, he thought.

"So you can just forget that nonsense about the major publisher that he was unfortunately prevented from saying anything about. It was a typical John publisher. Existed only in John's head."

"Might one be able to read that letter that he wrote to you?" Johansson asked.

"No," said Sarah, shaking her head. "You can't because I've thrown it away. I threw away all his letters, and you would have done the same."

The key that was in the hollow heel, thought Johansson.

"Those papers," said Johansson. "That he was supposed to have in a safe-deposit box. Do you know what they are?"

"Not a clue," said Sarah. "The only thing I know is that it's my safe-deposit box."

A little more than six months earlier, a month or so after John's uncle had died, John got in touch with Sarah and asked her to rent a safe-deposit box in her name but for his use. He needed it to store certain "secret and very sensitive documents" with which he was working. Sarah had refused at first but because he nagged and nagged and nagged she had finally given in. Under certain conditions, however.

"That I kept one of the keys and that if he put the least little thing whatsoever into it that might be suspected to contain something illegal, then I would personally carry all of it to the police."

"And he went along with that?" said Johansson.

"Of course," said Sarah. "I guess that was what he was hoping for. That I would go and snoop in his little deposit box and become his own little secret coconspirator."

"Did you ever check what he had in the safe-deposit box?" asked Johansson.

"Yes," said Sarah. "It had been about a month since I'd rented it and because I was at the bank anyway on other business I actually did that."

"Well," said Johansson, smiling. "What did you find then?"

"It was empty," said Sarah. "It was a typical John safe-deposit box."

But after that she hadn't checked the safe-deposit box. When she received the letter that she threw away she hadn't even thought about doing so. When she found out that he had died she still hadn't thought about doing so. And when she read John's letter to Johansson, it was a Friday evening and the bank was closed for the weekend.

"They open tomorrow at nine o'clock," said Sarah. "So you can get your papers then."

Since I'm here anyway I might as well do it thoroughly, thought Johansson.

"Is there a nice hotel here in town?" he asked.

"Yes," said Sarah, smiling. "The Weissman Excelsior is the very best and you can even sleep in dear Dad's bed."

"I don't want to be a nuisance," said Johansson.

"Not a nuisance in the least," said Sarah. "But there is one thing I'm wondering about."

"Yes?"

"I actually tried to phone you yesterday," she said. "When I'd read the letter that John sent to you, I tried to call you at home. In Sweden."

"I have an unlisted number."

"I know," said Sarah. "I spoke with directory assistance in Stockholm. Then I called your office too. The Swedish National Police Board, the Swedish FBI. John wrote that you were head of an FBI. The Big Boss."

Oh, well, thought Johansson and smiled weakly.

"And what did they say?" he asked.

"That I should call on Monday during office hours and talk with your secretary. I also spoke with someone on duty and he was very polite but no one was allowed to talk with you."

"Did you tell them your name?" asked Johansson. Where do all these curious women come from? he thought.

"Of course," said Sarah, smiling broadly. "I said that my name was Jane Hollander and I worked with the state police in Albany and that it was an urgent official matter."

Sigh, thought Johansson.

"Jane and I are old classmates," said Sarah, giggling. "She actually is a police officer and works with the state police, so it was almost true, but it still didn't help."

"Nice to hear," said Johansson and smiled.

"But you just show up and knock on my door. Just as easy as pie."

"Yes," said Johansson.

"So how did you do it?" said Sarah, looking at him with curiosity. "How did you actually find out about that letter with my address? I'll die of curiosity if you don't tell me."

"Pure chance," said Johansson modestly, "just pure chance."

"Pity," said Sarah ironically. "And here I'd gotten the idea that you were pretty smart."

"You said something about John's uncle," said Johansson, who wanted to change the subject.

"Yes, he was a really horrible person. Fortunately he died last spring. I thought we might go to his house so you could see how he lived. John was living there too the past few years."

"And that won't be a problem?" said Johansson.

"Not in the least," said Sarah happily. "It's my house now. First John inherited it from his uncle, and now I've inherited it from John. I was thinking about donating it as a summer camp for young black drug-users from New York," said Sarah delightedly.

"Sounds interesting," said Johansson neutrally.

"It sure does," said Sarah. "They were the people John's uncle thought the very worst of. It's true that he hated almost everyone, but young black drug-users from New York were the ones he hated the very most. He's going to twirl like a propeller in his grave when he finds out about it. Then we can have dinner afterward. I know a really good place right in the neighborhood, a Vietnamese restaurant."

Vietnamese, thought Johansson. Good thing Jarnebring isn't along.

Practical business. First Johansson borrowed her phone and called his hotel in New York. After a certain amount of discussion and financial compensation, it had been arranged. It was good enough if he was out of his room before three o'clock the following day and because he was supposed to check in at Kennedy by six o'clock he at least had the time worked out. First the bank as soon as it opened in the morning, after that the train to New York, then the hotel to pack, pay, and check out. Then it would have to be a taxi to Kennedy to check in, a little quick Christmas shopping, and after that the evening plane directly home to Stockholm, where he would arrive on Tuesday morning. A completely feasible schedule, thought Johansson, and if he only had a little time left over he would phone work and see to it that one of his colleagues picked him up at Arlanda and drove him directly to the office.

Then he shoveled snow. Sarah had a car that was snowed in, in the garage, and all things considered, not least considering the next day, it was a better alternative than a taxi. Johansson started shoveling dressed in a sport coat; when he was through he was in his shirtsleeves, and despite the fact that the temperature was almost zero, he felt markedly refreshed. The garage door had frozen stuck, but after a few hefty pulls with his feet solidly on the ground it had come unstuck and could be opened. Inside was his reward: an almost new Volvo station wagon.

"You have a Volvo," said Johansson delightedly. "Why didn't you say so?"

"Surprise, surprise," said Sarah, smiling.

It was Johansson who got to drive, which was practical considering that his hostess had packed herself into an ankle-length red wool coat with hood, lined leather boots, and thick knitted mittens. For the most part only the tip of her nose protruded.

"I got the car from Dad," she said. "He wanted me to drive safely, but I think it's way too big."

"It's one of the safest cars there is. Your dad seems to be a very wise man," Johansson stated.

"Big, safe, and Swedish," said Sarah, beaming. "I'm glad you got to meet a relative."

Wonder if she's interested in me? thought Johansson.

On the way they stopped at a good-sized shopping center where Johansson bought a set of clean underwear, a shirt, and a toothbrush. For some reason all of these articles were on the same shelf right before the checkout counter.

What a peculiar country, thought Johansson. Wonder how many unplanned overnights there would have to be for it to be profitable to give them a shelf of their own, in Albany, more than three hours' drive north of New York, of all places?

"Can I help you, detective?" said Sarah and smiled inquiringly. She had lowered the hood of her winter coat and her frizzy red hair was like a halo around her head.

"No," said Johansson and nodded toward the shelf by the checkout. "There was just one thing I was thinking about."

"Planning for the unplanned," said Sarah and smiled.

This must be the cleverest woman I've ever met, thought Johansson, for of course he was like that himself as well.

Then they drove out to the house where John had lived before he went to Sweden, where he died.

What an extraordinarily lugubrious place, thought Johansson, who made it a point of honor to constantly expand his vocabulary. The house stood on a rise fifty yards from the road. It was built of brick that had turned black with age and was large enough to hold an entire summer camp of young drug-abusers. Turn-of-the-century American neo-Gothic, a mausoleum of gloominess that concealed its secrets behind tall lead-cased windows.

"What do you think?" said Sarah, smiling with delight. "It sure is cozy."

"I think you should sell it," said Johansson. "Otherwise those poor kids will take an overdose."

On the lower floor was a large hall that opened onto an even larger living room. Dark men's-club furniture from the era before the war, and rows of framed photographs crowded together on the sooty mantelpiece above the fireplace. On the brown-spotted wallpaper were light rectangular and square areas, evidence of paintings that had previously hung there. On the facing long wall was a pair of half-open double doors into a neighboring dining room, where merely sticking his head in caused Johansson to lose his appetite. It was untidy with a vengeance. Ashtrays overflowing with cigarette butts, crumpled cigarette packs, and dried-up apple cores, newspapers tossed on the floor, piles of books that had been taken off a bookshelf that was still leaning precariously. In the middle of the floor was a motley pile of outdoor rattan furniture barely covered up by a worn-out Oriental rug.

"Elegant, isn't it?" said Sarah.

The only thing Johansson looked at closely were the photographs on the mantelpiece. Twenty-some photos of one or several persons with frames of silver, pewter, and wood, and judging by the motifs they had been taken over a period of about fifty years. A man was pictured in all the photos except one, a portrait of a woman in early middle age. She was high-busted, had her hair set in a bun, wore a dress with a collar, and was staring sternly at the photographer.

"John's mother," said Sarah. "The reason she's staring like that is that as usual she's dead drunk. All the others are of his uncle, the colonel, visiting fine people that he's met."

"You say colonel," said Johansson. "I thought you said he was a professor."

"We'll discuss that later," said Sarah. "After you've looked at all his photos where he's visiting fine people that he'd met."

Not a bad summary, thought Johansson. In the photo where he was the youngest, the uncle was dressed in full academic regalia with a flat hat, black robe, and chain, courteously bowing toward a white-haired skeleton in the same getup. In the others as a rule he was dressed in uniform or double-breasted suit with broad lapels, and depending on the outfit he was either saluting or shaking hands with other men, without exception older than himself and, judging by their appearance, higher class as well. Two of them Johansson even recognized. The first from his school history textbook, for it was President Harry S. Truman, who, politely leaning forward, was shaking hands with Uncle Colonel-Professor, who, despite the broad-striped suit, was standing at stiff attention with his chin thrust forward and a steely glance. Who the hell is it that he resembles? thought Johansson.

In the other photo he was standing in dress uniform, saluting a small bulldog-like man who seemed to be looking at something else, unclear what but in any case outside the picture, and who quite recently, in a historical sense, had been host to Johansson and his colleagues: the legendary head of the FBI, founder of the FBI Academy in Quantico, J. Edgar Hoover. He resembles someone, thought Johansson with increasing irritation, and it wasn't Hoover, for he only resembled himself.

One of the photos was more informal. The colonel in his forties with a somewhat older man, both in double-breasted striped suits, smiling broadly toward the photographer with their arms around each other's shoulders. There was also summer and sun glistening on the waves of Strömmen in Stockholm with the palace in the background. It must have been taken outside the Grand Hotel, thought Johansson with surprise, and from force of habit he turned the photograph over. A brief handwritten text: "Comrades in the field, Stockholm, June 1945."

"My hometown," said Johansson delightedly, despite the fact that he had been born in the sticks north of Näsåker, and handed the photo over to Sarah. "This is Stockholm. You can see the Royal Palace in the background."

"Very nice," said Sarah politely. "Do you know who he's hugging?" she asked, giving the photo back.

No one I know, thought Johansson, shaking his head. "Not a clue."

"But Hoover you recognized," she said and smiled teasingly. "The fact is, here at home this man is almost as big a legend as Hoover. His name was Bill Donovan, known as Wild Bill. He was the first head of what in time became the CIA, although during the war it was called OSS, Office of Strategic Services. I believe it was in 1947 that they changed the name to CIA."

So that's how it was, thought Johansson and nodded. Who is it that he resembles? he thought. It wasn't Wild Bill Donovan, even if he and Uncle Colonel were rather like one another.

He thought of it on the stairway to the upper story. Of course, it's that human disaster Backstroem, thought Johansson with delight. Apart from the difference in age they could be identical twins, he thought.

"Special Agent Backstroem," said Johansson out loud to himself.

"Pardon?" said Sarah.

"It was nothing," said Johansson. "I was just thinking out loud."

It's strange how often you think of things when you're on a staircase, he thought.

On the upper story there was a hallway, and past that a narrow corridor with rows of doors to a half dozen bedrooms of varying size, besides one larger and one smaller bathroom.

"I was thinking about starting by showing you the colonel's room," said Sarah.

The colonel? The professor? A man with at least two strings on his lyre, thought Johansson.

Colonel John C. Buchanan had obviously had the use of the largest bedroom in the house, with his own bathroom. The furniture also provided a picture of the man who had lived there, even if a very curtailed one. Against the one short wall stood a tall, narrow bed with a mahogany headboard and frame that still held a mattress, although the linens were gone. On each side of the bed stood a nightstand of the same type of wood and on the one to the right of the pillow was an old-fashioned iron bed lamp with a parchment shade.

On the opposite wall stood an English desk and a desk chair in the same style with a high back and broad arms, upholstered in green leather. On the wall above the desk were ten or so lighter areas where paintings or photographs of various sizes had clearly been hanging, and the desktop was also completely empty of objects with the exception of an electroplated penholder.

The room had two high windows out toward the street, where Johansson could see Sarah's black Volvo. A cornice hung over heavy dark curtains, running on tracks, that could be pulled closed. On the opposite long wall toward the corridor stood a large green safe of 1970s vintage with a combination lock and the solid door standing ajar. Inside it was empty.

Empty, thought Johansson and looked at Sarah.

"You call him the colonel," he said, "but first you told me that he was a professor at the university in this city."

"Yes," said Sarah. "He was, in the formal sense—professor, that is. He wrote a dissertation in political science right before the war. I've never read it but Dad did when I started seeing John, and Dad was completely crazy for a whole month. He was as crazy as he usually gets when you award the year's Nobel Prize in economics."

Now she's smiling again, thought Johansson.

"Although he really was a colonel, I guess," said Sarah. "He became an officer when we entered the war and I believe he retired sometime in the early sixties. It was then he got that position at the university. It was an open secret that it was in gratitude for his time in the military. It's true they created a new professorship for him, in contemporary European history or something like that, and the lectures he gave attracted a certain amount of attention, to put it nicely, and he was always just called the colonel."

"What did he do in the military?"

"Intelligence officer," said Sarah, nodding decisively. "To put it simply, he worked for the CIA, or its precursor, the OSS. I said that already, didn't I? He did his service in Europe, among other places in your home country. He was at the embassy in Stockholm for several years. You saw the photo yourself down in the living room."

"You're quite certain that he worked for the CIA?" said Johansson.

"Quite certain," said Sarah, shrugging her shoulders. "That's what everyone said. John harped on it constantly and what other reason would there be to stand and hug someone like Wild Bill Donovan?"

And why did they take a photo when they did it? thought Johansson. I would think it must almost have been considered official misconduct in those circles.

"Did you ever meet him?" asked Johansson.

"I met him a few times when John and I were together. He was just as unhappy that John was seeing me as Dad was that I was seeing John, so on that point they were in agreement." Sarah smiled and shook her head. "He didn't like me," she continued.

"Why is that?" said Johansson. "Was he as crazy as his nephew?"

"Because I'm Jewish," said Sarah.

"I understand," said Johansson. How the hell do you respond to that, he thought.

Then they were in John's room. Considerably smaller and without a bathroom, but for the most part furnished along the same fundamental principles minus the safe and the heavy curtains but plus a TV, VCR, and radio cassette player. Clearly someone had lived in the room until quite recently, a person who wasn't especially orderly, at that.

"Housecleaning was never John's strong suit," declared Sarah.

That's not the problem, thought Johansson. Where are the traces of the person who's been living here?

On the wall above the desk hung an old oil painting depicting some horses grazing in a meadow, quite certainly something inherited from his uncle and of highly questionable value as a work of art. In addition a few framed posters, the most memorable of which was a photograph, grainily shot against the light, of a young, vulnerable Marilyn Monroe leaning over a balcony railing.

On the nightstand beside the bed was a clock radio. On the desk were some of the things usually found on a normal desk. An unwashed coffee cup, paper clips, brads, coins, and a number of pens, a cheap watch with a worn-out band, typing paper, and envelopes. A tall, adjustable table lamp screwed tightly onto a strong iron plate. A few paperback books, all of them mysteries or thrillers. But no bookcase, no calendar, no notebooks, no neatly organized albums with photographs, no private video-tapes or cassette tapes. Nothing at all.

It looked the same inside the large brown armoire on the short wall across from the bed: jackets, jeans, and shoes, shirts, undershirts, under-wear, and socks, stored all over the place, clean clothes mixed with dirty. On the floor was a golf bag with a half dozen clubs and stuck down among the clubs a Remington short-barreled semiautomatic 12-gauge shotgun. Loaded with a full magazine and to be on the safe side with a shell fed into the bore.

"What did he have this for?" Johansson asked as he drew the shell out and locked the safety catch.

"I don't know," said Sarah, shaking her head without the least hint of a smile. "He was just like that. Take it away, please."

Finally they walked around the house. They were even up in the attic and down in the cellar, and the first impression was also the only lasting impression that Johansson had. Most memorable was the enormous pile of empty bottles that they found in the cellar. A mountain of glass: bour-bon, Scotch, and Irish whiskey bottles plus a few hundred extra that had contained American vodka, and when Sarah saw the mountain she didn't lose her cheer.

"Did I mention that the old man drank a bit?" Another giggle.

Then they locked up and went to a Vietnamese restaurant only a few hundred yards farther down the street, lit up with paper lanterns and with its own Christmas tree before the entry.

Phenomenal food, although hardly something you would dare offer Jarnebring, thought Johansson a little more than an hour later. They had started with a soup made of something that looked like seaweed and that according to Sarah *was* seaweed, a very special and good-tasting sea-weed. After that they ordered some kind of Vietnamese ravioli filled with thin strips of smoked duck breast. Johansson drank beer while Sarah drank white California wine and talked and smiled for the most part the entire time.

First he asked her about the house they had just visited. Where were all the paintings, books, art objects, and other personal belongings that ought naturally to have been found in a house of that size? Sold, according to Sarah, over a period of years and apparently for the same reason that had brought about the death of their owner.

"I don't know what kind of pensions the CIA has," said Sarah. "I guess you'll have to call their office in Langley and ask."

It had been ten years since Sarah had been a guest in the house; according to her recollection it hadn't been so remarkably furnished even during the time when the colonel had also drawn a salary as a professor.

"It was mostly junk. Not that many books, and the art was roughly like that painting of the horses you saw in John's room. What I recall the best is that he had a lot of scrap metal with a military connection that he collected, a lot of helmets and swords and medals and that kind of thing. He himself was terribly proud of his collections. I doubt that he got millions for them, but it's clear they weren't completely worthless, I guess. This country is full of crazy people who collect such things."

Then Johansson had led the conversation on to John, and he'd done so using John's room as a starting point. What had bothered him, "as a cop," was not that the person who was living there seemed to be a real pig, for Johansson had seen considerably worse, but rather a pig who seemed to lack personal qualities and interests. You didn't like things like that if you were a policeman, which Johansson was.

Sarah had nodded in agreement. John was a slob who at the same time was conspicuously uninterested in generally accepted human means of enjoyment; a bed was something you slept in, clothes something you put on yourself because it was warm or cold or rained or snowed, and eating was something you did when you were hungry.

"Drinking beer, on the other hand, was something you could do all the time."

"He must have had some interests, don't you think?" Johansson persisted.

Few, according to Sarah. What he read were mostly just mysteries, spy novels, and other similar junk, and when he watched TV he seemed to change channels the whole time.

"He wasn't even interested in sports. That golf bag in his closet must be something he got from the colonel. I know that he was a member of a golf club for awhile, but that he resigned his membership when they started to accept black people."

Nice guy, thought Johansson, but he didn't say that.

"John didn't even like walking; he thought it was a waste of time. When we went out during the time we were together he used to station himself in the darkest corner of the bar and drink beer while he checked out girls and looked mysterious. He thought that was really exciting."

"But he must have done something," persevered Johansson, who was starting to get seriously interested.

"John was only interested in John. I don't think he was even interested in women, in spite of all the conquests that he bragged about. I believe it ran in the family. His uncle was completely uninterested in women. Everything he said and did only concerned other men. Women weren't part of the equation for him."

So that's how it was, thought Johansson, who had worked for more than twenty years as a policeman.

"A true member of the homoerotic society," Sarah summarized. "Of course he hated gays too."

"Did John have any friends?" asked Johansson.

"Lots," said Sarah and giggled. "What do you think?"

John had lived in his own little world. "The John World," in which there was no place for friends. There were only scoundrels great and small, spies and terrorists, and because he himself was one of the few remaining white knights, his life was in reality a mission.

"To unmask them and see to it that they ended up in jail. That was what life was all about for someone like John. Although he liked men like you. Big, strong cops, and if you'd met him I'm convinced that you would have kicked him in the butt within five minutes."

I see, one of those, thought Johansson, who had been a policeman for all of his adult life but had still never kicked anyone in the butt, for he used to let his best friend, Bo Jarnebring, take care of that detail for them both in those days.

"I'm quite certain that's why he became a journalist," Sarah concluded.

John had worked as a journalist for several years, and for a while he had even been employed as a reporter of some fame at the local TV station.

"He looked so good that no one heard what he said," Sarah explained. "But then he got ambitions and started at our largest local paper as an investigative journalist, and it was then that the shit hit the fan."

According to Sarah, that the shit hit the fan was ultimately due to the restaurant where they were eating, and the one who had seen to it that it hit where it did was actually not John but his uncle the colonel. The restaurant was owned by a Vietnamese family who had come over as boat people at the end of the seventies. They had quickly found economic success in their new homeland and today they owned and ran more than ten businesses in Albany and the surrounding area: restaurants, laundromats, and convenience stores as well as a building supply store and a large motel.

In the early eighties they had opened the restaurant where Johansson and Sarah were sitting, only a couple of stones' throws from the house where the colonel lived, and it was then too that the colonel had gone seriously crazy. Vietnamese were the Enemy, and as the Enemy they were riffraff, according to the colonel. "Not real warriors, just common gangsters," and as for the almost two hundred thousand of them who had fled to the United States, they were either communist infiltrators or common deserters who ought to have been shot on the spot. First he'd risen up from his drinking bench and gone around the neighborhood with a petition, but the interest among his neighbors had been tepid and instead it was getting more and more crowded at the newly opened restaurant. It was high alert and red alert and the colonel had succeeded in converting his nephew to the cause.

"Which unfortunately was not that difficult, I guess," Sarah said and sighed. "However it happened, John succeeded in getting the newspaper to start publishing a series of articles that we had a Vietnamese mafia on our hands. After two articles, publication was interrupted and to make a long story short, the newspaper had to pay a lot of money and John was fired."

"Was there anything that he wrote that was true, then?" Johansson asked, occupationally injured as he was.

"I can't imagine what," said Sarah. "It was certainly a typical John disclosure."

Then they had fruit for dessert, but when Sarah ordered green tea Johansson felt more than a slight hesitation.

"Do you think they have coffee at a place like this?" he asked, lowering his voice.

"Of course they do. Vietnamese aren't numbskulls. If I were you I would order a double espresso."

She's actually really pretty, thought Johansson. Although a little sharp perhaps.

It was Johansson who drove the black Volvo home to Sarah's. It's true that he had had two beers, but because they'd been sitting in the restaurant for almost three hours, and because he would never dream of doing it at home, it wasn't such a big deal. When they came back they had sat down in the living room and talked awhile. Sarah had asked him if he wanted to have wine, whiskey, or something else, but he had declined. Why—he didn't really know himself; he had just said no thanks, and therefore things had turned the way they had. After a rather short time the conversation had run out. She had shown him to his room, said good night, stood on her tiptoes, and given him a light kiss on the cheek as she smiled and nodded, and that's how it was.

Johansson brushed his teeth, put on his clean new American underwear, and crept down into her dad's bed, which was both large enough and hard enough for Johansson's requirements. Five minutes later he was sleeping, on his right side and with his arm under the pillow as he always did when he was at home, but without having followed his older brother's advice. How would that look, in her papa's bed? thought Johansson just before he fell asleep.

CHAPTER X

Free falling, as in a dream

Stockholm in November

In spite of everything Berg felt a certain confidence, even a certain increased confidence. True, this Krassner affair was not good, but up till now nothing had come out that was directly alarming. The signals he got from Waltin seemed to indicate the opposite. The fellow clearly abused narcotics, and considering the quantity he'd purchased it appeared not entirely impossible—if required, if it appeared that he was sitting on some essential secrets and the matter was going to become public anyway—that the police and the prosecutor would be able to sell him to the media as a cynical narcotics dealer and not just some ordinary drug-abusing academic. In such contexts it wasn't really a matter of whether what was said was true or false but rather of who was saying it.

According to Waltin and his officers there were also many other things indicating that Krassner was not in his right mind. High-strung, suspicious, almost paranoid: These were hardly qualities that furthered his objectivity and clarity, if things were so bad that his uncle had let the cat out of the bag about something that might have consequences for Berg and the interests he was employed to protect. Whatever that might be, thought Berg. With all due respect to Swedish security policy, regardless of whether you were talking about the official or the factual accounts, Krassner's uncle had ended his active service almost thirty years ago. He was dead, besides, so in that respect Krassner couldn't count on any active support from that quarter. You should take care not to see ghosts in the daytime, Berg decided, and at that point he had also started to view the situation more positively.

In the best case, perhaps this story could be turned to the advantage of Berg and the operation. It had already contributed to normalizing his relations with the prime minister's special adviser, and that was good enough. That this depended on the fact that, at least for the time being, he needed Berg more than Berg needed him was nothing to sulk about. Instead it gave him an opportunity to take the initiative, go on the offensive, and, he hoped, be able to win back some lost territory. At the first weekly meeting with his superiors in November, therefore, Berg had decided that he would only bring up two matters, and both were chosen with care. By himself of course.

However, he had not been able to avoid the brief introductory description of the situation. First he mentioned the ongoing survey of antidemocratic elements within the police and the military. "It's not going quickly, I'll be the first to admit that, but it's moving forward," said Berg, nodding confidently. None of his superiors had any questions or raised any objections.

After that something about the Yugoslavs—"it appears the situation is calm just now"—and finally the usual mantra about the Kurds, and it was then that the minister had come to life and everything started to go completely wrong, despite all of Berg's exertions.

"This Kudo," said the minister. "How's it going for him? It's been a while since we heard anything from that front."

Thank the good Lord for that, thought Berg without changing his expression.

"It's rolling along according to plan," said Berg. "I've told them to try to penetrate a little deeper into the special ethnic aspects of . . . yes, their communication, if I may say so. How they exchange secret messages and those kinds of things. We're often up against difficult questions of interpretation."

"Yes, it would be interesting to get to meet them some time," said the minister. "Yes, this Kudo here and his closest associate . . . what was it he . . ."

"Bülling," Berg interjected quickly, because he wanted to put an end to the misery.

"Exactly," said the minister and brightened noticeably. "Bülling, that sounds almost German."

"Or assumed," declared the special adviser with a light sigh.

"You mean as in *byling*, slang for 'cop,' " said the minister delightedly, for he was not stupid in that respect. "Rather inventive, it might even be said, almost a little bold."

"Bülling is actually a very bold person," said the special adviser, looking at the minister with almost closed eyes and a heavily corroborative nod. "Without exaggeration I would maintain that Bülling is probably the absolute boldest and bravest police officer in the corps."

"You don't say," said the minister, leaning forward in order to hear better. "Is there anything you can tell us about this?"

"It will have to stay in this room, then," said the special adviser, with a certain apparent hesitation. "Yes, he was the one who saved all those kids from that burning day-care center out in Solna a few years ago."

"Now that you mention it," said the minister with his forehead deeply creased. "I have some vague recollection."

"The whole day-care center was burning like a beacon, but Bülling rushed straight into the sea of fire and carried out every single kid. Fourteen times, a kid under each arm, in total about thirty kids if I've calculated correctly, but if he hadn't been able to borrow the Phantom's fireproof undies probably not even Bülling would have managed it."

"You're pulling my leg," said the offended minister.

"Why would you think that?" said the special adviser, looking at the minister as though he were an interesting object and not a person of flesh and blood. And at last Berg had been able to get to the point.

Berg had prepared himself carefully. First he had an up-to-date list made of persons who in various ways might be thought to constitute a threat against the prime minister and those closest to him. He had also been very selective in his choice and only included those who, according to his coworkers, "deserved to be taken seriously." All those who'd only been drinking at their neighbor's and seen the prime minister on TV and sworn that "I'm going to personally shoot that bastard's head off" had thus not been taken seriously. Not even if they were in the national guard and had an AK-4 in the closet, or devoted their time to hunting or competitive shooting, which by the way evidently many of them seemed to do. So many that there were even grounds for suspicion that such activities formed an essential part of their personal profiles.

Their neighbors and other close associates also appeared to form an interesting group, because daily more or less anonymous tips came in to the police authorities, and even directly to the secret police, about normal, honorable Swedish citizens who "in an informal social context promised to take the life of the prime minister." But "all of these drunkards, nut jobs, and big talkers"—at any given point in time there were hundreds of such pending cases piled one on top of another in Berg's surveillance register—Berg had chosen to leave out. Remaining were twenty-two persons who at the moment could be imagined going from words to action, and those whom Berg himself looked at most seriously were of course those who hadn't talked very much about their wishes or intentions.

Viewed as sociological material they formed an interesting group; among other things, they were distributed across the entire social spectrum. There was a count with his own castle, large forests, and landholdings who, it was true, said little for the most part but who at the same time possessed considerable personal and material resources. In addition he had an ominous history. He was demonstrably prone to violence and risk-taking, and capable in practical matters. In the B-annex on Polhemsgatan where Berg spent most of his time he was long referred to as "Anckarström"—the notorious assassin of King Gustav III in 1792—and on one occasion Berg had personally intervened in a rather delicate matter. When he'd found out that the prime minister had accepted an invitation to an exclusive dinner to which "Anckarström" had also been invited, he had contacted the government office building. At the last moment the prime minister had had a conflict and Berg had avoided both a personal headache and an unnecessary assignment for the bodyguard unit of the secret police.

In this material there was also a Swedish billionaire who resided in London. He had left a tax suit behind at home in Sweden in which the government was demanding several hundred million dollars from him, and with London as a base he had spent large sums over the past several years to support various campaigns directed against the Social Democratic Party, the government, and not least the prime minister personally. At a private dinner at the West India Club in London he had also expressed more far-reaching ambitions than that and promised ten million to the person, or persons, "who can see to it that the Gustav III of our time meets a logical end." According to Berg's informant, who had been a guest at the same dinner and had a long history within the industry's own security organization, the presumptive ringleader had been stone sober, serious, and low-voiced when he laid out his offer. "He seemed almost slightly amused as he said it," the informant summarized.

In Berg's organization the billionaire had been given the cover name Pechlin, after one of the conspirators against Gustav III; it was Berg himself who'd chosen it for him. Berg was interested in history, and most of what he read outside his work were books dealing with Swedish history. There was something soothing about the subject, thought Berg. Regardless of how depressing it had been and how badly things may have gone, it was already history and nothing that he could be expected to do anything about. However, these two, and a few others besides, were still exceptions, and the center of gravity was of course where it always was in such matters. Exactly half of the twenty-two were dangerous criminals, and two of them were serving life sentences for murder.

One of the two was a Yugoslav terrorist, and because he was where he was, it was not he but rather his associates who constituted the practical concern. He had ongoing contacts with at least three of his countrymen, all of them known criminals who seemed to have a lot of hair on their chests and had complete freedom of movement. They were also difficult to keep an eye on, extremely taciturn in a hard-to-understand language, almost Mafia-like in their behavior and choice of associates.

The other murderer was a dogmatic Swede who harbored a deep, implacable hatred for the Swedish authorities in general and the judicial authorities in particular. He was no ordinary dogmatist, either. Among other things he was technically knowledgeable and had during his active period pieced together a number of bombs that functioned well enough to earn him his life sentences. Among those who were like-minded he was a model and a leadership figure, and because almost all of his supporters were still running loose he ached like a thorn in Berg's awareness. Most recently he had also shown an ominous interest in the prime minister and at least two of his governing colleagues.

What the remainder had in common was that they were all men without a previous criminal record, but who otherwise constituted a delightful mixture. Two of them were, in context, more interesting than the others. Pure nightmares from a secret police perspective, Berg used to think in gloomy moments. One was a former paratrooper and junior officer at the paratrooper school in Karlsborg. Ten years earlier he had been discharged from the military and simply disappeared, it was unclear to where. A girlfriend of his had reported the disappearance to the police, but the investigation had been discontinued when she received a postcard from Turkey on which he briefly reported that he didn't intend to see her again, thanked her for "at least one memorable lay," and asked her not to bother the police on his behalf as he was "doing great" and didn't intend to "return home any time soon." The girlfriend had shown the postcard to the police, who had asked the usual questions, compared the handwriting on the postcard with previous messages, and closed the case. Of what the "memorable lay" consisted had never been discovered, but according to local gossip the ex-girlfriend was said to have parachuted on at least one occasion in her life.

A little more than a year later he had shown up in Sweden again and been observed, purely physically, in connection with a large-scale surveillance effort against a Swedish political organization on the extreme left wing. It was also by pure chance that he had been noticed—the SePo spy who did so had had him as a commander when he did his military service as a paratrooper, and the spy described him as the person who would end up lowest on his list if he had to choose an enemy. The object's background, the context in which he was observed, and the opinion of the person who had done so had quickly increased interest in his person at the secret police's surveillance squad.

"For Christ's sake, we're talking about a guy who can kill half this squad with his bare hands," the somewhat bad-tempered chief inspector summarized the surveillance matter that had landed on his desk.

Because neither he nor his colleagues in the military intelligence service had sent him there as an infiltrator—the very thought had been absurd—it was definitely the right man in the completely wrong place. Left-wing activists should have eyeglasses with lenses thick as bottle bottoms. They could happily go around in workman's shirts and carpenter's pants, for that made both surveillance and identification easier, and as long as they had office-workers' hands with arms that weren't any thicker than those of the squad's female office assistants, they could squawk as much as they wanted that the working class that they nowadays represented would violently overthrow society.

As long as they couldn't jump-start a car, much less screw together a functioning bomb, or even bloody one of his colleagues' noses. To that extent they left him cold. The ex-paratrooper did not.

Regardless of this they'd drawn a blank. The ex-paratrooper had disappeared without a trace, and because he could also shoot a hole in a five-crown piece at a distance of five hundred yards, the bad-tempered chief inspector decided that it was high time to go outside the building.

"This is truly not a person you invite home for a cup of tea, so I believe it's best that we talk with the Germans," decided the boss, who was both an educated man and mild-mannered, despite the fact that he was a police superintendent.

The Germans had made contact six months later when they sent a surveillance picture that, according to their own image analyst "with a certainty bordering on likelihood," depicted the former paratrooper. The picture had been taken by a rather craftily placed surveillance camera that covered the parking lot outside the agricultural bank in a small town by the name of Bad Segeberg thirty-five miles outside Hamburg. Just that day an amount corresponding to a little more than a million U.S. dollars had been in the till, and right before closing time three masked men had come in and taken it all with the help of their automatic pistol, probably of the Uzi brand and of Israeli manufacture. A robbery "with clear terrorist connections," declared the head of Constitutional Protection's division in Schleswig-Holstein. The three robbers were obviously *putz weg*, and it would be highly desirable if the Swedes could help out with their own countryman.

The following day the former paratrooper had been the object of an operational effort by the Swedish secret police: Operation Olga. The reason this name had been chosen was not that they wanted to mislead the enemy, which they would gladly do, but rather that the object of surveillance had gone by the nickname Olga during his time as a paratrooper. True, it wasn't something you called him when he was listening, for then you were dead, but the reason he'd acquired this particular nickname was flattering enough, for there was only one person in the entire paratrooper school in Karlsborg who was even tougher than the object in question—namely Olga, who was the manager of the paratroopers' cafeteria.

Six months later Operation Olga had been concluded, and at that point for the most part everything about the person who was being investigated was known, up to when he'd finished military service. After that almost nothing was known other than that "with a certainty bordering on likelihood" he had robbed a bank in northern Germany six months earlier and clearly had a fairly close connection to a Swedish group on the extreme left wing with the Palestinian question topmost on its order of business. But it was as if he himself had been swallowed up off the face of the earth. Until two months ago, when he, with the same appearance despite all the years that had passed, tanned and in seemingly perfect physical condition, had shown up in a picture taken by a rather craftily placed surveillance camera at the little park outside the government building, Rosenbad.

Operation Olga had immediately been brought up from the archives, assigned a new project number and a new budget. Berg had elevated the guard level for Rosenbad and the key persons who worked there and had informed the person responsible for security at the government office. He had also had a conversation with the prime minister's special adviser, who had been markedly uninterested in the matter itself but as usual generous with both sarcastic remarks and expressions of doubt.

"I don't believe in such characters," he stated behind his heavy, lowered eyelids. "As soon as they've acquired a face they're almost always uninteresting. I don't believe in your connection either," he continued. "It's probably as simple as the fact that you've confused him with another or several others, and it wouldn't be the first time in that case, would it? And if you haven't done so, we can be thankful for the fact that he went to the right meeting."

"Right meeting?" said Berg. "I don't really understand what you mean."

"Don't worry," said the special adviser with his usual wry half-sneer, for this was before Krassner had come into the picture and forced them to approach one another. "It's not that I'm trying to convert you to the Palestinian cause. What I mean is only that if he'd gone to a political meeting of the sort to which his type is expected to go, there would scarcely have been people from your group who could've caught sight of him."

So that's what you say, thought Berg sourly, but because this was before Krassner had brought them closer to each other he had kept his thoughts to himself.

A former paratrooper who had been observed on three brief occasions over a period of ten years and had otherwise disappeared without a trace. The other person who was of particular concern to Berg was the owner of a nursery outside Finspång in the province of Östergötland. It was the government office's own security department that had reported him to Berg, and normally he would only have become one more case in the large pile of such cases that they were content to simply register.

A little more than a year earlier the man had written to the prime minister personally and asked for his help. After a divorce his ex-wife had gotten full custody of the couple's then six-year-old son. In spite of the fact that she was a whore, in spite of the fact that her new husband was both an alcoholic and a criminal, and in spite of the fact that he loved his son more than anything else in the world. Could the prime minister intervene and put things right? Obviously he could not. The nursery owner had received the usual friendly letter of refusal from the female adviser in the prime minister's office who took care of such matters and could rattle off the legal arguments in her sleep. Then he'd written again and received the same reply as the previous time. In his third letter he had sharpened his tone, become personal, unpleasant, even threatening. Then he'd started phoning, and about the same time as he landed on Berg's desk he'd ceased making contact. From sheer momentum, however, the matter had gone on to the secret police's office in Norrköping, where they either had little to do or money left in their account. The gardener was both a marksman and a hunter and had a license for eight weapons in total: a revolver, two pistols, three rifles, and two shotguns. Fourteen days after a surveillance file had been set up on him with the secret police in Norrköping he had shown up at a political meeting in Åtvidaberg where the prime minister was the main speaker.

When the meeting was over he had sneaked around in the parking lot outside, and when the prime minister and his guards drove away to have dinner at the Freemasons Hotel in Linköping he'd followed them in his car. He had parked a distance away from the hotel, walked back and forth on the street outside, and after awhile went into the hotel lobby. At that point he was already surrounded by a hastily doubled surveillance group of, in total, four plainclothes detectives from the secret police in Norrköping.

"Do we know if he's armed?" asked the group leader on the radio.

"Answer don't know," said one of the detectives who was best situated to see the object at the same time as he himself moved his service weapon from its shoulder holster to his right coat pocket.

"Okay," said the group leader. "If he moves even one yard in the direction of the banquet room we'll go in and take him."

But he hadn't. Instead he had quickly gone out onto the street again, gotten into his car and driven back to the house where he lived. The following day, after the leadership team meeting, he'd received the code name Immortelle.

As a surveillance matter, Immortelle had developed in a promising manner, but as a human being he appeared to be steadily feeling worse. It seemed as if he'd suddenly given up hope of getting his son back. He hadn't even tried to contact him. He'd let go the employees he'd had previously, and the business he was running had been put on the back burner. His contacts with the outside world, by telephone and other means, had been drastically reduced. He isolated himself from other people. Instead he started cultivating certain of his earlier interests and acquired at least one that was completely new and at odds with his history. He could spend hours at the shooting range, where he put shot after shot into a torso target at a distance of three hundred yards with the aid of his hunting rifle and a newly purchased high-powered telescopic sight. When he'd started he was a good shot. Now he was at the same level as the police department's own sharpshooters.

Early in the morning he disappeared out into the terrain dressed in running shoes and jogging clothes. A few months earlier he had needed more than a quarter of an hour to make his way around the cross-country track where he worked out. Nowadays he ran his two miles in less than nine minutes. In the evenings he lifted weights. He had taken a weightlifting bench, barbells, and weights to one of his greenhouses and his nightly training sessions usually lasted for two hours most days of the week. He was strong, he was fast, he could shoot, and taken all together this was not good at all.

On top of all that he had joined the Social Democratic Party. Scarcely from conviction, for there was nothing in his background that pointed in that direction. From the careful markings that he made with a pencil in the party newspaper, the local chapter's member newsletter, and various mailings that had been rescued from his garbage can, he seemed most interested in where the prime minister was to be found, in a purely physical sense, in the immediate future. He had a motive, and he was also in possession of the means. Now he was just searching for a suitable occasion, and there was touching agreement about all this not only among the secret police in Norrköping but also among their superiors up in Stockholm.

Berg's account had made an impression on his listeners. The minister of justice had been almost shocked. "Yes, I'm a little shocked when I hear this sort of thing," he concluded. "You'd rather not think about the fact that such people exist."

After that he got caught up in an extensive exposition of how things had been during the old king's time. Back when he was only a young boy who went with his father to Palmgren's Leather behind the Royal Theater to fetch Papa's new riding boots, when the king suddenly came in, nodding amiably at everyone in the store.

"He walked around all alone, yes, not counting his aide-de-camp, but that was mostly so he could avoid paying himself, I guess. He walked around all alone in the middle of Stockholm and no one would have dreamed of even saying something rude to him." The minister shook his head mournfully.

Even the chief legal officer had spoken up. When Berg—without naming names—had given a short description of the provincial count, the chief legal officer had suddenly opened his mouth for the first time outside his judicial preserve. He himself was an aristocrat on both his father's and mother's side of the family.

"He is regrettably a relative of mine," the chief legal officer stated dryly. "By marriage, of course," he added quickly when he saw the special adviser's pleased smile.

The special adviser had said exactly what Berg had expected he would *not* say.

"How many people would you need to be able to carry out a complete surveillance of these characters?"

"Complete surveillance?" asked Berg in order to make clear to himself that the person who had posed the question also understood its import.

"Full surveillance. I'm talking about twenty-two surveillance teams." The special adviser nodded.

"We can just forget that," said Berg. "I don't have that many people. Besides, they have a number of other things to do, as you gentlemen are certainly aware." Why is he asking that? thought Berg. He surely must know to the penny how many resources we have, and he can count too.

The special adviser had been content to nod.

"One more thing," he said. "How many others are there that you are aware of? Besides this especially qualified group that you've reported on?"

"Hundreds," said Berg. "Certainly hundreds." He's not asking on his own account, thought Berg. He wants me to say it to the others. Why does he want that? he thought.

Then he recounted the information that the head of his bodyguard unit had compiled and he took the field with flying colors and fluttering banners.

"I've had a compilation done," said Berg. "Of the guarding of the prime minister during the last thirty days before this meeting."

.   .   .

The prime minister had been traveling inside and outside the country during seventeen of those thirty days, and if the decision had been up to Berg, he could just as well have been gone the entire time, for then he was always guarded by his own regular group of bodyguards, often augmented by reinforcements from the operations bureau as well as substantial resources from the local police. Best of all was when he was abroad, for there they had completely different experiences and the security forces were as a rule enormous compared to what Berg had to work with. It was worst when he was at home, at work, or in his own residence.

"During eleven of these thirteen days he hasn't had any physical protection during the night, other than the guard from the security company that we've placed outside his entryway. On every one of these days he has on one or several occasions been alone outside Rosenbad or his residence. Altogether this amounts to more than twenty occasions, as it appears, everything from a quarter of an hour to several hours. He has walked away from and back to his residence; he has been out having dinner or in town shopping. That's the situation," said Berg, nodding with all the seriousness that the situation demanded.

"Naughty, naughty, Berg," said the special adviser, chuckling with delight.

"I have not, repeat not, had him followed," said Berg. "This is information that I have put together in other ways, and there is only one reason that I have done so. The prime minister is an object of protection for which I and my people are responsible and, moreover, one of our six highest priority objects. You are aware of the background that I have reported on and the rest you can certainly figure out for yourselves."

"I'll talk with him," said the special adviser, and he sounded neither ironic, uninterested, nor even weary. "But you should probably not expect too much. He is who he is—and then, he is my chief," he added by way of explanation.

"I'll talk with him too," said the minister of justice. "I really will."

"You can of course explain to him that it's not like it was in the old king's time," said the special adviser behind his lowered eyelids, and when he said that he sounded exactly as usual again.

. . .

For the past fourteen days Waltin had been planning a break-in. The first time he'd done a break-in he was only fifteen years old and still in junior high school. And he hadn't intended to steal anything that time either. He just wanted to look around a little. He'd made his way into the apartment of a schoolmate who'd gone away with his family during midwinter break. It hadn't been especially difficult. He'd gotten hold of keys long before and he'd visited his schoolmate at home on several occasions so that he was well oriented in the family residence. Actually it was his mother that Waltin was interested in. A small, slender, beautiful woman with a lot of class and not the least like her piggish son.

It had been a marvelous experience. He'd walked around for hours in the large, silent, dark apartment. He'd had surgical gloves on, a little practical pen-like flashlight that he'd bought at the hobby store, and he'd had a hard-on almost the entire time. He had proceeded systematically without leaving any traces. In a photo album in the parents' bedroom he'd finally found what he'd been searching for. It was a photo of his friend's mother. Without a stitch on her body she stood, smiling in the most shameless way toward the photographer, and judging by the background this was out at their summer place in the archipelago, for he'd been there too. At the same time it had been a great disappointment. She was holding his classmate, who already looked like a little pig ten years ago, by the hand, and besides she had much larger breasts than he'd thought. At least at that time.

At first he had nonetheless considered taking the photo with him, trying to cut away the little pig and making a copy of the remainder which he could send to her anonymously with a few well-formulated lines hinting that there was more, and worse, and that perhaps they ought to meet . . . but those breasts were much too repugnant in their fat, white tangibility, so her photo had remained in the album and while he masturbated he tried to cover the little pig and the breasts with the fingers of his left hand. It had gone rather well, even if it had taken a while, and when he was done he had vigorously rubbed sperm over both pig and breasts.

When he left he had taken along a few pieces of gold jewelry and a few bottles of very good French wine. He had pawned the gold jewelry bit by bit and been paid handsomely. He had enjoyed the wine alone in the seclusion of his room while dear Mama, as usual, lay dying in the next room. Everything also indicated that he had conducted himself creditably. It didn't even seem as if they had discovered that they had had a secret visit. The pig had been exactly like he always was, equally sniveling and pushy, and if he'd had a break-in at home the whole school would surely have known about it before lunch break.

That was then. Nowadays he was only occupied with legal break-ins, and his professional capacity had never been questioned among the taciturn few who had the honor of helping him with the practical details. Although this time it didn't feel right. For one thing he wasn't especially motivated. What could someone like Krassner actually produce if scrutinized? If it had been a question of ordinary bet-making he wouldn't have put a dime on the fool. It was not a simple task, either. Entry codes, alarms, detectors, and surveillance cameras were one thing—they could be as sophisticated as anything, for that just it made more fun—but seven watchful youths living squeezed together in a shoe box was something quite different and seven times worse.

A necessary condition was that he get them out so that the place was empty. Little Jeanette would take care of the South African, even if Waltin didn't like the fact that he hadn't come up with a better solution. It also appeared as if he would be rid of the five remaining students. Two would be going home to their parents and a third to his girlfriend. Two had intended to stay home and at least meditate a little before possibly going out, but because Jeanette had managed to arrange the pop-concert tickets, he would be rid of them too. Probably would be, and that just left his greatest concern, Krassner himself.

It was only right and appropriate that that old duffer Forselius get to help out with this matter. It was, after all, his fantasies that were the basis of the whole thing. But naturally he had dug in his heels like a restive mule when Waltin had called on him to talk about the matter.

"I hear what you're saying," he said sourly when Waltin explained what it involved. "I hear what you're saying."

"You're the only one I can trust," said Waltin. "True, he has contacts with some journalists, but I don't want to take that risk. I'd rather let it be."

"That's nice to hear," said Forselius, sounding a trifle more energetic. "That rabble should just be mowed down."

Certainly, thought Waltin. Fine with me, but what do we do instead?

"Couldn't you invite him here and relate a few war memories about you and his uncle?" Waltin suggested.

"To someone like that?" snorted the old man. "You don't think it's bad enough the way it is?"

What is it now? thought Waltin, who didn't have any idea what this was actually about.

"Not real ones, of course," said Waltin with well-acted terror. "God help me, no, I was thinking that since we were at it anyway we might cook up a good story. If you understand what I mean?" He had leaned forward in the well-worn leather armchair and nodded as ingratiatingly as his precarious position allowed.

"You're thinking about the days when it was Professor Forselius who held up the mirrors," grunted the old man while he reached for the carafe of cognac. "Those were different times."

What mirrors? thought Waltin. What's he raving about? Suddenly satisfied and contented?

"Certainly, certainly," said Forselius. Downed a substantial gulp and wiped away the remaining drops with the back of his hand. "But how the hell do I get hold of that damn person, for I'm guessing he doesn't have a telephone at that damn place he's living in?"

"We'll have to write a letter," said Waltin.

So they had written a letter in which Forselius invited Krassner to his apartment, at nineteen hundred hours on Friday the twenty-second of November. Forselius had gone through old files since meeting Krassner the last time and he had found some that might possibly be of value to his work and that he actually thought his uncle should have received if he'd still been alive, but if Krassner himself was interested, then . . .

"Then we just have to hope that piece of shit replies," said Forselius.

"I'm sure he will," said Waltin warmly.

"And if he doesn't, then you'll have to think of something else instead," said Forselius slyly.

"I'm sure it will work out," said Waltin, getting up.

"I remember there was a Pole. It was right after the war. We were short on time then too. And it was important as hell."

"Yes," said Waltin amiably. "I'm listening."

"It's not important," said Forselius, shaking his head. "It was right after the war and we were playing by different rules at that time, but we sure did get him out of the way. That we did." Forselius sighed heavily.

Wonder if they killed that Pole the old geezer was mumbling about? thought Waltin when he'd come down onto the street. In that case it had probably been quite practical, but because times were different nowadays he'd decided on a different alternative. To his surprise Berg had bought it as well. Even more surprising, he'd suddenly appeared to lose interest in the entire business.

"If there is no other solution," said Berg, holding his palms out at an angle. "I'm assuming it's one of our own that will take care of it."

"Yes," said Waltin. "I think we arrest him, and then the narcotics investigators can handle the rest without revealing the sender. I have an old contact I can discuss it with."

Then he'd spoken with Göransson and Martinsson. No problems whatsoever, since they would only be doing what he told them. Post themselves outside the student dormitory, and if Krassner came out before nineteen hundred hours on Friday evening they were to follow him and see to it that he made his way to old man Forselius. Watch him while he was there and warn if anything went awry. And when everything was over and Krassner was on his way home, they could call it a day.

If he didn't come out they were to go up and arrest him. Take him to the police station on Kungsholmen and put him in jail, suspected of narcotics offenses or, alternatively, aggravated narcotics offenses. As little paperwork as possible and a quick turnover to the guys on the narc squad, and they definitely didn't need to think about a search of the premises, for others would take care of that.

"Are we clear with one another?" asked Waltin.

"Sure," said Martinsson, surreptitiously flexing his biceps in the mirror behind Waltin's back.

Göransson had been content to nod, but on the other hand he'd been around considerably longer than Martinsson.

Can't forget to take care of Forselius's letter, thought Waltin.

True, Waltin hadn't said very much to Assistant Detective Jeanette Eriksson, but because she was twenty-seven years old and far from being a numbskull she could figure out the rest herself.

Clearly there's going to be a search of the premises, she thought. The kind that doesn't usually get talked about. But then she hadn't thought about it any further, for she had other things to think about that she felt were more urgent and more worrisome. The tickets that she'd arranged for the pop concert on Friday evening had been the least of her problems and easy enough to take care of. It was actually Waltin who'd arranged the tickets, but it was her idea.

She and Daniel had been sitting in the kitchen, drinking coffee, when Tobbe and Patrik had come in to keep them company. They'd known each other since high school and played in the same band, which was several years before they'd managed to end up in the same student corridor. Now they were sour as vinegar, for despite the fact that they'd taken turns standing in line for hours, they hadn't gotten hold of any tickets to the concert by their favorite band next Friday. She'd never heard of this band, but she grasped the opportunity in flight.

"I'm sure I can arrange that," she said, nodding at them.

"Forget it," said Tobbe, shaking his head and swilling a few generous gulps from the bottle of strong beer he had with him.

"For real?" asked Patrik doubtfully.

"I have an ex who works for a record company," Jeanette lied. "He always used to be able to arrange tickets."

Krassner himself was a considerably greater problem. One day when she was sitting in the common kitchen, reading, Krassner had suddenly come in and sat down right across from her. And despite the fact that he was smiling at her, she understood at once that it wasn't going to be especially pleasant.

"What's that you're reading?" he said, grasping the cover of her book.

"It is a book about criminality," Jeanette said in her best schoolbook English, at the same time trying to appear appropriately offended by his pushiness.

"Criminology is a required subject at the Swedish police academy," said Krassner, and it was more of a statement than a question.

Watch out, you little shit, thought Assistant Detective Eriksson while trying to appear only seventeen years old.

"I don't know," she said. "I don't believe so, but they have it at the university in Stockholm. I'm in my second year."

Krassner sneered like someone who knew better than to let himself be fooled by someone like her.

"You mostly sit out here in the kitchen," he said.

"It's so Daniel and I will be able to study better," Jeanette said innocently. "I hope it doesn't disturb you?"

Krassner shook his head, got up, stood in the doorway, and looked at her with his unpleasantly insinuating smile.

"Take care, officer," he said. Turned around and disappeared into his room.

Jeanette had not replied. Only looked at him surprised, like someone who didn't understand. What was he driving at? she wondered. Does he know something? Scarcely possible—in fact, highly improbable. Does he suspect something? Surely, for he's that type. What does he want? He wants to test me, she thought.

"He seems completely screwy. I promise you, the man's not healthy, you can see it in his eyes," Eriksson summarized when she met Waltin that same evening.

"He can't know anything," said Waltin.

"No," said Jeanette, "but I think that's completely uninteresting to him."

"You don't look like a typical police officer, exactly," said Waltin, smiling paternally. "He's trying to test you."

"Sure. He's trying to test me, despite the fact that I look like I do. That says a great deal about him, doesn't it?"

"You have to sit in the kitchen? There's no other option?"

"No." Jeanette shook her head. "Not if I'm going to be able to pass his door and try to hear what he's up to."

"It'll be over soon," said Waltin and smiled consolingly with all his white teeth. "And there isn't anyone else who could manage it better than you."

Then there's one more reason to sit in the kitchen, thought Assistant Detective Eriksson, but you certainly don't want to hear about that, and because it will soon be over I guess I'll have to live with it.

The essential reason that she always sat in the kitchen was Daniel, or M'Boye, as she called him when she was talking with Waltin and her colleagues. Regardless of the fact that it would soon be over, she and Daniel were in their sixth week now, and he was a completely normal young man to whom she at most had given a light kiss and an occasional hug, in spite of the fact that they had gotten together more than twenty times and spent numerous hours in his room, where they had been occupied with everything between heaven and earth except what they ought to have been devoting themselves to.

He must think I'm completely nutty, thought Eriksson. Good thing he's the way he is.

Daniel was not only big, strong, handsome, and talented. He was also both kind and well brought up, and as soon as he understood that Jeanette was not the usual "Swedish girl" he had also mobilized an attentive and patient side of his personality. Regardless of that, to put it simply, Assistant Detective Eriksson had still had to work like a beaver to avoid making use of that part of the body that Daniel—in a Freudian moment when even he had lost his footing—called her "little beaver." Jeanette didn't like what she was doing. She was exploiting a decent person who liked her. When the air in Daniel's room got thick as mayonnaise, she used to rescue herself by fleeing out to the student corridor's common kitchen. Her pretexts for doing so were no longer even far-fetched, they were worse than that, but fortunately it would all soon be over. Then she would disappear from his life, he would go home to South Africa and continue to live his life, and hopefully the marks that she left would not be all that deep.

Forselius had not phoned Waltin until late Thursday evening, and when he'd finally done so Waltin had already started planning his alternative in detail. Berg had called him that afternoon and at that time he'd said that it was probably leaning toward being a narcotics arrest in any event because Forselius had not been heard from. Berg seemed to have reconciled himself to the thought. "Yes, yes," he had declared simply, "perhaps it's just as well."

But then Forselius called, and he sounded both energetic and conspiratorial.

"Yes, it's me here," said Forselius on Waltin's secure line.

Hello to you, you old bastard, thought Waltin. And here you are calling in the middle of the night and sounding like the Third Man.

"Nice to hear from you," Waltin said politely.

"I just called to say that everything will go off as planned," said Forselius. "We've just spoken on the phone."

"How nice," Waltin said cordially. "I'll be in touch."

Wonder if I ought to phone Berg and tell him we're back to Plan A, Waltin thought. It can wait, he decided, and instead he decided to call up Hedberg and give the all clear. He, after all, would be pulling the heavy load, and Waltin didn't want to let him wait for word unnecessarily.

My best coworker, thought Waltin with warmth. Hedberg, who never said a word but always did exactly what he should. Sometimes it almost felt as if they were brothers. Imagine how many bad things his colleagues have said about that man, thought Waltin.

CHAPTER XI

Between Summer's Longing and Winter's End

Albany, New York, in December

[MONDAY, DECEMBER 9]

The local weather report promised milder weather after the weekend, but forgot to mention the snow. When Johansson woke up on Monday morning, it was coming down heavily outside the window of the professor's bedroom, and, Norrlander that he was, he realized that there could be problems driving. Sarah seemed to have drawn the same conclusion, even though she was born in Manhattan.

"Jesus," she said. "Have you seen the kind of weather we're having? Now we've got to get a move on so you don't miss your train."

Johansson had showered, gotten dressed, and packed his few belongings in the practical shoulder bag he'd bought cheaply in the gift shop at the FBI. It took a quarter of an hour, and when he came down to the kitchen he was met by his hostess, who was busy with breakfast. Newly showered, fresh, and energetic judging by her appearance, she had apparently dressed in a shorter time than Johansson, for when she'd come in to wake him she was still in a nightgown.

A highly remarkable woman, thought Johansson, which in his native dialect was a mark of great respect.

"How would you like your eggs?" asked Sarah.

Scrambled eggs, fried ham, toast, fresh-squeezed orange juice, and a large cup of coffee while he was entertained by Sarah, who talked happily about snowstorms and other local bad weather in Albany and its vicinity that she'd experienced during her not altogether long life. And so far it had been very good, but then the subject of precipitation had come up and the misery had begun.

It was only a few miles to the bank—Sarah made use of Citibank's local branch—but because the Volvo didn't have snow tires and the world outside the windowpanes was white with snow, it had required a good deal of skidding and zigzagging from one side of the road to the other before they finally arrived. Inside the bank it was calm and silent, with almost no customers.

"Some weather," said Sarah happily as she lowered the hood of her ankle-length red wool coat.

"It looks like we'll be having a white Christmas," the female cashier concurred, smiling amiably. "Are you going to stay home or are you driving to New York?"

Know each other from before, thought Johansson automatically. Just so they don't start babbling a lot, he thought, nervously glancing at his watch.

The babbling had been confined to a polite minimum. Then Sarah filled out a slip of paper with her name and safe-deposit box number and shot off a big smile at an older uniformed guard who was posted at the entrance a few yards away, at the same time as she nodded toward Johansson in explanation.

"He's with me," said Sarah. "He's my new assistant."

The guard had been content to smile paternally toward Sarah and more neutrally toward Johansson, and two minutes later they were standing down in the bank vault where Sarah set the key in the lock of the largest type of safe-deposit box.

Wonder if that's the key that was in the shoe, thought Johansson.

"Now let's see," said Sarah.

She winked conspiratorially at Johansson while they helped each other pull out the box and place it on a nearby table.

"Should you or I look?" Sarah asked, giggling.

"It's your box," said Johansson. "You look."

Sarah shook her head and smiled.

"You get to look first," she said. "It's my Christmas present to you."

Paper, nothing but paper, and considerably less than he'd imagined, but in any case a pile about eight inches high that was divided in plastic sleeves and between thin cardboard folders, at least one of which looked old.

"This is clearly the manuscript of his book," said Sarah, who had already started rooting in the pile. "It's actually thicker than I thought." She handed over a bundle of more than a hundred typewritten pages encased in a plastic sleeve.

Johansson took it and quickly leafed through while he eyeballed the pages. The title and author's name in large letters on the cover page. "The Spy Who Went East, by John P. Krassner," Johansson read. Foreword, table of contents, and completely written out pages at the beginning. Chapter headings, typewritten outlines, and difficult-to-decipher handwritten notes on the otherwise empty pages toward the end.

He writes the way he cleans his room, thought Johansson, weighing the thin bundle of papers in his hand.

"A typical John manuscript," said Sarah, smiling. "Exists for the most part in the author's head. I have a suggestion," she continued, nodding toward the pile on the table. "Put everything in that practical little bag with the fancy emblem and read it in peace and quiet when you have time. But I don't believe you should expect too much. John was not exactly a Hemingway, to put it mildly."

"He wanted you to have copies," Johansson objected. So I'll probably miss that eleven o'clock train, he thought.

"Forget it," snorted Sarah and suddenly seemed upset for the first time since he'd met her. "Not on your life. I don't give a hoot about his damn copies."

Oops, thought Johansson. She's a redhead all right.

. . .

In the car en route to the station she explained how she viewed the matter.

"Perhaps you think I'm the surly type," she said, shaking her head, "but for the past ten years I haven't wanted to deal with John. For me he was a finished chapter when I broke up with him, and as I said that was more than ten years ago, but because he could never take no for an answer I've had to put up with him anyway. Despite the fact that I've been sick of him and all his fantasies the whole time, and despite the fact that I'd had it up to here with him and his old fascist uncle." She measured a few inches over her flowing red hair with her hand.

"And yet you were his heir," said Johansson, smiling wryly.

"Sure," said Sarah. "He was like that. Refused to take no for an answer. But I've never wished him dead in earnest, and I'm truly sorry that he is dead, for I don't wish that on anyone. Do you know what I'm thinking about doing?" she continued.

Johansson shook his head.

"I'm going to give it all away to charity."

"You haven't thought about seeing it as personal compensation?" Johansson suggested, for he could look out for himself when it really counted. That shack ought to be worth quite a bit, if it's not too heavily mortgaged, he thought.

"It's out of the question," said Sarah. "Besides, I have enough to get by. I don't want to have anything to do with John anymore, much less his ridiculous papers and his silly fantasies. John is dead, okay. I intend to let him rest in peace and I definitely don't intend to contribute to his being able to continue stirring up trouble from the place where he is now. He's certainly in heaven, after all. If you're going to be God to Irishmen, you probably have to have a forgiving nature."

Now she's herself again, thought Johansson.

"I propose that we do it like this," said Johansson. "I'll read the papers at my own leisure, and if there's something that I think that you absolutely need to hear about I'll contact you."

Sarah shrugged her shoulders.

"Okay," she said. "Although I find it extremely hard to think what that might be."

Once they arrived at the station, Johansson's train should already have left, but because it was delayed a half hour they actually had plenty of time. They had left her car in the parking lot and when Johansson handed her the keys he felt a stab of guilty conscience.

"Can you manage getting out of here?" he asked.

"I'll take a taxi," said Sarah, smiling. "Then I'll fetch the car when the weather gets better. They say it will warm up."

She shrugged her shoulders and smiled again.

"Take care of yourself too," she said. "You have a considerably tougher journey than I have."

Then she'd lowered the hood of her red coat, stood on tiptoe, hugged him, and with lips puckered gave him a big kiss right on the mouth.

"Take care, detective," she said. "And don't forget to call if you should happen to be in the area."

On the train people were standing in the aisles. Reading Krassner's papers wasn't even to be considered. The trip to New York took almost five hours instead of less than three, and when he arrived there wasn't much time to play with if he was going to make it to his flight. But once he found his way out of the underworld and out of Grand Central Station it had stopped snowing and he understood that his earthly problems were over for now.

At seven-thirty the SAS evening plane from New York, destination Stockholm, leveled out at its cruising altitude right according to schedule. The warning signs in the cabin had been turned off, and he heard the clinking from the beverage cart behind the galley curtain just as he sensed a faint aroma of food. He had packed the papers he'd gotten in his suitcase. He'd be able to read them when he was home.

That must be the cleverest woman I've met in my whole life, thought Johansson. She was rather pretty too, and yet she'd been together with that nutcase Krassner.

I don't understand women, thought Johansson, sighing.

CHAPTER XII

Between Summer's Longing and Winter's End

Stockholm in November and December

[FRIDAY, NOVEMBER 22]

Hedberg arrived well in advance. He liked to arrive well in advance, even on simple assignments like this. He and Waltin had lunch together, discussed the requirements and the goal, went over who should do what and a few other practical details.

"I want to find out what he's up to, quite simply," Waltin summarized. "And when you've taken care of things I don't want him to find out that you've done so."

"He's writing something," said Hedberg. "That's all we know?"

"No doubt something shocking," concurred Waltin, smiling wryly. "Which according to certain political thinkers might possibly have significance for the security of the realm, which in turn entails your and my modest participation in this little project."

"Okay then," said Hedberg, getting up. "I'll be in touch as soon I'm done."

After lunch he'd returned to the apartment that Waltin had arranged for him. Clearly better than staying at a hotel with lots of people who might notice you at the wrong moment and in the wrong place. You also got a receipt if you stayed at a hotel and if you paid cash you could almost be sure that someone would think that strange, become suspicious, and make a mental note of your appearance. Almost as bad as credit cards, which were a pure paper trail that your opponent could pick up by electronic means even years later if things went badly. But if you were camping at Waltin's you never got a bill, and if you ran into a neighbor when you were coming in or going out it was almost a sensation. He had lots of vacant apartments too. Hedberg had seldom needed to stay at the same place twice, and the refrigerator was always well stocked in accord with his wishes.

Hedberg slept a few hours. He liked to be well rested when he went to work. Then there was less carelessness.

Seven o'clock was the agreed-on time. At that time the corridor should be empty and he would be able to do his part, hopefully as quickly as possible. He was already on the scene at six o'clock to reconnoiter; the first thing he saw was the blue delivery van someone had parked at just the spot where you had a complete view of the dormitory lobby.

Fucking amateurs, thought Hedberg with irritation and returned to his own car, which he'd placed some distance away. Why hadn't they gotten themselves a well-situated lookout where they could sit without risk of being discovered? He himself had no intention of being photographed, regardless of whether it was his former colleagues who were holding the camera. Least of all then.

"There he is. Damn, he's early," Assistant Detective Martinsson declared a second after Krassner had stepped out briskly through the entryway.

"Eighteen thirty-two," Göransson said, making a little note on the pad that sat on the instrument panel. "I guess he just wants to arrive in good time."

Nothing bad that doesn't bring something good with it, thought Hedberg. First he'd seen Krassner's back, but because the light was poor out on the street he was uncertain if he'd seen right. But then the blue delivery van had suddenly shown up and taken a new position less than a hundred yards behind the man who was disappearing down the street. Okay then, thought Hedberg. No rest for the wicked.

Krassner had clearly decided to walk over to Sturegatan. He'd also been so kind as to select the correct sidewalk. He was walking fast too, so it was no great art for them to keep a suitable distance despite the fact that they were shadowing him from a vehicle.

"Fucking amateur," snorted Martinsson. "If I'd been him I would've walked on the other side of the road. They never learn that you should walk against traffic."

"If I were you I would just be thankful," said Göransson. "It must be close to ten degrees outside. Be glad that you can sit in a warm car instead."

With you as chauffeur, thought Martinsson, for it was hardly by chance that Göransson was sitting in the driver's seat just this once. You really need to move a little, you lazy bastard, thought Martinsson, but he didn't say that.

Looks good, Hedberg noted, inspecting his own image in the mirror while he took the elevator up to the seventeenth floor. Typical worker with blue overalls, tool belt, and a small metal toolbox where he had put his camera and the walkie-talkie that he needed so those two amateurs who had driven off in the blue delivery van would be able to warn him if Krassner was suddenly inspired to come up with some tomfoolery.

"He's twenty minutes too early," Martinsson observed as Krassner's back disappeared through the entryway to Forselius's building on Sturegatan. "Should we report that he's arrived, or what?"

"Yes," said Göransson. "And then I think we should drive around the block and position ourselves a little farther down. Better to stay on the same side as the entryway."

"Okay," said Martinsson, pressing the send button on the portable radio three times.

I see, thought Hedberg when a crackling sound came from the radio in his toolbox. The object is at a secure distance and we're almost twenty minutes ahead of schedule. So what do I do now? he thought.

"A hamburger would sit nicely," said Martinsson.

"The hell it would," objected Göransson.

"There's a stand up at Tessin Park," said Martinsson innocently. "It'll take five minutes at the most."

"Okay then," said Göransson, sighing. "I could go for one too. With cheese and raw onion and a lot of mustard and ketchup. I want coffee too. Coffee with milk."

Take a chance, Hedberg decided. He'd stood in the stairwell between the sixteenth and seventeenth floors for almost five minutes, observing the glass door to the corridor where Krassner was living. True, the lights were on inside, but that's how it should be and it looked empty. Leaking faucet, thought Hedberg, smiling wryly as he took the keys out of his pocket. You should never wait with a leaking faucet.

Nothing here, nothing there, but here, thought Hedberg while his sensitive fingers probed the crack between the door frame and the door to Krassner's room. He moistened the little scrap of paper against his tongue, carefully unlocked the door, pressed the scrap of paper back where it had been, sneaked into the dark coat closet and slowly pulled the door closed after him while he held the door handle down. Empty, thought Hedberg, slowly releasing it again. And high time to carry out a little work.

. . .

"Damn good burger," said Martinsson contentedly, belching to give emphasis to his judgment.

"So-so," said Göransson.

He still sounds grumpy, thought Martinsson.

"It's not the end of the world," he said. "For Christ's sake, it's only five past seven. Five minutes more or less isn't the end of the world. Better than raw hamburger."

"Sure, sure," said Göransson. We're well situated, in any case, he thought. Scarcely a hundred yards down on the street and with full view of the entryway, and five minutes isn't the end of the world, nor ten either, for that matter.

"I can take the first hour if you want to lean back," Martinsson suggested. Instead of smoking a peace pipe with you, you grumpy bastard, he thought.

"Okay then," said Göransson. "You take the first hour."

Why didn't I decide that we should meet in his room instead? thought Assistant Detective Jeanette Eriksson, glancing nervously at her watch. Seven minutes late, and the guy who's going to do the job is probably already frantic. Lay off, Jeanette, she thought. You know very well why you didn't want to meet him in his room. Drink your beer, which you've ordered and paid for with government money, and try to appear normal. Quarter past, she decided. If he hasn't shown up by quarter past I'll have to make radio contact.

Hedberg had started in the shower room. Shower, toilet, sink, medicine chest with mirror, tiled walls, and a plastic mat that looked almost new and appeared to be solidly glued to the floor. Plastic gloves on his hands, plastic covering over his shoes, and the very first thing he did was to place his walkie-talkie on the desk inside the room so he would be quite sure to hear it if someone needed to warn him. Between the medicine chest and the wall he found a plastic bag with a few carelessly rolled cigarettes. Marijuana, thought Hedberg, sniffing in the bag. He placed it back carefully where it had been. Coat closet next, thought Hedberg.

Hat rack, three wall-mounted closets with overhead cabinets. This is going like a dance, he thought.

Come sometime then, thought Jeanette, glancing at the clock, and just then he arrived. Fourteen minutes late and with an embarrassed smile.

"I'm really sorry I'm late," said Daniel as he leaned over, giving her a hug and a kiss on the cheek.

"It's okay," said Jeanette, trying to appear just irritated enough.

"I have a suggestion," said Daniel, sitting down on the stool next to her. "There's a good Mexican restaurant down on Birger Jarlsgatan. What do you think?"

Five, maybe ten minutes' walk, thought Jeanette. She herself would have preferred to stay in the vicinity in case something happened, but on the other hand Waltin hadn't said anything that prevented her from doing it. Only that she should see to it that M'Boye was kept away from the student dormitory for at least an hour and that she should make contact as soon as everything was done. Okay, she thought. Have to move a little, walk off the tension.

"Okay," she said, smiling. "That's okay."

The closets were mostly empty, screwed solidly tight against the wall, although one of the skirting boards against the floor was coming loose. Hedberg got down on his knees, took a knife, and poked carefully with the blade between the skirting board and the linoleum. I see, thought Hedberg with satisfaction, removing the molding and sticking in his hand. Papers, he thought. A rather thick bundle encased in a plastic sleeve.

Hedberg carefully coaxed out his find. Got up and read the text on the first page. "The Spy Who Went East, by John P. Krassner." Is he spending his time writing a mystery? thought Hedberg, bewildered, leafing through the manuscript. It wasn't that long and was far from finished, judging by the amount of handwritten additions and corrections. How will I have time to photograph this? he thought, and at that moment he heard steps in the corridor outside the door.

Waltin was sitting at home in his large apartment on Norr Mälarstrand watching porn. It was one of his favorite tapes and originally part of a large confiscation that Berg's coworkers had made at the home of some crazy Yugoslav, but because it was altogether too good to be shown at personnel parties at the bureau he'd pinched it for his own use. A private American production in which the play's leather-clad hero had hung up a real prize sow from a pair of ceiling hooks in his rec room. A well-narrated and very morally instructive story, although for Waltin it was nevertheless mostly about the play's female protagonist. Exactly the type he hated, with large, fat white breasts that bobbed up and down as soon as she moved, and now she was getting exactly the treatment her type deserved.

The steps in the corridor outside had died away. Then he'd heard the door between the corridor and the stairs slam shut. It was supposed to be empty of people here, thought Hedberg, exhaling. He tiptoed into the room and over to the desk and quickly started laying manuscript pages out on the available surface. Desk lamp or flash? he thought as he took the camera out of his tool bag. Desk lamp, he thought. It goes more quickly and is less visible. He arranged the light so it was balanced and started to photograph. It must be over a hundred pages, he thought with irritation. Wonder if I have enough film? It went quickly, in any case. The first roll was done in a few minutes, and just as he stood putting in a new one he heard it again, the slam of the door to the corridor. Someone's on their way in, thought Hedberg, turning off the desk lamp and tiptoeing quickly out into the coat closet.

Strange that he puts up with me, thought Jeanette, trying out her shy smile at her table companion. They had been seeing each other for almost six weeks and all he'd gotten was a kiss and a hug, and he hadn't even nagged at her, much less tried to wrestle with her. What she had been thinking about most the past few days—for her assignment would be over this evening if you could believe Waltin—was how she would extract herself from this without hurting him unnecessarily.

"You must think I'm really boring," said Jeanette.

"No," said Daniel, shaking his head seriously and placing his large hand over hers. "You're not like other girls I've met, but I respect your attitude toward . . . well, you know."

Daniel smiled wryly and shrugged his broad shoulders.

"Besides, I like you. A lot," he added, squeezing her hand and nodding.

Damnation, thought Assistant Detective Eriksson, but she didn't say it. Instead she just nodded with a shy smile and her gaze directed at the tablecloth. Sort of the way little Jeanette would have done.

Waltin moaned lightly with pleasure and sipped his malt whiskey while the whiplashes echoed from his black Bang & Olufsen speakers and the female protagonist shrieked like a stuck pig.

"There's more to come, there's more to come," Waltin hummed with delight, for he was both exhilarated and the tiniest bit intoxicated, and just then of course his red telephone rang. His secure line.

Typical, thought Waltin, sighing as he paused the film. Quarter past eight, he thought, looking at his watch as he picked up the receiver. It must be Hedberg, and it could only mean that everything had gone according to plan.

"Yes," said Waltin. "I'm listening."

"In a little less than three weeks I'm going home," said Daniel. "Do you want to go along?"

He smiled at her, that big white charming smile, but it was probably mostly to conceal the seriousness of his question, she thought.

"I don't know, maybe later. I have that exam that I just have to take care of and then I'm going to spend Christmas with my parents." The latter was true in any case, she thought.

"You must come to South Africa," said Daniel and smiled. "It's amazing."

I'm sure, thought Assistant Detective Eriksson. And how do I get myself out of this? But she didn't say that either.

"Everything went well?"

"Yes," said Hedberg.

"Anything interesting?" asked Waltin.

"Nada," said Hedberg.

"Nada? Nothing?"

"Messy student's den, a lot of papers, and most of the ones that had something on them lying on his desk. A few miscellaneous handwritten notes."

"And that was all?"

"Yes," said Hedberg. "I took a few rolls of what was on the desk. I got the idea that he's writing some kind of mystery."

"Mystery? Why do you think that?" asked Waltin.

"I found a page," said Hedberg. "I have a picture of it. Typewritten. Looked like the cover to a mystery or something. The Spy Who Went East, by John P. Krassner."

"The Spy Who Went East?"

"Yes, The Spy Who Went East. Supposed to be the Russians, I guess."

The spy who went over to the east? Strange title, thought Waltin. Went over from what?

"And there wasn't anything else? I mean the book itself or anything?"

"There were a number of pages with more or less text on them and those I took pictures of. Most of what was there was on the desk, but there wasn't too much. I got it all on three rolls, so he doesn't seem to be any great author."

"Were you able to check the ribbon in the typewriter? How much had he written?"

"Yes. Appeared almost unused."

An old bastard and his crackpot fantasies, thought Waltin.

"I'll talk to you tomorrow," Waltin suggested.

"Sounds fine," said Hedberg. "I was actually planning to go and turn in, so you can call me early if you want."

. . .

First Waltin thought about calling the security police's own central liaison and asking them to inform Göransson and Martinsson that they could call it a day. But then he started thinking about that idiot Martinsson and decided that they might just as well sit where they were, at least until they themselves made contact. It was below zero outside, and in all likelihood it would soon be the same temperature inside that old delivery van he'd loaned out to them. It was only to be hoped that old man Forselius entertained himself half the night with that scatterbrain Krassner while Martinsson froze his dick off on the street outside, Waltin thought contentedly. Besides, he really wanted to see the end of his film. True, he'd seen it more times than he could recall, but it only got better and better every time. So be it, thought Waltin, pouring a fresh malt whiskey and reaching for the remote control.

They sat at the restaurant for almost two hours, and once they came out onto the street she thought about leaving, saying that they could talk tomorrow, and going home, but for some reason that didn't happen. Instead they walked home to Daniel's, a brisk walk—they even raced a little—and when they strode in through the entryway to the dormitory he looked at her with his big eyes and his gentle smile and asked if she wanted to have a cup of tea. And she nodded and followed him into the elevator. What is it you're doing? thought Assistant Detective Jeanette Eriksson.

What do you mean, first hour? thought Martinsson, glancing at the blanket-wrapped, snoring bundle in the back of the delivery van. Almost three hours, and the last two hours he'd been cold as a dog despite the fact that he'd wrapped his legs in a blanket and even stuffed a couple of old copies of *Expressen* under his rump in a desperate attempt to alleviate the cold that forced its way up through the seat.

Like some damn homeless person, thought Martinsson. And that damn Göransson must be built like an Eskimo despite the fact that he'd taken almost all the blankets that they had in the car. And that damn druggie who sat gorging himself in a big Östermalm apartment. He would slice the arms and legs off him as soon as he stuck his nose outside the door and then . . .

"Jesus!" Martinsson swore out loud and sincerely as he turned the key in the ignition.

As soon as she stepped into the corridor she saw them and all her alarm bells starting ringing in her head. What is going on? she thought. But fortunately Daniel took over so she had time to think. Another Daniel than the one she knew. Big, black, and threatening, a person who didn't step back and who quite certainly hadn't grasped that the men whose way he was blocking were police. Jesus, thought Assistant Detective Jeanette Eriksson despite the fact that she almost never swore, what is going on and what am I doing here?

The film was over. The whiskey wasn't, and there was more available if that had been the case, but Waltin didn't feel like it. A really good red wine is better, thought Waltin. Softer, more balanced, and you didn't lose your clarity in the same way regardless of the degree of intoxication, but just now he didn't feel like wine either. The only thing he felt was a slight irritation. Waste of resources, thought Waltin. What was important now was to bring home little Jeanette and see to it that somewhat more essential things were accomplished. And at that moment the phone rang. Past ten, thought Waltin with surprise, for some reason it was that old bastard Forselius that he was picturing. However he might have gotten the number here, thought Waltin, picking up the receiver.

"Yes," said Waltin. "I'm listening."

"For Christ's sake, Martinsson, turn off the engine," said Göransson, sticking his rumpled head between the seats. "We can't sit with the engine on, you know that well enough."

Hope your sleep was good, thought Martinsson, but before he had time to say anything really cutting on the same theme they called them on the radio.

"Yes," said Martinsson, turning off the engine. "We're listening."

"You can call it a day, boys," said the officer on the radio. "I was just speaking with the Alpha dog."

"Call it a day," said Martinsson. This is God help me not true, he thought.

"Yep. He wants you to call it off. Then he wants to meet you tomorrow, but he'll be in touch early in the morning regarding the time."

Göransson had already reached out his hand and turned on the ignition, despite the fact that he hadn't managed to crawl out between the seats.

"Do you mind driving?" he asked.

"Where are you calling from?" asked Waltin. Calm down, he thought.

"From a pay phone down in the vestibule at . . . well, you know," replied Assistant Detective Eriksson.

"Okay," said Waltin. "So do the following. Walk a little ways down toward town and take a taxi to my place, so we can talk in peace and quiet."

What the hell is going on? thought Waltin.

While Waltin was waiting for little Jeanette he had taken the opportunity to freshen himself up. He had washed himself—hands, face, and armpits—brushed his teeth, and sprayed over any lingering scent of whiskey. Then he'd changed his shirt, to a loose and comfortable cream-colored linen with his monogram embroidered in blue silk on the breast pocket. And while he was polishing his feathers he had been thinking sharply the whole time.

There was a significant risk that the shit would hit the fan, thought Waltin. In addition there were several things that didn't add up. According to the conversation with Hedberg at approximately a quarter past eight, when he called from the apartment that Waltin had arranged for him, he was supposed to have carried out his assignment without complications, between seven and roughly a quarter to eight. Between thumb and index finger and it will work out, thought Waltin.

According to Göransson and Martinsson, a double misfortune that he must do something about at once, Krassner had walked through Forselius's doorway on Sturegatan as early as twenty minutes to seven, and when they were sent home three and a half hours later he should still have been there.

Truly very peculiar, thought Waltin, because according to the Stockholm police command center, Krassner had fallen out of a window from the sixteenth floor of the Rosehip student dormitory on Körsbärsvägen at five minutes to eight in the evening and approximately half a mile from the place where he was supposed to be sitting shooting the breeze with a confused old bastard from the days of the cold war. Moreover, the information as to time and place were certain, because he himself had checked them, obviously in a completely secure but devious way. Had he even been at Forselius's at all? The simplest thing would no doubt be to ask directly, thought Waltin, but at the same time that could just as well wait. Having come that far in his thoughts he was interrupted by the discreet signal from the doorway telephone. Little Jeanette, thought Waltin, and he felt both exhilarated and capable of action.

Good Lord, thought Jeanette confusedly as she looked around Waltin's living room. How can a police officer afford such an apartment? Even if he is a superintendent?

"How are you doing?" asked Waltin. He looked at her, smiling a little but with a touch of seriousness and with a sympathetic wrinkle in his forehead.

"I'm okay," said Jeanette, nodding. "I understood of course that he was crazy. And I've said that. But that he was crazy enough to jump out the window, that I didn't believe."

"We'll discuss that later," said Waltin soothingly. "Would you like something to eat?"

"No. I ate a while ago."

"Then perhaps I might offer you something to drink? A glass of wine, perhaps?" Waltin looked at her with the same slightly worried smile.

"A glass of wine would be nice. If you're having one too."

"We both probably need one," said Waltin confidently. So that we can finally get to the point, you and I, he thought.

A quarter of an hour later the pieces started falling into place. Little Jeanette sat curled up on his big sofa; she was already working on her second glass of wine. She seemed collected but at the same time vulnerable and a little dejected in a way that was both attractive and arousing.

"If I've understood the matter correctly, you meet M'Boye at the student restaurant a little after seven. Then the two of you walk to a restaurant on Birger Jarlsgatan. Eat dinner for two hours and return to his apartment at the dormitory. You're there at about nine-thirty."

Waltin looked at her with mildly inquisitive eyes. Whatever it was you had to do there, you little bitch, he thought.

"Yes," said Jeanette, nodding. "And that was when we ran into the guys from Stockholm. They were done with Krassner's room and were just leaving but Dan— M'Boye got angry and asked who they were and what they were doing there. I guess he didn't realize that they were police. For a moment I was worried that he would attack them." Jeanette nodded, mostly to herself, apparently, taking a gulp from her wineglass.

"What did they say then?" asked Waltin. "The police," he clarified.

"Well, there was a rather heated discussion between them and M'Boye. They said that it was a suicide, that they were completely sure of that but they didn't want to explain why and M'Boye refused to buy it."

"Do you know why?" asked Waltin. "Why didn't he believe it?"

"Presumably because they were policemen and because he doesn't like the police," said Jeanette, shrugging her shoulders. "Well, and because it was skewed from the start. One of the cops was actually not very nice. The other one was more normal. He was a technician. He even introduced himself."

"And you?" said Waltin.

"No." Jeanette shook her head. "I tried to keep myself in the background. I didn't even need to say my name. They seemed to be in a big hurry to get out of there, actually."

"And neither of them recognized you," asked Waltin.

"No," said Jeanette, and for some reason she smiled.

"And you're quite certain of that?"

"Yes, quite certain. When they left I heard the one from the after-hours unit, he was the short fat one who was actually rather awful, he called me a typical student whore."

"Sad," said Waltin without smiling. "Sad to have such officers. You don't know their names?"

"The short fat one never introduced himself, but the other one showed his ID."

"Do you remember his name?"

"Yes, his name was Wiijnbladh. Detective inspector."

This isn't true, thought Waltin delightedly. Wiijnbladh, that wretched little shit.

"Is it anyone you know?" asked Jeanette.

"No," said Waltin, shaking his head. "It doesn't ring any bells. Don't believe I've even heard the name."

It's not anything I'm thinking about telling you, in any case, thought Waltin.

"You know what," he said. "This is a very sad story that we've landed in, because of a poor person who actually appears to have been seriously mentally ill, and if there's anything I blame myself for, it's probably that I didn't listen carefully enough to what you said about how bad things were with Krassner. . . ."

"I don't think you should do that," objected Jeanette. "Unfortunately I wasn't especially clear, but . . ."

Waltin shook his head negatively.

"Jeanette," said Waltin. "You and I are police officers. Our duty is to protect the security of the realm, and unfortunately it's the case that most of what we encounter in our job is more or less crazy. But we're not social workers, we aren't doctors, and we're definitely not spiritual advisers. Do you hear what I'm saying?"

Clearly, thought Waltin, for she nodded in agreement and looked both serious and collected.

"We won't get involved in the investigation of Krassner's suicide," Waltin continued. "The Stockholm police can take care of that. That will take its own course, even if I will, naturally, see to it that we're kept informed. But as far as we're concerned I have a definite feeling that this entire sad story is over. And unfortunately, unfortunately it had a bad ending, but there's nothing we can do about that. What you and I should do is the following."

She looked at him and nodded. Attentive, listening, willing to do what he said. Excellent, thought Waltin.

"What we should do is simply one thing," said Waltin. "We should lie low." And I'm going to lie between your legs, thought Waltin, but he didn't say that, for she didn't have anything to do with it.

[SATURDAY, NOVEMBER 23]

When Waltin woke up early on Saturday morning, little Jeanette was lying next to him in bed. As a seducer he had been faced with considerably more difficult tasks. She had seemed almost compliant when he led her into his bedroom, and because it was the first time, he'd held back and contented himself with performing a couple of for the most part normal acts of intercourse. He had been just determined enough but not more, and when he woke up she was sleeping curled up in a fetal position with her head boring down into the pillow, holding yet another pillow pressed against her belly. Waltin had lain looking at her a while, and he was still very satisfied with what he saw. This can be completely perfect, he thought. All that was demanded now was precision, clarity, and a perfectly executed acclimatization, and because the conditions were good he could happily take the time such things took when they were worth the effort.

Then he went out to the kitchen and prepared breakfast, set the table over by the window with the view, and exerted himself both in how he did it and what he set out for them. When everything was ready he'd wakened her with a light kiss on the forehead, and now she was sitting across from him. In one of his altogether too large bathrobes, newly wakened, with tousled hair and a bare, unadorned face. And she looked both surprised and delighted when she understood that the cup in front of her contained neither coffee nor tea.

"Chocolate with whipped cream," tittered little Jeanette. "God that's good! I don't think I've had that since I was a kid."

Which is the very idea, thought Waltin, stroking her lightly across the back of her neck.

"I was thinking about inviting you to dinner this evening," said Waltin, at the same time letting his thumb stop at the base of her neck. "I would have preferred to have spent the whole day with you," he continued with the exactly right charm-filled apologetic smile, "but unfortunately there are certain practical matters that I must take care of before we can relax."

Little Jeanette had nodded with a serious expression. Just like children always did when they understood that they'd become a part of something important.

"Now here's what we'll do," said Waltin, lacing his powerful, suntanned fingers in hers, which were half their size. "I don't want you to return to the student dormitory. On the other hand, I want you to keep track of that M'Boye so he doesn't get you dragged into something. Can you phone him?"

"He was going to call me at home this morning," said Jeanette. "He doesn't have a phone of his own. Just the one that goes to their corridor."

"Avoid that," said Waltin. "Lie low. Keep track of M'Boye. See to it that he doesn't start anything. Can you manage that?" Waltin smiled warmly and squeezed her hand.

Jeanette nodded.

"Good," said Waltin. "Then I'll find out what this sad story is really about."

First he arranged a meeting with Hedberg in the small sleepover apartment at Gärdet that he'd loaned out to him. Hedberg seemed fresh and rested and offered fresh-brewed coffee. Waltin had decided to wait to discuss Krassner's suicide.

"Tell me," said Waltin, taking a sip of the hot coffee.

.   .   .

According to Hedberg there wasn't much to tell. He had seen Krassner leave the student dormitory at six-thirty, and when he got the all-clear signal on the radio ten minutes later he had started to work. One hour later he was finished and then he'd taken his gear, left the place, driven home, called Waltin, and reported.

"A messy little student apartment; he didn't have too many things. A few papers and those you have on film."

Hedberg nodded toward the three rolls of film that were lying on the table.

"Well, what more was there?" said Hedberg, looking as though he was thinking deeply. "He'd hidden some marijuana cigarettes behind the medicine cabinet. He got to keep those." Hedberg smiled wryly.

"What impression did you get of him?" asked Waltin. "As a person, I mean."

"Impression," said Hedberg. "Well, I guess I almost got the impression that the person living there was a little crazy. Looked like an ordinary junkie pad. Things tossed everywhere, sheets bunched up at the foot of the bed. Nothing that you would have appreciated," said Hedberg, smiling faintly.

So there, thought Waltin who had difficulty with intimacies, even when they came from such a highly valued colleague as Hedberg.

"A little crazy, you say?"

"One of those paranoid junkie types," said Hedberg, nodding. "That door alert, the piece of paper on the door frame, I found right away, for example."

"And you put it back when you left," said Waltin.

"All according to orders and established routines," said Hedberg.

"No complications," asked Waltin, lightly and just uninterested enough.

"So-so," said Hedberg. "If I were to complain, there was actually someone left in the corridor after seven o'clock. Right after seven I heard someone going out through the door to the vestibule. Then there was someone who came in right after and turned and went out again. I got an impression that it was the same person and that he'd forgotten something that he came back and fetched."

M'Boye, thought Waltin, who had Jeanette's account fresh in his memory. Goes to show that blacks can never learn to tell time.

"I'm sorry about that," he said. "It was one of those people who can't keep track of time."

"It's not the end of the world," said Hedberg. "I heard him and he didn't see me, so I'll give you that one."

Okay then, thought Waltin. Then there's just one problem remaining.

"A little problem has come up," he said.

Hedberg contented himself with nodding.

"Krassner has taken his life."

"Oh, lay off." said Hedberg, surprised. "When?"

"Five minutes to eight yesterday evening," said Waltin. "He did a double full gainer out the window at the student dormitory."

Hedberg hadn't been easy to convince, and his objections were both logical and completely understandable.

"I think this sounds strange," said Hedberg. "It was almost twenty till eight when I left his corridor. That was just a quarter of an hour before he would have jumped out through the window."

"Yes," said Waltin. "There isn't much time to play with."

"Then he's supposed to have written a suicide note as well? It can't have been a very long epistle, otherwise we would have run into each other."

"He might actually have written the letter before and had it with him," said Waltin, who was thinking out loud.

Hedberg shook his head and still seemed to be full of doubt.

"I still think it sounds strange," he said, also sounding like someone thinking out loud. "He must have left that meeting over on Sturegatan at least fifteen minutes before he jumped out through the window. And in that case he can hardly have done more than come in and left. His meeting, I mean. What kind of strange meeting was it?"

"Yes," said Waltin. "There's a lot here that's strange."

"Sure," said Hedberg with emphasis. "And then if he was on his way back, how is it that the guys who were supposed to watch him didn't make contact and warn me?"

Interesting question, thought Waltin.

"It'll work out," said Waltin, putting the rolls of film in his pocket. "I'll be in touch when I know something."

What is it that I've forgotten? he thought, getting up. Is there something I've forgotten?

"There was something else," said Waltin. "Help me."

"You mean that letter?" asked Hedberg. "The letter about the meeting?"

"Exactly," said Waltin, "Krassner's invitation to the meeting with Forselius. Did you find it?"

"No," said Hedberg. "It wasn't left behind in his room, in any case. Of that I'm quite certain. Neither a letter nor an envelope."

Damn, thought Waltin, despite the fact that he almost never swore.

"We'll just have to hope that he didn't have it with him," said Hedberg, smiling wryly.

Waltin was not the type to take unnecessary risks. If Krassner had indeed had Forselius's letter in his pocket when he jumped out the window, it was too late to do anything about that. On the other hand there was almost certainly still time to warn Forselius so that he could keep his mouth shut if the investigators from the Stockholm police were to contact him. In addition there were of course a number of other major reasons to find out what he and Krassner had really been up to at the meeting, which in any event must have been considerably shorter than planned.

Forselius seemed even less pleased than usual to encounter Waltin. After the usual grumbling about Saturday morning and "important business," he finally yielded and received him in his darkened apartment, as usual and despite the time of day wearing a dressing gown and holding a brandy snifter. Waltin pretended not to notice and turned on the charm, being careful not to show his cards from the start.

"How did the meeting with Krassner go?" Waltin asked with a conciliatory smile.

"The meeting with Krassner," said Forselius, with a calculating look at Waltin. "You're wondering how the meeting with Krassner went?"

"Yes," said Waltin, smiling amiably. "Tell me how it went."

"So kind of you to ask," Forselius grunted. "It went just fine."

"That's nice," said Waltin. "What did you—"

"The little snake never showed up," Forselius interrupted, fortifying himself with a generous gulp from the snifter.

"He never showed up?"

"I'm happy that your ears are functioning," Forselius said amiably. "As I said. He never showed up."

"What did you do, then?" Waltin asked with interest. Idiot, he thought. The old man is a complete idiot.

"I waited a while. Then I read a good book, an excellent book, in fact, about stochastic processes and harmonic functions. I have it here somewhere if you're interested." Forselius made a sweeping gesture in the direction of the bookshelves behind his back.

"It never occurred to you to make contact?" asked Waltin. As we'd agreed on, you miserable old bastard, he thought.

"No," said Forselius, looking as if he'd never given it a thought. "On the other hand I did make a call to your boss."

What else would you expect? thought Waltin.

"And what did he say?"

"Not too much," said Forselius. "Either he wasn't at home or he didn't want to answer."

"Did you leave a message?" asked Waltin.

"I never leave messages on answering machines," said Forselius haughtily. "It goes against the nature of the operation."

When Waltin told Forselius that Krassner was dead, the old man nodded approvingly. It was an excellent opportunity to find out in peace and quiet what "the little snake" had been up to. The information that he must have taken his own life was received with amused indulgence.

"Took his own life, of course," said Forselius, winking. "So now the superintendent wants me to testify that he seemed deeply depressed when we met, if our colleagues from the open operation should knock on my door."

"If that should be the case I only want you to say how it was," said Waltin with forced courtesy. "That he wanted to meet you for an interview but that he never showed up." And that you can keep yourself sufficiently sober not to mention us, he thought.

"So it was then that he"—Forselius grunted with enjoyment while he drew his index finger across his wrinkled neck—"took his own life."

Sigh, thought Waltin, and five minutes later he said goodbye, correct yet courteous.

After the visit with Forselius, Waltin took the road past the firm's garage. The blue delivery van stood parked in its usual place and it had been cursorily cleaned. However, in the trash can by the garage door only five yards away someone had been recklessly careless. The black garbage bag was almost empty, but on the top was a paper bag and inside it an empty can, a crumpled coffee cup, and various scraps of paper that were evidence of a hamburger dinner for two, plus a receipt for the whole party from the hot-dog stand up by Tessin Park at Gärdet.

What kind of world is it we live in when a police superintendent is forced to use his weekend to root through garbage cans? thought Waltin gloomily while with distaste and the help of his pen he poked through the leftovers. What do I do now and how do I get rid of these two lightweights?

First he returned to his office and spoke with an acquaintance who was responsible for certain security issues at the ministry of foreign affairs. No problem, because Waltin promised to pay the costs, and the joint decision on a quickly arranged extra exercise under realistic conditions could be made immediately. One hour later he met Göransson and Martinsson in his office. Both appeared to have slept well, and one thing was obvious right from the start: Neither of them had any idea about Krassner's demise.

"Tell me," said Waltin, nodding and smiling amiably while he leaned back in his large desk chair and formed his fingers into a church steeple of the classic Gothic model.

"Yes," said Göransson, clearing his throat and leafing through his little black notebook. "Well," he continued after another throat clearing. "The object left his address on Körsbärsvägen at eighteen thirty-two hours. After that he walked at a brisk pace down Körsbärsvägen, then Valhallavägen on the sidewalk on the west side. He arrived at the appointed meeting place, Sturegatan 60, at eighteen forty-two hours and went directly in through the doorway. Ten minutes later, that is," Göransson summarized with a discreet throat-clearing and a slightly nervous side glance at his younger colleague.

"I see," said Waltin blandly. "And what did you do then?"

"We positioned our vehicle approximately one hundred yards further down on Sturegatan," said Göransson, giving Martinsson another glance. "It was the best position according to our collective judgment."

"What else?" asked Waltin heartily. "Was it you who was driving, Martinsson?"

Martinsson tore himself unwillingly away from his image in the large mirror behind Waltin's back and shook his head.

"No," said Martinsson. "It was Göransson who drove."

Göransson glared acidly at his younger colleague, which wasn't easy, as he was trying to do it on the sly.

"And at what time had you taken up your position?" Waltin asked innocently.

"About eighteen forty-three," said Göransson. "About eighteen forty-three more or less, that is."

This is getting better and better, thought Waltin, but he didn't say that.

"And so then what happened?" Waltin asked with curiosity, at the same time leaning forward across the desk in order to further indicate his deep interest.

Not a thing, according to both conspirators. They had just sat there—true enough, in the front seat of a Dodge delivery van but watchful as two eagles—until the radio operator had made contact and told them to break it off and call it a day and then it was past ten o'clock.

"Twenty-two-zero-eight hours," Göransson clarified with a fresh throat clearing and after another look in his little black book.

"It's all in our surveillance memo," Martinsson assisted obligingly. "It's sitting in the usual folder."

"But that was very good, wasn't it?" said Waltin, nodding and leaning back. Lying with all the practice that the profession had given them, he thought, and now it was crucial to just be rid of them before the natural stupidity that qualified them for this same profession also made a mess of things for him.

"I have a special assignment for you gentlemen," said Waltin. "A very urgent one, abroad, might take a week, maybe two. The thing is that the ministry of foreign affairs needs help with a little discreet surveillance of a somewhat mixed delegation of politicians, people from the foreign ministry and the military, and I have to have a couple of lads that I can really rely on. Through thick and thin," he added gravely.

"Yes," said Göransson. "We're listening, chief." The thought of a fat foreign per diem had put life into his tired eyes.

"Abroad," said Martinsson, who was younger, had a harder time concealing his enthusiasm, and was already packing his bathing trunks.

"We can be at Arlanda in two hours, packed and ready," Göransson agreed obligingly.

"That won't be necessary," said Waltin dryly. "It's good enough if you can be at the central train station before six o'clock." For further transport to a place where there aren't any hamburgers and where it's guaranteed that you'll be freezing your asses off, thought Waltin, but he didn't say that.

"Train," Göransson burst out, and the light in his eyes had gone out.

"Train," echoed Martinsson, who seemed so taken aback that he forgot to check his reaction in Waltin's mirror.

"I think it's going to be a very interesting journey," said Waltin, nodding with conviction, "and you'll receive further information accordingly and on a need-to-know basis."

It will be a fantastic journey, he thought. In the middle of a bitterly

cold winter on one of those fine old Russian trains and with all the service that has made their hosts famous among their Western visitors.

"He who makes a journey always has something to tell," said Waltin,
smiling amiably. "In addition the ministry of foreign affairs has arranged
passports for you, so you don't need to mess around with visas," he
added consolingly.

In the afternoon Waltin made quiet inquiries about how it was going
with the Stockholm Police Department's investigation of Krassner's
death. According to his contact, who had spoken with the head of the
after-hours squad, the investigation was already done. A few practical
details remained that the local precinct at Östermalm would take
care of.

"Seems to be a rather typical suicide. However it is that you can jump
from the sixteenth floor—but he was after all some sort of student, so he
was high, of course," Waltin's contact summarized.

That was nice to hear, I guess, Waltin thought sympathetically and
decided that the rolls of film that Hedberg had taken could wait until
after the weekend. So could contact with Berg, who was out of the
country meeting important people and was only to be disturbed if
something happened that was even more important, and in Waltin's
ledger Krassner didn't merit an entry. Finally, thought Waltin, who had
more essential things on the program.

Assistant Detective Jeanette Eriksson had done her part as well. Daniel
had called her right before lunch and as usual he was friendly and obliging, and this time also worried about how she was doing. Jeanette had
said the things she was expected to say. That it felt sad despite the fact
that she didn't know Krassner and had mostly perceived him as a very
strange character who hadn't even been particularly nice. Whatever the
case may be, it was still a strange feeling since she'd said hello to him as
recently as a few days ago. One thing was important; she absolutely did
not want anything to do with the police. True, she hadn't said anything
to Daniel earlier, but her previous experiences with the Swedish police

were far from good. Despite the fact that she'd never done anything criminal.

"They treat all people like criminals, even if you're completely innocent," said Assistant Detective Eriksson.

According to Daniel she had no reason to be concerned. She could trust him unconditionally. He would really not drag her into anything if the police were to come around again. This Krassner was truly a strange person and Daniel himself was certain that he'd also been a racist. And as far as the Swedish police were concerned, he had unfortunately been struck by the fact that they were obviously like the South African police, and he couldn't even bear to go into his experiences regarding the latter.

"It's a particular kind of people who become police officers," Daniel maintained. "It doesn't seem to matter where they come from, and I've never met one who seemed normal and humane."

Because Jeanette would as usual be meeting her sick mother over the weekend, one of her early lies and the emergency exit she made use of most often, they decided that they would talk after the weekend, perhaps meet in town and have lunch together.

Okay then, thought Assistant Detective Jeanette Eriksson as she put down the receiver. And now she could finally start planning her evening.

Okay then, thought Waltin as he strode into his apartment on Norr Mälarstrand. High time to plan the evening.

[MONDAY, NOVEMBER 25]

When Waltin came to work on Monday morning he felt sharp in mind, strong in body, and with a pleasurable weight in his crotch. He had spent the last thirty-six hours with Jeanette Eriksson, and they hadn't even set foot outside the door. With the exception of a few brief meals and a few hours' sleep, he had also been for the most part screwing her the entire time, and everything had gone according to plan. Women were naturally submissive. Waltin had known that for a long time from his own extensive personal experience, but with many women—and strangely enough this often concerned those who were a little younger—there might still be problems stemming from the rampant delusions spread by certain media and groups on the left fringe. Something that in its turn might create mental blockages that prevented them from full enjoyment in what was for a woman the obvious way.

Little Jeanette had, however, responded in a natural way to the signals he'd given her, although it was still mostly a matter of intellectual influence, and her physical qualifications were extraordinary. The slender boyish body, her closed eyes when he was working his way through her erogenous zones, the pathetic little attempts to hold back her reactions before she achieved orgasm. The only thing that bothered him now was the black triangle of tightly curled hair that covered her little womb, but that was a detail he looked forward to being able to attend to the coming weekend.

High time to tighten the thumbscrews, thought Waltin contentedly, and just then his red telephone rang.

Berg had spent the weekend together with some colleagues at Constitutional Protection. The meeting had taken place at an exceedingly comfortable spa hotel twenty or thirty miles outside Wiesbaden, and for once he'd had the opportunity to bring his wife along. The Germans had arranged a charming ladies' program so that he and his colleagues had been able to work completely undisturbed while their wives visited various attractions along the Rhine, and in the evenings they had taken their meals together. Exceedingly nice parties where the host had escorted his wife to the table for the somewhat simpler and more informal welcome buffet on Friday evening, and Berg himself had been given the place of honor at the gala dinner on Saturday.

You can really count on the Germans, thought Berg. They were a people who were careful about both content and form in their relationships with their fellow human beings.

.　.　.

On Sunday evening he and his wife had taken the flight to Copenhagen. His wife had continued with a connecting flight to Stockholm because she had classes at the school where she worked on Monday morning. He himself had taken the hydrofoil to Malmö, checked in at the Savoy, eaten a simple dinner at the hotel, and gone to bed early.

On Monday morning he had set up a meeting with his colleagues at the department in Malmö, but before they sat down at the conference table he had called his secretary in Stockholm. It had after all been two and a half days since he'd last had access to a secure telephone.

"Waltin wants you to call him," said his secretary. "It's about Citizen Kane," she added. Where had she heard that name before? she thought.

Krassner, thought Berg, and much later, when he thought back to this incident, he recalled that he'd had an unpleasant foreboding about something even then. Unclear why, but real. He remembered that distinctly long afterward.

Waltin's voice sounded utterly unconcerned. Almost as though he had nothing to do with the matter.

Of course Berg also thought about that. Both then and long afterward.

"How has it been going?" asked Berg.

"Just fine," said Waltin. "It appears we've been worrying ourselves quite unnecessarily." Not me but you, he thought, but he didn't say that.

"What do you mean?" said Berg.

"I've just been looking through the results of his so-called intellectual efforts, and it seems to be pure rubbish."

Despite the fact that he'd been sitting at his typewriter several hours a day for a month and a half, thought Berg, but he didn't say that.

"Tell me," said Berg.

"Fifty-some pages with highly confused notes. Some assorted texts, a few drafts of something that might possibly be a thriller, possibly a documentary history, but presumably something in between."

"What's it about?" asked Berg.

"I suggest that we take that up when we meet," said Waltin, his voice sounding rather pleased. "Let me put it like this. Both you and I and many of us here in the building have probably indulged in the same line of reasoning."

I see, thought Berg. So that's the way it is. He'd already suspected as much.

"Has anything else happened?" he asked.

"He killed himself on Friday evening," said Waltin, and judging by his tone of voice, he wasn't one of the chief mourners.

"I'm coming up," said Berg. "See to it that someone picks me up from the flight."

One more scatterbrain, thought Waltin.

Berg and Waltin had spent the whole afternoon together, and when they went their separate ways neither of them was especially satisfied with the other, despite the fact that they both concealed it well.

There's something careless about him, thought Berg. Something childish, something immature.

"We'll lie low," he said. "I'll take this over starting now. I will of course keep you informed."

Waltin shrugged his well-tailored shoulders. Berg might soon start working in the Kurd unit, thought Waltin. Along with both those other loonies.

"Fine with me," he said. "Although you're worrying yourself unnecessarily."

First Waltin had described the work they'd done. It had actually gone completely according to plan, if you could believe him. The operative had made his way in, done what he was supposed to, and made his way out, observed by no one, and that was just what the whole thing was about. True, Göransson and Martinsson had messed up and lost track of Krassner, but luck had still been on their side. It was a fact that Krassner had taken his own life, and he'd done it under his own steam. Whether he'd been high and only wanted to try his new wings or had suffered a sudden insight into his lost life was beyond Waltin's judgment. Regardless of which, the question was not their concern. Krassner was not a security matter anymore and had actually never been one. That was Waltin's firm view.

"If we're going to blame ourselves for anything, maybe it's that, I guess. That we didn't really see how crazy he was," said Waltin, shrugging his shoulders. "The guy seems to have been completely confused. I suggest you look at his posthumous papers." Waltin slid the bundle, including photographs, to Berg.

You can be quite sure that I will, thought Berg.

"Where are Göransson and Martinsson?" he asked.

"On an educational trip," said Waltin, smiling wryly. "I thought it was safest to take them out of action."

"How much do they know?" asked Berg.

"They don't know about Krassner's suicide," answered Waltin. "They'll no doubt find out about it sooner or later. They don't even know that they managed to lose him. And of course they have no idea that I know what they'd been doing instead of being on the job."

Berg contented himself with nodding.

"Eriksson?" he asked.

"Keeping an eye on the situation. I'd thought about bringing her in as soon as Stockholm has written up Krassner. I've told her to keep herself out of the loop." You don't need to worry about her, thought Waltin.

Berg nodded again.

Waltin and I, he thought. That's two. Plus Göransson, Martinsson, and Eriksson, that makes five. And Waltin's operative, whoever that might be, which incidentally was yet another question that could wait at least until he himself had found out the answer, which made six people altogether. And Forselius, he thought, and suddenly that was far too many. What is it those motorcycle hoods always say? he thought. That three can keep a secret if two are dead?

As soon as Waltin had left, Berg had gone out to his secretary and asked her to phone for a taxi. He'd already dismissed the thought of sitting there at work. Better to go home to his wife and the house in Bromma and think over the situation in peace and quiet. Perhaps try to sleep on the matter and in the best case dream positive dreams that Waltin was maybe right despite the carelessness that doubtless was the main ingredient of his boyish charm.

"Have we had any calls?" asked Berg, making an effort to smile at her cheerfully. A rock, he thought. A true rock.

"The prime minister's special adviser wants you to contact him as soon as possible," she said.

Eight, thought Berg gloomily.

[TUESDAY, NOVEMBER 26]

Brooding all night, little sleep; but when he came to work early in the morning he had nonetheless gotten a few days' respite. The special adviser had called—he'd thought they should meet but then other things had come up and he was sitting in political discussions that most likely would be long drawn out. So he'd spoken with the minister of justice, who by the way would be making contact with Berg directly during the day, and they had agreed to postpone the weekly meeting until Friday. A bad day in and of itself, but it would be just fine if he and Berg could meet a few hours before the meeting.

"An old friend called me over the weekend and told me," said the special adviser.

Might his name possibly be Forselius? thought Berg, and I'll be darned how communicative you've suddenly become.

"That'll be just fine," said Berg. "I can meet Friday morning at nine o'clock."

"Great," stated the special adviser. "And should anything happen you can reach me down at Harpsund."

Berg promised to contact him at once if such were the case. Them up there and us down here, he thought as he put down the receiver.

Berg devoted the entire day to Krassner. True, at first he'd thought about whether he should turn the whole thing over to one of his more reliable coworkers, but after careful consideration—there was something in this story that didn't feel quite right—he'd decided to do it himself. At least to start with, and until he could be completely certain that it wasn't heading off in the wrong direction.

He started by looking at the pictures from the secret search of Krassner's student apartment. In total there were just under a hundred pictures, enlarged and of excellent quality. A dozen of them showed various parts of the interior from various angles. Untidy and littered with a vengeance, much like the addicts' pads he'd seen during his time as a young uniformed policeman out in the field, and the messy desk was scarcely evidence of uninterrupted work under harmonious conditions.

The remaining pictures depicted only papers, white typewriter paper with varying amounts of text, sometimes typewritten, some longhand. Several papers crumpled up, smoothed out to be photographed and, he hoped, crumpled up again and returned to their original position. And it was now that Berg started having problems. Krassner's handwriting— for you had to assume that he was the one who'd held the pen—was hard to decipher, and what was actually written there was cryptic, often abbreviated, and obviously in English throughout. Same thing with the typewritten pages: short sections and lines of text without a single context, more like drafts and directions for an outline than parts of a narrative. This is no manuscript, thought Berg—with one exception, which was possibly a basis for something that was probably meant to become a book.

The exception looked suspiciously like the title page to a book, and without being particularly familiar with the matter Berg assumed that it was a not entirely unusual expression of the agonies of authorship. "The Spy Who Went East, by John P. Krassner," Berg read, whereupon he made a neat little pencil mark in the upper right-hand corner of his copy. Easier to see when you leaf through it, thought Berg, who had an idea that he should first try to arrange his material in some sort of logical narrative sequence. What the whole thing was really about would be a question for later.

In total eighty-five pages with varying amounts of text, Berg thought after a second count, using a moistened index finger. Sixty-one of them, folded, wrinkled, crumpled up, seemed to emanate from the pile on his desk and the floor around it, while the remaining twenty-four, judging by one of the interior pictures, had been more or less organized on Krassner's otherwise not especially well-organized desk.

Berg first sorted the papers into two piles—wrinkled versus more or less orderly—in order to try to ascertain whether the written material in each pile possibly indicated some separate context or intellectual development, but it hadn't made him any wiser. After more than an hour of reading, his only conclusion was that clearly this dealt in part with things that the author was already done with or had rejected and thrown away, and in part with things that he hadn't gotten around to throwing out, but that the distinction was simply not clear from the written text. The fellow actually seems to be extremely confused, thought Berg, and for some reason he also happened to think about Waltin. Well-tailored, smiling, and in his eloquent way convinced that Krassner was a completely uninteresting nutcase who was only wasting their time.

More than once during the afternoon he pondered his poor English. In an absolute sense, and definitely in a relative sense as well, it was true that he spoke better English than the majority of his colleagues at a corresponding hierarchical level within the police operation. Not compared to Waltin, of course, for he had a quite different background, but by comparison with real police officers. In a normal, social context he managed well enough, but here he felt hopelessly handicapped. English was not his language, period, and more than once he'd been surprised by the fact that certain of his fellow workers had the temerity to maintain that they spoke fluent English. And they obviously believed it, despite the fact that their English was even worse than his.

Even before he'd started his go-through, his secretary had supplied him with a thick English-Swedish technical dictionary that he'd used before in similar connections. After lunch she'd been able to fetch a few more books that dealt with American technical expressions and common abbreviations, American colloquialisms and American slang, and after several more hours of fruitless linguistic efforts he finally gave up. He underlined those words, expressions, and passages that he didn't understand, had his secretary copy them, and called in one of his linguists from the analysis section.

Reminds me a little of Marja when she was younger, thought Berg, who often thought about his wife, and he smiled at his hastily summoned assistant.

"You couldn't help me with a little translation, could you?" said Berg, handing over the list of hard-to-decipher words and expressions. "From English to Swedish," he added, and for some reason he almost sounded apologetic as he said it.

The female linguist quickly looked through the copy he'd given her, nodded, and smiled.

"I think I can manage this," she said. "When do you want it?"

"As quickly as possible," said Berg, and an hour later she was back in his office.

"Well," said Berg, smiling. "How did it go?"

"I think I've managed most of it. In a few cases I've provided alternative interpretations. The most likely ones are on top." She handed over a few neatly typewritten pages in a red plastic folder.

"Tell me," said Berg. "Who wrote this? What kind of person?" he clarified.

"Goodness," she said, smiling. "Linguistic psychology is not really my strong suit."

"Try," insisted Berg.

"American," she said, "definitely American. Neither young nor old, somewhere between thirty and forty, I'd say. Academic, seems to have written a bit, might even be a journalist, and in that case I think I can guess who his idol is."

"I see," said Berg. "Who?"

"Hunter Thompson," said the translator. "You can see the Gonzo journalism in his way of writing, even if I would say it's the wrong context in which to use it."

"Gonzo journalism?"

"How to explain," she said, smiling. "Let's put it like this. If you're going to describe an event or a person, what's important journalistically is not the event or person itself but rather the journalist's feelings and thoughts in the presence of the event or person. What's interesting is what goes on in the head of the journalist, if I may say so."

This sounds extraordinarily practical, thought Berg.

"That sounds awfully practical. Must save an awful lot of time."

"Certainly," said his coworker, giggling. "Although if it's a good head then it can be both interesting and entertaining. Like Hunter Thompson, for example, when he's at his best. When he's bad he's just incomprehensible."

"Sounds a little doubtful if it's the truth you're after," Berg objected.

"The best Swedish example is probably Göran Skytte. Of a Gonzo journalist, I mean."

Skytte, thought Berg. Wasn't he that tall, unpleasant, self-centered, boring Scandian who ran around with that dreadful Guillou?

"So Skytte is a Swedish Hunter Thompson?"

"Well," his coworker objected, "I have a boyfriend who plays hockey in Division Four, but I guess he's not exactly a Gretzky. Although he would no doubt really like to be."

"This here, then," said Berg, pointing at the papers in the red plastic folder.

"With the qualification that my basis for comparison is perhaps a bit thin, then I think I would still maintain that Skytte is better."

"Skytte is better," said Berg. Than Krassner, he thought.

"Definitely," said the translator. "If we're talking Gonzo journalism, then Thompson plays in the National Hockey League, Skytte is in Swedish Division Four, while this guy here still has major problems with ice-skating."

"Despite the Gonzo journalism?" said Berg. And its practical relationship to the truth, he thought.

"Perhaps more accurately, just because of that. May I ask a question?" She looked at Berg with a certain apparent hesitation.

"Yes," said Berg. "Although I can't promise that you'll get an answer."

"These things that you wanted me to translate. This much I understand, of course, that it's the basis or draft or texts for some kind of book."

"Yes," said Berg. "That's right."

"What I'm wondering," she continued, "is if it's a nonfiction book. A factual description?"

"Yes," said Berg. "At least that's certainly the author's intention." And an exceedingly annoying one, he thought.

"And the remaining material looks the same?"

"Yes," said Berg. "More or less." In all essentials, fortunately, he thought.

"In that case I think the author is going to have major credibility problems," said the translator. "And besides, I don't think he writes very well."

Gonzo journalism, thought Berg as she closed the door behind her. And for the first time during this dreadful day he felt really enlivened.

When Berg could finally call it a day and go home, it was almost ten o'clock. With the answer sheet in hand, it also seemed he could have used his time on other, much more essential work, but considering the results he could still be content. He had summarized his observations and conclusions in a special memorandum a few pages long, just enough to be the basis for the oral presentation he was thinking of making on Friday morning when he met the prime minister's special adviser. And yet, because the content of Krassner's posthumous reflections was what it was, he was actually looking forward to this. Quite apart from the objectivity in what was clearly, despite everything, intended to be a factual description.

"The Spy Who Went East," thought Berg. Who Krassner's spy was he had already figured out before he started reading, for he himself had heard it ad nauseam during his years in the big building on Polhemsgatan. During those years when the present government had been in opposition there had even been powerful forces within the closed operation working to open a preliminary investigation into the matter. Something that Berg had fortunately been able to avert with kind assistance from the then chief of national police. Although he was still not really clear about the title of Krassner's intended book. The spy who went over to the east, thought Berg. From where, then? he thought. From the north, from the south, from the West? In all likelihood from the West, despite the fact that Krassner hadn't given any direction whatsoever on that point in his papers, and although he'd had an uncle who worked for a number of years within the American intelligence service. Hopefully blessedly departed in accordance with the rules that applied to the cause that he served, thought Berg and decided that he'd probably been unnecessarily worried after all. The fellow actually didn't seem to have been all there, he thought as he leaned back in his seat and closed his eyes.

"Excuse me, chief," said his chauffeur with a careful throat clearing. "But we're home now."

"I must have dozed off, so I guess I'm the one who should beg your pardon," said Berg.

[WEDNESDAY, NOVEMBER 27]

Finally a night of uninterrupted rest, and by breakfast time Berg had already decided that he'd been unnecessarily concerned, that he had more important things to do, and that the explanation of the immediate circumstances surrounding Krassner's suicide could well be turned over to a reliable coworker. Persson, thought Berg, and just then the sun peeked in through the kitchen window.

"Good morning, good morning," said Berg, in an excellent mood, to his secretary as soon as he strode through the door to his office. "Can you ask Persson to come in to see me?"

Berg had known Persson for more than thirty years. They'd been in the same class at the police academy and a few years later they'd shared the front seat of one of the Stockholm Police Department's radio cars during a not particularly eventful summer while their older, regular colleagues enjoyed their vacations in the country with their families and other colleagues and their families. Then Berg had started his climb toward the top of the police pyramid while Persson had played it safe and chosen to remain down below. Twenty years later, and in Persson's case twice as many pounds around the middle, they ran into each other by chance in town. Persson was working as an investigator on the burglary squad, and true, there were better jobs, no doubt, but because life was as it was . . . A week later he'd started with Berg, and it was a decision that neither of them had had reason to regret.

"I'm listening," said Persson, sitting down in the visitor's chair in front of Berg's large desk without asking for permission first, because he and Berg were old constables who'd worked like dogs together and such nonsense didn't apply to him.

"This concerns a few discreet inquiries about an apparent suicide that occurred on Friday evening," Berg explained.

"Hmm," said Persson, nodding.

Five minutes later Berg had familiarized his former classmate with all the details and was essentially ready to go ahead with more essential matters than this lunatic Krassner.

"Is there anything you're wondering about?" asked Berg amiably.

"No," said Persson. Shook his head, got up, and left.

A real old-time constable, thought Berg affectionately when he saw Persson's fat rear end disappearing through the door. Just as meticulous, taciturn, merciless, and kind as his father, the rural constable, had been during his time in the corps.

Two hours later everything was back to normal again and his good mood was shattered. Kudo and Bülling had requested an immediate meeting because their "analyses of certain telephone traffic clearly indicated that an assassination aimed at a highly placed but not more closely identified by name Swedish politician was imminent."

"There's one thing I'm wondering about," said Berg with as judicious a tone of voice as he could summon despite the situation. "It says here"—Berg rustled the papers he'd just received—"I quote, not more closely identified by name, end quote."

"Exactly," said Kudo energetically.

"That's right," Bülling assisted with his gaze glued to the fringe of the carpet.

"Not more closely identified by name, what does that mean? Do we have his first name?" Or hers, or his or her initials? thought Berg, a little confused, while a rapid-onset headache started to feel its way out toward his temples.

"Answer no," said Kudo briskly.

"In other words, we lack the first name of the politician in question," mumbled Bülling.

"Do we have his last name?" asked Berg. Fälldin, he thought hopefully. If it were the former prime minister, it would certainly facilitate a possible surveillance assignment.

"Answer no," countered Kudo. "Last name negative."

"So in other words we have neither the first nor last name of this . . . not more closely identified by name . . . politician?"

"Exactly," said Kudo, nodding with emphasis.

"He's highly placed, in any event," Bülling clarified in a mumble.

Then we devoutly hope it's not Santa Claus, thought Berg, but he didn't say that.

"I think we'll do the following," he said instead.

Five minutes later he had returned to his office, where he informed his secretary that he intended to work at home the rest of the day and could only be disturbed in event of war, naval attack, or coup d'état. Although obviously that wasn't how he put it.

"I'll call for your car," said his secretary. Poor thing, she thought. He seems completely worn out. Why doesn't he ever take a vacation?

[THURSDAY, NOVEMBER 28]

On Thursday, the twenty-eighth of November, Chief Inspector Persson wound up his discreet inquiries in Bureau Head Berg's office regarding the immediate details in connection with the Stockholm Police Department's investigation of the suicide of the American citizen John P. Krassner that he had initiated the day before: "probable" suicide, as it read in the initial review of the case. And as his old friend and colleague who had given him the assignment was on a visit to the secret police's office in Luleå, the debriefing would have to wait until the following morning.

All the same, thought Persson, deciding to take off early.

[FRIDAY, NOVEMBER 29]

First he met with Persson. He had set aside an hour for their meeting, but because Persson was the way he was, they were done in twenty minutes. Krassner had taken his own life; there was quite simply no latitude for any other possibility. Suicide was also the conclusion arrived at by the investigators from the Stockholm police. In reality the case was already closed, aside from the fact that the formal decision might drag on a few more days.

"I was thinking about his movements right before . . . well, before he jumped out the window," objected Berg, whose constant worry was gnawing inside his head. "He seems to have made his decision awfully late."

Not the least bit strange, according to Persson, but actually classic suicidal behavior. Trots off to a meeting set up beforehand and right when he gets there he changes his mind and leaves. Mucks about town, returns home, and settles the matter.

Well, thought Berg. He doesn't appear to have been particularly rational.

An embarrassing detail remained, according to Persson. If you were to dig into such things, Göransson and Martinsson had actually messed things up big time and it was no thanks to them that Waltin's operative was already finished and had managed to leave before Krassner showed up at home in his apartment.

"Damn blind bats," summarized Persson, and should Berg decide to send them back to the open operation at once, he could personally see about scaring the shit out of them before they got kicked out.

"Well," said Berg, "I'd been thinking about maybe waiting a little while until everything has a chance to settle down."

He's starting to get soft, thought Persson, but he didn't say that.

Then Persson got up to go, but before he did so he did something completely unexpected.

"There was one more thing," he said, looking at Berg.

"I'm listening," said Berg, and as he said it he heard alarm bells start ringing in his head.

"Waltin," said Persson.

"What about him?" asked Berg.

"Get rid of that piece of shit," said Persson.

"Is there anything in particular?" The alarm bells were ringing louder now.

"No, nothing in particular," said Persson, shrugging his broad shoulders. "I just don't trust him."

"Have you heard anything?" persisted Berg.

"No, but there isn't one single thing right with that bastard," Persson said as he left.

What do I do now? thought Berg, and the alarm bells in his head were now pealing.

Then he went to Rosenbad and met the prime minister's special adviser, who appeared heavy and worn-out and was disquietingly red around the eyes. He doesn't look well, thought Berg, and something must have happened with their relationship, for the thought that his old tormentor was feeling poorly made him depressed in a hard-to-explain way. Berg proceeded gingerly and started by recounting the immediate circumstances surrounding Krassner's suicide. The technical investigation at the scene, his posthumous suicide letter, the forensic doctor's report, questioning of the witnesses, and the observations that his own detectives had made during the time they had kept him under surveillance—everything, absolutely everything, pointed unambiguously in the same direction: suicide.

The special adviser was content to nod and smile his wry smile with the heavy eyelids lowered.

"We must try to endure the sorrow," he said, laughing a little.

Now I recognize you, thought Berg.

"Well well, then," continued the special adviser, mostly sounding as if he was thinking out loud. "A mutual acquaintance maintains that you killed him."

I must do something about Forselius, thought Berg. He seems to have gone completely gaga.

And then they finally got to the point.

"Tell me," said the prime minister's special adviser. "What was he up to?"

The result of the search that Berg's coworker had carried out—Berg was careful to underscore that this was a matter of a house search and that it had full legal support in the partially secret legislation that governed his operation—showed that Krassner was in the process of writing a book, that he didn't seem to have gotten especially far in his work, and that the little there was to study was incoherent, not to say incomprehensible. In addition, with his suicide the entire affair was no doubt over.

"What was it about?" The prime minister's special adviser suddenly seemed a bit more alert and looked at Berg with curiosity.

"It was about your boss," said Berg. "Or, to put it more correctly," he added judiciously, "I think it was intended to be about your boss."

"Explain," said the special adviser.

The material that Berg had studied mostly contained drafts of background descriptions: of the Social Democratic Party's frightful history, with its constant zigzagging between capitalism and communism; how during the war the party had been closely allied with the Nazis; and that from the beginning the party had been led by lechers and bribe-takers. Branting kept mistresses and was really just a capitalist in disguise who wanted to cover his own rear end just in case. Per Albin also had mistresses and moreover took bribes from the executives that he used to play poker and drink with. Krassner had this from a reliable Swedish source, whose grandfather had himself been one of the bribe-givers and told it in confidence to the source's own mother. In addition he was a multimillionaire by virtue of the fact that he'd organized a national fund on his fiftieth birthday whose proceeds had gone straight into his own pockets.

"Just imagine," said the special adviser with delight. "I've always thought that Per Albin was a wise man. But Tage, then? What kind of mischief was he up to?"

"Erlander is not mentioned whatsoever in the material that we have inspected," Berg declared.

"That's fishy," said the special adviser. "People from Värmland have always been crafty types. And they drink, and they're damn lazy, just like the slaves in *Uncle Tom's Cabin*. It was dancing at the crossroads and all that kind of thing."

Say that during an election campaign, thought Berg, but he didn't say that.

"Well," said the special adviser, looking urgently at Berg. "I realize you've saved the best for last. My highly esteemed boss: What kind of criminal activities has he gotten himself into?"

"Apart from the fact that he's been a Russian spy since the mid-1960s he seems to have conducted himself quite well for the most part," said Berg dryly.

"And what is the evidence for that?" said the special adviser.

"Nothing that you couldn't read between the lines in *Svenskan*," said Berg. Or that I haven't heard at work, he thought, but naturally he didn't say that.

"And that's all?" asked the special adviser, sounding almost disappointed.

"That's all," said Berg, "and the only reasonable conclusion is that we've been unnecessarily concerned."

But then the objections had come and suddenly Berg recognized his old self.

"There are four things that I don't really understand," said the special adviser. "In general there are lots of things I don't understand, but in this case there are four."

"I'm listening," said Berg, and now he was hearing the alarm bells again. Faintly and way back in his head, it was true, but clearly.

"The reason that we got unnecessarily concerned was not Krassner of course, but his uncle. Where is he in this?"

Nowhere, according to Berg.

"I recall you saying at the beginning that he was sitting for entire days writing at his typewriter, and all you find are less than a hundred pages of unsorted and mostly rejected notes, despite the fact that he'd been at it for six weeks? Has he hidden something, and in that case, where?"

According to Berg there was nothing to indicate that he had hidden away either documentation or material that he'd written himself. In any case not here in Sweden.

"The material you looked at seems to deal primarily with the party and its leadership. To me that sounds like a typical background description to something else. And a completely plausible reason to come here and get down to work."

"You mean he ought to have more material at home in the U.S.," asked Berg. Concerning your boss, he thought.

"Yes."

"I am withholding judgment," said Berg, "but if it is of the same quality as what we've found here, I still don't think there's any reason for us to worry."

For you don't really want me to ask the Germans to pose the question to our colleagues across the pond, he thought.

"And then I don't understand the title of his book," said the special adviser. "The spy who went over to the east?"

"I don't either," said Berg.

Nice to hear, thought the special adviser, for that was exactly the answer he wanted.

The ensuing weekly meeting went completely without friction, and the minister appeared mostly to be thinking about the approaching weekend. Berg had devoted most of the time to briefing them about two ongoing investigations of foreign embassies. One dealt with suspected refugee espionage and one with an unfortunately already completed case of industrial espionage in which the foreign office was resisting deportation. None of those present had any questions. On the other hand, the alarm bells in Berg's head were still ringing.

It is as it is, thought Berg when he got into his car outside Rosenbad. It's nice that the weekend's almost here.

[THE FIRST WEEK IN DECEMBER]

So, what's really going on? thought Assistant Detective Jeanette Eriksson as she settled down on her usual chair at work on Monday morning after having spent the weekend together with her new—and secret—boyfriend, Police Superintendent Waltin. For wasn't that how she was expected to view him, despite the difference in age? Her rump was sore too, which was awkward because the seclusion of her own office was now only a memory. Moreover, the whole Krassner project was already history, of the type that could never be told and with the lid painstakingly screwed down by the highest boss himself. And everything had started so well just a week ago, or ten days, to be exact, thought Eriksson, who was still careful about time regardless of whether it concerned work or her private life. Or, as in this case, something that had started as the former and continued as the latter.

Krassner was definitely history and Daniel would soon be. The last time they'd spoken she'd told him a tall tale about her constantly ailing mother suddenly becoming so much worse that she was now compelled to go home to Norrland to help her dad take care of her and her younger siblings. Daniel's sympathy as usual knew no bounds and she herself had felt even more reprehensible than usual. All that actually remained was Waltin, for it was he who now decided in detail how she should cover up after the assignment with Krassner, and it was he who now occupied her private life and clearly intended to do so in such a way that she didn't have the least desire to talk about it with anyone. Like that bag of candy that he'd first given her and then taken back for reasons that would scarcely be publishable even in Aunt Malena's little column in the big evening paper.

What is really going on? thought Assistant Detective Eriksson as she carefully adjusted her bottom to find the least painful position before she went to work on the day's routine assignments.

On Tuesday, the third of December, the Stockholm police closed the investigation of John P. Krassner's sudden death. His suicide was now explained beyond all reasonable doubt, there were even papers on the matter, and before the day was over Police Inspector Persson in his discreet way produced a copy of the entire investigation.

On the other hand, he had missed Krassner's belongings, the few things he'd left behind, for the embassy had already sent those home to the United States. This clearly bothered Persson, who among other things asked for some invitation that was not found either in the confiscation record or on the list of things sent home, but Persson had not been the least bit concerned. You throw away that kind of shit as soon as you get it, don't you? Persson thought, and he'd said so as well.

"You throw away that kind of shit as soon as you get it, don't you?" said Persson.

Berg contented himself with nodding in agreement, but to be completely sure he also requested an expert opinion from one of the bureau's psychiatric consultants. An extraordinarily competent doctor of the old school who had helped him on several previous occasions and who hadn't disappointed him this time either. Clearly Krassner's posthumous letter indicated that among other things he had a "strong depressive disposition" and that the "suicidal thoughts that had tormented him a long time" had finally acquired an "almost compulsory and occasionally hallucinatory character."

Finally, thought Berg, and high time to place this sorrowful story with the other secret files.

The weekly meeting had a mixed agenda in which the prime minister's somewhat eccentric awareness of security had once again been discussed.

"I took the matter up with him after our most recent government meeting, as I promised," reported the minister of justice, nodding with poorly concealed pride.

"And what did he say?" asked the special adviser avidly from behind half-closed eyelids.

"He promised to think about it," answered the minister.

"That is truly exceptional progress. I really must congratulate you," said the special adviser, chuckling. "Then I won't ruin the whole day for you gentlemen by relating what he said to me when I brought up the same question."

And that was as far as they got.

After the meeting the prime minister's special adviser took Berg aside to ask a simple, personal question.

"This Waltin," he wondered. "This is a person that you trust unconditionally?"

I must do something about Forselius, Berg thought with sudden irritation. I can't have it this way.

"I understand that you have spoken with Forselius," said Berg.

The special adviser made a difficult-to-interpret gesture that clearly was to show he didn't intend to say boo on that subject.

"Let me put it like this," said Berg carefully. "I think it mostly concerns a lack of personal chemistry, and were I to give a direct answer to your question I can only say that up till now I haven't had any concrete reason whatsoever to mistrust Police Superintendent Waltin." Apart from his private, childish little antics, which there's no reason to go into here, thought Berg.

This time the special adviser contented himself with a slightly dismissive gesture.

"And you are of course aware of the structural problem?"

"I'm not quite sure I understand what you mean," said Berg, still careful.

The rest of the conversation proceeded on a so-called level of principle. That was, after all, what it was called when someone like the special adviser intended to tell someone like Berg off. According to the special adviser, Berg's structural problem was a logical consequence of the manner in which he had built up the supervision of his operation. Who would supervise the final supervisor in the chain? Especially if he were as well concealed as Waltin with all his external functions?

"It's an insoluble problem," said Berg. Like the kind that you love to talk about, he thought.

Not insoluble at all, according to the special adviser from his elevated position. Instead, what it involved was simply adopting a dialectical attitude in his view of the organization and its operation. Building competition and oppositions into the structure was an excellent way to also check what the various parts of it were actually up to.

"And what will happen to a peaceful work environment?" objected Berg. Dialectical, he thought. Wonder if he's a communist? True, there was nothing in his papers, but his manner of reasoning was undeniably suspicious.

"Think about it," said the special adviser with a dismissive shrug of his shoulders. And suddenly Berg's inner alarm bells started ringing again.

On Friday Berg informed Waltin that Krassner was now a closed case, and despite the fact that this concerned what was fundamentally a serious story that might have ended considerably worse, Waltin was his usual irresponsible self. A well-tailored shrug of the shoulders, thought Berg, and if I don't do something about that I may well have a new parliamentary oversight round my neck.

"What were you thinking about doing about that senile character with the cognac?" asked Waltin, who was not one to let things pass.

"I'm hard at work on it," said Berg, who had already decided to change Forselius's clearances and hadn't the slightest intention of announcing it to anyone. Least of all Waltin.

"If you want you can send him an invoice," said Waltin, smiling like a satisfied wolf. "He's cost me almost a thousand man-hours."

"Oh well," said Berg, changing the subject. "It'll work out." And in the worst case I'm sure you can pawn your watch, he thought, but naturally he didn't say that.

Instead he contented himself with giving a few general directives for the ongoing work: the survey of antidemocratic elements within the police and the military, the Kurds and other terrorist organizations, threats against the prime minister and other pillars of society—just to mention the general overview.

Knife ourselves in the back, gnomes and trolls, Krassner and other loonies—sounds like an excellent agenda, thought Waltin, but obviously he didn't say that.

"Fine with me," said Waltin. And he himself had more important things to get to work on.

On Saturday the prime minister's special adviser met his old teacher and mentor, Professor Forselius, at the Turing Society's annual Christmas dinner at an exclusive gentlemen's club. An informal society, to be sure, but the guests were in tails and full academic regalia in memory of one of the greatest who had also lived his life between the promise of summer and the cold of winter and chosen to finish it by his own hand when the chill around him had become all too apparent.

The annual Christmas dinner was always enjoyed on the first Saturday in December, because it was preferable to be done in good time, and the ceremonies, the pace, and the majority of the members had been the same since the days of the cold war. First a simple buffet and a few shots of aquavit without preamble so that even the gout-afflicted professors could mingle easily with one another. Then a traditional, bourgeois dinner, which always ended with the carafe of port going clockwise around the table before they headed to one of the inner rooms for coffee and cognac.

Forselius had taken his old pupil aside and placed them both in chairs in the corner that he considered most suitable for informal conversations about such things as were included in the secrecy laws of the realm.

"Do you still have your professorship or do the socialists pay so damn little that you can't afford to buy a new tuxedo?" grunted Forselius, nodding toward the wreaths of oak leaves around the special adviser's black velvet collar.

"I still have the appointment and I have the salary to keep a horse, kind of you to ask," said the special adviser. You're your usual self, you old bastard, he thought with the warmth that naturally ensued from a fine dinner.

"You should watch out for those devils," warned Forselius. "Next time it may be you who goes out on your ears through your window."

"Those that I've spoken with maintain that he took his own life," said the special adviser. And I promise to watch out as soon as we start the election campaign, he thought.

"Obviously," snorted Forselius. "Is it the one with the gold watch who says that?"

"Correct me if I'm wrong," said the special adviser, "but wasn't it you who made contact with him?"

"With Berg, yes," said Forselius. "Berg is a good fellow, a little stupid, it's true, like all policemen, but simple and pleasant and good to deal with. Always does what you tell him."

Give me a break, thought the special adviser, who belonged to a different generation than his mentor.

"What do you think I should have done, then?" he asked.

"Seen to it that the staff took care of it. That's what we always did in my time. I'm sure you know what SePo thinks about people like you and your boss? He of all people ought to know that, shouldn't he?"

Sometimes you're awfully tedious, thought the special adviser, but he didn't say that.

"Why in heaven's name should SePo kill someone like Krassner?"

"Sometimes I actually worry about you," said Forselius, looking sternly at his old pupil. "In order to get their mitts on his papers, of course."

"His so-called papers contained mostly nonsense—only nonsense, actually."

"So that's what they say," said Forselius. "And you, what would you say if you thought about it?"

That it was just nonsense, thought the special adviser, but he didn't intend to enlighten Forselius about that in any case.

Waltin had chosen to spend this weekend on the estate he'd inherited from his father in Sörmland. True, his apartment on Norr Mälarstrand was very good for meeting his normal needs, and he had laid out a good deal of money both to soundproof it and install the technical equipment that he needed for his private documentation, but for the sensitive initial phase greater isolation than that was required.

Comfortable and off the main road. The fields and forests had long been rented out, and, considering the times, at a respectable price. The employees who had always been there had been laid off and moved, and nowadays there were no human eyes or ears in the vicinity that might see or hear things that didn't concern them. No help to be had, in a nutshell, and his training of little Jeanette was going completely according to plan. Because she had no idea of the reality in which he lived, and that would soon become hers, she also seemed to perceive the whole thing as some type of sexual role play which enticed her more than it frightened her.

The previous weekend he'd actually already reached a breakthrough in their relationship. He complimented himself for the stroke of genius with the bag of candies: her all too ravenous appetite for salt licorice and gummi bears, the subsequent punishment, and the spontaneous opportunity that this in turn had given him to remove the annoying growth of hair between her legs with the help of a razor. Now she looked most attractive: small and slender with her thin, almost boyish body and her totally naked vagina. If only the hair on her head were allowed to grow a little, she could be almost perfect, with two small braided pigtails. Little Jeanette, age thirteen, thought Waltin with all the love and all the hope for the future of which only he was capable. Even the documentation of their budding relationship had succeeded beyond expectations. He already had enough video and audio sequences both to satisfy his own fantasies when he was alone and to nip possible attempts at rebellion in the bud. Everything indicated that Jeanette might become one of his most successful projects ever.

Why can't he fuck like other people anymore? thought Assistant Detective Jeanette Eriksson, who this weekend was spending more time bent forward across his knees with her redder and redder backside straight up in the air than her lover, Police Superintendent Claes Waltin, was spending between her legs. She felt dejected and generally confused, and not even Krassner, who had after all been dead for more than fourteen days, was leaving her in peace. There was something that didn't add up, and finally she plucked up her courage and asked him, if for nothing else than to get a little peace and quiet. In the best case to get him to think about something other than various ways of paddling her rear end.

"There's one thing that I don't understand," she began hesitantly, with the shyly downward look that she realized that her situation now demanded.

"There is so much that you don't understand," said Waltin with both warmth and malt whiskey in his voice.

"There was something that Dan—that M'Boye told me that evening when we came back and we discovered that Krassner had killed himself," she continued.

"Yes," said Waltin with an irritated wrinkle on his otherwise smooth and suntanned forehead. Wonder if she's fucked that damn black guy, he thought, but because the very thought was so unpleasant he quickly pushed it aside.

"When he spoke with the cops," she added quickly. "That Wiijnbladh from tech and that horrible little fat guy from homicide."

For some reason that she didn't understand the wrinkles had smoothed out and Waltin suddenly appeared both pleased and curious.

"I'm listening," he said.

Daniel had arrived late. They were to have met at seven o'clock, but he hadn't shown up until a quarter of an hour later. In the lobby of the student dormitory on his way out to the meeting with Jeanette he had run into Krassner, who was on his way into the building. The time would have been, oh, about ten or twelve minutes past seven. Briefly and in summary, she couldn't get those times to agree with the times that the team had planned for carrying out their inspection of Krassner's residence.

"Well thought out, Jeanette," said Waltin approvingly. "We actually had better luck there than we deserved."

Then he related to her how their operative had violated his instructions and had already begun the operation at twenty minutes to seven, while M'Boye was still in his room. Krassner's home was both small and empty of interesting material, and the house search for which they had set aside an hour had been finished in less than half that time.

"Good thing they didn't run into each other," said Jeanette, feeling a genuine sense of relief.

"Must have been a few minutes at most that separated them," Waltin agreed, looking at her greedily.

Nice try, Hedberg, but you're not fooling me, thought Waltin, and suddenly he felt as exhilarated as that time when, completely by chance, he'd run into dear Mama as she stood staggering on the Östermalm subway-station platform.

Five minutes later everything was back to normal again.

Naughty, naughty Hedberg, thought Waltin contentedly while he energetically penetrated little Jeanette from behind to the stimulating and muffled sounds that she was emitting through his professionally applied muzzle.

What is really going on? thought Jeanette, for of course she couldn't say anything.

CHAPTER XIII

And all that remained was the cold of winter

Stockholm in December

[TUESDAY, DECEMBER 10]

Finally home, thought Johansson as he stepped off the plane, feeling real ground under his feet after ten days. His colleague Wiklander had used his police identification to meet up at baggage claim and help him with his suitcases. The rest had been a pure formality, as always when police officers and customs officials meet under collegial conditions, and a quarter of an hour later they were sitting in Johansson's service vehicle on their way into the city.

"Did you have a good trip, chief?" asked Wiklander as he changed lanes like a car thief.

"Completely okay," said Johansson. "The food was decent and I learned one or two things that I hadn't heard about before." And a few things that I'll try to forget, he thought.

"I was slaving at the after-hours unit over the weekend," said Wiklander with an innocent expression. "Some female American cop phoned who wanted to get hold of you at any price."

"So what was her name?" said Johansson, even though he already knew the answer.

"Detective Lieutenant Jane Hollander, I think she works for the state police in New York," said Wiklander. "Seemed awfully urgent."

"I see, her," said Johansson. "Yes, I spoke with her before I left. On the phone," added Johansson completely unnecessarily. You're starting to lose your grip, Lars, he thought.

"She sounded nice," said Wiklander neutrally. On the phone, sure, give me a break, thought Wiklander, who'd been around awhile.

"She was part of that course at the FBI," Johansson lied.

"She sounded good-looking," persisted Wiklander, who among other things was also one of the boys.

"So-so," said Johansson. "She was nice, that is, but we sure have better here at home," he declared with a trace more Norrland in his voice. "Moving on," he continued by way of diversion. "Has anything in particular happened in old Sweden while I was away?"

Not too much, according to Wiklander. Färjestad was way ahead in the hockey standings and had most recently played the pants off Brynäs, which was especially gratifying for a Värmlander such as himself, but otherwise nothing of consequence had happened.

"For the most part I guess that's all," Wiklander opined. "Well, and then Edberg creamed Wilander in the final at the Australian Open, but I guess you've already heard that."

No, thought Johansson, and now I'm going to try to forget it.

"How's the weather been?"

"Cold," said Wiklander, shaking his shoulders demonstratively. "Damn cold, in fact. The pundits are saying it's going to be a really severe winter. That old man with the perch fins was on TV the other night and according to him it's going to be merciless."

"I was thinking about asking you for a favor," said Johansson, whose thoughts were elsewhere.

"I'm listening."

"It's a little sensitive," Johansson continued. "A Stockholm matter," he clarified, to further indicate how sensitive it was to meddle in such things if, like he and Wiklander, you were now working at the National Bureau of Criminal Investigation.

"I understand," said Wiklander, smiling wryly. "What have they come up with this time?"

"It's already been written up and dismissed as a suicide," said Johansson.

"You suspect foul play, chief," said Wiklander, smiling a little more broadly.

"Actually I don't suspect anything," said Johansson. "It's more a feeling that I have."

"I understand exactly," said Wiklander, nodding.

He suspects that it's a murder and that's not good, since Johansson actually is Johansson. Hooga hooga, thought Wiklander, who viewed his boss as both a spiritual and professional role model.

Judging by the pile on his desk, Wiklander's description appeared to be more or less correct, and Johansson's world had definitely not fallen apart despite his absence. In the case of the overlooked Turkish murder victims the doorman had found in the elevator shaft, the ombudsman had acted with unusual speed and issued a reprimand along the lines of on-the-one-hand-on-the-other-hand, which those most closely concerned would certainly be able to live with. So far so good. But new misery had occurred, and this time unfortunately it concerned his own organization.

During an unusually merry company party at one of the squads, one of his chief inspectors was said to have tried to force himself on a female civilian employee. The person making the report was anonymous—as usual, thought Johansson with a dejected sigh—but was quite obviously to be found in their own corridors. The man singled out as the perpetrator had taken sick leave on the advice of his boss, and the alleged victim didn't want to talk about it at all. The matter had now been turned over to the district prosecutor in Gothenburg—for the usual geographic distance to maintain objectivity—and in any event hadn't been leaked to the media. And when it finally was, with any luck his successor would be sitting at his desk.

Ten days, thought Johansson hopefully. Then he would have vacation over the Christmas, New Year's, and Epiphany weekends, and when he finally returned he would just clean out his office before he left for a more tranquil existence at the personnel office of the National Police Board. And a nice dinner or two with the old comrades from the union, thought Johansson, who in spirit was already sitting in his own neighborhood restaurant with his counterpart, making toasts with Aunt Jenny's crystal shot glasses.

After lunch—because he hadn't felt especially hungry he had been content with a cup of coffee and a sandwich—the jet lag caught up with him and struck with full force. True, he'd slept a few hours on the plane home, and where he was sitting it was only two o'clock, but in his head it was suddenly bedtime after a long, strenuous day.

"Now I'm going to go home and turn in before I faint," said Johansson to his secretary. "If you can call a taxi for me, then I'll see you tomorrow."

At home on Wollmar Yxkullsgatan everything was as usual. The neighbor had watered the plants, fed his two fish, and sorted his mail. The pile of newspapers was much higher, but that could wait. Instead he set the suitcases down in the hall, went straight to his bedroom, took off his clothes, crept down between the sheets, and fell asleep at once. When he woke up, it was eight o'clock in the evening and he was as frisky as a squirrel. He was ravenously hungry too, despite the fact that the contents of his refrigerator offered a man with his appetite faint hope. Beer, mineral water, and way too much aquavit, thought Johansson gloomily, and what do I do now?

First he thought about pulling on his clothes and slipping down to his beloved neighborhood restaurant, but instead he got into the shower and let the water run so he could think better, and an hour later it had all resolved itself for the best. All that had been required was a systematic ransacking of the refrigerator, freezer, and pantry, and a little creative thinking as well as various practical measures à la Kajsa Warg, thought Johansson contentedly as he filled the coffeemaker and poured a tall cognac as a reward.

First an open-faced sandwich with egg and anchovies on hardtack; after that a few slices of moose filet, which he'd thawed quickly in the microwave and simply turned in a hot iron skillet so that they were still thoroughly red and juicy under the browned crust; add to that raw-fried potatoes and homemade garlic butter, all in all a classic Swedish meal worthy of a genuine Norrlander who had once again returned to his native soil after completing exertions abroad.

After that he pulled out the phone jack in order to be in peace, and took his coffee, cognac, and the thick bundle of newspapers into the living room, where he lay down on the sofa in order to evaluate, in peace and quiet, his colleague Wiklander's summary of what had taken place in the realm during his absence.

Färjestad had taken a comfortable lead in the ice hockey finals and it had been unusually cold for that time of year. Some days the temperature in Stockholm had been between 10 degrees above and 10 degrees below zero, but as for the rest everything seemed to have been rolling along as usual at this time of year.

Christmas sales should break records—on this point merchants and consumers were in touching agreement—despite the fact that the times obviously could have been better. The minister of finance, on the other hand, was unusually optimistic, and in a widely publicized interview he maintained that Sweden was now finally on its way to removing itself from the ensnaring debt the country had landed in due to the previous conservative administration's mismanagement.

The minister of finance was a popular person and possibly the chief explanation for why things were going well for the ruling party. In Sifo's December opinion polls, support for the social democrats had risen to forty-four percent, an increase of one percent over the previous month, despite the fact that an overwhelming majority of the party's supporters simultaneously "completely or partially lacked confidence in" the leader of the same party, the country's prime minister.

Poor devil, it can't be easy for him, thought Johansson with a sympathy that in any case was uncharacteristic of the rest of the police in the nation. News reports, political analyses, editorials, cultural articles, humor columns, and the usual gossip, page up and page down, all shared a common preoccupation with the prime minister's character deficiencies and various human shortcomings.

During the short time that Johansson had been away, the prime minister had managed to be assessed for back taxes and promised "an impending tax charge of considerable proportions"; had "seriously damaged Nordic cooperation by his arrogance"; had "expressed opinions that are completely alien to a unionized democratic philosophy"; and had "vacillated disquietingly" when information about the Russians' shameful treatment of their political dissidents was demanded of him.

In addition he had "incited a struggle against the tax collectors" when, at a lunch with a number of journalists, he had discussed the latest turns in his own tax case. But in contrast to anyone else, who would have been met with standing ovations, by the next day the evening papers had already forced him into full, disorderly retreat. "An unfortunate joke at a private, informal gathering," the prime minister explained.

How the hell does he keep it up? thought Johansson from the depths of his police experience; the only possible consolation in the misery was that there were others in the same arena who didn't seem to be having it so easy either. The Center Party's nominating committee had fired its party leader six months before the convention, which mortified Johansson even more, for two reasons. For one thing, they were both natives of the province of Ångermanland—according to Johansson's firm conviction there were far too few representatives from Ångermanland in national politics—and also because he seemed to be a decent fellow.

True, Johansson had never met him, but he'd seen him on TV, and you didn't need to be a policeman to understand that he was decent, honorable, and completely normal. In contrast to most others in the same business, thought Johansson, who was clearly irritated despite the fact that he would never dream of voting for the Center Party, for there were more than enough others in his family who did so. This country is in the process of going completely to hell, thought Johansson gloomily, consoling himself by pouring another splash of cognac into his almost empty glass.

Within the so-called cultural sector, on the other hand, the picture was more divided and at first glance not particularly easy to understand. *The Charter Trip II* was still the number one movie, in its fourth week now with over a million viewers, while the country's second most esteemed director was in a state of severe personal brooding due to a lack of financing for his next film. The planned staging of *Swan Lake* at the Stockholm Opera had had to be postponed because of a simple broken leg, and at the same time Sidney Sheldon and the Collins sisters were topping the Christmas best-seller charts and selling more books than "almost all serious authors combined."

High time to go to bed, he thought, as the jet lag again made itself known, resulting in a large yawn.

Krassner can wait, thought Johansson as he brushed his teeth. He could unpack his suitcases tomorrow, because apart from Krassner's posthumous papers they contained mostly clothes that needed to be laundered, and as far as Krassner's papers were concerned he already had a gnawing premonition of what was there, and the only thing he felt about that was a growing unease.

We'll have to see what Wiklander comes up with, Johansson decided, adjusting the pillow under his head, and a minute later he was sound asleep. On his right side with his right arm under the pillow, as always.

[WEDNESDAY, DECEMBER 11]

Johansson's internal clock had been upset. Normally he always woke up at six in the morning, but now it was only four o'clock and Johansson was both alert and in need of a substantial breakfast. First he showered and got dressed, but creativity was no longer sufficient. He'd polished off the only egg in the house during yesterday evening's festive dinner, and the remaining filets in the can of anchovies didn't tempt him, not at this time of day at any rate. So he had to be content with a cup of black coffee and a few slices of hardtack with butter while he read the morning paper.

Damn, thought Johansson, staring crossly at his clock. Only five-thirty despite the fact that he'd almost memorized *Dagens Nyheter* and even squandered his life by reading the sports section.

He thought about unpacking his suitcases, sorting the laundry, and at least laying Krassner's papers on the desk in his study, but for reasons that weren't entirely clear to him he had not yet made up his mind to do that. Instead he took a brisk walk to the office—piercing cold and raw dampness along the piers that bit into his cheeks and the tip of his nose—and when he strode into the reception area on Polhemsgatan right after six a.m. the guard looked both worried and red-eyed.

"Has something happened?" he asked.

"Early to bed, early to rise," said Johansson with feigned heartiness, despite the fact that his stomach was rumbling and it would be another hour yet before he could quiet it in the cafeteria down by the swimming pool.

When his secretary arrived right before eight o'clock as she always did, he had cleaned his desk, the calendar pages were white as snow, and before him lay an entire workday during which he could wander around in his own corridors and shoot the breeze with his colleagues. As long as nothing especially critical and pressing happened that demanded his elevated participation, of course. Why would that happen, for it never did, thought Johansson, nodding toward his closest female coworker.

"You don't have a few minutes?" she asked, and from her guilty expression he knew at once what it was about.

She's changed her mind, he thought.

"Of course," said Johansson. "Why don't we go into my office and sit down."

She had changed her mind, and it took her five minutes of circumlocutions to get it said.

"It's clear that you should stay here," said Johansson kindly. "Who knows how long I'll remain at the personnel office? I hardly know that myself."

Women, he thought.

"Let me know if you think of someone else," said Johansson. "I'm not asking for miracles; it's enough that she's half as good as you," he added, with a little extra Norrland in his voice.

It's all the same, he thought as she went out through his door.

After that he devoted a good hour to looking in on his old colleagues and talking about this and that and mostly about robbers old and new. When ten a.m. approached he excused himself, returned to his office, and called his accountant at the bank's trust department.

"I want you to sell my Fermenta shares," said Johansson.

The accountant wiggled like an eel in a saltcellar, but Johansson, who looked out for number one when it came to things that were his, was unrelenting.

"You want me to hold on to them?" asked Johansson.

"I'm sitting here with the latest report from our analysts and they see a continued, very strong growth potential. They're firmly advising against selling—instead they're recommending buy even at the current level."

Wonder if those are the same bean counters who firmly advised me against buying three months ago? Although it's clear, then I got them for a song.

"Okay," said Johansson heavily. "Let's do it like this. I want you to sell all of my shares in Fermenta, and I'm going to stay on the line until it's done."

"Now it's done," the accountant said sourly after about half a minute of mumbling next to the receiver.

"Excellent," said Johansson. "I'm sure you know what old man Ford used to say? The one with the Model T?"

"No," said the accountant. He still sounded hurt.

"Profit is profit," said Johansson and hung up.

Okay then, thought Johansson. So what do I do now? He looked at his watch and leaned back in his desk chair. Just past ten and nothing to do. First he had a random idea that he should give Wiklander a buzz and offer his services, but then the police superintendent in him immediately put his foot down. He shouldn't even think about it, for it was altogether too sensitive for a man in his position, and considering the probable significance of the matter, unnecessary as well.

Johansson drummed his fingers on the desk crossly. The policeman in his soul had suddenly come to life, refusing to back down, and he felt a strong urge for a little old-fashioned honest detective work. What was it that piece of shit wrote in that letter, the one I was never supposed to read? thought Johansson. That he'd gotten my home address from a very well-known Swedish journalist? Johansson could only think of one such person, and for lack of anything else it was just as well to get the matter cleared up.

Wendell, the editor of the large evening paper, sounded both flattered and interested when Johansson called and suggested lunch the same day.

"Are you up to something interesting?" asked Wendell with curiosity, because he knew from experience that Johansson usually dealt in hard goods.

"No," said Johansson. "Just thought it might be nice to get together. It's been a while."

"I understand," said Wendell cryptically. "We'll discuss it when we meet."

I doubt that, thought Johansson, but didn't say it out loud.

All real police officers disliked journalists, and in that respect Johansson was no exception. It was Wendell who was the exception, and Johansson had recognized it many years earlier when he'd started his climb to the top of the police pyramid and felt the need of someone like Wendell. They had started exchanging back scratches with each other and up to now they had both profited from the trades. Wendell was also the only journalist who had gotten Johansson's home address, strictly for his own use and for sensitive deliveries. But he'd probably betrayed that confidence and turned it over to Krassner, and because Johansson was not about to move on account of Wendell's loose lips, it was just as well to make an early, clear indication of this.

Otherwise he didn't have anything against him in particular. He was a pleasant guy, just like Johansson fond of the good things in life, such as food, drink, and women, and just like Johansson he had his own favorite Italian restaurant, where they'd gotten a large tray of mixed Italian cold cuts as a little appetizer before things got serious.

Business first, thought Johansson, leaning forward and nodding amiably at Wendell.

"Do you know an American journalist named Krassner, John Krassner?" asked Johansson.

Wendell suddenly looked rather wary. Then he nodded.

"I've met him a few times down at the press club on Vasagatan. He's working on some project here, writing some book, very hush-hush, but I haven't seen him in a good while now, so he's probably gone back to the States. The fact is that we talked about you at some point."

Johansson nodded to him to continue.

"Don't know how we got onto that subject. I seem to recall that he asked me if there were any honorable cops here." Wendell smiled weakly and raised his beer glass before he took a gulp.

"So what did you say?"

"I seem to recall that I said something to the effect that I knew one at any rate," said Wendell. "I no doubt mentioned your name too—in fact, I'm sure I did. It was right at the time when you were making headlines in the media as the foremost champion of justice."

"Why did he want to get hold of someone like me?" said Johansson. "Was there some information that he wanted to get?"

Wendell shook his head doubtfully.

"Don't think so. Just between us he's a mysterious type. It was never really clear to me what he was doing, other than that it was a great revelation, of course." He shook his head in sympathy, then asked, "Has he been in contact with you? If I were you I'd be a bit careful with the good Krassner."

"He sent me a mysterious letter," said Johansson. "I actually didn't understand a thing, but because he sent it to my home address I thought I should ask."

Wendell shook his head dismissively. "Forget it," he said. "I would never dream of giving out your home address. All he got was the address to your office. To the bureau, the National Bureau of Criminal Investigation. I think I said it was in the phone book."

Hmm, thought Johansson.

Then they talked about other things besides Krassner, had pasta with veal, and tiramisu for dessert.

In addition they drank both beer and wine, and at coffee Wendell excused himself as usual.

"Small bladder," said Wendell, smiling wryly. "Shall we have one more small grappa?"

As usual too he'd hung his sport coat on the back of the chair, and as soon as he left to go to the restroom Johansson stuck his hand in and fished his address book out of the inside left pocket. Well organized and neat handwriting, and he himself was under "J" with his home address, the address of his office, and all three of his telephone numbers.

The details are starting to fall into place, thought Johansson. He put the address book back and tried to make eye contact with a waiter.

"Can we each get a grappa?" said Johansson just as Wendell came back, and then they continued talking about everything else but Krassner.

It had been really nice. Johansson insisted on paying, and afterward he indicated that it was on his own account by leaving the check behind on the table. Then he'd excused himself to go to the restroom before they left, and Wendell had of course palmed it the way he always did. The newspaper could easily take this, and to his credit it should be said that he never wrote the names of his various informants on the back. Wendell was just looking out for number one; besides, it was almost Christmas and in this case it didn't hurt any poor people.

When they separated, Wendell returned to the newspaper office while Johansson took a taxi and went home. Regardless of the fact that it was almost Christmas he had no intention of returning to his workplace to exhale strong beer, wine, and grappa on his coworkers. Others besides him could do that, in other places with other rules than the ones that applied to him.

Finally he unpacked his suitcases. He sorted the dirty laundry, dividing it between the two laundry baskets in the bathroom, hung up what didn't need to be washed in the closet, and set the Christmas presents he'd bought on the desk in his study. Remaining were Krassner's papers; the unease he'd felt earlier had not lessened after the meeting with Wendell. When he'd packed his suitcase at the hotel in New York he had put them into the plastic bag that he'd gotten when he bought his new shoes, and they were still there.

What do I do now? thought Johansson, weighing the bag in his hand, a few pounds at the most. He still had the same unpleasant premonition of what he would find when he finally made up his mind to read through them. He didn't want to take them to work, for they had no business being there, and besides, they were his. He'd gotten them from the person who had inherited all of Krassner's earthly belongings, and that if anything made them a legal acquisition.

Problems, thought Johansson, and since they didn't concern him they might just as well wait. I'll take them with me up to my big brother's, he decided. Then I can read them in peace and quiet. If he was going to do it anyway it was just as well to do it thoroughly. That's how it will be, he decided. Folded up the bag and laid it on the bookshelf in his study alongside the books that he'd also thought about taking with him to read during the Christmas holiday. He'd found what he was look-ing for, he'd had the good fortune to do so, and now it wasn't going to run away from him, so the work that remained could just as well wait until he felt ready for it.

Having the luck to find what you're looking for: among archival researchers—a profession that is best practiced as a calling—this is some-thing so great and unusual that there is a special word for it: *Finderglück*. A German expression that can't readily be translated but whose original meaning is that you have the luck that is also required for your efforts to be crowned with success. On the other hand it doesn't mean that you're going to be happy once you do, for that's far from always the case.

For a professional archival researcher, Johansson's reaction was not especially noteworthy. Researchers are well aware of the feelings that usually surface when this uncommon grace befalls you: the ambiva-lence, the doubt, the spiritual hangover or, in severe cases, even anxiety and remorse that can appear when you're sitting there with the find in your meager hands. And obviously the possibility that what you've found will unfortunately show that you've had it all wrong with your theories or hypotheses.

Johansson was no archival researcher, but during his years as a detective he had devoted hundreds of hours to what in police talk is called internal surveillance: seeking the truth or traces of the truth in various police and other registers, and he was well acquainted with the feelings that went along with both the uncommon successes and the constant failures. One time he had even found a murderer that way, and because the victim was an especially big son of a bitch while the perpetrator was an ordinary and pleasant person, afterward—and to himself—he'd cursed the union of intuition and judicious precision that had led him correctly where all his other colleagues had gone astray. Without even needing to leave his office and while his colleagues were as usual running around out in the field.

Those papers aren't running away from you, Johansson repeated to himself, nodding in confirmation in his solitude. Besides, he needed to take a little nap, after the time change and the heavy Italian lunch, which he'd paid for with his own money to boot. He'd already done the necessary shopping for his survival on his way home to Wollmar Yxkullsgatan.

When he woke up it was only seven o'clock in the evening but he was both alert and clear in the head and didn't give a thought to Krassner and his papers. Then Jarnebring called as he stood in the shower, and because it was almost Christmas he continued the entertainment program already under way and invited him to dinner at his very good neighborhood restaurant. Jarnebring didn't have any particular objections but rather contented himself with suggesting the same menu as the last time so as not to take any unnecessary risks, and a good hour later they were sitting across from each other, raising Aunt Jenny's crystal glasses over a very good baked toast with anchovies, tomatoes, basil, and mozzarella.

"Brilliant," said Jarnebring, aahing audibly after the shot. "These spaghetti guys aren't your usual gooks."

No, thought Johansson. They'd probably never dream of serving boiled sausage with white bread and shrimp salad.

"Tell me," said Jarnebring while bolting yet another anchovy toast and nodding knowingly toward his empty glass. "Spare me no details, like Bogart used to say."

So Johansson told about his visit to the FBI and the meeting with the police in New York, but as to the rest he didn't say a word about meeting Krassner's old girlfriend Sarah Weissman or about Krassner's posthumous papers that he'd brought home with him.

"You gave up on that crazy American?" asked Jarnebring.

"Sure," said Johansson. "I've given up on that, although yesterday I figured out how he got hold of my home address, and you were just about right there. He got it from one of our Swedish talents. I talked with him today. Krassner clearly wanted to make contact with the Swedish police. Not that I understand why, but he clearly did."

"They always do, damn guys," snorted Jarnebring, who hated journalists. "You should have made glue out of that bastard who gave out your home address."

"I let mercy precede justice," said Johansson, smiling wanly, "so he was allowed to live. How's it been going for you, by the way?"

The sun was shining on Jarnebring's home front. The colleague with the Achilles heel had shown promising signs of recovery and should be coming back half-time after the holidays. Someone other than Jarnebring could take care of the other fifty percent, so he would get back to the bureau and a little real work. And his live-in—for that was no doubt the way he had to view her, since he mostly lived at home with her, despite the fact that hers was the only name on the apartment lease—had been unusually kind and good recently.

Hultman had also offered a happy surprise. It wasn't enough that he'd shown up with the promised mixed case. He'd also had the good taste to supplement all the liqueurs and other shit that women were so fond of with a whole carton of Jarnebring's favorite bourbon. But naturally he hadn't mentioned that to Johansson. True, Johansson was his best friend, but in the thin air where his friend was living nowadays there were a few things that he would feel better about not knowing. Instead Jarnebring chose a different solution and invited him home for a small pre-Christmas dinner.

"What do you think about next Thursday? Me and my old lady are both off then. I've bought two kinds of aquavit," Jarnebring assured Johansson, for that was another way of looking at the matter.

"Suits me fine," said Johansson, for it did.

"She has a damn pretty girlfriend too." Jarnebring for some reason lowered his voice and leaned across the table. "A colleague, working temporarily at Norrmalm. What do you think about that?"

"Well," said Johansson. "It sounds nice. Is it anyone I know?" What should I say? he thought.

"Don't think so," said Jarnebring. "She's been put on duty for a few months. Works in Skövde with the uniformed police, fresh gal, no kids, nothing steady."

"How old is she?" asked Johansson.

"Well," said Jarnebring, shrugging his shoulders. "Like mine, in her prime."

So that's how it is, thought Johansson, and for unclear reasons he suddenly became a little depressed. Perhaps it was his tightening pants lining and his still only half-eaten and in and of itself extraordinarily good-tasting roast pork with marsala sauce and polenta. It must have been something.

"That'll be nice," Johansson repeated.

It'll have to be the swimming pool early tomorrow, he decided, pushing his plate to the side.

"If you're not having any more I can take that," said Jarnebring greedily.

They remained sitting, talking, and drinking until the restaurant closed, and then Johansson called off the traditional follow-up, pleading a combination of jet lag and early business matters. Jarnebring's protests were surprisingly mild.

"You work too much, Lars," he said. "And exercise too little. Come along and work out sometime, why don't you?"

Then he did something highly unusual. He leaned over and put his burly arms around Johansson's shoulders and gave him a hug.

"Take care of yourself, Lars. We'll see you in a week."

It must be the Italian food, thought Johansson with surprise.

When he came home and went to bed he had a hard time falling asleep for once. A feeling of depression that didn't want to go away. Women, thought Johansson. Must get myself a woman. Then he dropped off as usual.

[THURSDAY, DECEMBER 12]

Johansson had started his day at work with an hour in the swimming pool, but when he emerged from the sauna after an additional half hour his waist measurement unfortunately appeared to be the same as before. On the other hand he'd acquired a ferocious appetite that he felt obligated to alleviate at once. He had two cups of coffee and a substantial slice of rye bread with meatballs and red-beet mayonnaise down in the cafeteria in order to put a stop to the worst of it before he sat down behind his desk.

Muscle-building, thought Johansson; he would certainly be able to solve the woman problem during the course of the day. First he thought about the post office manager he'd met when he was poking around on the fringes of the Krassner case. A really splendid woman, who seemed wise as well, whom he'd already made use of in his fantasies on a few occasions when he followed big brother's advice, but the practical problems were considerable.

You can't just call her up and ask if she wants to go to bed, thought Johansson. However much you'd like to. Besides, that was inappropriate for other reasons as well. Consider, for example, if the Krassner case were to take an unfortunate turn and get new life and she were to be called in as a witness in a new investigation, and he himself were to be . . . something he'd rather not imagine. You've chosen the wrong profession, thought Johansson, feeling the despondency coming back with renewed force, and what was that wretched Wiklander up to anyway? Almost two full days since he'd told him to check on whether the pieces in Jarnebring's investigation really were in place, and since then he hadn't heard a peep from him.

Six weeks without naked skin, thought Johansson. And the fact that he was crawling in his own hide wasn't so strange. In a week he would be meeting the female friend from Skövde that Jarnebring had announced, but quite apart from the fact that that was an eternity away, his feelings about this encounter were, to say the least, mixed. Say what you will about his best friend, his view of women was different from Johansson's.

After lunch he sneaked away from the office to shop for Christmas presents, and when he came home it was already evening and he was dead tired. First he had a simple dinner alone and idly watched TV for an hour. Then he went to bed and fell asleep without any fuss, and during the night his post-office manager visited him in his dreams and it was quite obvious that she didn't work for the police.

[FRIDAY, DECEMBER 13]

When Johansson woke up he was in an excellent mood despite the fact that no candle-adorned Lucia appeared to sing for him; in the shower he followed big brother's advice. Seeing that it was Friday the thirteenth, when no one ought to stick his neck, or any other body part, out unnecessarily, this was, moreover, a risk-free and attractive form of erotic practice. While he made coffee he hummed an old Sven-Ingvars song, great fan of dance-band music and real policeman that he was, in contrast to those fictional opera lovers who seemed to populate every single made-up police station from Ystad to Haparanda. Despite the ominous combination of date and weekday, he felt instinctively that this was going to be a really good day.

. . .

When he got to work his faithful coworker Wiklander was already sitting in the corridor outside his office waiting for him, but before he let him in he sent him to fetch coffee for both of them. There had to be some system; he himself had fetched numerous cups of coffee for older colleagues when he was Wiklander's age.

"Let's hear it," said Johansson, leaning back in his desk chair and sipping the day's second cup of coffee. Freshly brewed, thought Johansson contentedly, biting into a saffron bun with raisins. Good, he thought, despite the fact that he didn't really like saffron buns with raisins.

"It's a suicide," said Wiklander. "On that point I'm in complete agreement with our colleagues."

"I'm listening," said Johansson and nodded.

True, the initial measures that the police in Stockholm had carried out left a great deal to be desired—everything, actually, if you wanted to be that way—but then their colleague Jarnebring, acting head of the local detective unit at Östermalm, had gone in and brought order into the case. Wiklander's line of reasoning and conclusions sounded in other respects quite like that which Johansson had heard from his best friend fourteen days earlier.

"Jarnebring is really good, so you don't get past him too readily," Wiklander observed. "Though for that matter, chief, you know that better than I do."

"Was there anything at all strange?"

"Well," said Wiklander, smiling wanly. "The gumshoes in the building next to us have also gone in and checked."

SePo, thought Johansson.

"You're quite sure of that?"

"Yes," said Wiklander. "Do you remember Persson, chief? The one who worked on aggravated thefts down in Stockholm a bunch of years ago? He's working at SePo now. Big, fat guy, surly type, though good, really good policeman. I know one of the gals in the archive and she told me that Persson had been down last week and copied the file and told her to keep her mouth shut because otherwise there'd be hell to pay."

"But she didn't do that," said Johansson.

"No," said Wiklander, grinning. "She doesn't like Persson. Thinks he's an uncommonly surly old geezer."

But she clearly likes you, thought Johansson.

"Was it Krassner they wanted to check on?"

"I thought so at first," said Wiklander. "But I'm not so sure anymore. Where I'm leaning is that it was someone else they were interested in. A foreign student from South Africa, a black guy who'd gotten a scholarship from the union federation. Belongs to some radical group of civil-rights activists down in South Africa. That's no doubt why they brought him here. The union, that is."

"What does he have to do with Krassner?" asked Johansson.

"Nothing," said Wiklander. "They were just living in the same corridor. Don't seem to have known each other."

"And why do you think that it was him they were interested in? The colleagues at SePo, that is?"

"They seem to have put an overcoat on him," said Wiklander.

"Huh?" said Johansson.

Wiklander had among many other things made a few discreet inquiries among the students who lived on the same corridor as Krassner. That was how he'd found out that one of them had a girlfriend who came by often. Louise Eriksson, nice-looking girl, around twenty, who'd said that she was studying criminology or some similar easily digested trendy subject, when she wasn't together with Daniel M'Boye.

She and M'Boye had clearly run into each other more or less by chance in the middle of October. After that they'd started getting together regularly, and they'd kept on that way at least through November. Although then the whole thing seemed to have run into the sand and lately he'd only spoken with her on the phone. Young Miss Eriksson herself had disappeared out to the fringes, according to her own information to go home to her parents and take care of her sick mother.

"Have you spoken with this M'Boye?" asked Johansson.

"Yes," said Wiklander. "Although he's actually rather difficult to talk to. Especially as it concerns that girl Eriksson. Unrequited love, perhaps," said Wiklander, smiling wryly.

"Is there any reason for us to bring him in?" said Johansson. Whatever that would be, he thought.

"That would be rather difficult, I'm afraid," said Wiklander. "He went home to South Africa yesterday morning."

Sigh, thought Johansson. "The girlfriend," he said. "Louise Eriksson, is she a police officer, does she work at SePo, or does she just freelance?"

"Jeanette Louise Eriksson, twenty-seven years old," said Wiklander. "Left school six years ago and disappeared almost immediately to SePo. I'm guessing she's in their detective unit. Really good type, actually, looks like she just left preschool. First name Jeanette, except when she's studying criminology at half speed at the university, for there she calls herself Louise."

"You're quite certain," Johansson persisted.

"Yes," said Wiklander, his voice not sounding the least bit offended. "You can be completely calm, chief. She works at SePo, lives alone in an apartment in Solna, studies criminology at half speed. The home telephone number she gave to M'Boye ceased to exist only a few hours after he'd departed from Arlanda. Secret number from the start and now they're just shaking their heads at the phone company. Typical SePo account and a heavy-duty sign that she's done with what she was supposed to do. I've checked on her mother too. She's as healthy as a horse, and if the passport photo matches she looks like she's her daughter's age."

"Do you have a picture of Officer Eriksson?" asked Johansson.

"Yes," said Wiklander with a somewhat broader smile. "Absolutely up to date. Took them myself the other day."

Wiklander handed over a bundle of photos taken with a telephoto lens and at a secure distance.

Nice-looking girl, thought Johansson, and she doesn't appear to be a day over seventeen.

Jeanette Louise Eriksson, stepping out of the doorway of the building in Solna where she lived. The same Jeanette Eriksson getting out of a car in the garage of the police headquarters in the basement in the Kronoberg block. Little Jeanette in the courtyard of police headquarters, facing toward the restaurant Bylingen within the courtyard, despite the fact that she looked as though she were on her way to school when the camera captured her obliquely from above.

"And you think that they put her on M'Boye," said Johansson. "As a girlfriend, with all that that entails these days?"

Doesn't that take a bit of gall even for those crazies? thought Johansson, who had a past within the police union and was still protective of his colleagues' work environment.

"Yes," said Wiklander, smiling broadly. "I actually asked M'Boye if she'd been anything special in bed but then he got a totally offended look. He's a really burly type, so I only asked once."

"And there's no possibility that M'Boye might have had something to do with Krassner's death?" persisted Johansson, who just happened to think of the letter that he actually shouldn't have read.

What was it that he'd written, the piece of shit? That if he died he would have been murdered either by the Swedish secret police or by the Swedish military intelligence service or by the Soviet military intelligence service GRU. By the way, didn't the Russians used to make use of operatives from African resistance movements when they were going to be really nasty out in Western Europe? In the back of his mind he had a vague memory that he'd read something like that in some classified memorandum that the gumshoes in the adjacent building had decided to share with their colleagues within the open operation.

"No," said Wiklander, shaking his head.

"Why then?" said Johansson. "They can't have got everything wrong, can they?" Every time, he thought.

"He has an alibi," said Wiklander and chuckled. "When Krassner jumped out the window, M'Boye and Eriksson from SePo were sitting in a Mexican restaurant down on Birger Jarlsgatan."

"You're quite sure?"

"I've checked with the owner. He's a Spaniard and doesn't seem to be particularly fond of blacks, if I may say so. He remembered them, maintained that he'd actually thought about phoning in a tip to the police, a big burly black guy and a little Swedish girl who looked like she was still in school. Where he came from there was the death penalty for such things. It took a good while when I talked with him before he realized that she hadn't been murdered."

This is too much, thought Johansson. SePo? Scarcely believable even in his gloomiest moments when he was still a young radical and had drunk too much red wine. For a policeman, that is. The Russians? Possibly, for everything he'd heard and read couldn't simply be nonsense? SePo and GRU. Impossible, thought Johansson. Not even the TV news editors would come up with something so preposterous.

"What do you think is going on?" demanded Johansson, looking challengingly at his younger colleague.

Krassner's suicide and SePo's interest in M'Boye had nothing to do with each other. It was a pure coincidence. Krassner had taken his own life. Beyond crazy, he drank and did drugs too. Plus there were all the other objective police circumstances that became known through the technical investigation and the forensic medical report. Not least the suicide note he'd left behind.

"A perfectly clear-as-a-bell suicide," Wiklander declared. "You can think what you want about our colleagues at SePo, but that's not in their repertoire. Besides, they would never carry it out that well if any of them got the idea to try."

"Do you have any idea why SePo was so interested in M'Boye?" said Johansson.

"Well, black, South African, a student, young, radical, member of some local resistance movement, here on money from the union federation—that's more than enough for them, I guess."

Yes, thought Johansson. I'm sure it is. Typical Friday the thirteenth, and now it had started to snow too. As if the snow they'd already gotten wasn't enough, even though it wasn't yet Christmas.

Before Johansson left work he phoned a female colleague who worked at the foreign nationals unit in Stockholm. She was the same age as him, divorced like him, with children who would soon be adults just like his. He'd called her a few months ago on a similar errand.

"What do you think about that?" said Johansson with a touch more Norrland in his voice.

"Sure," she said, and sounded clearly delighted, although with a Stockholm accent.

"Shall we say the restaurant at seven o'clock?" said Johansson.

"What do you think about at my place in an hour?" she said, and giggled. "Then we can eat dinner afterward? I think you get so tired from all that Italian food."

Easy as pie, thought Johansson, suddenly feeling just as young as when he used to think like that.

[SATURDAY, DECEMBER 14–SUNDAY, DECEMBER 15]

Johansson had spent the weekend with his two children. They would be celebrating Christmas and New Year's abroad with their mother and her new husband, "new" for the past ten years. This weekend offered the final chance to safeguard the remnants of tradition their present circumstances had left them. Apart from that they'd had a nice weekend. On Saturday they'd taken a walk in the city. True, it was cold, but with sparkling sun from a clear, pale-blue sky; his children had appreciated it in a way he hadn't expected. It turns out that way, I guess, if you live in a big house in Vallentuna, thought Johansson.

Then they'd shopped for food in the Östermalm market, had lunch at McDonald's on Nybrogatan, and bought a Christmas tree at Maria Square that they carried home to Wollmar Yxkullsgatan, where they decorated it with red glass balls and silver garlands. True, a small and rather sad-looking tree that was already shedding seriously, but it smelled like Christmas, in any case, and the youngsters were satisfied and happy. They'd made dinner together and his son had shown unexpected domestic talents while his daughter set and decorated the table. No Christmas food, for neither Johansson nor his children were especially fond of it. Good Swedish food, quite simply, which they all helped each other select and prepare. Favorites in reprise, Johansson had thought contentedly while he carefully turned the veal burgers in the frying pan and his son attacked the potatoes with the potato masher.

First a little Swedish smorgasbord with a discriminating selection of domestic classics: smoked eel, lightly salted lox, caviar, and a few well-chosen types of herring. Johansson had taken shots, one for each leg, from Aunt Jenny's glass, and when he noticed that his son was glancing furtively at him as he raised the first glass he realized that sooner or later he would have to ask the question. The boy would, after all, soon turn seventeen.

"Would you like a half shot?" Johansson had asked. It is Christmas, he'd thought.

"No, good Lord," his son had said with genuine feeling.

"You shouldn't swear, you little bastard," Johansson had said prudishly. "Though it's good if you can leave the aquavit alone as long as possible," he'd added paternally.

After the meal they'd exchanged Christmas presents in front of the tree and both his daughter's and son's eyes had twinkled. The decal-inscribed sweatshirts that he'd bought at the FBI had aroused especially great enthusiasm. Considerably more than the metal-studded leather jackets that for good money he'd dragged home from the suggested shop on Fifth Avenue in New York. He himself had received a Vikings' greatest hits collection and a book that, judging by the back cover copy at least, ought to be completely readable. Plus a padded hunting vest with leather facing and large pockets, which was a present from both of them and had certainly dug deep holes in their collective capital.

"So dear old Dad can keep on exterminating all the animals in the forest," said his daughter, smiling gently.

On Sunday the youngsters had slept the whole morning while Johansson idled around the apartment in last Christmas Eve's dressing gown. He'd showered, had coffee, read the newspaper, and thought a bit about Krassner and the remarkable coincidence of his suicide and SePo's interest in his neighbor from South Africa. But despite his own cherished rule that in situations like this you ought to hate chance, it must nevertheless still be a pure coincidence. The exception that proves the rule, he decided in order to finally get some quiet in his head, and because the youngsters had started to show signs of life he prepared a substantial American breakfast instead.

Pancakes with maple syrup and juniper-smoked bacon. His son had been just as delighted as his dad and loaded in double portions despite his sister's vociferous warnings about cholesterol and being overweight and high blood pressure and sudden, premature death.

"I don't understand how you can eat that kind of thing," she'd said, stirring her breakfast yogurt. "It's not enough that it tastes disgusting, it smells disgusting too, and it's pure poison besides. Don't you understand that you can die?"

"Although it is awfully good," Johansson had said gently, stroking her on the cheek.

In the afternoon he'd sent them home to Vallentuna in a taxi, and because he'd gotten his statement of account from the bank for his stock sale the day before, he hadn't even thought about what it cost for two teenagers to go home that way.

It's clear they should have it good, thought Johansson. I have it good myself, and it will be theirs by and by anyway. Then he drew a hot bath, mixed a giant highball with a little gin and a lot of ice and Grappo, which he placed within comfortable reach before he himself stepped in to relax, not to wash himself, as it was best with hot water, an ice-cold drink, and plenty of time.

What a splendid weekend, thought Johansson contentedly. It had started well too. True, not with a great lifelong love, but shared urges were clearly good at putting temporary loneliness to flight. They hadn't even gone to the restaurant afterward. A simple sandwich and a glass of wine at the kitchen table had been every bit as good as an Italian three-course dinner.

Wonder if you can live that way? thought Johansson, drawing more hot water in order to preserve his philosophical state of mind. Life as a bearable division of pleasure and tedium with occasional temporary efforts as soon as loneliness became too marked? Although in the long run it probably wouldn't work, thought Johansson, taking a sip of his highball. It has to lead to something more lasting. How was it he'd put it, the poet Vennberg? "Cry of loon and knife toward open eye / anything at all just not the same loneliness anew."

He's a good poet, that Vennberg, thought Johansson. He wasn't alone in thinking that, either. He was the prime minister's favorite poet too, for hadn't he read that in some book whose author and title he'd otherwise forgotten? Some political journalist at *Aftonbladet,* and types like that were a dime a dozen at that rag, thought Johansson. Although Vennberg was all right. He's probably never shot a loon, thought Johansson and smiled, for he himself had shot a good many, even when he was a little boy—he could still hear Papa Evert's curses ringing in his ears when he'd come home with his illegal contribution to the dinner table.

Wonder if the prime minister has ever shot a loon, thought Johansson, and in that moment he understood exactly what had happened when Krassner died.

When Johansson climbed out of the bath he dried himself extra carefully, for now was not the time for rushing ahead. Then he put on his dressing gown and went into his study and took out the plastic bag with Krassner's papers. Set them on the desk and decided to start with the bundle that contained the manuscript to Krassner's book, "The Spy Who Went East."

He found it almost at once. First the title page with the author's name. Then a table of contents with chapter headings that extended over two pages, still incomplete and with handwritten corrections and additions. Then he found what he was looking for. On a page of its own, a quote that served as an introduction to the text that followed in the first chapter.

Johansson translated as he read, which was no great art because for the most part he could reproduce the short passage by heart both in the English original and the Swedish translation.

"I have lived my life caught between the longing of summer and the cold of winter. As a young man I used to think that when summer comes I would fall in love with someone, someone I would love a lot, and then, that's when I would start living my life for real. But by the time I had accomplished all those things I had to do before, summer was already gone and all that remained was the winter cold. And that, that was not the life that I had hoped for."

Now there was an additional reference. On a separate page with foot-notes that had been inserted after the chapter: "Extract of letter from Pilgrim to Fionn, April 1955."

Johansson put the manuscript aside and took out paper and pen. What was it that she'd said, Sarah Weissman, that extraordinarily talented woman, when they'd met? Only a week ago, but it already seemed like an eternity. This was nothing that Krassner had written himself; on the other hand it might very well be something he'd pinched from someone else. On that point she'd clearly been quite right, and now when Johansson was sitting with the key—or at least the start of a key—it didn't seem as if he'd intended to conceal that relationship, either. The author was clearly a person who'd chosen to call himself Pilgrim and who, more than thirty years ago, had written a letter addressed to another pseudonym, Fionn.

What else had she said about the author? That it was a man, obvi-ously, for women didn't write like that; a man who was neither Ameri-can nor British but who spoke the language fluently for the most part; an educated, talented man with a poetic disposition, or rather a poetic ambition, perhaps. Johansson had an excellent memory, this memory in particular was recent, and without having made any notes he recalled that this was exactly how she'd expressed herself.

"I have lived my life caught between the longing of summer and the cold of winter . . ."; "Cry of loon and knife toward open eye / anything at all just not the same loneliness anew." Vennberg's poem must be of considerably later date, thought Johansson, but that was actually quite uninteresting, for this dealt with something else, a poetic disposition, a poetic ambition, a way of seeing, experiencing, and formulating, and a favorite poet was not something that you chose by accident.

The prime minister, thought Johansson. This he'd already under-stood, and it was a conviction so strong as to leave no room for other alternatives. The prime minister was Pilgrim, or more exactly . . . he had been, more than thirty years ago.

And who is Fionn? thought Johansson. Who was it that Pilgrim was writing to? Easy as pie, thought Johansson, for he'd already figured that out, and when he pulled out the relevant volume of *The Swedish Reference Book* from the bookshelf it was mostly to get confirmation in print. Finn, he thought. Fionn must be Finn in English.

"Finn, Anglicized form of the Gaelic name Fionn, hero in ancient Irish saga literature, see Finn cycle," Johansson read.

John C. Buchanan, Krassner's uncle, he thought, who in the spring of 1955, when the cold war was at its coldest, must have had his ass full as a CIA agent in Europe and Sweden. How was it Sarah had described him? One of those shrewd, lying, really thirsty, and naturally prejudiced Irishmen. But he must have had something else, thought Johansson, for this was certainly no shabby agent he'd managed to recruit.

This is the only reasonable explanation, he thought, for it was a farewell letter sure enough, but hardly a farewell to life. Only a former external collaborator with the world's fourth-largest security organization who, in an educated, talented, and, considering the context, unusually poetic manner, was stating that he no longer wanted to be part of it. A still-young man who had other plans for his future life.

What do I have to do with this? thought Johansson with irritation, looking around for his highball, which he must have left behind in the bathroom. Not a thing, for regardless of what Pilgrim and Fionn had been up to more than thirty years ago, it was still a good five years too late for someone like Johansson to even lift his little finger. Statutes of limitation are not a stupid invention, thought Johansson. They save a lot of unnecessary running around. So what should he do now? For a police officer like himself there was actually only one problem remaining, and that was Krassner himself. What was it Sarah had said? That he would rather die than take his own life, and on that point she had probably been right as well, thought Johansson. What remains is just to find out how it really happened.

Obviously it was Krassner that SePo was interested in the whole time, and quite certainly it was pure coincidence that M'Boye got to function as a hanger for Krassner's overcoat. Not even the secret police were so dumb that they didn't understand that it was a matter of a tiny window of happiness for the white regime in South Africa, and that someone like M'Boye might very soon be sitting in the new government. The trade federation has clearly realized that, for otherwise why would they have brought him here? Presumably SePo hasn't even given a thought to him, thought Johansson, and from what he'd heard from Wiklander he didn't seem to have realized anything either.

Rule number one, thought Johansson, leaning back in his desk chair. You have to like the situation. During his more than twenty years as a policeman he could not recall any situation that he disliked as intensely as the one in which he now found himself.

Rule number two, thought Johansson. Don't complicate things unnecessarily. He hadn't encountered anything as complicated as Krassner's so-called suicide, either. And what the hell do I say to Jarnie? he thought with a deep sigh. Quite apart from the fact that he's my best friend, he's going to think I'm not all there.

Rule number three, thought Johansson. Hate chance. There at least it seems that you were quite right. He gave a wry smile toward Krassner's pile of papers on his otherwise well-organized desk. And because that pile was now his own, he could start by finding out what it was really about. What was it he'd written in that letter that he'd probably never seriously believed Johansson would ever receive? So I can see to it that justice is served in my own country, thought Johansson.

[MONDAY, DECEMBER 16]

On Monday morning right before eight o'clock Johansson phoned his secretary and reported that he planned to sit at home and work during the day and that he preferred not to be disturbed.

Unless all hell breaks loose, of course, although why would that happen? thought Johansson.

"Yes, unless something totally new comes up," he said.

"But you'll be in tomorrow?" asked his secretary.

"Sure," said Johansson. "I'm coming on Tuesday morning as usual." Quit nagging, he thought.

"And you haven't forgotten that you're going to a conference on total defense on Tuesday and Wednesday?" she continued.

"No," said Johansson, and finally he could put down the receiver.

It took him a couple of hours to go through Krassner's manuscript. If even a portion of what was written in it was true and could be substantiated, it would be tricky enough for the person it dealt with, but just now it wasn't the actual contents of the papers that interested him. What started the police alarm bells ringing in his head was the extent, the volume, and above all else the structure of what Krassner had written, combined with the imagined contents of what he still hadn't had time to write.

What was there was just under one hundred fifty typewritten pages that dealt with the book's protagonist, the prime minister, and regardless of whether what was written there was true or false—for that was a later, subsidiary question—it was a manuscript in sufficient condition that a professional editor could manage to make a book out of it. A book of roughly two hundred fifty to three hundred printed pages, assuming the author had been able to realize the ambitions that he had recorded in his table of contents and transform what remained to be done into written text.

Even more interesting was what was still unwritten. What that would deal with was evident from a rather detailed outline, which seemed to assimilate all the chapters with headings and brief descriptions underneath, and last but not least from the frequent handwritten notations that Krassner had made in his manuscript. Thus, among what was missing were chapters that would deal with Swedish social democracy and the history of social democracy, previous social democratic leaders and their wheelings and dealings, Sweden's role in the Second World War, the Swedish policy of neutrality, the security situation in northern Europe, and the threat from the great neighbor to the east.

A background description, plain and simple, thought Johansson, and he also realized from the handwritten notes under the still-unwritten chapters that Krassner had intended to complete that part of the work in situ—that is, in Sweden. It stood there plainly in a number of places and in Krassner's own, barely legible handwriting, "Sweden!" "to be written in Sweden," "write in S.," and there were also handwritten references to the places he would be seeking his material: "Labor Movement Archives," "Social Democratic Archives," "Parliamentary Protocols," "Kungliga Biblioteket (Royal Library, Humlegarden)," and so on.

Most interesting of all was the conclusion that followed from the fact that the manuscript on his desk, with the exception of about twenty pages, consisted of photocopies. There must be an original and possibly one or several copies somewhere else. Those pages that weren't copies showed up more or less randomly in the running text; possibly it was as simple as that they'd just landed in the wrong pile when Krassner sorted them after copying.

True, Johansson was not an author, but if he had been one and had flown four thousand miles to write an already-determined background description for a book that he, both mentally and in terms of content, surely thought he was already pretty much done with . . . if such had been the case, thought Johansson, then I would have so help me God brought along what I'd already written. In order to have a baseline when I was writing those final obvious sections that nonetheless needed to be there so that it would look one way and not another if you'd gotten it into your head to write a book.

Hence the alarm bell that was ringing in his head. When his colleagues had done the house search at Krassner's place right after he was supposed to have jumped out the window, it had simply and summarily been swept clean of the sort of things that ought to have been found there, namely Krassner's collected working materials. What he'd brought with him from the States and what he'd gathered together during his six weeks in Sweden. True, he didn't expect any great feats from Bäckström and Wiijnbladh—he was well acquainted with both of them and if he'd had any say neither of them would have been a police officer—but they weren't completely blind. Besides, Jarnebring had been there and the only, obvious conclusion from the fact that he hadn't found any papers either was that there weren't any to find. And who in that case had cleared them away? For Johansson was completely convinced that they'd been there from the start.

The guys at SePo, thought Johansson, and, considering what had happened since, there were two alternatives that appeared more credible than any others. In the first case someone had taken the opportunity to do a so-called covert house search while Krassner was out running around town, on his own initiative or because someone had lured him away, and this someone had gathered up his papers and taken them along when they'd left the place. And so far all was well and good and most likely even legal. True, Johansson had no particular insights into the classified legislation that governed the more sensitive aspects of the work of the secret police, but the little he knew still suggested that that was how it had been.

Then Krassner comes home right after seven, for Jarnebring himself had told him about that, which suggested strongly that it was probably true. And when he comes into his room and discovers that all his papers are gone, he becomes so depressed that he steals a few last farewell lines, from the protagonist in his work in progress, and jumps out the window. The same prime minister who, according to Krassner himself in several places in his manuscript, "makes me wanna puke" gets the honor of formulating his last words in life?

Forget that, thought Johansson. Not Krassner, who has multiple copies of all the essentials in his safe-deposit box back home in Albany and most likely an original too that he's tucked away somewhere else. Not Krassner, who has a loaded, unsecured automatic weapon in his bedroom in Albany. Not Krassner, who even in his youth was capable of beating up the woman in his life. Not SePo either, for that matter, for what would be the point of doing a covert house search if the person you did it to would discover it as soon as he came home? In that case there were other, considerably easier solutions. Concoct a suitable suspicion, arrest the piece of shit, and put him in jail while you go through his belongings in peace and quiet. Johansson himself had done that more than once, so here he had solid ground under his feet.

But . . . what if despite everything there hadn't been any papers? Perhaps he stored them some other place? What if the secret police had never done a covert house search? What if Krassner quite simply had taken his own life? If, if, if, thought Johansson with irritation. Maybe a necessary prerequisite for getting any reasonable order into all of these reservations would be for him to go there and speak to the former neighbors. Forget that too, thought Johansson, for apart from everything else he simply didn't have time.

Instead he phoned Wiklander, who had already been there and was not completely incapable as a police officer.

"I'm home," said Johansson. "I want to talk with you. You'll get a cup of coffee."

Fifteen minutes later he and Wiklander were sitting in Johansson's living room, each with a mug of freshly brewed coffee. He had closed the door to his study.

"There's one thing I'm wondering about," said Johansson, sniffing the steam rising up from the mug.

Wiklander contented himself with nodding. What is it he knows that I don't know? he thought.

"That evening when Krassner jumped out the window," Johansson continued, "how many of them were living on that corridor?"

"Seven, including Krassner," said Wiklander. "Normally there would have been eight but one seems to have moved home. There was some relative who had suffered an accident. His father, I think. Or maybe it was his mother?"

"How many of them were at home?" said Johansson. "When he jumped, I mean."

"At home," said Wiklander, looking as though he was thinking intently. "Krassner himself was out on the town of course. He came home around seven. That black guy must have run into him when he was on his way out. I have the idea that there's something about that in the investigation. Yes. So there was him, the black guy, M'Boye, who was on his way to the restaurant to meet his girlfriend, our colleague Eriksson." Wiklander smiled wryly.

"The other five, then," said Johansson.

"Three of them seem to have gone home over the weekend. The students living there were mostly from the country," said Wiklander, who himself was from Värmland and went home to his dear mother in Karlstad whenever he had the chance.

"That leaves two," said Johansson. "Were they at home?"

"No," said Wiklander. "They were supposed to have been . . . wait now, this is how it was. First they were going to go to some concert, but then they didn't get any tickets, and then they had planned to start partying a little at home before they went out later . . . but then they got tickets anyway. . . ."

"It wasn't by any chance our colleague Eriksson who arranged that detail for them?"

"Now that you mention it," said Wiklander. "I recall that I thought that she must have worked pretty hard to weasel her way in. Although I doubt if she paid—it was probably the firm that did."

So it was empty in the corridor when Krassner died, thought Johansson. And it was our colleague Eriksson who saw to that. Nothing so complicated.

"What's the problem?" said Wiklander, looking tentatively at his boss. What is it he's keeping to himself? he thought.

"No problem at all," said Johansson, smiling. "Now I have all the pieces in place, many thanks to you, by the way."

That leaves alternative two, thought Johansson when he'd let Wiklander out after the anticipated quarter hour of coffee-drinking and police chitchat about this and that. Alternative two was not a pleasant alternative. Lunch, thought Johansson, but first a refreshing walk so I can clean out the dross I have in my skull.

The hills of the South End, the water and the city below, were cold and windy with snow in the air; but it could scarcely be more beautiful than this in a person's life, thought Johansson. Krassner had had his papers at home, the guys at the secret police had made a covert house search. For reasons that Johansson didn't understand they had taken his papers with them. Then Krassner is supposed to have written his suicide note, with words he'd borrowed from someone else—and on a completely new, unused typewriter ribbon, despite the fact that in all likelihood he already had the same text in his manuscript, all ready and written out, and despite the fact that in all likelihood he ought to have typed many thousand keystrokes during the time he'd been here. And no used typewriter ribbon in the wastebasket either, despite the fact that cleaning was hardly his strongest suit.

Something must have gone completely to hell, thought Johansson while a cold hand brushed against his heart. He considered it out of the question that a Swedish secret police officer would have murdered Krassner in cold blood and feigned a suicide. That just doesn't happen, thought Johansson. We're talking about Sweden, for God's sake. And considering who Krassner was out to get in his book, and if it was really SePo that grabbed his papers, it was a complete mystery why his manuscript wasn't already in circulation as a best-selling news item in all of the media, thought Johansson with a certain heat. There must be another explanation, and the only one he himself could imagine was that one or more of the operatives who carried out the operation itself had made such an awful mess of things that a feigned suicide was the only solution at hand.

That would explain the silence in the media. It wasn't out of solicitude for the person that Krassner was out to get in his book, it was about their own rear ends. That would also explain the considerable dexterity required to transform the murder of Krassner into a suicide. Wonder who their chief operative was, thought Johansson. Jeanette Eriksson was out of the question. This he realized from the pictures he'd seen—and besides, she had an alibi. M'Boye. Think how strange it can get, thought Johansson with a wry smile. Besides, she was completely the wrong type.

What do I do now? thought Johansson and sighed. If I talk about what I believe, everyone, including my best friend, will think I've gone completely screwy. There's no one I can ask, and if I trot over to SePo and do so anyway, I'll be sitting in the parking bureau in Västberga the next day. And I don't have the least legal basis for even the tiniest bit of surveillance, despite the fact that I'm still the head of the country's most powerful detective organization. At least on paper.

All I have are my own papers, thought Johansson. For they're mine and mine alone.

Plus I'm hungry, he thought. Really hungry, the way you get when you've already done a whole day's work in the morning and you still haven't gotten a bite to put in your stomach. I can take care of that, in any case, thought Johansson, setting a course toward his beloved neighborhood restaurant, where excellent lunches were served even on a normal Monday a week before Christmas.

After lunch Johansson returned to his office, set Krassner's manuscript and other notes to one side, and instead went through the remaining files. That was how he found the letter that Pilgrim had written to Fionn in April 1955, or more correctly stated, a copy of that letter.

It was a very old copy, certainly not much younger than the letter, on thin, shiny, yellowed photo paper. It was taken with a copying machine from the time when you took a picture with a regular camera firmly mounted onto a copying table, processed the film, and copied the pictures at the desired size.

It was with a number of other, similar copies in an old red cardboard binder that had a white label pasted in the upper-right-hand corner. The label had three lines. On the first someone had written the owner's name with ink and nib in a neat, old-fashioned handwriting: "Col. John C. Buchanan." On the line below and in the same handwriting, what was intended to be stored in it: "private notes, letters, etc." Damp stains that had dried at various times were on the cover, rings from glasses—probably whiskey, thought Johansson with a grin, visualizing the pyramid of bottles in the colonel's basement.

Pilgrim's letter to Fionn was handwritten in ink with a fountain pen, the handwriting expressive and aggressively slanted forward, yet completely legible; there was no location and no date. The paper was unlined and folded horizontally in two places with the same distance between the folds, the paper quality unknown but judging by the folds probably high. There was a notation written in ink on the letter in a neat, old-fashioned handwriting, and this with a steel nib as well: "April 1955, exact date unknown, arrived during my visit to G." The colonel, thought Johansson, without knowing why; despite the fact that the lack of an envelope bothered him, he also had an idea that Pilgrim had sent the letter to Fionn's home address.

The text was direct, yet it also had a literary touch, a poetic tone, and if the poet in him had been uppermost as he held the pen he still hadn't forgotten what he wanted to get said. It was a short letter. Scarcely ten or so lines longer than the concluding portion that Krassner had quoted in the book he was writing and that someone else most probably had used as his final words.

Johansson translated the entire text into Swedish and wrote it down on a piece of paper. Then he read it and carefully pondered what was written there, and only after that did he draw his conclusions. The man didn't want to be involved anymore, thought Johansson. For he had clearly been involved for some years at least, and it appeared to have been a rich life as well if you could really take him at his word.

Fionn,

I would be a scoundrel if I pretended that your generous offer didn't make me both happy and moved, and a liar if I even suggested that those years that I've worked together with you—for a great and noble cause—haven't also been the ones which have meant the most to me and my purely personal development. A few times it has even been so exciting and so critical that when the whole thing was finally done and I'd come out the other side, I've been a different person than when I went in. And at least once I've been granted the grace, while still young, to fall freely, like in a dream.

But everything has its time. My decision is irrevocable and is simply due to the fact that my task has also taken over my life and hasn't left anything else behind. For that's how it's turned out. I have lived my life caught between the longing of summer and the cold of winter.

> *As a young man I used to think that when summer comes I would fall in love with someone, someone I would love a lot, and then, that's when I would start living my life for real. But by the time I had accomplished all those things I had to do before, summer was already gone and all that remained was the winter cold. And that, that was not the life that I had hoped for.*
>
> Pilgrim

You can really accomplish a lot with small means, thought Johansson; specifically it was the altered paragraph division in the quotation that irritated him, even if it had improved the poetic substance.

The spy who gave notice, thought Johansson. For being a mere twenty-seven years old when he did that—Johansson had looked up the prime minister's year of birth in one of his many reference books—he seemed truly sardonic. Buchanan could probably keep from laughing, and if he'd been the way Sarah had described him, Pilgrim's eloquence had probably been wasted effort.

After that he gathered together Krassner's papers and put them back in the bag. The rest that was there could well wait, because he was a policeman, not a historian. Perhaps they ought to be donated to the archives of the labor movement, thought Johansson. Or I could forget about the whole thing, have a tall highball, and call up some nice woman, for this of course wasn't the life I had imagined either. Wonder if they've gone home at the foreign nationals unit? he thought, looking at his watch.

[TUESDAY, DECEMBER 17, TO WEDNESDAY, DECEMBER 18]

It was the Defense College that acted as host for the conference where questions of total defense were to be discussed from and including luncheon on day one until and including luncheon on day two. An exclusive affair with only a dozen hand-picked delegates who ordinarily worked as high-level bosses within the media sector, industry, and the governmental administrative apparatus.

The first meetings had been held as early as the late 1940s; according to the official history it was then–prime minister Tage Erlander himself who had hatched the idea of gathering representatives of both private industry and the public sector under the aegis of the defense department for the purpose of strengthening the country's defenses. Thus the new concept of "total defense": a Europe crisscrossed by new borders, new alliances and power constellations, a cold war between East and West, a strongly questioned Swedish policy of neutrality. In that situation it seemed both logical and obvious that the country's prime minister would decide to try to create peace in his own backyard at least.

This time they would be gathering at a comfortable and well-situated conference center in the archipelago south of Stockholm, and for some reason it was Wiklander who was to drive Johansson there.

He wants to talk about Krassner, thought Johansson, but because he himself didn't intend to open that discussion, he sat in the backseat and read through his conference material. It was only when they'd started heading east at Järna, and there wasn't much time left to play with, that Wiklander spoke up.

"There's something I've been thinking about," said Wiklander. "If you have time to listen, chief?"

"Of course," said Johansson, making the effort to sound as though he really did.

"It struck me when we left each other yesterday. I don't know if I'm on the wrong track, but your questions got me thinking. I suddenly got the idea that maybe the colleagues at SePo took the opportunity to do a little house search in that guy M'Boye's room and that was why our colleague Eriksson had carted him away to the restaurant."

"The same thought struck me," said Johansson. "That was why I asked you." Only a half lie, he thought.

"And while they're doing that, that wretch takes the opportunity to jump out his window," said Wiklander, his voice actually sounding rather gloomy.

"I've thought about that too," said Johansson, trying to slip in a little extra authority in the service of the lie and of credibility. "They did their thing and Krassner did his and then they left without having any idea that Krassner had already jumped or was just about to jump out his window."

"Can it really be that bad?" said Wiklander doubtfully. "I mean, they must have had people outside keeping an eye on the situation, don't you think?"

"They must have been standing outside the entrance at the back in that case, while Krassner jumped out on the front side," said Johansson, who had decided to preserve Wiklander's misunderstanding.

"Yes. Well," said Wiklander, but he didn't sound especially convinced. "It doesn't appear to have been very professional."

"I think we're in complete agreement about that," said Johansson without needing to sound uncertain, "but personally I think they probably never did a house search."

"You mean . . ." said Wiklander.

"That Eriksson and M'Boye went out and ate and that was all," said Johansson.

"Hmm," said Wiklander, nodding. "That's sort of what I've been thinking. That it's a coincidence, plain and simple."

"And I also think that was why they wanted to check out the investigation of Krassner's cause of death," said Johansson. "To be sure that M'Boye didn't have something to do with Krassner in some mysterious way."

"Well," said Wiklander, sounding considerably happier. "There's probably no doubt he took his own life. There's simply no other possibility."

"No," said Johansson. It's nice to hear that you've arrived at that insight, he thought.

Johansson was the only police officer at the conference, and when he'd read through the list of participants a few days earlier he'd thought that by God this wasn't cat shit they'd scraped together—with certain reservations about himself. The list contained two chief executives, a supreme court justice, six managing and deputy managing directors from industry, two editors in chief, plus a police superintendent who, to be on the safe side, had been propped up with the addition of "and head of the Swedish Bureau of Criminal Investigation." All in suits and ties, of course, because it was only the Scots who made war in skirts.

It had been a very civil affair. True, it had started with a war game where first the participants drew lots and swapped occupations, not in order to go to the front lines but rather to see to it that communications, the food supply, and the medical and legal systems were functioning. In other respects as well the conference had primarily dealt with just that: how you got roads and telephones, electricity and water, to function, how you saw to it that people didn't starve to death and that they had clothes on their backs. And how you got them to behave like "people" even if the worst were to occur.

The final morning had been devoted to a seminar drill under the leadership of a "special adviser to the prime minister," the latter's own éminence grise, who also bore the highest responsibility for security questions affecting the government and the central administration. Considering that, he'd been unusually specific when he handed out his assignment. He wanted the course participants to write down the names of the three living Swedes who ran the greatest risk, ranked by likelihood of personal attack. Not just anybody, obviously, but those who were in high positions in politics, industry, or the bureaucracy. Or were celebrities for other reasons such as, for example, the queen, Astrid Lindgren, or Björn Borg.

In total the delegates had written down twenty-some names, and the country's prime minister had landed overwhelmingly in first place, having received twice as many risk points as the remaining names combined. All of the delegates had placed him topmost, and one managing director of a large fashion company, himself far from unknown, had written the prime minister's name three times to be on the safe side. Despite their seminar leader's title.

"So the result appears to be quite unambiguous," said the special adviser as he began the concluding discussion. "It would be interesting to hear your reasons," he continued while he observed the delegates behind half-closed eyelids and with a sardonic smile.

Peculiar type, thought Johansson. If he hadn't been so fat you could easily take him for a viper lying in the hot sun, only pretending to be asleep.

"Politicians of course often become a bit controversial," one editor in chief began tactfully, because someone had to begin.

"Good God," moaned one of the executives, who, judging by his complexion, ought to do something about his blood pressure. "If people like you read what you yourselves were writing, you must surely understand that he doesn't seem the least bit controversial. You just have to read back what you're writing."

"What do you mean?" said the editor in chief with a faint smile.

"I think it's touching that you all appear to agree that the fellow is a real son of a bitch. I myself have no idea, for I've never met him," he added, glaring acidly at the editor in chief.

"Which I have," clarified the editor in chief, looking for some reason rather superior.

"So he is a real son of a bitch, then," said the executive, and the ensuing laughter drowned out the weak protests of his opponent.

Then things had broken loose in earnest: "arrogant," "upper-class type," "rotten," "malicious," "holds a grudge," and "very un-Swedish." In addition he was "much too intelligent," "much too educated," "much too verbal," "much too talented," and all in all "much too unreliable."

"And let's not forget that he's obviously spying for the Russians too. How he manages that between all his tax evasions," said the executive with the blood pressure, looking sternly at the second editor in chief for some reason.

The only one who hadn't said anything was Johansson. He hadn't even changed his expression but was content to surreptitiously observe their seminar leader, whose body language, apart from the wry smile and the lowered eyelids, was not completely unlike his own. But now he had the chance.

"I think that's all nonsense," said Johansson suddenly, and because he was who he was and looked the way he did, the room suddenly went completely quiet.

"What do you mean?" said the special adviser, with a faint twitch of the eyebrow.

Good, thought Johansson. Here's a nibble, and it's the big fish who's circling the hook.

"Well," said Johansson leisurely and with a lot of Norrland in his voice. "Quite apart from all the logical and rational reasons that argue against that . . . and you know that sort of thing better than someone like me," he added good-naturedly, nodding toward the rest of the assembly.

"Speak up, man," hooted one of the younger executives who'd been on a survival course abroad. "If you've said A then you have to say B."

"Purely from a police perspective, then," said Johansson hesitantly in order to secure the bait thoroughly around the sinker and the line. "Purely from a police perspective, then . . . he's simply the wrong type, as we say. The type who would never spy for the Russians. Not him, no." Johansson shook his head heavily and everyone who saw him understood that the very thought was impossible.

"It is quite nice to hear that opinion from such an esteemed representative of the police," said their chairman. "It's not always what I've heard being whispered among his colleagues."

"What do you mean?" asked Johansson.

"That the prime minister would *not* be a spy," said the special adviser with clear emphasis.

"I didn't say that," said Johansson with well-acted astonishment while he carefully traced the line between his thumb and index finger.

"I thought you said he was completely the wrong type?" Now the prime minister's special adviser had hoisted up his eyelids at least halfway.

"No, there I think you've got me wrong," said Johansson like a peasant, shaking his head. "As a spy he's probably a rather good type, at least when he was younger. Today no doubt he has too much to do, and then he's probably pretty much under observation too. If it's the case that he has spied for someone, then I believe that it was long before he became prime minister. And he would never dream of doing it for the Russians."

"That is very nice to hear. You don't have any tips on who it might have been in any case?" asked the special adviser.

"Quite certainly for the Americans," said Johansson. "For the CIA, if I were to speculate."

And there you bit, thought Johansson when he saw the shift in the special adviser's look.

"I've understood that within the police your political preferences differ from mine and my boss's," said the special adviser, sounding a little bit too offended for someone like him.

"Well," said Johansson and nodded. "That's no doubt correct. Although I personally think that he appears both educated and . . . well, intelligent."

"But a spy? For the CIA?" said the special adviser, and got a few giggles as reward.

"It's so easy to get into things," said Johansson, letting him savor his heaviest police look. "And the kind of intelligence I'm thinking of here doesn't have anything to do with it. On the contrary. What attracts a person the most is the sort of thing you're already suited for; otherwise it would be no big deal to abstain. It's easy to get into things, but it can be considerably trickier to get out." Johansson nodded again, mostly to himself as it appeared, and in the room where he was sitting it was dead silent.

"I don't believe we'll go any further than this," said the special adviser with a light hand movement and a suave expression. "Besides, I understand from the agreeable aromas wafting their way in from the kitchen that it's almost time for lunch. I think it's high time to adjourn. Gentlemen . . . personally I think that this has been both extraordinarily pleasant, interesting, and even exciting, and if I now may . . ."

What if I were to ask him to extend greetings from Fionn? thought Johansson as he gathered up his notes. Although that's probably not necessary, for now he could read him like an open book. Despite his heavy, unmoving face, his reclining posture, the half-closed eyelids, despite all of his body language, his phlegmatic self-assuredness and well-formulated speech, Johansson could see that he appeared truly terrified. Wonder how much he knows? he thought.

[THURSDAY, DECEMBER 19]

When Johansson came to work on Thursday morning, it was as if the pre-Christmas calm had been blown away and a state of total war prevailed between his own narcotics squad and its counterpart at the provincial police department in Dalarna. They'd been working together on a large case for several weeks. The head honchos were in Borlänge and Falun, and it was there that it had started, but the case had quickly expanded and appeared to have offshoots both in the rest of the country and abroad. Finally the chief constable in Dalarna had slammed his fist on the table and put his foot down. No more travel or surveillance outside their own turf, and it was high time to bring in a partner if he wasn't going to get the auditors around his neck.

After an agitated meeting, in which the head of the province's narcotics squad had called his chief, the chief constable, "a fucking accountant," the commander had nonetheless had the last word, and for the past three weeks the case had been divided between the police authorities in Dalarna and Johansson's own national bureau. And no one was happy.

As far as the police in Dalarna were concerned, it was their biggest narcotics case since the gold rush years in the midseventies, and they had no intention of sharing the returns on their own efforts and exertions with some "Stockholm-area-code hotshots." So the collaboration might have been better.

At the National Bureau of Criminal Investigation it wasn't the travel allowance or even the budget in general that constituted the inhibiting factor, for in that respect new angles kept popping up. There was nothing wrong with their creativity, either, and because "the peasant police out in the sticks" were always just "scratching the surface," the joint case had grown like a mold culture until it finally landed "in the competent hands of real policemen."

"This could become a really big deal," explained Johansson's traveling companion from his visit to the United States.

"But the colleagues in the province want to go in now?" asked Johansson.

"Sure, so they can celebrate Christmas in peace and quiet, those lazy bastards," said the head of the bureau's narcotics squad with a certain heat.

"Still, I'm thinking they must have some other reason," said Johansson, who'd been around awhile and had heard this and that before.

"A few of the local crooks are heading to Thailand over Christmas. Those provincials have gotten it in their heads that they intend to stay there for good, which is pure rubbish, and besides they're not the ones who are interesting. It's our usual guys who are behind this, the Turks and then those Polacks I was telling you about, they've been with us of course for several years now. Those damn Dallanders are just retailers," snorted the head of the bureau's narcotics squad, who was from Stockholm and didn't know better.

"Let Dalarna bring them in then, if they aren't of interest to us," said Johansson.

For the sake of household peace—and our own crooks don't seem to be running away from us either, he thought.

"But it's going to spoil our own job with the real head honchos," objected his former traveling companion, and he didn't sound at all the way he had the last time they'd met.

"I hear what you're saying," said Johansson.

And I've heard it ad nauseam, he thought.

"It's been their case from the start," said Johansson, "so it's hard for me to see how we would be able to stop them." Or why, he thought.

"Well, you're the one who decides, of course," said the narcotics chief inspector sourly, standing up.

"Yes," said Johansson and contented himself with smiling with his mouth only. I'm the one who decides. And sometimes that's awfully practical, he thought.

Childishness, thought Johansson, which had taken the entire morning from other things that he'd needed to do instead. Such as slipping out and shopping for a few backup provisions as a present to Jarnebring, who would surely require extra contributions of both liquid and dry goods for dinner, despite his energetic protestations to the contrary. Besides, he himself needed more exact information as to the time and place.

Now that had been solved, at any rate. Jarnebring had phoned after lunch and given the address of his latest girlfriend.

"I was thinking it's more practical that way," said Jarnebring. "You know girls, they love to fuss. And then I've loaned out my pad too. To Rusht, if you remember him?"

"Is there anything I can bring?" asked Johansson. To Rusht, he thought with surprise. Wasn't he that long-fingered character with the bad breath who managed the coffee fund at the bureau? Surely that was going too far, despite the fact that he was a colleague.

"No," said Jarnebring. "I've arranged everything. His old lady kicked him out," Jarnebring clarified, "and I can't really let the poor bastard celebrate Christmas at the local mission. Besides, I've hidden the silverware in my toothbrush case, so he'll never find it."

"And you don't need any aquavit?" said Johansson, who was not one to take risks and especially not right before Christmas.

So our colleague Rusht had a girlfriend, despite the fact that he reeked like a cadaver in a well and had six fingers on each hand, he thought.

"No," said Jarnebring emphatically. "I've got lots of liquor at home. Well, at home with my girlfriend, that is, I'm not stupid that way, and he seems to have something more permanent going for the week after Christmas. Rusht, that is," he clarified.

"Decent of you," said Johansson, who had always thought that Rusht was a real son of a bitch regardless of the season.

"So you don't need to think about aquavit," Jarnebring concluded.

Strange, thought Johansson as he put down the receiver. Wonder if he's won on one of those horses he bets on?

That Jarnebring had a new girlfriend was nothing strange. He almost always did; to be on the safe side he usually recruited them from his own ranks. Considerably younger than he, strawberry blonde, high-busted colleagues who as a rule were doing service with the uniformed police when they weren't fussing around Jarnebring. And so far that added up this time as well, thought Johansson when she opened the door after the second ring and smiled broadly at him. More interesting was the fact that this particular example had clearly survived spring, summer, and autumn, and that this time Jarnebring seemed to have brought pillow-case and blanket with him and, at least for awhile, abandoned his own bachelor pad in Vasastan. She's probably both motherly and patient, despite the fact that she looks like she does, thought Johansson.

Her friend from Skövde who'd been called in was also on the scene, and as far as her exterior was concerned she might very well have been a sister of the evening's hostess. When they said hello he also noted interest in her eyes. Wonder if it's something she's heard, he thought, or if it's just my blue eyes? For it can't be due to the fact that I exercise too little and eat too much. Because of my blue eyes, Johansson decided, and as soon as he decided that it turned into a very pleasant evening.

It became very clear when they sat down at the table in her small kitchen that he didn't need to worry about the food and drink that he hadn't brought with him. Excellent assortment of pickled herring, gravlax, and smoked eel, an excellent potato casserole with just the right creaminess, golden-brown meatballs, and little sausages that sizzled as the hostess lifted them out of the oven. There was lots of beer and wine besides. She must be rich too, thought Johansson, loading up another spoonful of scrambled eggs with finely chopped fresh chives. Nice to look at and fun to talk with. Prepares food like Aunt Jenny herself, motherly as well, patient, and . . . probably wealthy.

"I didn't think people like you existed," said Johansson, toasting his hostess. "Speak up if you want to meet a real guy." Wonder if she reads books too, he thought.

"I didn't think you knew anyone besides me," said Jarnebring good-naturedly. "What do you think about chasing with a really old gin?" he asked, fishing up a bulging clay jug from the rows of regular bottles.

Wonder where he's gotten hold of all the liquor? thought Johansson. Regardless of whether she had money, she didn't seem to be the type to buy liquor for them. Not in such quantities, in any case, and quite apart from how much of a guy she'd now gotten hold of.

"Sounds good," said Johansson, who'd only had three stiff ones, the effects of which he didn't feel in the least. Must be some horse, he thought.

Coffee and cognac were set out in the living room, along with masses of liqueurs and other oddities, and when Johansson saw the whole lot he immediately abandoned his theory that his best friend must have won at the track.

"Coffee and cognac will do for me," said Johansson when his host started rummaging among all the bottles. Now he was feeling the effects of the drinks with dinner and he didn't intend to pour sugar on the fire.

Jarnebring's girlfriend and her friend drank cream liqueurs with obvious enjoyment—they probably don't read books, thought Johansson—and it was then too that he got an answer to his musings.

"God, this is good," said the female friend from Skövde, letting the tip of her tongue feel her upper lip. "Can you ask your contact to arrange a few bottles for me too?"

"I'll ask him," said Jarnebring, smiling and raising his glass.

Hultman, thought Johansson. Wonder what Jarnie has helped him with? he thought, and if Jarnebring hadn't been his best friend he would certainly have been a little worried.

The time had gotten to be past midnight before Johansson finally stopped to think that it was high time to go home. Not because he felt out of sorts exactly—for the last hour he'd been content simply with mineral water—but in twelve hours he would be sitting at the steering wheel. Best to break up when it was the most fun.

"Now it's time for me to say thank you," said Johansson. "You haven't done this in vain and you must speak up in good time before the wedding so that I can repay you."

Jarnebring had kept a good face but still rolled his eyes when no one else could see them. The hostess had been giggly and delighted and kissed him right on the mouth, and her friend had clearly also decided to think about getting along.

"I heard you live on the south end too," she said, giving Johansson a smile and an assessing glance. "If you don't have anything against it, maybe we can share a cab?"

"Sure," said Johansson. You're rolling in it, lad, he thought.

[FRIDAY, DECEMBER 20]

He'd packed his suitcases the day before. His clothes, Christmas presents for his relatives, books to read, plus Krassner's posthumous papers, if he were to have an extra day and didn't have anything better to do; everything was in his suitcases. In the morning before he went to work he'd picked up the car that his brother had arranged for him. What remained was to go around at work and wish everyone merry Christmas and drink way too much coffee. He'd decided to eat lunch on the way. Right before the stroke of twelve he gave a Christmas present to his secretary, got a surprised smile, neither more nor less surprised than what he'd counted on, and a cool kiss on the cheek in thanks.

Then he took the elevator down to the garage and sat in the large rented car, which didn't cost a cent, for his big brother, who was in the business, had seen to that, loaded the tape player with some nice dance-band music, and set a course northward. Just under 240 miles makes just under four hours, thought Johansson as he turned onto Essingeleden, at a good time judging by the sparse northbound traffic.

CHAPTER XIV

And all that remained was the cold of winter

Stockholm in December

December had started unusually well for Bäckström and his colleagues in homicide. At the beginning of Lucia week, they'd taken the boat to Finland for the squad's traditional Christmas conference. They'd gotten thoroughly primed even before going on board, and when Bäckström and the others went to piss away most of it before sitting down to eat lunch, Danielsson was in his cups on the shit-house stairs, even before they'd passed Lidingö on the way out.

This is, God help me, too good to be true, thought Bäckström. What a fucking phenomenal start!

First he and his colleagues just stood silently and looked at Jack Daniels where he was lying, motionless and with his drunken head at a mysterious angle against his chest, but then Rundberg, that ingratiating bastard, took him by the shoulder and shook him and raved that someone had to fetch a doctor, and then Jack Daniels suddenly sat up ramrod straight and stared at them with his bloodshot eyes.

"You cowardly bastards," he hissed. "I don't hear any applause."

Then everything went back to normal again. At lunch Lindberg started nagging that no one ought to take more than one schnapps, given the afternoon meetings, but then old Jack Daniels, who was also back to normal again, told him to shut up and eat. After that he made a toast with Bäckström. First he just sat and glared at him the way he usually did, but then he suddenly grinned and raised his glass.

"Skoal, Bäckström," said Jack Daniels. "Better luck next time we go to the can."

Say what you like about old Jack Daniels, but he's a tough bastard, thought Bäckström, who was already into his fourth and starting to get a little sentimental.

"Skoal, chief," said Bäckström, "and I'm not one to complain."

Clearly that had been the right answer, for Jack Daniels had grinned like an old killer bear and treated him to his fifth.

When they got to Helsinki, Bäckström slipped away from the rest of the company. He called up a Finnish friend, a cop who had good contacts and was made of the right stuff. They went to a nightclub where they picked up two Estonian girls whom they took home to the colleague's place. Bäckström gave his specimen a real all-round lube job. She was a small, fat brunette with big tits and good speed on her little mouse. Both she and her friend were in Finland illegally, so neither of them had been particularly difficult to negotiate with when they were going to settle the price, and the colleague told them what he and Bäckström did for work. Before they left she even asked Bäckström if they couldn't meet again sometime. Perhaps in Stockholm?

Dream on, you horny little cunt, grinned Bäckström as he staggered on board again in good time before departure. Out of pure curiosity he'd also trotted down to the meeting room and there sat Lindberg playing the conference game along with Krusberg, another ingratiating bastard, and a couple of the younger talents who probably didn't have much choice. Bäckström sat down for a while to rest his weary feet, but Lindberg was carrying on about some meaningless statistics that no real policeman could bear filling in. Then he left and looked up the others, who to a man sat gathered in the bar, getting warmed up before departure. Then everything was as normal again.

When they came back to the precinct the day before St. Lucia's Day, old Jack Daniels took Bäckström aside and asked him if he couldn't arrange the practical details around the Lucia celebration so it wouldn't be so damn expensive. Bäckström understood exactly what he meant, and even though it was at the last minute he succeeded in getting hold of his contact at the coast guard, who'd gotten a meeting with his own contact, who in turn had produced a whole case of mixed goodies at a reasonable price.

"No need to pay for the whole damn geriatric system because you want to have a drink," said Jack Daniels contentedly when Bäckström returned with his booty after a well-executed assignment.

Then they celebrated Lucia according to good old traditions, and Bäckström didn't even need to slave at the after-hours unit over the weekend. Danielsson, that decent old drunk, had given him a special assignment and written out all the overtime forms required so he would be able to rest his weary head and take the weekend off with a good conscience.

Monday didn't start off badly either. He'd hardly managed to stick his foot in the precinct door before one of the younger talents came rushing in all out of breath to say that there'd been a double murder out in Bromma that demanded Bäckström's immediate professional assistance.

Unfortunately it wasn't as good as it sounded. Despite the address it was an ordinary gook murder. A crazy Iranian who had shot his wife and young daughter. True, the wife was Swedish, but what the hell could she expect when she'd gotten married to someone like that and told the poor bastard that she wanted a divorce besides? How fucking stupid can you be? thought Bäckström.

When the camel driver was done with the old lady and the kid he'd clearly tried to do himself in too, but that hadn't gone too well. As so often with those types, his courage had failed him as soon as it concerned his own well-being. First he'd tried to shoot himself in the head, but naturally he'd missed and only parted his hair, and when the uniformed police had gotten there, he was sitting out in the kitchen whittling his wrists with an old bread knife. In other words, a completely ordinary gook murder, and the most shocking thing was perhaps that the poor bastard had a license for two weapons, a moose rifle and a shotgun. Clearly he'd taken the hunting test, and those morons at the licensing unit had licensed the hunting rifles to him. How the hell could a bastard like that get a license to hunt? In Sweden besides, thought Bäckström.

The rest was pure routine. Fortunately he'd got hold of that little fairy Wiijnbladh in tech, so the actual crime-scene investigation had gone quickly enough, and he'd gladly turned over the gook to a younger colleague who might need a few easy cases to practice on before things got serious, and it was then of course that the whole thing had gone to hell. As always when the real pro isn't nearby. His younger colleague simply dropped the ball, and the good doctor had of course been smart enough to take the opportunity to stuff so many pills into the poor bastard that he hadn't been able to talk. How fucking stupid can you be? thought Bäckström. And now his colleague had the chance of a lifetime to squeeze a proper confession out of the guy as he was lying there in intensive care with his eyes crossed and tubes in both arms.

"Have you thought about starting at the City Mission, lad?" said Bäckström, fixing his eyes on the little moron from hell when he came back from the hospital and stood in Bäckström's office, whining that he couldn't cope with his job.

The good doctor was clearly one of those intrepid citizens who took themselves too seriously. He'd admitted the murderer to the psychiatric unit, and the guy was simply lying there keeping his mouth shut. "Deeply depressed, beyond communication, and with apparent risk of ending up in a long-term psychotic state," according to the fax that His

Highness sent over to the squad as an answer to Bäckström's own friendly question of whether he couldn't be allowed to talk with the poor bastard. They intend to snatch the gook away from me, those bastards, and then they'll release him for Easter as usual and he'll suddenly be free as a bird and healthy as a horse, thought Bäckström, who'd been there before. But we'll see the hell about that, he thought, and went in to Jack Daniels to procure a little extra help.

Unfortunately it appeared as though he might have chosen a better occasion. A hangover had clearly caught up with his honored boss, which no doubt only proved that not even a drunk like him could cope with partying the way they usually did before Christmas. Jack Daniels had gone completely nuts and Bäckström got the whole blame, despite the fact that he was innocent. Any more special assignments before Christmas were out of the question. And so were a large number of other things, if Bäckström, who came back from the hospital without a confession, understood the matter correctly.

"How fucking stupid can you be?" bellowed Jack Daniels in his sympathetic way, pounding his fist on the desk.

So Bäckström had to make the best of a bad job, gather together his bag and baggage, and drive himself back up to the hospital and question the gook. Late in the evening, besides, so he could be certain that that damn doctor was sitting at home celebrating his victory over justice along with the rest of the red-wine leftists. Although there you shit in your pants, thought Bäckström while he rigged up his tape recorder next to the bed. The gook himself was playing the nut-house game, looking at the ceiling with empty brown, tear-filled eyes and hands folded on the bedcover as if he really didn't have anything to do with the matter but was just a completely ordinary psycho case in a large pile of innocent people.

This will be fun, thought Bäckström delightedly. He switched on the tape recorder, did the usual introductory tirades, and looked gently at the gook while he held out the photo he'd brought with him.

"I understand that you're not feeling well," said Bäckström amiably, patting him on the shoulder. "But I think you're going to feel a lot better if you unburden your heart."

It wasn't a bad photo, in color, of course, and with good sharpness in all details, and it functioned completely perfectly. The daughter was two years old and had clearly been asleep when little gook-papa had come in to say goodnight for good. She'd had on white pajamas with big Mickey Mouses on them, and according to another photo, which Bäckström had seen in an album at home at the crime scene, she'd been really cute like all those gook kids always were.

Now, on the other hand, she didn't look funny. Her dear father had clearly stuck the barrel of his moose rifle in through the slats of her little bed, set the muzzle against the base of her skull, and pulled the trigger. The bullet had gone diagonally down through the body and out through her belly. On its way it had taken with it the entire package of the small intestine, which was lying like a neat, pale pink ball outside her pajamas, covering at least one and a half Mickey Mouses. It was not a bad photo, as stated, and the gook only needed to cast one brown goat eye on it in order to reconnect sufficiently for the damn doctor to be up on charges for his crazy diagnosis.

His mouth started going like a sewing-machine needle while the tears and sweat sprayed off him. Broken Swedish, of course. For long intervals he'd been completely incomprehensible, and for awhile he of course tried to put the blame on his wife, but Bäckström nonetheless got it done, although he had to toil like a galley slave with the tape recorder when not being forced to keep his interrogation object in bed where he should be if he was ever going to get healthy. It only took an hour to put all the pieces in place. Then the nurse was allowed to come in and stick a sturdy injection into the poor bastard as a reward, and before Bäckström left he took the opportunity to give him a few parting words.

"I'm certain that you're going to feel much better now that you've spoken up," said Bäckström kindly, patting him on the arm and smiling mournfully toward the nurse. "Tsk, tsk, tsk, it's too bad about some people."

It was clearly strong stuff she'd poked into him, for when Bäckström left he was just lying there staring at the ceiling again. Just like he'd done an hour earlier.

But ingratitude is the world's reward. The following day Jack Daniels came into Bäckström's office and raged and was not the least bit grateful. The gook had evidently taken his own life during the night after Bäckström's visit, despite the fact that he'd been given all the chances in the world to relieve his inner pressure. So it turned out to be the afterhours unit anyway, and considering how his finances looked after the most recent partying he didn't have any choice other than to slave over both Christmas and New Year's. What a fucking world, thought Bäckström gloomily. What fucking people there are and what fucking lives they live.

Wiijnbladh had a lot to do, chairman of the party committee that he was, and when he was finally starting to put all the details in order, that fat loudmouth Bäckström in homicide called and nagged that he needed help with a double murder. Nice as he was he naturally joined in, despite the fact that he had more important things on the program. This was a tragic family affair. Two spouses had quarreled, the man had clearly met a new woman and wanted to separate, and in her agitated and deranged condition the wife had taken his moose rifle and gone upstairs where she first shot their little daughter and then herself. Normally it was the other way around, i.e., it was the husband who shot the wife and children, but Wiijnbladh thought that the trace evidence spoke clearly, even if Bäckström refused to listen to that version. And as he neither had the time nor the inclination he settled for finishing his own business, and then he returned to his real assignment, organizing the celebration of the boss's sixtieth birthday.

The boss, whose name was Holger Blenke, was something of a legend within criminal investigation. To start with he'd been a cadre commander in the cavalry—that was at the end of the Second World War—but as soon as the war was over he'd applied to the police department. Had to patrol his way up like everyone else to eventually end up in the tech squad, because he was a handy fellow who not only had a good way with horses but generally liked to fiddle around with things.

Blenke had already been around during the old boss's time, when the technical squad was established; it was with him that Blenke had earned his spurs. You might well say that it was the old boss who'd broken ground and after that it was Blenke who had administered the forensic fields that the old boss had plowed up, thought Wiijnbladh, hurrying to put this well-thought-out formulation down on paper. In the midst of everything else, of course, he was to make the speech in honor of the boss. Unfortunately it hadn't gone so well for the old boss in the autumn of his years. Instead most indications were that in a drunken delusion he had beaten his oldest son to death in connection with a garden-variety apartment break-in, but because Blenke had been in charge of the crime-scene investigation, it had nonetheless finally been resolved for the best. The case had been written off as an accident, and if nothing else the efforts Blenke had made then indicated his qualifications to be the old boss's obvious successor. But to bring up such unpleasant details in a birthday speech was of course completely out of the question, and Wiijnbladh had decided early on to stick to the more general and all-embracing features of the history of the squad when the time came. That was still the most interesting, while the other things were just the usual police-station gossip, thought Wiijnbladh.

The work of planning his big day had unfortunately not proceeded without friction. Differing ideas and conflicting desires had demanded their tribute of compromises in matters both high and low, and at times Wiijnbladh had to mobilize all the diplomatic ability he was capable of in order for anything to get done. First they'd argued about the present for which they were going to collect money. Olsson, who never missed a chance to make himself seem important, had suggested that a travel stipend should be established in the boss's honor, but considering the relevant amounts the whole idea was ridiculous to start with. Including a short stay, the money would hardly be enough to take you round trip to Växjö or Hudiksvall, quite apart from the question of what exactly you might be able to pick up in terms of knowledge of criminal investigation in such places.

Instead Wiijnbladh had underscored that in a context like this it must obviously be a personal gift, and the only natural thing was to proceed from the boss's personal interests and hobbies. That was why they had finally decided to buy a chain saw, for the boss had a little summer place out on Muskö south of the city, and his major free-time interest was felling trees on his property.

After this they'd gone over to planning the party itself, and that was when things had gone seriously wrong within the committee. First Olsson, who was always the same, had developed an extremely peculiar idea that amounted to devoting the whole day to lectures and seminars where various problems and methods of criminal investigation were elucidated, but an otherwise united party committee had fortunately voted him down at once, even if one or two—considering the context— had perhaps not expressed themselves so well.

"The Chimney Sweep doesn't give a damn about such novelties" was how one of the really old foxes on the squad summed it up.

Chimney Sweep was the boss's nickname, even if it wasn't what you called him when he was listening, and the reason he'd gotten this nickname was that he had always been a warm adherent of the classic old technique of searching for fingerprints with the help of brush and coal powder. Fingerprints in particular were Blenke's great professional passion. The one time he could get really engaged and worked up was when he got onto the subject of what he called the Great Betrayal. As early as the beginning of the century, and throughout the Western world, apparently, the technique of using coal powder had been abandoned in favor of various other mysterious powders, liquids, light rays, or even gases that reacted chemically with the prints you were seeking, and which were completely incomprehensible to regular, normally constituted people.

"Gas me here, gas me there, the only gas we policemen need is tear gas," as Blenke himself had so pointedly concluded the discussion when the question had been on the agenda during a morning meeting at the squad.

And as always, of course, it was that loser Olsson—Doctor Olsson, as his colleagues called him, even though he'd probably only gone to elementary school like all the others—who recommended that perhaps one ought to take a closer look at these new methods. Who was going to do that, since all the books were in foreign languages? Olsson seemed to have good contacts, in any case, as was shown most recently, when the ombudsman's office had courted him despite his miserable efforts in connection with the murders of those three Turkish narcotics dealers.

But clearly it had been that careerist Johansson, who was head of the National Bureau of Criminal Investigation, who had chosen to write an amazingly lax statement that the ombudsman's office had obviously accepted.

The whole thing was inexplicable, thought Wiijnbladh. What interest could a bigwig like Johansson, known for stepping over colleagues' bodies if needed, have in supporting a lightweight like Olsson? Probably it was just an expression of the general arrogance and laziness that characterized people like Johansson, the Butcher from Ådalen, as certain members of the uniformed police called him. Personally Wiijnbladh had only met one leader within the corps who possessed the moral stature, the knowledge, and the capacity for practical action that one ought to have the right to demand of every person at that level. Police Superintendent Claes Waltin with SePo, thought Wiijnbladh with warmth. A man who had also personally sought him out to ask for advice on various technical questions of interest to the closed operation.

If he'd only had the opportunity he would have sent him a personal invitation to Blenke's dinner, but for cost reasons the number of invitations to persons outside the squad had been kept to an absolute minimum. And considering the locale and the remaining arrangements that the party committee's majority had voted through against his express wishes, it was surely just as well. Waltin on a Finland boat, thought Wiijnbladh with a shudder.

For all too many of his colleagues it was unfortunately the case that the boundary between a normal party and a conference was fluid. A work conference was a party that your employer was paying for, and the most popular locale for the Stockholm Police Department's conferences was the boat to Finland, which regrettably—in the midst of the drunkenness, spending, and common immorality that were its essence—provided conference rooms. As a sort of alibi, thought Wiijnbladh, and the sorrow that was always with him could sometimes turn into pure impotence and despair.

Obviously his colleagues had also gone behind his back and made contact with the travel agent in advance. Because the technical squad had already been one of the shipping company's steady customers for many years, there hadn't been any problems in negotiating various benefits when it was finally time to celebrate the squad's boss. Wives, fiancées, live-ins, and regular girlfriends would thus be allowed to come along for free, Blenke himself would have the shipowner's cabin, the price of both liquid and dry goods had been heavily discounted, and the matter was already decided. A trip with the wife on a Finland boat, thought Wiijnbladh, and the hopelessness he suddenly felt was without limit.

They sailed the week before Christmas. The entire squad, including partners both formal and informal, as well as the birthday boy himself, bringing along his wife and a half dozen close friends; in total a good sixty people, and to start with everything had gone according to the program. First a reception with champagne, which the shipping company had paid for, a few short speeches along with the presentation of gifts. Blenke was very happy with his chain saw, and so far all was well and good.

But then everything reverted to the norm again. First there were free activities until the evening's celebration dinner, and all too many of the participants, exactly as he'd feared, used that time in the usual unfortunate way and for the usual unfortunate reasons. And when it finally came time for Wiijnbladh's celebration speech—minutely prepared for several months—the atmosphere was at such high volume that only those sitting closest to him were able to make out what he was saying. After dinner his wife disappeared, as usual and for the usual reasons, as usual unclear where and with whom. And when she returned to their little cabin late that night he—as usual—pretended to be asleep.

I'm going to murder her, thought Wiijnbladh while she, giggling and intoxicated, reeking of alcohol, sweat, and sex, undressed, lay down in her bunk, fell asleep immediately, and started snoring loudly. But then he must have fallen asleep himself, for when he woke up their boat was already at the dock. This he understood from the sounds and voices and the water that had stopped moving against the wall of the cabin where they were lying.

I must see how the weather is, he thought, and as silently as he could he pulled his clothes on and sneaked out on deck. It was overcast and gray and very cold, despite the fact that there was snow in the air. He didn't feel sorrow any more, just hopelessness and despair. Impotence naturally, because he was the type who couldn't even manage to kill his own wife. He couldn't even kill her.

The closer it got to Christmas, the tighter the clouds had massed over Berg's head. At the final weekly meeting of the year—they usually took a break over Christmas and New Year's, since everyone was off anyway and nothing in particular was usually going on—he was once again compelled to take up the question of the prime minister's personal security and his awareness of the issue. Nonexistent awareness of security, thought Berg, but naturally he didn't say that, and fortunately he'd forgotten how many times he'd kept it to himself.

The old threats against the prime minister remained. The only thing that had happened was that new threats had emerged. The Harvard affair, with attention from the media, seemed to have released a pure spirit of readiness among the country's ideologues, and a day did not pass without new reports coming in of fresh lunatic recruits to the ranks.

"I'm not going to make things worse than they are," said Berg with unexpected frankness, "and I'm not trying to maintain that these characters can be compared with the Jackal or other professional terrorists and hired killers"—Berg paused before he continued—"but at the same time let us not forget that the most common attacks against highly placed politicians and other similar persons are actually carried out by the so-called solitary madman. A simple man who works with simple means and unfortunately can attain gruesome results."

"I have understood that my esteemed boss has declined all security over the holidays," said the special adviser behind half-closed eyelids and with the usual irritating smile.

"Yes," said Berg curtly. "He wants to be in peace and celebrate Christmas and New Year's with his family and a few close friends."

"The blessed Christmas season," nodded the special adviser under cover of his half-closed eyelids and his wry grin.

"What worries me most," continued Berg, who didn't intend to let himself be sidetracked, "is that he clearly intends to spend almost a week at Harpsund."

"I know, I know, for grace has even befallen me in the form of a small invitation," sighed the special adviser.

"Harpsund is a security nightmare," said Berg, nodding with emphasis at everyone at the table.

"You're thinking of that cook they have," said the special adviser. "Yes, she's really a nightmare. If I actually accept, I'm thinking seriously about bringing my own food."

"I'm not thinking of the cook," said Berg, who was not inclined to witticisms. "I'm thinking about one or several assailants, and considering the way things are down there, none of them needs to be particularly well qualified."

"I actually brought that matter up with my dear boss," said the special adviser. "That head of personal security you have can be extremely tedious and finally I gave up. So I talked with him, but he simply wants to be left in peace. It's been a little much lately, if I may say so, and if I should be so indiscreet now as to quote him he doesn't think that the crime rate in municipal Flen during the approaching holidays constitutes a major problem in his existence, not right now anyway. He just wants to have a few days off, wife and children, peace and quiet, presents and tree, pleasure and enjoyment, no bodyguards, no police whatsoever, not even a little guard in a red Santa suit lurking down by the gate." The special adviser chuckled with delight.

"I too am hoping for a peaceful holiday," said Berg seriously.

"Yes, we all are, I guess," said the minister of justice, sounding unusually engaged. "Personally I'm going to celebrate Christmas with my old mother, and considering that she's almost a hundred I'll really have to decline . . ."

"Can you arrange it so that he avoids having them in the house?" interrupted the special adviser.

"Yes," said Berg. "I can do that. I can arrange it so that he doesn't even need to see them." Even if that requires more than twice as many resources, he thought.

"Then that's what we'll do," decided the special adviser. "I'll warn the boss so he doesn't take out his moose rifle and shoot them by mistake if they're sneaking around in the park."

"That would certainly be practical," Berg agreed.

"Although I can't guarantee that he won't try to invite them in for mulled wine and ginger snaps," said the special adviser. "My dear boss easily turns sentimental this time of year, and we shouldn't underestimate his ability to adapt himself to . . . what is it you policemen say? . . . his ability to like the situation."

"Ginger snaps and mulled wine, that would certainly be fine," said Berg, smiling.

"Not a lot, of course," said the special adviser, raising his hand in a slightly dismissive gesture.

After the meeting they had lunch at Rosenbad, which had been a tradition for many years. During the bourgeois administration it had often been really nice, with ample refreshments and conversation that had been both frank and agreeable. And you didn't need to sit and wonder the whole time what they really meant when they said something, thought Berg. Although this wasn't a bad lunch either. Everyone except Berg, who was going back to work afterward, had schnapps with the little Christmas plate that had been served as an appetizer. The minister had two, the special adviser probably three by filling up his glass on the sly when he didn't think anyone was looking, while the chief legal officer was content with a half to indicate solidarity.

With coffee the minister and chief legal officer excused themselves, having other urgent business, but the special adviser wanted to talk with Berg alone.

"Damn it, Erik," he said. "Considering that it's almost Christmas and everything, can't I treat you to a cognac with coffee?" Suddenly he also seemed completely different. Almost like a young boy who was in a quandary and wanted the help of an adult.

"A little one, then," said Berg, smiling. "If you're going to have one too?"

"Sure I will," said the special adviser, sounding normal again. "It's possible that I'll have two, but that's a question for later."

"I'm listening," said Berg, nodding and leaning back. Perhaps there will be Christmas this year despite everything, he thought.

"Have you heard of a police superintendent named Lars Johansson?" asked the special adviser. "Big burly Norrlander, my age, works as head of the National Bureau of Criminal Investigation? I believe he is going to be a bureau head after New Year's."

Have I heard of Lars Martin Johansson from Näsåker? thought Berg. And how do I respond to that? he thought.

"Yes," said Berg.

"What's he like?" said the special adviser with curiosity, leaning forward.

Berg nodded thoughtfully, taking a bigger gulp of the cognac than he had intended, to have time to think.

"What's he like? What do you mean?"

"I mean, what's he like as a detective?"

"He's the best," said Berg. For he is, of course, he thought with surprise at the same moment as he said it.

"What's he good at?" The special adviser nodded at him to continue.

"At figuring out how things stand," said Berg. "Actually, it's almost a little uncanny. Sometimes you get the idea that he's one of those people who can see around corners," he continued, smiling. Ask me, he thought. Despite the fact that it must be almost ten years ago.

"You sound almost as if he can walk on water," said the special adviser.

"I'm almost certain he can't do that," said Berg. Nor would he ever dream of doing it, either, he thought. Not Lars Martin Johansson.

"Is there anything else he's good at?"

"He's taciturn," said Berg with more feeling than he intended. Ask me, he thought, for on more than one occasion he had thanked God that Johansson was clearly made that way.

"Not a telltale, exactly," the special adviser clarified.

"If he's decided not to say anything, then nobody hears anything," said Berg, nodding emphatically. "The problem I guess is rather that he follows his own mind when he makes a decision." What are you getting at? he thought.

"Sounds like a thinking person," said the special adviser, sighing lightly. "He has none of the faults or deficiencies of us normal mortals?"

"Well," said Berg. "On some occasions I've gotten the idea that when he's finally figured out how things stand, then the rest of it is less important to him." Fortunately, he thought.

"That justice must take its course and all that?"

"You might possibly put it like that," said Berg. "Are you looking for my successor?" he continued, smiling wanly.

"Certainly not," said the special adviser, sounding almost a little shocked. "Haven't I said that, by the way? Both I and my eminent boss are extraordinarily satisfied with your contributions. As far as we're concerned, we'd be glad if you would stay until your dying day." And if this Johansson is as you say, then he's the last one we're going to take instead, he thought.

"Nice to hear," said Berg, smiling. "And if I could be completely forthright now, then I haven't exactly always had that impression."

"I know, I know," said the special adviser, looking almost guilt-ridden. "I've always had problems with that bit. You should hear how my ex-wives and children describe me. It's really terrible. But we're working on that. It's almost the only thing that Ulla-Karin and I are working on."

"Ulla-Karin is your current wife," said Berg with a certain hesitation, because he only had vague recollections of these rather muddled aspects of the special adviser's personal file.

"No, for Christ's sake," said the special adviser with feeling. "Ulla-Karin is my psychiatrist—my therapist, that is. Excellent person, lecturer at Karolinska, smart as a poodle, as a whole kennel of poodles, actually."

"That's nice to hear," said Berg neutrally. Wonder if he's pulling my leg? he thought.

"My wives have always been completely crazy," continued the special adviser, seemingly mostly to himself. "Completely stark raving mad."

"It can't have been easy," said Berg sympathetically.

"What do you mean by easy?" said the special adviser vaguely. "Who the hell said you should have it easy?"

Yes, who said that? thought Berg, glancing quickly at his watch.

"Now to change the subject," continued the special adviser. "This Waltin, he worries me, actually."

And now he looked as he always did again although without the least suggestion of a smile.

There were four primary reasons for this unease that the prime minister's special adviser expressed. The first was in regard to Waltin's personality. Simply and summarily, without having met him, without being able to speak more particularly of why or even who he'd spoken with, he didn't trust Waltin.

"I understand what you mean," said Berg, and discovered that he sounded more compliant than he ought to have.

Wasn't someone like him expected to defend his closest coworker?

"Waltin is not a typical police officer, if I may say so," continued Berg.

"Nice to hear," grunted the special adviser.

"But this much I think I can say," Berg concluded, and this was no doubt an expression of the concern that he as boss had to show, "that during all the years that we have worked together, I have never had reason to criticize him for anything that he's done in service."

"Think about it," said the special adviser.

The second reason was in regard to the so-called external operation. The special adviser had thought about that and come to the conclusion that it was not a good solution to the secret police's completely legitimate demand for supervision of its own operation. And whether the head of the operation was good or bad as a person was actually less interesting when looking at the big picture, but if he was like Waltin it could go really badly.

"You don't want to say more," said Berg, trying to make his voice sound completely neutral.

"I was thinking that we could take that up after the New Year," said the special adviser. "I'm actually still thinking."

So that's what you're doing, thought Berg, who suddenly felt a familiar, insidious weariness.

The third thing concerned the Krassner case. Completely disregarding whether he'd actually taken his own life—as an old mathematician, the special adviser was aware that chance could sometimes provide the most unexpected results—this was nonetheless an affair that filled him with both wonder and displeasure. What was written in Krassner's posthumous papers was of course only confused nonsense, but quite apart from the fact that he was hardly a budding Pulitzer Prize winner, was there nothing in his history that indicated that he should have been this confused and incompetent? Where, by the way, were the traces of his uncle who had had a central position with the American intelligence service for many years? At the embassy in Stockholm to boot. For while he had irrefutably held that post, he was conspicuously absent from Krassner's posthumous papers.

"Not a trace of the old bastard. Nowhere," said the special adviser emphatically.

"There's unfortunately a risk that he might have put such papers as he might have received from his uncle somewhere else," admitted Berg, who had thought about the matter himself. "In that case I'm pretty certain that they were left behind in the States."

"There's no risk they might have disappeared along the way?" The special adviser looked at him seriously.

"I really don't think so," said Berg with a certain emphasis. "Even if I'm only speaking for myself, I really don't think so. We're usually rather meticulous about that sort of detail."

"Hmm," said the special adviser, looking as though he was thinking deeply.

The fourth reason dealt with a very unpleasant story, and if it was true, Berg had been nurturing a snake in his bosom. Fortunately it was also so concrete that he ought to be able to check it out. And if there was something to it, then Waltin's days were numbered, at least with him. The only question that remained was where in that case he would get to number the rest of them.

"You don't want to talk about where you've gotten your information?" asked Berg.

"Far be it from me to insult a man of your intellectual abilities," said the special adviser, smiling.

"Thanks for the compliment," said Berg. The military, he thought. Who else?

"One last question," said the special adviser, indicating that that was the case by pushing his coffee to one side and making an effort to get up from the table.

"I'm listening," said Berg.

"Waltin and that Johansson," said the special adviser. "There's no possibility that they're in it together?"

"No," said Berg. "I take that to be completely out of the question." What is it he's saying? Berg wondered to himself.

"Why? Why is it out of the question?"

"I don't really know how I should put it," said Berg thoughtfully. "Let me say this. If what you believe about Waltin is true, then Johansson is probably the last person that he would be in league with. As Johansson would have seen to it that he landed in jail long ago."

"If it isn't true, then? Might they possibly see each other socially?"

"I know they've met professionally at some point," said Berg. "And I'm as certain as you can be that they've never met or even talked to each other in the private sphere. No," said Berg, shaking his head. "I think you can forget that."

"Why?" persisted the special adviser.

"Johansson is a real policeman," said Berg. "He would never dream of socializing privately with Waltin."

Like Persson, thought Berg. Or me too, for that matter.

"But Waltin himself? I understand the fellow can be frightfully charming if he shows that side of himself?"

"Waltin doesn't like real policemen," said Berg seriously. For that's of course how it was, he thought; he'd figured that out early on. We're probably not refined enough for him, thought Berg, smiling wanly.

"Interesting," said the special adviser, suddenly looking happy. "He actually thinks that you real policemen are real rabble, some sort of garbagemen of the legal system," the special adviser clarified with obvious enjoyment.

"More or less," said Berg. I'll be darned how happy you've turned, he thought.

When he was sitting in the car to go back to the office he suddenly changed his mind and asked his chauffeur to drive him home. Following up on that story about Waltin that the special adviser had told him required more quiet than his place of employment could provide. Then he had to think about that strange, concluding question that the special adviser had asked. That Johansson and Waltin could be in it together, completely disregarding what "it" might be, was an impossible idea. It was quite simply wrong, because they didn't do anything together, never had and never would, thought Berg.

The special adviser, on the other hand, was not a nitwit. If you were to believe the test results in his personal file, he was as little a nitwit as was humanly possible in a purely statistical sense. But he had nonetheless asked the question. There must be something he's heard and gotten wrong, thought Berg. Rather recently, besides. At that conference on total defense, thought Berg. For that was certainly where he'd met Johansson. What was it Johansson had said that disturbed the special adviser so much that he was forced to go to Berg to get help? Johansson must have said something about Krassner, thought Berg, and as soon as he'd had that thought his whole line of reasoning became incomprehensible. What in the name of heaven could someone like Johansson know about someone like Krassner? thought Berg.

. . .

As soon as Berg stepped inside the door of his cozy house in Bromma he sat down with the telephone and called his faithful coworker Persson. Berg had two things that he wanted him to find out.

"If you can drag yourself here I'll even see to it that you get a little food," said Berg with the gruff solicitude that naturally ensued when you'd shared the front seat of the same radio car for a long time.

"You've just made me an offer I can't refuse," said Persson, and twenty minutes later he was standing on Berg's front stoop.

When Berg had fed Persson, they moved to the study with coffee and a cognac each to be able to sit in peace. First Berg told the story about Waltin he'd heard from the special adviser and that he in turn had probably gotten from the military intelligence service. That was taken care of in less than ten minutes, and Persson didn't make a single notation in his little black book.

"Well," said Berg. "What do you think?"

"I'll believe anything at all about Waltin," said Persson. "But you knew that already, of course."

"Yes," said Berg, smiling faintly. "I think I've understood that much."

"I'll check it out. You had something else," said Persson.

"Yes," said Berg. "It concerns that dreadful Krassner. At least I've gotten the idea that it does."

"The do-it-yourselfer," said Persson.

"Exactly," said Berg.

"I'm listening," said Persson.

For some reason it took Berg almost a half hour to explain and to recount the conclusions he'd drawn from the fact that the special adviser had asked him whether Johansson and Waltin might be in this together. Persson sat silently the whole time, and he did so even when Berg was through.

"Well," said Berg. "What do you think?"

"I'm thinking," said Persson, holding out his glass. "May I have another cognac?"

When Persson had gotten his cognac, he sat silently for another few minutes without even sniffing the expensive drops. He just sat there, sunk in his chair with his gaze turned inward. Finally shook his head, looked at Berg, and raised his glass.

"Naw," he said. "Both you and that socialist in the government building have gotten this wrong. So I think we'll just forget that."

"What do you mean?" said Berg, with his faint smile.

"Someone like Johansson wouldn't even touch someone like Waltin with a ten-foot pole," said Persson. Johansson's a real policeman, thought Persson, but he didn't say that. And a good fellow, he thought, but he didn't say that either, for Berg could certainly figure it out all on his own.

"So if Johansson were to have said something about Krassner, in any case he hasn't heard it from Waltin," said Berg.

"We can just forget that," said Persson. "If indeed he has said something . . . for that's of course just pure guesswork on your part." Persson smiled and nodded at Berg. You need a vacation, he thought.

"You don't think he might have heard something from Jarnebring?" Berg persisted. "They're both still like two coats of paint."

"Whatever he might have heard from him," said Persson. A good fellow, Jarnebring, thought Persson. And a real policeman, just like him and Johansson, or like Berg when he was young. Before he became the boss and started looking under his own bed for ghosts that were never there.

"So you think we should close the case," said Berg, smiling. Peculiar, he thought. Suddenly he felt both calm and happy, despite all the special advisers and strange colleagues with Rolex watches who took the joy out of existence.

"I don't even think we have a case," said Persson. "If you don't believe me I suggest you ask Johansson if he's said something about the Krassner guy to that socialist in the government building. For that matter, perhaps you should question all three. Johansson, Jarnebring, and the socialist. Good luck," he said and chuckled.

"I give up," said Berg. "I'm on the wrong track."

Persson shrugged his fat shoulders.

"He might well have heard something," he said. "Given how much shit all the police are talking the whole time. He might well have said something to that socialist. If for no other reason than to test him," said Persson, who was a real policeman. "Or to mess with him. I've heard that he can be as annoying as his boss."

"Skoal," said Berg, raising his glass. "And merry Christmas, by the way." And peace to both great and small, he thought.

Berg and Johansson had a story in common, and Berg hoped that Johansson, despite his sometimes uncanny ability to be able to see around corners, was unaware of this.

Almost ten years earlier Johansson, who at that time was working with the Stockholm Police Department's central detective unit, developed suspicions about someone in the bodyguard unit of the secret police. According to Johansson—for likely his old armor-bearer and best friend Bo Jarnebring had been acting as travel companion—one of Berg's officers (granted, one at the base of Berg's high pyramid) robbed a post office in connection with a security assignment. And as if this wasn't bad enough, he tried to cover his tracks by murdering two witnesses who had recognized him.

Briefly and in summary, it was quite a hair-raising story, and how Johansson—who truly lived up to the epithet "a real policeman"—was able to think along such uncollegial lines at all was a complete mystery. Possibly here as well it was a matter of his ability to sometimes be able to see around corners. In any event, there were unfortunately many things that indicated that he was correct in all the essentials. This even Berg was forced to admit, although it still pained him every time he did so. The investigation had been closed rather quickly and the man concerned had not even been questioned, much less informed that he was under suspicion in the matter. He hadn't even been fired—however that could have been arranged—but after a few more years he had chosen to leave of his own free will, and instead of returning to the open operation he had quit the police force. Where he'd gone after that Berg had studiously avoided finding out.

His own role in this sad story was not something he was proud of, despite the fact that he'd been able to turn it into an advantage for the operation instead of the catastrophe that would have otherwise been the alternative if Johansson had prevailed. Actually it also concerned far more important issues than one policeman who ought never to have been allowed to become one. Important matters that Berg was assigned to protect and in which the price, regardless of how the whole thing came out in the end, would always be too high. For all that, the only one who had acquitted himself creditably in the matter was Johansson, despite the fact that, measured by any objective legal standard, he had failed completely.

During the years that followed, Berg had been worried about how things would go for Johansson. Would he run around like a rabid dog telling his story to anyone who had, or didn't have, the energy to listen? Would he, like so many before and after him—completely disregarding whether they were right or wrong—go to the media to get help?

Johansson had shown himself to be exactly what he seemed to be, a real policeman. He had never said a word. Just held his tongue and shook himself and continued as though nothing had happened. Instead he'd made a career within the same operation that had betrayed him. Certainly not a bad one, and the way he'd gone about it fit in well with the reputation that had always surrounded him. Say what you will about Lars Martin Johansson from Näsåker, and there were many of his colleagues who did, no one would even think that he was anything but "a real policeman." There were plenty enough who'd arrived at a painful insight in that regard.

And Berg would never think so, for he himself was "a real policeman." Or had been, in any case, before the bureaucracy that he was now appointed to lead had started to eat him up from inside. He had tried to do what he could for Johansson, and as far as such things could be done in secret. He'd tried to become his secret mentor, his "rabbi," his "padre," his "godfather," as his foreign colleagues used to describe the situation. Why isn't there any good word in Swedish for that, by the way? thought Berg. Because such things are un-Swedish, naturally, and in any case nothing you can talk about openly. Especially not in these times.

But with Waltin it was much simpler, for regardless of what he might be, in any case he was not "a real policeman." Berg and Waltin also had a history in common. It went even further back than his one-sided secret contacts with Johansson. Most recently it had unfortunately developed less well, and by the day after his meeting with Persson, Berg decided that it was high time to change that. Despite the fact that it was almost Christmas.

"So, here we sit like two little birds on a branch," said Waltin with a conciliatory smile while in passing he adjusted a crease in his new trousers of classic English tweed. And you're only getting sadder and grayer, he thought, nodding toward his boss.

"There are a few things we need to talk about," said Berg.

It certainly did not turn out to be a pleasant conversation. The subjects that Berg had chosen didn't allow for that.

First he brought up the Krassner case. It was as though he couldn't avoid the misery, despite the fact that Krassner had taken his own life. Despite the fact that their own covert house search was only an unfortunate coincidence. Despite the fact that they had done exactly what they were expected to do and what their employer actually had the right to demand of them. Which he actually had demanded of them, even if the special adviser hadn't left any paperwork about the matter.

"What I'm trying to say," said Berg, "is that we could have avoided a great deal of trouble if you had followed my advice and made an ordinary narcotics arrest. I'm not ruling out the possibility that he might have tried to take his own life as soon as he'd been let out of jail, but then this wouldn't have ended up as close to our table as it does now."

I don't believe my ears, thought Waltin. He seems to have become as gaga as old man Forselius.

"With all respect I seem to have a different recollection," said Waltin with a friendly smile. "I seem to recall that when I suggested that we should do it like that, you rejected the whole idea." And I never found out why you did, he thought.

"Then I am afraid that our recollections diverge," said Berg, digging out a paper from the pile on his desk. "I have a notation here that we discussed the matter the day before; it was Thursday, the twenty-first of November, at sixteen zero five hours in the afternoon and I was the one who called you. . . ."

This isn't true, thought Waltin, but he didn't say that. He was content to smile and nod, for if it was really going to be like this it was important to keep a good countenance.

"And according to my notes," Berg continued, "you then told me that you had planned a narcotics arrest the following day. I've also noted that I approved that."

"Sure, sure," said Waltin. "But that was at the point when Forselius had not yet made contact, but then he did late in the evening and we went back to our original plan."

Berg moved his shoulders regretfully.

"I have no notes about that," he said. "Why didn't you call and tell me about your change of plans?"

My change of plans? thought Waltin. This is not true, dammit, he thought.

"I seem to recall that you'd gone to the Germans," said Waltin.

"That wasn't until the following day," said Berg. "And if so, wouldn't it have been possible to call me there too? Or what?"

"Yes," said Waltin, smiling despite the fact that it was starting to be an effort. "Somewhere there seems to have been a breakdown in communication."

"Yes, unfortunately that does appear to be the case," said Berg. "A completely different matter," he added.

Then he discussed the department's view of the external operation and that he himself would not be opposed to an inspection if one were to be requested. There was no one outside pulling on the door handle exactly, but sometime during the spring it would certainly come up.

"We'll have to set aside a few days and go through all the papers," said Berg. "Sometime at the start of the new year."

"Fine with me," said Waltin, getting up.

He's not smiling anymore, thought Berg.

Wonder how it's going for Persson, thought Berg, leaning back comfortably in his chair after he'd been left alone in his office. The only light in my firmament; wrong, he thought, for there was actually one more, faintly glistening in the distance like the Star of Hope. The hope that he would finally be rid of Kudo and Bülling.

The Stockholm chief constable and Kudo and Bülling had found one another. Given the police context it almost resembled a love story. Not because they slept with each other or even cuddled a little, for they were all fully reliable homophobes, and in that respect no shadow fell on any of them, despite the chief constable's secret literary leanings, Kudo's recurring observations of gnomes, and Bülling's general peculiarities. What was involved instead was a very strong, almost transcendental spiritual communion of the type that can only arise when highly gifted people are united by a common interest even greater than themselves.

"The Kurds," said the chief constable with ominous emphasis on both words. "Gentlemen," he continued solemnly, nodding toward his two visitors. "We are talking about what is at the present time the most dangerous terrorist organization in the entire Western Hemisphere. So give me some good advice. What do we do?"

Finally, thought Kudo. Finally someone in the leadership who realizes the seriousness of the situation. Necessity trumps the law, thought Kudo, for he'd read that somewhere, and purely concretely it was the incomprehensible secrecy rules of the secret police that this very necessity had in mind. Then he and Bülling related everything to their new ally, but first they had naturally given him the necessary background.

The very first thing they had related was their secret language. About weddings and other events, about poets and about lambs who were to be butchered. About cakes, pastries, and rolls and all their difficulties in working out what this actually meant.

"We will have a wedding, we will butcher a lamb, we will have two poets, cakes, pastries, and rolls. . . ." The Stockholm chief constable nodded with pleasure while he savored every word. . . . "Exactly like myself, you gentlemen have paid notice to the strongly ethnic character of the codes they're using."

"Exactly," said Kudo. "Exactly."

"Exactly," said Bülling, nodding toward the chief constable's newly polished floor.

"So it's hardly by chance that they have chosen these particular codes for their operations here in the West," stated the chief constable. "Tell me," he said as he rubbed his hands with delight. "Tell me how you've solved this ethnically oriented problematic."

It was Kudo then who told about their new informant. He was himself a Kurd. Political refugee like all Kurds, but in contrast to the rest of their informants he had applied of his own free will. He was a baker besides, and had a brother who was a butcher, and together they ran a little catering business whose customers were almost all Kurds too. For many years they'd been delivering their wares and services to countless Kurdish weddings, funerals, and parties.

In such a context that particular background was unbeatable, Bülling had thought as he made the preparatory analysis. Their new informant knew everything about what deliveries and other arrangements were part of a real wedding, a normal funeral, or an ordinary party. Apart from his special knowledge he could see directly if there was something strange when their surveillance objects were planning their activities, and as a result they were sitting in a tight spot, thought Bülling. Planning a political murder based on the orders for a real wedding was naturally impossible. The operation would be doomed to fail.

The fellow had another quality besides, and it was not so strange that it was his best friend and closest colleague, Kudo, who had discovered it, considering that he himself had received the same gift: Their new informant was also a seer. He could see contexts, connections, and occurrences that were hidden to normal people, and this regardless of whether they were already a fact or were still in the future. At first Bülling had resisted the very thought that it might be like that. Considering his informant's other qualities, it was almost too good to be true, and Bülling's critical bent and analytical mission made him generally skeptical of such possibilities. Therefore Kudo had proposed a scientific test, and it was Bülling himself who had set it up and carried it out. Down to the least detail and in order not to leave any imaginable explanation untested.

First he'd pulled out a number of cases that he and Kudo had succeeded in clearing up and of which their new informant could not have the least knowledge. Based on these cases he had then formulated twenty or so specific questions that had taken him and Kudo months to reach a solution to. Their new informant had only required a little less than an hour to answer all the questions, and all of his answers had been correct.

Before they'd told the chief constable about their new weapon in the struggle against Kurdish terrorism, they had discussed whether they should reveal to him that their new informant was also a seer, that he had the gift. It was unfortunately the case that many people resisted such possibilities for primitive, emotional reasons, and because their own worldview was then at risk of collapse. This had solved itself quite naturally and obviously. Toward the end of their lecture, Kudo had nodded toward their new ally, and when he saw the look in his eyes, those gentle, wise, boundary-crossing eyes, he had simply said it. Straight out.

"And besides, he has the gift," said Kudo. "He can see things that others don't see."

The Stockholm chief constable only nodded at first. Mostly to himself, it seemed. Then he looked at them with great seriousness and great sincerity.

"They're the best," he said. "And the most difficult."

Finally they told about their most recent and most urgent surveillance case. On the planned assassination of a "highly positioned but not more closely identified Swedish politician."

"He has given us the name," said Kudo.

"I'm listening," said the chief constable.

"The prime minister," said Kudo.

· · ·

When Kudo and Bülling had left him, the chief constable decided that he must warn the prime minister. The prime minister was still his personal friend from long ago; he himself was the only police officer that the prime minister could trust. He had helped him before and at a time when he wasn't even the prime minister. Most important of all: If the prime minister met with a political assassination, it was the chief constable's personal responsibility to see to it that it was cleared up and that the perpetrator was brought to justice.

I must warn him in good time, thought the chief constable. Before something happens, he clarified to himself and in order to rule out any possibility of a mistake.

If Kudo and Bülling and the Stockholm chief constable had seen the light, it was all the darker in the world where Göransson and Martinsson were nowadays. First that mysterious work trip to Petrozavodsk in the middle of a biting-cold Russian winter, where they were both about to freeze their rear ends off. When they'd come home, a series of freezing-cold, meaningless surveillance assignments, one after another, which never seemed to end.

The news that they would be moving back to the open operation after the New Year had almost come as a relief. Naturally they hadn't been told the reason that it had turned out that way, but in the squad there were rumors of yet another reorganization. The week before Christmas they were called in to the top boss's own stable boy, Chief Inspector Persson, in turn—Göransson first because he'd been serving the longest—and as usual in these contexts he'd had the company of the bureau's attorney. There they had to sign the usual papers, which promised secret legal proceedings, multiyear prison sentences, financial ruin, and personal disgrace if they uttered a word about their time with the closed operation. More terrifying than the documents they signed was Chief Inspector Persson himself, and before Martinsson left the room he gave him a parting word.

"You've had damn good luck, lad. If I'd been the one to decide we would've boiled you for glue."

Whatever, and you can shove it up yours, you fat asshole, Martinsson thought, and that evening he went to the local bar and got royally drunk.

Obviously it had been the usual old dive down on Kungsgatan, and as it was right before Christmas there was no lack of police officers in the place. The line wound all the way down to Vasagatan—a few guys who were working in radio cars had been in such a hurry to get there that they still had their uniform trousers on—and when Martinsson finally got in there was so much going on that the floor, walls, and ceiling shook. But despite the fact that he got drunk as a lord, he couldn't summon up the right mood. After a while he spotted young Oredsson, who was sitting with a couple of girls in a corner, and because they seemed unusually sober it was there that he sat down.

He'd met Oredsson last summer. They went to the same gym and had run into each other while exercising, lifting weights, and sitting in the sauna and male bonding, and one thing had led to the other and rather quickly it had become clear to each of them where the other stood. Because he himself was working quite a lot with the survey of the police at Norrmalm, he had also tipped off his chief about Oredsson. Here was a budding officer who shouldn't have any difficulties making his way into the circles they were working with. There was nothing really wrong with Oredsson, thought Martinsson. There was nothing really wrong with his opinions either, for most of what he said was both right and reasonable and everyday police fare, for that matter. As an infiltrator he would have passed like a hand in a glove, but just before he was to give him the invitation, the boss had suddenly blown off the whole thing, and as usual he hadn't been told a damn thing about why. And considering what he himself had met with it was no doubt the best thing that could happen, thought Martinsson.

When he was standing in the john relieving the pressure, Oredsson came in and stood at the urinal beside him.

"How's it going, Strummer?" said Oredsson, sounding worried. "You seem a little down."

"It's okay," said Martinsson, shaking the artillery piece before lifting it into his trousers. With just one hand, thought Martinsson, for he always thought that.

"How'd it go, by the way, with that job you were talking about last summer?" said Oredsson. "You never got back to me."

"It got fucked up," said Martinsson. And you should probably thank God for that, he thought.

"Too bad," said Oredsson. "That thing with SePo sounded exciting."

"I've quit," said Martinsson.

"Did something happen?" said Oredsson, taking him by the arm.

"Fucking fifth columnists," said Martinsson, and then he pulled Oredsson into the john. Locked the door and told him everything about what Berg and the other bastards were doing.

Afterward it felt much better. Oredsson stood him a few beers and they made a toast in silent collusion. And that stable boy Persson could shove those fucking papers up his fat ass, thought Martinsson.

Bäckström celebrated Christmas at the after-hours unit. It wasn't the first time and certainly would't be the last, either, especially now that old Jack Daniels was completely off the wall, but on the whole it wasn't too bad. The union had clearly celebrated a victory, for they'd gotten yet another nap room since last year. Not that Bäckström cared. He used to sneak up to the homicide squad when he needed a nap, for it was a lot quieter there, but the union rep was proud as a rooster and because he was a tedious bastard Bäckström made sure to take a potshot at him while passing through.

"I thought we were here to work, not to slack off," said Bäckström. "But correct me if I'm wrong."

The poor bastard just glared at him, despite the fact that it was Christmas and everyone should be happy, and then the safety rep took over and nagged for a quarter of an hour about that new disease A-I-D-S. Doesn't concern me, thought Bäckström, for he didn't poke assholes, blacks, or drug addicts, and if he needed to touch someone there were always plumber's gloves that he could put on.

The cases were mostly shit as usual. Nothing worthy of a real pro such as himself. Mostly thefts and drunken driving, and who had the energy to care? Not Bäckström, in any case, so he took the opportunity to nap for a few hours. Although there was naturally a bright spot or two despite the fact that the Christmas food in the break room had disappeared rather quickly. Three Finnish tramps—real geniuses from Karelia—had broken into a shoe store on Sveavägen and emptied the Christmas display of fifty left shoes, and when the police cars came with their blue lights one of the Finns had almost cut his own throat as he was trying to finagle his way out through the window. So when they came to the after-hours unit there were only two of them, but every little bit counts, thought Bäckström as he locked up the remaining two, each in his own barred compartment.

Then the riot squad came in with a little gypsy lad who had been siphoning gasoline up on Karlbergsvägen. It was Ornery Adolf's squad—dear colleagues have many names—and he and his guys were sour as vinegar, for the rest of the tribe had managed to escape. He was a funny little guy, thought Bäckström. With Goofy shoes, trousers a foot too long—where had he pinched those?—and the tribal chieftain's cap on his curly little head. He was bent over like a poker and moaning that he'd gotten gasoline in his little belly and had to go to the hospital, so Bäckström arranged a barred compartment for him too. Farthest in, to be on the safe side, so he wouldn't disturb the others who were there.

But then the boss started to make a fuss about the gypsy's age, and that perhaps it would be best if someone sat with him in a normal room until the old ladies from the social services after-hours office had time to drag themselves there and take over.

"It's cool," said Bäckström. "I've counted his fingers and there are six on each hand."

The boss, who was a Pentecostalist, was a humorless bastard, so he didn't want to hear that, and for a while it looked rather critical. But then

the tribal chieftain himself showed up with half of his numerous relatives to talk the lad out, for he was only thirteen according to Papa
Taikon, and then it became a real circus. For clearly they'd missed the
fact that Ornery Adolf and his lads had taken the opportunity to stay
and chow down a holiday snack. And then they suddenly had six folk
dancers arrested instead of one. This is a pure Christmas week sale,
thought Bäckström.

Then of course a bunch of old hags came in too who'd gotten a little
well-deserved Christmas whipping. One of them wasn't half bad. True,
her face looked like a Lappland owl, but she had rather nice tits and was
only half as old as the other drunken hags who'd gotten a beating. High
time for a case of my own, Bäckström decided, took her into an interrogation room, and turned on the red light on the door in order not to be
disturbed.

First the usual sniveling, but Bäckström had paper napkins on hand, so
that would no doubt work out.

"I understand that this is awfully difficult for you," he said with his
most sympathetic tone of voice. "You shouldn't feel any pressure, so
take your time and start from the beginning. You can take my card, by
the way, in case you need someone to talk with." So you can get your little mouse greased up too as soon as you look human again, he thought.

A few hours earlier she'd gotten the bright idea to toddle over to her ex-
boyfriend's to give him a Christmas present. True, it was over because
he drank too much and ran around with other women and was generally crazy, but he should get a little Christmas present in any case, and
when he got it he'd evidently started wrestling and seen to it that he got
a lay as a bonus. How fucking stupid can you be? thought Bäckström, for
in the preliminary report the officers from the uniformed police had
filled out there wasn't any mention of a rape.

"You don't have his name and address?" Bäckström asked as
he leaned forward and patted her consolingly on the arm. Out in the
cold, he thought gloomily, and close up those tits weren't especially

noteworthy—who the hell gets turned on by Dachshund ears? Wonder if I can ask to get my card back? he thought.

First he spoke with the boss and told him about the rape the colleagues had missed, and because the chief was that type, he got so worked up that Bäckström was worried he would get the big police medal.

"Nice to have a few people who've been around a while," said the boss, nodding. "Good, Bäckström, good," he repeated. "I'll take care of the victim and make sure that the doctor has a look at her, then you see to it that you bring in the perpetrator."

What the hell kind of justice is there in this world? thought Bäckström gloomily fifteen minutes later. The victim had gotten a lay and now she was lying in a warm doctor's office resting up. The perpetrator had gotten both a present and a lay and was no doubt sitting at home boozing in that good ol' cottage warmth. He himself was sitting in the dark in a bumpy service car in the middle of an ice-cold Christmas Eve, together with that surly guy from the union, to collar some crazy bastard who was nesting far out in the southern suburbs, and if he was even still at home Bäckström would certainly get to celebrate Christmas in the hospital with a Mora knife in his belly.

Plus the union guy sat and nagged the whole journey that they had to see to it they got backup from the uniformed police before they went into the apartment.

"Perhaps we should check if he's at home first," said Bäckström wearily. "Or what do you think?"

The union guy was content to nod. True, he was surly, but still he did have the good taste to keep his trap shut. The ex-boyfriend was home. Bäckström listened at the mail slot and heard sounds both of the TV and of someone going to the can. And because he was there anyway he rang the doorbell and the perpetrator opened, let them in, and asked if they wanted anything. A cup of coffee or something? On the other hand he couldn't offer them any aquavit for he'd stopped drinking. There was something here that didn't add up, thought Bäckström.

A dark, rather husky fellow in his mid-thirties, completely sober as far as Bäckström could determine. His apartment was small and neither tidy nor untidy. The bed in the only room was covered with a throw but it didn't appear arranged. The TV in front of the sofa was on; clearly he'd been sitting and watching when Bäckström rang the doorbell. Nothing arousing either, a normal American flick—Bäckström had seen it himself when it was at the theater.

The only thing that gave a little hope was all the books he had and a few posters on the walls that clearly seemed political, even if they weren't exactly Chairman Mao. Wonder if he's a communist? thought Bäckström, and while their host, the perpetrator, was making coffee, Bäckström took the opportunity to snoop around a little. It was then that he found the dartboard that was hanging on the door to the bathroom. Damn, thought Bäckström. That was the face of our dear prime minister, with hook nose and everything. Damn solid workmanship, too, with the picture printed directly on the target itself, and the majority of the thrown darts appeared to have landed just right and straight on the nose of the poor bastard.

There's something that doesn't add up, thought Bäckström, for of course he couldn't be a communist.

"Damn amusing dartboard you have," said Bäckström when they were sitting on the sofa drinking coffee. "Where can you buy one like that?"

"You mean of the traitor?" said their host, and here there was definitely something that didn't add up. "You can have it if you'd like. I can get more."

"That's okay," said Bäckström, for that damn union guy he had with him had already started to purse his lips. "There was another thing that we wanted to talk about with you."

So then they did that and as so often before it appeared that the little whore had made it all up. They'd been together, but otherwise there wasn't a thing that was right. He was the one who'd left her, and it would soon be six months ago, for he couldn't put up with her constant boozing and yelling; he himself had tried to quit drinking alcohol. Suddenly she'd shown up at his place on Christmas Eve and the present she had with her was a bottle of whiskey and two glasses.

She'd sat down on the sofa and started hitting the bottle, teasing him because he didn't want any, and because he'd felt the need he'd suddenly gotten extremely angry. Taken the whiskey and poured out what was left into the sink and told her to leave. Then she'd attacked him and tried to smack him with a vase and he'd taken hold of her and gradually he'd succeeded in carrying her out.

"And you didn't screw her?" asked Bäckström, who was eager to be clear about that little detail. And besides, it was the reason he was sitting here wasting his young life.

Of course he'd screwed her, although not for six months, not since he'd left her, but before that he used to be on her approximately five or six times a day. Perhaps a little more when it was a holiday and they'd partied really hearty.

There, there now, thought Bäckström, who hadn't gotten any since he'd greased up that little Estonian whore with the big knockers, and feeling a certain draft in his crotch.

"Why'd you smack her, then?" asked Bäckström, who didn't mind being a bit direct about things if it would save time.

"Hell, I didn't smack her," said their host, looking at them with honest blue eyes.

"Lay off," said Bäckström. "I talked with her half an hour ago, and her face looked like a Lappland owl."

"She did when she came here too," said their host, "but when I asked her she didn't want to talk about it. You can ask my neighbor, by the way. He was the one who helped me get her out of my apartment."

Then they talked to the neighbor, and when they'd done that they thanked him for the visit, got in the car, and drove back to the after-hours unit.

"My God, what fucking whores there are," said Bäckström with feeling. "I've got a good mind to give her a going-over myself."

"Think about what you're saying," said his colleague indignantly. "It's not appropriate to say that kind of thing if you're a policeman."

"Shit in your pants, you fucking amateur politician," said Bäckström, for he'd thought about saying that for a long time, and when he looked at his watch it was already a quarter past twelve in the morning and his Christmas celebrating was over for this year.

Early on the morning of Christmas Eve, Berg had been compelled to get into a taxi and go down to Rosenbad to inform the special adviser of an embassy case that had taken an unexpected turn. The special adviser seemed to be in an excellent mood despite the early hour. He offered him coffee, and the case itself went both quickly and painlessly.

"Okay then," said Berg, making an effort to get up. "Then I guess I should wish you merry Christmas and hope that I don't have to disturb you anymore this year."

"I wish the same to you," said the special adviser. "And good luck with the reorganization. It must be the best Christmas present you've gotten in a long time," he said, looking unusually cheerful.

What does he mean? thought Berg, sinking back into the sofa.

"Now I don't understand," said Berg.

"Then you aren't aware either that the Kurds are thinking about murdering the prime minister," said the special adviser, pouring more coffee for them both.

The Stockholm chief constable had phoned a few days earlier and wanted to speak with the prime minister at any price. Because it wasn't the first time and the prime minister had more important matters on his hands, he had to be content with the special adviser. The story that the chief constable had told went in brief along the lines that "he'd gotten reliable information from a completely reliable and intimate source that the PKK was planning to murder the prime minister."

"So I thanked him for the tip," said the special adviser, "and to myself I congratulated you for finally getting rid of them both."

"I'm afraid they're probably still with us," said Berg, sighing. And perhaps it wasn't this that I'd imagined, he thought.

"It'll work out," said the special adviser, raising his coffee cup.

Then Berg took a taxi back to his wife and the house in Bromma. They had lunch together with his sister and brother-in-law, and after that all four of them drove to Roslagen to celebrate Christmas Eve with his aged parents. A calm and pleasant family Christmas, thought Berg when he was back in Bromma and he and his wife had gone to bed, each with a book that they'd given one another as a Christmas present. Then he fell asleep and for some reason dreamed about the child that they'd never had, and at three o'clock in the morning he had to get up as usual and take a leak.

Oredsson and his comrades had celebrated Christmas in the country. A real midwinter sacrifice according to ancient Swedish custom. They'd managed to rent an entire vacation establishment with a lodge and everything up in Hälsingland, and despite the fact that there were almost twenty of them, the majority of them police of course, they'd had plenty of room. First Berg, who was their leader, had called a general meeting where Oredsson had informed them of what their colleague Martinsson had told him.

"As I'm sure you know," said Berg, looking at them seriously, "that traitor at SePo is my own uncle, and if there are any of you who have a problem with that then I'd like us to take that up now. Personally I can only apologize for the relationship."

No one had any problems. On the contrary, all of them took the opportunity to express their sympathies and indicate their loyalty.

"Good," said Berg. "So what do we now? Do you have good suggestions? Thanks to Oredsson, here, we are of course forewarned and thereby armed."

They agreed to lie low for the time being.

"We lie low, we close ranks, and we keep our eyes and ears open," Berg summarized, and then they ate whole roast pig and drank a great many beers. Perhaps a few too many in some cases, considering that joint exercises had been planned for both Christmas Day and the day after Christmas.

· · ·

As the wee hours approached, Berg took Oredsson aside and thanked him for his good contribution. Then he told him about his father, who had also been a policeman and was killed in an accident when Berg himself was only a child. In a car chase he'd lost control of the vehicle that he was driving, ended up in the water, and drowned. Service car with bad brakes, two crooks in a stolen car who succeeded in getting away and were never caught, a policeman who died on duty. Things can be so different, thought Oredsson, clearly moved by what Berg had related. Two brothers, one who died a hero's death and one who became a traitor.

Oredsson's colleague Stridh had taken a good many comp days over the holidays. He'd celebrated Christmas Eve with his sister, who was his only living relative and an excellent human being. She was also single, worked in accounting at a small advertising agency, and was both bookish and interested in cooking.

A pity really that she's my sister, thought Stridh as he took yet another portion of her home-preserved Christmas herring. For otherwise we might have gotten married.

Bo Jarnebring had celebrated Christmas as a twosome, the other person being his new girlfriend. Sort of new; after all, they'd been together since last summer and it had only gotten better the whole time. A few weeks earlier they'd decided to get engaged on New Year's Eve, but for reasons he wasn't really clear about he hadn't told Johansson, despite the fact that he'd had more opportunities than in a long time.

Why is that? thought Jarnebring. Because you're a coward, thought Jarnebring.

"Darling," said Jarnebring, going out to the kitchen where she stood, cheeks red from the heat. "I've been thinking about something."

"You're hungry," she said, smiling. "It'll be ready soon."

"No," said Jarnebring, shaking his head. "I was thinking about this thing with the engagement."

"You've changed your mind," she said, moving a casserole dish from the burner.

Didn't she look a little worried? thought Jarnebring, grinning like a wolf.

"No," he said. "But what do you think about doing it now instead?"

"Now?" she said, giggling. "You mean now . . . now?"

"Yes," said Jarnebring, putting his left arm around her waist and pulling her to him while she turned off the stove with her right hand.

"What are you doing? Aren't we going to eat?"

"Now, we can do it like this," said Jarnebring. "First we'll take off all our clothes so that all the new gold shows to best advantage, then we'll exchange rings, then we'll screw each other, and then we can eat. Then you'll get your Christmas present too, but that will be a surprise."

"Okay," she said, nodding and pulling her blouse over her head.

Then I'll call Johansson and tell him, thought Jarnebring. What do you mean, coward? he thought.

The day before Christmas Eve, *Svenskan* had a big advertisement with a special offer from Åhlén's department store: KNOCKOUT PRICE ON SEXY LINGERIE! TANGA, TEDDY, AND FISHNET STOCKINGS ONLY $10.

Svenskan is really starting to go downhill, thought Waltin with slight distaste while he decapitated his hard-boiled egg with a well-timed tap with his right hand.

"Available in red, black, and white," Waltin read, sighing and savoring his breakfast tea. Black for normal people, red for the lower classes and upstarts, white for those who don't dare. The things you have to put up with on an empty stomach, thought Waltin, sighing again.

The following morning he took the opportunity to slink in to Åhlén's, as he happened to be passing through the city center anyway. He purchased a half dozen in various sizes, all in black, of course, and the female clerk gave him a smile that was only a hair's breadth from a highly unprofessional come-on.

"Should I wrap them up in different packages?" she asked, smiling flirtatiously.

"No," said Waltin, smiling slightly. "Just put them in one bag." And if you can't behave properly then I'll put you across my knee, he thought.

With the necessary commodities in a bag under his arm, distracted by the female clerk and with his thoughts elsewhere, he made a mistake that someone like him couldn't afford to indulge in. When he stepped out onto the street he ran right into Wiijnbladh and that fat, red-haired sow who was his wife.

"Police superintendent, what an honor," said the little fairy, who was about to tie himself in knots. "May I perhaps introduce my wife?"

"How nice," said Waltin, noticing the rapid shift in her eyes and the secret understanding in her expectant smile.

She's not going to say anything, he thought, extending his sinewy, suntanned hand.

"Claes," he said, flashing all of his white teeth. "Nice to meet you, and merry Christmas too."

"Lisa Wiijnbladh," she said as she shook hands. And then the little whore had the gall to draw the red-painted nail of her pinkie against his palm.

"It would be nice to meet again sometime," she said, and that idiot she was married to had naturally not understood a thing. How could he? thought Waltin, smiling the whole time, as he took back his hand and felt his crotch tightening up.

It must have been sometime last spring, thought Waltin as he disappeared down Hamngatan moving just fast enough, heading in a safe direction. Big fat white breasts with freckles on them and rather small nipples? I'll have to look at my notes, he decided.

"That was a colleague of yours," said Wiijnbladh's wife with a neutral tone of voice, somewhere between a question and a statement.

"A very highly placed man at SePo," nodded Wiijnbladh, trying to sound unmoved. "We know each other from before," he added with a look of importance.

How nice for you, old man, thought Lisa Wiijnbladh while she felt the usual contempt bubble up inside her. Personally I've only slept with him, she thought.

"What was his name again?" she asked.

When his inner pressure became too strong he always tried to get as far away as possible to release it. It didn't always work out, overworked by a demanding schedule as he was. On some occasions he'd been forced to take risks. One such occasion was last spring, and it was then that he'd run into Wiijnbladh's wife without having any idea that she had a husband, much less that he was a policeman.

"But you've never worked at SePo, have you?" said his wife suddenly when they were sitting on the subway a while later on their way to her sister's. For what use would they have for someone like you? she thought.

"No," said Wiijnbladh, trying to sound as mysterious as the circumstances allowed. "Not in a formal sense, no."

So you're a secret agent, she thought. In that case they can't be right in their heads.

He'd gone to a simple place in the city. Simple clientele, many women by themselves, middle-aged or on the way to being so, already passed over or on their way down. Abandoned, vulnerable, searching, desperate in their hunt for something better, or at least a few hours' company. He'd found her in the bar where she sat, showing her generous cleavage for anyone who cared to look. Considering the competition she was the beauty of the place, red-haired, white-skinned, busty, twenty pounds overweight, heavily made up, intoxicated, and Waltin had felt a completely irresistible desire to hurt her.

Is that why you're always so nervous that you can never get it up? thought Lisa Wiijnbladh while feeling how the shaking of the subway car touched the inside of her thighs.

398

"I'll be darned—you're so secretive, old man," she said. Smiled, leaned forward, and patted him on the cheek.

"Well," said Wiijnbladh, suddenly feeling both happy and embarrassed. "There are certain things in my job that are hard to talk about." She touched me, he thought.

"You and he have met socially," said his wife, trying a mischievous smile on him. It's not talking that's your major problem, she thought.

"Perhaps you might say that," Wiijnbladh nodded. "We've met privately."

"Where does he live, then?" asked his wife.

Waltin had taken her to one of the front addresses he used for the operation, choosing this one because there were no neighbors and the bed had sturdy corner posts. He'd brought everything else he needed with him.

"You're awfully curious," said Wiijnbladh evasively. What was it he'd said that time he'd approached him at work? he thought nervously. He'd mentioned it in passing.

"Admit that you don't have a clue," said his wife, looking exactly as she always did.

"Norr Mälarstrand," said Wiijnbladh, suddenly remembering.

First he'd spread her out, binding her hands and feet to the four corners of the bed, and as usual he'd used his leather straps. Pulled a little tighter because she was rather drunk, because she needed it, but mostly because he was in the mood for it. Pulled her top and bra up over her head, pulled up her skirt to her waist and cut apart her panties. It was simplest that way, he liked doing it, liked the sound when he did it, and he felt as if he was going to burst apart from within when he entered her.

· · ·

"Norr Mälarstrand," repeated his wife. And why would someone like him invite a little shit like you home? she thought.

"Fantastic apartment," said Wiijnbladh, nodding. "He had a really fantastic art collection," he added, nodding again. What was it Waltin had said when he showed him that Matisse forgery? he thought.

It was not that she hadn't played along. She went along, she was a part of it. The fat sow was actually enjoying it, and despite the fact that she was as drunk as she was she had suddenly achieved orgasm, just shrieked flat out and arched her body in the bed despite the fact that he'd tied her up. And he had immediately folded up; all his strength had suddenly simply run out of him.

"I had no idea that you were an art lover," said Lisa Wiijnbladh sourly.

"Art is really nice," said Wiijnbladh evasively. Now she's her usual self again, he thought.

He'd put the muzzle and blindfold on her and tightened her a little harder. But that hadn't helped either. Then he shaved her between her legs, for that usually helped, but all that had happened was that she'd come to climax one more time while he was at it.

And then he gave up.

"Perhaps you ought to start painting yourself," said Lisa Wiijnbladh. "Like that Zorn." Wasn't that his name? she thought.

"Oh well," said Wiijnbladh, stealing a glance at his watch. "When would I have time for that?" Won't we be there soon? he thought.

When they were sitting on the sofa afterward he'd poured her a hefty drink. She'd needed it, for she'd looked unbelievably awful. The makeup that had run all over her face, the large white sagging breasts, the skirt bunched up around her waist, and her legs spread while she looked at her shaved sex. Suddenly the tears had started to flow.

"What have you done?" she'd whimpered. "What will I say to my husband?"

"That might be a nice surprise for him," Waltin had said lightly, and suddenly the familiar feeling had returned. You have a husband, he'd thought.

"Or draw naked women," persisted his wife. "What is that called, when they sit and draw naked women?" Although you'd hardly be able to manage that either, she thought.

"Life drawing," said Wiijnbladh sourly, for he'd learned that on the job. "It's called life drawing."

"My God," she'd sniffled. "What will I say to my husband?"

Now the tears had sprayed out of her and she'd suddenly appeared quite inconsolable.

"You can surely think of something," Waltin had said helpfully. Otherwise I'll have to help you, he'd thought, for now the feeling had come back again, just as strong as before. Before, she wasn't able to behave the way she should.

"He's never going to believe me," she'd sobbed. "He's a policeman."

Policeman, Waltin had thought. This is too good to be true. It had felt as if he were going to burst again as he pulled her up and forced her down across the arm of the sofa. Then he'd entered her from behind and she had howled like a banshee the whole time and before he drove her home he'd tied her up on her belly in the bed and given her a good going-over with his belt.

"Maybe you think that's really fun," his wife teased. "Lots of naked women. Drawing them shouldn't be all that hard."

"We're here now," said Wiijnbladh evasively and got up. "It's here we change trains," he said. Actually I ought to kill you, he thought.

Because he had snooped through her handbag when she went to the bathroom, and because her name was what it was, a look at the Stockholm Police Department employee register had been sufficient to find him.

Detective Inspector Göran Wiijnbladh with the technical squad. I must meet him, Waltin had thought, feeling almost as enlivened as that time when he'd seen his dear mother take the escalator down to the subway at Östermalm Square.

The prime minister's special adviser celebrated Christmas together with his old friend, teacher, and mentor, Professor Forselius. True, both had a number of ex-wives, even more children, and in the case of Forselius an almost unbelievable and quickly increasing number of grandchildren and great-grandchildren, but when it was finally time to celebrate Christmas, for various reasons they only had each other, and it had been like that for a number of years.

It wasn't so strange either that they always convened at the home of the special adviser. Forselius either ate canned food or went to the exclusive gentlemen's club Stora Sällskapet, while the special adviser had access to all the resources that his secret life could offer. If you looked in the phone book—he was actually in the phone book with both first and last name, but without title—he had a very modest address on Södermalm where he never set foot other than to fetch his mail, and the telephone number that went there had been forwarded from the first day to the large home in Djursholm where he actually lived. In addition he had a housekeeper, a wine cellar, a party membership book, and several million dollars that he'd buried abroad with all the care of which only people like him and Forselius were capable. Strangest of all, he'd earned all his money himself and he'd done it before he'd turned thirty-five.

Forselius loved him more than his own children, while the special adviser's feelings for Forselius were more mixed. He liked his children best anyway, he used to think, for actually Forselius was only a grumpy old bastard who could be totally and uniquely self-absorbed. He did have one characteristic, though, that was hard to beat. Forselius was the only person that he could talk with about the kinds of things that no one else understood, and because questions of that type made up the essential reason for his continued existence, the answer was also a given.

And who the hell wants to toast themselves in a shaving mirror on Christmas Eve? thought the special adviser, raising his glass toward his only and recurring guest.

"Skoal, professor," said the special adviser. "And merry Christmas."

"Skoal, young man," said Forselius, savoring the wine in his glass. "And merry Christmas to you too."

"Well," said the special adviser, looking at him with curiosity.

"Petrus," said Forselius. "1945."

"My birth year," said the special adviser.

"A great year in Bordeaux," said Forselius.

"A great year here, there, and everywhere," said the special adviser generously, thinking of his own inception.

"Have I told you about that Pole?" said Forselius. "It was the same year."

"The one you killed," said the special adviser, chuckling so that his fat belly jumped.

"Oh well," said Forselius. "What the hell choice did we have?"

Appetizer, main course, cheese, and dessert, but not a herring butt, slice of ham, or Christmas pudding as far as the eye could see. A skinny, middle-aged, black-clad woman who moved like a lost soul between the kitchen, the serving corridor, and the enormous dining room table, never saying a word. Now she stood in the door between the dining room and the library, exchanging a glance with the master of the house.

"I believe that coffee and cognac are waiting," said the special adviser, setting aside his damask napkin, pushing his chair back, and getting up with a certain effort.

Forselius nodded, cleared his throat, winked meaningfully, and leaned forward.

"Is she mute, man?" he whispered. "Is she really mute?"

"I really don't know," said the special adviser. "She's never said anything."

. . .

With coffee and cognac they usually exchanged Christmas presents. Always the same kind of Christmas present, yet always different than the one they'd received and the one they'd given the year before. Each a folded-up slip of paper that they gave to each other and then unfolded and read. A frighteningly long row of numerals on both pieces of paper, different numerals, wrinkled brows. Forselius's brow smoothed out first and his wrinkled old man's face split into a contented grin.

"I won again," he said with delight.

"You and your fucking prime numbers," said the special adviser sourly. "I've got a job to take care of, you know. Besides, I'm sure you're cheating with the military's big computer," he added indignantly.

"Why do you think that?" said Forselius slyly. "Perhaps I just think better than you do?"

"Ha ha," said the special adviser, who was a poor loser and a completely insufferable winner.

Then they played billiards and drank highballs half the night before Forselius staggered up to his guest room on the second floor early on Christmas morning. There he fell asleep immediately after he'd kicked off his shoes and despite his advanced age flung himself on top of the bedspread.

Waltin had prepared himself carefully. First he'd found out everything that was worth knowing about that fat red-haired sow and her miserable husband. Neither background, money, nor schools, but no one would have expected that, he thought contentedly. Dreary four-room apartment in a suburb, no children, the sow clearly worked at the phone company and was otherwise best known for kicking herself weary under men other than the one she was married to. Certainly started as one of those old-time switchboard operators who sit putting things in small holes the whole time and then it had just gone on from old habit, he'd thought, giggling with delight.

. . .

As soon as he was bored he used to take out the pictures he'd taken of her as she lay tied up with muzzle and blindfold and everything, and for a while he'd seriously considered sending the best picture as a reader's contribution to those miserable porno rags you found in pretty much all places where there were lower-class men, but on further reflection he'd refrained. Perhaps I might need her again, Waltin had thought, and the thing about her husband appealed to him much more.

He'd called him up a month or so after the encounter with the sow, and when he'd said who he was the miserable little shit had been so flattered that Waltin regretted that he hadn't recorded him on tape.

"As I said," Waltin had said, "I need to freshen up my technical knowledge without blabbing about it to the whole operations bureau."

"Of course, of course," Wiijnbladh had gushed. "Then I propose Saturday morning, for I'm at the after-hours unit then and for the most part I'm usually alone there," he had said officiously. Wonder who gave him my name? This can lead who knows where, he had thought, and in his mind he had already seen himself as head of the secret police's myth-shrouded, covert tech squad.

"Fine with me," Waltin had replied in English. "Shall we say ten o'clock on Saturday?" Wonder if he understands English, he'd thought.

"Discretion a matter of honor," Wiijnbladh had said, unknowing procurer that he also was.

Wiijnbladh had met him dressed in white coat with a sash; only the stethoscope was missing. Plus the education, of course, but altogether it was better than Waltin could even have imagined in his wettest, most secret dreams. Then they'd walked around the unit and Wiijnbladh had shown and demonstrated and babbled like a little windmill while Waltin had had a half erection practically the whole time.

"Here, for example, we have a Matisse that came in last week," Wiijnbladh had said, showing a painting that someone had set on a workbench. "Forgery, of course," he'd said, sighing like the art connoisseur he surely was.

What do you say? Waltin had thought. I thought he'd painted that with his feet.

"I have a few pieces myself," Waltin had declared with the bon viveur's matter-of-factness. "Feels nice to hear that you keep a close watch on those kinds of things."

Of course he had gotten on a first-name basis with him as soon as they'd shaken hands. That was half the fun. Then he'd made little snide remarks during the course of the journey whenever there was an opportunity.

"It's just horrible that someone could do that to a child," Waltin had said, shaking his head mournfully while Wiijnbladh showed him a little pair of undies on which one of Wiijnbladh's colleagues in the forensic vineyard had evidently succeeded in identifying semen stains.

"Ugh yes," Wiijnbladh had said.

"You have kids yourself," Waltin had said; this was more a statement than a question, and of course he'd already known the answer.

"Unfortunately," Wiijnbladh had answered, "my wife and I have not had any success in that regard."

And in no other regard either, it appears, despite the fact that she can hardly be accused of a lack of willingness, Waltin had thought, making an effort to preserve an indifferent and sufficiently regretful expression.

"I myself don't even have a woman by my side," Waltin had said, shaking his head. I hardly have time to screw everyone else's, he thought.

"Yes," Wiijnbladh had said, and suddenly he'd seemed to have his thoughts somewhere else. "Although marriage can have its drawbacks."

What is he saying? Waltin had thought. This is almost too good to be true.

Finally Wiijnbladh had shown him the weapons room: hundreds of weapons of all imaginable sizes and manufacture. Military and civilian automatic weapons, rifles and ordinary shotguns with whole or sawed-off barrels, revolvers and pistols, shootable walking sticks, pen pistols, bolt pistols, nail pistols, even a regular slaughtering mask.

"Mostly confiscations we've made in connection with various crimes," Wiijnbladh had explained. "Although we purchase quite a few as well, to have in our weapons library."

Yes, for you probably can't read, Waltin had thought. What an unbelievable mess, he'd thought. Weapons on the walls, on shelves, in boxes and cabinets. Weapons and parts of weapons in an old shoe box that someone had clearly started sorting into smaller piles before he'd found something else to do. Weapons and parts on tables and benches and even a sawed-off, disassembled shotgun that someone had set aside on the seat of a chair before he'd run off to do who knows what.

"Seems to be quite a lot," Waltin had said, nodding, as a telephone started ringing in the background.

"We have almost a thousand weapons here in the unit. Excuse me a moment," Wiijnbladh had said.

"Sure," Waltin had replied, and as soon as he'd heard him lift the receiver in the room outside, and without understanding how it really happened or why he did it, he'd stuck his hand down in a half-opened drawer, fished up a revolver with a short barrel, and let it glide down into his very deepest pocket.

"Excuse me," Wiijnbladh had said when he came back, "but that was the after-hours unit that called."

"Not at all," Waltin had said. "If there's anyone who should beg pardon it's I, who am taking you away from more important tasks. I'd like to thank you greatly for the visit. It's been very instructive."

Almost as good as that time he'd seen dear Mother come out of the doorway where she lived and with the help of her canes and the usual antics limp away toward the stairway to the subway.

Wiijnbladh and his wife as usual celebrated Christmas with his sister-in-law, her semi-alcoholic husband, and their fourteen-year-old son in the town house in Sollentuna where they lived. It was exactly as wretched as it always was. First they ate and then they watched TV and then they passed out Christmas presents, and after that they watched TV again.

Then his brother-in-law fell asleep on the sofa after the usual intake of beer, wine, and a dozen shots, spiked coffees, and highballs. His head leaned back against the sofa at a ninety-degree angle, mouth wide open, violently snoring. His wife and her sister disappeared out into the kitchen, where they sat and giggled and drank wine behind a closed door. The son remained sitting, glaring furtively at Wiijnbladh when he thought he didn't see him. Judging by his look he was retarded and undependable, thought Wiijnbladh, the only consolation in this connection probably being that he would soon turn fifteen and then Wiijnbladh would be able to look him up in the crime registry to see what he was really up to when he was expected to be in school or sitting at home doing his homework.

"Perhaps we should think about moving along," said Wiijnbladh, and as soon as he opened the door to the kitchen his wife and sister-in-law fell silent. It was his wife who was telling something, he'd heard that, and clearly she'd been laughing till the tears ran while she did so.

"I believe your dear husband will have a lay . . . too," said the sister-in-law after a stage pause, and then they both laughed so hard the tears were flying around them.

I ought to kill the both of them, thought Wiijnbladh.

As soon as Waltin came home to his apartment on Norr Mälarstrand, he made a decision and called up little Jeanette.

"Change of plans, my love," he said. "It looks like we'll have to celebrate Christmas here in town. A few things have happened at work, so I have to stay within reach," he clarified.

"When do you want me to come?" asked Jeanette. Lovely, she thought. Then perhaps I can sit normally during the week after Christmas.

Wonder if she's going to try to make contact with me, thought Waltin. Or if I should make contact with her. And suddenly he became so aroused that he was compelled to take out those old photographs he'd taken of her last spring and go into the bathroom and release himself.

. . .

What the hell is happening? thought Jeanette with surprise. First champagne and Russian caviar, then foie gras and that sweet French wine she loved, filet of sole and more champagne. Now they were eating black currant sorbet. And he was just as tender, courteous, and entertaining as the first time. And better looking than ever despite the fact that he'd been damn good-looking the whole time.

"Skoal, my love," said Waltin, raising his glass. "By the way, I've bought a Christmas present for you."

An ankle-length mink coat with a hood, and when can I wear that? she thought. In another life, wonder what it cost? One or two or several years of my salary before taxes, she thought.

"I heard it would be a cold winter," said Waltin, smiling. "And I don't want you to have to freeze."

What is happening? thought Assistant Detective Jeanette Eriksson, who would soon turn twenty-eight.

I must get hold of Hedberg too, thought Waltin while he looked at little Jeanette, who was sleeping in the bed by his side. Unpunished, without being rocked to sleep after a few too many glasses of champagne and with his Christmas present as the only covering over her slender body. Then I must see to it that Berg calms down, he thought. For his own good if nothing else.

Right before midnight Jarnebring mustered his courage and called his best friend to tell him.

"I've gotten engaged," said Jarnebring.

"What's her name?" said Johansson, who sounded unusually happy and in high spirits and certainly had a few under his belt. "Is it anyone I've met?"

"Stop it, Lars," said Jarnebring, who wouldn't let himself be disturbed by such boyish nonsense on his great day.

"Many congratulations, Bo," said Johansson, "and merry Christmas to both of you. And take care of yourself. And of her too," he added, suddenly sounding serious again.

You sentimental old Lapp bastard, thought Jarnebring when he put down the receiver. Christ, I must've gotten something in my eye, he thought, rubbing the corner of his right eye with his fist.

"Was he happy?" asked his fiancée.

"Hmmmm," said Jarnebring, nodding.

I must get hold of Hedberg, thought Waltin, but then he must have finally fallen asleep, for when he looked up again it had already started to get light outside his bedroom window.

CHAPTER XV

And all that remained was the cold of winter

Sundsvall over Christmas and New Year

Johansson's oldest brother lived by the sea about ten miles outside Sundsvall in a big old wooden palace that had been erected as a summer place for a rich country squire during the golden years in the middle of the nineteenth century. It hadn't gotten smaller since his brother had taken over.

Let's see now, thought Johansson, who was an old detective and had a good memory. He's asphalted the driveway, extended the parking area, and bought a new car for his wife.

On the morning of Christmas Eve they hunted hares on one of the islands. It was an old tradition from their upbringing at home on the farm outside Näsåker, and the only thing wrong with it had been that the foxhound used to run off more often than not and that Mama Elna was usually good and angry at them when they finally came home, whether they had a hare with them or not.

This time it went better. The sea was not frozen over, so neither the foxhound nor the hare had any choice but to keep on dry land. On the other hand, the dog was still chasing flat out when his brother looked at his watch and reported that it was time to go home if they weren't going to miss Christmas Eve lunch.

"What do we do with the bitch?" said Johansson, who would happily have stayed behind to shoot one more.

"The hunting boy will take care of that," said his brother, nodding in the direction of the wooded hillside where their dog driver had been stationed for more than an hour.

"I had no idea there were so many hares out here on the islands," said Johansson, jerking his chin toward the three chalk-white corpses that lay on the bottom of the boat as they went home.

"Christ, there aren't any hares out here," said his brother, grinning.

"Where did these come from, then?" asked Johansson, who had shot one and almost gotten another.

"The boy set them out last week," said his brother, grinning. "Who do you take me for?"

Nice to hear you haven't changed, thought Johansson.

The luncheon on Christmas Eve was not just the opening but also the high point of the Christmas celebration at home with Johansson's oldest brother, and they always ate in the kitchen. By knocking out the ceiling and the walls between the attic, the original kitchen, the serving areas, and the old dining room of the forest squire, his brother had created a great room large enough for the latter-day Viking chieftain that he of course was. The buffet was spread out on the table to avoid unnecessary running, a log fire blazed in the open fireplace, and Johansson's brother sat as usual in the high seat at the short end with Mother to his right and Father to his left, all of his children along the long sides, and his wife and Lars Martin at the opposite end.

"Merry Christmas to you all," said Johansson's big brother, smiling with his strong, yellow horse-trader teeth and raising his brimful schnapps glass.

You haven't changed, thought Johansson.

Papa Evert and Mama Elna, seven children, three sons-in-law, three daughters-in-law, twenty-one grandchildren, five great-grandchildren, and even with outside additions in the third generation, not even big brother's kitchen would have been sufficient if they had all come. But despite the fact that annual family reunions had been held at home in Näsåker going back several generations, the majority of the large Johansson family had chosen to celebrate Christmas elsewhere, at their own places, as always happens when family feelings have cooled and other feelings and commitments have intervened, even without serious conflicts or quarrels.

For obvious historical reasons, Johansson's parents chose to celebrate Christmas with their eldest son when they themselves had gotten too old to gather the family at home with them. That was why Papa Evert sat at his oldest son's left side. Nowadays he was only half the size of "Little Evert," and with every Christmas more and more like something that had been hung to dry at home in the sauna on the family farm north of Näsåker.

After lunch there had been an exchange of presents in the living room, yet another blazing log fire, and enough sofas, armchairs, and other chairs to accommodate even those who hadn't come. Johansson had as usual been Santa, wearing a red stocking cap but refusing to wear a mask, pleading the heat from the fire, far too many shots at lunch, and the decisive circumstance that the youngest member of the company was actually fifteen years old and clearly old enough to lace his Christmas cider with one or two strong beers when he thought his parents weren't watching. Although of course he hadn't said that last thing. It was Christmas, after all, and what did he have to do with it?

At last, however, it was over, and all the food and all the drinks were beginning to have their effect in earnest. The final present from the last of the rows of bast-fiber laundry baskets was doled out; as always to the woman of the house, from the master of the house and without Santa's assistance. As always more expensive than the rest of the arrangements combined, and as always it was passed around so that everyone could express their proper admiration for the host's generosity, warm heart, and magnificent financial condition.

"Not too bad," said Johansson in order to make his brother happy while he held up the glittering necklace. And certainly long enough to go around her waist, thought Johansson, smiling approvingly at his nicely shaped and nowadays, regardless of the season, always suntanned sister-in-law.

"Yes, I'll be damned how good we rich people have it," his brother chuckled jovially, waving his thick Christmas cigar and puffing smoke on his youngest brother.

Watch out, thought Johansson, or I'll sic the business squad on you, and then he withdrew to a corner to talk with his old father in peace and quiet.

"How are you feeling, Papa?" said Johansson in a loud voice as he carefully patted him on the hand.

"Don't shout, boy, I'm not deaf," said Papa Evert, grinning with delight at his favorite son and at the same time pushing him in the stomach with his free hand. "It doesn't look like you're in want of anything, in any case," he stated contentedly with a glance at Johansson's ample middle.

"Papa seems spry," said Johansson at a normal volume and with filial concern in his voice.

"Oh hell," said Papa Evert, shaking his head. "It's probably a good while since I did that sort of thing, and that's not really something you talk about with your children," said his papa, who heard what he wanted to hear. "Although I'm spry and sharp, yes indeed, despite all the crap you hear on the radio and read about in the newspaper."

Almost ninety, almost deaf, half the size he was in his prime, and thin as a rake. But spry, thought Johansson, and you could have it worse than that.

Then Papa Evert got onto his favorite subject—the increasing crime rate that nowadays was more and more often afflicting even Näsåker and its vicinity. There had been a break-in at the school and someone had put their mitts on one of the forestry company's machines.

"Although with that business at the school I'm damn sure that it's Marklund's little bastard, despite the fact that he's never there otherwise," said Papa Evert.

It was worse, though, about the forestry machine, considering that such a thing cost several hundred thousand crowns—it had been almost new—and that it was probably someone from outside the district who'd been at it. Lars Martin should send up a few good fellows from the national police in Stockholm. Norrlanders preferably, but it would be best of course if he could come himself.

"You can always ask that brother of yours if you can borrow that bitch of his so you can take the opportunity to do a little hare hunting at the same time," said Papa Evert, who gladly mixed business with pleasure.

He himself had gotten rid of his hunting dogs the year he turned eighty.

"That'll be good," said Papa Evert in order to underscore the weight of his argument, nodding toward his youngest son.

Johansson sighed, not simply from longing for another life than the one he was now living. But before he got involved in a discussion that he preferred to avoid, two of his nephews took over and he went and sat down with his mother.

From the frying pan into the fire, thought Johansson five minutes later, for Mama Elna was not only small, thin, spry, and without the least thing wrong with her hearing, she was worried besides.

"You don't look healthy, Lars," said Mama with her head to one side. "You seem overworked, and then I do think you've lost a lot of weight since I last saw you."

Always something, thought Johansson, and at first he almost felt a little encouraged, but that was before she got onto her personal favorite among all the things that worried her where little Lars Martin was concerned.

"You haven't met anyone," said Mama Elna, tilting her head from left to right in order to truly show how concerned she was.

"You mean women, Mama," said Johansson, smiling like a good son.

"Yes, what else would I mean?" said Mama Elna watchfully.

"I guess you always meet one or two," said Johansson evasively, because he didn't have the slightest desire to tell his mother about the school of two where he'd wallowed around like a killer whale last week.

"You know what I mean, Lars," said Mama Elna, who didn't intend to give up. "I mean something solid, something steady, something like . . . well, like Papa and me."

No, thought Johansson. Not like you and Papa, for that kind of thing doesn't exist anymore.

A while later he excused himself, wished a merry Christmas and good night to all, took his Christmas presents with him—mostly books, including several that clearly appeared to be readable—and went up to his room to read awhile before he fell asleep. For reasons that weren't entirely clear to him, he also thought about the woman he'd met at the post office up on Körsbärsvägen almost a month ago. Pia, thought Johansson. Pia Hedin, that was her name. Maybe after all, thought Johansson, and then he fell asleep.

The quiet life in the country, Johansson thought a few days later. And for reasons he wasn't clear about either, and without knowing anything about it, it was life in the Russian countryside he had in mind. The life that was lived in the time of the czars, before the revolution and by a small number of landed gentry. Must be something I've read, thought Johansson. Perhaps it was the birch groves down toward the sea, the stillness, the lack of activity while he read his books, took long walks, ate and slept, and watched his brother drive away and come home again in his constant business affairs, the particulars of which he preferred not to think about. No sleigh rides with blazing torches, of course, but no wolves howling in the winter night, either. No balls with champagne and women with plunging necklines who flirted wildly behind open fans in order to keep the cold at a distance. But no anxiety, either, that the cold you caught while you were doing that would also end your brief life.

Days came and went, and he himself was only an ordinary, temporarily appointed police superintendent who would soon become a bureau chief and in the meantime was charging his batteries. That was how you ought to look at it. On Saturday, the twenty-eighth of December, the Stockholm chief constable was the birthday child of the day in the big evening tabloid, and because Johansson had met him on several occasions he devoted almost a quarter of an hour of his usual walk to thinking about the day on which his birthday fell. Holy Innocents' Day, thought Johansson, and regardless of what you thought about the fellow—he had a definite opinion—he was hardly an innocent. Neither in the original meaning of the word nor in the general, everyday pejorative sense it had gotten later. I'm afraid it's probably worse than that, thought Johansson as he lengthened his stride. For whatever reason, it was certainly the most exciting thing that happened that day.

On New Year's Eve his brother and sister-in-law had a big party with champagne, hired serving personnel, and a number of female guests with plunging necklines and men in tuxedos.

"I forgot to say that," said Johansson's brother. "It's formal, but if you want you can borrow my old one, which I don't use anymore. In the worst case you can just say to hell with buttoning it."

How nice, thought Johansson. So I don't have to rent one.

Buttoning it had also gone well. Despite the fact that the jacket was double-breasted it felt roomy, and when Johansson observed himself in the mirror in his room, he looked like any other middle-aged car salesman.

"Christ, little brother, you almost look human," said his brother contentedly when Johansson came down to the living room a while later.

"Pity you have such short legs," said Johansson. "Otherwise it would have fit perfectly."

"You can keep it," said his brother generously. "I have several."

"You don't know a dwarf who's sufficiently short and fat?" said Johansson.

"Christ, little brother," said Johansson's big brother, putting his arm around his shoulders and hugging him. "Tonight we're going to have fun. We'll eat and drink and dance and be nice to the ladies. By the way, did I say that I've arranged a surprise for you?"

Johansson's surprise had arrived approximately in the middle of the crush of guests, which was quite all right considering who she was and who the other guests were. And in a low-cut dress, which she hadn't been wearing the last time they'd had dinner at his neighborhood restaurant.

"Lars," she said, sounding both happy and surprised. "What are you doing here?"

"I live here," said Johansson.

Because Johansson's big brother was not one to leave anything to chance, not least if he was in cahoots with Mama Elna, for that's what must have happened, thought Johansson. Obviously they were seated next to each other at the table and had lots of time to talk about both this and that.

"You never called me the way you promised," said Johansson's table companion, sounding almost a little hurt when she said it.

How about you, then? thought Johansson, but he didn't say that. Instead he looked at her with his honest blue eyes and lied.

"Of course I did. I called you the same week I came home from the U.S., and at the switchboard they promised to leave a message," said Johansson, who knew from experience just how certain such a thing was.

"They're completely hopeless," said his table companion with feeling in her voice.

"And then I've been really busy," said Johansson.

Which was at least a bit more true, he thought.

"How do you know my brother, by the way?"

They had evidently met at a Rotary meeting where the police had been discussed, and only a week later the invitation had come in the mail.

Still, you must have said something else, thought Johansson.

"And because my ex-husband and I had finally decided to go our separate ways, then . . . well, here I am anyway," she said, smiling in a manner that could hardly be misunderstood.

He ate and drank, quite a lot even, and then he danced, and he mostly danced with his table companion, and more than once he noticed his big brother's shrewd grin in the throng behind his back. At the stroke of twelve he gave her a kiss and got a kiss in return, but instead of replying to it he gave her the same wolfish grin that his best friend used to give women when he needed time to think.

"I didn't think they let women into Rotary," said Johansson.

"Rotary?" said his table companion, confused and more than a little drunk. "Rotary? You're probably thinking of the Masons."

Then a light supper was served in the large kitchen, and even though she didn't have a fan her intentions were clear enough. And what the hell do I do now? thought Johansson, who suddenly was not the least bit interested. Much less here at home with his own older brother and his gingerbread-colored wife.

"When are you coming to Stockholm next time?" asked Johansson distractingly while he removed his hand from hers, which was only half as large. He could always give the baseball cap he'd bought at the FBI to someone else, he thought.

But it finally resolved itself, and the farewell kiss she gave him before she left in the taxi along with several other guests was sufficiently cool for him to understand that this was probably not the moment for him to change his mind.

"Christ, Lars," said his brother crossly when they were sitting alone in the large living room in the middle of all the rubbish that the guests had left behind, "you're starting to lose it."

"I have a hard time with thin women," said Johansson, who both knew his brother and knew that his sister-in-law had gone to bed.

"What do you think I've said to the wife?" said his brother with feeling. "Thin women are an abomination. But do you think she listens? Hell, no," he sighed gloomily.

"Skoal," said Johansson, and then he finally went to bed.

On New Year's Day after dinner he and his brother sat in front of the TV, not really watching, sipping highballs, and exchanging small talk the way you do when you know each other well and most everything has already been said. On the evening news there was a long, live-broadcast New Year's interview with the prime minister. According to the introduction, which sounded peaceful enough, it was to have been about what had happened during the year just passed and what was going to happen during the year that had just begun, but it quickly changed to being only about the prime minister himself and his various private doings, and of course it took this turn in a way that was clearly planned from the start. The reporter pulled and tugged at the prime minister like an angry terrier with a trouser leg while the interview victim tried to protect himself with his usual arrogant eloquence; without his having seemed to grasp it, this was the very point of the whole performance.

Those bastards probably can't even spell "Christmas peace," thought Johansson, who was just as fond of journalists as all real policemen, but his brother seemed greatly amused.

"Poor devil," big brother chuckled with delight. "He never learns."

"You've stopped voting for the social democrats," said Johansson innocently.

"Don't be an ass, Lars," said his big brother good-naturedly while he reached for the remote control and switched off the TV.

"I had a salesman once," said his big brother, "and he was, so help me

God, exactly like that wretch that they always come down on so hard as soon as he shows himself on TV."

"I see," said Johansson. What should I say? he thought. "So, what was he like?" asked Johansson.

"He was probably the friendliest devil this side of the Dal River," said Johansson's brother, laughing a little at the memory as he poured more whiskey into his glass.

"Friendly?"

"Well, he could barely manage to open the hood on the damn car he was showing before he was practically on top of them. Babbling like a windmill about the family and the weather and serving them coffee and almost tying himself in knots to please them. Although they just wanted to buy a car. He was completely unbeatable, the poor bastard."

They don't sound especially alike, thought Johansson. "You'll have to excuse me," he said. "It must be all the Christmas food, but I don't really understand."

"What is it you don't understand, little brother?" said Johansson's big brother indulgently.

"They don't sound especially alike," said Johansson. "Your salesman and the prime minister, I mean."

"So help me God he was exactly like the prime minister, except the other way around," Johansson's brother clarified. "They were alike as two peas where it counts."

"I still don't get it," persisted Johansson.

"And you're supposed to be a policeman," sighed big brother. "Neither of them could keep their distance," he clarified. "That damn salesman I had was like a Band-Aid without you even having to ask him, and that wretch we just saw on TV with his well-oiled yap would risk making an enemy for life out of any old idiot just to have the last word, when he ought to have the sense just to keep his mouth shut and nod and go along because everyone knows that he knows better."

Finally, thought Johansson.

"I understand what you mean," he said. "Did he sell any cars?"

"He must have sold one occasionally," said Johansson's brother, shrugging his shoulders. "He got fired. No one can afford that type if you're going to make a living from it," he added, taking a good-sized gulp from his glass. "People who aren't like everyone else, I mean."

I understand exactly, thought Johansson, who had been to a course and heard the same thing, although expressed in a different way and in other words.

Krassner, he thought. I must do something about that wretched Krassner.

"I'm going to need to work for a few days," said Johansson. "Do you have a free desk in the house?"

"You can borrow my farm office," said Johansson's brother. "No one will disturb you."

If you're going to do something anyway, it's just as well to do it methodically, Johansson always thought, and he did so this time as well, despite the fact that he had seldom felt so ambivalent and poorly motivated. The day after New Year's Day he carried Krassner's papers down to the farm office, and when he could finally pack them in his suitcase again it was already Epiphany and high time to go home to Stockholm.

There hadn't been much vacation, either, between sessions at his borrowed desk. True, every day he'd taken a long walk, but it was Krassner and his papers that occupied his thoughts the whole time. At the family meals he became more and more monosyllabic, and when his brother suddenly had to go away on business for a few days he almost experienced it as a liberation, despite the fact that they seldom had time to meet.

He'd been forced to drive in to Sundsvall twice to go to the library, and he'd made several calls to Stockholm; he'd spoken on the phone three times with a more and more perplexed Wiklander. But on the day before Epiphany, he was done; he'd even written a long memorandum on how he viewed the matter. What am I really up to? thought Johansson. It was of course not a matter of an ordinary crime investigation, even though he was now convinced that Krassner had been murdered and even though he felt he had a more than reasonable conception of why and how it had been done. He had learned a great deal about the prime minister, he certainly had. He knew just about as much about him as about the perpetrators and victims whose lives he used to survey when he worked investigating especially violent crimes. And a great deal, besides, which only a very few knew about.

The problem, thought Johansson, was simply that however he twisted and turned the matter, the prime minister was neither the perpetrator nor the victim in the part that dealt with Krassner. With the exception of himself, the perpetrator, and a probable few shadowy characters whose existence he could only intuit, everyone else was ignorant not only of this but probably of the entire story. It'll work out, thought Johansson, for he already had an idea of how he would be able to leave Krassner and his papers behind him.

He devoted the first day to reading through Krassner's manuscript and the remaining documentation that he'd come across—to get an overview and because he always used to do it that way. That was also the most frustrating day of all, and what irritated him above all else was the author's way of writing. With the exception of the first chapter, each section was introduced by a text in which the author, at length, with great seriousness and unshakable confidence in his own importance, recounted his feelings and thoughts about the various facts and other circumstances that he later described. And even in the running account there were reflections and passages inserted according to the same pattern. And what a cockeyed style, thought Johansson with irritation, traditional reader that he was, and firmly convinced that a factual condition is best described with facts and only facts, the colder the better. Crap, thought Johansson acidly, pushing aside the piles of papers and deciding it was high time to call it an evening. Besides, his belly was growling seriously.

The following day he finally went to work on the factual questions themselves. From everything that he'd read, what was true, what was false, what was questionable? Krassner's manuscript began with a sensational story said to have played out in March of 1945 in Stockholm. It was a detailed narrative with names, places, times, and several persons involved in the action. If nothing else that bit could be checked out, thought Johansson.

There were quite certainly several aims behind Krassner's choice of introduction. A good way to whet the reader's appetite for what was to follow, besides being a simple and effective presentation of two of the book's main characters, his own uncle John C. Buchanan and a Swedish mathematics professor by the name of Johan Forselius. The actual aim, however, was quite certainly different—namely, to describe how the Swedish military intelligence service in the final phase of the war had collaborated fully with its American counterpart, and the way in which that might have been done.

The protagonist of the story was a Polish captain by the name of Leszek Matejko. When the Germans attacked his country in September 1939, Matejko was a young lieutenant of the Polish cavalry with its fine old traditions, which was crushed under the treads of the German tank divisions in a matter of days. Matejko had escaped with no more than a fright and a bloody rag around his head, and when the Polish defeat was a fact he succeeded in making his way to England by dangerous paths to continue the fight. Once in London he became one of the first Polish officers enrolled in the "free Polish armed forces."

Their need of cavalrymen had been limited, but because Lieutenant Matejko was a talented young man he had quickly been made into an intelligence officer, and in that capacity he remained in London during almost the entire war. It was also here that he got his anglicized nickname, Les. In the fall of 1944, when the Russians had driven the Germans a good way back into his old homeland, Captain Les Matejko was moved to the British embassy in Stockholm as a liaison officer, you "hardly needed to be a military person to understand why," wrote Krassner. Of course, thought Johansson, nodding, for even he understood that, even though he always considered himself highly civilian in outlook. What he didn't understand, on the other hand, was why Krassner hadn't continued to write the way he'd started. This could have been really good, thought Johansson, sighing disappointedly.

At about the same point in time the American major John C. Buchanan showed up at the American embassy in Stockholm where he, almost immediately and apparently quite without embarrassment, seems to have initiated cooperation with his "colleagues" in the Swedish military intelligence service. One of the Swedes he met, with whom he even started to socialize privately, was the professor of mathematics Johan Forselius. According to his nephew the author, and not described particularly respectfully, the friendship was primarily due to the fact that they had another great interest in common besides intelligence activity, namely alcohol. A commodity to which Buchanan, accredited to the American embassy and in contrast with his dried-out Swedish comrade-in-arms, had free and unlimited access.

One more lush, thought Johansson, and before he could read on, for some reason he saw the glass pyramid in Buchanan's coal cellar again.

Forselius was an interesting person, thought Johansson, making a note on his pad.

Born in 1907, a mathematician and clearly not a bad one: He defended his dissertation at the age of twenty-seven and was named professor at Uppsala University at only thirty-three, approximately the same time as the Germans occupied Denmark and Norway. That was also the point when he had to leave the academic world. Forselius was called up as a regular, noncommissioned officer assigned to the intelligence department at army headquarters as an analyst and code breaker. When he was discharged at the end of the war, in 1945, he was still just a sergeant. At the same time he was a legend among code breakers the world over.

What do you mean, sergeant? thought Johansson, making a new note on his pad. A Swedish sergeant who is a drinking buddy with an American major, professor of mathematics, world-renowned code breaker. . . .

And is discharged as a sergeant? There's something here that doesn't add up, thought Johansson, who had done military service himself and been discharged as a master sergeant.

Late winter in Europe, 1945. A broken-winged German eagle had fallen to the ground. The United States and England and their Soviet allies were perfunctorily striking final blows from their respective positions while their strategic thinking was headed in a completely different direction. How should you position yourself for the decisive test of strength that military logic said must come soon, the struggle between the democracies of the Western world and Stalin's dictatorship in the Soviet Union?

Late winter in Stockholm in 1945, the agents of the Western world flocking together, and here it seemed the choice had already been made, for Forselius and Buchanan and Matejko and all their associates on the right side of the field were completely at home with each other while the talk was of their great new joint concern: the powerful neighbor to the east. It's then that things started to happen.

Clearly it was Buchanan who sounded the alarm. Despite his anglicized nickname, there was intelligence from the OSS indicating that Captain Leszek "Les" Matejko's heart was with the Russian comrades-in-arms who would probably soon be the main enemy in the decisive test of strength between good and evil. Considering Matejko's background and origins, and considering the overall strategic situation, it was not a simple problem they'd been presented with, and the first decision that had been made was to keep the Englishmen out of it and turn the whole thing into a purely Swedish-American operation.

Forselius got to set the trap, and he'd done it in a very cunning way, by distributing coded messages to various presumptive suspects, then trying to intercept them through the usual radio surveillance to see which way they'd gone.

The suspicions against Matejko had been strengthened, but it was far from being the case that the trap had closed on him, and there were several in their own ranks who not only expressed uncertainty but even pleaded his case. But time was starting to run short, and information came in indicating that Matejko was intending to disappear to his old homeland securely behind the Russian front. In that situation they decided to take no chances, and on the evening of March 10, 1945, an expedition embarked from the military's secret building on Karlaplan in Stockholm to Matejko's residence two flights up from the courtyard on Pontonjärsgatan on Kungsholmen.

The mission of the expedition was far from clear. Who had actually dispatched it was shrouded in mystery because in principle of course it concerned a suspected case of espionage, with suspicions directed against a person with diplomatic status. Considering who he was, Matejko was to be approached as carefully as the situation allowed. Try to ascertain his intentions and sympathies, in any event secure his person, and as far as possible do so by peaceful means. Whose decision this actually was, however, is not evident from Krassner's manuscript. He doesn't seem to have even understood the problem.

The expedition had five members, and its composition was strange, to say the least: professor and conscript Sergeant Johan Forselius and Major John C. Buchanan, both in civilian clothes; Second Lieutenant Baron Casimir von Wrede; Second Lieutenant Sir Carl Fredrick Björnstjerna; and Captain Count Adam Lewenhaupt, all three of the last-named officers in the intelligence service's security detail, dressed in uniform and armed with service pistol model 40. The whole company rode in a gasoline-powered black 1941 Buick, Buchanan's service car from the embassy, and it was Buchanan who drove. What the others possibly didn't know was that he had also brought along "his only friend in life," the American Army's .45-caliber Colt pistol.

After fifteen minutes' drive through a depopulated, darkened Stockholm, they arrived at Matejko's home address on Kungsholmen, walked up, knocked on the door, and were let in. Buchanan concisely, "in his laid-back, amiable way," recounted the reason for their visit, whereupon Matejko—Polish cavalry officer and gentleman that he was—told them to go to hell and leave him in peace. In that situation a tumult arose in the small apartment as Second Lieutenants von Wrede and Björnstjerna tried to calm Matejko down. Kicks and blows were delivered. Captain Lewenhaupt drew his service pistol and placed himself in the doorway, whereupon Matejko, clad in dressing gown and pajamas, promptly jumped out of the window from the third story straight down to the courtyard.

In contrast to the unfortunate Krassner, he escaped with a sprained foot and limped out onto the street. His pursuers took the stairs down and when they came rushing out of the entryway, the limping, swearing, and shouting Matejko had gotten a good head start in the direction of relative security up on Hantverkargatan. Then Major John C. Buchanan drew his Colt pistol, dropped to his knee on the sidewalk, gripped it with both hands, aimed, and shot him in the back.

This hadn't lessened the confusion. They somehow dragged the still wildly swearing and now profusely bleeding Matejko into the car, forced him down in the backseat, and drove away. Wild palaver now broke out about where they should take him. Despite the fact that he seemed to be in good condition verbally, there was no doubt that Matejko was badly wounded. There were two fully equipped civilian hospitals right in the vicinity, Serafen and Sankt Erik, but for various reasons of discretion and secrecy it was decided to drive him to the naval garrison hospital out at the Waxholm Fortress.

The atmosphere in the car was also less than good. Matejko was not happy, and when they came out onto Norrtäljevägen, Captain Lewenhaupt started to express doubts about the suitability of Buchanan going along out to Waxholm. Buchanan, an officer but not a gentleman, asked him to shut up and shove it, and at approximately the same time Matejko stopped swearing, gave up the ghost, and died.

The rest of the group were quite naturally seized by a certain dejection. They stopped at the turnoff to Waxholm for a brief war council, during which they decided to drive back to town and turn over the concluding parts of the operation to Major Buchanan. Buchanan let his comrades out on Valhallavägen and continued alone with the corpse. Unclear to where, but according to his nephew and biographer, he and his colleagues at the American embassy were said to have taken care of the body "in accordance with customary routines and in an established manner." Sounds like a normal body at sea, thought Johansson. On his pad he made note of four names in alphabetical order by last name: Björnstjerna, Forselius, Lewenhaupt, and von Wrede, and after that he called Wiklander at work.

Sweet Jesus, thought Johansson as he leaned back in the desk chair to collect his thoughts. If you were to believe Krassner, it was clearly those two lunatics Forselius and Buchanan who made a secret agent out of his own prime minister.

The main character of the piece delayed his entry until the second chapter of Krassner's manuscript, and apart from the introduction it was a section that Johansson could very well have written himself. A concise description of the prime minister's personal background, childhood, and upbringing, which correlated with the more or less official descriptions that Johansson had studied elsewhere.

Fine background, fine family, fine upbringing, went to a fine school where he'd taken his diploma with fine grades, and all this fineness was also the very point of Krassner's introduction. The prime minister was, namely, no common traitor to his country who only made the author "ready to vomit"; there was a deeper idea underlying Krassmer's gastrointestinal pains as well. In contrast to common traitors who only betrayed their country—and possibly fundamental human freedoms and rights, if they came from the West and not the East—the traitor/ prime minister was playing across a considerably broader register. He had also betrayed his class, his childhood environment, his family, even done violence to his own "natural personality" and the particular "ethos" that, according to Krassner, characterized people like him—that is to say, not this prime minister in particular but rather the kind of person he would have been if he hadn't been a traitor after all.

Johansson was content to sigh deeply over all this sordidness that supposedly characterized the country's highest political leadership and instead, hardened as he was, leafed a few pages ahead, for now things were starting to get seriously interesting. The war ended the same month the future prime minister began his compulsory military service with the cavalry. The Germans had had enough, cremated their self-shot leader at the Chancellery compound in Berlin, and thereafter surrendered unconditionally. The victors initiated the dividing up of the European continent and an eighteen-year-old Swedish cavalryman began building his life.

First sixteen months of military basic training; out as a sergeant, fine marks, of course, and directly to the university for more academic pursuits. Scarcely two semesters later, back to the military for six months of reserve officer training, and at some point during that time one of the secret recruiters from the military intelligence service must have taken notice of him. On July 5, 1947, Professor Forselius sent a letter to his armor-bearer Buchanan. It was written on a typewriter from that era with the usual sprinkling of uneven keystrokes, individual worn-out letters, and an "a" that continually leaned to the left. A rather short letter in English, barely a page, and the introductory lines about summer drought in Stockholm and the "damn rationing" suggested that the recipient, Dear John, was already at home in the United States.

After the usual greetings and a little manly grumbling, the letter writer had quickly gotten to the point. "I've been thinking a great deal about our conversations concerning the intellectual aspects of our offensive in Europe, which has further confirmed our common conviction that this is a question of the utmost strategic importance, and I have come to the conclusion that we ought to proceed to practical action very soon. I also believe that I have found a person who can be of great value to us in the execution of regular field operations."

Forselius had received a tip about the person in question from one of his contacts at the Swedish intelligence service a few months earlier, and he had used the intervening time to personally take a careful look at the person mentioned. Obviously his inspection had turned out to his great satisfaction, and the letter concluded with his warmest recommendations: "True, he's a slender little lad, but he seems to have a hell of a big heart and a damn bravado when it really counts."

As if this weren't enough, he was also "highly gifted, far above the average for his fellow officers," with "stable conservative views," spoke "several languages fluently," appeared to have "the exact right mental disposition for the type of work that we've talked about," and in addition intended to "go to the U.S. already this autumn to study for a few semesters at an American university," which gave them "a heaven-sent opportunity to proceed to action," according to a very contented Forselius.

At the end of August that same year the future prime minister began his studies at a first-rate university in the Midwest, and when Professor John C. Buchanan had suddenly shown up at the same place a few months later to give a series of guest lectures on the theme "Europe after the Second World War, the politics of Soviet occupation, and the risk of a third World War," the secret thought behind this event was sufficiently enticing for a twenty-one-year-old future politician to sign up for them.

Forselius had obviously been correct in his judgment of the prime minister's "mental disposition," for just before Christmas Buchanan wrote to thank him for his assistance with a successful recruitment to the CIA's "more intellectual operations in the European field."

"Just a few short lines to thank you for your help with Pilgrim. We had lunch last week after he'd returned from the introductory training, and I must say that he is developing in a way that exceeds even my wildest dreams." The photocopy of the handwritten letter was found among the rest of the papers.

I see, and you got a code name too, thought Johansson, and then he interrupted his study of Krassner's intellectual inheritance to consume a good lunch from the Christmas and New Year's leftovers that his ginger-bread-colored sister-in-law had set out. After lunch he napped for an hour, because she had forced both beer and two aquavits on him—she herself kept to mineral water—and when he woke up he took a brisk walk in the dense twilight to clear his skull before he returned to his borrowed desk. Damn, this is starting to get really exciting, thought Johansson as he stamped off the snow in the entryway to his brother's farm office.

Late in the summer the following year, Pilgrim returned to Sweden, obviously bringing with him very fine American grades, resuming his studies at the university as well as beginning a career as a student politician that was so successful that his new employer, Sweden's United Student Corps, chose just a few months later to send him to West Germany for an extended "study and contact trip." Despite the fact that he was clearly "a particularly talented young man," it was nonetheless a career that was a bit on the fast side for Lars Martin Johansson, with his more traditional police officer's disposition, and it was Krassner who fueled his suspicions.

According to Krassner, as soon as neutral Sweden had become clear about which way things were leaning, this was the way that military cooperation with the United States had been initiated. This had also gone so far that it was now becoming possible to extend things covertly, without openly doing violence to the official position of a "continuously maintained strict Swedish neutrality." In general this had concerned military intelligence operations directed against the traditional Swedish enemy and previous ally of the United States, the Soviet Union.

The United States provided the Swedish military with money and technical equipment while the Swedes contributed their geographic position and the personnel required for the job itself to get done. Krassner needed only a few pages to describe—mostly in passing, as it appeared—both the overall features and a number of astonishing particular events in this unofficial (to say the least) Swedish foreign policy.

A primarily defensive military cooperation, just in case. The other side of the coin was the more offensive and intellectually oriented strategy that enthused both Forselius and Buchanan along with their spiritual brethren within the Western world's intelligence organs. For Forselius and Buchanan the underlying thought was simple and obvious and, of course, axiomatically elitist in a way to which a thinking person with stable conservative values didn't need to give any thought.

What would decide the future of Europe was the direction in which the young, developing elite would go in a political sense. Because the work of influencing that issue, like all other superior and essential human endeavors, was best carried on in organized forms and preferably with organized tasks and goals as well, the student movements had become both the new armies of the cold war and the field where the battle was fought.

Against this background it wasn't so strange that it was the American military headquarters in Frankfurt that had taken care of Pilgrim in matters both large and small when he'd finally arrived to "begin his studies" and "make his first international contacts."

Certainly an interesting time, thought Johansson. Pilgrim had clearly not been a bad haul. As soon as he'd gotten his feet wet he'd started running like a shuttle behind the iron curtain that had just been pulled down: East Germany, Poland, Czechoslovakia. International symposia, conferences, lecture tours, study visits, debates, and ordinary simple gatherings were sandwiched with secret nighttime meetings, smuggled-out messages, agents to be recruited, and sympathizers to be won over to the right cause. But also the sort of people they hadn't been successful with, who had become suspect and uncovered, who had let them down. One or two had even disappeared or died.

And the whole time Buchanan had held his fatherly, protective hand over his young favorite Pilgrim. They had frequent and ongoing contacts by letter and telephone and in all the customary secret ways, and all of a sudden Buchanan might suddenly show up, nod at Pilgrim, and take him out to a restaurant regardless of whether it was in Stockholm, Frankfurt, Berlin, London, or Paris. But never in Warsaw, never in Prague, never on the wrong side of the curtain.

An exceedingly generous father figure with almost inexhaustible resources, it appeared, if one were to believe Krassner's writings and the documentation he'd received from his uncle. Pilgrim had been active as an agent for the CIA within the international European student movement for almost five years, from the autumn of 1948 to the summer of

1953, and during all of that time Buchanan had had his spending hat on and his wallet wide open. Among Krassner's papers was a neat, handwritten compilation of the amounts transferred to "Pilgrim and/or Pilgrim Operations and/or Pilgrim Operatives" during the years in question: Buchanan's handwriting, the usual type of copy, the amount of the sum, whether it was disbursed by check, postal order, or in cash, as well as the date and year of the disbursement.

In addition to this compilation there were also twenty-some copies of both Swedish and foreign checks and postal orders that were either drawn blank or to "the holder" or "the bearer," and none of them had been issued by the CIA or any other official, semiofficial, or covert American authority whatsoever. Instead the money came from American institutions, foundations, and not-for-profit organizations: from the Ford Foundation, the Rockefeller Foundation, from the Beacon, Borden, Edsel, Price, and Schuhheimer foundations, most often from the last named.

Generous guy, thought Johansson, a perception clearly shared by Krassner himself, who in one of his messy and partly handwritten footnotes had scribbled that "Bartlett K. Schuhheimer was a true American and patriot who willed his entire fortune to the fight against the red menace" at the same time as he named his "good friend and comrade-in-arms Col. John C. Buchanan to oversee and distribute the assets of the foundation."

The whole thing had started on a relatively modest scale. During November and December 1948, Pilgrim had received $1,248.50 for "board and lodging, travel costs and expenses."

He would hardly have anything to complain about, thought Johansson.

However that might be, by the following year Pilgrim, judging by the costs, had evidently really gotten the operation going. Buchanan had transferred more than $30,000, or almost a 150,000 Swedish crowns in total—a sum corresponding to the combined average annual salaries of fifty-some Swedish industrial workers in the same year. Johansson knew that because he had just refreshed his knowledge of economic history with the aid of a book he'd borrowed from the library in Sundsvall.

During the following two years it had gone even better; almost $60,000 during 1950 and more than $70,000 the following year. But then something dreadful must have happened to Pilgrim or his operation or the branch as a whole, for only a year later the costs had gone down to about $25,000, and by 1953 they were broadly speaking back to where they'd started, a piddling $9,085.25 for the whole year.

According to Krassner it was Pilgrim himself that was the explanation. He had found other, more important things to do and started winding down his involvement both as a student politician and as a secret agent. The operation that he'd built up would be turned over to others, and all of it, by the way, happened with Buchanan's consent.

High time to call it an evening, thought Johansson, for the clock in his stomach had already said it wanted to have dinner, and the one on his wrist as usual had no objections.

His brother had returned from his business dealings and after dinner they sat in front of the fireplace in the living room to have a quiet high-ball before going to bed.

"Well," said Johansson's big brother demandingly and with a look of curiosity. "How's it going?"

"What do you mean?" said Johansson, smiling amiably.

"I've heard from the wife that you're sitting by yourself fiddling around all day long," said his brother. "Is it something secret you're working on?"

"No," said Johansson, shaking his head. "I'm just sitting, reading a book."

"I didn't know they made books with loose pages," said his brother, chuckling.

"It's not printed yet," said Johansson.

"I peeked in through the window before I left yesterday morning," his brother explained. "But you didn't see me or hear me. So is there anything interesting in it?"

"So-so," said Johansson. "Do you remember that DC-3 the Russians shot down out in the Baltic when I was a little boy?"

"Yes," said big brother, nodding. "I remember, that was when Papa started cleaning his moose gun even though there were almost three months left till moose season. Did they shoot down any others as well?"

"A Catalina plane that was out searching for the DC-3," said Johansson. "It was the sixteenth of June, 1952. The DC-3 was three days earlier, the thirteenth."

"I do remember that," said Johansson's big brother, smiling wryly. "Papa Evert was damn tipsy and considering what a bad shot Papa is, I guess we were really lucky the Russkies stopped messing with us."

"The reason that the Russians shot them down was that they were out spying on the Russians on behalf of the Americans," said Johansson. This is going to be interesting, he thought.

"You shouldn't read that kind of shit," said his big brother, sighing dejectedly. "I remember you were the same when you were little. You read a lot of shit and then you believed it too. For a while I thought there was something seriously wrong with you."

"It was a joke," said Johansson. "Skoal, by the way." That you believed, he thought.

"You shouldn't read a lot of shit," his brother repeated. "Look at me. I haven't eaten porridge or read a damn book since I started being able to defend myself, and I'll be damned if I don't make just as much in a month as you pull in in a year. Skoal, then."

Certainly, thought Johansson, marking his agreement with his glass. I guess that's precisely the point, he thought.

The following morning—he'd just sat down to start the day's work on Krassner's papers—Wiklander called him despite the fact that it was Saturday.

"I got the number from your brother," Wiklander explained. "It was those counts and barons you were wondering about."

"Are you at work on a Saturday?" asked Johansson. Wiklander can go places, he thought.

"I'm slaving at the after-hours unit," Wiklander explained. "Thought about going to the Canary Islands in January but the holidays can really put a draft in your wallet."

"I'm listening," said Johansson, who had never been to the Canary Islands in his entire life and had no intention of ever going there, despite the fact that he was a real policeman.

It had taken awhile even for Wiklander, for none of the subjects of inquiry were in the police's own register or archives, and for a time he'd almost believed that he would have to go outside the building, but then fortunately he'd happened to think of his colleague Söderhjelm.

"But then I happened to think of our colleague Söderhjelm in the fraud unit," Wiklander explained, "and it struck me that she's one of them."

"One of them?"

"Yes, one of the nobility, that is," Wiklander clarified. "They usually know everything about each other."

Personally Johansson had only a faint recollection of a younger, female colleague. Well trained and at the same time courteous but without being the least bit ingratiating, which was actually an all-too-rare combination in the world where he'd chosen to live his life.

"I'm listening," he said.

"Yes, those people clearly know everything about each other," Wiklander repeated. "She is supposedly distantly related to that von Wrede too. She arranged for me to chat with someone she knew at the House of Nobles. It's an organization they have," he clarified for his obviously commoner boss.

"I'm listening," said Johansson. Get to the point already, he thought, feeling a slight irritation when he saw the piles of paper in front of him.

"They're dead," said Wiklander. "All of them except for that math genius are dead. Although he's not nobility, of course. Some old family of clergy from Västergötland, the Söderhjelm woman thought. Semi-refined, if you like."

. . .

All of the aristocrats involved were dead, and no normal causes of death either, according to Wiklander. First out was Captain Count Lewenhaupt, who had passed away as early as 1949 from the complications of a tropical disease that he'd picked up during a safari in Africa.

"Some mysterious worm that crept in under his skin and took up residence in his liver. He died at some special clinic for tropical diseases in London," Wiklander summarized.

Bilharzia, thought Johansson, who was not the usual policeman and knew a little of everything.

Second Lieutenant Baron von Wrede had died in a traffic accident in 1961. According to Wiklander he'd evidently driven his convertible sports car right into the stable on the estate where he lived.

"The word on the ground is that he was drunk and had argued with his wife," said Wiklander, who was also a real policeman of a more usual type than Johansson.

"Björnstjerna, then," said Johansson. "Where, when, and how did he die?"

"Seems to have been a completely normal death, actually," said Wiklander, his voice sounding almost a little disappointed. "Died at the Sophia Home; in 1964, of cancer. He wasn't particularly old, either. Born in 1923."

"Forselius, then," Johansson pressed. "What have you found out about him?"

"He's still alive," declared Wiklander. "Although he was considerably older than any of the others. Seems to be an interesting type. He's even in the encyclopedia. I trotted down to the public library. Took the opportunity to peek at a few books that he's written."

"So was there anything interesting?" said Johansson in a friendly tone.

"Sure," said Wiklander. "Although it was pure Greek plus a lot of numbers, so I'll reserve my judgment."

"Interesting type?"

"If I've understood things correctly, I believe he's worked quite a bit for SePo," said Wiklander. "Even in later years, actually, despite the fact that he's as old as the hills. If I haven't gotten the matter completely turned around, I believe he's the one who built their computer program for codes and encryption and all that stuff they work with."

"You haven't talked to anyone?" said Johansson, and for some reason he felt a faint stab of worry.

"Not my style," said Wiklander dismissively. "I found it out on my own."

"Except for Söderhjelm," said Johansson judiciously.

"She's like me so, she doesn't count," said Wiklander curtly.

"That's good," said Johansson. "What else were you thinking about doing this weekend?" he added familiarly, and as a suitable and diplomatic conclusion.

"As soon as I get off I thought about asking Officer Söderhjelm to dinner," said Wiklander. "Nice lady, actually."

Nice to hear that someone is normal, thought Johansson, looking at his paper-strewn desk.

"There's one thing I'm wondering about," said Wiklander, sounding a little cautious. "If you'll excuse me, chief."

"Shoot," said Johansson. "I'm listening."

"What is this really about?" said Wiklander. "Is it something I ought to know about, or what?"

"Well," said Johansson. "If it stays completely between us?"

"Obviously," said Wiklander.

"I'm actually in the process of writing a mystery," said Johansson. "I just needed some good characters."

"So that's how it is," said Wiklander, whose voice suddenly sounded very wary. "Too bad they were dead, then."

"You can't have everything," said Johansson tranquilly, and then he thanked him for his help and finished the conversation.

In a normal mystery isn't everyone dead sooner or later? he thought as he put down the receiver, and you can't have everything. Or can you? And for some reason he started thinking about the woman he'd met at the little post office up on Körsbärsvägen.

During 1953 the prime minister had changed the direction of his life. It wasn't a dramatic change, but rather a course correction, and he seemed not only to have retained his interest in secret activities but also to have developed them in more conventional, national forms. And according to Krassner, this had all happened not only with Buchanan's consent but with his clearly expressed approval and support.

First he had begun phasing out his involvement with student politics to switch his sights to greater political goals. As a natural consequence of this, among other things, his activity within the CIA decreased sharply, and after the summer of 1953 there was nothing in either Krassner's text or Buchanan's documentation to indicate that he carried out any direct assignments whatsoever on their behalf. On the other hand, according to Krassner, he still had close, recurring contacts with Buchanan all the way up to the spring of 1955, when he'd sent his strange, poetically worded notice that his life between the longing of summer and the cold of winter was now to be seen as history.

During the same year he'd also gotten a steady job—two steady jobs, in fact. Right before the summer of 1953 he'd gotten a position as an "analyst" with the intelligence department at army headquarters, and only a few months later he'd started working as an assistant to the then prime minister. Not a bad job for a highly talented young man with great ambitions in life, and not a bad employer, either. Not least as his professional connection to the twenty-five-years-older prime minister soon appeared to those around them like an almost classic father-son relationship.

The prime minister as a young man, Pilgrim, Johansson's own prime minister, seemed to have had a genuine interest in security work and intelligence operations. His work as an analyst also appeared to have been relatively unbound by the label his employer had put on his assignment. Whether that was in order to mislead the devil, or only a simple expression of the fact that he actually was a free operator, was beyond Johansson's ability to judge, and Krassner no longer had any substantial contributions to make, either. But there was hardly anyone trying to rap the old prime minister's personal assistant on the knuckles, thought Johansson.

To start with, according to Krassner but without particular details or evidence in the form of documents, he was said to have worked on the regular military cooperation between the Swedish and American intelligence services; what this actually involved was to analyze security requirements and in the end to exchange personnel, services, and the necessary material to satisfy those requirements. Here on several occasions he was said to have turned to Buchanan for assistance in both word and deed, but it was unclear what this would have consisted of in concrete terms. Krassner also pointed out that because Buchanan was working in a different branch of CIA operations, his contribution had mostly concerned arranging contacts and generally functioning as a type of door-opener and personal guarantor that Pilgrim was both "a good kid" and of "the right stuff."

Of the prime minister's alleged role in the building up of IB, the Information Bureau, Krassner had little to convey beyond what had come out or been suggested in the domestic public debate. Krassner recounted these briefly as generally known, clear facts, and that was all. Pilgrim had played a central role when the secret organization whose primary task was to keep the political opponents of the social democrats under supervision was established, and according to the same source, in a conversation with Buchanan as early as the fall of 1954, he was said to have made it completely clear that he considered his social democratic organization the "natural governing party in Sweden."

Viewpoints of that type naturally disturbed Buchanan. Especially as they came from a "highly talented young man" with "stable conservative views," and among his posthumous papers there was also a photocopy of his notations from the conversation with Pilgrim. Judging by the handwriting and the copy, written by Buchanan at the time when the conversation was supposed to have taken place, but as a piece of evidence nonetheless of secondary value because when all was said and done it was Buchanan's version of what Pilgrim was supposed to have said. Not to mention being generally hard to interpret and cryptic in places.

All the same, thought Johansson, for by this time even Pilgrim was starting to show clear signs that his passion for intelligence operations was in the process of cooling. Instead it was his political activity and ambitions that had come to the fore, and it was also now that his career caught fire and started taking off in earnest. His political assignments started to be piled high and he'd gotten more and more say in his own job in a formal sense as well. At the start of the sixties he'd become head of the prime minister's chancellery, and only a few years later he'd taken a seat in the government. During the following years he'd exchanged ministerial positions in the direction of the short end of the table, and when his own boss retired, at the end of the 1960s, it was time: prime minister, despite the fact that he was one of the very youngest members of the government and almost an alien species as a social democrat, considering his background, upbringing, and education.

I see then, thought Johansson, looking at his watch. The clock in his stomach had not started seriously ticking, mostly due to the fact that there were still several hours left before dinner, but he felt a strong desire to get out and move about. Not a walk, thought Johansson, for then melancholy would strike him in earnest. Drive into town, he decided, and return the book about economic history he'd borrowed from the library.

Once he was at the library he also took the opportunity to make a few inquiries of his own, and although he was only at a public library in Sundsvall, he more or less stumbled across an interesting piece of information about the mysterious Forselius that Wiklander evidently had missed. Not so strange in itself, thought Johansson, considering what he knew and what Wiklander didn't know.

First he found a book with the title *Great Swedes in Mathematics,* and there he retrieved both Sonya Kovalevsky—despite the fact that she was Russian—and Professor Forselius, whose secret activities were passed over in complete silence and in which the further significance of what he'd otherwise done was in any event beyond Johansson. True, he could count, but higher mathematics left him cold. On the other hand there was nothing wrong with his eyes, and he noticed quite quickly that Forselius clearly had a disciple who was no slouch either. Who moreover shared the same name with the prime minister's special adviser and approximately the same age too. So that's how it is, thought Johansson, and then he returned home to his brother's to have dinner.

Johansson lay awake quite a while that night and thought about his knowledge of the country's prime minister, and for some reason he felt almost exhilarated as he did so. Hardly the man who's described in the bourgeois press, thought Johansson, smiling as he lay in bed. More like some hero of the Western world out of a random issue of *Reader's Digest*. He used to read the magazine cover to cover when he was young, "Humor in Uniform" and a little of the cold war's musketeers, but no lettres de cachet, for here it was more likely a question of messages written with invisible ink, and no frothing horses but rather an old Buick V-8, rumbling along through dark and stormy nights, and if there were trapdoors they were probably in people's heads. Although the hollow oak trees where you hid things would have been the same. Oaks could get as old as anything, after all.

There must have been a great deal worth writing about, thought Johansson, for he'd also read that in *Reader's Digest*. The scoundrels from the East used to have pens that were actually pistols, umbrellas with poisoned ferrules, and innocent-looking walking sticks that with a quick tap on the handle could be transformed into shining rapiers with razor-sharp blades. But what had Pilgrim actually had, aside from his noble intentions and a good cause?

He would have needed someone like my big brother, thought Johansson. A slightly simpler companion like big brother with his shrewd head and his huge fists and his completely unsentimental ability to punch anyone and everyone on the jaw as soon as things didn't suit him. Or like Jarnebring, perhaps? True, he wasn't as shrewd as his brother, far from it, but when it came to genuine hand-to-hand fighting he was unbeatable. Not even James Bond could have managed him even by escaping, for then Jarnebring would have caught up with him and chopped him on the neck and given him a going-over until he was no more than an empty suit coat and a pair of limp trousers from some tailor on Old Bond Street and. . . . About then he fell asleep, and when he woke up in the morning it was with the same smile on his lips.

Sweet Jesus, thought Johansson, laughing a little to himself. Pilgrim and Jarnie, what a radar unit.

High time to tie up my sack, and the sooner the better, thought Johansson, because it was Sunday, Epiphany Eve, and the day before his journey home. It had been a quick shower and an even quicker breakfast, and at six-thirty he was already at his place at the large desk in the farm office.

The piles before him had thinned out and most of it he'd been able to sort out. Of the documentation only a letter with its envelope and a condolence card with a black frame and a three-line poem remained. But these were original documents, not copies, they were handwritten, and according to Krassner it was the prime minister, Pilgrim, who had written them, after he'd become prime minister, and according to Krassner he had written them in May 1974. They were postmarked Stockholm and sent by express mail to Buchanan's post office box at home in Albany.

Almost twenty years after he'd written his farewell letter, thought Johansson. An entire lifetime, considering all that had happened and all that he'd experienced. Peculiar, very peculiar, thought Johansson.

We ought to be able to check on these, he thought from force of habit while by turns he held the letter, the condolence card, and the envelope between the nails of his thumb and index finger, twisting and turning them. Perhaps there are prints too, he thought. American technicians had succeeded in securing fingerprints that were decades old—he'd read that in the FBI's monthly journal—and it was almost always a matter of prints left on paper. Where would I get his fingerprints from? thought Johansson with a wry smile.

The letter first: It was short, written by hand with Pilgrim's characteristic, expressively forward-leaning penmanship—like a cavalry charge on paper, thought Johansson, smiling again. The stationery was thick and certainly expensive. When he held it up against the light he saw the Lessebo watermark.

> *Fionn,*
>
> *Heard about Raven's tragic death yesterday. I truly hope that you put away the bastards who did it. Because I'm guessing that you intend to go to his funeral, I would be grateful if you could deliver the enclosed final greeting from me. Don't ask me why, but Raven was a true lover of Icelandic sagas. Take care!*
>
> *Pilgrim*

Then the condolence card, which he had sent in the same envelope.

If this is Snorre then I'm Japanese, thought Johansson while he read the three lines on the card, written in Swedish:

> *Death is black like a raven's wing,*
> *Sorrow is cold like a midwinter night*
> *Just as long and no way out*

Must be something that Pilgrim wrote himself, thought Johansson. Perhaps something that only he and Raven understood the meaning of and which now served as a final greeting. What was it she'd said, that extraordinarily talented woman he'd met a month before? A man with a poetic disposition, or rather a poetic ambition?

Johansson leaned back in the desk chair while he stretched his back with his fingers laced together behind his neck in order to think better. But this time it didn't help. Instead he took Krassner's manuscript and continued to read. Now only a third of it remained, a thin bundle that already felt limp in his hand and whose written contents seemed to promise little more. According to Krassner, during his active period Buchanan recruited almost a hundred agents in the struggle for Europe's young, developing elite. He'd had two favorites, and according to his nephew they were the only ones who really meant anything to him. One was Pilgrim and the other was Raven. The first had betrayed him; the other had been faithful to him unto death.

Raven was Salomon "Sal" Tannenbaum, same age as Pilgrim. Born and raised in New York in a prosperous intellectual Jewish family, and according to the "Irishman" Krassner, that was just about the best background you could have in the international intelligence world, regardless of whether you "opened your brown eyes" in Moscow, Warsaw, London, or New York.

Must be your German father, thought Johansson grimly while he hurried through the sparse text.

He'd gotten his agent name, Raven, from Buchanan, an obvious and simple choice, as he looked like a raven and was as wise as two. After studying law at Harvard and an early involvement in the American student movement, he'd met Buchanan, been recruited as an agent for the CIA, and gone over to Europe in order to make a few introductory brushes with the communist student organizations.

In Frankfurt, in November 1948, Raven met Pilgrim. Not unexpectedly, they took a liking to each other.

Raven's contribution on the European front, however, had not lasted long. Instead he'd returned to the United States and started working as an attorney for just about every worthy, politically correct purpose whatsoever that could be found in the great land to the west. Sal Tannenbaum had represented the civil-rights movement, the Black Panthers, Mexican farmworkers, Native Americans, and even Eskimos. He had "stood up" for racial integration, union rights, peace in Vietnam, and of course for world peace. He had thundered against organized crime and capitalist exploitation of the black underclass. He had almost always done it pro bono—and according to Krassner he'd been one of the CIA's most effective infiltrators of the "radical, socialist, and communist movements" on the American home front for more than twenty years.

Sweet Jesus, sighed Johansson. If this is true he can't have had it too easy.

In May of 1974 a man, probably in early middle age, probably white, probably dressed in a suit, with an everyday appearance, had come into Tannenbaum's office. Calm, quiet, and unobserved he walked past the receptionist, who was on the phone as usual, opened the door to Tannenbaum's office, and shot a bullet right through his head. Then he'd left the place, and considering who the victim was and how little the witnesses had seen, the whole thing was a police nightmare.

Must have been crawling with motives and possible perpetrators, thought Johansson. And if it really was as Krassner alleged, and someone else must have come to the same conclusion, you probably have to multiply them by two, he thought.

According to Krassner it was much simpler than that. The murder of Raven was a contract killing. The person who had ordered it was Pilgrim, and those who'd helped him with the practical aspects were the new masters he was serving, the Soviet Union and its military intelligence services. (Hence the title of Krassner's book, "The Spy Who Went East.") Krassner's explanation was long, complicated, and thin. Firm evidence was completely lacking and instead Krassnerian logic held unrestricted sway. During his twenty years with the police, Johansson had heard a number of Swedish variations on the same theme discussed ad nauseam in police break rooms and among friends, although he'd never heard anything even remotely similar to this.

Fair is fair, thought Johansson while reviewing in his mind's eye several of the most rabid characters among the colleagues he'd had, all of whom had in common that they never ought to have been allowed to become policemen. Russian spy? Yes, because "everyone knew" that. Murderer? No, and there wasn't anyone who suggested that, either. And personally he'd always thought—regardless of how he'd voted, for that of course had varied over the years—that the whole thing was pure nonsense. That the prime minister would spy for the Soviet Union was just as improbable as he now found it probable that for several years in his youth he'd been an agent for the CIA. I'll buy that from you, thought Johansson, and the "you" he was thinking of was that wretched Krassner and his thirsty uncle. But the rest you can just forget.

Having come that far in his musings, he was interrupted by the phone ringing, even though it was only eight o'clock on a Sunday morning. It was Wiklander, and as a real policeman should he'd found something out. Namely that the mysterious Professor Forselius not only knew highly placed persons in the secret police but also was a close friend of the prime minister's special adviser, the same man responsible for security issues that affected the prime minister and the government.

"Interesting," said Johansson mendaciously. "How'd you find that out?"

"Our colleague Söderhjelm," said Wiklander. "Didn't I mention that we were going to have dinner together yesterday evening?"

Evidently one thing had led to another, and without going into details Wiklander had ended up somewhat later in front of Söderhjelm's well-stocked bookshelf, inherited from an uncle with literary interests, where by pure chance a book about great Swedes in mathematics had caught his eye, and with Forselius freshly in mind one thing had led to another.

"Pure chance," said Wiklander modestly.

"So how was dinner?" said Johansson as a diversion.

Nice, according to Wiklander. So nice, in fact, that he was now considering forgetting about the Canary Islands and going instead with Söderhjelm to Thailand on a three-week-long diving expedition.

"Sounds nice," said Johansson neutrally. "Say hello from me, by the way, and thanks a lot for the help."

I am her boss, after all, he thought as he set down the receiver and returned to Krassner and the concluding and messiest part of his manuscript, which had been messy from the get-go. And because he'd instinctively mistrusted everything in it when he'd done the first run-through, he decided to read it extra carefully now.

Concurrently with his growing political success, Pilgrim had also acquired international ambitions, and by the end of the 1960s he had already actively expressed his support for just about every movement or conflict hostile to the United States that could be found on the political map. First he'd turned against the U.S. struggle for peace and freedom in Vietnam, then he'd started to give support to Castro in Cuba and various South and Central American rebels, and as the cherry on the cake he'd stood up for Arafat and his Palestinian terrorists.

According to Krassner he'd done so because he was now, and had been for a long time, an agent of influence for the Soviet Union—he hadn't mentioned even a word about his possible political convictions—and whatever the case he'd driven his old comrades-in-arms Buchanan and Raven crazy. Raven was the more furious of the two because he wasn't the person everyone believed him to be but was rather merely an ordinary, hardworking, true American CIA agent. And he was also a Jew, so it was the support of Arafat and the Palestinians that vexed him the most.

Raven wanted to strike back and reveal Pilgrim's past. Buchanan was hesitant. Accustomed as one easily became in his line of work to doubters, defectors, normal traitors, and double agents, regardless of the factual background it was "bad for business" to expose old agents. As things were, with Raven exerting pressure and wanting to retaliate by messing with Pilgrim, and Buchanan trying to hold him back while other solutions were being considered, the whole thing had solved itself at the beginning of May 1974, by way of the "probably white," "probably dressed in a suit," "probably early middle aged," and quite certainly "everyday" man who walked into Raven's office and shot his head off.

.   .   .

"On the usual inscrutable roads where the intelligence agents of the world travel," wrote Krassner, Pilgrim's Russian comrades had evidently intercepted what was going on, and Pilgrim's friend and agent contact, the Russian KGB general Gennadi Renko, member of the Politburo and the Central Committee, had quickly seen to cleaning up Pilgrim's history. This was the situation in which Buchanan made his decision. Regardless of the fact that he was now risking his life, his temporal support, and his posthumous reputation, he didn't intend to take this lying down, and what made him the most furious was that Pilgrim had had the nerve to send a condolence card to a man he'd had killed. Therefore he told his story to "his nephew, young friend, and faithful squire," and "demanded of him a sacred oath" to see to it that "justice was served and that perhaps the greatest traitor in European postwar history got his just punishment."

"And this was the only, the simple, and the obvious reason that I've written this book," Krassner concluded his manuscript. The end of the very last sentence he'd evidently decided to cross out, possibly from false modesty or because he'd gotten cocky, but as it was carelessly done with the aid of a ballpoint pen and the last page, like the page before it, was an original and not a photocopy, Johansson could still read the original typewritten text from the back side of the paper: "despite the fact that I am obviously well aware that I am thereby running a considerable risk of being murdered myself."

On Epiphany Johansson drove home to Stockholm in a car that he'd borrowed from his brother and that he was to deliver to a car dealer on Surbrunnsgatan of whom he had a vague police memory that he would rather not think about. Instead he thought about other things, mostly about Krassner and the papers he'd gotten from him. He was in an unusually good mood the whole time, mostly pondering a small detail in Pilgrim's farewell letter to which Krassner hadn't given him an answer. Not even the hint of an answer.

That time when he'd fallen free, like in a dream?

· · ·

What was it that had really happened back then? thought Johansson. And before him, in the twilight land of his imagination, he saw a rebuilt Lancaster bomber with sound-muffled motors that in the middle of the black night was searching under Polish radar. The jumping hatch was already pushed open and there stood Pilgrim in black overalls and a tight-fitting leather hood with only his hawk-nosed profile sticking out. Every muscle tensed while he held tightly to the cable on the roof. Now, now he got the high sign, and after a decisive nod he jumped straight out just as he released his hold on the cable and fell freely, like in a dream, through all the blackness, toward all the unknown down there.

Think if a real writer got to sink his teeth into Krassner's material, sighed Johansson. What a story it could have been. It wouldn't even have to be true, he thought.

CHAPTER XVI

And all that remained was the cold of winter

Stockholm in January and February

Waltin never tried to get hold of Hedberg. Instead he was seized by boredom while the days simply slipped away without his being able to get anything reasonable accomplished. He even broke off the training of little Jeanette, despite the fact that now was when he ought to have had the time to seriously attend to it. Instead he just sat there brooding about all the idiots who surrounded him fixated on only one thing—how to get at him and hurt him. Berg, for example, who quite obviously was trying to put the blame on him for the fact that that crazy junkie Krassner happened to tumble out his window. And he would rather not think about what that lunatic Forselius was up to along with his bosom buddies in the government building. Then that red-haired sow and her miserable husband—that is what they were called, regardless of whether or not they were fulfilling their marital duties—who had more or less accosted him on Christmas Eve. What she was in the process of cooking up he would rather not think about either.

Of course he stayed away from work—a benefit of the external operation—because he'd heard through the grapevine that Berg's fat stable boy, Chief Inspector Persson, was sneaking around, asking strange questions. If there was anyone he didn't want to encounter it was Persson. Primitive and brutal and completely unscrupulous, fully capable of coming up with just about anything as soon as the master snapped his fingers. Not Persson, anyone but Persson, thought Waltin.

For a few days he tried to get some temporary relief by fussing with his collections. He had hundreds of Polaroids, and quite a few regular pictures as well, which to be on the safe side he'd had processed abroad, and almost as many hours of videotapes and tape recordings, so as a private collection it ought to be the finest in the country, but there were also irritating imperfections and blemishes.

Take, for example, the pictures of that red-haired sow he'd seriously considered sending as a "reader's contribution"—where did they get them all, those jerk-offs, for you know they couldn't read?—to one of the working class's many pornographic publications, but on closer consideration he'd refrained, because you actually couldn't tell from the pictures that she was the subject. A fat red-haired sow lying tied up to the bedposts, before and after the removal of a portion of red bush; true, you could see that, and for many people perhaps that was good enough, but you actually didn't see that she was the one it depicted, and that was of course the whole point of publishing the pictures.

Because she had wriggled so infernally his meticulously applied muzzle had slid up so it covered half her face, and unfortunately he'd missed correcting that little detail during the photography, overworked and stressed as he was due to Berg and his incessant paranoid fantasies.

All the inactivity and idling at home in the apartment finally almost made him crazy, and because he was in the process of jerking himself dry just to get a little peace and quiet, he hadn't had any choice. Despite the fact that the risks were considerable, for they always were, and with the bad luck he'd had lately they would scarcely have lessened, he nonetheless decided to go out into the field again. Sink or swim, thought Waltin, but I have to find something sensible to do.

First he deliberated whether he should arrange a wiretap on her—he'd done that before and it was simple enough to sneak in an extra number when you were turning in the usual monthly lists anyway—but because that madman Persson was running around loose somewhere out in his own terrain he didn't dare take the risk. Instead he had to reconnoiter himself—in and of itself he'd done that before and he did it better than most—but the problem was that it was so doggone boring. It was only policemen and ordinary brain-dead people who endured sitting for hours in the front seat of a car staring at the same entryway while the object of surveillance was lying at home in bed playing with himself or looking at videos or gobbling down pizza, so he did what he usually did. He improvised a little and chanced it a little to get the time to pass, and one way or another it always worked out for the best.

But not this time.

Instead of sitting the whole day outside her office, he crank-called her a half hour before she quit in order to make sure she was there, and when she answered he just put down the receiver, got into the car, and took up a suitable position outside the exit to her office. It took only a quarter of an hour before she suddenly stepped out onto the street, her coat unbuttoned despite the cold, so that no poor, overworked wretch who only wanted to go home to suburban misery would be able to miss those fat breasts straining under her yellow sweater. The stuffed sow is always the same, thought Waltin, giggling as he visualized her, how she sat there rubbing against the seat of her chair all day while she stuck things into small holes.

But instead of disappearing in the direction of the subway—he planned to approach her right before the intersection—she remained standing. She just stood there, then she looked at her watch, and suddenly that well-known excitement started to sneak up on him. The one he always felt right before he found out something about someone that he could make use of. She's waiting for someone, thought Waltin.

And at the same moment someone knocked urgently on the windshield of the car, pulled open the door, and stuck a police ID in his face.

"Move over," said Police Inspector Berg, nodding with narrowed eyes toward the passenger seat.

Berg's nephew, thought Waltin. Hadn't he just been taken out of service for those reports of brutality? The jeans and the jacket seemed to indicate that, but why in that case hadn't they taken his ID away from him?

"What's this about?" said Waltin guardedly. He already knew, though, for in the corner of his eye he saw that the stuffed sow on the other side of the street was almost jumping with delight. She's fucked him too, of course, he thought. She's certainly fucked all of those cavemen.

"Are you deaf or do you want me to help you?" asked Berg.

And because his eyes looked the way they did, despite the completely improbable situation, Waltin nonetheless did as he was told and wriggled over to the passenger seat.

"I'll make it brief," said Berg. "Lisa is a good friend of mine. Stop messing with her, or I'll see to it that things get fucking disagreeable for you."

"I don't know what you're talking about," said Waltin, sticking his hand in his pocket in order to take out his own ID to get him to understand the seriousness. You don't threaten a police superintendent with the secret police, thought Waltin.

"Stop persecuting Lisa, or I'll see to it that she reports you, and don't try to say that you're here on duty," said Berg, pushing aside Waltin's hand with the ID card.

"I don't understand what you're talking about," said Waltin. The guy is completely crazy, he thought. You can see it in his eyes.

"You and I both know," said Berg. "She reports you, my colleagues and I who've seen you stand up and testify. Do we understand one another?"

"I would encourage you to leave my car immediately," said Waltin. Completely crazy, he thought. Totally crazy.

"This isn't your car, it's the department's car, just so you know," said Berg as he opened the door to get out.

Waltin didn't say anything, for the threat in his eyes was so real that he could touch it.

So he just remained sitting and watched Berg go over to the stuffed sow and take her by the arm. They both disappeared up the street. Only then did he drive away. I'll kill them, thought Waltin.

After Berg had followed Lisa to the subway he met his comrades. It was a meeting that they'd already planned during the Christmas holiday, and it was also then that they'd set up the tactics for how to find the traitor who had wormed his way into their ranks. They already had their suspicions, so now it was only a matter of setting the trap and seeing to it that it closed on the right man.

Lisa's a good girl, he thought. Really good lay too, and a jerk like that Waltin should just be killed. It was clearly enough to poke at him to make him shit in his pants, so it probably wouldn't be all that difficult, thought Berg.

At the meeting he "surprised" the assembly with a few well-prepared little semi-red viewpoints that he and the group had agreed on, and it was the very guy that they'd guessed in advance who started to carry on and go on the rampage. Damn overacting, thought Berg. We'll get you soon. Then they had coffee and he only needed to exchange a glance with the comrades to know that they'd understood exactly the same thing he had. The traitor had worked like a beaver to ingratiate himself and provoke people to say wrong things, but of course that hadn't gotten him anywhere.

On the first day of the new job, Johansson noticed a newspaper clipping on the internal bulletin board next to the cloakroom. It was the annual New Year's greeting from the Stockholm chief constable to his faithful personnel, which someone had clipped out of the Stockholm Police Department's personnel newsletter, and to be on the safe side marked it, with the help of a felt pen, with a thick black frame.

It was no ordinary New Year's greeting, especially not within the police. True, he'd heard whispering for a long time about the chief constable's literary ambitions, but he really hadn't counted on this. People didn't usually throw themselves headfirst out of their private closets when they'd finally made up their minds, thought Johansson, while he muttered his way through the poem's seven short lines. One of them he happened to recognize from some other context, but he'd forgotten from where, and on the whole it was all the same.

> Black asphalt,
> shining neon,

> *the stench of urine from the tile of the subway,*
> *in the station john a junkie dies of an overdose,*
> *Stockholm, city of cities,*
> *A dove pecks on the window ledge where I live,*
> *there is Hope!*

Under the chief constable's poem someone had written with the same black felt pen, "Give me a real policeman from Ådalen," and when Johansson saw the brief assertion something touched his Norrland heart. Nice to know you're welcome.

An unusual lot of poets around lately, he thought as he walked down the long corridor in the direction of his office. Prime ministers and police chiefs and God knows what. Perhaps you ought to write something yourself, he thought, but because that idea was so absurd he immediately dismissed it. A real policeman never wrote poems, and personally he'd already quit that kind of thing when he was a kid. Long before he became a policeman.

Bureau Chief Berg used to think about Swedish defense as a cheese, an unusually hollow, large-holed cheese of the classic Swiss model, and the primary reason for this was the stable and resistant foundation of stone on which the nation rested, for in it you could make holes, and in holes you could put things. He was more hesitant about the hedgehog the military used to talk about, and when they sometimes pulled out the Swedish tiger from the days of the cold war he was definitely not with them anymore. A taciturn Swedish tiger? The very thought was preposterous, Berg used to think, because if the Swedes really had been taciturn there would be no need for people like him. Berg existed, for good reason, because certain people talked too much, and it wasn't any more complicated than that.

The hollow cheese was a better image than both the hedgehog and the tiger because it was there that all the necessities of war were stored, from coffee and underwear to fuel and grease, plus an artillery piece or two that must be on hand when you wanted to strike back. The good Swedish rock foundation was crisscrossed with mile after mile of secret passages and ten million square feet of secret spaces where everything that would be needed could be stored, just in case.

The practical problems connected with this choice of strategy dealt in all essentials with the requirements for heat, ventilation, air humidity, and dehumidifying, and it was hardly by chance that Swedish industry was also the world leader in these technical areas. In Sweden there were thus two multinational corporations that produced and sold everything from fans and pumps to air-conditioning and dehumidifying installations, with customers over the whole world, regardless of whether their requirements were military or civilian.

These products were sold on an open market and protected in the usual way through patents and licenses, and so far didn't involve spies, but as soon as they were installed in military installations it became a completely different matter. For the materiel to be put into place and function demanded a thorough knowledge of the installations where they were to be placed, and based on this knowledge a number of interesting variables could then be calculated: site, size, and range of application, type of materiel, and quantity of various products and commodities, in order to codify those that concerned military capacity, strategic direction, and endurance. Depending on who the purchaser was, a banal, ordinary industrial fan might quickly be transformed into an espionage assignment of the first order.

A good year and a half earlier, detectives in the secret police conducting routine surveillance of an official with the Soviet trade delegation had gotten wind of a previously unknown Swede who, after the customary checks, was shown to be working as a sales engineer at the smaller and faster growing of the two multinational Swedish companies in the business. When the alarm had been sounded Berg had been on vacation, the first real time off he'd had in several years, and it was Waltin who filled in for him. When Berg came back the case was already closed and evidently disappeared, for however Berg rooted in his memory, he couldn't find the least trace of it.

· · ·

"And you're quite certain that it was in June of the summer before last," asked Berg.

"Quite sure," said Persson. "Waltin took it over just as soon as it came in. It was the sixth of June, National Day, in fact. It was concluded less than a month later, the first of July."

"So what did he do?" said Berg. "Waltin, that is." While Marja and I were in Austria, he thought.

"Unclear," said Persson. "The person involved quit rather abruptly, so the basic tip-off is that Waltin contacted the company executives. We don't seem to have done anything here in the building, in any event."

"This sounds completely unreal," said Berg. "Why in heaven's name did he do that?"

"Personally I can only think of one reason," said Persson.

"Yes?"

"Their single largest export market is the United States. How do you think the Yanks would have reacted if they'd found out that the company was the object of an espionage investigation? That concerned the Russians?"

"But why on earth would Waltin do something like that?"

"There's only one reason," said Persson, suddenly looking rather satisfied.

"Yes?"

Persson held up his large right hand with the back of his hand toward Berg and rubbed his thumb against his index and middle fingers.

"Maybe he needed to buy a new watch," Persson grunted contentedly.

I don't believe my ears, thought Berg.

"We have to talk with him," he said.

They had the first weekly meeting of the new year the third week in January. None of the issues Berg chose to bring up were especially important or urgent. He did not touch on the prime minister's personal security awareness in any way. Most likely because he was now beginning to resign himself to the thought of having to live with it as it was— that is to say, nonexistent, or at best insufficient.

Kudo and Bülling as usual reported a great number of questions "of the utmost importance for the security of the realm" during the operations bureau's preparation of those cases that he needed to take up with the government, but personally he'd been content to communicate to his political superiors that all appeared calm on the Kurdish front. Contrary to his habit, the minister of justice didn't come up with any moronic follow-up questions, either, contenting himself with nodding in concurrence.

Berg devoted most of the time to the ongoing survey of extreme right-wing elements within the police and military, but even there he was able to provide reassurance. According to the operations bureau's informants, activities within these groups appeared, if anything, to have decreased, and the future would show whether that was due to the fact that they'd eaten too much Christmas food or to something else.

Then final questions remained, and because that point traditionally was given over to a somewhat more lighthearted summing-up and give-and-take, it came as a total surprise when the minister of justice started asking questions about very sensitive command-and-control procedures in connection with the work of the secret police. As a breach of etiquette it was almost shocking, but etiquette was clearly the thing they were least interested in talking about.

"I guess I'll get right to the point," said the minister of justice, who suddenly sounded like a completely different person than the one Berg had become accustomed to, "for unfortunately it is the case that this so-called external operation has concerned us a great deal."

Then the chief legal officer took over. The legal officer, of all people, who had hardly opened his mouth during all these years, thought Berg, and from the papers that he started to shuffle and from what he then said, Berg understood two things. That he of course was not one to speak unprepared, and that he must have a very large bone to pick with Berg and his operation.

"To summarize," said the legal officer with a crackling-dry voice and as though he were addressing a child, "the business-enterprise element of the external operation is not in accord with the instructions of the government. Quite apart from the entire construction, it must be considered utterly dubious as an instrument of control."

"When this came up the first time during the previous administration," Berg objected, "I was of the distinct impression that they were completely in agreement with us that it was only a question of a cover in order to protect the actual operation. And as you gentlemen perhaps recall, we also briefed our parliamentary committee."

From their facial expressions Berg could tell that they didn't share the previous administration's understanding of the matter, and that none of them had any memory of any information from their time in opposition.

"Because you've done business with both private and public clients, it is quite obviously a question of a business operation in the legal sense, and thereby inconsistent with your instructions," the legal officer repeated.

"Well," said Berg, swearing to himself about how compliant he sounded, "but that's of course in the very nature of the matter. How else would we be able to maintain a credible front?"

"It sounds as if it's high time to close up shop," chuckled the prime minister's special adviser behind his half-closed eyelids. "I have a vague recollection that you and I talked about this previously, by the way."

So that's how it is, thought Berg.

"It's naturally regrettable that the previous administration's attorneys didn't pay attention to this little complication," the legal adviser stated contentedly. "If you had asked me I would have been able to enlighten you on the fact that the entire arrangement was unthinkable from the start."

"Naturally we're not demanding that you immediately close the whole thing down," said the minister of justice amiably. "The control function naturally must remain, and we understand fully that you may need a certain transition period in order to find a . . . how shall I put it . . . a more correct legal form for the whole thing."

"By Monday would be good," said the special adviser, laughing so that his fat belly bounced.

"Oh well," said the minister of justice sourly, because it was he who actually had a seat in the government, and he had the right to demand a little good manners even from the prime minister's confidant. "You surely need a little longer, but if we might get your thoughts on how such an oversight should be set up by the next meeting or perhaps even the following meeting then I'll be completely satisfied." The minister of justice nodded affably.

How generous of you, thought Berg. Not enough that I'm expected to cut off my right arm myself. I also have to decide where, when, and how it should be done. Provided that it goes quickly, of course.

It was at that point that he decided to try a different angle of attack, and afterward he deeply regretted having done so. He ought to have understood better, he thought. This was something they must have prepared with all the precision required for a successful ambush.

"I have heard it suggested," Berg began hesitantly and carefully, "that the government is planning a new parliamentary oversight of the entire closed operation . . . and it would be far from me to have any opinions about that," he continued just as carefully as he'd begun, "but am I to understand from what you are now saying that you have abandoned the idea of a more comprehensive inspection?"

"Certainly not," said the minister of justice, sounding just as jovial as if it was an ordinary present that was going to be given out. "Certainly not," he repeated. "When we discussed the matter at the higher governmental level, we were only in agreement on the fact that it would be advantageous to deal with this question in particular before we set to work on the somewhat broader oversight."

"We don't want to embarrass the opposition," the special adviser clarified with his usual wry grin.

"Not at any price, certainly not," emphasized the minister with a cordial voice. "Let others score such crude political points."

So there's no help to be had, thought Berg. Wonder how many they've talked with?

"I will put together a proposal as quickly as is possible," he said, nodding curtly. "If there's nothing else, then . . ."

He understood by their satisfied head shaking that they all thought he'd gotten as much as he could tolerate for one occasion.

Despite repeated attempts, Waltin hadn't gotten hold of Hedberg. After the shocking attack he'd been subjected to by that fat red-haired stuffed sow and Berg's deplorable nephew—actually he ought to report him, but justice would have to be tempered with mercy, and first he wanted to discuss the problem with Hedberg, who always used to have good ideas when it was a matter of retaliating with interest—he'd felt anxious and phoned Hedberg on his secret number far into the night. The phone had rung and rung, but no one had answered, and finally he'd gone to bed after a few stiff malt whiskeys.

The explanation for Hedberg's absence came in the mail the next morning. On the hallway mat below the mail slot lay a single postcard: blue sky and blue sea, white sand and green palms. When he turned over the card and saw the only word written there he understood exactly: "Diving," read Waltin, smiling. Hedberg was clearly at his favorite place, devoting himself to his favorite hobby, and just like all the times before he would soon return from Java to relative civilization and his little house on northern Mallorca, where he'd settled many years ago when he'd had enough both of his fatherland and of the secret police he'd worked for.

Hedberg, thought Waltin, nodding with approval as he always did every time he thought about the brother that his constantly sick little mama had denied him, and when he did so this time he suddenly got a totally brilliant idea how he might use him to shut his deplorable and clearly paranoid boss up. For it was of course Berg who had supported Hedberg that time almost ten years ago when those lunatics at the Stockholm Police Department's assault unit were after him like a pack of howling bloodhounds. We all have a history, and I'll see to it that you don't run away from this one, thought Waltin contentedly.

It must have been almost ten years ago, thought Waltin. Those so-called detectives in Stockholm wanted to get Hedberg for a post-office robbery and two murders. The whole story was absolutely absurd and obviously quite worthy of police thinkers like that Norrland tramp Johansson and his violence-worshipping best friend, Jarnebring, who were the ones who'd let the pack loose.

First Hedberg supposedly slipped away from a bodyguard assignment, where he was guarding the minister of justice while the latter was screwing a slightly more high-class prostitute to exhaustion, and took the opportunity to rob a post office not far from the security object's love nest. Then he supposedly killed two witnesses who recognized him and wanted to extort money from him. True, he'd only run over the first one with his car, but the other one he'd killed in a rather more old-fashioned and honest way, dumping the body out at the Forest Cemetery. An ordinary old bum, so that was no doubt both pious and practical, but the peasant police had persisted anyway, even though it would have been best for all concerned just to bury the wretch and forget the whole thing. They were going to get Hedberg and that was that.

Until the minister of justice stood up and provided an alibi for his bodyguard. Hedberg had not budged an inch from the minister's side during the entire day. That's how it stood and the whole so-called case had fallen apart like a house of cards. Hedberg hadn't even been questioned for information, and all the files in the case had been carried up to Berg for forwarding. Wonder just where they went? thought Waltin with delight.

A both interesting and morally instructive story on the importance of not sticking your nose into other people's business and with a clearly humorous point. It wouldn't do to remove Hedberg, but as he was the active type that liked to move around, he wasn't all that easy to have in the office, either. Especially as there was a great deal of talk even internally. To put it briefly, Berg had had a little problem, and as so often before it was Waltin who had solved it for him. You can't expect gratitude in this world, thought Waltin, while at the same time feeling more exhilarated than in a long time. And because Hedberg clearly was good enough to get a recalcitrant minister of justice (nowadays forgotten and removed from politics) under control, then he certainly was still good enough to get Berg to fall in line.

When Hedberg wanted to quit and Berg was about to end up in an acute phase of his chronic control mania, Waltin offered to shift Hedberg over to the external operation in order to see to it, under tranquil and well-controlled conditions, that he was kept in a good mood by using him as a so-called external consultant. Berg not only supported this, he thanked him warmly, and because Waltin, in contrast to his so-called boss, was no ordinary wooden head, he'd naturally seen about documenting his gratitude. It'll work out, thought Waltin, and at the same moment the doorbell rang on his front door.

Outside stood Berg's own stable boy—he saw that through the peephole—although just now he appeared more fat than terrifying, thought Waltin as he quickly checked his morning getup in the hall mirror before opening the door.

"The earlier in the day the finer the guests," said Waltin tranquilly as he let the fat man onto his expensive rug. "What can I help you with, chief inspector?"

"Berg wants to talk with you," said Persson curtly. Don't put on airs, you stuck-up devil, he thought.

"What does he want?" said Waltin. Since he's sending his fat household slave, he thought.

"You can take that up with him," said Persson. You pompous little bastard, he thought.

"Has he forgotten to pay his phone bill?" asked Waltin innocently.

"Don't know," said Persson. "Why do you ask that?"

"Because he's sending you, chief inspector," said Waltin conciliatorily. "At this early hour."

"Shall we go?" said Persson. Or should I drag you out, although I probably won't have such good luck, he thought.

"Tell him that I'll see him in his office in an hour," said Waltin, holding the front door in a way that even someone like that ought to understand.

He evidently had too, for he only grunted something before he turned on his heel and left. And Waltin himself whistled under his breath while he stood in the shower and pondered how he would set the whole thing up. High time that he did something about little Jeanette too, he thought. He'd actually been neglecting her lately.

"You chose a preventive effort, you say," said Berg, looking at the dandy sitting on the other side of his good-sized desk, pinching his eternal trouser creases.

"Not the hint of suspicion of a crime, products that can be purchased freely on the open market and that even the Russians might need. . . . So at that point I chose to inform the corporate executives and recommended a number of preventive measures to them," Waltin summarized. Instead of injuring our exports, he thought.

"These crime-prevention measures," said Berg. "What did they consist of?" He seems completely unmoved, Berg thought as he heard the alarm bells in his head start to ring. Faintly, to be sure, but nonetheless clearly enough.

"That it was probably best they move their employee, for his own sake if nothing else, and then I arranged it so they had contact with one of our external consultants, who helped them with an analysis and a security program—forward-directed preventive measures, quite simply. I don't recall the details, but I'm assuming it was managed and invoiced in the customary way, and I definitely know that from the company's side they were very satisfied with our efforts." You should have seen the check they gave me, he thought.

"An external consultant?" asked Berg, although he ought to have listened to the alarm bells, for they were ringing louder now.

"You surely remember Hedberg, whom you asked me to take over a number of years ago," said Waltin, smiling cordially. "An extraordinary person, as it turned out, even if at the time I no doubt felt a certain hesitation regarding your decision. Yes, considering his earlier difficulties, I mean," said Waltin with the right worried smile. "So I was wrong, you were right," said Waltin, allowing his well-manicured fingers to illustrate how wrong he'd been and how right his boss had been.

Hedberg, thought Berg, and now the alarm bells were booming in his head.

"Hedberg." Waltin savored the name as though it were a fine wine. "I owe you a great debt of gratitude there, considering everything that man has helped us with over the years." Not least with the Krassner case, he thought. He almost started to giggle out loud when he saw Berg's face. I'll wait to mention the Krassner case, he decided.

That's enough now, thought Berg. That's more than enough.

"There's been a lot of talk, as you understand," said Berg, exerting himself not to sound compliant.

"Yes, I can imagine that," said Waltin empathetically, "and considering that Hedberg must have been completely innocent, I recall that you told me that the minister of justice at the time personally vouched for him, so it's really rather frightful." And let them talk, he thought, for the money I got neither you nor anyone else is going to find.

"I hope you weren't offended," said Berg. Does the trap feel like this when it closes? he thought. A week, at the most fourteen days until he had to inform Waltin that his operation would be shut down. Waltin, who certainly would not hesitate for a second to strike back and use Hedberg and his story against him.

"Certainly not," said Waltin with conviction, smiling with his white teeth. "I think your questions were completely legitimate, and considering that it's your old protégé Hedberg who has helped us, then I hope that you understand that everything has been managed in the best way." For now the shit has finally hit the right fan, and considering the context, that was probably an unusually apt description, thought Waltin.

Enough, thought Berg. And the alarm bells were thundering so it was impossible to even think.

"I understand what you mean," said Berg. What do I do now? he thought.

A little over a week at the new job and Johansson had never felt so frustrated in his entire professional life. He'd of course been aware that he would no longer be working as a police officer. It was the price you had to pay if you wanted to advance, and Johansson could actually imagine life as a high-level bureaucrat. He was good at getting people to feel comfortable and do their part and see to it that there was order in existence, even within the police department. But unfortunately that wasn't what he was working on. He'd become clear about that after a few days, and there was nothing that even suggested a different, and better, future. During the week that had passed he'd only worked on reassigning bad police officers to higher positions with the help of their extraordinary ratings, and arranging it so that good police officers got to quit early because they'd already had enough. One of them he remembered from his time with the surveillance squad. An officer fifteen years his senior, who not only was a real policeman, but who had gladly shared with a young and inexperienced Lars Martin. Johansson called him up and asked him out to lunch. If for nothing else than to get to see him and see what had happened, and—if nothing had happened after all—to try to persuade him to stay.

"It wasn't yesterday," said Johansson, nodding with warmth toward his older colleague. He looks a hell of a lot friskier than I do, he thought enviously.

The officer had clearly made the same observation, for their lunch had started with the obligatory joke about all the superintendent muscles that were swelling around Johansson's waist nowadays.

"You crossed my desk the other day," said Johansson. "Saw that you were thinking about quitting."

"And then you got the idea that you could convince me to stay," declared his older colleague.

"Yes, you see," said Johansson, smiling, "despite your advanced age you appear both clear and energetic."

"That's not the problem," said his lunch guest, shaking his head. "Do you know why I became a policeman?"

"Because you knew that you could become a good policeman," said Johansson, who already sensed what was going to come.

"Because I wanted to put crooks in the slammer so ordinary decent people could live in peace."

"Who doesn't want that?" said Johansson, and suddenly he felt gloomier than in a long time.

"I didn't for Christ's sake become a policeman to sit for days on end filling out forms that I stuff into a binder," declared the older man with a certain intensity.

Me neither, thought Johansson. I became a policeman because I wanted to be a policeman, not because I wanted to become head of the personnel bureau of the National Police Board.

"How's it going for you, by the way?" asked his guest. "I guess you'll soon have more binders to put things in than anyone else on this sinking ship."

And then they proceeded to talk about old times.

The only bright spot in Johansson's existence was the lively debate that had broken out on the personnel bureau's bulletin board over the fact that the Stockholm chief constable was nowadays swinging his pen with his visor lowered. When Johansson returned from his unsuccessful lunch mission he took a look at the latest contributions.

There was a little of everything, from various commentaries and suggestions arising from the chief constable's problematic living situation to mixed literary viewpoints: "It can't be fun to live like that" declared "A concerned colleague," while the contribution from "Unlicensed real-estate agent within the corps" was both clear and constructive: "I can arrange a studio in Sumpan for you off the books for just twenty-five bills so you don't have to spend the night on your windowsill."

Police humor is crude without exactly being warm, thought Johansson, proceeding to the literary portion: "This year's Nobel Prize winner?" speculated the pseudonym "I write too in my free time" while "Poetess in a blue uniform" was more to the point in her appreciation: "Write more! Release my longing! Slake my thirst!" Even a completely innocent Johansson was included in one corner as "Old Man from Ådalen."

Oh well, thought Johansson, sighing as he settled down behind his even bigger desk, despite the fact that the one he'd had before had been more than large enough.

It was considerably worse for himself. In a formal sense he was still a policeman, and if he was doubtful on that point he only needed to dig his police ID out of his pocket and look at it. A small national coat of arms in yellow and blue, the word "Police" in red block letters, and the only thing that might confuse a badass was possibly his highly suspect title "Bureau Head." Although on the other hand they never did look very carefully, and when by the way would he have an opportunity to flash it, for this was actually only a friendly gesture from his employers' side to keep him, and people like him, in a good mood.

Already the object of social therapeutic measures, thought Johansson, and that was when he decided. High time to clean up Krassner, he thought, taking the government office telephone book off its shelf. Next highest up on the first page, thought Johansson, and with a longer title than anyone else in all of Rosenbad. "Special adviser at the disposition of the prime minister," he read, and he dialed the number.

Not completely unexpectedly, it was the special adviser's secretary who answered his telephone.

"My name is Lars Johansson," said Johansson. "I'm bureau head at the National Police Board. I would like to speak with your boss." An extra lot of Norrland in his voice, however that might have happened, he thought.

"I'll see if he's in," said the secretary neutrally. "One moment."

Do that, thought Johansson, silently sighing, and to be on the safe side check that he hasn't hidden under his desk. And then he answered.

"We've only met in passing," said Johansson, "but now the matter is such that I would like to meet you again."

"I remember, I remember," said the voice in Johansson's telephone, and he could picture him, poured out in an easy chair and with the heavy eyelids at half-mast. "It was an interesting discussion we had."

"Yes," said Johansson. And you aren't going to be any happier this time, he thought.

"You don't want to say what it concerns?"

"There are a number of papers that I want to unload," said Johansson. "It's a long story and I'm not calling on official business."

"Yes?"

"They're about your boss," said Johansson. But it's clear, just say the word so I can heave them over to the colleagues at SePo, he thought.

"You have a hard time talking about it on the phone?" asked the special adviser.

"No," said Johansson, "but I thought it would be best if I came over so we could deal with this privately."

"Now I'm getting really curious," said the special adviser. "You don't want to . . ."

"There are greetings to your boss from Fionn," Johansson interrupted.

"One moment," said the special adviser, "just one second."

It took longer than that, more than two minutes, but then things progressed rapidly, and less than an hour later Johansson was sitting across from the special adviser in his office on the eighth floor at Rosenbad.

He's his usual self, thought Johansson. Although the smile on his lips was friendlier than the last time. An interesting smile.

"It concerns these papers," said Johansson, pushing across the bundle with Krassner's manuscript and documentation.

The special adviser nodded amiably but without even a hint of a movement in the direction of the papers he'd just been offered.

"I received them without having asked for them," said Johansson. "It's a long, involved story that, moreover, I don't intend to go into."

The special adviser nodded again.

"I've read them, naturally," said Johansson. "They deal with your boss. A few of the papers he's even written himself, and because I haven't received them as part of my job and I have no reason to suspect him of any crime, I thought that you could give them to him. I think it's really not my department," said Johansson.

"You want to relieve yourself of a worry," said the special adviser understandingly.

"Because it isn't my worry," said Johansson. "And if someone else wants to worry about it, I don't intend to get involved."

"I understand," said the special adviser, nodding.

"I've written a little memorandum on the whole thing," said Johansson, handing over the short summary that he'd written on his brother's typewriter, without signing it.

471

Obviously he'd thrown away the ink ribbon and the typing element, so his brother's electric typewriter would be of no help if someone happened to think of that.

"If you don't have any questions then I can wait while you read it," said Johansson.

"If you don't have anything against it," said his host. "Perhaps you'd like more coffee after all?"

Experienced reader that he was it had only taken him five minutes, and when he was done there were two things he had noted in particular. Forselius had clearly been right all along, and Berg's judgment of Johansson seemed to fit to a tee.

"Are you certain that SePo killed him?" asked the special adviser.

"Not SePo," said Johansson, shaking his head. "I believe their operative landed in a situation he wasn't able to handle and so he killed him and then solved his own problems by feigning a suicide."

"In that case that's shocking," observed the special adviser, without showing any particular feelings. "In that case they've made themselves guilty of a murder," he continued.

"Not they, but he," said Johansson. "My colleagues have written it off as a suicide, and the only reason they've done that is that they're convinced it was one. And should this person not appear and confess, then I see no possibility at all of opening a preliminary investigation into the case. All possible evidence of anything else is unfortunately already gone."

And what you've gotten from me isn't sufficient for that in any case, he thought.

"Do you know who the operative is?" asked the special adviser.

"Not the faintest idea," said Johansson. "You'll have to ask SePo about that." Then you'll have to see if they answer, thought Johansson.

"Correct me if I'm wrong," said the special adviser. "Your colleagues have written off the case as a suicide, from conviction you say, and there is no evidence whatsoever that might give support to suspicion of anything else, not the least reason to open a preliminary investigation. You can't even open a preliminary investigation, if I've understood the matter correctly."

"Quite correct, couldn't have put it better myself," said Johansson, smiling.

"Excuse me if I appear tedious," said the special adviser, "but you yourself are still convinced that he was murdered."

"Yes," said Johansson. "He was murdered all right."

Not my department anymore, he thought a quarter of an hour later as he stepped out into the winter sun outside Rosenbad, and the relief he felt was noticeable even in the weather. What if I were to call up Jarnebring? Go out and eat a little and ask what they want for a wedding present. If she'll let her new fiancé out, of course, and for some reason he'd also started thinking about that dark woman he'd met at that little post office up on Körsbärsvägen just two months ago. I really ought to look her up, he thought. Now that I'm a free man.

As soon as he'd said that about Fionn, the special adviser had excused himself and gone out to his secretary and called Forselius on her telephone, and unexpectedly enough he had answered at once and sounded completely sober, despite the fact that it was already late morning.

"Who is Fionn?" asked the special adviser.

"Fionn, Fionn," teased Forselius. "Why are you asking, young man? That was long before your time."

"Please excuse me," said the special adviser, "but we'll have to discuss that later."

"Fionn, alias John C. Buchanan," said Forselius.

"Buchanan was Fionn," said the special adviser in order to avoid misunderstanding.

"Fionn was Buchanan's code name, one of them," said Forselius, "and the only reason that I'm saying it on the telephone is that he's dead. Not because it's you who is asking."

"Thanks for the help," said the special adviser.

"Thus I would never dream of saying what your boss had as a code name," Forselius droned contentedly. "Regardless of what I think about him."

"We'll discuss that later," said the special adviser.

As soon as the peculiar Norrlander left, he said to his secretary that he didn't want to be disturbed for a couple of hours, and then to be on the safe side he locked himself in, in the event that his boss might nonetheless come rushing in as he had a habit of doing when he wanted to talk about something important or just socialize in the most general way.

With the help of the memorandum he'd received, his own reading habits, and the mental capacity that a generous creator had given him when he must have been in an especially good mood, it only took him a couple of hours to go through the papers he'd received. Wonder how long it took him, he thought, leafing through Johansson's memorandum, which in itself was quite uninteresting since his own problem was a different one: that he couldn't arrive at even a marginal objection to what was there. Berg was right about that business with the corners, he thought. So it was only to be hoped that he was also right about his being taciturn, he thought.

I have to think, the special adviser decided, and then I'll have to see what I should do. As things were now, there was only one thing he knew for certain. Regardless of everything else, he certainly wouldn't say anything to his boss. What he doesn't know won't hurt him, he thought, and factored into this was an awareness that he now knew things about his boss that he had never known for certain before. He'd sensed it, figured out how it probably must be, which was not so strange considering his own background and Forselius's habits with alcohol and all his more loose-lipped confidences, but at the same time he had no reason to believe that his boss suspected that he knew anything. And it has to stay that way, he thought. Out of pure concern for him, he thought, for he would prefer not to think about himself.

· · ·

The secret police operative had not only killed Krassner. In order to arrange a credible suicide in the way that he'd chosen, he must have gone through Krassner's papers and taken with him anything that might in the least jeopardize the credibility of Krassner's suicide note. Probably it was as simple as that, thought the special adviser, that he'd come across a largely finished manuscript. What Johansson had received by unclear means plus the parts that Krassner had written during his time in Sweden, which hopefully were not as scandalous as what his uncle had supplied him with.

At the same time it didn't appear particularly believable that Krassner had any documentation with him of the type that Johansson had gotten hold of. For one thing it wasn't required for the work he was doing in Sweden; for another he appeared careful to the point of paranoia, so his basic source material was certainly not something he was dragging around. Probably a largely finished manuscript—true, à la Krassner bad enough—but probably no documentation, the special adviser concluded.

The documentation Johansson had received was mostly copies, but the simple explanation for that was that Buchanan probably hadn't had anything else to give to his nephew. The few original documents were those that had been sent directly to Buchanan and that he, quite certainly against his instructions, had chosen to retain. The probable conclusion was that Buchanan's employer, the CIA, was sitting on the originals of at least the majority of the documents Buchanan had copied, certainly also counter to his instructions, and then turned over to his nephew.

In some mysterious way that Johansson hadn't wanted to go into, which he himself had avoided asking about, and which he hadn't succeeded in figuring out, the same papers had after Krassner's death ended up in the hands of Johansson, who had chosen to turn them over to him. So that he in turn could give them to his boss? On that point Johansson had not been especially clear, much less insistent, so it was probably as simple as he'd said. He had just wanted to be rid of them, and that also spoke strongly against the fact that he himself would have copied the files. It also appeared highly improbable that he could be sitting on any more originals. Not least considering the antique appearance of the document copies and that he'd actually turned over originals originally emanating from the prime minister himself.

You shouldn't complicate matters unnecessarily, thought the special adviser, who'd had William of Occam as one of his philosophical favorites ever since he was in grade school. So forget Johansson, he thought. He could probably also forget the CIA. There were papers in one of their archives but this by no means meant that they had any active knowledge of the prime minister's doings almost forty years ago. Tricky, thought the special adviser, they might know something but they don't necessarily have to.

On the other hand, if they did know something, things got simpler. Considering the security situation in northern Europe, they must be hoping Buchanan's spiritual inheritance didn't become public knowledge. Perhaps during the days of the conflict in Vietnam, and in the inflammatory conditions that then prevailed, but hardly now when the wounded relations between Sweden and the United States had been allowed to heal for many years and even the scars had started to fade. Then they had themselves to think about as well. You weren't allowed to do what Buchanan had done, never mind how incensed you might become at a former agent. Bad for business, thought the special adviser.

The problems you have are here at home, thought the special adviser, and the operative who was the cause of it all was probably the person he needed to be least concerned about. Krassner's so-called suicide note was hardly something the operative had an interest in reading about in the newspaper. Then Johansson need not be the only one to figure out what had actually happened, and Krassner's murder was actually almost the whole point.

If you started swinging that scythe, then the murderer would not be the only one to wind up in the rake. He would have company all the way up, but while he himself and Berg and Waltin, and possibly others that he didn't know, would only be forced to leave their jobs and be ass-whipped in the media in the usual way, the murderer would go to prison on a life sentence, and even though the drop in social status was relative, that could hardly be what he was hoping for. On the contrary, the suicide that he had so dexterously and cold-bloodedly arranged indicated that he absolutely did not want to get caught and that he had a considerable capacity to avoid doing so.

His dear boss would naturally have to go, despite the fact that he had no idea either of Krassner's existence or that his youthful convictions were threatening to catch up with him. For once that happened, his ignorance would be almost worse than his active involvement. The political ripple effect would of course be considerable, and the nation, the party, and the opposition would certainly be able to contain their laughter. Certain people would of course be greatly amused, but it was always that way.

We'll take that up later, for it doesn't need to get that bad, thought the special adviser, and he returned to Berg and Waltin. It was these two lightweights who had initiated, carried out, and been responsible for this entire extraordinarily poorly managed affair. Did they know anything about what had actually happened? Probably not, thought the special adviser. He was almost certain that Berg didn't know anything. True, he'd never met Waltin, but if Forselius's description was correct he hardly appeared to be the most assiduous laborer in the security vineyard. They probably neither know nor suspect anything, thought the special adviser. And if they do, they ought to have a strong and natural interest in keeping quiet about it. Out of pure instinct for self-preservation.

Provided that no one started giving them a bad time, of course, and drove them into a corner so that they stopped behaving rationally and instead started striking wildly around themselves. We actually have a little problem here, thought the special adviser, because it was he who had been the main driving force behind the secret political agreement to close down or in any case recast the so-called external operation, and as if in passing teach Berg and his coworkers to behave themselves by darkening their lives with yet another parliamentary investigation of the secret police. Good thing Johansson showed up in time, thought the special adviser, feeling almost a little energized at the thought of how he would have to convince those around him of the importance of making a complete reversal.

Forselius, he thought. What do I do with him? And considering what he now knew, he already regretted that he'd called him and asked that question about who Fionn was. True, the old man was almost eighty and drank like a fish, but there was nothing really wrong with his head. Perhaps I ought to invite him to dinner, thought the special adviser; in the worst case I can always poison his food.

The special adviser had devoted days, months, and years of his life to thinking about how one might politically defuse the security politics that Sweden had carried on in secrecy during the years after the end of the Second World War. He and Forselius had even arranged seminars where this was analyzed and discussed. Those invited had been few in number—at the most there had been seven people around the table—and everyone who came had to sign the usual confidentiality agreement.

Obviously these were only the sort of people who already knew how things stood, so you avoided wasting time on that question. At the same time there were hundreds of people who knew. Politicians and military people naturally made up the largest group, but there were also historians, journalists, and corporate executives who had acquired knowledge of the matter in various ways, as well as the usual small number of thinking people who on their own steam had figured out how things were. Of course you couldn't invite all of these people in—that was contrary to the mission and would have been both counterproductive and dysfunctional—but because the special adviser and Forselius only wanted to meet the sort of people who had something essential to say, and obviously according to their own way of viewing the matter, the number called in had not caused any problems whatsoever.

As far as Sweden was concerned, in a political-security sense the years after the end of the Second World War might best be compared with a long walk on ice that has formed overnight. What would the great neighbor in the east think up? At its heart was an almost four-hundred-year history of constant wars with and political opposition to the Russian archenemy. A country then led by Joseph Stalin and that in a geopolitical sense had never before stood so close to Swedish territory. The Russians were in Finland, in the Baltic states, in Poland, in Germany, even on the Danish islands in the Baltic Sea. Wherever you turned you only saw the Russian bear with his mighty paws, ready to deliver the final embrace.

Which way could they go? If it was a matter of flight, there was only a wounded Norway to make for, but considering how the Scandinavian peninsula looked, the only advantage of Norway was that in such a case it was a very short sprint. There was no question of throwing themselves into the arms of the West, either. First, the West wasn't interested—they had more important things to work on—and the Swedes' cooperation with the Nazis was well remembered by far too many people. Second, the Russians would naturally never allow such a thing and wouldn't even need to declare war in order to make clear to the Western powers why that wouldn't work. The West had already figured that out on its own, and considerably greater values than Swedish neutrality were at stake on the European continent. And just see how things had gone for the Poles, despite the fact that they'd allied themselves with both England and France even before the war.

The idea of a Nordic defense alliance also had to be abandoned early on, and since neither the Norwegians nor the Danes were anything to count on in a pinch, one could live with the fact that it never came to be. In that case the Finns were better, both historically and in other ways, but the Russians had already made sure of them. In such a situation only political double-dealing remained: Wave the placard of "strict Swedish neutrality" amiably toward the Russians—until your arms went numb, if necessary—and at the same time play under the covers with the American military. Take in all the help you can without being discovered. For what choice did you really have?

By and by conditions in Europe had started to normalize. The new borders that had been drawn on the map started to solidify in people's awareness. The two large power blocs had put themselves in balance. People out in Europe started believing in peace and becoming reconciled to all the new things that were the prerequisites for peace. Both Stalin and Beria were dead, and say what you will about those who replaced them, it no longer seemed completely obvious that the Russian leaders started the day with a breakfast of small children.

In the world of rationally managed politics there was no room for any feelings, and as soon as the pressure from the East had started to lessen, it came time to slacken the ties to the West in order to gradually cut the most critical lines. And bit by bit Sweden had started to execute the policy of neutrality to which it had given not much more than lip service in the previous ten years. If the date for the prime minister's farewell letter to Buchanan, April 1955, had been a coincidence determined by his personal situation—you could get that impression when you read it—it was in any event a timely coincidence. Talk that the policy being conducted should also have been "strict" was of course pure nonsense intended for the audience in the sixth row. No rational politician let himself be directed by emotions, but only pure lunatics tried to be strict.

In the mid-1950s it was high time to set up a new game plan. Swedish society had been Americanized at a brisk pace and in a confidence-inspiring way for the Americans. A country where the youth drank Coca-Cola, listened to Elvis, and had their first sexual experiences in the vinyl backseat of a Chevy convertible from Detroit was necessarily a good country. And from the Swedish side, of course, there was nothing to fear. The United States was at a secure distance geographically, and not even the Communist Party leader Hilding Hagberg believed in all seriousness that there was any risk of being attacked from that direction. That was just something he said when he went to Moscow to bring home his periodic support payments: that the Swedish military intelligence service let him be supported year after year was quite simply due to the fact that it served Sweden's security and political stability on the Scandinavian peninsula.

All that was thirty years ago, and because the special adviser lived and worked in the present, it wasn't history that was his problem. The constant postwar cheating under the cover of the wet wool blanket of neutrality was a given fact, and for him it was a matter of how the country would be able to free itself from that history without jeopardizing the policy of neutrality, which with every day that passed became an ever better and cheaper alternative.

This was the problem that his and Forselius's seminars had dealt with exclusively. The other thing was already known, so why waste time on it? Instead they had devoted all of their power to trying to propound the required conditions so that the policy that had actually been conducted during the postwar period could be openly discussed. Not with the aim of any higher measure of historical or political insight within the population—on the contrary, they were grateful that interest had decreased with the passing years—but rather because there were simply still very strong political and security reasons to do so.

Despite the fact that the secret Swedish military and political cooperation with the United States and the other Western powers was thirty years old, and that in all essentials it had ceased twenty years ago, it still had considerable political explosive force. Describing the Russian bear as more and more moth-eaten was one thing. It wasn't true, however, for his paws had never been more powerful than now; the fact that certain small teddy bears in his own winter lair had started talking back and nosing longingly in a westerly direction as soon as the wind was right only made him even more irritable.

Liberalization in the Soviet Union, the increasingly open opposition, the clearer signs of a faltering economy, had more and more often given the special adviser sleepless nights. As a thinker and strategist, given the choice between a stable dictatorship and one in democratic transformation, he obviously preferred the former because then the problems were much easier to calculate and solve. What the people who lived there thought and felt about the matter left him cold. It would be best for him if they didn't think at all. And best for them if they assigned him and people like him to think for them.

Obviously neither he nor Forselius lived with the illusion that the

Russian military intelligence service had been successfully deceived. Their political leaders had been informed long ago of the Swedish double-dealing. The Russians knew, the special adviser and those like him knew that the Russians knew, and the Russians obviously knew that the Swedish intelligence service knew that they knew, too. Everyone who knew something knew everything they needed to know, and obviously it was also known that in general terms this was an ineffective means for anyone who wanted to bring political pressure to bear to do so, as long as that knowledge could be met with total denial from the one who was being subjected to it. And as long as ordinary people only knew who they could trust.

It was the public knowledge and public questioning in Sweden in particular that were the critical factors. Simply put, it was the Swedish population that must first discover that their leaders had deceived them; as soon as they were convinced of that, they would also make it possible for the opponent to exploit the knowledge he'd had all along and transform it into a sharp-edged political weapon. From Krassner to the Swedish media to the citizens of the nation, thought the special adviser.

There was one prerequisite for the special adviser to be able to solve his problem in a risk-free way for the country and its citizens, and it was more important than all the others combined. First the Russian bear must be neutralized. To just shoot him was no longer imaginable—that possibility had passed almost fifty years ago, and if the Swedes themselves had been holding the shotgun it would probably never have existed—rather it was a matter of waiting for the time when the bear, for other reasons, had become so old, feeble, and toothless that it was completely harmless.

Only then might the people begin to uncover Sweden's secret history from the time after the Second World War. They might do that themselves, seeing to it that it happened under controlled circumstances and at a sensible pace. Preferably on the basis of new historical research, debates on the cultural pages of the newspapers, and strategically published memoirs written by old politicians whose names no one could even recall. You might even offer the occasional daring, youthful journalistic revelation.

But before that it was unthinkable, and the combination of the prime minister's youthful risky undertakings as a secret agent and Krassner's considerably later ambitions as an investigative reporter was a time bomb ticking under the sofa where the special adviser used to lie stretched out while he solved his problems. And right now he was heartily sick of them both. Furthermore, it was high time to take a shower and change clothes, for in an hour he would be feeding his old friend, mentor, and comrade-at-arms Professor Forselius.

"How is it, Bo?" said Johansson, nodding toward the broad gold ring on Jarnebring's ring finger as he helped himself from the plate of cold cuts they'd ordered as an appetizer. "I thought she was supposed to give you one with a skull on it?"

"Like before," said Jarnebring, smiling and shrugging his broad shoulders. "Damn good gal, actually. The ones with the skull were sold out, so it ended up being an ordinary plain one," said Jarnebring, spreading his fingers.

"Nice to hear, considering you're going to get married," said Johansson. "That she's a damn good gal, I mean."

"Well," said Jarnebring evasively. "That's for sure, but it's not going to be tomorrow, exactly."

"You're trying to stall for time," Johansson teased. "Skoal, by the way."

"No," said Jarnebring with a certain emphasis, as soon as he'd set down Aunt Jenny's glass. "But it's for sure that there'll be a certain adjustment."

"I thought you said it was like before," Johansson teased.

"What is it with you, Lars?" said Jarnebring. "Are you having problems at work or are you holding an interrogation, or what?"

"I guess I'm just jealous," said Johansson, sighing. Perhaps you ought to take a swing by that post office, he thought.

"And here I thought you were jealous," said Jarnebring, winking and smiling his usual wolfish grin. "Skoal yourself, by the way."

Then everything had been as usual again. A little too much aquavit, perhaps, for Johansson to feel good from it—as usual it appeared not to have
the least effect on Jarnebring—plus the usual stories in old and new ver-
sions about things that had happened since they'd last met.

"So how's your new job?" said Jarnebring.

"You want a truthful answer?" asked Johansson, sighing.

"Obviously," said Jarnebring with conviction. "How the hell would it
look if people like you and me sat and lied to each other?"

"It's probably the dreariest damn job I've had in my entire life," said
Johansson, and as he said that he felt it was the truest thing he'd said in a
good while.

"Quit, then," said Jarnebring. "You've got enough to get by. You can
start in surveillance. Become one of those old owls."

"Yes, in essence I do," said Johansson, "but that's not the problem."

"What is it, then?" asked Jarnebring. "Do they have to shut down if
you step down?"

"No," said Johansson. No, he thought. "They could certainly find
someone else."

"Know what?" said Jarnebring, patting him on the arm. "I'll give you
some good advice."

"I'm listening," said Johansson, nodding. I really am, he thought.

"Stop whining. It's only old ladies who whine, and that doesn't suit
you," said Jarnebring. "Give some real thought to how you want it to be
instead, and then it's just a matter of seeing to it that it turns out that
way. Write it down on a piece of paper and clip it securely to your big
snout so you don't forget what you've promised yourself."

First you decide how you want it to be, and then you see to it that it
turns out that way, thought Johansson. Sounds rather obvious, actually.

"Sounds good," said Johansson, nodding, because he really thought
so. "I'll think about doing that. Seriously," he added.

"That's not good enough, Lars," said his best friend, shaking his
head. "You already think too much. Just do as I say, then it will work out
famously."

"I'll do as you say," said Johansson, nodding. "Although I'll lose that bit with the piece of paper."

I'll do it. It's starting to be high time, he thought.

A simple weekday dinner with only clear lobster soup, lamb filet, and a mango sorbet; with it a Chablis, which unfortunately was perhaps a bit on the heavy side, an excellent Chambertin, and a good port wine from 1934. Far from the best of the meals they'd enjoyed together, but their conversation had as usual stayed on a very high level.

"Did you know that Queerlund was a spy for the Russians?" asked the special adviser, sniffing in his glass of red wine. Orange, he thought. Orange, and a scent of perishability.

"Do the Turks have brown eyes?" Forselius snorted. "I've warned them about that damn fairy for forty years now, but do you think there's anyone who listens?"

Queerlund was not from Denmark. He was a Swedish diplomat, now retired after a long and extraordinarily successful career. In addition he was homosexual, but in contrast to most others like him he had never made a secret of it. Within the secret police and the military intelligence service it was also an open secret that from the beginning he had sandwiched his diplomatic career with his mission as a spy for the Russians. Obviously his name was not Queerlund, for no Swede was named that. It was his code name among everyone who had tried in vain to put him away, and perhaps not well chosen, because even Queerlund used to find great enjoyment in telling everyone what they called him.

Queerlund was included in Krassner's book in the form of a concise, routine declaration of his espionage and sexual orientation and the consequences the latter could have—"a sitting duck for the KGB Call Boys"—but in contrast to everyone else, Krassner also had an explanation for why he'd never been caught. He was the prime minister's envoy to the Russians, and thereby also protected.

"Wonder why he's never been caught," said the special adviser with an innocent expression and his half-closed eyes directed toward a distant crystal chandelier. "If he's been at it so long, I mean?"

"Bah," grunted Forselius. "Hell, people like that are protected."

Oh well, observed the special adviser. No bite that time.

Then they had proceeded to talk about other things, and only when it was time for the port and Forselius was thoroughly soaked with wines from Burgundy that he baited and threw out the hook again.

"I was thinking about that Pole you told me about," said the special adviser with the same innocent expression. "The one you killed a few days before I was born."

"You can be completely calm, young man," clucked Forselius. "It had nothing to do with your mother, that I can assure you."

Watch yourself, old bastard, thought the special adviser, who didn't like it when someone spoke about his mother that way.

"I seem to recall you telling me that he'd dropped out through the window and broken his neck when he tried to flee? May I have the port, by the way?"

"Yes, what about it?" said Forselius, glaring suspiciously as he set the carafe beyond the reach of his host.

"I've heard that you shot him. May I have a little more port, please?"

"So that's what you've heard," said Forselius cunningly as he reluctantly pushed over the carafe.

"Yes," nodded the special adviser while he poured more port both for himself and for his tablecloth. "Your old friend Buchanan shot him in the back out on Pontonjärsgatan on Kungsholmen."

Forselius slid down a little in his chair, set aside his glass, and clasped his veined old man's hands over his belly while he inspected his host.

"Congratulations," he said, nodding with approval. "How did you get hold of Krassner's manuscript?"

"How'd you get hold of it yourself?" countered the special adviser. Forselius slowly shook his head and tapped his broad forehead with his index finger.

"I haven't seen a line," he said. "Who do you take me for? I knew John. I was there, I can count. It's no more difficult than that."

Nice to hear, thought the special adviser. I still don't need to worry about him.

"Tell me," said Forselius with curiosity.

Then the special adviser told him everything, except how he'd gotten Krassner's papers and who had given them to him. That was naturally the first thing that Forselius had asked.

"I understand that you don't want to say how you got them, and I also understand that it's not through the usual channels."

The special adviser smiled and nodded in agreement. For then you wouldn't have needed to ask, he thought.

"Do you believe them?"

The special adviser had thought a great deal about this but nonetheless took a good while to answer.

"I have confidence in the supplier," he said. "I've thought a great deal about the delivery. Considering who the supplier is, I'm inclined to buy the delivery as well. Yes and yes." The special adviser nodded with as much emphasis as someone like him might allow himself.

"Okay," said Forselius, and then they moved into the library where the special adviser's deaf housekeeper had set out coffee and cognac and lit a fire in the fireplace.

Then they talked business.

Forselius shared the special adviser's evaluation. Within the secret police it was probably only the operative himself who knew what Krassner knew. And if he'd understood the contents of the papers he'd taken with him at all—the suicide he'd arranged unfortunately pointed in that direction—at the same time he ought to be the one with the greatest interest in keeping quiet.

"What do you think?" said the special adviser. "Should I try to find out who he is?"

Forselius shook his shoulders hesitantly.

"I think that wouldn't be very wise," he said. "Who wants to wake a sleeping bear? And what would we do with him without being dragged along ourselves?"

So right, so right, the adviser thought and internally he sighed deeply. For if you really thought about it, it was so bad that it was he and Forselius and a number of retarded secret policemen—one of whom was clearly more actively disturbed—who had ennobled Krassner from one ordinary loony in the pile to a person of great significance for the security of the realm.

Krassner's material? Now that they both knew what was there, just how dangerous was it really?

"At the Ministry of Foreign Affairs they can certainly contain their laughter," declared Forselius. "They're no doubt working night and day to prepare the fifty-yard-line negotiations with the Russians."

New boundaries were to be drawn in the Baltic. Arriving at the negotiating table with a fresh public questioning of Swedish neutrality policy would hardly contribute to their Russian counterparts' willingness to compromise.

"What do you think if we burn the whole thing up ourselves?" asked the special adviser.

"What do you think your boss would think about that?" clucked Forselius.

"He would probably not be too happy," said the special adviser, smiling wryly.

"And what do you think he would say when he found out about Krassner and his so-called suicide?" asked Forselius with a chuckle.

"Not happy, sad, and really, really tired," said the special adviser, laughing till his fat belly jumped.

On that point they were in complete agreement. By itself they would certainly have been able to deal with Krassner's material, leaving aside whether a competent editor had put order into the messy manuscript in the meantime and transformed it into a book with hard covers from a reputable publisher. They ought to have been able to manage that too with the usual juggling between denial, silence, and undermining the author, his morals and motives. A few bruises, a few scrapes, perhaps. But that could have worked out.

But not now. Definitely not now.

"Why the hell should he fall out the window?" said the special adviser with irritation.

"Oh well," said Forselius, emptying his glass. "You don't have any more, by the way?"

He pointed toward the now-empty bottle of Frapin 1900.

"Are you joking with me?" said the special adviser. "You bet your ass I have more. I have lots and lots. You don't want to have whiskey, then?" he added, for he really had no desire to rummage around in his wine cellar in the middle of the night, with a lot of spiders and shit that he hated, and his housekeeper had let him know that she was going to slip away to visit her daughter as soon as she had set out the coffee and cognac and cleaned up in the kitchen.

"Whiskey," said Forselius with distaste. "I'll give you a piece of good advice, young man. You should never pour malt on top of grapes."

What choice did he have? First he had to go down into the wine cellar and fetch the cognac. Then they played billiards the whole night, and Forselius mixed a highball of Frapin 1900 and soda pop, great connoisseur that he was. And when the special adviser woke the next day he was compelled to phone his secretary and say that he was poorly and had to stay home.

"Poor thing," she said with genuine sympathy. "Now you must promise me you'll get better so we can see you on Monday."

Finally someone who understands, thought the special adviser, and then he took two headache pills and a large glass of water and went back to sleep again.

Waltin had finally gotten over the apathy that had lately plagued him severely. He had quite simply decided to remove the fat red-haired sow from his awareness. Simply not worth the trouble, and as far as Hedberg was concerned he would surely be in touch when he finally returned to Europe. He usually did so, if for no other reason than that he needed money.

Instead he resumed the training of little Jeanette, who had been so sadly neglected recently. They spent the weekend together down in Sörmland, where he saw to it that she had a number of new, mind-expanding experiences. When he drove her home he also assured himself that they'd left the fur coat he'd given her as a Christmas present behind—pure madness, really, when he thought about it, now it was in safe keeping, *his* keeping. High time to look around for something different and plan something new, Waltin thought as he left her off outside the doorway to her pathetic little apartment in that miserable suburb where she lived. There were any number of them out there, and in order to avoid future mistakes with types like that fat red-haired sow he also decided to confine his reconnaissance from now on to slightly better establishments. A little lower middle class, thought Waltin, for there is sure to be a lot of unredeemed longing there.

Berg wanted to meet him on Monday; he had on his funeral face right from the start. First he informed him that they were up against a new parliamentary oversight of the entire operation, but that the social democrats in the government office also wanted to get rid of the external operation. He himself had understood this all along since he, unlike Berg, wasn't an idiot, and this was the moment he'd been waiting for.

"I was thinking about asking you to develop a preliminary study so we could start by jointly considering how we should organize it instead," said Berg evasively.

"I don't understand why they have to be so impossible," said Waltin innocently. "You don't think this can have anything to do with that unfortunate story involving the Krassner person."

"I have a hard time seeing that," said Berg, and just then the alarm bells started ringing in his head again. Faintly, true, but what should he do? He couldn't of course just ask Waltin to shut his mouth and do as he was told.

"I've actually gone through the matter one more time with Hedberg, whom we had as an operative, yes, you remember him," said Waltin in a light and casual tone of voice. "And I'm completely convinced of the fact that there's nothing in this affair we need to be ashamed of. Hedberg is probably without comparison the most competent person we have access to, isn't he? I completely share your opinion of that man. He's a rock."

Hedberg, thought Berg as the booming increased in his head; he'd probably sensed it the whole time, but he hadn't thought of asking. Why must he always talk about the wrong things? thought Berg. Sometimes I get the idea he's a complete idiot, he thought.

"Krassner is history," said Berg, making an effort to sound as though it really was that way, "so I don't think we even need to think about that. Do you think you can get a preliminary study to the meeting with them next week?"

"Of course, no problem at all," said Waltin courteously, and then they moved on to talk about other things. Berg was almost preoccupied and looked as though he needed a long vacation, which suited Waltin just fine.

When he came out of the police building after the meeting with Berg he was in such a good mood that, despite the cold, he decided to walk down to the city center, where he could meet completely normal people who wanted him to help them increase the security of their economic operation and were willing to pay for it. He hadn't even left the block before one of the Stockholm Police Department's riot-squad vans glided up alongside him. Next to the driver sat Berg's retarded nephew, and the only reasonable interpretation of this was that he and his simian friends had been let off on all the complaints and had now gone back to duty. Young Berg sat with the window rolled down and his burly arm supported against the door frame, and the cold was unlikely to be the reason he was also wearing black leather gloves. And because Waltin was a civilized person he was finally compelled to say something.

"Is there something I can help you gentlemen with?" said Waltin without slowing his pace.

"Just checking that everything's calm," said Berg. "Trying to maintain general order and security."

"Feels reassuring to hear that we're on the same side," said Waltin, congratulating himself for his imperturbability.

"Makes us happy too," said Berg, suddenly sounding as sullen as a child. "We haven't always had that impression."

It was then that Waltin got his idea. A pure impulse, for how in the name of heaven could psychopaths be able to injure him, and it was high time he made that clear to them.

Waltin just stopped, and because the driver hadn't managed to put on the brakes he was forced to back up a yard before Berg again had eye contact with Waltin.

"It's probably not me you should be worried about," said Waltin lightly, glancing at his watch. "And if you gentlemen are going downtown anyway you can drive me to Norrmalmstorg," he said. And you should certainly be careful about playing poker, thought Waltin when he saw the surprised shift in Berg's expression. Of course he also waited until the driver jumped out and held open the door for him. It's not just your uncle who can shut things down, thought Waltin as he climbed into the van.

When Berg arrived at the weekly meeting the special adviser wasn't there. Berg glanced inquiringly at his empty seat as he sat down, and the minister of justice nodded with a worried expression.

"Unfortunately he had to run off," said the minister. "It was a close friend of his who passed away. He sends greetings, by the way, and regrets that he couldn't be here."

Close friend of his, thought Berg, astonished. Wonder what such a person is made of? But naturally he hadn't said that. Saying such a thing would probably be the last thing he'd do, he thought.

First he took up the ongoing survey of extreme right-wing elements within the police; he started by recounting the disturbing observations that Waltin had reported to him the day before.

"We unfortunately have encountered certain problems with our data collection," said Berg cryptically.

"Is it the computers that are causing trouble again?" asked the minister without the slightest hidden motive.

"If it were only that good," said Berg, shaking his head. "No, unfortunately it's worse than that, I'm afraid."

And when he'd said A he might just as well say B, he thought.

"A couple of our field agents, infiltrators, as certain people say, have expressed concern that they might be at risk of being unveiled, so we've been compelled to bring them home to the building and break off," said Berg. "We must find some way to regroup before we can continue."

"Good Lord," said the minister with genuine concern. "There isn't any risk that something will happen to them, is there?"

What would that be? thought Berg. We're living in Sweden, after all, and it's policemen we're talking about. Both my own men and the ones they're spying on.

"It probably needn't turn out that badly," said Berg soothingly.

"Nice to hear," said the minister, appearing sincerely relieved.

Under the "remaining questions" point, and before they departed, Berg only let it be known that they were in the process of putting together the requested preliminary study about the external operation, giving it the highest priority, and that he counted on being able to submit it at the next meeting. The minister of justice seemed almost embarrassed as he said that, and the chief legal officer suddenly excused himself and took off.

"I believe perhaps our friend from the Cabinet Office expressed himself less well than he might have the last time we met," said the minister, clearing his throat and casting a meaningful glance at the relevant person's empty chair.

"Far be it from me to question either your viewpoints or your motives," said Berg courteously. For I'm not that stupid, he thought.

"I haven't thought that, either," said the minister cordially, "but I have tried to speak with our mutual friend in order to get him to understand that this is such a complicated affair: It really is something that bears thinking about in peace and quiet. It's not something you should be rash about, I mean."

The minister leaned forward and lowered his voice. "Without being indiscreet," he continued, "it was actually he who asked me for advice on a related matter, and so I also took the opportunity to say what I thought about this."

I see, thought Berg. So that's how it went.

"And I actually succeeded in convincing him," said the minister contentedly.

"Nice to hear," said Berg, despite the fact that the only thing he was really hearing were the alarm bells ringing in his own head.

"It will have to take the time it takes," declared the minister with a confirming nod. "For me it will be just fine if we can clear this up sometime during the spring."

What is it they're really up to? thought Berg as he stepped out through the doors to Rosenbad. At an internal seminar they'd had at work, the lecturer had described something that was evidently called Anderson's Confusion Strategy, after the American psychologist who had invented this method, which was dubious, to say the least. Evidently what the whole thing amounted to was that you continually sent contradictory messages to the person you were out to get, while at the same time oscillating between cordiality and threats. According to the lecturer, in a normal case it only required a rather small dose of this before the object was ready for both the pillbox and the straitjacket.

That can't be what he's up to, thought Berg, and the one he was thinking about was the prime minister's special adviser. Although it's clear. He's certainly capable of most anything, thought Berg.

It was Forselius's Polish cleaning woman who had found her employer. He was lying dead right inside his own front door when she opened it, and as she had studied medicine at the university in Lodz before she finally succeeded in getting from there to Sweden and the Swedish social home service, she had no problem at all with that. Forselius was dead; everything indicated that he had died rather recently and that he had probably suffered a stroke. In addition, as usual he was wearing his stained dressing gown and reeked of cognac.

His cleaning woman had dialed the telephone number she was supposed to dial if something happened and almost immediately a number of people had arrived. All of them men, all of them both friendly and taciturn, and one of them certainly also a doctor.

So it figured that he'd been some sort of high-ranking spy, she thought, but with her background this wasn't something you talked about. Then one of them had driven her home, told her she shouldn't worry, that she would be off work the rest of the week, that she would nonetheless get her pay as usual, that she wasn't to talk with anyone about what had happened, and that he or one of his colleagues would get back to her if there was anything more.

That suited her fine. Forselius had been more troublesome than all the others she cleaned for combined. She'd gone to the day care and fetched her little boy and then they'd played the whole afternoon in a park that was in the vicinity of their apartment.

The special adviser arrived right after the people from the military intelligence department but a good while before the bunglers from the secret police, who, unfortunately, had to take care of the formalities.

They'd known each other for more than twenty years, but when he looked at the old man there on his own hallway rug he was forced to ask himself what he really felt. Sorrow? Regret? Worry? Nothing in particular?

"Do you have any idea what he died of?" he said to his own doctor, who was kneeling over the body.

"You mean what he didn't die of," said the doctor, smiling wryly and shaking his head. "Well," he continued, sighing dejectedly. "That will no doubt be seen in the autopsy, but if you want a preliminary guess I believe he had a massive cerebral hemorrhage. He was actually almost eighty, even if he refused to realize that."

A shame about a brain like that, thought the special adviser.

When they went through the contents of Forselius's wallet, a sturdy, old-fashioned affair of brown leather that he always carried in his back pocket, they found a folded-up envelope with a handwritten text in Forselius's handwriting: "In the event of my death." In the envelope was a slip of paper with another brief, handwritten message, "You should die when it's the most fun, JF," and judging by the usual forensic indications he might very well have written that a half-century ago when he was sitting in the secret building on Karlaplan, breaking codes.

I'll be damned, thought the special adviser. I miss him already.

CHAPTER XVII

And all that remained was the cold of winter

Mallorca in February

Hedberg had returned from the humid heat on Java to his little house on northern Mallorca where he'd been living in forced exile for almost the past decade. When he landed at the airport in Palma he'd been met by a cooling, early summer wind—it was almost seventy degrees even though it was only the first week in February—so in any event he couldn't complain about the weather. He picked up his car from long-term parking where he'd left it a good month earlier and then drove home to the house in the mountains north of Alcudia. There were worse days than this, he thought.

Not all his days had been good. Considering that he hadn't even been called for questioning, much less indicted or convicted, he'd nonetheless been subjected to a shocking assault on his rights. Naturally he'd been allowed to retain his job, but all the whispering in the corridors, the sudden silence when he came into the break room, colleagues who openly avoided him, all this had nonetheless made it impossible for him. Besides, he didn't feel at home behind a desk. And all just because he'd tried to protect himself against a small-time gangster and a bum who tried to extort him for money that was rightfully his.

When he got the invitation to come over to the external operation and work for Waltin it almost felt like a liberation. There had been plenty of money too, a few times there had actually been quite a lot, and he liked Waltin. He was a talented guy with a lot of charm and quite a few interesting ideas. Besides, Hedberg knew that he could trust Waltin, almost as if they'd been brothers and grown up together, despite the fact that they really didn't see each other all that often.

So he'd been all the more surprised when he went through the papers that he'd taken from that American journalist and at first had intended to get rid of in some secure way. Not that his English was like Waltin's, but in any case he knew enough to understand most of what was there, and for a while he'd even gotten the idea that Waltin had duped him.

But the more he thought about it, the more unbelievable it seemed. It was probably no more complicated than that Berg and those social democrats in the new government that he worked for were in league with each other and that Waltin had been duped just as much as himself. Berg with his sanctimonious exterior and his well-oiled mouth was naturally the one they'd turned to in order to remove the embarrassing files the American was sitting on. Documents that showed what every thinking person ought to have been able to figure out on their own: that the country was being run by a traitor and a Russian spy. True, Hedberg hadn't been aware that in addition he'd managed to worm his way in with the CIA in his youth, but considering all the other things he'd done, such as have his best friend murdered, for example, that had hardly come as a surprise. Nor that he got away with it that time either. Of course people like that always get away with it.

Waltin was probably as fundamentally duped as he was, and considering what had happened it was just as well. How would he have been able to discuss this with Waltin? It would have been the same as signing your own life sentence. If only he'd been certain that he could trust Waltin completely, then he wouldn't have hesitated a moment to tell him the whole thing. The problem was that during his entire life he hadn't met a single person who had shown themselves to be completely reliable when it really counted. So it was also wisest to keep quiet about what he knew. At least until he could be sure that not only Krassner but the whole affair really was dead and buried.

· · ·

Actually it was he who was the real victim. He would never have dreamed of even defending himself against such a person as Krassner, if he'd only known who he was and what he was working on. On the contrary, he would have treated him to a beer or two, for he'd earned it, considering the job he was working on. He hadn't had any choice, and exactly like the time before he'd only tried to defend himself.

Suddenly he'd just stuck the key in the lock and stepped right in, and because Hedberg had been standing on the other side of the door in a narrow coat closet there hadn't been anywhere to go. And instead of asking him what he was doing there—he was, after all, dressed like an ordinary laborer, so he ought to have thought of that—Krassner had just attacked him and started by trying to head-butt him, and then when he'd dropped him to the floor he'd first tried to knee him and then bite him, and in that situation Hedberg no longer had any choice. He'd been forced to defend himself, and unfortunately he'd happened to break Krassner's neck along the way. Pure self-defense, and if there was anyone who was a victim in this story it was he. To start with he had of course been duped into it, exploited in order to protect the greatest traitor in Swedish history.

The rest had been pure routine. He'd thought about throwing him out through the window from the start. For what else could he have done? The guy couldn't just lie there. But because he still had to photograph his papers, he'd happened to see that introduction that he'd written to his book, and when he'd looked at it it had suddenly struck him that this was a typical suicide note, and then there wasn't too much left to think about. He'd sorted a suitable pile for that traitor Berg and those other idiots, kept the rest for himself, and seen to it that it all appeared normal. Most of the time had gone to changing the ribbon in the typewriter and typing a new, similar suicide note, which he'd then put in his pocket and taken with him. He'd put the real one in the typewriter, and he'd seen that there were prints on it when he held it up against the lamp. Thank the devil for that, by the way. It was of course actually Krassner who had written it.

Then he'd broken loose the catch on the window, lifted him up, and thrown him out. Rather a grand sight, actually, as he fell straight down, and it was only when he hit the ground that he'd seen the bum who was prowling along the building exterior with his mangy pooch and almost got the whole package right in the face. When he'd pulled in his head so as not to be unnecessarily visible, he'd seen that one shoe had evidently fallen off when he was wriggling the body out through the rather narrow window. It wouldn't do to have it lying on the floor, so he'd picked it up to throw it out too, and because the bum had just been standing there glaring with his silly little dog he'd made a serious attempt to put it right in his cap. Although this time it wasn't exactly a quarter, like when the bums were sitting down in the subway begging change for liquor. Unfortunately he'd missed and instead hit the pooch, which had folded up and lain down flat on the ground. And nothing more than that had happened. He'd just packed up, made a final quick check, and left the place. The rest had been a question of maintaining a good face, which wasn't too difficult since Waltin was the only person he needed to talk to.

Typical suicide, if anyone were to get the idea of asking him. One of the most typical he'd heard about, actually, with a letter left behind and the whole shebang. Ought to sit like a sports cap on those retarded policemen in Stockholm, thought Hedberg, and then he hadn't thought about it again.

CHAPTER XVIII

And all that remained was the cold of winter

Stockholm in February

The Stockholm chief constable had received very positive reactions to his New Year's greeting in the police department's newspaper. Many people had contacted him, both inside and outside the corps, not least many women who had been tremendously appreciative. All this warmth coming his way had strengthened him in his conviction that perhaps it was high time that he realized yet another of his visions.

If you disregarded his literary activities—for there it was more a matter of an inner calling—the chief constable had two great interests in life: physical training and police problem-solving, or detective work, as it was usually more popularly called. Every year he spent hundreds of hours on jogging tracks and ski trails, and it was during one of these exercise rounds that he'd gotten the extraordinary idea of creating an internal training course in qualified police problem-solving. Obviously nothing for the hoi polloi, but an exclusive forum for the most promising and most qualified of his many coworkers. The actual training operation, lectures, and seminars that he saw before him, he intended to run himself. The lack of qualified forces from other quarters was unfortunately apparent and moreover was one of the reasons that he had developed his thoughts in this area.

He had devoted a great deal of his time to thinking about what he should call the operation. This business of sending the right signals was not only important but often completely decisive. Since it was quite clear that the great deficiency in all investigations of serious crimes was that the intellectual analytical work was neglected in favor of running around out in the so-called field, knocking on doors and talking to witnesses and family members and a lot of other peculiar, time-consuming activities, he'd first thought about christening his lecture series "The Armchair Detective," but because so few of his coworkers understood English he had dropped that idea early on.

It was then that he had his flash of genius: "The Scientific Detective"! At the first seminar he planned to take up the new systematic arrangement of police clues that he'd developed during all the hours he'd spent on the jogging trails out at the police academy in Ulriksdal to which he'd transferred his regular fitness training. A good system of classification as a foundation; that was the solid ground that must be laid before the purely analytical work could begin, and managed correctly, there wasn't a crime, however difficult it might appear, that couldn't be solved by correct intellectual operations. You wouldn't need to leave the meeting room where you were sitting at all other than to eat, go to the toilet, stretch your legs, and whatever else was necessary in a physical sense, but obviously had nothing to do with the work itself.

He had invited only ten participants to the first seminar, "A Systematic Classification of Police Clues." Kudo and Bülling, of course; his own Deputy Chief Inspector Grevlinge, who perhaps wasn't exactly God's gift to the police academy, but a very industrious and loyal force; an experienced and skillful technician by the name of Wiijnbladh, whom he'd never met—it was the head of the tech squad who'd given him the tip—as well as a few other officers. In addition there were a few external talents, for as always in an intellectual, analytic context it was imperative that you got new, fresh input from outside. It was his best friend, who was now an executive in state-owned industry but who had earlier had a long history as a consultant to the department, who had promised to ask a good friend of his, a former diplomat who had a very high position in the foreign ministry and solid experience of his own in police investigation. And this person had in turn contacted one of his acquaintances, a press spokesman with the National Police Board who also brought great personal experience of "forceful exertions in manly connections and environments," as the former ambassador summarized it in the very friendly letter that he'd written to the chief constable to thank him for the invitation to the seminar.

After he'd welcomed the participants he started with a little lecture on historical scientific detectives both in literature and in so-called real life, and he'd brought in Holmes, Bertillon, and Locard, and his own great predecessor in the subject, Georg Liljensparre. Only after that had he gotten onto the subject of his own system of classification.

"You must always have a main track," the chief constable began. "By main track I mean the clue that in the light of earlier empirical experience of similar criminal actions is in statistical terms the most probable."

No one had had any objections, and most of them had diligently taken notes.

"As far as the next most likely alternative is concerned," the chief constable continued, "I have chosen to characterize it as the alternative main track. This has among other things the advantage," he added, "that if new information should present itself that alters the original probabilities of various alternatives, then it's simple enough to make an alternative main track the main track and vice versa. Any questions?"

"What do we do about the broad unprejudiced effort?" wondered one of those invited, whose name he'd forgotten. He had to ask Grevlinge afterward.

"On that point there is no reason for concern," the chief constable, who had thought of everything, reassured him. "At the next level, the third level below the main track and the alternative main tracks, we have thus a greater or lesser number of so-called secondary tracks, and the great advantage with that is that we are free to have as many secondary tracks as might need to be mobilized based on the particular case."

The congregation had pondered this obvious point in deep silence.

"Imagine a pyramid, a logically constructed pyramid," said the chief constable. "Moving from bottom to top we have secondary tracks, alternative main tracks, and main tracks, and obviously we work in the opposite direction from top to bottom, digging down intellectually, so to speak."

"An excellent ground rule in all analytical work," agreed the retired diplomat.

"Exactly," assisted Kudo, who realized that it was high time to say something if he wasn't going to be run past by a bunch of civilians.

Strange characters, by the way. If it hadn't been an impossible thought he himself would have guessed that all three were homos. That character in the leather jacket who was some sort of spokesman at the National Police Board was hardly the type you'd want to run into in a dark alley. Especially not in Skeppar Karls gränd, for wasn't it there that they had their little society? thought Kudo, who had a history with the Stockholm Police Department's old vice squad.

"Agent Bülling and I already work like that," added Kudo.

"Always from the top down," mumbled Bülling, carefully pulling his foot in because there was clearly someone who was stepping on his toes the whole time.

"Excellent, excellent," praised the chief constable, who thought it was now high time that he unveiled one of his analytical innovations. "Gentlemen, if I say 'the wrong track,' what do you think of?"

"Well," said Grevlinge. "That's the kind of thing that crooks get up on the dupe front. To dupe you and your colleagues, that is." Grevlinge looked around with a certain hesitation, since it was a while since he himself had been involved.

I must do something about Grevlinge, thought the chief constable. Send him to a course or something.

"In a traditional sense, yes," said the chief constable. "But if I say 'police wrong track,' what do you think of then?"

Nothing, judging by the empty faces looking back at him.

"An innovation," the chief constable explained with a certain pride. "Everyone around this table has surely at some point landed in a situation where you want to confuse your opponent, lead him astray, deceive him, quite simply. Thence also the police wrong track or simply the wrong track, as I myself prefer to call it since it's we in the police who in this connection have both the initiative and the advantage of interpretation."

"Obviously," agreed Kudo. "If you lose the initiative you're lost."

"For the same reasons I would like to propose a change of termi-nology, namely that from now on we reserve the expression 'wrong track' for those consciously false clues that we ourselves choose to set out, while the earlier 'wrong track'—that is, what the crooks have set out—will be called 'false tracks' from now on. In addition this gives the right signals," the chief constable underscored with a certain emphasis. "The crooks set out false tracks while we ourselves set out wrong tracks."

"I have a suggestion," said his best friend.

"I'm all ears," said the chief constable, because his best friend was a highly talented man.

"I was thinking about suggesting that we complement your otherwise extraordinary analytic model with something I myself would like to call 'dead-end track,' " said his best friend.

Dead-end track, thought the chief constable, feeling the intellectual excitement growing in his head like the bubbles in a newly opened bottle of soda pop. Crystal clear but at the same time stimulating.

"Would you mind developing that?" he said.

This his best friend had done with both joy and all the brainpower of which he was capable. From his own activity in state-owned industry—it was there he'd gotten the idea—he had discovered that sometimes you were compelled to have a workforce in reserve in order to be able to meet what was new and unexpected or simply the strain of additional demand in general. So that these people wouldn't have to sit around dawdling in the meantime, or even worse get up to something, he created a reserve of duties of a purely make-work nature. A kind of completely harmless nonwork that at the same time had all the outward characteristics of work.

"The advantage with a dead-end track is that it doesn't lead anywhere," summarized his best friend. "At the same time it looks exactly like an ordinary clue," he added.

"What do you mean, exactly?" said the chief constable slyly. "If you could expand that somewhat in the police context, I mean."

"Imagine that you have a large surveillance force where you can't keep everyone occupied but at the same time you want to have a reasonable reserve just in case," said his best friend. "Drive them out onto a dead-end track until you need them."

Ingenious, thought the chief constable. His best friend hadn't become his best friend by chance.

"It would be excellent if you could write this down for the next time we meet," said the chief constable, nodding with genuine warmth. "Yes, gentlemen. Should we perhaps be thinking about moving along? Any concluding questions?"

There was only one who had raised his hand. He hadn't said anything the entire time. A skinny little character, the one who came from the tech squad, and whose name he hadn't even needed to learn since he was here for the first and the last time.

"My name is Wiijnbladh," said Wiijnbladh. "I work at tech and I have a small question."

Get to the point sometime, thought the chief constable sourly and contented himself with nodding. The fellow looks like a sparrow, he thought. How he got into the academy is a pure mystery.

"What do we do about the ordinary clues?"

What the hell is he saying? thought the chief constable. Ordinary clues?

"Ordinary clues?"

"Yes, fingerprints and bloodstains and that sort of thing," Wiijnbladh clarified.

"I see, those," said the chief constable. "Those I was thinking about coming back to in another context."

The sparrow was content to nod, which was a good thing for him since there were always vacant positions at the parking bureau out in Västberga, and instead the chief constable rounded off their meeting with a few well-chosen words.

"To quote the greatest detective that ever lived . . ." said the chief constable. "To quote the greatest of all detectives," he amended, for on closer thought he of course hadn't lived in a formal sense but rather only in a novel or two. . . .

"When we have ruled out everything that is obvious or merely believable and only the unbelievable remains . . . then, gentlemen . . . then nonetheless it's that which is the truth, however unbelievable that might seem," said the chief constable, nodding solemnly.

That man has The Gift, thought Kudo.

. . .

The special adviser didn't go to Forselius's funeral, but when all the others had left and before the cemetery workers had filled in the family grave where he would rest, he took the opportunity to lower a final greeting to him: an ordinary plastic bag with a couple of bottles of Frapin 1900 plus a copy of his own old dissertation on stochastic processes and harmonic functions. Then he drove back to Rosenbad, where there was a great deal to tackle, and from now on he would be forced to do it himself. What do I do about Krassner? he thought. After he'd spoken with the minister of justice he understood that the message to Berg had been delivered, and he hoped he would get a period of peace and quiet. Hopefully he wouldn't need to think about it at all.

He'd gone through a few economic analyses that he'd gotten from the military, and if he were to believe them the Russian bear was in the process of falling to its knees. The economy wasn't up to it, quite simply, and sooner or later something would happen. But what would happen? he thought. And when?

His boss didn't appear to be very cheerful either, and within the party there was a great deal of talk in more or less closed circles about the prime minister's falling approval ratings and how that would influence the party's possibilities in the next election. At the same time a palace revolution didn't appear particularly likely. Social democrats didn't get involved in that kind of thing, but it wasn't good, and sooner or later something would have to be done. The well-being of the individual was secondary to the well-being of the party, he thought, and for a moment—it must have been Krassner who flickered past in his awareness—he was a hair's breadth away from starting to think along the forbidden lines that solved the majority of both his own and the party's problems. Stop, he thought, for such things don't happen here. They were still living in Sweden, after all.

. . .

At the weekly meeting Berg confirmed that the ongoing survey of the extreme right-wing elements within the police had been put on ice for the time being, but given the situation he chose not to even comment on it. Now it was the doctrine of least possible disturbance that prevailed, and in that connection an abandoned survey of a number of unsuitable police officers was a low price for a little peace and quiet. After the meeting he took Berg aside—the minister was of course the way he was and this time he wanted to make certain that the message had really gone out—and saw to it that the most recent intentions regarding the future of the secret police really had been made clear enough. But Berg never ceased to amaze him. He appeared almost absentminded and mostly nodded in agreement regardless of what he said.

When Berg returned to work he'd decided something. Quite apart from what he'd just heard he had no intention of giving way to Waltin and his transparent attempts at extortion. It was sink or swim, thought Berg, and the advantage with people like him was that as a rule they swam and almost never sank, regardless of what happened. Waltin had to go and he knew exactly how he would get rid of him. So he called him up and reminded him of the financial data on the external operation that he wanted turned in. He also emphasized that he was especially interested in the economic aspect of the operation. The gold watch around Waltin's wrist perhaps helped him keep the time, but for Berg it was an indication of where he should look for his opponent's weaknesses.

He let Persson sit in on the entire meeting to take notes, but above all because he had a salutary and subduing influence on Waltin, and Berg didn't intend to listen to any more drivel about Hedberg this and Hedberg that.

"So it would be good if we could get the economic figures by next week," said Berg. "Then the auditors will have the time they require."

"Fine with me," said Waltin, nodding and smiling.

The gauntlet has been thrown, he thought, and personally he didn't intend to pick it up. On the other hand, he intended to bring home Hedberg in order to get his help with weeding out the stacks of papers and securing the money that was flowing around in the system and that was rightly his and no one else's.

Johansson had spent the weekend thinking about what he should do with his life. He wasn't exactly getting younger, and if life wasn't going to slip through his fingers it was high time that he took hold of it. The slip of paper that Jarnebring had recommended had rather quickly been scribbled full and needed to be recopied. Jarnebring had also phoned and asked how he was doing.

"How's it going?" said Jarnebring. "I have a front seat that's waiting for us both."

That time is probably past, I'm afraid, thought Johansson as he put down the receiver, and frankly he didn't miss it anymore. There were other things that were more important, and as a first measure when he came to the board on Monday he requested a leave of absence starting March 1.

The national commissioner contacted him by phone only an hour later. Might he possibly be able to speak with him?

How do you reply to that? he thought, and when he was finally sitting there and saw that the fellow really appeared sincerely sorry about the fact that he risked losing him, he had almost regretted it.

"I think it's as though I've come to a halt," said Johansson, putting on a little extra Norrland accent as he usually did as soon as the need arose. "So I've been thinking that it's high time that I get more education. Was actually thinking about registering at the university and studying a little."

Peculiar thing about all these academics that ran the police, he thought as he was leaving an hour later. They got all excited as soon as someone like him so much as hinted at wanting a little education, and if Johansson hadn't put his foot down he could certainly have taken half his salary with him to rest up at an institution of his own choosing with an ever-so-distant connection to the legal system. The national commissioner had for some reason recommended studying law, and Johansson had thanked him for the tip and promised to think about it. Whatever. His application would be granted and thus he'd set an end point for the professional misery that he'd landed in.

It was no longer of vital importance to wine and dine the union. Much less raise Aunt Jenny's glass in their company, he thought, and what he would like to do with them instead he didn't need to think about either. He intended to clean off his desk, but first of all it was high time that he do penance considering the casual attitude he'd evinced when his predecessor in the position—now surely a happy man—asked him for help and advice with that wretched Koskinen.

Officer Koskenkorva was now head of the Stockholm Police Department's command center and living proof of the fact that traveling testimonials were an infallible means of moving up within the corps. Koskenkorva had barely had time to set his rear end in his chair and hide his namesake vodka in the clothes closet before it was time again. The pile of appeals, complaints, union opinions, and the usual collegial beefs that was heaped on Johansson's desk was quite improbable considering that the person concerned never did a lick of work and to be on the safe side got drunk whenever he was supposed to do any.

The operational head of the uniformed police in Stockholm, an old hooligan who was both efficient and completely to Johansson's taste, had decided to carry out a large preparedness drill in order to find out what sort of people his personnel really were. A scenario had been outlined in which His Majesty had been subjected to an attack during a reception at the palace in Stockholm and the perpetrators succeeded in escaping from the crime scene and were now somewhere in the great cement city between the customs gates. The description of the wanted persons that would be sent out was both contradictory and highly believable, the vague description of their escape car and escape routes equally so, and altogether it looked to be an interesting test of what the police in the capital were actually capable of when what couldn't happen had nonetheless happened. Because the operational head also knew what they were made of, he'd chosen to plan the entire drill for Monday morning.

Koskenkorva had a central role in all this. Put simply he was the spider in the web if something were to really happen, and unfortunately he'd gotten wind of the whole affair. The misery had rolled along, the union had jumped onto the bandwagon, for this type of information might become a real murder weapon in the hands of the employers. And the introductory drizzle of objections had quickly turned into a hailstorm.

On the other side was a thin blue line: the personnel in the riot squad, of course. When Johansson thought about Berg's horrible nephew, who had now gone back into active duty despite Johansson's brave attempts to get him parked in a cell, where he naturally belonged, a shadow had fallen across his face. In addition there was the anonymous society called Still Functioning Uniformed Police in Stockholm, which had made contact with his predecessor when Koskenkorva's appointment had been in the works during the fall. Finally, a number of individual voices had been raised that in sum said it was "high time for a little action."

One of the few who didn't have anything to say about the matter was the Stockholm chief constable. He's no doubt writing in his little blue book, thought Johansson, but merely as a matter of form he nonetheless called him up to hear what he thought. His voice sounded guarded, thought Johansson, like all aesthetes when their circles are disturbed by simple types like himself. It's all the same, he thought, and then he briefly recounted his view of the matter.

"I've already solved that question," said the chief constable. "But thanks for your concern."

"Excuse me," said Johansson. "I don't really understand."

No, who would have thought that? thought the chief constable, sighing.

"The drill you were wondering about," said the chief constable, making an effort to speak slowly and clearly the way you would if you were speaking to a child. "I've had a simulation carried out instead," he explained. "A kind of police war game, if you understand what I mean."

"Actually not," said Johansson. "You wouldn't be able to explain—"

"Don't worry yourself," interrupted the chief constable. "And if you'll excuse me I actually have other, more important matters on my agenda."

The bastard hung up, thought Johansson, looking with surprise at the receiver in his hand. He hung up right in my ear.

The whole thing was really rather simple, and that kind of practical drill based on some sort of obsolete boot-camp model was not only violently overrated, costly, and risky, it also missed the essential, namely the honing of intellectual preparedness, while encouraging driving around street corners on two wheels with howling sirens and screeching tires.

The chief constable had also tried to explain that to the so-called operational head, but as usual the man had refused to listen. He'd let Grevlinge take charge and they would no doubt be able to find something for him, and if they didn't then it was his bad luck. Västberga, thought the chief constable, and then he'd decided it was high time to have a look at them even though it was Monday morning and he really had more important things on the program, like his workout session and that course in creative writing he'd had his mistress order from the community college.

Obviously he'd chosen an intellectual approach. The drill organizers had been allowed to borrow the police administration's conference room, and by moving a few tables together in the middle of the room they had been able to set out the large general map of the police district that usually hung on the wall. The necessary written information with the applicable assumptions had been passed out to all the participants, and when the alarm was given it was only a matter of going to work.

Chief Inspector Koskinen sat at a smaller table at one end of the room while the others walked around, moving the vehicles and other units as he directed and positioned and redirected, and at times it got rather hectic before the perpetrators could be arrested. Because everyone was in the same room they had also gotten by completely without radio communication. They talked and passed notes to each other, and it wasn't more difficult than that, even if purely verbally and for the sake of realism they had of course used the usual hailing codes.

"I would like to congratulate you on a well-performed job," said the chief constable, nodding graciously at Koskinen. Good Lord, he looks completely worn out, he thought. Must have been tough.

"Yes, it worked out," puffed Koskinen. "Despite the fact that it was Monday morning when it happened. May I offer you a throat lozenge, by the way?"

Koskinen was clearly a little under the weather—had a cold, he explained—and you realized that although the fellow reeked of menthol tablets, he'd nonetheless heeded the call to arms when the trumpets sounded. Which only showed that I was right the whole time when I refused to listen to all the whining about his appointment, thought the chief constable contentedly when he returned to his office. For that matter, high time to put on my running shoes. A sound mind in a sound body, thought the chief constable, and in the evening he thought seriously about drinking a few glasses of red wine while he tuned the strings of his inner lyre.

CHAPTER XIX

And all that remained was the cold of winter

Stockholm in February

Waltin was in the habit of keeping everything sensitive in his head. He'd learned that early on, and there would have to be compelling reasons to put something on paper within the operation where he worked. He had no great faith in auditors, either, and if you simply kept things orderly around you there was no reason to fear them. Nonetheless—and this he knew—people did make mistakes. This applied to him as well, and for that reason he was very careful about inspecting the papers that were to be turned over to Berg.

The money didn't worry him. Everything essential was already taken care of, and on that point he didn't have the least concern. Certain withdrawals and transfers could, however, still be made, an invoice or two might be supplied with the right date and inserted into the bookkeeping, and if you minded the pennies the dollars tended to take care of themselves. Hedberg's little foreign company in the security industry, the one that Waltin owned but with Hedberg's name on all the files, would shortly receive a substantial replenishment of liquid assets.

Because he was forced to do what he was doing, he'd taken the opportunity to amuse himself royally while he did it. He'd sorted and turned in the material in the most confusing way, attached hard-to-read handwritten scraps of paper with questions and opinions on everything between heaven and earth, which was innocent enough and totally uninteresting if it was really him that they were after. The auditors might as well have to earn their keep while they were at it.

Berg never ceased to surprise him. Waltin had been completely convinced that the coward would roll over when he tossed Hedberg out on the table. But he hadn't. Instead Berg had obviously thrown a wrench into his plans, even if he'd needed that fat-ass Persson in order to put up real resistance. Inspected closely, his own cards weren't especially good, either. What could he say? That he had reason to suspect that his own operative had killed Krassner and feigned his suicide? In which case, why had he kept quiet about the matter for more than two months? Not good, not good at all.

But apart from his mounting irritation at a totally incompetent boss, there was nothing to suggest that if everyone just sat quietly in the boat, things would go wrong. As it was now, they were in the process of dismantling a perfectly functioning organization simply because some social democrats in the government office building wanted to be ornery with them. This was pure madness, and even wanting to discuss the matter at all showed how weak you were. He'd spoken with Hedberg on the telephone several times but he seemed almost evasive. Did he suspect anything? Did he have any clue that Waltin was trying to lure him home to Sweden in order to lock him up in prison? Hedberg was far from being a genius, but he was sufficiently intelligent for the kind of thing Waltin usually used him for. He was a calm, likable person, and above all else he was reliable. In addition, considering their history together, he was the very last person Waltin wanted to quarrel with. Anyone at all, but not Hedberg.

Finally he'd been forced to take the bull by the horns and explain to Hedberg that he now so help me God had to come home to Sweden to help clean up. There were things that Waltin didn't understand and that Hedberg might possibly help him with. The sort of things that you couldn't discuss on the telephone, for they both knew that so-called secure lines only existed in the believer's imagination. And perhaps if he now distrusted Waltin, he ought to take a look at the amounts that had flowed into the company's account recently. Money that Waltin had turned over to Hedberg with full confidence and that he would naturally never be able to demand back if Hedberg turned difficult. Clearly he'd bought that argument, for the last Saturday in February he'd suddenly phoned from Arlanda on Waltin's secret number to report that he was on the scene.

Waltin had put him up in the apartment at Gärdet where he'd lived when he'd come over most recently to help with Krassner. Not to remind him in any way, but simply because that was the most secure he had to offer at the moment. It was at the disposal of the external operation and only he knew about it. Berg obviously had no inkling about it, and it was a so-called secure address. It was not a place where people from the open operation might come rushing in at any moment. Besides, it was a nice place to stay. Waltin himself had made use of it on a few occasions, and if it was good enough for him with his demands for seclusion and comfort, then it was more than good enough for Hedberg.

When they met, Hedberg said little, as usual, but there must have been something more that was weighing on him because he started by saying that he could only stay until next Saturday. Partly because he'd been planning to return to Java for a long time, partly because he had to see to getting his boat in the water.

"Fine with me," said Waltin good-humoredly. "Then we'll just scrape together as much as we have time and energy for."

During the work-filled days that followed they also started to find each other again. Hedberg softened, and Waltin started to regain his confidence. On Thursday, when they were done for the most part with what they needed to do, Waltin treated him to a nice dinner at an out-of-the-way place, and when they were sitting with their coffee Hedberg opened up.

"At first I thought you intended to set me up," he said suddenly, looking at Waltin.

"Oh well," said Waltin, making an effort to sound both relaxed and sufficiently uninterested. "If anything it's probably the case that you know considerably more about this than I do. The only thing I've understood is that wham-bam Berg has my head on a platter."

"Yes," said Hedberg, smiling wanly. "I got that. And I certainly think you understand that I'm not the type to set you up."

No, thought Waltin with feeling, for in that case you'd no doubt dream up something considerably worse.

"Sometimes it's best not to know something," said Hedberg cryptically.

You're telling me, thought Waltin.

Then Hedberg sat quietly for almost a minute while he twirled his spoon in his coffee cup, and that must have been when he decided, for he'd spilled everything that up till that moment Waltin had been forced to figure out for himself.

"There wasn't anything really wrong with that American," said Hedberg, for some reason choosing not to refer to him by name. "It was those fucking social democrats that were after him to protect that traitor they had as a boss." He didn't go into how he now knew that. "He'd managed to worm his way in with the CIA and sold them out too. To the Russians, of course, since they were the ones he was working for the whole time. Ever since he was a little snot-nosed kid," clarified Hedberg.

"I guess I've suspected a thing or two over the years," said Waltin, sighing. Would have been fun to read those papers you took with you, he thought.

"Then he had his best friend murdered too," said Hedberg, nodding.

"My God," said Waltin with well-acted disgust. "Are you sure of that?" Clearly had more balls than his voters, he thought with delight.

"Quite certain," said Hedberg, nodding. "A murder-for-hire that the Russians arranged for him. I guess he didn't dare pull the strings himself," said Hedberg with a snort.

"No, my God," said Waltin with emphasis. "I hope you'll excuse me but I at least have to have a little pick-me-up. Will you join me?" Sounds like a book that just has to get published, thought Waltin with delight. That manuscript must be worth millions.

Hedberg hardly drank at all. Something that Waltin had been glad to note right at the start of their acquaintance, but what he had just related had clearly made an impression.

"I'll have a small whiskey," said Hedberg. "Something inexpensive is fine."

Before they parted they decided to meet the next evening to clear up the final details before Hedberg went back.

I don't need to worry about him, in any case, thought Waltin as he sat in the taxi on the way back home.

Late on Friday afternoon Waltin had taken the opportunity to drop by Berg's office in order to turn in yet another thick pile of painstakingly unsorted documents so that his boss would have something to upset his weekend with, and on the way into Berg's office he almost ran into a chief inspector with the prime minister's security detail, who was on his way out. Red under the eyes and clearly so upset that he neither saw nor heard.

"Heavens," said Waltin, smiling with his white teeth toward Berg. "He didn't seem happy. Have you been mean to him?" As well, he thought.

Berg didn't seem especially upbeat, either. He sighed heavily and shook his head absentmindedly. He'll soon be ready for the madhouse, thought Waltin contentedly. We're only counting the days.

"No," said Berg. "If only it were that simple. He's just gotten a touch of his usual headache."

"So that's how it is," said Waltin as he set his papers on Berg's desk. "Brought along a little reading for you before the weekend, by the way. What's the big boss come up with this time, then? Is he going to go over Niagara Falls in a barrel?"

"If only it were that good," sighed Berg. "No, he's going to the movies with his wife."

"Here in town?" said Waltin with genuine astonishment. On a Friday evening after payday and thirteen drunks for every dozen and without a guard? The man must have a very strong death wish, thought Waltin, and considering how many years he'd heard everyone complain about the prime minister's nonexistent security awareness, it was a pure miracle that no one had taken advantage of the opportunity. Must be all the TV-watching, thought Waltin. People just sit and stare at their televisions instead of doing something sensible with their lives.

Berg sighed yet again and then he said something that he really wasn't allowed to say, not even to Waltin, despite the fact that Waltin was a police superintendent with the secret police and both security-classed and equipped with a muzzle both lengthwise and crosswise.

"He called a few hours ago and canceled his bodyguards. He and his wife were thinking about going to a movie, and before that they were going to have dinner together at their residence."

"Clint Eastwood's latest, of course," said Waltin, clucking with delight.

"No idea," said Berg, uninterested, for personally he never went to the movies. He didn't say that; it wasn't decided for sure. Not even that, he thought dejectedly.

Well, well, thought Waltin when he left Berg. You can't have everything, but nonetheless he felt the same tingling expectation as that time when he saw dear Mother standing there wobbling on the platform with her silly canes.

High time to go home, thought Berg, looking with distaste at the papers that Waltin had left on his desk. Considering the orderliness that Waltin was clearly capable of, it was his good fortune that he wasn't compelled to support himself for real by running his own business. When the auditors had reported to Berg they'd been almost white in the face, and what had shaken them the most was that they were completely convinced that Waltin had genuinely exerted himself to do his very best. Anyway, that was completely uninteresting, considering what happened later.

During the years that followed Berg devoted hundreds of hours to ransacking his consciousness. Honestly, sincerely, and ruthlessly he tried to recall down to the smallest detail what he'd done, said, and thought during the days in question that would change his life as well. He obviously remembered the short meeting with Waltin, as well as the reason that Waltin had dropped by his office. In order to deliver a bundle of papers that, it was true, were classified at the highest level of secrecy, but in any case had nothing to do with what happened later. That was all, and there wasn't anything more.

When Hedberg showed up in the apartment at Gärdet he was late. It was going on seven-thirty and Waltin had waited for half an hour and more or less given up on the idea he'd been thinking about. Whatever it was, thought Waltin in his usual superficial way, but just at that moment Hedberg put the key in the lock.

"Unfortunately I have to cancel our little meeting," said Waltin, "but we were through with each other for the most part anyway."

"That's okay with me," said Hedberg, shrugging his shoulders. Perhaps I should stop by Café Opera and see if there's anything worth screwing, he thought. It's actually been a while.

"I heard a funny thing at the office an hour ago," said Waltin. Just in passing like that, he thought, so we'll have to see if there's anyone who'll rise to the bait.

"Yes?"

"Our mutual acquaintance seems to have phoned and canceled his bodyguards. He's supposed to be going to a movie with his wife. In the middle of town on a Friday evening after payday when there are thirteen drunks to the dozen," said Waltin, smiling.

"The Swedes are a patient people," declared Hedberg. "I'm sure he's figured that out. Kept in the dark and put up with just about anything."

"Unfortunately that's how it is," sighed Waltin.

"Does he still live there?" said Hedberg suddenly.

"Yes," said Waltin as he looked at the expensive watch that he'd stolen while dear Mother was still alive and he himself was far too young to be able to use it. "Yes, he still lives there.

"From one thing to another," said Waltin as he stood up. "Because I'm forced to close down, I bought some goodies and put them in the fridge. If there should be anything left over, just leave it so I can take care of it tomorrow after you've gone. I was thinking about stopping by anyway."

"It'll work out," said Hedberg.

As soon as Waltin had left, Hedberg went out to the kitchen and took out the plastic bag with mixed delicacies that Waltin had placed in the fridge. The revolver was under a foil container from the Östermalm market with prepared veal burgers, cream gravy, small green peas, and mashed potatoes.

Who the hell does he take me for? thought Hedberg crossly as he weighed it in his hand. Buffalo Bill?

Then he looked at his watch and it was almost eight, so perhaps there wasn't so much to think about, but since he'd planned to go into town anyway he might just as well take a look past Old Town where the traitor lived.

CHAPTER XX

For a great and noble cause

Stockholm, February 28–March 1

Taking a taxi to Old Town was out of the question. Regardless of the fact that he was short on time, it would have to be the subway. Running to catch the train was out of the question too, so he'd missed the first, and when he finally arrived at Old Town it was eight-thirty and he'd already decided to give up the whole project and take a swing into town and do something else instead. He could always toss the antiquity that Waltin had slipped him into Strömmen, for it was hardly something he wanted to carry around with him, much less leave at the coat check if he went to a bar.

It'll have to be a brisk walk, thought Hedberg, and when he strode out of the subway the first thing he saw was them, walking straight toward him from the alley. Almost a hundred yards, and they hadn't seen him, in any event, so he turned on his heels and went back up onto the platform. A rather risk-free long shot, for if they were going to the movies it was probably at Hötorget or Rådmansgatan, and if it should turn out that he was wrong then he would have to live with that too.

The alley would have been perfect, he thought, but now it was the way it was and then there were other conditions that applied: keeping his distance and hoping for luck. So he jumped onto the train that had just come in, even though he knew they wouldn't make it. He rode past the central station, but at Hötorget he got off and positioned himself on the platform, pretending to read the newspaper while he was waiting. He had a fool's good luck, for when the next train pulled in there were enough passengers where they were sitting that he would be able to melt into the crowd.

Being in the same car was naturally out of the question. Instead he took a chance again, got into another one, and was among the first to get off at Rådmansgatan. Because he'd devoted hundreds of hours to shadowing people he wasn't the type to follow them if he had the choice. He went out onto the street ahead of them, and as soon as he was certain that they were going to the Grand Cinema he went into the lobby and placed himself in the ticket line for a film that plenty of people would see but not them. Wrong film for people like them, and as soon as he was sure which film they would see instead he left. He already knew when their movie would end, for he'd got that from the poster in the lobby, so he didn't even need to slink past a well-stocked newsstand to check it in a newspaper. And he obviously never even considered asking the cashier.

He didn't consider hanging around outside the cinema for two hours, either. That it was bitterly cold was uninteresting, for his job was to keep his distance and minimize risk, and the price of that was that he had to take a chance. So again he took a chance. Took the chance that they would watch the movie to the end, for people like that usually did; took the chance that they would then head home; and took the chance that they would take the subway, for they usually did that too.

If he really was going to shoot someone, he didn't intend to do it on an empty stomach. He hadn't eaten a thing all day. So he slipped into a Chinese restaurant on Drottninggatan, with just enough people, just drunk enough and occupied with themselves, and no coat check where he needed to hang his jacket. Then he ate and read the newspaper in peace and quiet. Paid cash, gave a respectable tip, and left the place with enough time, not too early and not too late. And exactly like the first time, when he saw them it was at a distance of a little less than a hundred yards, and they were walking at a brisk pace straight toward him.

Unfortunately they were walking on the wrong side of the street. On the west side of the street along Adolf Fredrik's cemetery and in the direction of Kungsgatan, a lot of people were moving in both directions and there was no question of getting anything accomplished there. He had just decided to hurry down into the subway, ride ahead of them to Old Town, and wait for them in the alley where he'd seen them the first time, when he had a fool's luck again. For suddenly they crossed Sveavägen and walked up to a shop window, and on that side of the street there was hardly a soul. It's almost enough to give you religion, thought Hedberg, crossing and positioning himself on the same side of the street at the corner of Tunnelgatan.

This is too good to be true, he thought. A dark little cross street with construction trailers and narrow passageways and a number of escape routes to choose from, right close by. If it had been his to choose, this was exactly where he would have arranged to encounter them. For what he intended to do there was no place better, and for them there was no place worse. So he waited for them while he pretended to look in the shop window, and when they were passing him he just walked up behind them, pulled the revolver from the right pocket of his jacket, cocking the trigger with the same motion, placed his left hand on the traitor's shoulder, and fired a loud and almost point-blank shot right down the edge of his collar.

His legs just folded up and he fell headlong to the street on his face. Dead, thought Hedberg, for he knew from experience, even though he'd never shot a man in his entire life.

And at the next second he backed up a step in order to get a better firing line, cocked the trigger with his thumb since the weapon was sluggish, aimed at the same place on the upper-class whore that the traitor had been married to, and fired again. She sank down on her knees with a sagging head and eyes that didn't seem to see. And presumably she must have twisted at the very moment that he fired, just when the flare from the muzzle blinded him, because he hit her in the lung and not in the spinal column where he'd aimed.

He was content to look at her for a few seconds, for in a minute at the most she would be dead, and in any event by then he intended to be somewhere else. Then he turned and because it was icy and slippery he ran straddle-legged and jogged along the stone border between the street and the sidewalk, and as he ran toward the stairs up to Döbelns-gatan he put the revolver back in his jacket pocket.

For a great and noble cause, he thought, and he couldn't have said it better himself.

When he came up onto Döbelnsgatan he stopped running, crossed the street at a normal pace, and continued straight along down the hill. At Regeringsgatan he turned right and took the stairs down to Kungsgatan, and as he was walking down toward Stureplan and the subway and saw all the people around him he knew that the flock gave him all the protection he needed and that he'd already gotten away. When he stepped into the apartment at Gärdet the time was only ten minutes to twelve. He took off his shoes and all his clothes and put them in an ordinary black plastic garbage bag, on top of which he set the revolver, and then he carried the sack out to the kitchen and placed it next to the refrigerator.

After that he showered and washed his hair, and when he'd rinsed off all the lather he did the same thing over again, letting the hot water run the whole time. Only after that had he gone to bed. He hadn't thought about anything in particular, and he fell asleep almost immediately.

The next morning he took a taxi to the airport bus and the airport bus to Arlanda, and if there were policemen out chasing a murderer they weren't at Arlanda, in any event. For once his plane took off on time, and when he landed in Palma it was almost seventy degrees, and for the first time since he'd moved there it felt like coming home.

CHAPTER XXI

Falling free, as in a dream

Stockholm, February 28–March 1

Oredsson and Stridh had been standing at the hot-dog stand down by
Roslagstull when the roof came crashing down on their heads. Stridh
had gone crazy, asking on the radio if they should attempt to cordon off
the main road at Roslagstull themselves while waiting for reinforcements, but instead they were ordered to drive to the crime scene and
help out with the practical aspects.

What is happening? thought Oredsson, while they drove down
Sveavägen toward the city center with spinning blue lights. He didn't
understand a thing, and if this was the beginning of something
bigger that he and his comrades were part of, shouldn't he have heard
something?

"This is complete madness," Stridh hissed. "What will we be doing
there? Someone has to cordon off the main roads. Even that drunkard
down in the pit must understand that!"

He seems completely crazy; must be a social democrat, thought
Oredsson.

When they finally arrived there were police and ordinary civilians
everywhere, and everyone was running around like headless chickens.
First they helped set up a cordoned-off area, but as people were in the
way the whole time—it had to be done quickly—it wasn't a very large
one. It actually turned out roughly like a sheep pen—in any event, it

was the smallest cordoned-off area he'd seen, thought Oredsson. And after that they just remained standing there while waiting for further instructions.

Because it was Friday evening and Bäckström was still behind on his finances, he had as usual been slaving at the after-hours unit, and when the alarm was sounded he understood immediately that this was the great moment in his life, and before anyone had gotten other ideas on his behalf he'd thrown on his coat and driven down to the crime scene. For where else should an old experienced homicide detective like him be?

Unlike everyone else, Bäckström also tried to get a few things done. First he took a peek at all the ordinary citizens who were in the general vicinity to check out if he saw anyone remotely suspicious, but they all just looked completely down in the mouth, and a few old ladies had even turned on the waterworks, whatever good that would do. Then they started chucking flowers inside the cordoned-off area (God knows where they'd gotten hold of them at this time of day), and then he trotted down to Tunnelgatan to get a little peace and quiet and see if he could find any tracks or anything else interesting. There were God help me tracks everywhere. Must be a millipede that shot him, Bäckström thought, grinning.

Then he expanded his investigations and took the opportunity to chow down a sausage with mashed potatoes at the stand on Sveavägen, and when he came back the Chimney Sweep himself was just getting out of a taxi along with that little fairy Wiijnbladh, and because he didn't have anything better to do he went up and said hello to them.

"How's it going?" said Bäckström.

"Under control," said the Chimney Sweep, who was a stuck-up bastard.

Kiss my ass, thought Bäckström.

"The chief and I are standing here, analyzing the situation," said Wiijnbladh, who was an ingratiating bastard.

And I'm on my way to the Nobel dinner, thought Bäckström.

"What have you come up with, then?" said Bäckström smoothly. This will be fun, he thought.

"That the crime scene obviously leaves a great deal to be desired," said the Chimney Sweep haughtily.

And what were you intending to do about it? thought Bäckström.

"So unfortunately there's not really much we can do," sighed Wiijnbladh, shaking his head in distress.

Sure, and it's damn cold too, thought Bäckström. And who doesn't want to come in out of the cold?

Then they got into a taxi and drove away, but because he was a real policeman he hitched a ride with a patrol car that happened to be passing by.

"Good that you came, Bäckström," said the boss as soon as he stepped inside the door. "We have a tipster who's contacted us, but she refuses to talk with anyone other than you." The boss handed over a telephone message slip.

"It'll work out," said Bäckström, heaving a large manly sigh. Seems to be a reasonable woman, thought Bäckström. Certainly someone he'd screwed, even if he didn't remember the name.

"How was it down at the crime scene, by the way?" asked the boss.

"Heavy," said Bäckström. "This can get heavy. Really heavy."

Then he got coffee, closed the door behind him, and called up the female tipster with the good judgment.

"Am I speaking with Chief Inspector Bäckström?" she hissed excitedly.

"Yes, it's me," said Bäckström with manly confidence. Just a matter of time, he thought.

"We met on Christmas Eve," she whispered. "I was the one who was raped by my old boyfriend."

This is God help me not true, thought Bäckström, moaning to himself. That fucking Lapp owl who ratted out her poor guy. The one who had that priceless dartboard with the victim on it, thought Bäckström. Too damn bad he hadn't taken it with him after all. Now it would be worth a lot.

"You'll have to excuse me," said Bäckström curtly, "but I'm sitting here with—"

"Good Lord," she whispered. "He's the one who's murdered him. I don't know what to do."

What the hell is she saying? thought Bäckström.

"Murdered who?" asked Bäckström.

"The prime minister," she whispered.

She is, God help me, off her rocker, thought Bäckström, but then he suddenly thought about the dartboard, so he didn't say that.

"Why do you think that?" he asked.

"Good Lord," she said dejectedly. "He's been planning to do it as long as I've known him."

"Do you know if he has access to weapons?" Bäckström asked carefully.

"Weapons, he has lots of weapons," she whispered.

This might be worth checking out, thought Bäckström, and since the after-hours unit mostly resembled the locked ward at a psychiatric hospital, he borrowed a service vehicle and drove to her place.

She lived in a messy little apartment on the south end, but he'd figured that out from the start. On the other hand, what she had to say didn't sound so stupid. Her old boyfriend, the one with the dartboard, was evidently a mean devil when it came down to it, and he had evidently hated the prime minister and then some. She mostly whispered and sniffled and snuffled, but they always did that, so it was no surprise.

"You said that he had weapons," Bäckström reminded her.

"Yes, he showed me one time."

"What were they?" asked Bäckström. "Do you remember that?"

"It was one of those like they have in western movies. One of those cowboy pistols."

What do you say? thought Bäckström, feeling the excitement rising, for before he'd left the after-hours unit he'd heard that one of the eye-witnesses from the crime scene had maintained that the perpetrator had fired a revolver.

"You mean a revolver," said Bäckström.

"Yes," she said, nodding. "A revolver, it was one of those."

Doesn't look good for the damn dart-thrower, thought Bäckström contentedly, for soon he would have a real pro breathing down his neck. Not good at all, he thought.

It had been the worst night in Chief Inspector Koskinen's life. And it had all started so well. Despite the fact that it was Friday after payday, the streets had been quiet all evening. Severe cold and biting wind were always the best way to maintain general order and security on streets and squares, thought Koskinen, deciding that it was high time to say hello to a dear old friend that he kept in his locker.

Fortunately he'd had time to knock back a few good-sized stiff ones before the roof fell in. He'd just locked away his best friend and fresh-ened himself up with some menthol lozenges when suddenly one of his operators came rushing in looking like seven years of famine.

"There you are. The devil himself has been let loose in the pit," said the operator, staring at him.

"The pit" was the internal name for the Stockholm Police Depart-ment's command center, and at first he hadn't understood a thing, but looked around in the dressing room to see if he might discover some-thing or someone.

What's this about loose? thought Koskinen.

"They've shot the prime minister," said his operator.

"What kind of nonsense is that?" said Koskinen. "It's one of those fucking drills, don't you understand?" I'll have to take it up with the union again, he thought. Must be that lunatic who's the head of operations.

His younger colleague just looked at him. Then he shook his head several times. Just stood there shaking his head while he looked at him.

"No, no, no," he said. Then he turned on his heel and went back in to the command center.

The rest was an absolute nightmare. Like that time last summer when he'd gotten the D.T.'s and wrestled with a squid for several hours despite the fact that he was only lying there sleeping and had almost strangled himself with his own sheets. Although that time it had worked out. He'd taken leave for a few weeks and the doctor had prescribed something a little extra strong for him. This night was worse, for it would never come to an end.

First he ran out of throat lozenges, which wasn't the end of the world since he had a cold anyway and it made sense to keep a little distance. But then he ran out of schnapps too, despite the fact that he'd stocked up extra since it was Friday. And then every single boss in the whole fucking district started barging in in the middle of the night, and what they all had in common was their demand to be immediately informed of the situation so that they then could devote themselves to being in the way. Situation here and situation there, and the only consolation was that the majority of them seemed to have celebrated so substantially that nobody noticed that he didn't have any throat lozenges to offer. And say what you want to about the chief constable, he thought, he was actually the only person who hadn't disturbed him. He hadn't made any contact whatsoever.

"The situation is as follows," said Koskinen for the fifty-eleventh time the same night. "The prime minister has been shot and the perpetrator has succeeded in fleeing the scene."

But otherwise nothing was the same and least of all did it have anything in common with that incomprehensible drill that the chief constable had arranged. And only on Saturday afternoon did he finally get to drop into his bed.

The Stockholm chief constable's leaving Chief Inspector Koskinen in peace was not due to the fact that he wasn't interested in what had happened. He'd taken leave over the weekend and driven up to Dalarna with his mistress in order to ski in Vasaloppet, and considering the delicate nature of this he had carefully avoided informing anyone of his whereabouts.

He had quite simply no idea that the prime minister had been shot in his own backyard. It was the porter at the hotel who told him when he came down to breakfast in the morning. The chief constable had obviously packed himself, his ski equipment, and his mistress into his car and immediately set a course toward Stockholm.

He could always ski in Vasaloppet next year, but the assassination of a prime minister was a more unusual event, so it was crucial to seize the opportunity that the occasion offered. What a unique opportunity, he thought as he sat behind the steering wheel, to be able to test the new intellectual methods of investigation that he'd developed for the first time on a real case. This is almost too good to be true, he thought, and while he drove, his mistress took notes on his various thoughts, ideas, and plans. Quite in order, for she was of course a police officer too, of a rather simpler type, it was true, but nonetheless a police officer.

Even before they passed Sala on the way home she had written down thirty-five different tracks divided into the three main categories of main track, alternative main track, and secondary tracks. He'd decided to wait with the so-called dead-end track that his best friend had so meritoriously suggested to him. For one thing he still hadn't got his promised memorandum on the matter, and also, naturally enough, he didn't know how large a part of his investigation force he would need to keep occupied with other things while waiting until he needed them.

"May I ask something?" said his mistress.

"Of course, dear," he said. She really sounds surly, he thought.

"It's the main track. How do you know that?"

"Know what?" the chief constable countered patiently.

"That it's the Kurds who shot him," she said. "How do you know that?"

"Because it's statistically the most probable," said the chief constable.

"They've never shot a Swedish prime minister, have they?" she said sourly. "They usually just shoot each other, don't they?"

"Yes, my dear, but it's really not so strange," said the chief constable, and he really exerted himself to be as amiable and pedagogical as possible. "That's something no one has done, of course. Neither Jew nor Greek nor . . . well, ordinary Swede then, if I may say so, has ever shot a Swedish prime minister. So you can't very well cite that against them. Or can you, dear?"

Wonder why he didn't shoot his dear wife too? thought Waltin as he strode in through the door to the apartment at Gärdet to clean up after his spiritual brother and highly esteemed coworker. Perhaps he's starting to get soft, he thought, but because that thought was so ridiculous he immediately dismissed it and instead went to work on the practicalities.

First he packed up the clothes and shoes in a suitcase; he would see to it that they were thoroughly cleaned before he hid them in some secure place. He obviously hadn't even considered throwing them out. These were objects of great historic value, almost unique, and his mouth was watering when he thought about how much they might bring in the not too distant future at an auction at Sotheby's. Or Christie's, for that matter.

He tossed the food and all the other garbage into the wastebasket and what remained now was only the weapon itself. When he woke up he'd already gotten an idea that was so brilliant that he'd been thoroughly excited the whole morning and had been compelled to seek relief twice before he could go to work on the practical tasks.

First he emptied the chamber of the two empty cartridges and the four bullets that Hedberg hadn't needed, put them in a stamp envelope, and placed them in the suitcase with the shoes and clothes. He wiped off the revolver carefully before he put that in his pocket, and then he took the suitcase with him, locked up, and left the place. So only the revolver was left, thought Waltin as he sat in his car, and the thought of what he was going to do with it made his whole body tingle.

First the now-deceased prime minister's special adviser had thought about writing a formal resignation letter or at least requesting a leave of absence, but from the atmosphere in the corridor where he was sitting, and without anyone having said anything—for suddenly it was as if he no longer existed—he'd understood that this would be completely superfluous. So he'd been content to just go home. On the way out he'd stopped and written a few brief lines in the condolence book set out in the lobby. True, it was a quote, not something that he'd written himself, but for various reasons it nonetheless felt more suitable than anything else, and he remembered it word for word despite the fact that it had been a good month since he'd read it.

> Death is black like a raven's wing,
> Sorrow is cold like a midwinter night
> Just as long and no way out

Then he drove home to the house in Djursholm, and after he thought a while he finally made a decision. First he wrote a message in Russian, the language that he'd learned in secret in his youth and that therefore he could never keep alive and that now—despite his extraordinary memory—caused him greater problems than he could have imagined. In itself that meant nothing, he thought. The message was clear enough and the fact that the language limped precariously only increased the degree of difficulty.

Then he coded it with the prime number that he'd thought about giving to Forselius on his eightieth birthday; he'd actually cheated a little with the help of the military's computer, but because that wasn't relevant any longer he might just as well use it like that. When he was finished he hesitated a long time about whether he should sign his name to it, the name they'd given him when he was only a little more than eighteen years old, in order to flatter him but certainly also in order to show that they even knew about such things as what his two-years-older classmates had called him in order to tease him when he started in the first grade in elementary school.

Finally he made up his mind and signed his name to it. Because they didn't have access to the key, breaking the code of the message would require decades of their combined computer power. So that was really quite uninteresting, but he could always treat them to a few headaches, if they ever did.

They're welcome to that, he thought, and when he read through the line of numerals that he'd written down he experienced a feeling of deep satisfaction that what he'd read only had meaning for himself and perhaps a few isolated others like him. You're welcome to that, he thought as he coded his name under the message. He could send it later, as soon as there was a suitable moment.

To the Bear and Michael . . . DLJA MEDJEV I MICHAIL . . . The best informant . . . TOT KTO SAMOI LUTSHI INFARMA-TOR . . . is the one who hasn't understood the significance of what he's told . . . TOT KTO SAM NE PONJAL STO ON RASSKASOVAL . . .

then his name, the name they'd given him more than twenty years before . . . The Professor . . . PRAFESSOR. For how else could he pay them back?

Then he burned Krassner's papers in the fireplace, and when after a while he went to bed he fell asleep for once without thinking about anything in particular.

At about the same time as the special adviser was going out through the entryway to Rosenbad, Waltin had slunk in through the door to the tech squad. Complete chaos prevailed, which suited him just fine, because he'd been able to put back the revolver that he'd borrowed from them more than six months before. He'd simply placed it on a bench and left the place without even needing to ask about that miserable little shit Wiijnbladh whom he'd had in reserve in case one of his dense colleagues had had the nerve to ask what a police superintendent with the secret police was doing there on a day like this.

But no one had heard, seen, or said anything, and he had simply left the place. And the feeling when he came out on the street again had been almost as fantastic as that time when he sneaked up behind dear Mother, who was standing there staggering with her pathetic canes just when he saw the train come thundering in alongside the platform. How he had passed behind her back, hardly even needing to brush against her, and continued in the direction toward the train and the escalators up to the street. How he'd heard the drawn-out metallic screeching from the braking train, the quick muffled thuds . . . and the seconds of silence before some hysterical female subway rider had started shrieking like a lunatic.

Johansson got the announcement of death on the radio as he prepared breakfast, and he'd been compelled to sit down and look at the clock. Up until five o'clock yesterday afternoon he'd been bureau head at the National Police Board. And when he stepped out through the door on Polhemsgatan it was on a leave of absence for the time being. When he'd come home he'd had dinner and devoted the evening to pondering how he should arrange his new life. Then he'd gone to bed early. Fell asleep immediately, slept securely and undisturbed the whole night, and when he woke it was with a smile on his lips. Now it was eight o'clock in the morning, no one had phoned him or pounded on his door in the middle of the night, because he'd pulled out the phone jack, and he suddenly understood that now he was someone completely different than he'd been yesterday.

Jarnebring phoned in the evening. He'd been away on vacation along with his fiancée and avoided the crash itself, but now he was called home and in service along with all the old comrades at the bureau. Plus quite a few new ones that he didn't much care for.

"How's it going?" Johansson asked automatically.

"It's going to hell," said Jarnebring with both conviction and feeling. "Do you know what they've got us doing?"

"No," said Johansson. How would I know that? he thought.

"We're going through old parking violations and suicides and hotel bookings since last summer," said Jarnebring. "Fucking academics. If you killed yourself last summer you can't God help me have shot the prime minister, can you?"

"They don't seem to know what to do," said Johansson. For that matter, how could they? he thought. Then they concluded their conversation and each returned to his own business. Johansson sorted his dirty laundry and threw out old papers. Then he went to bed and fell asleep more or less as usual.

When the chief constable strode into his office they came rushing like a flock of sheep, all bleating at the same time. But he only needed to stop and raise his hand with a commanding movement to silence them.

"Gentlemen," he said, "I'm taking command and hereby call the investigation force to its first meeting at fourteen zero zero hours in the large auditorium in the Kronoberg block. Proceed, carry out."

It takes so little, he thought as he strode into his office and closed the large double doors behind him.

At about the same time as the Stockholm chief constable was withdrawing in order to commune with himself in private, Police Superintendent Waltin sat down across from Berg on the other side of his large desk.

Good Lord, thought Waltin with delight when he saw him. He seems in a state of complete dissolution.

"How are you doing, Erik?" said Waltin with a worried expression.

"I'm sure I've had better days," sighed Berg. "The only consolation just now is that his wife made it."

"Yes, he clearly spared her," said Waltin with a pastoral expression. Must talk with Hedberg when we meet, he thought.

"Spared," snorted Berg. "He missed, the bastard, the bullet grazed her back and she's alive only by God's providence."

Perhaps I ought to send him to an eye doctor too, thought Waltin.

"You wanted to talk with me," said Waltin, adjusting the crease in his trousers. In honor of the day he'd chosen a simply cut dark-gray suit with matching monochrome tie. Dark gray, almost black, very appropriate considering the circumstances.

"I was thinking that you can manage the liaison with the investigation down in Stockholm," said Berg. "You'll have that as your only assignment for the time being." Then I'll have to try to see to it that we're still here when this is over, he thought.

"Fine with me," said Waltin. "How did you intend to organize this?" This is almost too good to be true, he thought.

"We'll have to start by giving them the material on threats to the prime minister," said Berg.

"Of course," said Waltin, making a note in his little black book that he'd taken out. I'll see to it that it gets thoroughly sorted first, he thought with delight.

"Yes, they've already gotten the Kurdish material, as I understand it, for Kudo and Bülling have no doubt already arranged that," sighed Berg.

"Nice to hear," said Waltin diplomatically. This really is too good to be true, thought Waltin.

"Yes, I guess that's all," said Berg, barely suppressing a sigh.

"What should we do about the oversight of the external operation?" asked Waltin with an expression of appropriate interest. Perhaps high time to close it down, he thought.

"It might as well continue as usual, the operation that is," Berg clarified. "I can't imagine that anyone is interested in any oversight whatsoever at this point." Don't show off, he thought wearily.

"And the Krassner case is probably history too, if I've understood correctly?"

"Yes, really," said Berg. Whatever that matter could possibly have to do with this, he thought.

"Yes, we may as well take the good with the bad," said Waltin sanguinely.

Where does he get all this from? thought Berg. What's wrong with this guy? Or is there something wrong with me? "Although we're hardly likely to escape a parliamentary investigation when this affair is finally cleared up," he said.

Especially if they clear it up, thought Waltin, on the verge of starting to giggle out loud. Although it doesn't need to go that badly, he thought.

"We'll cross that bridge when we come to it," said Waltin consolingly.

Between Sala and Stockholm the chief constable had already worked out the completely new investigative organization that he intended to set up. It was both logical and self-evident and took the form of a rather flat pyramid. At the bottom he had the investigation force itself, and according to his preliminary calculations he would need at least six hundred men if he were to be able to create a sufficient reserve just in case. Then he obviously needed a staff of all the heads of the various departments and the various observers from the ministry of justice and the remaining authorities within the legal system that he'd thought of calling in. Plus the secret police and the National Bureau of Criminal Investigation, obviously, and just so they wouldn't get any ideas in their little heads he now made a small notation about "observer status" in the margins. At the most, forty-some people in the investigation command itself, he thought contentedly.

Then remained the most important part of his organization: his secret brain trust, to which he only intended to invite his best friend along with his good friend the former diplomat (considering possible connections to foreign countries), a wide domain for himself, along with that first-rate spokesman at the National Police Board whom his best friend's good friend the diplomat had tipped him off about and whom he'd actually already met at the introductory seminar on the scientific detective. And if the need arose then it surely ought to suffice if representatives of the main track at any given moment were called in? It's logical to start by calling in Kudo and Bülling, thought the chief constable, making yet another notation in the margin in his neat handwriting.

Well, I guess that's all, he thought contentedly, and Grevlinge would have to take care of the purely practical aspects as usual. Organizational questions were really rather boring, he thought, especially for an artistic soul like his, so he quickly moved on to more exciting ones.

Because this was a historic event, by the time he had passed Morgongåva he had already been clear about the need for a historian. Or more correctly stated, a female historian, because he immediately, and for essentially different reasons, happened to think of a female journalist at the large morning newspaper whom he'd known for a while. Considering who had been taking notes while he drove, however, not much had been said about this during the ride itself.

Someone who continuously chronicles my thoughts and other reflections, thought the chief constable, nodding to himself. A kind of silent conversation partner, quite simply.

Someone should begin sketching out a large group portrait of the investigation leadership. Most indications argued for a rather imminent arrest. Considering that it was already known who the victim was and when, where, and how the crime had been committed, the only thing that remained was the perpetrator himself, so in a purely intellectual sense the whole thing was already eighty percent cleared up, thought the chief constable, and because those group portraits certainly took a good amount of time, it was perhaps just as well if Grevlinge were to make the first moves now. The chief constable made another notation.

This left the most important question of all, namely his personal security during the work of the investigation. Already in the car he'd sketched out the renovations of the office that would have to be made: bulletproof glass in all the windows, secure locations, strategically placed caches of weapons, and a few other little goodies, but the most pressing thing would be to build up a personal bodyguard unit. Making use of the guys in the secret police's bodyguard unit was naturally completely out of the question considering what had happened to the prime minister, the chief constable thought, and at the same time he congratulated himself on having already set them up as one of his many secondary tracks. Fortunately he also had access to competent and reliable people closer at hand. In his own riot squad there were certainly plenty of loyal officers who stood ready to take their daily allotted shower of bullets with chests bared in order to protect their boss.

Then he'd been struck by a thought. A completely new thought, for it was remarkably often that he was struck by such thoughts while working on something completely different. It is undeniably a strange coincidence, he thought, that the prime minister happens to be murdered the same weekend that I'm out of town to ski in Vasaloppet. On closer reflection this was really a question of yet another track, he thought, and closed his preliminary notations at once with a thirty-sixth entry: "Vasaloppet track."

Bäckström had landed another lead, and though he differed somewhat in body type, in dedication he was just like a hunting dog. His colleagues in the uniformed police had brought in an old junkie who was running around at the scene of the crime and acting out, and when they'd taken the goods off him he'd started howling that he was willing to "make a deal," and his offer this time was a detailed description of the perpetrator, who had just about run him down as he fled the scene.

"Jan Svulle Svelander," said Bäckström, in order to show that he was a man with a knowledge of people.

"So what?" said Svulle, shrugging and trying to squeeze a pimple on his nose.

"My colleagues in the uniformed police say that you saw the perpetrator," said Bäckström.

"Could be," said Svulle. "Depends."

"I don't know exactly how large a reward there might be," said Bäckström, "but we're certainly talking about a million."

"A million," said Svulle with eyes like saucers.

"At least," said Bäckström, nodding heavily. "Might it have been this old guy?" he asked, holding up the photo of the dart-thrower he'd taken with him from the Lapp owl.

"Yes," said Svulle. "Dead certain. That's him."

"And this isn't something you're saying just for the sake of the reward?" said Bäckström slyly.

"Who do you take me for?" said Svulle, offended. "It was him. Dead certain. Hundred percent."

At fourteen zero zero hours the chief constable welcomed the investigation force. The room was chock-full. People were sitting and standing on each other, and a younger detective had even climbed up and lain down on the hat shelf out in the lobby in order to be part of this historic event. It was mostly just Bäckström who was missing, for he was sitting at the after-hours unit and didn't have time to come because he was completely occupied with clearing up the murder of the prime minister. He was quite convinced of this since he'd found the dart-thrower near the top of the lists of threat-makers that the secret police had sent down to them.

The whole thing had gone quickly and efficiently, and Grevlinge could take care of the purely practical aspects, thought the chief constable when he stood up and demanded silence with a commanding gesture.

"Yes, gentlemen, that's about all for now, and in order to give you a few parting words from one of history's great personalities, I thought I would simply say in conclusion"—the chief constable made a precisely calculated stage pause that he'd rehearsed in front of the mirror in his office—"that this, gentlemen . . . this is not the end . . . far from it . . . and this is not the beginning either . . . but," said the chief constable, making another stage pause, "one thing I can promise you for sure . . . this is the beginning of the end."

CHAPTER XXII

Falling free, as in a dream

Stockholm in March

On the Sunday after the murder the chief constable held his first press conference, and considering its national significance it had been decided to broadcast it live on TV. It was with a certain excitement that Waltin settled down on his large sofa, since he'd already understood at the investigation command's first meeting what the major news that the chief constable intended to present would consist of.

Little Jeanette was also on the scene, despite the fact that he'd already decided to get rid of her. She had aged noticeably recently, and that sort of thing just didn't work, but be that as it may, this event demanded an audience, so she had to put on her little rose-colored slip while she served him the malt whiskey that he needed in order to get into the right mood.

As the whole thing dragged on for a while Waltin unfortunately got more than a little intoxicated, so when it was finally time he was forced to lie down and cover one eye with his hand in order to focus right. The advantage on the other hand was that he avoided seeing little Jeanette, who was sulking as usual. But at last it was finally time. The chief constable leaned forward, nodding seriously but nonetheless smiling toward his audience, and after a well-timed pause he held up two revolvers in front of him while he was met with a veritable cascade of flashbulbs, wave after wave streaming toward him.

"These, ladies and gentlemen," said the chief constable, "are two revolvers of the same type as the one that the perpetrator used when he shot our prime minister."

You don't know how right you are, thought Waltin with delight. After the investigation command's meeting he had seen with his own eyes how that little pompous ass Wiijnbladh demonstrated them for his top boss.

"I'm guessing it's the one in your left hand," Waltin had yelled, "the one with the short barrel," and when he did so he'd been overcome by a violent fit of laughter. Exactly like when he'd stood on the escalator that time and thought about dear Mother, who'd just left him for good on the tracks down below.

He is, God help me, not all there, thought Assistant Detective Jeanette Eriksson, age twenty-eight. And he can't fuck like a normal person, either. And now I'm going to forget the lunatic.

By Monday Bäckström's little investigation was already wrapped up, and all that really remained was to collect the murderer. But because everyone clearly had so much going on, a few more days went by before he finally got an audience with the chief constable. Evidently he was working all night too, for it was almost ten before that little nausea-inducing Grevlinge finally let him into the chief constable's office.

What the hell are all these homos doing here? thought Bäckström when he saw the three civilians who sat in shirtsleeves and red suspenders around the chief constable's conference table. True, he already knew that business with Babs, for Babs himself had told Bäckström that he was best friends with the chief constable when Bäckström had questioned him that time Babs had been robbed by a seaman that he'd brought home to play Donald and Daisy Duck with, but those other two? Where did they come from?

The older one was suspiciously like that Queerlund that SePo used to run around and drone on about, and that somewhat burlier character was even more like the man who was a cashier at the Society for Swedish Leathermen down on Skeppar Karls gränd, where the board of directors used to hang members up on hooks from the ceiling the whole night. Damn, this doesn't add up, thought Bäckström, for the chief constable himself had a reputation for being a real threshing machine with the ladies. What the hell is going on? thought Bäckström. I must warn him, he thought.

"Sit down," said the chief constable cordially, indicating an empty chair with his hand.

"Yes, don't be shy, now," said Queerlund, winking, while Leather Man only looked damned eager. The only one that behaved himself was actually Babs, who doubtless still remembered the investigation that Bäckström had conducted.

"Thanks," said Bäckström, sitting down on the edge of the chair as he felt the sweat start running inside his shirt collar. "Yes, I believe I've found the one who did it," he said, clearing his throat nervously, for he hadn't felt this uncomfortable since the time when that half-monkey Jarnebring had attacked him and snatched his beer.

"We're all ears," said the chief constable, nodding benevolently. And if this doesn't add up, we always have the Kurds, he thought confidently.

At about the same time as Bäckström was sitting with the Stockholm chief constable, another meeting about the murder of the Swedish prime minister was starting. Four thousand miles west (in round numbers) at CIA headquarters in Langley, Virginia, and if nothing else this was an illustration of what a small world we humans live in.

It was the head of the Office of Scandinavian Affairs, Mike "The Bear" Liska, who called the meeting, and the reason was that they wanted to make a summary of the case that at the bureau—and for several years— had had the code name the Buchanan Papers. The agency's analysts thought that a connection probably existed between the Buchanan Papers, the murder that the Swedish secret police operative had in all likelihood perpetrated on Buchanan's nephew John P. Krassner, and— possibly—the murder of the Swedish prime minister.

What was worrying the analysts was that if such were the case they couldn't understand either the motive behind the murder of the

Swedish prime minister or which persons were behind it. Everything they had been able to produce up till now argued strongly instead that it must have been the work of a so-called isolated madman. A bewildering case, thought Liska, and despite his long-term experience of the Swedish field he felt completely at a loss. The story quite simply didn't hang together. It was "un-Swedish" in some way, he thought, and now of course he had no one that he could ask directly.

Present at the meeting was also the responsible field agent, Sarah J. Weissman, who normally worked as a language expert at the National Security Agency, under the cover of being a freelancer in the publishing industry. Quite naturally, moreover, considering that it was she who had originally sounded the alarm on Buchanan's increasing talkativeness and the book that her ex-boyfriend from younger days was clearly in the process of writing about John "Fionn" Buchanan and his agent from the cold war, "Pilgrim."

Given that she had had Krassner's entire confidence it was also she who had really conducted the case. She'd had a full view right from the start, and NSA had had no objections whatsoever against loaning her out to their colleagues at the CIA. She had even had the decisive responsibility for the screening as well as the preparation of those documents that had finally been turned over to the Swedish former police superintendent Lars M. Johansson, previously head of the Swedish National Bureau of Criminal Investigation.

Regrettably, the case had developed in both a dramatic and unexpected manner through the security measures that Krassner had taken on his own initiative, and of which they had been completely ignorant up until Weissman had the opportunity to read Krassner's letter to Police Superintendent Johansson, which had been returned to her address, arriving twelve days after the news of his death.

The knowledge of Police Superintendent Johansson's existence had quickly raised the temperature at the office and generated some extensive activity at the CIA's unit at the embassy in Stockholm. When it then came to their knowledge that Johansson was evidently in the United

States—true, for other reasons, which one might reasonably conclude had nothing whatsoever to do with the Buchanan Papers, as his business trip had been arranged several months before Krassner went over to Sweden—the tension had approached the boiling point.

It had not been reduced by the fact that there were two circumstances that were hard to reconcile. Johansson could not possibly have gotten hold of Krassner's letter, but at the same time he was inexplicably interested in both Krassner and Weissman. Could it be that he had simply developed suspicions about Krassner's suicide? They knew about his close friendship with the policeman who had investigated the case, as well as the fact that Johansson was a very competent police officer.

Regardless of the reason for his trip, the analysts' wrinkled brows had not contributed a thing until Johansson suddenly knocked on the door of Weissman's home and she herself a full day later had told the whole, improbable story about "a shoe with a heel with a hole in it."

The jubilation at the bureau had known no bounds when Weissman, in her inimitable Swedish-influenced Minnesota accent, had again related Johansson's story. Liska himself laughed until the tears ran. Despite thirty years in the business this was the absolute best story he'd heard up till now that he could never tell.

"Jesus, guys," giggled Sarah, "you should have seen that big Swedish cop just sitting there on my sofa . . . so full of that country-boy confidence . . . the real McCoy of the North Pole."

So as far as Krassner was concerned the matter seemed to be more or less clear, even quite clear. He had actually been murdered because he had most unfortunately been confronted with a Swedish secret police operative, after which the latter tried to save his own rear end. Something that apparently he had also succeeded in doing. Regrettably by taking with him the rather discreet and innocent message they were trying to send to the Swedish secret police to be forwarded on to the person that it ultimately concerned.

. . .

On the other hand, the murder of the Swedish prime minister was quite a different story. That they had let Krassner carry on at all depended on the fact that all along they had counted on his being caught in the net of the Swedish secret police, which in a certain way he had been. In that way, without unnecessary drama, a "friendly warning" could be sent to Pilgrim—they did have a history in common, after all—the significance of which was that perhaps they were not always unreservedly willing to accept his constant criticism on questions that naturally belonged to the sphere of the political interests of the United States.

Which was why they'd allowed the completely preposterous accusation of the murder of Raven to remain in the papers that Johansson was allowed to take home with him. They themselves knew better, and the only reason the FBI hadn't arrested the perpetrator was that he was already dead, and that it might have disturbed an ongoing and considerably more important investigation of a Mafia family in Cleveland, which had had a conflict with one of Raven's clients and solved it by shooting the client's representative when the latter had become too troublesome.

They had sat for several hours before they had finally come to agreement and decided to place the Buchanan Papers in the files under the usual seventy-five-year secrecy rule and with a special notation that "they, in all probability, had no connection with the murder of the Swedish prime minister" but rather "that this, in all probability, was an action of an isolated madman. Conceivable murderers of the prime minister within the circle of Swedish secret police officers and intelligence agents who had knowledge of Krassner are thus lacking, as are conceivable motives. The case is hereby closed, and no further actions will be taken by the bureau." Liska noted it all on the cover of the file folder before it was carried down to the archive.

After that the meeting had been concluded on a high note and the majority of the participants had gone out and had two or even more beers together.

CHAPTER XXIII

And that wasn't the life that I had imagined

Stockholm, March 12

When, on his birthday, Johansson turned on the TV to look at the daily press conference about the latest police progress in the hunt for the murderer of the prime minister, he understood immediately by the body language of the chief constable as he took his place at the podium that great things were in the making.

"Yes," said the chief constable, smiling his usual solemn smile. "Today I have the pleasure of reporting that we have taken a person into custody as a suspect in the murder of the prime minister. It will be requested later today that he be arrested. This is a man in his thirties with connection to a known extreme right-wing organization . . ."

And when Johansson suddenly caught sight of Bäckström, who was clearly about to burst with delight, at the outer edge of the TV screen, he understood both how it had gone and that it couldn't possibly be true. So he turned off the TV and decided that it was high time that he took himself by the collar if he was going to straighten out the loneliness that was actually in process of leading him away from himself.

It doesn't cost anything to ask, thought Johansson, and considering that it's your own birthday and not even the kids have called to congratulate you, you really don't have much to lose. So he took a taxi to the little post office on Körsbärsvägen, and as soon as he strode in he caught sight of her and she of him. In addition she looked happy when she did so, and she immediately stood up and went to the counter.

She is no doubt the most beautiful woman I've seen up to now, thought Johansson, and she still has no ring on her finger, and the worst that can happen is that she says no.

"Police superintendent," she said, smiling. "Come, let's go into my office so we can talk in peace and quiet.

"I was listening to the radio," she continued. "Perhaps I should say congratulations. I heard that you've gotten hold of the man who did it."

"Well," said Johansson. "You never know." And we can take that up later, he thought, for regardless of everything else that doesn't concern me anymore. "I didn't come here to talk about that," he said, and for some strange reason he almost sounded as if he were still living up in that out-of-the-way spot in Ådalen where he'd grown up.

"Why'd you come here, then?" she asked, looking at him with her big dark eyes.

Sweet Jesus, thought Johansson, and despite the fact that he had after all made the occasional hazardous arrest in his day, this was almost too much.

"I thought about asking if I could invite you to dinner," said Johansson. It's my birthday, he thought, but naturally he didn't say that. For you didn't say such things.

And as soon as he saw the expression in her eyes he understood how she would answer.

"That would have been really nice," she said, "but I already have other plans." I've actually met a new guy, she thought, but naturally she didn't say that. For you didn't say such things.

"That's too bad. Perhaps another time," said Johansson, smiling. He felt as if someone were bracing himself against his rib cage, trying to tear his heart out of his body. Then he smiled and nodded and left the place, and considering that all he'd gotten was a no, and a very friendly no besides, he understood how little it took to do him in.

. . .

What a peculiar man, thought Pia Hedin, looking after him. And as different as they could be, despite the fact that they were both police officers. First that big burly Norrlander with his attentive eyes and his slow-moving manner, who never got in touch, even though she thought she'd given the clearest of signals that time they'd met more than three months ago. And then Claes, her new love, whom she'd met at the bar just a week ago when she was out with a girlfriend and had almost started to give up hope of ever meeting a normal guy. Claes with his perfect exterior and his devastating charm and all that sensitivity deep down inside, which she already knew was there the first time they looked at each other.

A NOTE ABOUT THE AUTHOR

Leif GW Persson has chronicled the political and social development of modern Swedish society in his award-winning novels for more than three decades. Born in Stockholm, Persson has served as an adviser to the Swedish Ministry of Justice and is Sweden's most renowned psychological profiler. He is a professor at Sweden's National Police Board and is considered the country's foremost expert on crime.

A NOTE ON THE TYPE

This book was set in Monotype Dante, a typeface designed by Gio-vanni Mardersteig (1892–1977). Conceived as a private type for the Officina Bodoni in Verona, Italy, Dante was originally cut only for hand composition by Charles Malin, the famous Parisian punch cutter, between 1946 and 1952. Its first use was in an edition of Boccaccio's *Trattatello in laude di Dante* that appeared in 1954. The Monotype Cor-poration's version of Dante followed in 1957. Although modeled on the Aldine type used for Pietro Cardinal Bembo's treatise *De Aetna* in 1495, Dante is a thoroughly modern interpretation of the venerable face.

Composed by Creative Graphics, Allentown, Pennsylvania
Printed and bound by Berryville Graphics, Berryville, Virginia
Designed by Virginia Tan